Land of the Wolf

A Novel of Viking Age England

Book Twelve of The Norsemen Saga

James L. Nelson

Fore Topsail Press
64 Ash Point Road
Harpswell, Maine 04079

Maps by Chris Boyle

ISBN- 979-8-9997291-0-1

To the once and future crew at Anchovy Meadows: Elizabeth, Nathaniel, Jonathan and Abigail. And to Lisa, still, after all these years.

PLATE 1

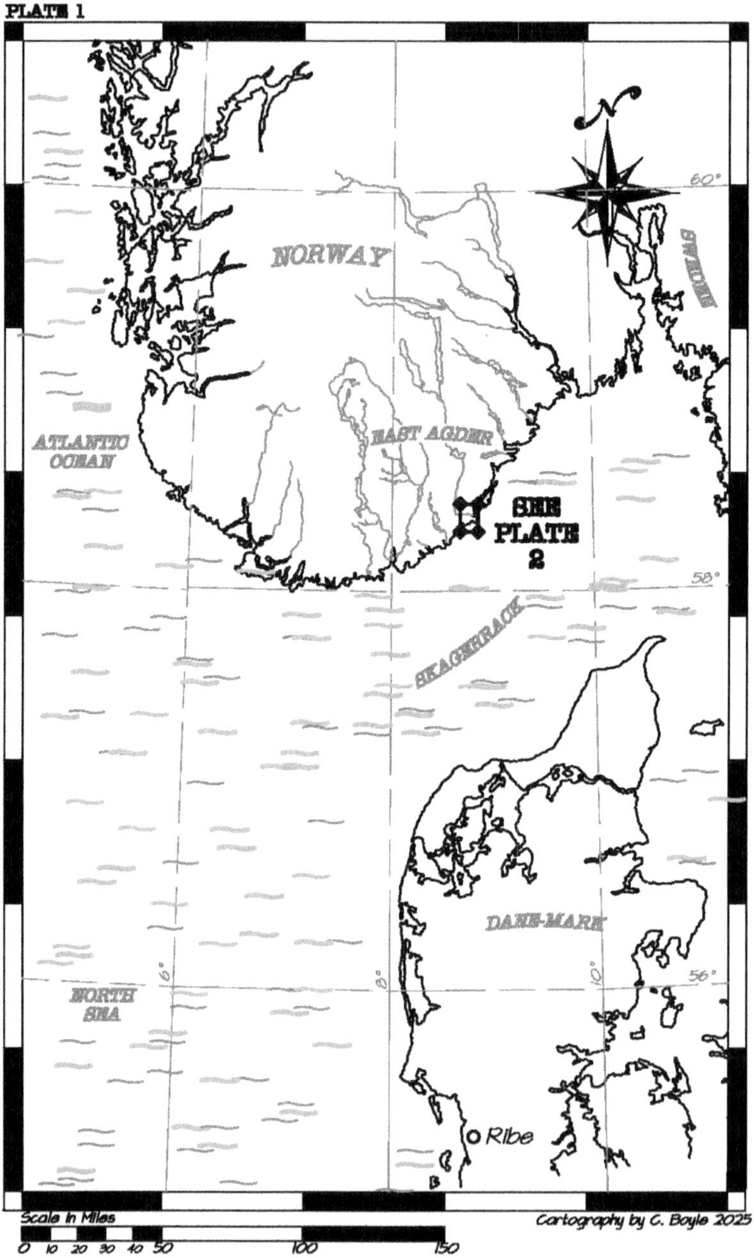
NORWAY
SWEDEN
EAST AGDER
ATLANTIC OCEAN
SEE PLATE 2
SKAGERRACK
DANE-MARK
NORTH SEA
Ribe
60°
58°
56°
6°
8°
10°
N
Scale in Miles
0 10 20 30 40 50 100 150
Cartography by C. Boyle 2025

PLATE 2

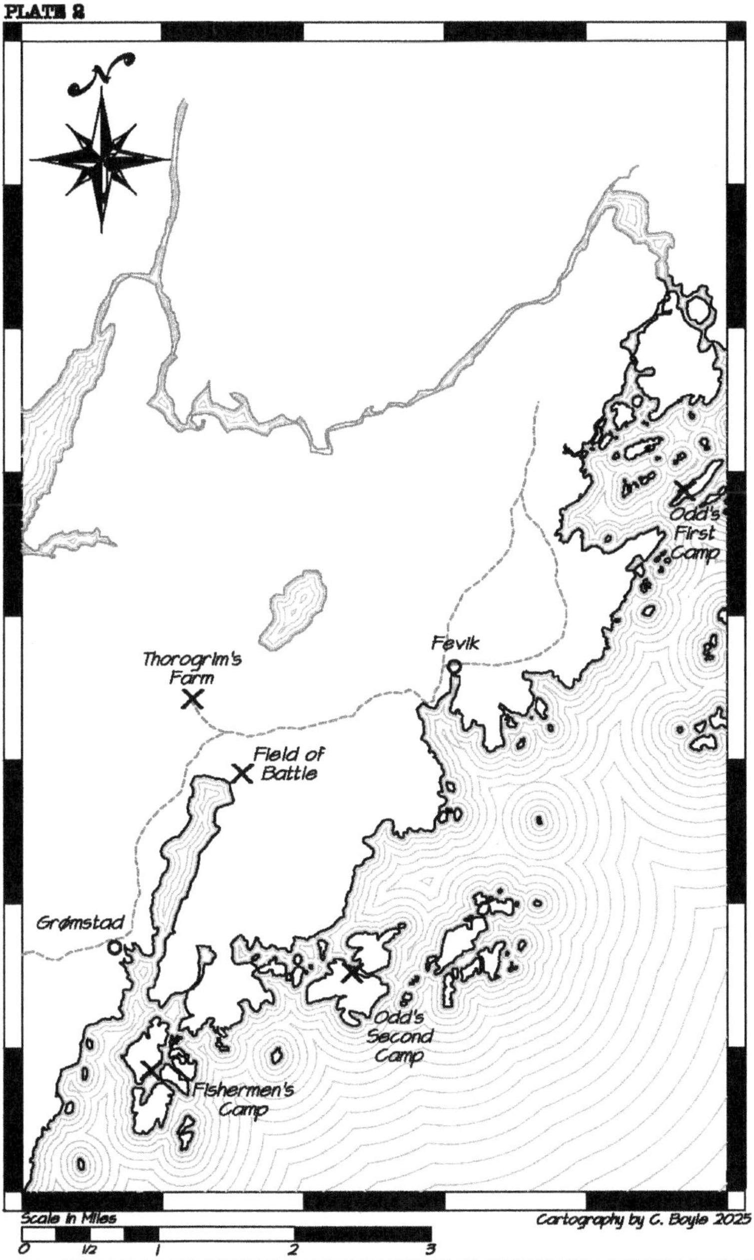

N
Odd's First Camp
Thorogrim's Farm
Fevik
Field of Battle
Grømstad
Odd's Second Camp
Fishermen's Camp
Scale in Miles
0 1/2 1 2 3
Cartography by C. Boyle 2025

The Viking Longship

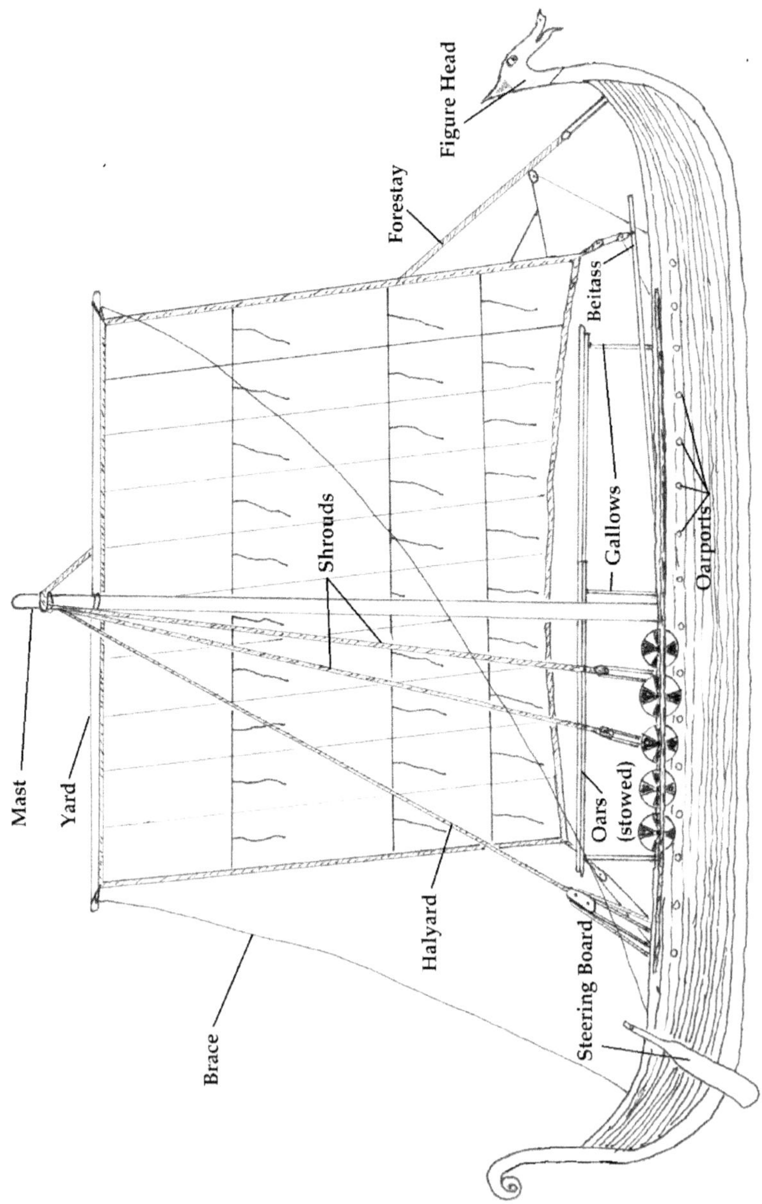

For terminology, see Glossary, page 432

Prologue

The Saga of Thorgrim Night Wolf

There was a man named Thorgrim Ulfsson who had two sons named Odd and Harald, and a daughter called Hild. Thorgrim was a wealthy man, having won riches in his younger days, raiding with a jarl named Ornolf the Restless, who was the father of Thorgrim's wife, Hallbera. After Thorgrim gave up raiding and married Hallbera, his farm prospered and Thorgrim grew more wealthy still, because he was hard-working and clever.

Now, Thorgrim came to be well-liked and respected by his neighbors, and his fame grew in East Agder, in the country of Norway, where he lived. Men often came to Thorgrim seeking his council, and Thorgrim was pleased to help as he could. However, on certain days, as the sun went down, Thorgrim's mood would turn dark, and he would shun the company of others, and men learned to stay clear of him then. It was rumored that when this happened, Thorgrim would take on the form of a wolf and prowl the countryside, and for that reason he came to be known as Keldulf, which means Night Wolf.

Thorgrim's farm and his herds continued to thrive, and his children grew strong and able, and Thorgrim took much satisfaction from this. Some years after Hild's birth, Thorgrim's wife Hallbera gave birth to another daughter, but Hallbera lost her life while bearing the child. With his wife's death, Thorgrim no longer found any joy in his life in Norway, so when his father-in-law, Ornolf, proposed they go a'viking once again, Thorgrim agreed. At this time his eldest son, Odd, was married with a family and a farm of his own in a village called Fevik, so Thorgrim did not bring him along. His younger son, Harald, known as Broadarm, was then fifteen years of age and still at home, so he accompanied his father on the raiding voyage.

Ornolf's ship was called *Red Dragon*, and in her the raiders sailed to Ireland, where it was their intention to win what plunder they could and return to their homes as the season for seafaring came to an end. But in that land they encountered many troubles and hardships. Ornolf was killed in battle, a good death which was pleasing to the gods, and so Thorgrim then took command.

Soon, other men and ships joined with him, and for some time they continued to raid in Ireland, until a great storm came and drove their ships, which now numbered five, to Angle-land. There they continued to find much fighting and plunder, but despite that, Thorgrim wanted only to return to his farm at East Agder and leave raiding and seafaring behind.

Now, at that time, there was a king in East Agder named Halfdan Gudrødson, who, because he had hair that was black in color, was known as Halfdan the Black. Like many kings, Halfdan was ambitious and wished for nothing more than to increase his wealth, power, and land-holdings. Since Thorgrim had been off raiding for several years, and no word of him had reached Norway, Halfdan claimed to believe him dead. He also claimed that taxes were owned, and said that he would take Thorgrim's farm in payment.

Thorgrim's son Odd, who had watched over the farm in his father's absence, knew that this was not true. He went to Halfdan and told him as much, but Halfdan wanted Thorgrim's farm for his own, so he sent Odd away. Odd then gathered all of the freemen who lived nearby and told them what had happened. They all saw what trouble might arise if Halfdan was allowed to take men's land from them, so they went to war with Halfdan, that they might stop him.

At first the gods showed much favor to Odd and his fellows, and they won several victories, but at last they found themselves trapped by Halfdan's army, so Odd gave himself up as prisoner so that the others might escape. Odd remained Halfdan's prisoner for some time, and was treated with great cruelty, until at last he was able to escape. Halfdan sent many warriors, under the command of a man named Skorri Thorbrandsson, to hunt him down, but through luck and cunning Odd kept clear of Skorri's grasp. Skorri finally trapped Odd at the farm of Ragi Oleifsson, but once again, and thanks to Ragi's cunning, they were able to escape in Ragi's ship. The captain of Ragi's ship was Bragi Shipslayer, who said he was the greatest ship's master who ever lived, but had wrecked many ships, which was why he was called Shipslayer.

While this was happening, Thorgrim and the others managed to cross the narrow seas to Frankia, where they fought to defend a man named Louis de Roumois, who was a Frank but had joined in with the Northmen on many raids. Now, rich with plunder and still meaning to return to his farm in Norway Thorgrim sailed to Frisia with his fleet of ships. In Frisia he met a man who had come from Norway, and who told Thorgrim of all the troubles his son Odd had suffered at the hands of Halfdan the Black. This made Thorgrim very eager indeed to return home and come to Odd's aid, who was said to be in great danger.

This is what happened.

Chapter One

The Sun grows dark, Earth sinks into the sea,
The bright stars fall from the skys.

The Poetic Edda

The sun had not quite crested the hills to the east, but there was light enough for Odd to see the water of the long, narrow bay, the ship's mast towering overhead, the yard with its furled sail resting on the gallows, and the two lines of men pulling at the oars with an easy rhythm. The western shore was well-lit now, while the eastern was still lost in shadow. Behind him, standing at the tiller, Bragi Shipslayer was singing softly to himself. Bragi seemed to hate quiet, and if there was no sound to fill it, he would provide it himself.

"There, do you see?" Bragi said, apparently to the company in general. "I took the ship right down the bay in full dark, and still our course is straight and true. I only wish the gods had held off the sunrise a bit longer. Then I'd show you lot how I could sail clean through these islands in the dark as well. Maybe I'll blindfold myself."

Odd made a face somewhere between a smile and a grimace. Just the night before — and it seemed incredible that it was just the night before — King Halfdan the Black's man, Skorri Thorbrandsson had burned them out of Ragi Oleifsson's hall, where Odd and his wife Signy, and Amundi Thorsteinsson and his wife Alfdis, and Bragi Shipslayer and his men Huginn and Muninn had been seeking refuge.

Skorri had set the hall on fire, but Ragi, anticipating such a thing, and stealing an idea from Odd, had dug a tunnel from the hall to a path down a hillside by the bay. Once clear of the burning building, they and Ragi's men had escaped in Ragi's somewhat derelict ship. They were bound to Fevik, Odd's home, where he hoped to rally men to his banner. But first they had to get there, which was no sure thing with the ship sinking under them.

"Well done, Bragi," Amundi said. "You yourself are a god where ship handling is concerned." Amundi knew, as they all did, that Bragi would not stop until he had received some sort of acknowledgement, and likely not even after that.

"I'm glad you recognize that, Amundi," Bragi said. "It's certain that the gods do, or they would have struck me down long ago. But it's possible that Halfdan the Black does not love me so, and he might not be so kind if he catches me. Or any of us. So we had best make this old girl trot."

Their foremost goal just then was to keep free of Halfdan and his men. Unfortunately, in sailing clear of the bay, they had no choice but to sail close by Halfdan's great hall at Grømstad. They would not be seen from the hall itself, which was set back from the sea, but they had to assume that Halfdan had ships keeping watch over the watery approaches.

"Huginn! Muninn!" Bragi called, and the two sailors who had been bailing amidships dropped their buckets with evident relief and came walking aft.

"I need you to look over the rig," Bragi said. "Shrouds, forestay, mast. Yard and sail as well. Let me know if we can even hope to set the sail on this sorry tub. Which is, as I said, a fine ship," he added, smiling at Ragi.

Huginn and Muninn nodded and headed forward. Huginn — Odd thought it was Huginn — hopped up on the larboard rail, one hand on the forward shroud, and peered close at the rope, picking at it with his fingernail and tugging it back and forth. Muninn pulled his knife from its sheath and began poking at the mast here and there, and then, apparently satisfied, climbed up onto the starboard rail and began inspecting the shrouds as Huginn was doing.

"Not much sea room for sailing, is there?" Odd asked.

"You let me worry about that, Odd Sheep-herder," Bragi said. "That is, if those two yanking on those shrouds doesn't bring this whole rig down around our heads."

Odd looked forward again. Huginn and Muninn had begun to climb aloft, legs wrapped around the thick, tarred shrouds, arms pulling them slowly up as they poked and tugged. Once they had reached the place where the shrouds were looped around the head of the mast they once again pulled their knives and started poking at the wood.

"Tell them not to poke too hard," Ragi said. "They might stick their knives clean through."

Odd pulled his eyes from the two men at the top of the mast and looked outboard. The shorelines to east and west were closing as the ship stood into the narrow stretch of water at the head of the bay. He searched the shores for any sign of activity, any riders watching the straits. He looked for fishermen or lumbering knarrs moving on the water. But there was nothing. It was daybreak and they were alone.

Forward, over the starboard side, the headland slipped past and the water opened up again into the harbor that fronted Halfdan's home. Odd pressed his lips together and felt his stomach tighten. The last time he had seen that place he had been in command of a small fleet of ships, an army of warriors. They had slipped in from the sea while Halfdan was away, hunting for them. They had anchored in that harbor and marched ashore.

It had all gone just as Odd planned it, at least initially. They had captured Halfdan's seat of power — his hall, his men, his servants, his wife and child, without a drop of blood spilled. The move was meant to force Halfdan to negotiate, to see reason. But Halfdan managed to capture Odd's young sister and promised to let her, and the men who had accompanied Odd, go free if Odd alone would give himself up. Which he did.

And now here he was again: not bringing the fight to Halfdan, but hoping to slink past.

He realized he was scowling. He forced his face to relax, but he couldn't untie the twisted knot of emotions in his head.

"Bragi!" Huginn called down from where he clung to the shrouds twenty-five feet above the deck. "Looks to be a ship of some sort up the harbor!"

"'Course there's a ship up the harbor, you wool-gathering fool!" Bragi called back. "That's what harbors are for."

"Couple of ships, in fact," Muninn replied. "But just the one's got men on it, and getting underway."

Bragi sighed, and all eyes turned toward the head of the harbor. The sun was just starting to peek over the hills to the east, but the harbor was still mostly lost in shadow and it was hard to make anything out from the deck.

"Getting underway, you said?" Bragi called back.

"Seem to be," Muninn called down. "Hard to see. Seems to be a bunch of the fools falling over themselves, getting oars out and such."

"Someone saw us from the shore…sent word," Ragi said. "Halfdan has eyes everywhere, and he certainly doesn't care to have ships that he doesn't know passing by his great hall. Odd, I think you made him nervous that way."

"I wish he had as much reason to be nervous as we do," Amundi said.

"Hey, you birds up aloft!" Bragi called to the men at the masthead. "Fly on down to deck, will you?"

Huginn and Muninn, their legs still wrapped around the shrouds, slid down in a controlled plummet, hitting the rails at the same moment and hopping down to the deck. They came ambling aft, and Odd was happy to see they were not splashing through ankle-deep water. The bailing, it seemed, had done some good.

"Well, what say you?" Bragi asked. "Will this rig stand up to a sail?"

The two sailors both looked dubious, their expressions nearly identical. "Might do," Huginn said. "The shrouds are old and stretched out, but they're not rotten."

"I wouldn't warrant it for a real blow," Muninn added. "But for the wind we'll get this morning, it might hold up. Or not."

"Thank you, that's very helpful," Bragi said. "But either way we best try. That ship, it's like to be Halfdan's, and it would be much better for our health if they didn't catch us. Go get the sail set, and any of these sorry farmers who are standing idle, get them to help."

The two sailors turned and headed forward. Muninn began to untie the gaskets that bound the sail to the lowered yard. Huginn rallied some of the men who were not pulling oars to do the same, then he began laying the halyard out for hauling.

"Not much wind, Bragi," Ragi said. "Not sure there's even enough to drive this sorry washtub."

Bragi turned his head slowly and regarded Ragi with a look of pity, touched with disgust. Odd had come to understand that look. It was one reserved for anyone Bragi considered ignorant about maritime affairs, which was anyone but him.

"Fear not," Bragi said. "I will conjure up the wind. I have the magic for such things."

It was not long before the sun had come free of the hills, rising at its dignified pace and spreading its light over the land and the water. They could see Halfdan's ship now as they rowed past the mouth of the harbor. It was not more than half a mile astern, and it was underway — even from the deck they could see that — the oars rising and falling, the bow aimed directly at them.

"Here, clap onto that halyard, there," Huginn called, and the men around him arranged themselves down the centerline of the ship, the thick rope held loose in their hands.

"Haul away!" Huginn called, and the men pulled, leaning into it, and the rope stretched and creaked and popped and the yard began to rise in jerks from the gallows on which it rested. As it rose, Muninn and a few others swung it around, dipping one end under the shrouds so it hung athwartships, not fore and aft.

"Hold!" Huginn called, holding up a hand, and the men on the halyard paused their heaving. He and Muninn looked back at Bragi.

"Yes, go ahead," Bragi called. "Set that miserable rag and we'll see how long before it tears itself to shreds!"

They continued to haul, and the yard rose and the sail spilled off the yard and a half-dozen men on each side hauled the sheets aft. The sail flogged and snapped and then filled, bellying out to leeward, and Odd realized that the breeze had increased with the rising sun, just as Bragi had suggested it would.

Well, he's no magician, he just got lucky again, Odd thought.

Bragi looked over his shoulder at Halfdan's ship, then out to windward, and then forward past the ship's prow. "We'll brace up sharp, starboard tack! Get that beitass run out and tack the starboard clew down! Come on now, are you all sheep-herders?"

The men forward moved to make that happen, running out the beitass—a heavy pole, twenty feet long—forward out over the starboard side and running the starboard corner of the sail down to it. These men did not earn their keep on the sea, but most of them had gone a'viking for a season or two at least and knew their way around ships. Indeed, there were few men in that country, or women either, who did not understand at least the rudiments of seafaring.

Once the sail was trimmed right, Bragi pushed the tiller away, just a bit, and the ship turned on a more southerly heading. The wind was coming over the starboard side now, and the ship heeled to larboard.

"Run those oars in, we're done with that nonsense!" Bragi called, and the grateful men on the rowing benches ran the oars in and stacked them on the gallows fore and aft.

With the ship heeling to leeward the water that was still aboard, most of it below the deckboards, came cascading down to the low side, creating a pool that rolled back and forth with the movement of the ship. Odd was disappointed to see how much water was still left onboard. That would not help them in their race against Halfdan's ship.

"Very well," Bragi called next. "Now that you men have nothing to do, you can all get to bailing! See, I've made it easy for you!"

The grumbling from the men forward made a soft sound like distant thunder, but they picked up buckets and helmets and whatever else was available and began flinging water over the leeward side. Odd looked aft once more. The men on Halfdan's ship were still rowing, and he could see no effort being made to set the sail. They may have no wind up in the harbor, he figured, or Bragi's move may have taken them by surprise, but either way he could see already that the distance between them was opening up.

The western side of the long bay was an unbroken shoreline as far as they could see, but on the eastern side the land devolved into miles of scattered islands, as if Thor himself had smashed the peninsula with his mighty hammer and left the shattered remnants there.

Bragi aimed the ship toward the eastern side, toward the nearest island, and as directly away from Halfdan's ship as he could. The breeze had built to a tolerable strength and the ship was heeling over and leaving a long wake astern, with the tree-covered heap of land, its granite base low in the water, directly ahead.

The ship drove closer: one hundred feet, fifty feet, the course unwavering, and Odd wondered if Bragi even saw the island under the bow. He fought the urge to say something, sure that he would be greeted by Bragi's scorn if he did. Twenty feet and Odd turned at last, unable to keep his mouth shut, when Bragi pushed the tiller away from him and the ship spun a quarter turn, running on a course parallel to the island.

"Huginn! Muninn! Trim that sail up!" Bragi called, then looked down at Odd, a wide smile on his face, that mischievous look in his eye.

"I hope you didn't shit your leggings, young master!" he shouted. "But the tide's flooding and we'll get less current here!"

Odd ignored him, tried to act as if he had not intended to speak. He looked back astern. They had certainly put some distance between themselves and Halfdan's ship, but he could see the men aboard the distant vessel were hauling their sail up now, the red and white striped cloth spreading as the yard was hoisted.

"Halfdan's men are setting sail," Odd said.

Bragi looked astern as well, then forward again. "Ha! Let them!" he shouted.

"You think you can outrun them?" Ragi asked, his tone amused, curious.

"What, in this tub of yours?" Bragi asked. "Halfdan should kill you just for the way you've treated this ship. You can bet his ship's not a wreck like this. No, I can't outrun them, but by all the gods I can outmaneuver them! Let's see how they play follow-my-leader though these islands!"

Odd shook his head in wonder. Bragi seemed to be genuinely enjoying himself, even with a powerful enemy in their wake, sailing a faster and more seaworthy ship. If he was feigning delight then he was as good an actor as he claimed to be a sailor.

The island swept past on the starboard side, so close Odd could easily have tossed a chunk of bread onto the rocks, but Bragi seemed unconcerned. The tide was low, the high tide line standing out sharp, with the blanched white rocks above, the dark, wet ledge below. Odd could see the current swirling and boiling as the tide came rushing in. Halfdan's ship, following in their wake, would have to cross the bay, and the flood tide would set them north, putting even more distance between them.

They continued running southeast, and Bragi set every man with a container to bailing. Everyone else, and the women as well, were sent to the windward side to keep the ship on as even a keel as possible. They passed the island and stood across the channel that separated it from the next, and the dozens of other islands beyond, humps of tree-topped stone that looked as if they had been scattered randomly over the water for as far they could see.

The red and white sail on Halfdan's ship was set now, bellied out and tacked down. Odd could see the occasional flash of white around her bow as she drove through the blue-green water. But he could also see her sideways motion against the land behind as the flooding tide pushed her north.

"Ah, Ragi, you may be a pretty one with a sword, but the gods of the sea will curse you for what you've done to this ship!" Bragi called.

"I told you, you great, blustering heap of blubber," Ragi said. "I told you she was in no shape to go to sea. I've become a farmer, may the gods help me. My raiding days are over. What need have I of a ship?"

Odd turned and looked forward. The water was over the deck boards now, up to the men's ankles, and swirling fore and aft with the pitching of the ship. The strain that the mast, sail, and rigging were putting on the hull was opening up the seams even wider and letting the water flow in faster than ever.

"Well, she just needs to stay afloat until midday or so," Bragi said.

"And will she?" Amundi asked.

"I have no idea, but I guarantee you we'll find out soon enough."

There was not much more to say, because there were not many options available to them. If they beached the ship on one of the islands to the east then they would be trapped there. If they crossed the bay and went ashore on the mainland then they would be at Halfdan's doorstep. There was nothing that they could do but continue to run, and hope that the ship did not sink under their feet.

Soon they were up with the next island in the chain, another hump of granite sporting low, scraggly brush, an island too small to support actual trees. Again, Bragi, confident in the depth of water, kept so close to the rocks that Odd felt he could lean over the side and touch them.

He looked out past the bow. He could see boats underway, fishing boats with their single sails set, making their way to the fishing grounds, or stopped in the water, casting or hauling nets. They seemed oblivious to the race for life and death going on in front of them. If they noticed at all, they seemed not to care. It was not their concern.

Odd knew those waters, at least a bit, knew them from the time he had led the fleet to Halfdan's hall. He knew that the archipelago they were passing to starboard ran for three or four miles down to the sea, and they would have to get through that chain of islands and then turn north and east to get to Fevik. But he knew as well that there were several ways through the islands, passages that would make the distance considerably shorter, but which were potentially hazardous, with tricky currents and hidden rocks and shoals. He wondered what route Bragi had in mind. He wondered what Bragi would say if he dared to ask.

Happily, he did not have to find out.

"We'll leave this next island to starboard," Bragi said, addressing anyone within earshot, "and then once we're past it you'll see a channel through. Not straight through, mind, but close enough. There's a fishing camp on one of the islands, I think, or at least some of these mangy dogs congregate there. Anyway, we shoot right past and into the open water beyond, and next thing we know young Odd Sheep-herder is buying us ale in Fevik!"

This was met with murmurs of approval. Odd leaned over the side and looked astern. Halfdan's ship had crossed the bay and was hugging the island, driving hard in their wake, half a mile astern. Closer than they had been. Noticeably closer.

"Fear not," Bragi said, seeing where Odd was looking. "Those sheep-biters, they won't dare follow us through the channel."

"I'm sure they won't," Odd said, though he was sure of no such thing, and he knew that Bragi wasn't either. It was easy enough to follow a ship into dangerous waters: if there were any hazards, the ship in the lead would find them first. The ship following had only to stay in their wake. Their best hope was that Halfdan's ship would give up the chase, that Halfdan had given orders that they not stray too far from their home port.

With a word from Huginn, the men who were not bailing trudged from windward to leeward and relieved those who were. The water, still ankle-deep, was coming in through the many open seams in the ship's bottom faster than they could scoop it over the rail.

"Once we turn and we bring the wind astern, it'll put a lot less strain on the hull, do you see?" Bragi said. "That leaking will stop quick as can be."

"You're a very hopeful fellow, aren't you?" Ragi said.

"I most certainly am," Bragi agreed. "It keeps me youthful."

The land on their starboard side slipped by and the quarter mile wide passage between that island and the next opened up, just as Bragi had said it would. The passage was bordered by a phalanx of smaller islands, but they could see directly through to the open water beyond, a mile away. In the channels between the islands, a dozen or more fishing boats were casting nets or rowing from one spot to another.

"Here we go!" Bragi called. "Huginn! Muninn! Look lively on those sheets and braces!" Bragi pushed the tiller away from him and the ship turned to larboard. Overhead the big yard swung around until it was nearly perpendicular to the centerline of the ship, and men on either side hauled away on the sheets, tugging the corners of the sail down.

With the wind now coming over their stern the ship stood more upright and the breeze seemed to die away, but the sail continued to fill and drive them ahead. They sailed into the wide channel running between the islands, and a moment later Halfdan's ship was lost from sight.

"These fishermen," Odd said, nodding toward the small fleet of boats, "are they from Grømstad?"

"No, not most of them," Bragi said. "Most live on these islands. They're a bunch of pirates, to tell the truth. Decent folk won't have them around."

"They sound like your sort of men, Bragi," Ragi said.

"Naw, too savage, even for me," Bragi said. "They hate everyone. But mostly they hate kings and laws and taxes and any of that sort of horseshit, which is why they hate Halfdan most of all. So I suppose they aren't all bad."

They sailed steadily past the islands, larboard and starboard, and past the fishermen working their gear. The boats from which they cast their nets were those substantial vessels known as faerings; double-ended, clinker-built, twenty or thirty feet long and each manned by half a dozen hard-looking men. Some of the fishermen glanced up as the longship moved silently by and offered no reaction beyond that, though most did not even bother to look.

"Now, here's Halfdan's ship, still right in our wake," Amundi said, looking aft. Halfdan's ship had come around the island and was standing into the passage, her sail bracing square with the change of course. She was a fast ship, apparently, and well-handled, and she had made up a shocking amount of distance very quickly.

"Well, they can bite my arse," Ragi said. "But it looks like we might have a fight on our hands."

"If it comes to a fight, we'll beat them into a porridge," Bragi said, "but they haven't caught us yet. Just watch what I do here!"

He pulled the tiller toward him, just a bit, and the ship's bow swung to starboard, running in closer to the scattered islands to the south. Odd could see the water swirling around the granite shores as the flood tide set up eddies and currents around the various brush-capped domes of rock.

He looked astern once more. Whoever was commanding Halfdan's ship did not seem in the least intimidated by the rocky passage or Bragi's latest change of course. They were still right behind, still making all the speed they could, which was clearly a lot more than Ragi's ship could make, with its foul bottom and hull half-full of water.

"Listen here," Odd said, loud enough to be heard down the length of the ship. Once everyone was looking his way he continued. "We'll leave off bailing and arm ourselves for a fight. Go ahead, now." It was not a request or a suggestion. He was done listening to Bragi's nonsense about out-sailing Halfdan's ship. Time to prepare for the inevitable.

"Do as you will, Lord Odd," Bragi said, "but I tell you…"

Whatever it was that Bragi meant to tell them they never found out, because in that instant their ship ran hard up onto a submerged granite ledge. The bow seemed to rear like a frightened horse and the air was filled with the horrible sounds of scraping and rending and cracking wood. The oars, stacked on the gallows, were pitched forward like so many massive spears, falling and tumbling on either side. The shrouds that held the mast vertical snapped like threads and the massive spar cracked five feet up from the deck, teetered, then came down on the starboard bow, crushing the uppermost strakes under its weight.

Odd was flung forward and he stumbled and tried to keep his footing, but failed. He went down, hands first, and was met by a great surging wave as the water filling the bilge came rushing aft. He spluttered and spit and pushed himself back up to his knees and then onto his feet.

The rest of the men and women aboard had been similarly thrown to the deck or knocked against the sides of the ship. Some were standing again, some heaving themselves up, some pulling the scattered oars off their fellows. Others were still sprawled in the bottom of the boat.

The bow of the ship was pointed up at an unnatural angle, but then it began slowly dropping, like someone easing themselves into bed. For a moment Odd thought the ship was slipping back into the sea, which would be a very bad thing, given that the bottom was clearly stove in. But then he saw that he was wrong. The ship was not sliding; the keel and the strakes were splitting as the vessel broke in two, the forward end falling and draping itself over the ledge on which it had run.

"Ha!" Bragi called, and Odd turned to see the burly man pushing himself back onto his feet after having been flung clean off the small deck aft. "Huginn, what's that?"

Huginn was at the base of the mast, untangling himself from the twisted ropes that had torn free. "Reckon that's nine, now!" he called.

"Nine! Well, let's see any son of a bitch beat that!" It took Odd a moment, but he realized that Bragi must be referring to the number of ships he had wrecked. Bragi Shipslayer. He sounded positively delighted.

Chapter Two

King Sigtryg, son of King Eystein...came out with his army against King Halfdan, and there was great battle, in which King Halfdan was victorious...

Halfdan the Black's Saga
Heimskringla

King Halfdan Gudrødson's great hall at Grømstad was a massive affair, an earth-and-board longhouse more than three hundred feet in length, with a great arched roof made of cut shingles. It stood near the center of some twenty acres of grounds — grass kept neatly trimmed by the grazing cattle, crisscrossed with packed earth roads and paths, all of it encircled by a wall twenty feet high, made of built-up earthworks and topped with palisades.

The great hall was the most imposing structure there, but it was certainly not the only one. Smaller buildings were scattered all around the grounds: stables, barns, thralls' quarters, a blacksmith, a bakery, barracks for the warriors who did not rate accommodations in the great hall itself. And of course a prison, because a man like Halfdan had enemies, and they needed to be kept under lock and key until more permanent arrangements could be made.

The prison was smaller than most of the outbuildings, but substantial, heavy-built of split logs and a roof of thick boards. The windowless interior consisted of one large common room, for those who posed a minor threat, and several smaller cells, for the ones who warranted special attention. It was on the floor of one of those smaller cells that Skorri Thorbrandsson sat, back against the wall, staring into the dark. There was nothing else to see, only dark.

When the sun was low in the west, he had discovered, a small sliver of light would come in through a chink in the wall near the edge of the roof. But there was no light now, so Skorri guessed it was nighttime. Or early morning. He did not know.

His ears could tell him nothing. The walls were too thick, the building too far removed from the rest of the compound, for him to hear any activity. The only sound, other than the scratching of the mice, was the muted talk of the few men currently held in the common room. But he had not heard from them in some time, so either they were asleep or no longer there. He did not know.

Skorri was not entirely sure how long he had been in the cell. Not long. A day, maybe. He had been given food twice, but that did not tell him much. Nor was he entirely sure as to why he was in the cell. The last words he had had with Halfdan gave him reason to believe he still enjoyed the king's favor. Perhaps even more than he had before.

He heard Halfdan's promise again and again in his mind, even spoke it out loud a few times: *You'll lead five hundred warriors to Fevik. You'll find Odd and any who are rallying to his banner. And you'll crush them like the vermin they are.* There was nothing else to think about.

The traitorous band he had once considered his men, Kolbein and that lot, had betrayed him in a surprise assault, dragged him bound to Halfdan's hall. Told the king lies about how he, Skorri, had turned against Halfdan, had gone rogue, gone off on his own.

It was not true, any of it. Everything Skorri had done, his single-minded effort to run Odd Thorgrimson to ground, he had done in service to Halfdan. And Halfdan had seen the truth of that. He had ordered his man to cut Skorri's bound wrists free, ordered Skorri, who had been kneeling before him, to stand. Halfdan was a wise man, and recognized loyalty when he saw it.

For that reason, Skorri did not understand why he was now in the prison. He had been willing to lay his head on the chopping block. He had expected Halfdan to take his life then and there, and was quite prepared to give it up for his king. Instead, Halfdan had offered to give him ships and men, to send him back out to finish the task of finding Odd, bringing him in, and crushing once and for all the intolerable embers of rebellion.

Skorri had felt a superhuman sense of relief when Halfdan spoke those words…*You'll lead five hundred warriors to Fevik.* He felt the way it must feel to have the Valkyrie lift you off the field of battle and up to the feast hall of Valhalla.

And just as Skorri was ready to belt on his sword and start laying out his plans for surrounding Fevik, where Odd and his band had surely gone, Halfdan ordered him locked in that black hole.

Halfdan is a just man…he appreciates my loyalty…means to reward me for it…. Those words, too, had been echoing around Skorri's head.

He heard something at last, a sharp sound, and knew it was the creak of the door to the prison's common room swinging open. He looked up, though he still could see nothing, and cocked his ear. He heard the door close again and heard the voices of the men on the other side, his fellow prisoners. He heard a louder voice, speaking in reply.

"Shut your mouths, or by the gods I'll shut them for you."

Skorri could see a narrow strip of light along the bottom edge of the door to his cell. Whoever had come in was holding a candle or a lantern or some such thing. And just as Skorri was starting to wonder if the newcomer was coming for him, he heard the key in the lock on his cell, and a moment later the door swung open.

Who it was standing there, Skorri could not tell. The light from the lantern in the visitor's hand, with its one candle burning, was blinding after so long in the lightless room. The flame, and the vague, dark outline of a man behind it, were all that Skorri could see.

"Skorri Thorbrandsson," the dark shape spoke, the voice deep and distinct.

"Thorgeir Sveinsson," Skorri said. He did not bother to stand.

The man moved a few steps closer and Skorri's eyes adjusted and he could make out Thorgeir's neat-trimmed beard, the light reflecting dully off his mail shirt.

"First, let me thank you for your treason," Thorgeir said. "I'm overseer now of the king's holdings, in your stead. His most trusted man. And look at you."

"*Most trusted man…*" Skorri repeated, with disdain. "I became overseer through brave deeds and loyalty. You became overseer by being the finest lickspittle in the land. There's the difference."

Thorgeir had been subordinate to Skorri once, charged with overseeing East Agder, when Skorri was the king's *sæslumadr,* the overseer of much of Halfdan's holdings. But when it came to kissing the king's hindquarters, no one, in Skorri's opinion, was subordinate to Thorgeir. And he had been rewarded well for that, it seemed.

"Stand up, Skorri," Thorgeir said.

Skorri briefly considered remaining where he was, demonstrating his lack of respect for Thorgeir, but he could see no advantage in doing so. He pushed himself to his feet, his joints and muscles aching from his prolonged sitting, from the beating he had taken from his men, and from his fall down the cliff in hunting Odd. The past week had been brutal for Skorri, the months before nearly as bad.

"King Halfdan said I was to have ships and warriors," Skorri said. "He said I was to keep hunting Odd. I'm not out of his favor, so I suggest you don't act like you're heir to Halfdan's throne."

Skorri had never liked Thorgeir, and he had always made that plain. And Thorgeir had made plain his dislike of Skorri, to the extent that he could, given Skorri's status. Now Thorgeir was very much enjoying this new situation, and it only added to Skorri's confusion. It was all very unsettling.

"Ah, yes, King Halfdan's promise..." Thorgeir said. "Of course he'll make good on it. Halfdan's a man of his word. Not like some lowborn worm such as you. But here's the thing of it. Even if Halfdan thinks you didn't betray him, the other jarls and the king's chief warriors still think you did. And for Halfdan to simply forgive such a betrayal might be seen as weakness."

"Is that so? And who, pray, put that idea into his head?"

"Are you saying that Halfdan is so easily led by the nose? That he's weak-minded?" Thorgeir asked, in something like a shocked tone.

"I'm saying only that...a day ago? Two? Halfdan was quite ready to send me to Fevik. And now it seems it will not be so simple. So I wonder who has been talking to him."

"Many men speak to the king, and he gives all his ear. So, Halfdan has decided you may have the men and ships that were promised, but only after you've received the proper punishment, and shown the proper deference."

Skorri pressed his lips together. He remained silent, because he did not know what to say. For one brief moment he had believed that all would be forgiven, that Halfdan had seen through the lies and seen him for the loyal servant and warrior that he was. But now he could see that the gods would not allow things to be that easy.

"Very well," Skorri said, sounding as unconcerned as he could, hoping to deprive Thorgeir of any satisfaction in this moment. "I'm loyal to King Halfdan and always have been. I'll be honored to do as I'm asked."

"Good. You may start by putting this on." Thorgeir tossed a heap of cloth at Skorri's feet. Skorri bent over and retrieved it, glad for the dark that partially hid how awkwardly he moved. He lifted it up and let it fall open. It was a crude, rough-spun wool tunic, a shapeless, knee-length garment with straight sleeves. A thrall's garment. A mark of humiliation.

Skorri scowled at the thing. He had never worn its like. And while the tunic and leggings he was wearing were torn and filthy, and his fine cloak was long gone, they had once been of the highest quality, clothes that carried some dignity. Not like this thing Thorgeir had given him. But clearly that was the point.

Still, Skorri would not give Thorgeir the satisfaction of protesting. Nor would he disobey King Halfdan. He would suffer whatever Halfdan required of him, as he had already suffered much, and at the other end of whatever was coming would be the reward that Halfdan had promised: the men and ships and the chance to crush Odd Thorgrimson at long last.

With some difficulty he pulled his tunic up over his head, and his shirt after that, then untied his leggings and let them fall. He managed to find the bottom of the thrall's garment Thorgeir had given him and shuffled into it. He could all but hear Thorgeir smirking as he held the lantern high and watched.

The rough cloth chafed against the various half-healed abrasions on Skorri's flesh, causing considerable pain, but Skorri gave no reaction as he settled the tunic in place. "Very well," he said. "Let's get on with it."

Thorgeir led the way out of the cell and past the few men in the common room who watched them with blank looks. He opened the door and Skorri could see that it was full daylight, sometime past *dagmál*, the time of the day's first meal. Half a dozen warriors stood waiting outside, spears held upright. An escort, apparently. Skorri did not think they were meant as an honor.

"Go," Thorgeir said. Skorri stepped through the door and Thorgeir locked it once again. "Follow me."

They headed off in the direction of the great hall, Thorgeir at the head of the band, Skorri following behind. Behind him he could hear the footfalls and rattle of weapons of the six warriors who marched in their wake.

There was already a bustle of activity around the grounds of Halfdan's royal compound. Bands of warriors were training with sword, spear, axe, and shield. Herders were driving small clusters of cattle here and there. From the smith's lean-to came the steady rhythm of iron pounding iron. Skorri noted it all as he walked, but mostly his eyes were trained on Halfdan's great hall, his thoughts on what awaited him there.

Two guards flanked the main entrance to the great hall, and they pulled the doors open as Thorgeir approached. He entered without breaking stride, Skorri behind him, the six guards bringing up the rear. The entrance was wide enough for them to remain in their two columns as they stepped through.

Thorgeir skirted past the benches and long fire pits that ran down the center of the great hall and stopped a third of the way down. At the far end of the hall stood Halfdan's massive oak throne, flanked by elaborately carved benches: seating for Halfdan's chief warriors and jarls when they were attending an audience with the king.

Halfdan was sitting on the throne now, and Skorri could see that he was wearing the thin gold crown that he wore on certain occasions. The sight of it made Skorri's stomach twist a bit, but he was not sure why. It seemed like a sign of danger.

Worse than the crown were the forty or so men between Skorri and the throne. Skorri recognized most of them: the chief warriors in Halfdan's *hird,* officials like Thorgeir who helped administer the kingdom, a few local jarls. They were seated on the benches on the sides of the great hall, but they stood as Thorgeir approached. Thorgeir, in turn, stepped aside, took Skorri by the arm, and pulled him forward.

The great hall was silent for a moment, the only sounds the rustling of cloaks and the crackle of the various fires burning in the pits. Then Halfdan stood, took a step forward, and spoke in a voice that filled the space.

"Skorri Thorbrandsson, you have been accused by many of treason to the crown, of fleeing from the duty you owed to your king, to whom you swore an oath. Now, I am a forgiving man, and a just one. I'm willing to allow you back into my good graces, but not before you have demonstrated, to me and to the company assembled here, your loyalty and your devotion to the crown. Is that understood?"

Skorri pressed his lips together. He wanted nothing more than to shout out that he had never been anything but loyal to his king, to say, once again, that everything he had done he had done for the benefit of Halfdan. But such protests, he knew, would not be heeded and they would not be appreciated.

"Yes, my lord," Skorri said.

"Good," Halfdan said. "You will come forward, then and beg my forgiveness. You will come forward on hands and knees, and you will make your way through the gauntlet of these good and loyal men. Do you understand, Skorri Thorbrandsson?"

Skorri glanced at the grim expressions of the men facing him in two long lines. He looked down the length of them to where Halfdan stood, his hand resting on the pommel of his sword, the crown glinting in the light of nearby flames.

"Yes, my lord. I gladly accept," he said.

The words had hardly left his mouth when he felt hands on his shoulders — Thorgeir's hands, no doubt — pushing him down to his knees. He came down hard on the wood-plank floor. The wound on his leg from the slide down the hillside fighting Odd, and the dozen other recent injuries he had suffered, were like so many knifepoints stabbing into him, but he made no sound.

Thorgeir's hands were on his back now, pushing him forward, and he came down on his palms and felt fresh stabs of pain. Then Thorgeir kicked him hard in the backside and said, "Go!" and Skorri could hear the delight in the man's voice as he started crawling forward.

The pain in Skorri's leg seemed to move in waves through his whole body, the rough cloth of his tunic tore at his various lacerations, his arms threatened to collapse under him from his injured muscles, but he crawled on. He clenched his teeth, tried to push the pain aside. His mind was so concentrated on that effort that he did not even realize he had reached the first of the men. Not until that man's foot came up under him and kicked him hard in the stomach.

Skorri felt the breath knocked out of him, felt the pain shooting through his gut and his chest and his arms. He fell on his side, gasping for air. He heard Thorgeir shouting, "Up! Move! Move, you coward!"

More shoes were kicking at him, at his back and his stomach and his chest. He could feel the agonizing blows from the flats of swords and he pressed his lips together hard to keep from screaming. He had the half-formed thought that there was still a dozen yards to crawl before he reached Halfdan, and that he could not possibly make it that distance. That he wanted to just lay where he was and let death come. But he also understood that doing so would somehow be worse.

He pushed himself over, forced himself back onto hands and knees. He was vaguely aware that men were shouting on either side of him, that Thorgeir was shouting behind him and kicking him in the rear, that others were kicking him in the legs and stomach, and the swords were raining down blows on his back.

He crawled, three steps, four steps. A leather shoe came up under his chin and kicked him hard. His teeth snapped together and he tasted blood, a lot of blood, in his mouth. His left arm collapsed and he went down and remained that way, face pressed to the floor planks, while the kicks and blows washed over him like a breaking wave.

"Go, you coward!" Thorgeir shouted again. And again, Skorri pushed himself up, and despite his certainty that he could not advance one more step, he continued on. He could no longer feel individual blows; it was an ocean of pain and he was immersed in it, and the shouting and the thump of shoes and swords and clubs on his body formed one big and amorphous cloud of noise.

He kept crawling, and the blows knocked him to his side and drove his face into the worn wooden boards again and again, and again and again he pushed himself up and forced himself on. His eyes were fixed on the ground directly in front of him, the feet and legs of the men on either side just a blur, barely visible, as his entire world was reduced down to each step, and to the extraordinary wracking agony that was his entire body.

He fell again, felt his head spinning, felt a kick in the gut, another in the face. He could feel the blackness coming over him and he was not sure if he was about to pass out or die, and he was not sure it mattered. But then something deep inside screamed at him, the thing that had been screaming at him all his life, that had been driving him on all his life, and he pushed himself to his hands and knees and crawled on.

Then suddenly the blows stopped, and there was something in front of him, but he could barely make it out, as one eye was already swollen shut and the other had blood running into it. He wiped the blood away and realized he was looking at Halfdan's shoes, and the hem of his bold, red tunic, embroidered with gold thread. Skorri stopped crawling then, and stared. He wanted to spit a mouthful of blood on the floor, but he still had presence of mind enough to know that spitting at the king's feet would not end well, so he swallowed and gasped for breath.

How long Skorri remained in that position of supplication, he did not know, but it seemed a very long time. With the pain rippling through him, every moment seemed a very long time. He felt the blackness well up again and again and he fought it off. Everything was spinning as if he was insensibly drunk. He thought he might vomit. Finally, Halfdan spoke.

"Kneel, Skorri Thorbrandsson."

It took Skorri a moment to understand what Halfdan was telling him to do, and another to consider if he was actually capable of doing it. Finally, he began pushing himself up, despite the burning agony that came with every movement. The great hall whirled around him, the pain came in waves. He was certain he would collapse to the floor and never move again. But he did not, and soon he found himself on his knees, looking up at King Halfdan the Black.

"You have proven your loyalty, Skorri Thorbrandsson," Halfdan said, his voice still loud enough to be heard throughout the great hall. "You have once again earned my favor, and I welcome you back into my household. And I will see that your loyalty is rewarded, as I reward all loyalty to my crown."

Skorri nodded. He was not sure if he should speak, or if he even could. He was not sure that he cared anymore about his loyalty to Halfdan, or whether or not he had earned the bastard king's favor.

Chapter Three

They leapt into the cockle-boat, but when they got a little way they found how the coal-blue sea poured into the boat, so they went back to the ship.

Laxdœla Saga

Ragi's ship splintered and groaned as it settled on the ledge on which it had run, now clearly visible two feet below the surface. Odd braced for the ship to slide off into deeper water and just keep going, and he considered what he would do. Grab his wife, certainly, though he knew Signy was a strong swimmer. Grab Amundi's wife as well.

But then the ship stopped moving as it came to a rest on the rocks, its back broken.

"Ha!" Bragi said. "I thought this miserable ledge was a bit farther to the south. Meant to trick Halfdan's ship into running up onto it. I guess the joke's on me!"

"No one's going to hit this ledge now, not with us marking it so well," Ragi said. "And the king's men don't seem any less curious about us." He was pointing with his thumb back over his shoulder. Halfdan's ship had not slowed. They were less than a quarter mile astern now, and coming fast.

"Yes, they're not like to go away, just 'cause this rock has slowed us up some," Bragi admitted. "So, time for the next great amusement! You fellows," he called forward, "you may as well do as Odd said; gather up your swords and spears and what have you."

The words were unnecessary. It was clear to every man aboard that they were going to have a fight on their hands, and very soon. The water was rushing in now through the stove-in planks and the men were splashing around, looking for their spears and axes and swords and what shields they had. The women, too, were gathering up any unclaimed weapons. This would be an all-hands effort.

Odd stepped up onto the raised deck and then onto the top of the rail, one hand on the high, arching sternpost to steady himself, and looked back. The sail on Halfdan's ship was coming down and the oars running out. The master was opting for greater maneuverability, or maybe he was not willing to go barreling through the passage under sail, not after seeing the fate of the ship he was chasing.

Odd turned and looked down into the waist of their wrecked ship and wondered if it would sink before their enemy could even get to them. It was half filled with water now, the men and women standing thigh-deep. But he could see that the water in the waist was level with the sea beyond, meaning the hull was as full as it was going to get. The ship had settled on the ledge and was resting there, and if it did not split completely in two, there it would stay.

The men were ready to fight, armed with swords, axes, and spears in hand, and a few shields here and there, whatever they had brought with them when they escaped from Ragi's hall. Halfdan's men, Odd imagined, would be better equipped than that. They would certainly have helmets and shields and likely leather armor, at least. Judging by the size of the ship, there would be more of them as well.

This is going to be a bloody business… Odd thought. He turned back toward Halfdan's ship and what he saw now surprised him. The fishing boats, which he had imagined would flee from the scene, or at most look on with curiosity, were gathering, and they were closing in on the approaching longship. Ten at least, maybe fifteen of them, all moving under oar, drawing cautiously nearer to the black ship, which was itself moving slowly ahead, driven by its sweeps.

"What by all the gods are they doing?" Odd asked out loud.

"Hoping to sell Halfdan some fish?" Ragi said. Odd was not sure if he was joking or not.

"Those pirates…" Bragi said. "They don't care to have a king's ship in their waters, and they see something ripe for the taking."

"What?" Amundi asked, incredulous. "Do they mean to attack a longship full of armed men?"

"These fellows, they have balls, I'll give them that," Bragi said. "And there's a lot of them. See there…there's more coming."

Sure enough, beyond the longship they could see more of the faerings converging on Halfdan's vessel, coming from between the islands and from where they had been working out in the bay. They looked like nothing so much as a pack of wolves closing in on a wary bear.

"They know this is Halfdan's ship," Bragi continued, "'cause Halfdan's man was dumb enough to fly his banner in these waters."

A long, pointed banner flew at the longship's masthead, a white field with a red border and the black silhouette of a falcon in flight. A banner Odd knew well.

"And like I said," Bragi continued, "there's no one they despise more than someone who styles himself a king."

"Halfdan *is* the king," Ragi said. "Too ambitious for his own good, but still the king."

"Not to these bastards," Bragi said. "They don't recognize anyone ruling over them, save for the gods of the sea."

Fore and aft, the men and women on Ragi's wrecked ship leaned over the sides and watched the gathering conflict a quarter-mile away. Halfdan's longship had been boldly coming on, the oars pulling hard, the water curling around the bow, but now they could see it had slowed as the rhythm of the strokes dropped off. Seven or eight of the fishing boats were clustered directly in its path, and more were coming up from the sides and astern. Each of the boats held half a dozen men, or more. Odd could see some brandishing spears, some axes.

"Will they actually fight Halfdan's men?" Amundi asked. "Are they actually reckless enough to try and take that ship?"

"Who knows?" Bragi said. "These fishermen, they're like wild animals…hard to know how they're going to react."

The oars on Halfdan's ship gave another stroke, then lifted out of the water and stayed there, like a bird drying its wings, and for a moment everything seemed to hang motionless; the ship, the fishing boats, the men and women in the wreck of Ragi's ship, even the sea around them.

And then the longship's starboard bank of oars came down and gave a hard pull and the ship began to spin around to larboard, presenting its long, black side to Odd and the others watching over the rails. Another stroke and the ship continued to turn until it was stern-to, and then both banks of oars came down and pulled together and the ship gathered way, heading back in the direction it had come.

"Ha! Those dogs!" Bragi shouted. "Running with their tails between their legs!"

"I wonder if these lunatic fishermen mean to attack her anyway," Amundi said. Odd was wondering the same thing. He hopped down from the rail and stood beside Ragi on the afterdeck, watching the longship pull away, her speed building with each stroke.

The fishing boats were following in her wake, but they were not pulling with anything like the gusto that Halfdan's men were, not rowing as if they were trying to catch her. They seemed more intent on escorting the longship out of their waters than launching a full-on attack. Ahead of the longship, the boats that had been heading into the fight now moved aside to give the ship room to pass.

"Seems they're happy just to chase them off," Ragi said, and the others nodded.

"They might have beat Halfdan's men if they attacked," Odd said. "Numbers alone might have done it. But it would have been a bloody mess."

"And no doubt Halfdan's men are happy to go back and report how they drove this ship up on a ledge," Amundi said. "But they'll have to fashion some excuse as to why they took no prisoners."

"Halfdan would burn them all at the stake if he knew it was Odd here they let escape," Ragi said.

The longship had put some visible distance between itself and the others by the time the fishermen gave up the chase, their faerings bobbing on the low swell. And then their oars came down and the boats closest to Ragi's ship turned on their keels and began pulling toward the ledge on which they sat.

"Well, Bragi," Ragi said, "you seem to be pretty familiar with these people. Are they coming to rescue us? Rob us? Kill us?"

"Like I said, it's hard to tell what this sort will do," Bragi said. "Like wolves, they move in packs. We'll just have to see who's the leader of the pack, here."

Odd and Amundi and Ragi and his men were already under arms, so there was nothing they could do now but wait and watch in silence as the fleet of fishing boats drew closer. Odd could see why the master of Halfdan's ship had opted to row away. There was something terrible and menacing about the pack's silent approach.

Like wolves, indeed…

Odd rested his hand on Blood-letter's pommel. He considered drawing the weapon, but resisted. No need to pull the sword until he knew he would have some use for it. No need to provoke a fight.

The boats were spreading out as they approached, coming on in the same slow, cautious way they had gone after Halfdan's ship. A dozen of them at least, but one was leading the way, advancing ahead of the others, coming right at the stern section of the wreck where Odd and the lead men stood.

There were more than half a dozen men in the boat: six pulling oars, a few up in the bow, spears in hand, one big man aft on the tiller. The oars moved with a hypnotic rhythm; the men were well-used to the work and their stroke showed the ease of long practice.

Twenty feet off the larboard quarter the oars stopped pulling and the blades dragged in the water and the boat drifted to a stop. For a long moment, the men in the boat and the men and women on the remains of Ragi's ship stared at one another. It was, not surprisingly, Bragi who broke the silence.

"Arnor? Arnor Knattarson?' he shouted. "You dog, is that you? I should have known! Who else would have the balls to go right after a longship of King Halfdan himself?"

Arnor Knattarson, if that was indeed the man in the boat, did not reply at first. He just stood largely motionless, staring back at Bragi and the rest, while his crew all turned and looked as well. Then he bent over, just a bit, and spit into the water.

"Bragi Shipslayer..." he said, his voice like heavy surf on a rocky ledge. "Looks like you did for another one."

"Number nine, I make it," Bragi said.

"Well, I wish you joy of it," Arnor said. "Since it's your last, and all. Going to be hard to sail a ship after I rip your lungs out."

"This fellow doesn't seem much disposed to help you, Bragi," Ragi said.

"Oh, we had a little disagreement, is all," Bragi said. "Nothing we can't work out like civilized folk."

A second boat had pulled up alongside Arnor's, stopping a dozen feet away, and the man at the tiller of that boat called, "Is that Bragi Shipslayer?"

"It is," Arnor said.

"Well, well, look what Njord has cast at our feet!" the second man called. "I'm going to rip that bastard's lungs out, and do it with pleasure."

"Arnor has already laid claim to his lungs," Ragi called. "But his liver is still there for the taking."

Odd frowned as he listened to this exchange, and his mind twisted with indecision. If these fishermen meant to kill Bragi, then Odd felt honor-bound to defend the man, regardless of how justified the fishermen's desire for vengeance might be. Bragi had, after all, come to Odd's aid when he most needed it.

But such a fight would be the death of them all: him and Amundi and their wives, Ragi and his warriors and the men and women of his house. Odd could not ask the others to lay down their lives for a fight that was not theirs.

Bragi spoke again.

"Now, now, no need for any of that! We may have had our differences, but now you'll honor me as a hero, I promise! You see who I have here? Who I saved from Halfdan the Black, who would have certainly killed him? This here is Odd Thorgrimson, son of Thorgrim Night Wolf! Odd, who led the rising against that bastard Halfdan!"

Those words had a strange but obvious effect on the men in the boats. Odd could see their expressions change, could see all eyes turn his way. Arnor said something to his crew, too quiet to hear, and the oars came down once more and the boat approached the ledge on which Ragi's ship rested. It moved silently, save for the creak of the tholes and the water dripping from the blades.

Ten feet from the stern, the faering came to a stop once more, all eyes turned toward Odd. Arnor seemed to be studying him, as if trying to decide if Odd was indeed who Bragi said he was. Then, slowly, he nodded his head.

"I seen you in Fevik," Arnor said, speaking to Odd. "After all that business started. When you were getting men to join you in fighting that bastard who styles himself king. Your beard was shorter then, and you had more meat on you, but I recognize you now."

"I lost some weight," Odd said. "Halfdan saw to that."

"So, you see?" Bragi said. "Odd and I are great friends, ever since I saved him from Halfdan's men on the road to Grefstad. You recall that, Odd, don't you? Halfdan's warriors all around you, and me and Huginn and Muninn, out we come, fists flying?"

Odd smiled. There was nothing else for it. "You're slippery as a herring, Bragi," he said, his voice low. "I can see how you've managed to live as long as you have."

"My luck has been decent enough so far," Bragi said, his voice low as well. He was still smiling, his expression unchanged. "Now, if these bastards don't kill me straight off, or leave us to drown when this ship goes under, then there's a fair chance I can go on living for some time yet."

Chapter Four

Water is required for the one who comes to a meal,
a towel and a warm invitation, a good disposition,
if he can get it, conversation and silence in return.

The Sayings of Hávi
The Poetic Edda

Bragi stood facing Arnor, his smile fixed on his face, his arms gesturing toward Odd as if he had conjured the man up from the spirit world like a wizard. And Odd could not help but smile as well, dire as their situation seemed to be. Then he forced a more serious look on his face and turned back to Arnor.

"Yes, it's true. Bragi stepped up when Halfdan's men would certainly have cut us down. I don't know what quarrel you have with the man, but I would be grateful if you didn't kill him, at least not anytime soon. And gratitude's pretty much all I have to offer just now."

Just as he finished those words, Ragi's ship gave another groan and settled a bit farther. "And if you were to get us off this ship before it goes under," Odd added, "I would certainly thank you for that as well."

Arnor frowned. He and the man at the tiller in the second boat exchanged glances. But they were no longer alone. Other fishing boats, seven or eight of them, were gathering, close enough to take part in the discussion. A man at the tiller of one of the new arrivals called out.

"Look there! Ain't that Bragi Shipslayer?"

"Yes, it is!" Arnor shouted, and now he just sounded annoyed. "But we're not going to kill him. Not yet," he added, which sparked a buzz of protest from the crews of the boats that had just gathered around.

"Shut your mouths, the lot of you, and listen!" Arnor called next and the buzzing dropped away. "This one here," he said, pointing at Odd, "this is Odd Thorgrimson…"

There was a pause, and then the buzzing started in again, a surprised and excited noise that left Odd completely bewildered.

How by all the gods do these bastards know who I am? he wondered. *And why would they possibly care?*

Since making his escape from Halfdan, Odd had thought quite a bit about what he would do next, and what he would do after that, whether he should try to raise the rebellion again, or just leave the country, make a new life elsewhere.

But this fight was no longer his alone. He knew that. Halfdan's ambition and iron rule had only grown worse since the uprising. Freemen like Amundi and Ragi and the others were also ready, eager, even, to stand up to him.

It had never occurred to Odd, however, that folk such as these fishermen might feel they had a dog in this fight, or that the name Odd Thorgrimson would mean anything to them. He had assumed that anyone who did recognize him would drag him to Halfdan's hall in exchange for whatever bounty was being offered.

"That's Odd Thorgrimson?" someone called from one of the boats. "Show yourself!"

Odd stepped up on the rail of the wrecked ship, one hand on the sternpost. He did not look much like a leader of men, he knew, in his tattered sheep-herder's clothing and mud-stained cape, now soaking wet from the wave of bilge water. He did not even look much like the Odd Thorgrimson who had stood up to Halfdan a year before. But he looked out over the men in the boats who were staring up at him and he saw heads nodding. They were apparently satisfied that he was who Arnor said he was.

The men in Arnor's faering gave another pull of the oars and the boat closed the distance, its keel bumping against the ledge as the bow scraped against the stern of Ragi's ship.

"I can take five of you," Arnor said. "Them other boats will come for the rest. Now get aboard before Bragi's latest wreck slides off this rutting ledge."

One by one the fishing boats came alongside the mortal remains of Ragi's ship and loaded their fill of refugees, then pulled away; a long line of boats wending their way through the scattered islands, going where, Odd did not know. He considered asking, but Arnor did not seem the talkative sort. He was as different from Bragi Shipslayer as night to day.

Wherever we're going, I guess we'll find out soon enough, Odd thought. *And it's bound to be better than being dragged to Halfdan's hall, or going down on Ragi's ship.* It was not as if Odd had a lot of choice or say in the matter.

The line of boats, with Arnor's in the lead, made its way through a channel between the two islands to the south. Half a mile along, a small cove opened up on the larger island to the west. Odd could see there was some sort of camp set up there, and its size surprised him. There were a few log-built, thatched-roof houses, and twenty or so tents hung over big A-frames scattered over the open ground. A few boats were pulled up and overturned on the shore, and smoke was rising from various fire pits. A series of wooden frames stood along the shore, covered with fish that had been cleaned, split, and splayed out to dry in the sun. A number of women and a few men were busy at various tasks, but they stopped and looked up as the fishing fleet approached.

Arnor's boat was the first ashore, running up onto the shingle beach with a crunching sound, and the two men in the bow hopped out and pulled it farther up. Then, one by one, the others made their way forward and over the bow, last of all Odd, Signy, and Arnor. Up and down the beach the other boats of the fleet were also coming ashore and likewise offloading crew and survivors of the wreck.

Arnor led Odd and Signy and the others up the short, steep, granite shoreline to the level ground above. "Helga, Isgerd, get some ale and some food for these men," Arnor called. "And these women."

Helga and Isgerd hurried off to obey. Arnor next led Odd and Signy, Ragi, and the others from his boat over to where a series of benches had been arranged around a firepit. He gestured for them to sit, which they did. Bragi, who had huffed up the shore behind them, sat as well. Arnor scowled at him, and seemed ready to tell him to leave, but then apparently changed his mind, and settled himself on a separate bench.

Odd looked around, curious. "Do you over-winter here?" he asked. The tents looked substantial, but he would not care to make one his home when the ice and snow were flying.

"Some do," Arnor said. "Some have homes elsewhere. Fevik. Grømstad. Vik. We'll go there in the winter months."

"I suppose in the decent weather you can fish here and you're left alone," Ragi said. "That must be a good thing."

Arnor grunted, but before he could reply several women came hurrying up with cups of ale which they handed around, and Odd and the others drank, deep and gratefully. More of Ragi's men came up the shore and found places on the benches, as did some of the fishermen, and more cups were passed around.

"We *were* left alone," Arnor said. "Not so much now. Halfdan demands his tribute, and he's been trying to collect. He hasn't had much luck, though, I can tell you."

Ragi laughed. "I'll wager he hasn't!"

"This tribute Halfdan demands, is that because of the uprising?" Odd asked.

"No," Arnor said. "Started before all that. But he's gotten worse. Much worse. Angry, I'd say, 'cause he's being defied. By you and by us. Sends ships down, now and again, try to catch some of us alone. But mostly we're able to drive them off, like we done today."

Odd and the others nodded. The women arrived with wooden bowls filled with what turned out to be fish stew. Odd had no great hopes for the quality of the food, and he did not much care, hungry as he was. But when he ladled some into his mouth he was pleasantly surprised.

As he ate, he looked around at the camp — village, really — hidden from the world beyond, and the men and women who called it home, for the summer months at least. The fisher-folk clearly were not given to putting themselves under any sort of rule. That fact notwithstanding, it was also clear that they looked to Arnor as a chieftain of sorts. Just how much authority that gave him, Odd could not tell.

"Here's the thing," Arnor said at last. "Halfdan knows we're here, and he has no control over us, and it drives him to madness. It won't be long before he sends half a dozen ships, more than we can fight. When your rebellion started, we thought that might be the end of Halfdan. We talked about joining you. Not that these whores' sons here can ever agree on anything. But then it seemed like the fight was over, and we figured it was just a matter of time before Halfdan came for us."

"So why don't you leave?" Amundi asked.

Arnor shrugged. "Where would we go?"

"And who would have you?" Bragi added. Arnor turned his head slowly, gave Bragi a menacing look, but Bragi just grinned.

Arnor turned back to Odd. "What about you? Where have you been all this time?"

"I was Halfdan's prisoner for a while. Taken prisoner after we took his hall at Grømstad."

"He wasn't taken prisoner," Amundi said. "He gave himself up to save the rest of us."

Arnor nodded. "That was the tale I heard. Never knew until now if it was true or not."

Again, Odd was struck by the words. *That was the tale I heard…* It would seem that stories of his doings were passing from mouth to ear, and more people than he would ever have guessed knew of his fight with Halfdan, its cause and the aftermath.

"Halfdan kept me prisoner for a while," Odd continued. "Figured I would serve as an example to the others." He thought of the whipping post set up at farm after farm, the beatings to the edge of death. He felt the fury and humiliation rising in him once again and he pushed them back down.

"Finally Amundi here and some others contrived to set me free," Odd continued. "We've been in hiding pretty much since."

There was more silence, more drinking. "But you're not hiding now?" Arnor said at last.

"No, we're not," Odd said. He wished he could tell the man that this was all part of some cunning plan he had devised, a carefully thought-out strategy, but of course it wasn't. They were just stumbling, it seemed, from one step to another. And Odd was sick of it. Time to regain his footing.

"So, what will you do?" Arnor asked.

"We're going to Fevik," Odd said. "That's my home."

"They'll rally to your banner in Fevik?"

"I don't know," Odd said. "I don't know what's going on in Fevik. But it's time to find out, because I don't mean to hide from Halfdan anymore, and I don't mean to keep running."

Arnor nodded again, but this time the gesture seemed to be one of approval. "So it could be that Halfdan's men are waiting for you at Fevik? Setting a trap, just waiting for you to come home?"

"It's possible," Odd admitted. "There's but one way to find out."

A man named Ref, sitting near Arnor, spoke next. "You're on an island, you know. You're not going anywhere, unless you swim."

"I know," Odd said. "Looks like it's you lot who'll decide where we go. If anywhere."

Arnor gave something that might be taken for a smile. "It's an unlucky man whose fate is in our hands. I might be willing to take you to Fevik, but I don't speak for anyone else."

"Who does?" Amundi asked. "Who's chief among you?"

"No one," Ref said. "No chiefs, no jarls, no kings. Each man commands his own boat, and his own fate. That's the only way we'd have it."

"But it's not how Halfdan would have it," Arnor said. "So we might be inclined to help you. But not with the moon as it is."

Moon? Odd wondered. What did the moon have to do with this business?

"Are you some sort of moon worshipers now?" Bragi asked, voicing the question forming in Odd's head.

"No," Arnor said. "We're herring worshipers. And the herring are running thick in this moon. Can't be away from the fishing now. Two days, three, and we'll see if we can't find men and boats enough to get you to Fevik. A fleet to bear you there, like some victorious chieftain."

Two or three days... Odd thought. He felt his stomach sink, his spirits sag like the branches of a tree weighted down with ice.

Two or three days was not long, but it certainly felt that way. After all the running, the hiding, the uncertainty, he had made a decision and he wanted to act on it. He *was* acting on it. And now, once again, he found himself in impotent exile, forced to bide his time. It felt like a nightmare.

Arnor and the other fishermen finished their stew and ale, and soon after, they set out again in their boats to resume the work that Bragi's ninth shipwreck had so interrupted. Signy, Bragi, Amundi, all of those who had escaped from Ragi's burning hall the night before, crawled off to some convenient spot to sleep, their bodies crying out for rest.

Odd, too, felt the press of exhaustion, but he knew that sleep would not come, that his mind was too much in a whirl for him to even close his eyes. So he wandered along the shore, watched the few men still in camp mending nets or boats, the women washing clothes in a spring-fed stream. He walked along trails beaten through the pine forest that covered the island, but the island was not so big that his explorations occupied him for long.

He sat by himself for some time, on a small point of land far from the camp, then joined the others for *náttmál*, the night meal. He said little. His dark mood pressed down on him, until at last Signy asked him in a low voice what the matter was.

"I'm troubled," Odd said, softly, so no one else could hear. "My mind is troubled. How could it not be?"

Signy nodded. She understood. She understood well enough to not ask anything more.

Darkness settled over the island, until there was nothing to be seen beyond the big fire, and the figures in orange light and deep shadow gathered around it, and overhead the shoals of stars, visible through the trees. The younger fishermen continued their festivities in a flood tide of mead, while the women and the older men made their way off to sleep.

Arnor found shelter and blankets for the castaways, and despite their having slept earlier, they were all still weary and sore, and more than ready to be off to sleep again. Odd, too, felt at last the exhaustion overtaking him, and he happily lay down beside Signy on the pile of furs they had been offered, under a borrowed blanket. He was too tired to remove anything but his sword, but yet he was not sure that sleep would come. He was still wondering about it as he drifted off.

He woke sometime later, bathed in sweat, confused, flailing in a tide-race of emotions. He did not recall where he was. He sat up and looked out into the dark. He could see the embers still glowing bright orange in the firepit, the dark shapes of trees that were visible in the light of the moon that had come up in the east. He could hear the lap of water, the rustle of animals out in the night, the buzz of late summer insects.

The fishermen's camp, he thought, and with that realization, his vague and galling emotions solidified into something more tangible: despair, gnawing worry, uncertainty. Misery. He had made the decision to go to Fevik and had felt a blessed sense of conviction about that choice. But now the momentum had stopped, and in the forced idleness Odd had begun to question the wisdom of his plans, such as they were. He wrestled with the morality of asking others to fight and die in a conflict that was of his own making, and a cause that might be hopeless from the onset.

He felt alone. Despite all the people around him — Signy, Amundi, Ragi, all of them — he felt alone.

He let out a low moan, giving voice to his agony, but softly, so as not to disturb Signy. This was the most anguish he had felt since the fight with Halfdan started. It was his moment of greatest doubt. He was not sure if he could go on. He pictured walking into the cold water that lapped against the shingle beach, just walking in and continuing on until it swallowed him up, and he found the thought strangely soothing.

There was a rustling just beyond the edge of the tent in which he and Signy were sleeping, some creature moving in the undergrowth. The night was filled with such sounds, and Odd knew that even small animals could seem big, scuttling across the forest floor, but this was different. Noisier, more substantial, but somehow stealthier as well. A danger, possibly. A genuine threat.

Odd stood and lifted his sword, Blood-letter, off the blanket beside him, taking care not to disturb his wife. His senses were sharp now, his ears picking out the various noises around him. Whatever it was, it was still there. Odd could sense it. He thought he could hear it breathing.

Bent over, he stepped carefully from the tent, looking around as best he could. The moon was higher now, and full enough for him to see the ground around him, and the various other tents, big and small, and the few log houses in the clearing up from the beach. He took another step, bringing his foot down silently and easing his weight onto it.

Behind him and off to his right he heard a sound like a low growl. He pulled Blood-letter from its sheath, tossed the sheath aside, and held the sword in front of him as he turned. He peered into the dark, but he could see very little beyond the trampled ground around him. He felt that single-minded focus and clarity that comes with such heightened and immediate danger. It felt good. Cleansing.

He took a step forward, Blood-letter held straight out ahead, muscles tensed. He saw something move. Nothing definable, just shades of dark against dark. He heard the sound of footfalls on soft ground. Man, animal, spirit, Odd had no idea what it was. He took another step forward.

He saw movement again, bolder this time, and he brought Blood-letter up and back, ready to strike. Then he heard footfalls, and the sound of something crashing into the brush surrounding the trees on the edge of the clearing. It was moving swiftly, but not, it seemed, in panicked flight.

Odd ran after it. He did not know why. He did not even think about it. He just ran. He reached the edge of the woods and pushed his way in, the bracken and the low branches whipping him and pulling at his tunic and threatening to knock Blood-letter from his hand. He pressed on, his soft leather shoes trampling the undergrowth. He could still sense the thing in front of him, and every once in a while he could see flashes of movement, but still he had no idea of what he was chasing — animal or man — or why.

Then suddenly he was out of the trees and standing in an acre or so of open ground. He recalled that place from his earlier exploration of the island: a bare patch where the granite lay exposed and no vegetation could grow. The moon had risen above the trees here, throwing is weak light over the clearing, and the forest stood like a palisade fence all around.

Odd paused, his body in a slight crouch, Blood-letter held ready. He looked slowly side to side. He felt very exposed, very vulnerable. The breeze had dropped off, nothing moved in the undergrowth, and the night seemed unnaturally quiet. The world holding its breath.

Then, a flash of movement to Odd's right, and Odd whirled, sword held low, left hand held out, ready for whatever might come. He could see it, twenty feet ahead and coming at him, swift and noiseless. Odd tensed, lips pressed together, legs braced. And then it stopped.

The moonlight washed over the gray rock, and in that weak illumination Odd could see at last what it was. A wolf. Black, barely visible, but without a doubt a wolf. Odd had seen many wolves, had killed more than he could recall, so he knew perfectly well what this was. Bigger than most wolves he had seen, maybe bigger than any. But a wolf, to be sure.

The creature was facing him, crouched, as if ready to spring, but somehow Odd knew it would not. They looked at one another, animal and man. Odd could make out little of the beast, save for its shape and the gleam of moonlight in its eyes. He would have expected the wolf to be snarling, or growling, but it was not. It was silent. He knew that he should be afraid, but he was not. He knew he should be ready for an attack, which would certainly leave one of them dead, but somehow he understood that such an attack would not come.

He straightened slightly, lowered Blood-letter a bit, but beyond that, he and the wolf remained motionless.

Lone wolf… Odd thought. *How strange…* One rarely saw wolves without their pack. To see a lone wolf on a small island was more unusual still.

Why am I not afraid?

The sight of a wolf always struck terror to some degree, no matter how brave a man might be. A wolf fifteen feet away, nearly invisible in the night, crouched and ready, should inspire more than a little panic. But this one did not. Rather, Odd felt a preternatural calm at the sight of the animal.

Then, with the slightest rustling of fur, the soft sound of padded feet on granite ledge, the wolf turned and raced off, running directly away from Odd. Odd straightened and watched it go. He did not chase after it, just watched until it vanished in the dark.

He stood there, motionless, for a long time, staring at the blackness into which the animal had disappeared. He felt the strangest mix of emotions wash over him, but the despair and loneliness he had felt earlier were not there. In their place was something else, something almost like hope. And the vague sense that he was not alone, and would never be alone again.

Chapter Five

A foolish man thinks he will live forever,
if he bewares of battle;
but old age will give him no peace,
even if spears give it to him.

The Sayings of Hávi
The Poetic Edda

Thorgrim Night Wolf was lying on soft earth and grass. Tall grass, stiff, like straw. He was bathed in sweat, but it was mostly dry now. He had a bad taste in his mouth, a copper taste. He was sore and tired, despite his just waking from sleep. But none of that was surprising, or new. They were old sensations, ones he had experienced for three decades or more. The aftermath of a wolf dream. And though they happened less frequently now, he still knew them well.

He opened his eyes slowly, and one at a time. Inches from his face was a small forest of thin, greenish-brown stalks, just as he had suspected. He was in some overgrown meadow, it seemed. Through the grass he could see the sinewy legs of Starri Deathless, clothed in torn and filthy leggings. He could see the hem of the man's tunic, which had once been a rich, deep blue, now faded to the color of a hazy sky.

"Night Wolf. You're awake." An observation, the sort Starri was wont to make.

Thorgrim grunted. He pushed himself up on one arm until he could just see over the grass. He looked around. It was dune grass, he realized, covering a high berm bordering a sandy beach a hundred yards away. Six ships were pulled up on the sand, the six ships of Thorgrim's small fleet: *Sea Hammer*, his own command, largest of them all, *Blood Hawk*, *Oak Heart*, *Black Wing*, *Fox*, and the smallest of the fleet, *Dragon*, commanded by Thorgrim's son Harald, who was seventeen years of age.

His men, three hundred or so, the crews of the ships, were spread out over the beach. Hard men, good fighting men, some who had been a'viking with Thorgrim for close on three years. Men who, like Thorgrim, were ready to return home and be done with their wandering ways. Or most of them, anyway. They were much wealthier now than they had been when they first set sail, and they had Thorgrim Night Wolf to thank for it.

"Where are we?" Thorgrim asked. His voice seemed strange to his ears, his words ragged-sounding.

"Two days' sail north of that town we were at. That Frisian town," Starri said.

"Dorestad," Thorgrim said.

"If you say so."

Thorgrim let the memories resolve in his head. Frankia, and the hard fighting against the enemies of Louis de Roumois. The easy sail north to Frisian waters. Dorestad, to make repairs to *Blood Hawk*. The last wolf dream.

"The gods are on the move, Night Wolf," Starri said. "Things are happening, I think. In Asgard and Midgard both."

Thorgrim was silent for a moment, considering that. Starri was not wrong, he thought, but still he asked, "Why do you say that?"

"The wolf dreams. Since I've known you, they've come less and less often. I was afraid the gods were not pleased, that they'd stopped talking to you. But now, two wolf dreams in…what? Half a dozen days? There's something going on."

Thorgrim grunted. *Wolf dream.* Again, Starri was not wrong. Since his early manhood Thorgrim had experienced the wolf dreams, when, come náttmál, his mood would turn foul, so much so that no one would dare be in his company. Then, he would go off on his own to dream his strange dreams. There were some — most, actually — who thought he shape-shifted as he dreamed, but Thorgrim was not so sure.

In all those years, Thorgrim could not tolerate anyone to be in his company when the wolf dreams came, nor would anyone try. Save for Starri Deathless. Starri, the berserker, touched by the gods, was the only one who could remain by his side during those times. He would sit, silent and alert through the night, as Thorgrim went off to the netherworld of wolves and spirits. Sometimes Thorgrim would tell him what he had dreamed, but Starri never asked.

Thorgrim thought about the dream from which he had just awoken. In some instances he could vividly recall what he had dreamed, in others he could not. This time, he remembered very little indeed. He had a sense of moving through the woods. He seemed to recall people, but they were asleep, mostly, and he had ignored them. All but one.

Often enough he would awake from a wolf dream feeling angry or vengeful, but that was not the case now. Now he felt worried, but at the same time hopeful. It was the strangest of sensations.

He looked down at the fleet, pulled up on the sand. A fire was burning in a fire pit, and men were moving slowly around. It was full daylight, but the sun was casting long shadows and hitting the back of Thorgrim's head, which was turned toward the east, and that meant that it had to be early morning.

Two days' sail north of Dorestad… Thorgrim thought. He was recalling more of the past week as he shook off the stupor of the wolf dream. He remembered meeting Hakon Styrsson there in Dorestad, hearing the news about Odd and his war with Halfdan. He recalled how desperate he had felt to get back to East Agder, and he felt that desperation welling up again.

*Two days' sail…*They were likely north of Frisia now, and into the country of Dane-mark. Another day's sail should get them to the market town of Ribe, though Thorgrim did not much care to go there. Too many temptations in such a place, for men with silver in their purses. It might be hard to get his people to leave in a timely way.

They were not so far from East Agder now. If they sailed from first light to last, they could bypass Ribe, find some beach to overnight as they moved north along the coast of Dane-mark. From there they had only to cross a hundred miles of open water to Norway. They could be home in three or four days if the winds held fair. Three or four days, after nearly three years gone. And what would he find on the shores of his homeland?

Thorgrim watched the smoke from the men's cooking fire blowing out over the water. The breeze was light and out of the east, which was good. It would help them get the ships back into the sea, and they should be able to make northing with their starboard tacks hauled tight.

"Come," Thorgrim said. He made to stand but Starri put a hand on his shoulder and kept him down. "What?" Thorgrim asked, his voice a whisper.

"There are men," Starri said, whispering as well. "I can smell them. And hear them." Like many berserkers, Starri's senses were far sharper than those of ordinary men.

Thorgrim scowled. "Men? How many?"

"A lot. And they're trying to be quiet."

Starri turned and went down on hands and knees and Thorgrim did as well. Wordlessly they crawled farther up the dune, the sound of their movement no louder than that of the breeze in the tall grass. They reached the crest of the dune and laid down. Thorgrim could feel the dry stalks poking at him as he and Starri reached out and parted the grass in front, just enough that they could see down the far side of the sand hill.

Starri was right. There were men, and quite a few of them. A couple hundred at least, gathered some ways away, where the hill concealed them from the beach. Most were crouching in the grass, though some were standing and moving about. Thorgrim could not make out much detail, but he knew that Starri could.

"What do you see?" he asked.

"Danes, to be sure. They're a sorry lot," Starri said, after he had watched them for a moment. "Spears and shields. Battleaxes. Not many wear mail or carry swords. A few helmets. They look like farmers, playing at warriors. But there's a lot of the bastards."

"Humph," Thorgrim said. "Some local chieftain. Must have seen the ships up on the beach. Probably not keen to attack us. Just wants to defend his land, in case we've come to raid."

"If they just meant to defend their lands, they would have stayed behind walls," Starri said, and Thorgrim knew he was most likely right. Whoever was lord of that patch of dirt probably saw a rare chance to gain riches, with these ships pulled up on the beach. Catch them by surprise, overwhelm them with numbers, take whatever plunder they had stowed down below the deck boards.

They can try if they like, Thorgrim thought: if they did, the surprise would be on them, and it would be an ugly one. Still, Thorgrim hoped very much that they would not.

"Here, look," Starri said, a bit louder. "The lazy dogs are standing now, getting ready." Thorgrim could hear a slight change in the man's tone. Starri's excitement was mounting in the face of so many armed men preparing to attack him and his comrades.

"Calm yourself, Starri," Thorgrim said. "We're not looking for a fight here."

"We're not?"

"No. We're trying to get home, quick as we can. It's what the gods are calling me to do. It's what the wolf dreams tell me."

Starri was starting to twitch a bit. His left hand was caressing one of the battleaxes thrust in his belt, the way another man might caress a woman's face. "Might not be much choice but fight, Night Wolf," he said.

That was true enough, though Thorgrim meant to do everything he could to avoid it. He knew he had to move quick if he hoped to get back to the ships without sparking a battle. He looked left and right. Whoever was leading the men at the bottom of the hill no doubt had lookouts hidden in the dune grass, watching the beach the way he and Starri were watching them.

"I promise," Thorgrim said, "when we reach Norway, there'll be more fighting than even you could dream of. Now, it's back to the ships for us, and underway." He gestured for Starri to crawl back the way they had come, and after a moment's hesitation Starri returned to hands and knees and crawled back down the dune, Thorgrim in his wake.

They crawled past the place where Thorgrim had spent the wolf dream, the grass flattened by his nocturnal thrashing, and continued on until the ground began to level out. Then Thorgrim stood and Starri stood as well.

"Don't run, Starri, just walk," Thorgrim said. If this chieftain had in fact brought his men out simply to defend against the raiders, Thorgrim did not want to do anything to alarm him. He did not think there was much danger of losing a fight with those men, but a fight took time. There was the battle itself, and after that there were wounded to care for, dead to bury, prisoners to loot and maybe bundle off for the slave markets. A day, at least, wasted. He had no time for that nonsense.

Soon the grass yielded to the sandy beach and Thorgrim and Starri continued on toward the water's edge. Thorgrim listened for any sounds behind him, orders given, or a battle cry, or the rustle of men getting in place to attack, but he heard nothing beyond the surf and the breeze in the grass and the sound of his own men up ahead.

"Easy, Starri, stay calm," he said. Starri's arms were starting to do that strange, jerking thing they did as the fighting madness descended on him.

They were a hundred feet from the shore when Harald saw them coming. He left off what he was doing and made his way toward them. He moved cautiously. Even after all those years he was never sure how to approach his father after a wolf dream.

"Father, good morrow..." Harald said as they met. Thorgrim continued walking and Harald fell in beside him.

"Listen, Harald," Thorgrim said. "There's a few hundred men on the other side of that dune, and they're likely making ready to attack us."

"I'll get the men under arms," Harald said, his wariness changed now to excitement. Harald liked a good fight almost as much as Starri. And more than that, he relished any chance to prove himself, which he had done often enough in his years raiding with his father.

"No," Thorgrim said. "No time for that. We have to get underway." As they drew nearer to the shore, Thorgrim could see his other captains — Gudrid of *Blood Hawk*, Asmund of *Oak Heart*, Halldor, who commanded *Black Wing*, and Hardbein, master of *Fox* — watching him approach, ready to move if they were needed. Thorgrim waved them over.

"On the far side of the dune," Thorgrim said, once they had assembled, "there's a few hundred armed men. Danes, I think. Seems we've crossed into Dane-mark. They might just mean to defend their lands, thinking we've come to raid hereabouts. Or they might mean to attack. Either way, we don't want a fight this morning."

He looked around at his men's expressions. It was clear that they did, in fact, want a fight, which came as no surprise. They were warriors to their souls. And even if they did not wish to fight, leaving might be construed as cowardice by the enemy facing them, and that was not to be suffered. But Thorgrim did not have the patience to indulge their concerns.

"Get the men and gear back aboard the ships, quickly," he said before anyone could raise an objection. "Any stores, meat or ale or bread, just leave it. We'll get more. I want to be underway immediately."

The others glanced at one another, and some gave desultory nods of their heads, though no one moved. Thorgrim felt his anger flaring, and that was rarely a good thing.

"Move. Now," he said, his voice like a growl, and that, at last, got the men going, but they did not get far. They were still turning away when they heard the cry from behind them, some ways off, loud and piercing.

As one, they turned and looked inland. A single man was standing on the crest of the dune. He was too far away for Thorgrim to make out much detail, but he could tell the man carried a bright-painted shield and was holding a sword aloft.

The Dane screamed again, a wild battle cry that seemed to roll along the beach. He was still shouting when the rest of the men came charging up over the crest of the hill, hundreds of armed men running in a long and ragged line. They were several hundred yards away, but they were moving fast as they poured over the top and raced down the other side.

Oh, Thor's arse, Thorgrim thought, even as he yelled "Weapons! Shields! Turn to!" loud enough for all of his men to hear. The captains raced off to their ships, shouting and waving at their men, leaving Thorgrim and Starri alone on the sand.

"Captains, defend your ships!" Thorgrim called next. "Form up in a shield wall around the bows of your ships!"

These Danish farmers would have a hard time breaking six individual shield walls, even more so when the defenders had their backs to the hulls of their ships. If Thorgrim's men could hold the Danes off, they might be able to shove their longships off and get underway, even as they fought.

"Come on, Starri, fight by my side," Thorgrim said next, grabbing Starri by the arm and half dragging him toward *Sea Hammer*. He could see that Hall was already forming the men up around *Sea Hammer*'s bow, shields interlocking, swords and axes and spears held ready. After years of successful raiding, most of the men had acquired mail as well — not so easy to come by — but few had had the chance to don it now, so quickly had this attack been launched.

Thorgrim and Starri covered the last hundred feet, and the men in the shield wall stepped aside, making a gap. Thorgrim thrust Starri through and followed behind. Hall handed him his shield. Thorgrim nodded his thanks and slipped the shield on his arm.

"Starri, you stand in the shield wall, you understand?" Thorgrim said. Starri had already pulled his tunic off and was starting to flail his arms and twirl around. In battle, Starri had a tendency to fling himself at the enemy. But Thorgrim wanted to put out to sea if they could, and he did not want to first have to extract Starri from some bloody melee.

"You understand?" Thorgrim asked again. Starri nodded his head, but it was not at all clear whether he was acknowledging Thorgrim's words or just twitching.

Thorgrim turned and stepped up to the shield wall, pulling Iron-tooth from its sheath and locking his shield with the others. He looked out across the beach. The Danes were still coming, a hundred yards off and running, their line scattering into six clusters of men going for each of the six ships.

Good, Thorgrim thought. The less coordinated their attack, the better.

He looked side to side. Hall was on his right, Vali on his left. "Starri's going to try and get at these bastards," he said. "Might try to climb right over us. You pull him down if he does."

Hall and Vali glanced at him. They seemed unconcerned about the coming attack, but the idea of trying to stop Starri Deathless gave them pause.

The Danes had halved the distance, and now they were screaming as they came on, spears leveled, axes held over shoulders, shields on arms. Not a very organized attack, but not the worst Thorgrim had seen. Farmers they might be, but like most farmers in the North countries they would be no strangers to battle.

"Ready!" Thorgrim shouted, digging his back foot into the sand to brace himself against the onslaught. He felt the blood pumping, the tightening in his muscles, the surge of energy: the old, familiar sensations.

Something brushed up behind him and he felt a foot on his leg, pressing down, threatening to collapse his leg under him: Starri, trying to leap clean over the shield wall.

"Grab him!" Thorgrim shouted, reaching up awkwardly with his left hand, the shield still on his arm. He managed to get a handful of Starri's leggings and pull, and on his right side Hall managed to get a handful as well, and they dragged Starri back and deposited him on the sand.

"Shield wall!" Thorgrim shouted at Starri as Starri thrashed on the ground. Thorgrim turned back, ready to lock his shield with the others once again, just as the Danes hit.

They did not come on in a wedge formation, or anything so neat. They hit in a line, wrapping around the half circle that Thorgrim's men had formed around *Sea Hammer*'s bow. They led with spears that drove into the men's shields and pushed them back against the hull, and from the sound of the yelling and the screams, their weapons hit flesh as well.

Thorgrim just managed to get his shield up and locked as a battleaxe came down over the top. Its hooked corner caught his shield's upper rim, and the man wielding it pulled back, trying to jerk Thorgrim's shield aside. Thorgrim gave him an inch, and a few more, until the man's head and shoulders were visible. Then Iron-tooth darted out like a snake, glancing off the edge of Thorgrim's shield, glancing off the edge of the Dane's shield, and driving into the side of the Dane's neck.

The pressure on Thorgrim's shield disappeared as the Dane released his grip on the ax, screamed, and fell back. Thorgrim slashed at the man to his right. A spear was thrust through the gap between his shield and Hall's, and Thorgrim ducked aside. Then suddenly Starri was there, grabbing the spear with his left hand and jerking it toward him. The Dane holding the spear did not let go, and he was dragged forward, slamming bodily into Thorgrim and Hall's shields, too close for either man to strike with their swords.

But they did not have to. Starri released the spear, stepped forward and brought the ax he held in his right hand down on the man's head, embedding it in his skull as if he was splitting wood. Thorgrim felt the warm spray of blood on his cheek as the man dropped and Starri pulled the ax free.

Thorgrim stepped to his left, just a bit, just enough to give Starri room to swing, not enough, he hoped, to allow Starri to break through the line and disappear into the crowd of struggling Danes.

He could hear shouting and screaming and the clash of shields on shields, and iron on shields, and iron on iron, all up and down the line. These Danes had plenty of fight in them, Thorgrim could see, and he cursed them, cursed this pointless bother that was putting more time between him and Odd. He thrust Iron-tooth around the edge of his shield and felt something strike the blade: an ax, another sword, he could not tell. He drew back, thrust again.

We have to send them running, Thorgrim thought. He had hoped perhaps to get underway in the midst of battle, to not waste time trying to run these bastards off, but he could see now that would not be possible. The Danes were putting up too much of a fight for Thorgrim and his men to just slip away.

Just as he realized that, Starri Deathless pushed through the space between him and Hall, a space through which only one as wiry as Starri could squeeze. With a shriek he was into the Danes' line, axes flailing, and this time Thorgrim let him go. Nothing would break the Danes' spirit like Starri bringing his madness to the fight.

And sure enough, Thorgrim could see the line of men in front of him suddenly waver, the shock of Starri's attack rippling out from his point of contact. The twin axes rose and fell and men around Starri threw their weapons away and ran, or they died where they stood. As the line wavered, Thorgrim's men pushed forward, pressing with their shields and hacking down with axes and swords, putting pressure on the Danish line.

Gaps were appearing among the Danes now, as men fell or fled, pushing against one another to get away from Starri. Here and there clusters of Danes were still exchanging blows with Thorgrim's men, but the enemy's line had collapsed. Thorgrim could see that.

But this was not the only fight. The battle, by Thorgrim's design, had been six separate fights at six separate ships, and he did not know how the others were faring. The ground was clear around him, the closest fighting men a dozen feet away, so Thorgrim stepped forward and looked off to his left, where the other ships were pulled up on the beach.

Through the press of warriors he could only catch glimpses of what was going on, but he could see that the battle around the bows of the other five ships was far from over. At *Blood Hawk*, Gudrid and his men seemed to have mostly driven the Danes away, but for the rest the fight went on.

Have to get to them, Thorgrim thought. *Come to their aid.* They had to finish this business at *Sea Hammer*, then roll up the rest of the Danish line.

He started to call an order to the men around him when he caught motion to his right. He turned and instinctively raised his shield. A big Dane, mail-clad, who seemed to have come out of nowhere, was charging at him, a battle axe raised and coming down at his skull.

Thorgrim stepped back and lifted his shield higher. The blade of the ax came down and split the edge of the shield, embedding itself in the wood, and the Dane jerked the shield aside.

Thorgrim twisted and thrust with Iron-tooth, but too late. The Dane had a seax, not a shield, in his left hand, and the blade shot in around the edge of Thorgrim's shield, the point driving into Thorgrim's chest, just below his shoulder bone. Thorgrim gasped as the iron ripped into him: it felt as if it was red-hot from the smith's forge.

The Dane pulled the seax free and drew the battle axe back again. Thorgrim watched the ax coming at him, but the seax wound seemed to have drained his strength, and he was unable to move. He saw Hall to his right thrusting his sword tip at the Dane. He felt the ax strike his head, the sensation like a bolt of lightning exploding in his skull, and then, nothing more.

Chapter Six

Many men are entirely friendly towards each other,
but abuse one another at a feast;
there will always be strife among men,
guest will fall out with guest.

The Sayings of Hávi
The Poetic Edda

There were many things going on in Halfdan's great hall and the grounds surrounding it, the acres contained within the confines of the high earth and palisade walls. A beaver pond of activity. The sounds and smells of the people's industry wrapped around the place like fog. But he could see none of it.

Cooking was a constant in the great hall: deer, boar, even whale, roasting on spits, stews of fish and carrots and onions simmering in cauldrons that hung from tripods over glowing coals. And from the smaller buildings beyond the great hall, bread baking, ale and mead fermenting.

The king's warriors practiced with sword, spear, ax, and shield, their shouts and the clash of arms rolling around the grounds. Carpenters hammered and sawed away, repairing old buildings, constructing new, or building wagons, wheelbarrows, benches. The smiths' hammers rang out from first light to last as they made weapons, repaired weapons, fashioned the myriad bits of ironwork needed for Halfdan's royal residence, his army, and his fleet.

All of this Skorri Thorbrandsson smelled and heard, but did not see, as he lay in the semi-darkness of his bedchamber, behind a closed door that opened onto the main part of the king's great hall. A thrall dabbed his face with a cool, wet cloth. His eyes were closed but he knew it was the young and attractive thrall, the one he would have been rutting with at another time, when he was another man. A less wounded man.

He winced as the cloth pressed down on a tender spot, and mumbled, "Stupid bitch," but not loud or clear enough to be heard. The thrall pulled her hand back, paused a second, and then began again in a different place.

Skorri did not know how long he had been in that room. In that way, it was like the time he had been in the prison cell, except now he did not even remember how he got there. Days and nights were lost in a blur of pain, of fevered sleep and agonizing periods of wakefulness. He had a memory of kneeling before Halfdan. Of Halfdan welcoming him back into his favor. But he did not know if that was real or a dream.

Thinking on it, as his strength grew and his thoughts became less fragmented, he had to guess that it was real. He was, after all, in one of the bedchambers in the great hall, and not back in the fetid prison. He had been told as much on waking, and the sounds and smells seemed to confirm it, though he did not know for certain. He had not actually left the room, had not even climbed from his bed save to use the pot provided for him to relieve himself.

But it looked like a bedchamber in the great hall, with its tapestries and furs and oil lamps, the bed, chair and table. Skorri was attended by thralls, and fed the same food that the king and his men might eat, and dressed in a fine linen tunic. His wounds, which were numerous and painful, had been bandaged and treated with poultices. Beyond the thin walls of wattle and daub he could hear the king's business taking place, and beyond that, the usual daily activity of the royal residence.

The thrall who was tending to him finished with her cloth and put it down beside the basin of water. "Would you eat now, my lord?" she asked.

Skorri opened his eyes and looked at her. Young, pretty, just the sort that Halfdan kept to attend those with status enough to live in the great hall. He had hardly spoken more than a few words to her, and those were mostly to curse her for this or that. He had not been in a very charitable mood, these past few days.

"What part of the day is it?" Skorri asked, the first question he had ever asked her, as far as he could recall. The girl looked up quickly, then down again.

"Just past dagmál, lord."

"How long have I been here?"

"Four days, lord."

Four days. Skorri felt the fury welling up again. It was coming back to him, bit by bit, the memories that had nearly been kicked and beaten out of him. He recalled Halfdan's promise of ships and men. He recalled the extraordinary relief he had felt on hearing those words, realizing that Halfdan understood and appreciated his loyalty.

And then, on the heels of that, being marched away to prison, locked up in darkness. Days of stewing in anger and confusion before that whore's son Thorgeir arrived to escort him back to the great hall. And the gauntlet.

Four days. You miserable idiot.

He was thinking of Halfdan when he thought those words. At one time he would never have directed such thoughts at his king, not even in his bleakest moments. He had always loved Halfdan. He had done everything in service of him. And Halfdan had rewarded him with the gauntlet.

Worse than the punishment was the time wasted. Skorri was certain that Odd and his band of outlaws were bound for Fevik. He told Halfdan as much. Halfdan had promised to send Skorri there to hunt them down. But rather that dispatch him and his warriors immediately — the only reasonable thing to do — he had forced Skorri to fester away in prison, and then beaten him half to death. And now they had wasted another four days just so Skorri could recover enough to walk. The gods alone knew where Odd was now, or what he had managed to accomplish in that time.

"Help me up," Skorri said. His words came out in a croak, which infuriated him, and he cleared his throat.

"Yes, lord," the thrall said, and she sounded uncertain. "Shall I get someone else to help as well?"

"No," Skorri said, and thought, *stupid bitch.*

He ground his teeth together as he swung his legs over the edge of the bed. The various bruises and lacerations pulsed and burned and pulled, but he made no sound. The thrall stepped up beside him and slipped her small hand under his arm. He stood, and she lifted as best she could, and with some difficulty he managed to gain his feet.

He stood for a moment, his head spinning, afraid that he was going to fall over. The thrall was still holding him under his arm, but Skorri was a big man and there was little she would be able to do to stop him from going down. But soon his head settled, the whirling stopped, and he felt confident that he could retain his feet.

"I'm fine," he said at last. He crossed the small room to where the basin sat on top of a wooden chest. He fished himself out of his leggings and relieved himself into the bowl. It crossed his mind to have the thrall pleasure him in some way before he left the room, but he dismissed the idea even before he was done urinating. He had too many other considerations at the moment, but he was pleased to realize that he had recovered enough to at least entertain such thoughts.

He finished his business, readjusted his leggings, and looked down at what he was wearing. The disgraceful garment that Thorgeir had given him was gone. Now he sported a tunic of green linen with embroidery around the hem and cuffs and neck. A decent article of clothing. He had no idea where it had come from, when it had been put on him, or by who.

He turned back to the thrall. "Where's my belt?"

Without a word she bent over and came up with Skorri's leather belt, his fine dagger still hanging from it. Skorri grunted, took it, and strapped it on. It was humiliating enough that he would have to step out into the great hall bruised and beaten like a slave. He was not about to do so with not one weapon on his person.

Skorri settled the dagger in place and crossed to the thin wooden door set in the wall. He stepped with care, not sure how his legs were functioning. His head swam a bit as he moved, but his steps felt steady, his legs sure.

Good…that's good.

He lifted the wooden latch, swung the door open and stepped out into the hall. Late morning, the hall was mostly deserted, only a few servants and thralls moving about, cleaning up from the morning meal and already preparing for náttmál. A knot of Halfdan's warriors were sitting at a table at the far end of the hall, drinking, playing at some game, and making quite a bit of noise about it.

Skorri looked around the cavernous interior, dimly lit by the few windows and the fires burning in the pits running down the center of the floor. Halfdan's overseer of the royal house, a man whose name Skorri did not know, was standing near the far end of the hall. He seemed to start a bit on seeing Skorri stepping out from his chamber, then he turned and hurried off.

"Is there something I can fetch you, lord?" The thrall was there at his elbow. "Food, drink?"

Skorri was about to curse at her again, but he realized he was very thirsty. "Ale," he said. "And be quick."

The thrall bowed and hurried off, and a moment later she was back with a horn filled near to the brim. Skorri took it and drank it down in a series of long, grateful gulps. He handed it back to the thrall, his mouth open to order more, when he heard the king's overseer call, "Lord Skorri?"

He turned. The man was ten feet away, hesitant in his stance, as if he was approaching a dog that might or might not be vicious. Skorri saw the man's expression change as he got a look at Skorri's face. Skorri had not looked at himself in a glass since his beating, but he could just imagine.

"What?"

"Lord Skorri, I'm pleased to see you up and about. I informed his majesty, and he would see you now."

Lord Skorri... Skorri wondered where that had come from, if the overseer had decided himself to use such a sign of respect, or if Halfdan had told him to. Either way, he seemed to be held in much higher regard now than he had been just four days earlier, when he was being kicked and spat upon.

"Very well. Lead on."

The overseer headed toward the far end of the great hall, where the king's throne sat on its raised platform. They made their way past the benches flanking the room, over the floor down which Skorri had crawled with kicks and blows raining down on him and Thorgeir yelling at him to move. Skorri felt his cheeks burn but he walked on, his head up.

"Please wait here," the overseer said as they approached the throne. Skorri stopped and the overseer continued on through the door to a chamber off to the side. Skorri wondered if he should bow or kneel when Halfdan appeared. But he did not feel like bowing or kneeling, so he decided to do neither.

A moment later, Halfdan swept out of the chamber, his movement, as usual, precise and elegant, almost as if he was dancing. He wore silver and gold arm rings and a cloak of purple silk, fastened with a gold brooch at his shoulder. His left hand and forearm were covered by a thick leather glove, on which perched the king's massive gyrfalcon, with its white breast and gray-spotted wings; a bird which Halfdan had named Valkyrie, and which he loved more than he loved any man or woman.

"Ah, Skorri, you are up, I see," Halfdan said as he approached. Skorri caught the heartbeat's hesitation as Halfdan looked at his battered face, but the king recovered quickly.

"Yes, your majesty."

"You've been well cared for?"

After the pointless beating, I suppose I have, Skorri thought, but said, rather, "Yes, your majesty."

"Good, good. Here, let us sit." Halfdan nodded toward one of the benches on the side of the throne room, then led the way over and sat down. Skorri joined him. He understood that the king was granting him a rare favor, the chance to sit beside him, and not before him. A privilege, but Skorri was unmoved.

The overseer appeared again, this time with a wooden dish holding chunks of raw meat, which he set on the bench between Skorri and the king. The gyrfalcon made a squawking sound and thrashed its wings, smacking the king on the back of the head. Halfdan held tighter to the jesses in his hand and made kissing sounds at the bird. He lifted a chunk of meat and gave it to the gyrfalcon, which quieted down as it ate.

For a moment the four of them, three men and a bird, were silent as the king's attention was on Valkyrie. The bird finished his piece of meat and Halfdan gave him another, then turned to Skorri.

"You understand, Skorri, why I needed to do what I did," he said, and his tone was matter of fact, as if his reasons were self-evident.

"I understand, majesty," Skorri said. That was only partly true, but it was also the only possible reply.

They were silent again as the king fussed with his bird. His eyes were still on the gyrfalcon when he started in again.

"Loyalty..." Halfdan said, pausing in thought, then continuing, "must be demonstrated. It's not enough for a man to say he's his king's man, that he is oath-sworn to his king. It must be shown in the bluntest terms."

Halfdan turned and looked Skorri in the eye. "Now, I never did doubt your loyalty," he continued. "But those others, the jarls, the chief men, those who lead my *hird*...to them it would seem like weakness, were I to simply take you at your word. Being a king is no different from being a wolf leading a pack. You lead through strength. Show weakness and there are those who would tear you apart. Do you understand?"

Skorri nodded. "Yes, majesty," he said, though in fact the entire thing seemed to him like a big, steaming pile of horse dung. Want to show real strength? He should tell the jarls and the chief men to kiss his arse, tell them that he, the king, he would do just as he pleased, and any who did not like it could die screaming, tied to a stake. That was what a real king would do.

"Good," Halfdan said. He reached over and patted Skorri on the knee, right on top of a massive bruise hidden by his leggings. It sent a bolt of pain through his leg, but Skorri did not react.

"Now," Halfdan continued, "I wish for you to see the men and ships I've assembled for your command. We still have this bastard Odd and his traitors to deal with. And I will not show to them the mercy that I have shown you."

With that, Halfdan called to the overseer, who escorted Skorri out of the great hall and onto the grounds surrounding the building. It hurt to walk, and it was difficult to keep up with the overseer and his frenetic pace, but Skorri managed. They crossed to where a band of warriors were running through drills with sword and shield.

"Koll!" the overseer called and one of the men left off the swordplay and came over to them. Koll Thorvaldson: Skorri knew him slightly, knew him to be a skilled and loyal warrior. He was a big man, about Skorri's size, with a neat-trimmed brown beard and long hair done up in a braid. He sheathed his sword and took off his helmet as he approached. His face was red and wet with perspiration.

"Grim," Koll said to the overseer, and Skorri recalled the man's name: Grim Grimsson. He still did not care.

"Skorri Thorbrandsson," Koll said next, nodding a greeting. His tone was flat, neither welcoming, nor suspicious, nor filled with disgust. He had no visible reaction to the state of Skorri's face, and for that Skorri was grateful.

"Koll," Skorri said, nodding back.

"King Halfdan set Koll to organizing your men," Grim said, "while you were…indisposed. He's drilling them now, as you can see."

"Good," Skorri said. He looked the overseer in the eyes. "You may go now." He suddenly felt that he could not endure the presence of this man, Halfdan's little toady, not while he was in the company of a real warrior such as Koll.

"Very good, Lord Skorri," Grim said, giving a bit of a bow and hurrying off, apparently as happy to be away from Skorri as Skorri was to have him gone.

"Is this all?" Skorri asked Koll, nodding toward the men still flailing at one another. "Is that all the men Halfdan has allowed me?"

"No," Koll said. He called for the men to take a rest from their practice, and then continued. "No, this is only part of them. I drill them in small units, so I can keep better watch over them. The rest are at other things…seeing to the horses, getting provisions ready for the march, that sort of thing."

"I see," Skorri said.

"Halfdan gave me leave to pick the men myself. That's the best of it. These are the cream of Halfdan's warriors."

"Hmm," Skorri said, as he looked over the men, now dropping onto benches or squatting on the ground, taking the ladles of water that the thralls offered them. He recognized a number of them. Judging from what he could see, Koll had chosen well. These men seemed to be excellent warriors indeed. "And ships?" he asked.

"Halfdan's allowed us five. Again, he gave me leave to choose. I hope that's all right by you. I chose the five best, as far as I could tell. Good ships."

Skorri nodded. This was starting to look agreeable. "We can use half of our warriors to man the ships, approach Fevik by the sea. Stop anyone trying to escape that way. March the other half around by land. Catch the traitors between the two. Hammer and anvil."

"Yes," Koll said. "Excellent." That was probably what Koll was planning all along, Skorri realized, and the man was just being polite. But that was fine. Deference, obsequiousness, it was what he would expect from a good subordinate.

"How soon before the men are ready to move?" Skorri asked next. But before Koll could answer, they were interrupted by the odious voice of Thorgeir Sveinsson.

"Skorri! You've recovered enough to walk, I see." Skorri and Koll turned. Thorgeir was approaching from the direction of the great hall. Skorri remained silent until Thorgeir had stopped five feet away.

"*Lord* Skorri," Skorri corrected. "That's how King Halfdan would have me addressed."

"Oh, to be sure," Thorgeir said. He looked at Skorri's face and made a wincing gesture. Then he nodded at the warriors who were taking a rest from their training. "How goes it with these men, Koll?"

"It goes well," Koll said. "They're good men."

"Yes, they are," Thorgeir said. He turned to Skorri. "I had Koll pick each of our men himself. The best of the king's army."

Our men? Skorri thought, but he did not ask the question, because he could see that Thorgeir wanted him to. Thorgeir answered it anyway.

"You look confused," Thorgeir said. "King Halfdan has given us command together. I'll take charge of the fleet going to Fevik. You'll take the men overland. Once we are at Fevik we'll be equals in making decisions."

Skorri knew that his anger and uncertainty showed on his face, but he was unable to stop it. He looked sharply at Koll. Koll's expression was sheepish, apologetic, but he pressed his lips together and said nothing.

"Oh, by the gods!" Thorgeir said, and he chuckled a bit. "After all that's happened you didn't think King Halfdan would give you free rein to do as you will, did you? What, and have you go rogue again? No, I think not."

Skorri did not reply. He just felt the humiliation burning inside of him. He felt the whole thing, which a moment before had seemed so promising, now collapsing into a heap of ash.

Chapter Seven

In the Land of the Slain
I warred and stirred up
Princes to strife without peace.

Greybeard and Thor
The Poetic Edda

There were two dozen men aboard the longship that was making its labored approach to Fevik. Sixteen of the men were rowing, eight to a side, their oars crudely shaped with axes from small trees felled on the south coast of Engla-land. Seven of the men were bailing, scooping water and flinging it over the side, barely keeping up with the inflow through the strained seams in the battered hull.

The ship could have held twice that number of men. It had, in fact, when it left from Fevik a year and a half earlier.

Aft, Bergthor Skeggjason stood at the steering oar, guiding the ship, *Wave Splitter*, on the last mile of a journey that had covered many hundreds of miles, and seen more than its share of disasters. Bergthor Skeggjason was not a lucky man.

That much had become clear to his men just a few months into their voyage. He had had five ships then, and about two hundred warriors under his command, but the raiding had not gone well. The towns and monasteries they tried to sack were more strongly defended than they had imagined, and those they managed to plunder were too poor to be worth the effort. The men had started to grumble. Quiet and mutinous discussions were taking place. Bergthor was sure of it.

But Bergthor's luck changed before any rupture appeared, or so it seemed. He crossed paths with his countryman, Thorgrim Night Wolf. Saved Thorgrim's idiot son, Harald, from certain death on the back of a whale, of all things. They had joined together, his fleet and

Thorgrim's, had fought the king of Wessex at a place called Hamtun, where Bergthor had lost his left ear to an English sword. Bergthor saved Thorgrim's life at Winchester. Their partnership had been profitable.

But then Thorgrim decided to make a deal with the Wessex king, to serve as his hirdman, to protect their fleet as they crossed the narrow seas. It was not a plan that Bergthor embraced, so he decided to follow a plan of his own making. Before he could act, however, Thorgrim and his men fell on them, took the oars off their ships and burned them, leaving them stranded on the beach until they could fashion more.

That was the end of Bergthor's brief streak of good luck. The men blamed him for their misfortune, and the four other ships in his company set off on their own. Bergthor and his men raided a village to the east of Hamtun, but the people there put up more of a fight than the Northmen would have thought they had in them. The Northmen left a dozen dead behind as they ran for their longship and escaped by sea.

By then the season was getting late and they had little choice but to go limping home. Each man still had a considerable hoard of silver, at least, which they had taken from the nobles of Wessex while in Thorgrim's company. They took some comfort from that, right up until they encountered the Frisian pirates a day's sail south of Ribe. Once again, they escaped with their lives, but just barely. The Frisians took everything else.

So here they were, making for Fevik, a year and a half after leaving from that port. Bergthor was returning with much less than when he left, including, once the tale of his bad luck had spread, the good reputation he had once enjoyed. He did not know if his farm was still there. Or his wife. Or his servants or animals. He did not yet know how much worse his situation could get. But he knew he was about to find out, and he did not relish that knowledge.

Bergthor kept his eyes on the town as they drew nearer. He did not care to look at his men, with their torn and filthy clothing, their lack of weapons, their hangdog, accusatory expressions.

Fevik did not seem much changed since the last time he saw it. It had always been a prosperous town huddled up to the edge of the water: a few score houses and workshops, plank-built, or wattle and daub, their thatched roofs like a series of hills covered in dried grass. There was a busy fleet of fishing boats. A long wharf serviced the trading knarrs that came from foreign ports and the raiding parties returning with plunder if they had been lucky, or with the taint of failure if not.

There were tradesmen and craftsmen's shops just inland from the water: woodworkers and blacksmiths, shipbuilders, comb-makers, goldsmiths, men selling weapons and men selling thralls. There were butchers and brewers. Merchants manned tables set up along the wide road that ran through the center of the town. There were taverns where food and drink and women could be had for silver or trade.

Beyond the town, and for many miles inland, there were farms of various sizes. One was the large and prosperous compound of Ornolf the Restless, who had been Thorgrim Night Wolf's late father-in-law. Ornolf had been one of the jarls in that region, a man who commanded much respect. Bergthor wondered what had become of Ornolf's farm, if the people even knew that Ornolf was dead.

He wondered who was now jarl, ruling over that small part of the world. He recalled a man named Gest Heggsson who was wealthy and favored by the king, second only to Ornolf in land and reputation. He wondered if Gest was now the one to be reckoned with in Fevik.

Several miles beyond Ornolf's farm was Bergthor's, much smaller, much less prosperous. But hopefully still standing, and still his.

One of Bergthor's men, one of those who had been bailing, straightened, turned, and looked out over the bow. They were half a mile from the waterfront, close enough to shore that even *Wave Splitter* was unlikely to sink before reaching land. With a grunt, the man threw his bucket aside and sat on one of the sea chests lashed to the deck, now empty thanks the Frisians. One by one the others did so as well. They had been bailing for days, and they were heartily sick of it.

A few of the erstwhile bailers, and some of the men pulling oars, shot ugly looks aft at Bergthor, but Bergthor ignored them. He nudged the tiller, aiming the bow toward a muddy patch of shoreline on the west side of the town. It was pointless to bring the ship up to one of the wharves. *Wave Splitter* would sink soon after it was tied up. Besides, the wharves were for ships that had business in Fevik. Bergthor and his men had no business there, save to make it ashore.

A few strokes more and *Wave Splitter* ran up onto the mud, touching Norwegian soil for the first time in a long year and a half, but there was no sense of jubilation or joy of homecoming aboard. No one said a thing. The rowers just stood, leaving their oars hanging in the row ports, and moved toward the bow, behind the bailers who were already there. One by one they jumped over the side and down into the soft mud, then slogged their way ashore. They did not collect up their belongings because they did not have any. They did not say a word to Bergthor as they left.

"Yes, be gone. And may evil spirits take you all and roast you alive, you bunch of miserable cowards," Bergthor said, though not loud enough to be heard by the men making their way toward the town.

He stood for a while on *Wave Splitter*'s afterdeck, watching the water swirl into the hull and looking out over Fevik beyond. He was not sure what to do next. Most men would head for their homes, but Bergthor did not want to do that. He did not care to tell his wife about his failure. He wondered if maybe his wife was dead, but he doubted it. He was, after all, not a lucky man.

Near the water's edge, just inland from a length of beach where fishing nets and split cod were drying in the weak light of an overcast sky, Bergthor saw the roof of a tavern he knew well, a place he had frequented, the owner of which he reckoned for a friend. The sight of the building made him realize how very much he wanted a drink. Many drinks, in truth.

He sighed and hopped down from the aft deck and made his way forward. Like his men, he had no belongings to collect. He had returned to Fevik with nothing of value save for the ship, and *Wave Splitter*'s only value now was as firewood. He hoped his friend still owned the tavern, and would be willing to let him drink on a promise of payment.

He climbed up onto the sheer strake at the bow and hopped ashore, into a foot of water, and below it, six inches of mud. With some difficulty and cursing he extracted his left foot from the muck, and then his right, but in doing so he left his shoe behind. He cursed again, fished the shoe out, and waded inland.

Bergthor paused on the rutted dirt road that ran along the waterfront and put his shoe back on, then trudged east, turning onto a side street that ran toward the town. The narrow streets were crowded the way he remembered: busy people going about their business, the air filled with the sounds of work being done and lives being lived. No one paid him any attention as he moved through the crowds.

He could smell smoke from a dozen fires, and iron heated red-hot in the smith's shops, and meat and bread cooking, and animal dung, and damp earth, and all those hundreds of smells that one forgets about when voyaging at sea. He paused at the door to the tavern, took a breath, and swung the door open.

The place looked no different than it had when last he saw it: cramped and dim-lit and crowded. Even the men at the tables and benches, and the soot-stains on the walls, and the trampled reeds and sundry bones and broken cups on the floor, all looked the same.

Bergthor closed the door and stepped farther in, searching for the tavern-keeper, but the tavern-keeper saw Bergthor first, and called out, "Ha! Thor's arse! Bergthor Skeggjason! You're still alive! I can't believe it!" The man was smiling, a wide smile.

"Hallbjorn!" Bergthor called back. "Yes, I'm alive! But not for long if I don't have some of your famous ale!" He smiled as well, and felt a sense of relief, the first such sensation he had felt in a long time. Hallbjorn was still here, still recognized him, and apparently did not despise him, as everyone else seemed to do.

"You've been gone a long time, if you think my ale is famous, or even drinkable," Hallbjorn said. "But it is strong, I'll grant you that! Come, have a seat, and I'll get you some!" He gestured to a bench and Bergthor crossed the room, aware of the squishing sounds his shoes were making as he walked, and sat down. A moment later Hallbjorn sat beside him and handed him a cup brimming with a dark and foaming brew, a second cup in his other hand.

"By the gods, what happened to your ear?" Hallbjorn began, and paused as Bergthor tilted the cup back and drained it off in one long swallow. The ale was yeasty and sharp, with the taste of barley and juniper. Bergthor could tell that it was strong indeed, and he was grateful for that. He smacked his lips, and Hallbjorn said, "Thirsty man," and handed Bergthor the other cup.

As Bergthor drained the second cup, Hallbjorn fetched two more, then sat again and continued. "So, tell me, what have you been about? How'd you get that wound? You've been gone for a year, if I recall. Off a'viking."

"Year and a half," Bergthor said. "Off to Frisia, and Frankia, and Engla-land."

"And how was the raiding, my friend?"

Bergthor took a mouthful of ale and shook his head. He had eaten little over the past few days, since they had little on board the ship to eat, and he was already feeling the effects of the drink. He felt a warm and soothing sensation coming over him, and he welcomed it.

"The raiding was not good. Not good. It's not like when we were young men, not at all."

"I'm sorry to hear that," Hallbjorn said.

"We had some luck, to be sure," Bergthor continued. "Had quite a bit of silver, at least for a while. That was in Engla-land. We met up with Thorgrim Ulfsson, who you might know, from Vik, and..."

"Thorgrim Ulfsson?" Hallbjorn interrupted. "Thorgrim, who's known as Night Wolf?"

"The same," Bergthor said, and he did not miss the change in Hallbjorn's expression, some strange mixture of surprise and concern.

"He's alive? Thorgrim's alive?"

"He was, when last I saw him. The bastard betrayed me, to tell you the truth. I hope he's dead. But he was alive when I last saw him in Engla-land...what? Two months ago?"

"You joined up with him, you say?" Hallbjorn asked.

"For a while. Until he betrayed me, like I said. But the raiding was good with him and me."

"Is he still there? In Engla-land?"

Bergthor squinted at Hallbjorn, wondered why the man was so curious about the doings of Thorgrim Night Wolf. Thorgrim was well known in that part of the world, to be sure, with a reputation as a clever man. And a dangerous man. He was well-loved and admired. But Hallbjorn's reaction suggested there was something Bergthor was missing.

"No, I don't think he's in Engla-land," Bergthor said. "He became oath-sworn to the King of Wessex, promised to sail across the narrow seas with the king's fleet. Protect them. Then he meant to sail for home, be done with raiding. That's why we had a falling out, and he turned on me. Why do you care so much about Thorgrim Night Wolf?"

"Ah," Hallbjorn said. He took a deep drink of his ale, breathed in again. "There's a great deal that's happened since you've been gone," he began. "Do you recall Thorgrim's sons? Thorgrim took the younger one, Harald, a'viking with him."

"Yes, I know them both," Bergthor said. "I saved Harald's life."

"Well the other, Odd, the oldest, he stayed behind, as you know, I'm sure."

Bergthor nodded, took another drink, and listened as Hallbjorn spilled out his tale of Odd's fight against Halfdan the Black, the uprising among the freemen of the country, Halfdan's brutal put-down of the rebellion. An astounding tale, and Bergthor listened with growing interest and mounting excitement.

"Thorgrim's in Frankia now, you say?" Hallbjorn asked as he finished his story.

"He may be," Bergthor said. "I'm not sure, really. He said a few other things about what he was planning, where he might go."

That, of course, was not true. Thorgrim had been unequivocal about his desire to get home, to never go a'viking again. He was bound for Vik, with hundreds of warriors, and as quickly as his ships would take him. But this was not information that Bergthor wished to spread, at least not to the likes of Hallbjorn. Not when he felt quite certain that Halfdan the Black would pay richly for that knowledge.

Chapter Eight

One should be a friend to one's friend,
and repay gift with gift;
men should requite laughter with laughter,
and lying with a lie.

The Sayings of Hávi
The Poetic Edda

Two days after waking in the bedchamber in Halfdan's great hall, Skorri Thorbrandsson led his column of men out through the tall gates in the earthen wall, bound away for Fevik. A long two days, but events in that time had done much to improve his mood. He was feeling more optimistic than he would have thought possible after learning that he would be sharing leadership with Thorgeir Sveinsson.

Initially, when Thorgeir had, with such delight, told him that it was Halfdan's decree that they be equals in command, Skorri had felt as miserable as he could ever recall. Once again his dreams of glory, of command, of recognition by his king, had been turned into a poisonous mix of confusion, fury, and humiliation. Even the gauntlet had not been so bad.

He was ready, at that moment, to just walk through the gates with nothing but the clothes he wore — which were not even his — and the weapons he carried, and just keep walking.

Thorgeir, it seemed, had sensed Skorri's dark turn, and the potential danger it represented. He seemed to understand that remaining in Skorri's presence just then might not be so good for his health.

"Good, then," Thorgeir had said. "This question of command, you and me, we'll discuss what it means. Later. I have business to attend to now." He looked nervously around. His eyes met Skorri's, just for an instant, before he turned away. "I'll be seeing to the ships."

He hurried off. Skorri watched him go. His mind was whirling with anger and shame. He had no sense for what course to set.

"Bugger him," Koll Thorvaldson said. He was standing at Skorri's side, watching Thorgeir walk quickly away. "He's of no concern to you."

"No concern?" Skorri looked doubtfully at Koll. "He's my equal in this, it seems. The king deemed it so."

Koll shook his head. "Not what Grim told me when he gave me Halfdan's orders to get the men ready. Grim said Thorgeir was to be your second. The command's yours. Halfdan knows better than to put two men in charge of one army."

"It doesn't seem like anyone told Thorgeir that."

"They did. Halfdan's order was that Thorgeir have command of the ships, but he's still to answer to you in all things. That's what Grim told me. Thorgeir just doesn't want you to know it. And he knows you won't go complaining to Halfdan or Grim. No better way to seem weak, or unfit for command."

"Thorgeir hopes I'll just take his word for it, that he's to be my equal?"

"That's my guess," Koll said. "He doesn't want you to come out of this looking better than him, and that's the only play he has. Because, here's the thing…the men mostly can't stand that bastard. I'll be honest, they're not so sure about you, but they truly hate him. So if it comes to it, I know who they'll follow."

Koll's voice had become softer, more conspiratorial. Skorri, as a rule, did not care for whispering and secrets and intrigue, but in this instance he was finding it quite agreeable.

"Would it be hard, do you think, to make the men more sure about me?"

"It would not," Koll said. "They know your reputation as a warrior, and that's what they most respect. Give them some reason to believe that it's in their interest to be loyal to you, and they're yours."

Skorri thought about those words. He thought about them all morning, watching the men at their drills. He thought about them as he addressed the assembled warriors, told them of the important mission on which they were bound. He considered what Koll had said as he decided to show Thorgeir that there was no question as to who had command.

It was well past noon when he finally called for a horse and ordered Koll to assemble a mounted escort of half a dozen men; not for protection, but for the gravitas they lent him. He had already ordered his servant to find him a mail shirt and helmet, both of the highest quality, the mail well-polished, the helmet tricked out with gold inlay, polished as well, until it gleamed. His sword and seax were strapped around his waist, fine calfskin gloves pulled over his hands.

Skorri Thorbrandsson was, for the first time since being dragged bound to Halfdan's hall by his traitorous men, fitted out like a proper warrior. His mood soared like a hawk on the hunt.

With his six mounted men-at-arms behind him, Skorri rode out the gate and covered the mile or so to the small harbor that served as the seaward approach to the great hall at Grømstad. The five ships of Halfdan's fleet, slated to sail to Fevik, were tied up to the two long wooden docks that jutted out into the water. Men were swarming over them — Halfdan's warriors — though they did not look like warriors just then, dressed as they were in leggings and sweat-stained tunics, with their sleeves rolled up, or bare-chested. They were heaving casks and bundles aboard, and setting up rigging, or lashing sea chests to the deck, or repairing this or that. The bustle of a fleet getting ready to put to sea, even if the voyage would be no more than a day or so north along the coast.

Skorri dismounted and his escort dismounted and they walked out along the dock, their mail making its distinctive jingling sound as they moved. They had left their helmets tied to their saddles, but other than that they came outfitted for battle. They found Thorgeir on the largest of the ships, aft by the tiller, in conference with someone Skorri did not know.

"Ah, Skorri!" Thorgeir called. He seemed to feel more confident now, among his ships and men, and his voice had its old, slightly mocking tone. "Come aboard, come aboard!" He waved for Skorri to approach, but Skorri remained where he was, silent, arms folded. For a moment Thorgeir said nothing, and then, as the silence grew more awkward, added, "You're not afraid of ships are you? Come aboard!"

Still Skorri did not move, just stood and looked at him, arms crossed over his chest, his six-man guard at his back. He could sense Thorgeir's growing unease in the way he glanced around, opened his mouth to speak, then closed it again.

Finally Thorgeir threw up his arms in a gesture of exasperation. "Very well then, I'll come to you!" He made his way amidships, where the longship bumped against the dock, and climbed up onto the worn planks.

"Skorri, I'm pleased to see…" Thorgeir began, but Skorri cut him off.

"What's the state of your readiness?"

"I…ah…" Thorgeir said, thrown off by the abrupt question, the gravity of Skorri's tone. "We're all but ready for sea, I should think."

"You should think?"

"We are all but ready for sea," Thorgeir started again. "We'll be ready by day's end." He looked at Skorri curiously.

"Good," Skorri said.

"I'll be manning each ship with sixty warriors," Thorgeir said next. "That will leave you…"

"You'll have thirty. Thirty men per ship."

Thorgeir paused, then frowned. He looked Skorri in the eyes. Skorri held his gaze and did not waver.

"Perhaps you didn't hear me," Thorgeir said, trying to regain the upper hand. "I'll take sixty men for each ship."

Skorri tilted his head back a little, looked down at Thorgeir, and rested his palm on the pommel of his sword. "Do you think this is a negotiation?"

"I think it's a…"

"Do…you…think…this is a negotiation?" Behind him, Skorri's men shifted a bit, the jingle of their mail punctuating Skorri's words.

Once again Thorgeir paused, unsure what to say. Skorri's new attitude, his assumption of command, seemed to catch him off guard. As Skorri had intended.

"I…" Thorgeir stammered a bit, but the wind was out of him now.

"Finish your work here," Skorri said. "Then I'll tell you what men you may have for the ships' crews." He turned on his heel and marched back toward the shore, his escort parting to let him pass. Thorgeir said nothing as he walked away.

The next day was filled with the final preparations. Food and ale, tents and spare weapons were loaded onto carts. Swords were sharpened, mail and helmets polished. Thorgeir was mostly absent, busying himself with the ships, avoiding Skorri to the extent that he could. And when he could not avoid Skorri, his demeanor was mostly deferential — deferential nearly to Skorri's satisfaction.

Koll knew the men far better than Skorri did, so he left it to Koll to decide who would go with Thorgeir to man the fleet. He gave Koll only one direction: allocate just thirty men per ship. That gave Thorgeir one hundred and fifty men in total: enough to sail or row or fight if he had to, while he, Skorri, would lead three hundred and fifty on foot. It seemed an appropriate division, given that the fleet should encounter no danger on their short voyage. And if Thorgeir thought it was unfair, he could whine and moan all he wished: that just made it all the sweeter for Skorri.

They moved out at dagmál the next day, a short time after breaking the night's fast. Skorri and Koll and a few of the captains were on horseback, the rest of the men on foot. Skorri was first out through the gate of Halfdan's compound, and he moved to one side to watch the men march past. They made an impressive sight: three hundred and fifty men in two loose columns, each with mail and iron helmets, spears over shoulders, swords on belts, shields slung over their backs. A frightening display of strength, enough to make Odd and those other rebel bastards piss their trousers. Enough to make anyone who saw them tremble at the power that Skorri could wield.

Here, at last, the army that Halfdan had so long promised, the army of which Skorri Thorbrandsson had so long dreamed. He smiled to himself.

They moved north through a country made up of rolling hills and stands of trees and open meadows. The summer had been dry, so the road was dusty, but that did not trouble Skorri, who rode at the head of the column. For those behind, the dust was choking, but it was better than trudging through mud. The army did not move fast — the carts of food and arms and tents slowed them up — but Skorri was not too greatly bothered. He did not want his men worn out by the march. And he was enjoying himself.

They passed by farms of various sizes along the way, each with its earthen wall surrounding the buildings, the humped roof of a farmhouse or hall visible over the top, fields where crops grew or cattle grazed. They saw no people. The dust from the marching column would be visible from some distance, and it was likely that word of the army on the move was traveling out ahead of them.

Skorri could picture the farmers and their wives and children huddling in fear, or maybe fleeing into the hills. Sure, it was their own king's men-at-arms, not some foreign enemy, but warriors were an unpredictable lot. Who knew what horrors they might visit on the innocent.

That, too, made Skorri smile.

The road ran northeast, roughly skirting the long, narrow bay on their right-hand side. Occasionally they would catch glimpses of the dark blue water and the far shore, where Ragi Oleifsson's farm stood. Or had, at least, before Skorri burned it to the ground. Where Odd Thorgrimson had once again escaped. Where Skorri's men had started their traitorous turn.

This was country that Skorri knew well. As King Halfdan's overseer he had been responsible for making sure the proper taxes were collected, and roads and bridges and such were maintained, and the king's peace was enforced. He had visited every farm and every village in a forty-mile radius, and he was known and generally hated by all. Such was the fate of the king's sœslumadr.

Fevik was not so far a march, and they might have reached it by nightfall with just a little effort, but as they continued deeper into the country, Skorri had another idea. He turned to Koll, who was riding at his side.

"There's a farm a little north of the road. Prosperous. An impressive great hall, or it was the last time I saw it. I think we'll spend the night there, give the men a proper rest before we continue on to Fevik."

"If you think that's best," Koll said. "Though I'm sure we could make Fevik by nightfall. Might have to leave the wagons with a guard to catch up, but the bulk of the column could make it."

"I'm sure we could," Skorri said. "But there's no need to tire the men out."

Skorri had been clear from the onset that he was eager to get to Fevik, and quickly, and Koll had acted accordingly. Now, Koll had to be wondering why Skorri was calling for an early halt to the march.

In truth, after all that Halfdan had put him through, and with this powerful army at his back, Skorri was feeling a bit less motivated to find Odd and put this business to rest, a fact he was only now coming to understand. Better to keep the warriors behind him happy. Better to secure their loyalty. And he had just thought of a lovely way to do that.

Half a mile on they came to a smaller road that ran off to the north, and Skorri turned the column that way, leading the men through rolling hills, with ledges of blue granite breaking through knee-high grass, and stands of oak, maple, and birch, and the ubiquitous pine and spruce.

They crested a hill and saw below them, and half a mile away, the farm that Skorri had in mind. It was clear even from that distance that the great hall was indeed impressive, its tall, arched roof stretching well over a hundred feet in length. A number of outbuildings were scattered around the larger structure, and it was all contained by a dirt wall of no great height, a wall intended to delineate the great hall's grounds and to keep wandering livestock in or out.

Beyond the walls were tilled fields lying fallow, and others, fenced in, where a scattering of cows and sheep grazed. There did not seem to be much activity around the place.

"Is this the hall you had in mind?" Koll asked, the slightest note of hesitation in his voice.

"Yes."

"This is Thorgrim Ulfsson's farm."

"Was. Thorgrim Ulfsson's dead."

"Yes, of course. King Halfdan himself said as much. He died owing taxes to the king. Which is why Halfdan claimed the farm for his own in the first place."

"Exactly," Skorri said. He was almost surprised that Koll, or anyone, recalled the misty origins of this bloody rebellion they were putting down. "The farm is by rights Halfdan's now. So who better to enjoy it than Halfdan's men?"

They continued on down the road, toward the wooden gate in the earthen wall, which was shut, and likely barred. Skorri was just wondering whether someone would open it for them, or if they would have to smash it down, when he heard it creak and saw it swing wide. They rode through and into the yard surrounding the great hall without breaking stride.

A lone man was standing halfway between the gate and the hall, and he approached as Skorri rode toward him. An older man, dressed in working clothes that had seen hard use. His hair was black and gray and long, his beard the same.

"I'm Skafti Hrappsson," the man said. "I'm the overseer here."

Skorri nodded to the man. He knew Skafti, remembered him from his days collecting taxes and keeping the king's peace.

"I'm Lord Skorri Thorbrandsson," Skorri said.

"I know who you are. King's overseer. Former overseer. The 'Lord' is something new."

Skorri ignored him, looked around the yard. "Where is everyone?"

"At their work."

"Well, we are their work now," Skorri said. He swung himself off his saddle and dropped to the ground in front of Skafti. Koll dismounted as well, and came around to join him.

"Me and my men, we'll need food and lodging for the night," Skorri continued. "We'll need our horses cared for."

Skafti turned and spit on the ground. "No one living in the great hall now. Got no food, no ale. No fires going."

Skorri fixed the man with a stare that would have made lesser men wilt, but Skafti just held his gaze. As king's overseer, Skorri had grown accustomed to this sort of silent insubordination. No one was happy when he arrived, and Skafti was probably even less happy to see him ride in with nearly four hundred armed men in search of food and shelter. Hence the stubborn lack of cooperation.

You're going to be less happy still, and soon, I should imagine, Skorri thought.

"I think you're a lying dog, Skafti Hrappsson," Skorri said. "Now, go see that the fires are stoked up immediately. Send men to fetch ale, mead, whatever you have. A few of my men will go with them, you understand, to make sure they don't overlook anything. Food as well. And get half a dozen of those sheep and butcher them up, right away. I want my men eating roast mutton by nightfall."

"Not sure we can do that," Skafti said. "Most of the men and servants are gone. Thralls sold off. Not many here to do as you need."

"Hmm," Skorri said. "That disappoints me, I must say. I was looking forward to my men having a comfortable night. But if you can't provide that, then this farm's of no use to us, so I suppose we'll just set it on fire and be on our way."

"This farm belongs to…" Skafti paused, unsure what to say next.

"Yes? Belongs to…?"

"Belongs to King Halfdan." Skafti spit the words. He did not try to hide his disgust at having to say as much.

"Exactly," Skorri said. "And I command King Halfdan's warriors. So see to it, or we'll burn the great hall to the ground, and you and all the rest of the vermin here with it."

It turned out there were more people still working on Thorgrim's farm than Skafti had suggested. Quite a few more. But that came as no surprise to Skorri. There was also considerably more ale, and mead, and hams, and salted meat, and dried fish, and bread, and all manner of foodstuffs than Skafti had led them to believe. Even in Thorgrim's absence, things had been well cared for, the great hall fully provisioned.

Thorgrim Night Wolf and Ornolf the Restless had planned to go raiding for a single season, but now three had come and gone, and nothing had been heard from them. Most took that to mean they were dead, though no one knew for certain.

But Skafti Hrappsson, who Skorri knew to be an honest and conscientious man, was not likely to presume his master was gone. He had been charged with overseeing the place in Thorgrim's absence, and no doubt did so and did it well, keeping the homestead ready at any moment for Thorgrim's return. That had been Skorri's guess, and it seemed he had guessed right.

Now, to continue keeping Thorgrim's farm safe, Skafti had to prevent Skorri from putting it to the torch, and that meant carrying out Skorri's orders promptly and well. He sent servants, with Skorri's men in company, to empty out the stores of food and drink. Half a dozen sheep were slaughtered and butchered and were soon roasting over the fires set roaring in the hearths on the floor of the great hall. The horses were brushed and fed and watered and bedded down in the stables with fresh straw.

By nightfall all three hundred and fifty of Skorri's men were seated at the various tables in Thorgrim's hall, which was easily big enough to accommodate them. The meat was cooked and served out, the wine and mead and ale flowing. Voices were loud, punctuated with laughter and singing: the sounds of men very much enjoying themselves.

Happy men are loyal men, Skorri thought, as he sat at the head of the table and looked out over his warriors, cups in hand, remnants of a feast scattered before them. He had not always believed that. Once, he had thought a good leader led by fear alone. But he was learning, revising his philosophy.

Rewards and punishment, he thought. Here were the rewards, in abundance. And more to come. When the time was right, and if he had to, he would apply the punishment. But not now.

One by one the men drifted off to sleep, or went face down on the table and stayed there, slumped over and snoring. There had been half a dozen women among the servants in the great hall, and Skorri noticed how they had vanished, one by one, as the evening wore on. Gone into hiding, no doubt, before the king's warriors became too drunk and too demanding in their desires. But none of the men were calling for women, so Skorri let it go.

Koll had picked twenty men to stand watch overnight, and when he reported to Skorri that they were in place and sober enough to do their duty Skorri thanked him and wandered off to bed. At the far end of the hall a few bedchambers were walled off from the main room. Skorri found the largest — Thorgrim's own, Skorri imagined — and that was the one he took for himself.

He carried a lamp into the dark room and looked around. After all that time, it was still clean and well-appointed, with blankets and furs on the bed, tapestries on the walls, chests which might or might not contain Thorgrim's personal belongings. There were swords and seaxes hanging from pegs, and silver candle holders, and a table with small chests of jewelry which Skorri imagined belonged to Thorgrim's late wife, and which Thorgrim had never had the heart to remove.

You live well, Thorgrim Night Wolf, Skorri thought. *Lived...* he corrected himself. He did not believe that Thorgrim Night Wolf was still alive. He hoped he was right.

If Thorgrim was alive, and if he managed to return in the middle of this uprising that his son had started over the king's claim to his farm, then it could be bad; very bad, indeed. There was no telling how the people might rally to Thorgrim, son of Ulf of the Battle Song, son-in-law of Ornolf the Restless, a man well-loved and admired in his own right.

But Skorri was not concerned about that. Because Thorgrim Night Wolf was dead.

He settled comfortably in Thorgrim's bed, covered by Thorgrim's furs, in the shelter of Thorgrim's great hall. As he drifted off to sleep, he realized that he found such accommodations quite agreeable. Found that they suited him well.

Skorri's servant woke him the next morning, just as the sun was coming up. Porridge was already cooking in a big pot over the hearth. Skorri had not ordered that done, so he guessed that Skafti Hrappsson had. Skafti was no doubt eager to please Halfdan's men, and to see them gone. And he would get his wish. Mostly.

Koll and the other captains roused the rest of the men, who were sleeping on the platforms along the sides of the great hall, or on the floor, or still face-down on the table. The servants brought basins of water, and the men washed their hands and faces and dug into the bowls of porridge offered them.

When they were done breaking their fast, they pulled their mail shirts back on, strapped their sword belts around their waists. Skorri waited until they were ready to move, then stood up on a bench so he could address them all.

"You are the king's men," he said, his voice loud and commanding. "My men. The finest in the land. You deserve more riches than the weaker sort. You deserve the spoils that come with being victors. This…" he spread his arms to indicate the great hall in which they stood, "…this was once the property of your enemy. Now it belongs to you. Before we leave, I want you to strip this place of anything of value. Anything you wish to keep, it's yours. All will be divided equally among you. But all is yours."

No one moved. Skorri looked down at Koll, who was staring up at him with a look of surprise, bordering on shock. Skorri looked out over the men once more.

"We march soon. If there's anything you'd take from this place, take it now."

That seemed to break through the fog. One man cheered, and then another, and then they were all cheering. And then they were rushing in every direction, snatching up everything that might be of any value: lanterns, and candlesticks, and tapestries off the walls, and swords, and spears, and seaxes, and battle axes. They tore into each of the sleeping chambers and came out with blankets, and furs, and jewelry, and mail, and tunics, and dresses, and shoes, and cloaks. And looks of confusion were long gone. Now Skorri saw only greed.

Skafti was standing beside him, he realized, though where he had come from Skorri did not know. His arms were folded as he watched the looting go on and on. He was frowning a bit, but otherwise his expression was unreadable. Skorri ignored him.

"King Halfdan lays claim to this farm," Skafti said at last. "And that means everything in it. You're stealing from your own king."

"You don't believe for a moment that Halfdan has any rightful claim to this place, you two-faced old dog," Skorri said.

Skafti spit on the floor. "Don't matter what I think. Matters what Halfdan thinks."

And I don't care a rat's ass what Halfdan thinks, Skorri thought, though he kept his mouth shut. He would never say such a thing out loud, and it surprised him that he had even thought as much. But it pleased him as well. He could feel his priorities shifting under his feet.

Chapter Nine

I know it, the eleventh: if I have to lead long-standing friends into conflict,
I chant beneath the shield-rims,
and they journey with strength,
safe to battle.

The Sayings of Hávi
The Poetic Edda

It was some time past midday when the fishing boats returned to the hidden camp on the island. They were early. Odd knew they were early because he had been on the island, in the fisherfolk's camp, for four days by then, and he had learned the rhythm of their work.

Every morning, just after sunrise, the men would load their nets and push their boats off the beach into the calm, protected water and row off between the islands. The women would turn to their tasks of cooking and cleaning and washing and mending. Odd and the other castaways would try to make themselves useful where they could. Bragi, Huginn, and Muninn helped mend nets and repair boats. Odd split firewood and gutted fish and laid them out to dry, not terribly pleasant work, but it was a help. Signy and Alfdis and the few women from Ragi's household joined the other women at their labors. Ragi and Amundi lent a hand where they could.

Odd tried to concentrate on the jobs at hand, but his thoughts kept returning to the wolf.

He had told no one about the encounter, not even Signy. He was not sure what the others would say about it, or if they would even believe him, or attach any significance to the event if they did. At times he was not even sure that it had actually happened. And he did not care. Because either way, it changed everything.

The entire thing, from his waking and running through the woods, to his standing face to face with the beast, to its running off, could not have taken very long. A few moments, maybe a bit more. He might have thought the whole thing was a dream, had he not found some small broken twigs clinging to his tunic, and scratches on his arms, when he awoke the next morning.

But, brief as it was, the strange event had shifted his entire attitude, like some huge rock suddenly yielding to pressure. He felt hopeful. He felt ready.

And that change stayed with him, even through the monotony of the following days. Every afternoon the fleet returned, the boats heavy-laden with fish, and Odd waited for Arnor to announce that the time had come for them to make their way to Fevik. And every day Arnor said nothing of the kind. Still, Odd's patience remained intact, and he hoped it would stay that way, though he was not entirely certain.

But he watched the boats now as they came pulling back into the little cove, earlier than was their wont, and clearly not as loaded down by their catch, and he felt hope flare up again.

Odd was standing by the water's edge when Arnor's faering ground up on the gravel. Silver and blue fish flapped in the bottom of the boat, but the catch, which did not even reach to the turn of the bilge, was smaller than Odd was used to seeing.

One by one Arnor's men leapt out and pulled the boat further ashore, and then finally Arnor himself stepped out. He looked around, scratched his beard, and said to Odd, "Tomorrow, we go to Fevik."

With that, Arnor made his way up the beach, leaving it to the others to empty out the boat and tend to the fish. Odd knew better than to press the man for more information. It would come, in Arnor's own time.

That time was náttmál, which was about what Odd had figured. Fish gutted and split, boats hauled ashore, nets laid out to dry, the men gathered by the fire for the nightly feast of fish stew and ale. The talk, as usual, was about the day's catch, but it was not the enthusiastic discussion of the past few days, a discourse on the extraordinary luck they had been having. The moon, apparently, was in a new phase, and the fish, while still running, were not doing so with the wild enthusiasm they had displayed over the past few weeks.

"Things are slowing down now," Arnor said to Odd. "And they'll get slower still, and stay that way for a while. So tomorrow we'll get you and your men to Fevik."

Odd nodded. "I'll be grateful for that."

Arnor turned and called out to the assembled men and women. "Listen here, you lot. Tomorrow we're bringing Odd and the rest to Fevik. We'll need…eight boats, I reckon. We got eight willing to go?"

He looked around and Odd looked around. Every head was nodding.

"What are we doing once we get to Fevik?" one of the fishermen, a man named Skidi, called out. Arnor did not answer. He just looked at Odd.

"Not sure," Odd said. "For a week now I haven't seen anything but trees, rocks, and fish. I don't know what's going on in Fevik, or anywhere. I don't know if there's anyone left who has the stomach to keep fighting Halfdan. That's what I want to find out. If you men can get me and my friends there, we'd be grateful. And if there is fighting to be done, and any of you wants to stay and join in, you'd certainly be welcome."

He looked around again. More nodding heads, but no one spoke, no one offered to fight. Odd had learned a bit about the fisherfolk in the time he had been on the island, and he knew they were not much given to promises and commitments. They were not much given to talking in general.

The fishermen ended their day the way they had every day since Odd's arrival, with ale and sad songs and more ale, and then Odd and Signy retired to their tent. Signy unfastened the brooches that held her dress up, stepped out of the garment, and lay down on their makeshift bed. Odd pulled a blanket over her, then removed his tunic and lay down at her side. Soon he was in a deep sleep. Ever since his encounter with the wolf, his sleep had been restful and undisturbed.

He woke just before dawn, though he was by no means the first one up. He never was. He stood, pulled his tunic on, and stepped out of the tent. The fire had been stoked to a blaze and a pot was hanging over it. Odd was pretty sure, from past experience, that the pot contained oat and barley porridge, hearty fare for breaking a fast.

A handful of men were sitting around the fire, which was not unusual, but now they were sharpening spears and axes and a handful of swords, which was. Odd had not seen any weapons in the camp before that morning, save for the knives that every man wore on his belt. But the fisherfolk were Northmen, and like every Northman they would not be without weapons nearby.

Odd made his way over to the fire and held his hands over the flames to ward off the morning chill. Arnor was there, and he left off running a stone over the edge of his sword and looked up as Odd came into the circle.

"We'll eat," he said. "Then load up the boats with food and ale and such. Get underway late morning. Won't take but a few hours to get to Fevik." With that he turned back to his sharpening.

"Good," Odd said. He thought about Arnor's words. "Shouldn't need much food and ale, for a few hours," he said.

"Take us a few hours to get there," Arnor said. "Haven't decided how long we'll stay."

Soon the rest of the men in the camp turned out, and once it was announced that the porridge was done they began digging in with enthusiasm. When dagmál was finished they began loading small kegs of ale and fish, and bags of coarse bread, into the boats. One by one they shoved off and took their places on the thwarts, oars held upright. Arnor had called for eight boats, but it seemed that every man in the fishing camp had elected to go to Fevik, and that meant more than enough boats to carry the survivors of Bragi's ninth shipwreck.

Odd and Amundi, Signy and Alfdis joined Arnor in his boat, while Bragi, wisely, chose another. Arnor took his place at the tiller. He grunted at the six men rowing and they brought the oars down, leaned forward, and took a long stroke.

The heavy faering began to gather way as the men fell into their rhythm and Arnor steered through the crowd of drifting vessels to take the lead. Arnor's boat left the camp astern, and the others fell in behind, a long line of boats, a couple dozen or so, moving at a steady and identical pace, as if they were all being pulled by the same rope.

Odd watched the islands as they passed. They were the same islands he had seen five days before on his way to the fishing camp, but coming from the opposite direction they seemed entirely unfamiliar. It was mid-tide and ebbing, and each island had along its base a stripe of wet rock where the water had fallen away, and above it, lighter-colored granite, gray-brown and dry.

He looked forward. He could see the wider channel ahead, the one Bragi was navigating when he ran Ragi's ship up on the rock. Once they reached that channel they would turn southeast and continue to work their way through the innumerable islands along the coast. He wondered if they would have to row the entire way, or if the wind would be fair to use the sailing rig that each of the fishing boats carried. He was about to ask when Amundi spoke first.

"Those others, what are they doing?" There was surprise and a trace of suspicion in his voice.

Odd turned. The rest of the fishing boats had stopped rowing and were sitting motionless, oars dragging in the water. Already Arnor's boat had left them a couple hundred feet astern.

"I'm going to take a look first," Arnor said.

Odd knew he would not elaborate, so he said, "Look at what?"

"We'll poke our nose out into the channel. See that none of that bastard Halfdan's ships are hanging about. If it's clear, the rest'll join me."

Odd nodded. That made sense.

A long cove came into view on the island to the west, and more of the channel was visible beyond the island's northern end. The boat pulled on, with Arnor looking toward the northwest, in the direction of Halfdan's home, the direction from which any of his ships might be expected to come.

Odd looked in the same direction as the island passed down the larboard side and more and more of the channel became visible. He saw nothing out of the ordinary. Until he did.

"Son of a whore, is that…?" he said, too surprised to finish.

"It is," Arnor said, and then, "Hold your oars."

The rowers stopped pulling and twisted around on the thwarts so they could see what the five people in the stern were looking at. Longships, a mile off, maybe a bit more, coming from the northwest and making way under full sail, their bows aiming for the same channel between the islands and the mainland that Arnor and the others were steering for. Five ships, and big ones, the striped patterns and diamond patterns on their sails bright in the morning light. A part of King Halfdan's fleet. They could be nothing else.

Arnor gave a bit of a sigh, as if suddenly faced with some minor inconvenience. He swiveled around until he was looking aft. The nearest of the fishing boats was about fifty yards astern and tucked up near the shore. Arnor gave a wave, pointed at the long cove off the larboard side, then faced forward again.

"Go," he said.

His own rowers took a pull and Arnor pushed the tiller over. The boat made a wide turn until it was pointing into the cove. To the south, the rest of the boats were filing into the cove as well.

The northern end of the island was a tall hump of rock and scrubby trees, and it hid the men and boats in the cove from the approaching longships, and hid the longships from them. The shores of the cove were mostly granite, and mostly steep, but there was one spot of gravel beach, and Arnor ran his boat up on that.

One by one the other boats approached and ran ashore as well, the men hopping out and pulling the boats farther up. No one spoke. The entire thing had an air of something well-rehearsed and oft repeated.

"Come on," Arnor said. Odd was not sure who he was addressing, but he said it loud enough for everyone to hear, and they all followed in his wake as he headed up the beach to where the gravel ended and the granite ledge began. Odd and Signy and their people followed as well, and Ragi and Bragi Shipslayer joined them.

"What's this all about?" Ragi asked.

"Looks like Halfdan's fleet's coming out," Odd said. "Or part of it. I think Arnor wants to have a better look, but I don't know."

The men and handful of women climbed up the smooth, sloping rock. They were a dozen feet from the crest when Arnor said, "Keep low." He bent down, approaching the crest doubled over, and the others followed suit. Soon they reached a place where they could see over the granite hill to the channel beyond. Arnor went down on one knee, eyes on the dark blue water and the gray, tree-capped islands to the north, with others kneeling on either side of him.

Halfdan's ships, running with a favorable wind, were noticeably closer now. Odd could make out the bright dots of color along their sides — the warriors' shields in the shield racks — and the flash of white under their bows as they plowed along. They were a handsome sight, Odd had to admit it, and a frightening one.

He looked off to the east. He could see a hump of rock about a quarter-mile away and he felt certain it was the ledge that Bragi had run their ship up on, but there was no wreck to be seen.

"What happened to Ragi's ship?" he asked, nodding toward the rock. "Isn't that where it hit?"

"It is," Arnor said. "Bragi, that dumb bastard. The wreck slipped off with the next tide. It's likely just under the water. You'll see it, once we get some more of an ebb."

They turned their attention back to Halfdan's ships. They were heading into the channel between the island and the mainland to the north, following the same route that Bragi Shipslayer had taken on his way to Fevik.

"Where do you think they're bound?" Odd asked. He had his own idea as to the answer, and he hoped he was wrong.

"On that heading?" Arnor said. "Most likely…"

"Just two real possibilities," Bragi interrupted. "Either they're coming to clean out this rats' nest of fishermen here, or they're heading to Fevik." Arnor glared at Bragi. Bragi pretended not to notice. "Isn't that right, Arnor?" he asked.

Arnor did not answer at first, and Odd thought he wouldn't. But finally he said, "That's right."

Odd said nothing, but silently he cursed his ill-luck. Had they left the fishermen's camp even a day before, he would already have been in Fevik, already gathering forces to stand against Halfdan. Now Halfdan's men would beat him there, and they would see to it that there was little enthusiasm for resistance.

How Halfdan could have known he was bound for Fevik, he could not imagine. He stared at the ships as they altered course a bit, passing between the island and the mainland, and the anger tumbled around in his mind.

Idiot! he thought. How hard was it for Halfdan to guess that he, Odd, would go to Fevik? Fevik was his home, the place where he was best known, the place where his grandfather, Ornolf the Restless, was still revered. He had taken the most obvious course of action imaginable, and then wondered how Halfdan might have guessed.

"They're not coming to clear out the fishermen," Bragi said, pulling Odd from his thoughts. Halfdan's ships were almost directly north of them now, and only about six hundred feet off the island's rocky shore. If the fishermen had been standing, rather than kneeling behind the crest of the hill, they would have been clearly visible.

"How do you know?" Amundi asked.

"Fast as they're going? If they meant to head for the fishermen's camp they'd have taken in sail by now, come in under sweeps."

Odd looked at Arnor, waiting for a reply, but Arnor said nothing. Odd suspected that he agreed with Bragi, a thing he was not inclined to admit.

Of all the cursed luck… Odd thought.

The five ships were just past the island now, sails full, Halfdan's swallow-tail banner — white, with the black silhouette of a gyrfalcon in flight — snapping at their mastheads. They had only the other string of broken islands to the east to navigate, and then they would be in relatively open water, at least until the next chain of islands along that ragged coast.

Odd was watching the ships, but his mind was elsewhere, thinking about what he would do now, what he *could* do now, with Halfdan sending this powerful fleet to Fevik. It occurred to him that the ships might not be all. Halfdan might also be sending warriors by land, with the hope of catching Odd and those following him between the two.

"Say, Arnor, do you think…" Bragi said, a hopeful note in his voice.

"Maybe," Arnor said.

What they were talking about, Odd did not know, but suddenly the lead ship in Halfdan's fleet came to a staggering halt, the bow dipping down, the mast swaying forward. The ship began to pivot on whatever it struck, turning sideways as the wind drove it on, listing hard to one side, though it remained otherwise immobile.

"Ha! Take that, sheep-biters!" Bragi all but shouted.

Odd looked at Arnor, who had the closest thing to a smile on his face that Odd had ever seen.

"What by all the gods happened?" Amundi asked.

"Ragi's ship, that Shipslayer ran up on that rock? Which I told you sunk?" Arnor said. "That stupid bastard driving Halfdan's ship just hit it."

Up and down the line, the fishermen hooted out jeers and shouts of derision, as loud as they could without being heard by the warriors two hundred yards away.

"Will they sink?" Signy asked.

"Doubt it," Arnor said. "It's not like they hit rock. They may be stupid bastards, but they're not as stupid as Bragi here."

They watched for a moment more, then Arnor added, "Still, looks like they hit hard, hung up pretty good, and on a falling tide. That ship's not likely to move any time soon. Not until the flood lifts it off."

"Well, that's something," Signy said. "I'm just sorry they won't sink."

Out on the water, Halfdan's small fleet seemed to have been thrown into chaos. The four intact ships went sweeping on past, but as they realized that the one had struck, they dropped sail as quickly as they could, which was not until they had been blown well past their stranded comrade.

They were still being set downwind and down-tide as the oars came out and they began the hard pull back. Aboard the ship that was hung up on the wreck, the crew was rushing fore and aft, struggling to pull in the sail they had hurriedly dropped, and leaning over the side to look at what they had hit. There seemed to be a great deal of confusion, yelling, and waving of arms.

"This is some fun, ain't it?" Bragi said. Huginn and Muninn agreed it was, and Odd did, too, though he did not say anything. The others were enjoying the show as well, judging by the ongoing comments and derision.

Halfdan's five ships huddled together, and aboard each there was more yelling and waving of arms and looking over the side. Two of the ships made a brief attempt to tow the stranded vessel off, but it was not in the least successful.

It was near midday when it became clear to everyone — the men and women on the hill and the warriors on Halfdan's ships — that the vessel hung up on the wreck was not moving until the tide flooded again, just as Arnor had first predicted. One by one the other ships pulled in their oars, raised sail, and gathered way back on their original course.

"Leaving the injured wolf behind," Ragi said.

"Injured, but still dangerous," Amundi said.

Dangerous, yes, Odd thought, looking at the stranded ship. The crew seemed to be sitting on their sea chests or on the low decks, resigned to their temporary fate. *Dangerous, but vulnerable.* He wondered if any of the others were thinking along the same lines that he was.

"Well," Arnor said at last, standing and stretching his cramped muscles, prompting the others to do the same. "They got about thirty men on that ship. We got about a hundred and fifty between all the boats."

"What are you thinking?" Amundi asked.

"Nothing. I think about fish. When it comes to fighting, Odd here does the thinking." He looked at Odd and everyone else did as well.

But Odd had already made his decision. "Let's take that ship from Halfdan," he said, "and see what use it might be."

Chapter Ten

News comes from the north:
The assembly is over,
Harsh sentence passed on me...

Gisli Sursson's Saga

Kjotvi Sighvatsson was talking. It seemed to Halfdan that he had been talking for a long time. Kjotvi was a jarl with extensive holdings to the north of Grømstad. He was loyal and paid his taxes without complaint and maintained a hird of two hundred excellent warriors, so he was a man who deserved Halfdan's attention. And he was getting it. At least, some of it.

Halfdan stifled a sigh. He glanced over at the other jarls and men of influence seated on the benches flanking his throne. They met like this every week or so, Halfdan and the important men of his kingdom, the men who, with their wealth and their warriors and the control they had over their people, helped the king maintain his power.

Their ranks, of course, were thinned. Amundi Thorsteinsson used to attend regularly, but he had turned traitor, as had several others. Some had been forgiven their treason, but were no longer welcome in the great hall. Others were being hunted. Thorgrim Ulfsson and Ornolf the Restless had attended once, but it had been years now since they had been heard from.

These gatherings were important, but they were also a bore, and generally devolved into a series of complaints about this or that, none of which interested Halfdan the Black.

That was the case now, as Kjotvi railed about a neighboring jarl, one who conveniently was not present, but who was apparently encroaching on Kjotvi's land. Halfdan did not care. In the best of times he would not have cared, and this was far from the best of times.

All the men sitting there believed that Halfdan had successfully put down the uprising led by Odd Thorgrimson and the other freemen to the east, that he had crushed the revolt the way a king should do. But Halfdan was not so sure. Odd was still out there, and Halfdan's people had brought him word of stirrings, rumblings, discontent. If Odd were to appear again, Halfdan was not sure what would happen. He would certainly look weak if the revolt he had crushed proved not to be so crushed after all.

Skorri will deal with that problem, he thought. *Skorri and Thorgeir.* But again, Halfdan was not so sure. He had been impressed by Skorri's loyalty at first, his refusal to abandon the hunt for Odd, his determination to catch the bastard. But Skorri, it seemed, did not take the punishment that was coming to him in the spirit it was intended, as an absolute test of obedience and a demonstration of his king's strength. His attitude seemed to verge on sullen anger. It was not good.

And Thorgeir. Thorgeir was loyal to Thorgeir, and whoever could do Thorgeir the most good. That, obviously, was Halfdan, which meant that Thorgeir was Halfdan's man. Unless he decided that someone else could do more for him. That was not so good, either.

It's not as if either of those two are any sort of threat to me, Halfdan thought next, and that was certainly true. Everything they had was given to them by their king. They were completely beholden to him. The worst they could do was fail in the task Halfdan had sent them to Fevik to carry out.

But if they did fail, and a genuine uprising ensued, then that might be a grave threat indeed.

"My Lord Halfdan?"

Halfdan looked up. Kjotvi had been addressing the assembly in general, but now he was looking directly at his king.

"Yes?"

"I hope your highness sees the justice in what I'm asking," Kjotvi said.

"Yes, yes, of course," Halfdan answered. He had no idea what Kjotvi was asking, or what he had just said. He looked to his left where Grim Grimsson, with his extraordinary memory, would generally be standing, keeping track of all that transpired. But Grim was not there.

Where is that fool, Grim? Halfdan thought. *He better have heard what this idiot Kjotvi just said.*

He wished desperately that all these people would just go away and leave him alone to exercise his gyrfalcon, but he knew, to his dismay, it would be some time before that happened.

Halfdan turned back to Kjotvi. "We'll see to making sure everything is settled in a fair way," he said, and his tone strongly suggested that he was done discussing the subject.

"Yes, highness, thank you," Kjotvi said. He sat down again, clearly aware that Halfdan had not been listening, but knowing better than to indicate as much.

"Now, what other business do we…" Halfdan began, when he saw Grim in the corner of his eye, standing in the posture he assumed when he had something important to say. "Hold a moment," he said instead, and called Grim over with a jerk of the head.

Grim hurried over, stood directly in front of the throne, leaning close so that none of the others could hear, though Halfdan knew they would be trying very hard to do so.

"Your highness…"

"Yes?"

"I have a man outside who would speak with you, lord. He's only hinted to me what he has to say…thinks he's being clever…but if I understand him, you'll want to hear it. You alone, lord."

Halfdan scowled a bit. He did not care for this sort of thing, for men keeping secrets close. If someone was playing coy with him, his natural reaction was to do violence to them. But if Grim said it was important, it likely was.

"Very well," he said. He looked up at the council, who were looking at him. "Some pressing business has come up. Go and find some food and drink, and we'll resume presently."

The jarls could not hide their curiosity, but neither did they hesitate to stand, bow, and disappear to the far end of the great hall. Grim hurried off, and a moment later he returned, leading a ragged, disreputable-looking man. His ill-fitting clothes suggested one who had once been stout but who had shed a lot of weight. The rents and patches suggested hard times. Most of his left ear was missing, but the wound was not recent.

The two men stopped in front of the throne and Grim whispered the word, "Kneel." The man hesitated, just for a heartbeat, then went down on his knees.

"Rise," Halfdan said, and the man stood.

"My lord, this man is named Bergthor Skeggjason and he says he's just returned from raiding in Engla-land and Frisia, and he has news he thinks will be of interest to you."

"Very well," Halfdan said. "Speak."

Bergthor looked up at Halfdan, looked him in the eyes, looked away, then found the courage to look him in the eyes again. "Ah…King Halfdan…" he began, stammering and hesitant. "Ah… yes, I do indeed have news. News of great importance… and…ah…news that, well, I think might be of some value to you. That is, your highness, news that you might want to…pay…gold…to hear."

Halfdan scowled at the man. He had obviously been rehearsing this demand for some time, probably had the whole thing quite polished on his way to the great hall. But now, standing in front of the king, his words and his courage were failing him. As well they might. The idea of extorting Halfdan the Black for money in exchange for information was remarkably bold, the kind of boldness that could quickly see a man held down and screaming out the last seconds of his life. This fellow Bergthor seemed to have realized as much, once the words started spilling out.

"You say that you have news that's important to me? And in order for you to give it to me, I should pay you in gold?" Halfdan said. His words were soft, calm, and they were turning Bergthor's bowels into some kind of putrefied liquid. He could see that. But, incredibly, the man continued on.

"Ah…yes, your highness, I think…that is to say…I would think that it might well be worth it…knowing what I do."

"I see," said Halfdan. "How about this? You tell me what you know, and I won't have my men cut your balls off and force you to eat them in front of me. How does that sound?" He looked up and called, "Guards!" and the two men standing close by came hurrying up, drawing seaxes as they did.

"No, lord! No, no need, no. Of course I'll tell everything I know! I was just…I…" Bergthor's words trailed off.

"Go," Halfdan said to the guards, with a wave of his hand. The men retreated back to their stations as Bergthor, well-motivated now, began to speak.

"Since I've been back, lord, I've heard tell of what that traitor, that scum, Odd Thorgrimson has done, rebelling and all. It's unthinkable. And I thought you should know…I understand that most folk believe that his father, Thorgrim…Thorgrim Ulfsson, known as Night Wolf…most think him dead. But he's not. I was with him, lord. We went raiding together, me and Thorgrim. Of course I had no notion of what his son was about."

The words were like a slap to Halfdan's face. *Thorgrim Night Wolf?* He felt his stomach tighten up, he felt sick as he considered the meaning of it. This had all started, this fight with Odd, because Halfdan had thought Thorgrim Night Wolf was dead, and he meant to take his lands.

It was not a move he had made lightly. Thorgrim was well-loved and well respected in East Agder. He was a powerful man. The people would rally to him. But Halfdan needed the income from Thorgrim's farm and property, enough that he had been willing to gamble that Thorgrim, who had been gone for nearly two years by then, and had not been heard from, was indeed dead.

Ever since then, and ever since Thorgrim's son had risen up against him, Halfdan had entertained one frightening thought: perhaps Thorgrim lived, and would return. As time had rolled past, he had convinced himself that Thorgrim was indeed dead, that the threat was gone. And now this.

It could change everything. It was bad enough, the way the people rallied to the son. How would they rally to the father? And what if it was not just Thorgrim?

"What of Ornolf the Restless? What do you know of him?"

"Ornolf's dead," Bergthor said. "Thorgrim told me so himself. Killed fighting in Ireland."

"Hmm," Halfdan said. That, at least, was good news. If the two of them had returned, there was no end to the trouble that might arise. Still, Thorgrim alone could create huge problems.

"Very well then, tell me what you know," Halfdan said.

"Yes, highness," Bergthor said. He seemed to have abandoned hope of payment, and now was just looking to get away with his life. "I was on the south coast of Engla-land, highness, me with four ships in company, and we came across Thorgrim Night Wolf, who had six ships and near three hundred warriors under his command. We went raiding together, at a place called Hamtun. That's where I got this, highness," he added, touching the remains of his ear.

"And?"

"And, highness, we fought with the king of Wessex, his fleet, and later Thorgrim and some others, they went to Wessex and they tried to…"

"I don't give a rat's ass what Thorgrim did in Engla-land, or what you did," Halfdan said. "I want to know where Thorgrim is, and what he intends."

"Ah, yes, of course, Lord Halfdan. Thorgrim and me, we parted company there, on the south coast of Engla-land, like I said, and Thorgrim, he took payment from the king of Wessex to protect them crossing the narrow seas. And he meant to return to East Agder after that, lord. That was all he talked of, returning to his farm."

Halfdan's scowl deepened. He looked off into the distance, considering this, vaguely aware of Bergthor fidgeting where he stood. He was tempted to tell Bergthor to stand still or he'd lose his other ear, but he guessed that frightening the man even more would be counterproductive.

"You did well, bringing this to me," Halfdan said, looking back at Bergthor and moderating his tone. "Thank you. Such information is certainly worth rewarding, and I'll see you're paid well for it."

Bergthor smiled, his expression a mixture of avarice and relief. "Thank you, your highness. My first loyalty is always to you, you may depend on that."

"Yes, yes, good. Now, tell me what you know of Thorgrim's whereabouts now."

"Well, highness, I know he was bound for Frankia, but I have no notion if he made it. Of course, there's no reason to think he didn't. The season was good, and he had six ships. Maybe the Franks turned on him. I don't know."

"When would he have been in Frankia?"

"We parted ways a couple months ago, highness. So, likely it was last month he was there? If he made it, like I said."

Halfdan nodded slowly as he thought about that. "And as far as you know, after Frankia he was bound for East Agder and his farm?"

"Yes, lord. That was certainly his intent."

Halfdan was silent again, staring off into a dark corner of the hall, until he became aware that Bergthor was fidgeting again. It seemed the man had told him everything he knew, which was precious little, but still of great importance.

"Have you told anyone else about this?" Halfdan asked next.

"Ah…no, lord. Certainly not," Bergthor said. He was lying, and not doing a particularly good job of it. "But the men who were with me, they knew, too, of course. About Thorgrim."

"Of course," Halfdan said, cursing to himself. *Of course…* Stories such as this were like vermin: once they started spreading they were near impossible to eradicate. Halfdan let his anger settle before he spoke again.

"Thank you, Bergthor, for this. You've done a great service to your king. You'll be rewarded, as I said. But I need you to keep this to yourself, and I'll need you to tell my man Grim the names of the men who were in your company. And, as further reward for your loyalty, I insist that you remain here, in Grømstad, as my guest."

"Oh, highness, that's very kind, but I don't think…" Bergthor began, fear and suspicion in his voice.

"No, no, I insist," Halfdan said, waving to the guards, who came hurrying over again. "Take Bergthor here and see he is housed in the barracks. Good quarters. See to it."

"Yes, highness," the guards said in unison, and one took Bergthor by the arm and turned him around and led him away.

Bergthor was certain that he was being marched off to his death, Halfdan imagined, but in fact he was not. He would indeed be housed in the barracks, and even paid gold for the information he provided. But Halfdan could not let the man loose in the countryside. He could not have Bergthor spreading tales of Thorgrim Night Wolf's imminent return. That would only inspire renewed resistance.

Once Bergthor was out of earshot, Halfdan gestured for Grim to approach. "What do you think?"

"I think, lord, it would be a very bad thing if Thorgrim Night Wolf were to return just now. When Skorri and Thorgeir are done with this Odd business, once the people truly understand that rebelling against the king will not go unpunished, then it might not be so much of a problem. But not now."

"I agree," Halfdan said.

"We should send ships south, lord. Try to find Thorgrim and stop him before he reaches these shores."

"We should," Halfdan said. "But we can't. I just sent five of my best ships to Fevik, and I need them there. Odd is the most immediate threat, and I don't have enough ships left to go searching all over the seas for that cur."

"Yes, lord."

"Strength of arms won't do, not in this situation. We must be clever, use our wits to head this off. If Thorgrim is coming north, he'll stop in Ribe. Any ship heading north from Frankia is bound to stop in Ribe." Halfdan was seeing a plan unfold in his head, even as he spoke. "I need one ship," he continued. "One ship commanded by a clever man. A loyal man. And if he's known to Night Wolf, so much the better. Do you know of such a man?"

Grim considered that. "I think I do, lord."

"Good. I'll speak with him. Go fetch him."

"Yes lord," Grim said, bowed, and hurried away.

Halfdan stared off once again toward the far end of the great hall. His attention, however, was not on what he was looking at, but what was forming in his head: a plan, coming into view like a longship appearing out of the fog. He smiled a bit, nodded to himself.

Yes, that could work…

Chapter Eleven

Hogni hewed seven with a sharp sword,
and the eighth he shoved into the hot fire;
so must a brave man defend himself against foes.

The Lay of Atli
The Poetic Edda

The fishermen made their way back to the small beach in the cove and collected up the weapons stored in the bottoms of their boats. Axes and spears mostly, and a few swords, wrapped in oiled cloth against the inevitable spray that would come over the sides. They had not imagined needing them so soon after leaving the camp.

Every man among them wore a stoic expression, but Odd could see the moods behind the blank looks. A few were nervous, or uncertain. Some, the youngest among them, seemed frightened. They were fishermen, after all, not warriors raised to the fight. But most looked eager, genuinely eager, to do battle with Halfdan's men, because they were not just fishermen, they were also Norsemen, and it was in their blood.

Once weapons were found, unwrapped, and tucked into belts, or strapped on, or laid back in the boats, the men, as one, looked over at Odd, and Odd realized with a start that they were waiting for him to give orders. Arnor had made it clear: when it came to fighting, Odd was in charge. For a year or more, since the start of this unlikely rebellion, Odd had found himself leading warriors into the fray, but he was still not entirely accustomed to it.

"We'll take to the boats," he said, loud enough for all to hear, "get underway in the order we left camp. We'll need a couple boats for the women, and we'll need some men to row them."

"No need of that," Helga said. Helga, Odd had learned, was Arnor's wife. "The women here can handle a boat as well as any of the men." Odd looked at Arnor, and Arnor nodded.

"Good, then," Odd said. "You women stay clear of the fighting. If the worst happens, then back to the fishing camp. Same for all of you."

That was all that Odd could think to say. He had learned, over the past year, that it was pointless to make elaborate plans. They did not last long.

The men and women pushed the boats out into the water and took up the oars. They pulled out of the long cove and back into the channel, then turned north. A hundred yards farther on, Halfdan's stranded ship came into view.

Arnor's boat was again leading the fleet. Amundi was with them still, though Signy and Alfdis had joined the women at the end of the line. In their place were Ragi and Bragi Shipslayer, the latter of whom was so eager for the fight that he was willing to get into a boat with Arnor.

"So what's your intention, Odd?" Bragi asked. He was rubbing his hands together, smiling. "Board the swine from all sides? Or just put me on board, let me go through them like some human scythe, let these sorry fishermen have what's left?"

"Once I think of something, I'll let you know," Odd said.

He was watching the stranded longship as they approached. He could see only a few men toward the bow, and a few more toward the stern. The rest must have been sitting down amidships, hidden from view by the row of colorful shields still mounted in the shield rack. The handful of men that Odd could see were watching the appearance of the fishing fleet with vague interest, and they clearly did not see it as a threat. They made no move to prepare, they did not even stir, as the line of boats came winding out from between the islands.

Then, as the fleet of small craft, loaded with men, continued its straight and unwavering approach, Halfdan's warriors seemed to realize that these were not just fishermen out for a day's work, but possibly a genuine danger. Fore and aft men leapt to their feet, pointing and rushing around. Odd could hear voices calling out, but they were still too far off to hear what was being said.

"Ha!" Ragi shouted. "We've kicked the hornet's nest now!"

One by one Halfdan's men lifted their shields off the racks, revealing the rest of the crew in the waist of the ship: men slipping mail shirts on over their heads, settling helmets in place, taking up swords and axes and spears. Arnor's boat was still fifty yards away when the warriors formed up in a loose line down the center of the ship, weapons in hand, shields in front, waiting to see if these oncoming boats were indeed the threat they seemed to be.

"Let's get close, twenty feet off or so, see what these bastards do," Odd said, and Arnor nodded. Odd swiveled around until he was looking aft. He waved to the boat astern and the man at the tiller waved back.

"We'll make a circle around them!" Odd called, pointing off to starboard. "Keep about twenty feet off! If you see us boarding them, you follow behind! And if we board, it's a fight to the death, them or us! Pass the word back!"

The man in the boat waved, turned, called to the boat behind him. Odd looked forward again. They had halved the distance to the stranded ship. The warriors were still in their loose line, stretching half the vessel's length, standing calm and ready. Two had stepped forward and were waiting at the ship's side; the master, no doubt, and his chief man.

Arnor's men were taking easy pulls at the oars, approaching slowly, giving the other boats time to get into position. The warriors aboard Halfdan's ship turned left and right as they watched the boats circle around them. If they had any questions before about hostile intent, they did not now.

This will be no easy thing, Odd thought. The fishermen outnumbered Halfdan's men two or three to one, at least, but Halfdan's men were trained warriors. In fact, they looked to be the elite of the king's hird. Each man of them wore a mail shirt and helmet, each carried a sword and a shield and a seax in a sheath horizontal at the waist. They were trained, experienced in combat, and they were not afraid of dying in battle. In fact, they welcomed it.

Odd's men, in turn, were fishermen, with a strange assortment of weapons, which, he suspected, they had rarely if ever used in a real fight. Not one of them had mail, not one had a helmet or shield. They would have to climb out of the boats and up and over the side of the ship just to get to the fight. He did not doubt that they would win in the end — numbers alone would likely do it — but it would be a bloody business.

Or perhaps not.

Twenty feet from the ship, Arnor brought the boat to a stop and it sat, rocking gently in the low chop. Odd was just getting to his feet when the master of the longship spoke.

"You men had best be about your business fishing," he said, his voice loud enough to be heard by all the boats. "You don't want to tangle with King Halfdan, and by all the gods you do not want to tangle with us. You try, and we'll rip the guts out of the lot of you." He banged his sword against his shield, once, and all the men behind him did the same, with impressive unison. It was meant to be intimidating, and it was.

"You look to be Halfdan's finest men," Odd called back. "Good fighting men. And you're right…we don't want to tangle with you. But we will have your ship. So you may give it up, or you may die protecting it. Your choice."

The master lowered his shield and took another step forward. He had something like a smile on his face.

"Odd Thorgrimson," he said. He sounded surprised, and even a bit pleased. "Well, you're just the one we're looking for. Why don't you come aboard and we'll discuss this."

"I might come aboard yet, but I won't do it alone," Odd replied. "I don't know you, friend, but let me make a suggestion. Don't throw your men's lives away. Give us the ship. We'll give you boats to get you back to Grømstad."

With that, the man actually laughed. "Oh, yes! We'll row back to Grømstad. We'll tell the king that we met Odd Thorgrimson and gave him our ship. Is that what you propose?"

"Yes, I suppose it is."

"You're a funny one!" The master turned to the rest of his warriors, who were also smiling with genuine delight. "What say you, men? Shall we give the ship up to Odd Thorgrimson and his terrible army of fishermen?" The men laughed, they hooted, they shouted, but Odd could not make out their words through the general cacophony.

"I don't think they're very keen on your offer, Odd Thorgrimson!" the master called. "Even if there was any chance of you killing us, which there isn't, we'd still prefer it. Rather be in Odin's feast hall than King Halfdan's prison."

The man had a point, Odd realized. There was no rational reason for Halfdan's men to give up the ship. A fight to the death was certainly preferable to that sort of surrender, and there was a very good chance that the longship's crew would prevail. It occurred to Odd that he might have made a big mistake, deciding to lead these men against Halfdan's warriors. Now his only choice was to suffer the humiliation of giving up even before the battle, or sending these sorry fishermen to an undeserving death.

"You're a clever man, friend, you make a good point," Odd called back. "There's no benefit in you giving up the ship, and little benefit in us trying to take it. But we certainly can't have you telling Halfdan that we're here, and we can't have his ship returned to him. So the best choice for us is to just burn it, with you aboard. That way we get most of what we want, even if we lose this fine vessel."

The master was still smiling when Odd finished, but Odd could see his expression had changed. It was subtle, but it was there: eyebrows a bit knitted, smile a bit forced. "How do you propose to do that? Light this entire ship on fire?"

"Oh, have no fear, we'll manage," Odd said. "You should be thinking about what it will feel like to be burned alive, and whether such a death will earn you entrance to the corpse hall. You understand…dying with no enemy in front of you, shrieking in pain." He shook his head at the horror of it all. "Doesn't seem like the Valkyrie will be much impressed by such a death."

"We wish you luck of it, Odd Thorgrimson," the master said. "We'll enjoy watching you try. And once the tide lifts us free, we'll hunt you down like the vermin you are."

Odd gave the master a friendly wave, then turned to Arnor, speaking low enough that he would not be heard aboard Halfdan's ship. "You have a fire-steel and tinder?"

Arnor nodded his head.

"Good," Odd said, but before he could get any further, Bragi interrupted him.

"You don't really mean to burn that ship, do you? And not fight?"

"I'm hoping they'll give it up, so that you can wreck it later," Odd said. "But if not, yes, we'll burn it."

Bragi looked at the ship, and then back at Odd, and he nodded. "Good, then. Reckon you get a fire going right under the bow, they won't be able to reach it to put it out. Looks like they just gave the hull a fresh coat of tar and resin, so that'll help." It seemed that Bragi found the idea of burning the ship nearly as inviting as battle.

Odd turned back to Arnor. "I'll thank you to get a fire going." He turned to the nearest boat, which was floating ten feet off the starboard side. "Row around to the other boats. All that oiled cloth they have on board, collect that up, and anything else that'll burn, anything they're willing to give up."

The men in the boat nodded, picked up their oars, and rowed off. Odd turned to the boats off his larboard side. "Row back to the island, gather up any dried wood or anything you find that might make for a decent fire."

The preparations did not take long. Soon Arnor had a fire burning in a small iron kettle, ready to ignite bigger stuff. The boat Odd had sent around to the fleet returned, loaded to the gunnels with heaps of oiled cloth. The two boats sent ashore came rowing back with stacks of dried wood, which they heaved on top of the pile of oil cloth.

"Hold on, now," the owner of the boat said, as the wood piled up. "Do you mean to burn my boat?" Why that had not occurred to him until just then, Odd could not guess.

"Yes, we're burning your leaking washtub of a boat, Thorlak," Arnor said. "And we're doing you a favor." Then, grudgingly, he added, "But I reckon we can build you a new one."

As promised, Halfdan's men did seem to enjoy watching the preparations. They jeered and hooted out suggestions and flung beef bones at the assembled faerings. The master stood up on the sheer strake, one hand on the shroud, and called, "You'd better hurry, Odd! The tide is near turning, and once it does we'll be down on you like Thor's hammer! You'll be the one shrieking out your life, I assure you!"

Odd gave the man a smile and a friendly wave. In a low voice he said to Arnor, "Is the tide near turning?"

"We have some time, yet," Arnor said. "Not much."

"Then let's be at it," Odd said.

They passed a line to the men in the sacrificial boat, who tied it off at the bow, and then a second, which they tied to the stern — why, Odd did not know. Then the men climbed aboard a second boat which had come to take them off. Arnor nodded to the rowers and they leaned into the oars, getting the boat underway, towing the fire-boat astern. They pulled around to a place where they could drift the boat down on the bow of Halfdan's ship, where the ebbing tide would hold it in place.

Halfdan's men were forward, watching the preparations, still flinging abuse, when Arnor tossed the kettle of fire onto the other boat. It disappeared into the bilge, and for a moment nothing seemed to happen. Then a column of black smoke came spilling up from the pile of cloth, and a moment later the entire thing burst into flames.

From the circle of boats around Halfdan's ship, the fishermen cheered with gusto. Arnor eased away on the rope made off to the fire-boat's bow. Beside him, another eased the rope made off to the stern, and in that way they were able to set the fire-boat directly under the bow of Halfdan's ship, perpendicular to the larger vessel, a prime spot for spreading the flames.

Halfdan's men were still yelling, still jeering, but not so loud, and there seemed to be a different tone to their mocking, as if their hearts were not entirely in it now.

The master of the ship was standing on the sheer strake up at the bow, trying to see the fire-boat around the flared sides of the ship.

"Here we go, friend!" Odd shouted. "It will take those flames a moment to catch, and you have until then to change your mind! Once it really takes hold, then there's nothing more we can do! After that, it's burn or drown for the lot of you!"

"We're not burned up yet, you whore's son!" the master called, his tone sharper than before. Behind him, on either side, the crowd of men parted as others came rushing forward, carrying oars like battering rams. They leaned over the side, thrusting the oars out ahead, trying to get at the burning boat and push it clear.

"Good luck with that, you dumb bastards!" Bragi called, and he sounded as delighted as he looked. But luck was not going to do Halfdan's men any good. With the burning boat tucked in close under the bow, the curve of the ship prevented them from reaching it with the oars, flail and curse as they might.

Soon they abandoned that attempt and moved forward until they were standing on either side of the prow, reaching straight down with the oars. From there they managed to get the oar blades onto the boat, but with the boat held fast by its bow and stern with the lines running to two of Arnor's faerings, and the pressure of the current pressing it against the ship, they could not make it budge. They shouted, and shoved with the oars, and the flames built higher, until at last the heat became intolerable and they retreated back aft.

Now it was the fishermen's turn to yell and jeer as the mounting fire roiled up from the boat and Halfdan's men appeared helpless to stop it.

"It's catching," Amundi said. "Looks like it's catching."

It did indeed. The fire-boat was burning fiercely, and the flames were spreading to the longship's hull. It was the tar and resin that were burning now, making the flames look impressive indeed. But it would not be long before the wood itself — thin, dried oak planks — would take, and that would be an end to it.

The men with the oars were making their way forward again, to try once more to push the boat clear, but the ship's master called, "Forget that! Forget that! Get me a rope!" His voice was loud even over the increasing roar of the flames.

A man appeared with a coil of rope in his hand and passed the bitter end to the master, who had climbed down from the sheer strake, driven back by the flames.

"Ah, may the gods take him, he's a bold one!" Odd shouted, seeing what the man had in mind. "Arnor, get us in there! Come on, now!" He jumped up and pushed his way toward the bow of the fishing boat, drawing Blood-letter as he did. The rowers, who were watching the flames with glee, turned and heaved back on the oars and the boat shot ahead, straight at the burning longship.

The master was over the side by then, foot pressed against the ship's hull, holding himself up with the rope in his left hand, drawing his sword with his right. He was working his way forward and under the bow, where he would be able to cut and shove the burning boat free, if he could get close enough.

With two strokes Arnor's boat closed with the ship. Odd could feel the heat of the flames on his face and hands, as if his skin was on fire, and he grit his teeth against the pain. The master looked up just as Odd was close enough to take a stroke with Blood-letter, and he raised his own sword as Odd's blade came at him, catching Odd's sword and turning it aside.

The master roared, a sound of fury and pain. He slashed at Odd, and Odd leaned back, let the blade pass, and thrust again. The master twisted sideways as the blade came at him, and with his forearm he knocked Odd's blade away, then thrust at Odd in turn.

Behind the master, and above, leaning over the rail, a knot of Halfdan's men, spears in hand, thrust down at Odd, and Odd knocked the shafts aside with a sweeping blow of his sword. The spear-men pulled their weapons back, held them up, arms cocked, ready to throw this time.

Oh, by the gods…

Odd had no mail, no shield. The spear-men were above him, just ten feet away, and they would not miss. He tensed, thought about turning and leaping for the bottom of the boat. He was still standing, frozen, when, of all things, a firkin of ale came flying over his head. It slammed into the spearmen and bowled them over like they were children's toys. From behind him, Odd heard Bragi Shipslayer yell, "There! Have a drink, you sorry bastards! It's getting hot up there!"

He was right. The heat was like nothing Odd had ever felt; as if he was in the flames themselves. He, too, was roaring in pain as the ship's master, still clinging to the rope with one hand, thrust straight and true. Odd tried to parry, but too late. As he twisted aside, the master's blade tore through the upper arm of his tunic. Even over the heat of the flames, Odd felt the burning sensation as the sharp edge of the sword tore through flesh: a painful wound, but not a deep one, he guessed.

The master shouted again, the sound now more like pain than rage. As Odd turned back he saw the man's tunic was on fire, the flames engulfing the hem, working their way up the cloth. His face was red and contorted, but still he fought on, one-handed, flailing at Odd as Odd caught the blade, turned it, and thrust.

This time Blood-letter found its mark, striking hard and straight on the man's chest, pausing for a beat as it hit mail and then driving on through. The master screamed again, louder, his eyes wide, and then he dropped.

If it was the sword blow, or the burning tunic, or his strength failing him, Odd did not know, but the man released his grip on the rope and fell straight down. He hit the water and did not slow, his mail shirt, helmet, and weapons pulling him under.

Odd turned and shouted aft. "Back! Get back!" He did not have to say it again. The rowers shoved the oars forward and the boat backed away from the burning ship, five feet, ten feet, and finally they were far enough from the flames that the heat was tolerable.

The crew of the longship was standing near the rail, some staring down at the water where their master had disappeared, some looking out at Odd or the other boats. Some still held weapons high, shields ready, but most had lowered them in a way that suggested they were confused and beaten, that the mounting flames and loss of the master had taken the fight out of them. No one shouted. No one moved.

Odd turned to Arnor. "Get me closer! There, amidships, away from the flames!" he called, pointing. The rowers pulled again, the boat shot forward, and Odd shouted up to the men on the burning ship.

"We can get you off the ship now, it's not too late!" he called. "But you have to move, or you'll burn or drown! This is no way for a warrior to die!"

Halfdan's men looked down at him, but still no one moved, no one spoke. They seemed stunned, as if they had each been hit hard in the head.

"Come on, now!" Odd shouted again, as Arnor's boat swept up beside the longship. "Throw your weapons down into the boat here! Weapons, mail, shields, quick, before it's too late!"

Still no one moved, and Odd began to wonder if they would, or if they would just stand there and burn to death. And then one man stepped up to the side of the ship and with a look of disgust threw his sword down into the boat, then his helmet after. He was still pulling his mail shirt over his head when the next man threw his sword and seax down, and then the next.

"Come alongside!" Odd called to the other fishing boats nearby. "Come and collect up these men's weapons!" A moment later they were underway, bumping up against the ship, as swords, helmets and mail rained down on them.

"Arnor!" Odd shouted. "Set some of those other boats to putting the fire out!"

"Too late for that, I think!" Ragi said, but Arnor called out to the fishermen nearby, shouting and waving.

"Get that fire-boat clear, set it adrift! And kill that fire if you can!"

Halfdan's men were down to tunics and trousers, and stripped of any last vestiges of defiance. "You men in the boats, back away!" Odd called next and the boats, loaded down with weapons and mail, began to draw away from the longship.

"Is this what your word means?" one of Halfdan's men shouted. "You'll leave us to burn anyway?"

Odd did not reply. The rest of the fishing boats were gathering around now, and he waved to them and pointed to the longship. "Get alongside!" he called. "Get those men into the boats! They're unarmed!" Odd had no intention of leaving the men to burn, but neither did he want them climbing into the same boats that held their weapons. Such a thing could give a man dangerous ideas.

In twos and threes the fishing boats pulled alongside, and Halfdan's men climbed over the sheer strake and dropped aboard. More boats were gathered around the bow. The fire-boat had been pulled clear and left to drift away. The crews of the fishing boats were furiously scooping up buckets of water, flinging them at the burning oak, and, incredibly, seemed to be gaining on the fire. The flames had started to grab hold of the oak planks, but not so profoundly that they could not be extinguished.

And then it was over. The manic activity of fire and battle and capitulation settled into a strange quiet. Odd called for the boats to gather together.

"We'll need four boats to give to Halfdan's warriors," he said, once the boats had all clustered around. "Which four of you want to give up your boats?" He waited. No one volunteered, as he suspected would be the case. He turned to the boats loaded with Halfdan's men, who were looking on with expressions of sullen defeat.

"None of these men seem much inclined to give up their boats," he said. "Which I understand. So we can put you ashore here, and you can walk back to Grømstad. Or maybe some of the fisherfolk would be willing to sell their boats."

Most of the warriors, Odd had noticed, wore silver bands around their arms, and some had rings and pendants of silver and gold. They were Halfdan's hird, and Halfdan rewarded them richly for their service.

"Well?" Odd asked a moment later, when none of Halfdan's men had made reply. He looked out at the angry faces of the warriors. Still, no one spoke.

"If that's what you wish," he said. Then, to the others, he called, "We'll set them ashore just to the north there."

That seemed to do it. It was a ten mile walk to Grømstad from the spot where Odd proposed setting them ashore. The distance was not so great, but the country through which they would be walking could be less than friendly. Halfdan's warriors were not well loved by the people, and the thought of trudging along those roads, unarmed, held little appeal.

"All right," one of Halfdan's men said at last, pulling his arm rings off. "We'll buy your miserable boats, and may the gods tear your liver out, you sorry bastard." He handed the rings over to the owner of the boat, who was now more than eager to part with his vessel, and Halfdan's other men did likewise. Soon the transactions were done, Halfdan's men settled in their new-bought boats, the former owners and their crews dispersed among the rest of the fleet.

"You can tell Halfdan we don't want this fight," Odd said as the warriors settled the oars into the tholes. "Tell him we just want to be left alone, as the freemen we are."

"We'll tell Halfdan where we found you," replied the one who had first given up his arm rings. "And we'll be there to watch your guts spill on the ground when he cuts them out. That goes for the lot of you."

With that he took a stroke of the oar and the others did the same and the four boats began the long pull back to wherever they decided to go. Odd did not think it would be Grømstad. He did not think these men would care to return to Halfdan's hall with news that Odd Thorgrimson and a bunch of fishermen had taken their mail, their weapons, and their king's ship.

"Enough talk!" Bragi called from the back of the boat. "Set me on this ship so I can see if she'll swim when the tide comes in!"

The rowers gave a few pulls and the boat bumped up against the longship and Bragi and Odd, Arnor and Ragi climbed aboard. They made their way to the bow, where the fire had scorched the planking on the outside and made the tar and resin inside bubble and smoke. Bragi took his knife from its sheath, and holding it by the blade began to thump the handle against the wood, listening to the sound it made as it bounced off the oak.

"Seems sound enough," Bragi said when he finished. "Don't seem like the fire ate through much of the wood. Now, when we float free, we'll see if enough of the caulking's left that we don't sink anyway, but my bet is we won't."

Arnor made a grunting sound. "Well, now we got a longship."

"We do," Odd agreed.

"So, what do we do with it?" Ragi asked.

"Not sure," Odd said. "But I suspect we'll think of something."

"And it'll probably get us killed," Bragi said. "At least, if it's something you think of. But I won't lie, that's why I like your company so."

Chapter Twelve

Bright land of wave's flame,
Goddess of gold, I came
To a hall where seven fires,
To my anguish, were burning.

Gisli Sursson's Saga

There was a face hovering above Thorgrim. It was all he could see when he opened his eyes. The face was familiar in its contours and coloring, but he could not make it out, as if he was looking at it through a thin sheet of ice. He frowned a bit and hoped it would resolve into something more recognizable, but it did not.

He was ready to close his eyes again, but then there was a voice as well, a voice to go along with the face.

"Father?"

*Harald...*Thorgrim thought. *Of course...Harald.* But that realization only made him wonder if Harald was really there, or if this was a dream. There had been so many dreams. And if he was there, where was he? Where were they?

It was too much. He closed his eyes again.

"He opened his eyes. You saw that, didn't you?" Harald again.

"Yes, yes, I did." That was Starri. Starri Deathless. "That's excellent. Most excellent. I've seen men, you know, take a blow to the head like your father did, and they sleep and sleep and don't wake up, and don't die, either. That is, until they do die. But it can be a long time."

"But they don't open their eyes? Like my father did, just now?"

"No, they don't open their eyes. They just lay there. So it's a good thing he opened his eyes. It means the gods are protecting him, the way we asked."

Thoughts were starting to form in Thorgrim's head, resolving into something that felt solid. He understood that he must open his eyes again if he wanted this ridiculous conversation to stop, so he let his head settle a bit, gathered his strength, then opened his eyes once more.

Harald was still there. Thorgrim let his head loll over to one side, and sure enough, Starri was there, too. They were more clearly visible now, as if the sheet of ice had melted away. He moved his head back amidships. He was looking up at the underside of a thatched roof, which he could just barely see. It was dark, the only light coming from a fire burning out of Thorgrim's sight, and maybe a lantern. He could smell woodsmoke, and meat cooking, and damp cloth.

"Father!" Harald said again, this time with more certainty, as if he was now sure that he recognized him. He laid his hand on Thorgrim's shoulder, a surprisingly delicate gesture for a boy who was decidedly not delicate. "How are you?"

Thorgrim blinked. He did not actually know. He considered the question. His head hurt, inside and outside. He seemed to have taken a blow to the left side of his skull, which would explain the vague throbbing, and the headache as well. But not so bad. He had a feeling that both throbbing and headache had been much worse at an earlier time.

His shoulder hurt as well, his right side, just below his collarbone. Sword thrust, or knife thrust, or spear thrust, one of those. He recognized the sensation, had felt it many times before. That, too, had the feel of a wound that was not particularly recent.

He ran a tongue over parched lips, but it gave him no relief.

"Water," he managed to croak, and he saw Harald and Starri react as if this was a command from Odin himself. Harald grabbed up a cup, and he and Starri put hands under Thorgrim's shoulders and eased him upright. And just as the water, the sacred water, Thorgrim's greatest desire at that moment, was coming toward his mouth, he heard a woman's voice calling, "Stop! Stop right there!"

Harald and Starri did stop, and their heads turned and they looked at some place behind Thorgrim's back. Thorgrim's eyes were locked on the cup. He wanted to shout, to tell the two men that he'd rip their hearts out if they did not give him a drink. He was trying to summon the strength to do so when a woman appeared in front of him.

She was not young, but not old, with yellow hair in two long braids, and cheeks that were pink and round like apples. She was pleasant enough looking, but she seemed to have stopped Harald and Starri from giving him water, and for that he wanted to kill her, though he doubted he could even lift his arms.

"Give me this," the woman said, taking the cup from Harald's hand. "You can't give him too much or you'll kill him, for sure." She brought the cup to Thorgrim's mouth and tilted it up and Thorgrim felt the cool liquid run over his lips, which were dry as hay, and run in a little rivulet down his mouth and throat. He could not recall a more wonderful sensation. He wanted to grab the cup and tilt the rest into his mouth, but he could not make his arms work that way.

Then the cup was gone, pulled away from Thorgrim's lips. Thorgrim opened his eyes and glared at the woman, and she stared back at him, looking him straight in the eyes. She did not seem in the least intimidated.

"Let's see how that sets," she said. She continued to stare at Thorgrim for a moment more, then nodded and put the cup to his lips again, and once again she allowed a little stream of water to run down his throat.

They repeated that ritual two more times before the woman said, "That's enough for now. More later."

Thorgrim made a small noise in his throat, though even he was not sure what he meant to say. He wanted more water, to be certain. But he was also desperate to close his eyes again, so he did that, and he felt Harald and Starri easing him back down on what he imagined was a bed.

He heard Harald say, "Is he all right? Was that too much water?"

He heard the woman say, "No, not too much. This is good, a good sign." And then Thorgrim was asleep again.

The next time he woke it was considerably lighter in the room. Daylight, coming in through a window or a door or some such. He was still looking up at a thatched roof, but he could make out details now: the rough beams supporting the roof, the individual strands of thatch, a swirl of smoke illuminated by the sunlight.

There were no faces.

He turned his head slowly and realized that the pain he felt before had largely dissipated. He looked to his right. There was a table with bread and meat and a pitcher laid out. There was a fire burning in a pit on the floor. There were tapestries of some description hanging on the walls. And there was the woman, the apple-cheeked woman, sitting on a bench beside him.

"Good morrow," she said, softly.

"Water," Thorgrim said.

"Of course." The woman stood and walked over to the table, filled a cup from the pitcher, and returned with it. She slipped a hand under his shoulder and lifted him to a sitting position and Thorgrim could sense the strength in her arm. She handed him the cup and he drank, two big gulps, and then, with gentle authority, she took the cup from his hands.

"How do you feel?" she asked.

Once again, Thorgrim had to consider the question. And when he did, he realized that he felt…not terrible. The pain in his head was considerably diminished. The wound in his shoulder was a dull ache, but nothing worse than that.

"I feel better," he said. His voice cracked as he spoke, and he cleared his throat.

"If you felt any worse than you did when you arrived, you'd be dead," the woman said. She was still supporting him as he sat up, one hand on his back. He looked at her face, no more than a foot away. A good face, strong jaw, a hint of cheekbones. Blue eyes. The same blue as the ocean when one gets far from land. He could see the fine lines etched around the corners of her mouth and eyes and across her forehead.

"Where am I?" Thorgrim asked.

"You're in my home."

Thorgrim looked around. It was a small house, but neat and nicely outfitted. The walls were wood plank and mostly covered by tapestries. Solid wooden platforms ran down either side, some covered in furs and blankets, some with implements for cooking or sundry pots and bundles. Embers glowed in a fire pit in the floor, and next to it sat a heavy-built table and benches. At the far end was a single room, divided off from the rest of the house by a wattle wall.

"And where is your home?" Thorgrim asked.

"On the market street," the woman said. There was a hint of a smile on her face. She was toying with him. He knew he should be angry about it, but he was not.

"And what town might the market street be in?"

"Ribe."

Ribe… At last, a real answer. *Ribe*… What by all the gods was he doing in Ribe? He had some vague sense of having wanted to not go to Ribe, but he could not recall why.

"How did I get here?"

"Can you sit up, do you think?" the woman asked, as if she had not heard him. She put a hand under his legs and eased him around and up so that he was sitting on the edge of the platform on which his straw-filled mattress lay. She took her hand off his shoulder and stepped back. Thorgrim's head swam a bit, but it settled, and he felt steady enough in his new posture.

"How did I get here?"

"Your men brought you. And your son. Before that, I don't know much. I'll let them tell you the rest." She crossed the room to where a pile of furs was heaped on the platform there and she laid a hand on it and shook it. It heaved and rolled and then an arm appeared from under, and then Harald was sitting up, blinking.

"Your father's awake again," the woman said. "He's doing better. Much better."

Harald looked around with the confused expression he usually wore when he was roused from sleep. He looked at Thorgrim and Thorgrim saw the understanding spread over his face.

"Father!" He pushed the furs aside and jumped up and all but ran the ten feet to where Thorgrim sat. "You're awake! You're doing better, Gyda said." He put a tentative hand on Thorgrim's shoulder.

Thorgrim nodded. "Yes. I feel…better. Not so bad. My head…" He paused a moment. "How did we get here?"

"Here in Ribe?"

"Ribe…this house? I don't remember anything." He could feel the old impatience rising up again, and he took that for a good sign.

"Do you recall the fight on the beach? With the Danes?"

Thorgrim looked at the floor. *Fight with the Danes?* He thought back, and as he did, it started to return. The beach, the ships pulled up on shore for the night, the stupid, pointless attack by…he could not remember who. Some local jarl, or bandits, maybe. He had probably never known.

"Yes, I remember now," Thorgrim said. "I'd been…sleeping. We were pulled up on the beach. On our way back to East Agder."

So we could help Odd. It was all coming back, including why he felt this strange, underlying sense of urgency.

"We were heading home to help your brother."

"That's right!" Harald said, smiling. "That's right. We…"

The door at the far end of the house opened and Starri Deathless came rushing in. "Ah, Night Wolf, I knew you were awake! I sensed it! And here you are! Awake!"

"Starri," Thorgrim said. "I'm happy to see you. Happy as I ever am."

"And me you! I knew the gods were not done with you, that they would not let you just die sweating and moaning in some sorry hovel in Ribe." He looked up at the woman. "No offence, Gyda."

"Oh, none taken," the woman said, and she sounded more amused than offended.

"Father was just saying he remembers the fight on the beach," Harald said.

"It was a good fight," Starri said. "Pleasing to the gods. Mostly. But you took that wound in the shoulder, and then this big Dane, he hit you right in the head with his ax. But the flat of the ax, do you see, not the blade. You'd be lucky if he'd hit you with the blade. You and Godi and Ornolf and all the others, you'd be fighting side by side in Valhalla, even now. Never a worry again. But he hit you with the flat. At least that's what Hall said. He was at your side when it happened. I think maybe I was in the middle of some swarm of filthy Danes just then."

Thorgrim nodded. He looked at Harald for a more coherent explanation.

"That Dane nearly killed you, like Starri said," Harald took up the tale. "But it was right near the end of the fight, just as the Danes were losing heart. Not long after that, we drove them off. I think it just stoked our men's anger, when they saw you fall. Of course, everyone thought you were dead, so they just fell on the Danes with a fury such like I'd never seen. Sent them running like dogs.

"We found you on the sand, and thought for sure you were dead, but then we saw you were breathing, so we knew you weren't. So we carried you aboard and we got underway, and we did what we could for you. But there's none of us who are so good at the healing arts."

"We took care of the wound in your shoulder," Starri chimed in. "Sword wounds, broken limbs, that sort of thing, we've all had plenty of experience caring for those, as you know. None better than you, Night Wolf. But the blow to your head? No one knew exactly what to do about that, except set healing runes around you, of course, and burn an offering to Thor."

"Then *Sea Hammer* started leaking, down by the garboard," Harald said. "Pretty bad. So with all that, we figured we had best put into Ribe. We knew you didn't want to go to Ribe, but we thought it best."

Thorgrim nodded. The words were spilling out of these two in a way that he had never seen before, as if they had been damned up while he slept, and now that he was awake the damn had burst and released a verbal flash flood.

"When we got to Ribe we ran *Sea Hammer* up on the beach and we asked the folk here if there was someone who was a healer, and they told us about Gyda. We fetched her and she said the ship was no place for you to get well and that you could come to her house. And so here we are."

Thorgrim was silent as he tried to sort all that out in his mind. So much had happened, and he had been aware of none of it. So very strange.

"How long ago was that, that we fought with the Danes?"

Starri and Harald looked at one another as they tried to reckon the passage of time. "Six days," Harald said at last.

"Yes, six days," Starri said, though Thorgrim was certain he did not really know.

"Six days...." Thorgrim repeated. He shook his head. He had been asleep for six days. This was not good, not good at all.

"We can't waste any more time," he said. "We have to get back to Vik. Odd needs our help, it can't wait."

He pushed himself off the platform and he saw Gyda move to stop him. His feet hit the floor but he kept going down, his legs buckling under him. The next thing he knew he was sprawled out, half on his side, and hands were grabbing onto his arms and lifting him up. He felt his feet come back off the floor as Harald and Starri set him on the edge of the platform again.

"Don't try to stand!" Gyda said, her face an angry scowl. "After six days in a death-sleep, don't try to stand! I'll tell you when you can stand."

I'll stand whenever I want to stand, you shrew, Thorgrim thought, but his head was swimming and he realized that he might pass out again, and, much as he wanted to, he could not make his mouth form the words. So instead he just nodded.

"Shall we lay him down again?" Harald asked. Thorgrim shook his head. He could not bear the thought of lying down again, but Harald was not asking him, he was asking Gyda. It seemed no one much cared what he thought.

"No," Gyda said. "He should be upright for now. Here, let's set him on this bench, with his back against this chest." She pointed to a bench pushed up against the long platform, where a heavy wooden chest could serve as a backrest. Carefully, Harald and Starri eased Thorgrim onto his feet, and Thorgrim took the weight slowly. Once he was upright, and well supported, and sure he was not going to pass out, he nodded, and the two men led him over to the platform and eased him down. He settled, leaned back against the chest, and let out a sigh.

"Good?" Gyda asked.

Thorgrim nodded. His head was still swimming, but not so bad. He felt a tiny spark of strength in his limbs.

"He needs food," Gyda said. "He's had nothing but broth since you brought him here. Do you want something to eat, Thorgrim?"

Thorgrim. It had been a long time since he had heard a woman speak his name. Not since Failend, and her strange Irish accent. It sounded good. He nodded again.

"Yes," he said. "Food." He realized that he was ravenous, as if the very word food had unleashed some powerful need.

"What can I fetch you?" Harald asked. "Bread? Meat? There's bakers and butchers nearby, I can get whatever you need."

Thorgrim looked at him, at his son, who wanted so much to help. He knew that Harald's eagerness came from the purest of motives, and he appreciated that, but at the same time he found it terribly annoying.

"Anything you need, we can get it, Night Wolf," Starri said, just as eager. "Ale, mead…"

Have I become some feeble old man? Thorgrim wondered. He was about to say something, something that would have been less than diplomatic, but Gyda cut him off.

"You two have been so kind, and so helpful. Honestly, Thorgrim would have died if not for you. But now I'm sure you have work to do. On your ship, or some such. I can see to Thorgrim."

"It's not a problem, really, I'm happy to…" Harald started in again, but Gyda let him get no further.

"No, really. I can see to Thorgrim." She stepped around behind the two men and gently pushed them toward the door. That, and her tone of voice, was enough to make them understand that they were, indeed, not needed just then. Reluctantly, they started walking.

"I'll see how the work is going on *Sea Hammer*," Harald said, turning back just as he reached the door. "And I'll be back to let you know."

Thorgrim lifted his arm and gave a little wave, a bit of a smile. Gyda shoved the two of them out and closed the door behind them. She went to the table and picked up a wooden bowl and spoon and scooped up some sort of stew from an iron pot hanging over the coals.

"Thank you," Thorgrim said.

Gyda nodded, a grim smile on her face. "You're welcome," she said. She came over to him, the bowl of stew in her hand. "They care about you, very much."

"I care about them," he said, and it surprised him. He could not recall having ever said anything like that before.

I am becoming a doddering old man.

"Good," Gyda said. "You should." She scooped up half a spoonful of stew and brought it to Thorgrim's mouth. It occurred to him that he should not let this woman feed him as if he was an infant, but he did not object. Instead, he took the mouthful of stew, chewed slowly, and swallowed. It was marvelous, the food of the gods. He heard his stomach growl. Gyda gave him another bite.

"This will do you a lot of good," she said. "It will build your strength back. Quickly."

"Good. I mean to sail on the tide."

Gyda smiled. "You're a stubborn man."

"I've been told that."

"You're also a strong man. Most men would have died days ago. Your strength saved you."

"It was my stubbornness. I'm too stubborn to die."

"That might be it," Gyda said. She scooped up another spoonful and Thorgrim took it and swallowed it down.

The stew, as Gyda promised, was rejuvenating. Thorgrim could feel the strength returning with each mouthful he swallowed. He wondered if Gyda had worked some charm or spell, mixed it in with the meat and carrots and onions. He was ready to eat the entire pot and then call for more. But, as with the water, Gyda only allowed him as much as she thought was safe.

He did not, however, feel the need to curse or threaten her this time. He found that even the small amount that Gyda fed him had much improved his mood.

When he was done eating he sat for a bit, reveling in the sensation of a partially full stomach. Life-giving. Gyda set the bowl and the spoon back on the table and gave him a cup of water, which he drank with relish. Then she sat on a bench a few feet away, facing him.

"Six days," he said. "How am I not dead of hunger?"

"We fed you broth, while you were in your death-sleep," Gyda said.

"How could I drink it?"

Gyda made a gesture with her hands to indicate that she did not know. "It's a strange thing. A person's mind can be shut tight, like a house with its windows and doors barred, and yet their bodies still do as they're supposed to. Or some of what they're supposed to. Breathing, obviously. But also drinking and such. We sat you up, held the broth to your lips, and you drank."

Thorgrim nodded. Strange. It was all so wonderfully strange.

Chapter Thirteen

Men of the warrior-host drank there — but concealers kept quiet
— wine in the foreign hall —
they feared the wrath of the Húnar…

The Lay of Atli

There was no room in the wagons for all the plunder that Skorri's men had taken from Thorgrim's great hall. The wagons, of course, were still mostly full, since they had not consumed any of the food or drink they carried, and had not needed the tents or weapons. But even if the wagons had been empty, there would likely not have been enough room for all that Skorri's men had carried away.

Happily, there were more wagons to be had: three of tolerable size sitting beside Thorgrim's stable. Even better, the draft horses needed to pull them were right there in their stalls, along with half a dozen other horses, not including those that had come with Skorri's column.

Skorri ordered Skafti to harness the draft horses to the wagons and tether the others to the back. All of it — horses, wagons and plunder — would be coming with Skorri and his men when they left.

Skafti said nothing. He just glared at Skorri for a moment, then turned and walked off. But by the time Skorri stepped out of the dim, smoky great hall and into the cool, sunlit morning, the draft horses were being buckled into their traces. Not by Skafti. The overseer was nowhere to be seen, unable to bear any more of this, Skorri guessed. But he had sense enough to set others to the task.

It was not long after that that Skorri led his men, his considerably wealthier men, back onto the road leading south. He did not look back. He had considered putting Thorgrim's hall to the torch, despite Skafti's cooperation, but in the end he decided against it. Eventually he might have to justify his actions to Halfdan, and that would be a hard one to explain.

They continued south, retracing their march of the day before, then turned east to continue on to Fevik, just a few miles distant. Once again it was a good day for marching, the weather dry and warm, not hot, the sky blue and cloudless. Skorri Thorbrandsson's mood was better than it had been in a very long time.

The road ran along high ground that gave them an occasional glimpse of the sea to the south, and tree-topped granite ridges to the north. Skorri's eyes were on the road ahead, but his mind was already in Fevik, already considering how he would root out the vermin, Odd and those still following him, what punishment he would mete out to those who gave him succor. Forfeiture of everything of value they possessed, to begin with. Beyond that, he was not sure. There was considerable opportunity here.

"Lord Skorri?" Koll broke into his thoughts. He was riding at Skorri's side, and had said little until then.

"Yes?"

"Where do you plan to quarter the men? There are fields just outside Fevik. We could set up camp there."

"Hmm," Skorri said. He had not really thought about it. Such basic logistics. He had been thinking on bigger things. "Perhaps make camp. Or perhaps we'll quarter in town, have the people there give the men lodging and food."

That would be a good way to keep an eye on things. The traitors in Fevik could not get away with much when his men were in their homes.

"We might find quarters for them in the village," Koll said, but he did not sound so sure. Fevik was not a big town, four or five hundred people at most. Skorri's army would almost double the population, meaning that his men would be packed into whatever miserable quarters they might find.

"Hold a minute," Skorri said, as another idea came to him. He smiled. He knew of two farms in Fevik that were unoccupied. One was Odd Thorgrimson's of course, but Halfdan had burned the long house to the ground. There was another one, however, and it was even finer than Thorgrim Night Wolf's.

"There's a great hall a couple miles from here that once belonged to Ornolf the Restless," Skorri said. "I think we'll house the men there.

Ornolf's long gone, of course, just like Thorgrim, but his great hall still stands. I saw it not two months back. Impressive place. Bigger than Thorgrim's."

"The men had no complaints about Thorgrim's great hall," Koll said.

"They'll have fewer still about Ornolf's."

The column continued east. Soon, over the trees, they could see the town of Fevik, downhill and to their right, half a mile away: geometric patterns of neatly bundled thatch with irregular columns of dark smoke rising up above, and beyond that, the long, narrow, bay stretching away south to the sea. Ornolf's farm and great hall lay a few miles beyond the village.

It was approaching noon when the roof of the great hall came into sight, rising up over the low hills ahead. It was over two hundred feet long, gray-shingled, a long, gentle arc, like the scaly back of some old mythical beast slumbering away in the midday sun. They came up over the rise and the rest of the building revealed itself, the walls built up of heavy vertical wooden boards, a series of buttresses supporting the massive beams that held up the roof. Fantastical animal heads, carved from oak, leered out from the gable ends.

Around the great hall stood the various outbuildings typical of a prosperous estate: stables, barns, workshops. Storehouses. A small temple. An earthen wall surrounded the grounds, separating the jarl Ornolf's residence from his fields and meadows beyond.

"By the gods," Koll said as they approached. "That fat old bastard Ornolf lived well, didn't he?"

"He did," Skorri agreed. "But he has no need of any of this now, wherever he is, so I reckon it's ours to enjoy. There's no telling how long we'll be in Fevik, running these traitors down. Hunting his grandson. So we may as well be comfortable."

There was quite a bit of activity around Ornolf's hall, more than there was around Thorgrim's. Thorgrim had left no family behind: his wife was dead, Odd was married, and off on a farm of his own, as was Thorgrim's daughter, Hild. The younger boy, Harald, had gone a'viking with his father and was probably dead, too. The other daughter, Hallbera, was somewhere. Living with her sister, perhaps. She had briefly been Halfdan's hostage, and since then she had made herself scarce. Skafti, and a few servants, and the men working the fields and tending the handful of cattle, were the only folk living at Thorgrim's farm now.

Ornolf's farm, however, was not in the hands of caretakers. Ornolf had left his wife behind, and no doubt other family members and hangers-on as well. They were not just biding their time, like Thorgrim's people. They were fully engaged in the business of running an estate. Even when Ornolf had been home, it was his wife who had managed things, leaving Ornolf free to do as he wished, which was eat, drink, sleep, hunt, and fornicate.

Skorri tried to recall the wife's name. She was a nasty, shrewish piece of work, he remembered that. Folk had always said that Ornolf went raiding just to get away from her. He certainly did not need the riches it could bring, at least not since the success he found raiding as a younger man.

Thurid... That was her name. As far as Skorri knew she was still alive. Too unpleasant to die. The gods would not have her.

The gate was open and they rode through, and all around the groundsmen stopped what they were doing and watched them enter. A servant girl sprinted for the small door on the side of the great hall, and Skorri knew that soon he would be facing down Ornolf's miserable wife, a thing he did not relish. He reined to a stop and slipped down off his horse, and Koll did as well.

"You there!" he called to a knot of servants who were standing nearby, watching with worried looks on their faces. "Come here."

Reluctantly, but quick enough to escape Skorri's wrath, they hurried over. "Fetch ale and food for my men. Tell the stable hands to get hay and water for the horses, and be quick about it, or by all the gods you'll be sorry." He was feeling less sure about taking over Ornolf's great hall than he had about Thorgrim's, and he was treating the people more harshly as a result.

"What...what is the meaning of this?" a voice called, shrill and demanding. "Who are you?"

Skorri turned. Thurid, mistress of the house, fat and red-faced, was hurrying toward him. She wore a wonderfully embroidered dress held up with massive, bright-silver brooches. Her gray hair was twisted in elaborate braids and pinned in place to encircle her head. Keys and a small knife and a pair of scissors hung from her belt on a silver chain, which swung wildly side to side as she came huffing over. A deep and apparently well-practiced fury seemed to radiate from her very core.

"I'm — " Skorri began, but Thurid cut him off.

"Skorri Thorbrandsson. King's overseer. Disgraced king's overseer, as I hear it. Had to crawl through the gauntlet, is the word. Yes…I can see that your face looks like it's been worked over with a cudgel. Disgraceful, you showing up here, and expecting a welcome, no doubt. Well, we most certainly will not be hosting you or these villains. As if we have food or drink to spare! Be gone with you."

She put her hands on her hips and stared at him, lips pursed, face even redder than before. Skorri started to reply, but then he realized that the moment he began speaking she was going to cut him off again and continue her harangue. And he realized that he had no patience for that. He had no patience for her nonsense, or anyone's nonsense. He had taken quite enough of it, and for far too long.

In his mind he saw a cup being filled with some noxious brew, and he knew that he was the cup, and for some time now the world had been pouring disappointment, humiliation, disrespect, into him. It started when his men had turned on him, continued as Halfdan patiently explained why Skorri's loyalty had been rewarded with the gauntlet. Thorgeir telling him they were to share command. Skafti's silent insubordination.

Oh, he had fought it, to be sure. He had put Thorgeir in his proper place, gave his men leave to loot Thorgrim's hall. It had brought him some relief. But now, he realized, he was full up. He was overflowing. He was done.

Skorri took a quick step toward Thurid and Thurid's scowl deepened. He could see the renewed outrage on her face, but he could not see fear, and that only made him angrier still. She started to speak, and Skorri drew his arm back across his chest. Thurid's eyes went wide as she realized what was about to happen, then Skorri swung and hit her backhand in the face.

It was not a warning blow, a slap to express displeasure. Skorri put all his strength into his arm, all his fury, and both were considerable. Thurid spun around, arms flailing, and tumbled to the ground as if she'd been kicked by a horse. She hit and rolled and finally came to a stop.

For a moment she lay there, face down. It was strangely silent. No one spoke, no one moved. Skorri wondered if he had knocked her out, or killed her. But it was just curiosity. He did not care, one way or another.

Then Thurid rolled onto her back and propped herself up on her elbows and glared at him. There was blood coming out of her mouth. Quite a bit. And, to Skorri's disbelief, she seemed ready to start in on him again.

He looked at the servant girl, standing open-mouthed in shock next to where Thurid lay, sprawled on her back. "Keep her quiet," he ordered. "Don't let her say a word."

Before the girl could react, Thurid started in, guttural sounds like half-formed words coming from her throat. Skorri drew his sword from its scabbard, but the servant girl, quick-witted enough to not be frozen in terror, dropped to her knees and whispered urgently to her mistress. Skorri could not hear what she said, but Thurid shut her mouth and just continued glaring at him.

For a moment more Skorri stood over her, sword in hand. If she had started in again, Skorri realized, he most likely would have killed her. Driven his sword right through her heart. The realization surprised him a bit, but it did not bother him at all.

He turned and slid the sword back into its scabbard. He was done with Thurid.

"Koll," he said, speaking loud enough for his voice to carry over the grounds. "Leave a captain and twenty men here. Have them keep care that nothing's removed, no silver hoards buried or carried off. This great hall belongs to the traitor Odd's grandfather, and we'll take from it what we like. And have them see that the servants start to ready a proper feast for us."

He turned and looked down at the servant girl, still kneeling at Thurid's side, and dabbing at the blood running down her chin. "You heard what I said? I'm sure the food and drink here is plentiful and good, and the best of it had better be laid out for us."

The girl nodded. Skorri looked back at his men.

"The rest of you men, you come with me and Koll to Fevik. We have business to attend to."

Soon they were underway again; Skorri, Koll and the other captains on horseback, the column walking behind on foot. They were weaker now by twenty-one men, but they were still an impressive force, certainly the most powerful within a day's march. Any uprising they met would be easily crushed. In truth, Skorri did not anticipate any, which he found disappointing.

With the wagons left behind, and with Skorri's greater sense of urgency, they moved faster than they had that morning, quickly covering the two miles back to Fevik. As they followed the road downhill toward the town, Skorri looked out over the streets and buildings ahead, looking for any sign of alarm, any sign that the folk there were making ready to resist.

Fevik was not a major trading center, not like Hedeby or Ribe, but it was one of the biggest on that stretch of the coast. The town sat at the head of a long, narrow bay, which ran south for a quarter mile until it emptied into a larger bay, and then the ocean beyond. Forty or fifty buildings of various sizes were scattered about, somewhat haphazardly, with plank roads running between them and yards delineated by low wattle fences.

Some of those yards were taken up by gardens, others served as smith's shops or woodworker's shops or boatbuilders' shops. Tables and stalls lined the main road, which was crowded with the usual assortment of carts and wheelbarrows and people on foot.

Skorri looked out over the roofs of the buildings toward the waterfront. There were many ships there, some tied to the docks that ran out over the water or along the shore, some riding at anchor farther out: longships and knarrs and fishing boats. There were ships pulling away from the docks, others floating nearby or making their way slowly under oar. Skorri turned to Koll, who was riding beside him.

"Do you see the ships from Halfdan's fleet in the harbor? Thorgeir's command?"

Koll was silent for a moment as he scrutinized what he could see of the waterfront over the tops of the houses. "Might be," he said. He sounded uncertain. "There are some big ships there. But from here I'm not certain they're Halfdan's."

"They better be there," Skorri said. "That miserable bastard Thorgeir had two days to move his ships five miles. I'll rip his guts out if he's not here."

The road leveled out as it ran into the town of Fevik, disappearing among the cluster of buildings ahead. Skorri reined to a stop a hundred feet from the nearest of them.

"I don't know why these roads are unguarded," he said to Koll, "but I mean to find out. Station ten men on each road leading out of Fevik. No one leaves. If anyone wants to come in, they may, but no one leaves. And send patrols all along the edge of town to make sure no one's sneaking out that way."

"Yes, Lord Skorri," Koll said. He turned his horse around and began shouting orders, and soon divisions of men were racing off in different directions to see that Fevik was sealed off to any vermin who might try to wriggle out. When that was done, Skorri continued on, Koll still at his side, a few hundred men still at his back.

They passed into the town, where the hard-packed dirt road became the plank-built main street, leading south to the waterfront. People stopped what they were doing and stared, silent, as they passed. Smiths stood at their forges, hammer and tongs in hand, eyes following the warriors. Women, bent over their gardens, straightened and wiped their brows and watched them go by. No one waved or smiled, but neither did they curse or fling ugly words, or anything more substantial.

Skorri did not stare back. His eyes were everywhere, because there were many things he was looking for. Some sign of ambush, or attack. Some furtive movements, indications of guilt, or fear of discovery. Some indication that Thorgeir had arrived, and had sent his men out into the town to look for traitors. He saw none of it.

He came at last to the place where the main road ended, and beyond that, a stretch of trampled ground ran down to the docks lining the water and the ships tied to them. Skorri was quite certain now that some of the vessels were part of Halfdan's fleet. A knot of men were standing on the shore, and Skorri saw Thorgeir among them.

He swung himself off his horse and turned to the men behind him. "Sit, rest," he said. "If you want food or drink, just take whatever you can find. But stay close. We'll have work shortly." He turned to Koll. "Come with me."

They crossed the trampled ground to where Thorgeir and the others were standing. Thorgeir had not missed the arrival of the warriors on the waterfront, and he was facing Skorri, arms folded, as he approached.

"Skorri, so glad to see you could attend here," Thorgeir started in, but Skorri ignored him, as if he had not spoken. He stopped and looked around the waterfront, at the ships moving about, the men idle on the dock. Finally, he looked at Thorgeir.

"I just rode into town, and there was no one to stop me," he said.

"Why…why would anyone stop you?" Thorgeir's eyebrows came together and he frowned.

"There was no one guarding the roads. No one stopping anyone from entering the town. Or escaping it. How long have you been here?"

"I…we arrived yesterday. Late."

"Yesterday… And what by all the gods have you been doing since yesterday?"

The frown on Thorgeir's face turned into a scowl. "Waiting on you, mostly. You and nearly all the men. Who might all have been here if you'd let 'em come by sea, as I wanted."

"You had five ships. One hundred and fifty men. You could have sealed this town like a grave with a hundred and fifty men."

"Not one hundred and fifty. *Dragon's Claw* hung up on a wreck of some sort and we had to leave her behind."

"You lost a ship? Between Grømstad and here, you lost a ship?"

"No, we didn't lose it," Thorgeir said, his anger mounting. "They went up on a falling tide. We had to leave them. The ship wasn't hurt. They'll float free soon enough and follow us here."

Skorri's anger was mounting, too, and he looked away before he lost control of it. Incompetence was second only to insubordination among the things he could not tolerate. Finally he looked at Thorgeir again.

"And what are you doing now?"

"Now we're trying to get all these fool merchants and fishermen off the docks so we can get our ships tied up," Thorgeir said, indicating the strange dance of vessels behind him. "And I'm speaking with jarl Gest Heggsson about how we might find these traitors."

Thorgeir nodded to the man standing beside him. In his single-minded anger, Skorri had paid the man no mind, had hardly noticed him, but now he did. He knew him, of course. Jarl Gest, lord of the lands around there since Ornolf the Restless had sailed off, never to return.

Gest was far from the wealthiest or most powerful jarl in East Agder, but he looked the part. His dark hair and beard were streaked with gray, and he wore numerous silver arm rings over the sleeve of his fine tunic. A cape, fringed in fur, was flung around his shoulders and held in place by an elaborately engraved brooch. The hilt of his sword was inlaid with gold. Behind him stood half a dozen men of his hird, all in mail and armed with swords, an ostentatious display for a minor noble.

"Jarl Gest. Of course," Skorri said, nodding. He recalled an incident, during his time as king's overseer, when Gest had not been as forthcoming with his taxes as Skorri had wished. That had not gone well, mostly for Gest.

"Skorri," Gest said.

"What can you tell me of these traitors, Odd and the rest?"

"Tell you? Nothing," Gest said, and Skorri felt the anger bubbling up again. "I don't know anything beyond what I've heard. Which is no doubt the same as what you've heard."

Skorri looked out at the water again, letting his anger settle once more. He wondered how many times he could do that before the anger took permanent hold, like a fire out of control.

"Fevik is Odd Thorgrimson's home," he said, speaking slowly and patiently, as if he had already explained this several times. "The people here are with him, so of course this is where he will come to reignite his uprising. And you're saying you know nothing of him?"

"That's what I'm saying. I haven't seen him or any of his people, and I know of no one who has."

"Impossible," Skorri said. "Maybe people need more persuasion. Maybe they're being forgetful."

"Well, here's something I have heard of late," Gest said. "Something you might not know. I was about to tell Thorgeir this. We had a fellow here not long ago, a few days past, I think, and he says he's seen Thorgrim Ulfsson. He says Thorgrim's alive and making his way back to Vik."

Skorri frowned and looked at Gest and tried to fathom what the man was saying. *Thorgrim Ulfsson? Thorgrim Night Wolf?*

"Who's this who says so? What does he know of it?"

"He's a freeman who lives inland a bit. Bergthor Skeggjason. Has a small farm. He went off raiding last year, and just came back. Didn't have much luck. He says he met up with Thorgrim Night Wolf in Engla-land and they sailed in company for a short while. He said it was Thorgrim's intent to return to Vik as soon as he could. Said it was pretty much all he cared about."

"Thorgrim Night Wolf…" Skorri said, mostly to himself. "And Ornolf? What of Ornolf?"

"Ornolf's dead. Killed in Ireland," Gest said. He did not even pretend to be saddened by that news.

"You spoke with this Bergthor?" Skorri asked.

"No," Gest said. "I heard all this from a tavern keeper here in Fevik named Thorhall. He seems to be the only one Bergthor spoke to. I sent for Bergthor after hearing this, but he was gone by then, and no one knows where. He went by land, wherever it was, since his ship's still on the beach, and half full of sand and water. I had my men search, but no luck."

"A tavern keeper?" Skorri said. "If you heard it from a tavern keeper, then I assume that everyone in Fevik has heard it as well."

"Yes, in Fevik. And well beyond, I would think."

"I don't see much call for concern here," Thorgeir said. "Some luckless bastard says he saw Thorgrim Ulfsson…what? Two months back? And thinks he's bound this way? And what if he is? What's that old man supposed to do?"

Skorri looked down at the ground. He heard Thorgeir's words, but he was not really listening. Rather, he was turning this news over in his head, and he found it a lot more worrisome than that idiot Thorgeir did.

Thorgrim's son, Odd, was well-respected in Fevik, and he had freemen from all over East Agder rallying to his cause. But Thorgrim was a legend in that country, a man who could inspire countless fighting men from farther afield to rise up and follow his banner. His skill as a leader in battle was well-known, and he might already have a powerful army to back him up.

"Did Bergthor say how many warriors Thorgrim had with him?" Skorri asked.

"He did not, not that I heard," Gest said. "But he said he commanded a fleet of six ships."

Six ships? That could mean well over three hundred men. Men hardened by years of raiding in foreign lands. Men who might have won immeasurable wealth, and the respect and admiration that went with it.

And what would Thorgrim do if he returned to find his eldest son at war with the king, just for trying to defend his father's farm? Whatever it was, Skorri knew they must be ready for it. And that meant dealing with Odd Thorgrimson quickly, and for good. He could not risk father and son joining forces.

He turned back to Thorgeir. "Have you searched the town?"

"No, I have not searched the town. I told you…"

Skorri turned to Koll. Thorgeir was still talking, but whatever he had to say, Skorri was not interested.

"Divide the men up into companies, twenty men each. Each company takes a street. Go house to house, search every inch of every building. The people can cry and moan about it if they like, it doesn't matter. We're not here to be gentle. Have the men look for any sign of Odd or any of the traitors. Question everyone. They're free to take whatever they please if it'll help them in their efforts."

"What do you think you're doing?" Gest said, his voice rising in pitch and volume. "I told you, Odd and the rest are not here. And you've all but given your men leave to loot the town!"

"Loot, is that what it is?" Skorri said. "They're looking for traitors. Traitors who might have been in your midst for how long, the Allfather alone knows. But you seem very eager to stop my men from searching for them. Maybe you know more than you're saying."

Gest shut his mouth for a moment, then began again. "I'm as loyal to King Halfdan as you are, you bastard, but I won't stand for a raiding party against my people! Who happen to be the king's people as well."

"You have no say here," Skorri said. His voice was calm, which he could see struck a nerve in Gest, like a warning bell. "I was sent by King Halfdan to do as I see fit. I was sent with five hundred men and five ships. He didn't send so powerful a force just so I could be gentle and soft with traitors. So unless you want to be thought of as a traitor yourself, which could mean your head ends up on a pike, I suggest you shut your mouth."

Gest did shut his mouth. He said nothing, and Thorgeir said nothing, as Koll organized the men into companies and sent them off to do as Skorri ordered. With considerable enthusiasm, they swept through the city, house by house, shop by shop, searching, questioning the folk who lived there, gathering up possible evidence of collaboration: silver coins, weapons, combs, jewelry, the better articles of clothing.

It was not entirely clear what they were searching for — Skorri's men would have recognized Odd Thorgrimson, but they could not tell one of his followers from anyone else. In truth, looking for Odd and the others was only part of what Skorri hoped to achieve.

More than that, he wanted to let the folk know that harboring traitors was a very bad idea. He wanted them to understand that he, Skorri, was willing to do whatever he needed to do to stop them. And he wanted his men to further enrich themselves by plundering these disloyal bastards.

Skorri mounted his horse and rode slowly up the main road and then back down another that ran parallel to it. He watched with some amusement the chaos that he had unleashed. His warriors were dragging women and children from their homes and forcing them to stand aside as they searched. Men stood and watched, and some held axes or heavy iron tools, ready to fight, but forcing themselves to remain still, because they were not ready to die, or the women who clung to them were not ready to let them die.

He headed down the main road again, moving through a surge of people trying to leave town.

"Back to your homes! No one leaves! Back to you homes!" he called as he rode, but none of them seemed to hear. Not that it mattered. They would find out soon enough, once they hit the line of men he had stationed around the town's perimeter. He wanted to smile, but he kept his face grim.

"Lord Skorri!" He heard a voice behind and turned his horse around. One of Koll's men was pushing his way through the panicked crowd. "Lord Skorri, Koll sent me. He says there's a ship approaching, and you should come have a look."

Skorri urged his horse forward, though the going was slow through the crowded street. Why the appearance of a ship should require his attention he did not know, but if Koll said it did, then it probably did.

He came to the end of the road, where it met the waterfront, and continued on to where Thorgeir, Gest, Koll, and a handful of others were staring out at the harbor.

There were two ships that Skorri could see in the distance, not one. The farther was about half a mile off and seemed to be having some difficulty. The yard was hoisted halfway up the mast and cocked at an unusual angle, the sail hanging limp and still partially tied to the yard. The ship itself was listing to starboard. It was making headway, but slowly, with only two oars pulling on the starboard side, and one to larboard. Skorri thought he could see men throwing buckets of water over the side.

The second ship was halfway between the shore and the newly arrived vessel, heading out to its stricken brethren, all oars pulling in unison.

"What's going on?" Skorri asked as he swung down off his horse.

"This ship out there, I'm quite certain it's *Dragon's Claw*, here at last," Thorgeir said.

"*Dragon's Claw*, the ship you lost?" Skorri asked.

"Clearly I didn't lose her," Thorgeir said. "Here she is."

"And apparently in some difficulty," Skorri said. "What happened?"

"How by all the gods should I know?" Thorgeir snapped. "She was fine when I left her. Something's happened. An accident or some such. I sent *War Hammer* out to tow her in."

Skorri watched them for a moment: *War Hammer* closing quickly on the wounded ship, *Dragon's Claw* all but stopped now in her progress, her three oars hanging limp in the water. He felt an uneasy sensation in his gut. Something here felt wrong. But *War Hammer* was well past the point where they might call her back, and there was nothing that Skorri or anyone could do now but stand and watch.

Chapter Fourteen

Hear a great wonder,
hear of peace broken,
hear of a great matter,
hear of a death
— one man's or more.

Gisli Sursson's Saga

They don't look much like fishermen anymore, Odd thought.

He was standing on the larboard side, the high side, of the heavily listing vessel. Along with Ragi's warriors, a couple dozen of the former fishermen were hunkered down in the bottom of the ship to starboard. They were wearing mail shirts over their rough working clothes, and helmets on their heads. They held spears in their hands, wore swords at their waists: the spoils they had taken from the ship's original crew.

There had been thirty men on board Halfdan's longship, which seemed to Odd a small crew for so large a vessel, but they probably were not expecting a fight. And why would they be, sailing in seas that were very much the domain of their king?

In the end, there had indeed been no fight. Just surrender in the face of a fiery death.

Now the fishermen were fitted out in the warriors' armor and carrying their weapons. Three were at the oars, and for appearance's sake, four more were bailing, and ostentatiously flinging the water over the side. Three were standing by with grappling hooks. The rest were hiding below the sheer strake, waiting. But they would not be waiting for long.

"Here they come, just like I said!" Bragi Shipslayer called from the tiller, just aft of where Odd stood.

Not what you said at all, Odd thought. It was Ragi Oleifsson who came up with the idea of bringing the ship to Fevik, making her appear disabled, to see what Halfdan's men might do. Bragi Shipslayer had scoffed at the idea. His chief objection, Odd imagined, was that he had not thought of it.

There had been some discussion on the matter. It struck Odd as a good idea. With surprise working for them they might pick up a second ship. Perhaps more than one. Arnor Knattarson and the other fishermen, eager to follow up on their one easy victory, agreed.

Odd leaned over the larboard side of the ship, the side not visible from Fevik and looked down. Four fishing boats were tied alongside, with another eighty or so men loaded aboard. Those men were armed, too, but with the crude assortment of weapons the fishermen had taken with them from the camp. They had no mail or helmets because there were no more to go around, though they hoped to acquire more shortly.

"A ship's putting off from Fevik," Odd said, just loud enough to be heard by all. "A longship." The men in the boats were hidden from shore, which was the point, but it also meant that they could not see what was going on.

"Just one?" Arnor Knattarson asked. Arnor had opted to lead the flank attack in the fishing boats.

"Just one so far. There doesn't seem to be any sort of alarm, and there doesn't seem to be many men on board, save for those at the oars." That was true, though it was hard to tell from nearly half a mile off.

"Stand ready, I'll give the word," Odd added, then straightened and looked back at the approaching ship.

"Fifteen oars per side," Bragi said. "I'll wager they double-banked 'em if they think they're going to have to tow us in. Sixty men."

"I don't see any crowd of warriors there. Sixty men who aren't expecting to fight," Amundi said. "Probably no mail or helmets."

"Probably not," Ragi agreed.

No mail or helmets, Odd thought. That was most likely true. It was hard to row while wearing mail, and it was not always the best choice in a sea fight.

He had told the fishermen as much, that they might be better off without it, but they had insisted. The novelty of donning a warrior's armor seemed to have been too much to resist. That being the case, Odd then suggested they would do well to avoid going overboard.

Of course, Odd was also wearing mail and a helmet. It was not what he preferred, at least not the mail shirt, but now he hoped to pass himself off as one of Halfdan's men, one of the ship's original crew, at least until the attack was launched. His tattered and faded tunic would never have fooled anyone, but with the mail covering it over, there was a chance.

He reminded himself that he, too, should avoid going over the side.

The approaching ship was a quarter mile off now, and they could see that Bragi was right, that the oars were double-banked. A couple of men were standing in the bow, and it was clear from the glint of sunlight that they were wearing mail, but the rowers seemed not to be. They were mostly hidden by the sides of the ship and the shields mounted on the racks, but as far as Odd could see they were in tunics only.

They would, however, have swords and seaxes, and perhaps spears. No Northman would step out of his door to piss in his yard without carrying some sort of weapon.

"You men with the grappling hooks, keep them out of sight, but stand ready. On my command," Odd called down the deck, and the men nodded. "And you men down there," he said to the fishermen sitting or lying on the ship's deck, "You don't show yourselves until I say. Understood?"

The men looked up at him and nodded.

The coming ship, driven by double-banked oars, closed fast, and soon Odd could make out the details: two men at the bow, rows of men pulling oars, lines of shields on the racks. The shields might be a problem.

"Hear me," Odd said to the men in hiding. "When I give the word, you stand and pull your shields from the rack. But you still won't be able to board the other ship, because their shields are in the way. You'll have to pull them free and throw them aside. Do you understand what I'm saying?"

Again, the men nodded.

A voice came from across the water. "Atli, is that you?" It was one of the men in the bow of the approaching ship, the ship's master, Odd imagined.

"Yes!" Odd called back. There was perhaps a hundred feet between the two ships, and closing fast.

"What by Thor's arse happened to you?"

"After we went up on the wreck we were attacked. Those pirates, call themselves fishermen. Like a pack of wolves."

Fifty feet between the ships, and a pause from the man in the bow of the approaching vessel. "You're not Atli," he called.

"Atli's dead, I told you," Odd said. "It's me, Ketil!"

Another pause as the longship came up parallel to Odd's ship with twenty feet between them, just enough space for their oars to avoid striking.

"Hold your oars!" the second man in the bow called to the rowers. The rowers stopped pulling and let the blades of their oars drag in the water, bringing the ship to a stop.

"Ketil?" the first man called. "Do I know you?"

Odd ignored him. He turned to the men with the grappling hooks. "Now!" he shouted, and the grappling hooks came up from where they sat on the deck, dangling from their seal-hide ropes, and each, with a single, expert twirl, sailed across the gap between the ships and dropped down behind the sheer strake. The men holding the ropes pulled them taught, and others leapt up to join them, and soon half a dozen men were heaving away on each line, pulling the ships together.

"What do you think you're doing?" the man in the bow called. He and Odd were separated by only fifteen feet or so, and Odd could see his eyes go wide in surprise. Then the air was filled with the sound of shattering wood, and curses, and shouts of outrage, as the vessels were hauled closer together, and Odd's ship ran up over the oars on Halfdan's and snapped them like twigs.

"Oh, you bastards!" the man shouted, realizing at last what was happening. He turned to call orders to his men, still seated at the oars, as Bragi Shipslayer suddenly appeared at Odd's side. He pushed Odd out of the way — nearly pushed him to the deck — then drew a spear up over his head. With a grunt he launched the spear across the space separating him from the master of Halfdan's ship.

The weapon flew arrow-straight, so fast it was just a blur. It struck the man mid-chest and did not slow in the least as it pierced his mail and flung him back onto the deck.

Odd recovered his balance, turned, and leaned over the side, shouting down at the boats below.

"Arnor! Go! Go!"

He straightened, turned back. The fishermen hidden below the ship's rail, whom he had told not to move until he gave the word, were already moving, leaping to their feet, pulling the shields from the rack and slipping them on their arms. The men on the grappling hooks were still heaving away, the ships just a few feet apart and closing.

I told you to stay down! Odd thought, but he did not say it, because there was no point. One of the fishermen stepped up on a sea chest and put a foot on the sheer strake, ready to launch himself up and over the gap between the ships. He was just pushing off when Odd grabbed his belt and pulled him back.

"Stand fast!" Odd shouted. "Wait until the ships touch!"

A foot, no more, separated the two when Odd shouted, "Get their shields! Pull them clear!" He reached out for the nearest one, and just as his hands were closing on the rim of the shield, a man appeared behind it, a man standing on Halfdan's ship, his face red with exertion, snarling through a thick beard.

The man grabbed the shield and pulled it out of Odd's hands. And as he did, Odd whipped the seax out of the sheath that was crosswise on his belt and drove the blade up and under the rim. He felt the point hit and drive in. He saw the man's eyes go wide and his mouth open in a scream. With his left hand Odd grabbed the shield and pulled it free as the man stumbled back, bent over, hands red with blood and pressed to the wound.

Odd was slipping the shield onto his arm when the ships struck, sheer strake to sheer strake, with an impact that he could feel in his feet.

"Tie off the grappling lines!" he shouted. "Get these ships lashed together!"

He saw motion out beyond the ship: Arnor leading the fishing boats around to the unengaged side of the longship to which they were now bound. The shields along the side of Halfdan's ship had been snatched away, but not by the fishermen, as Odd had told them to do. Rather, Halfdan's warriors had figured out quick enough what was going on, and they had abandoned their oars to stand with shields on their arms and swords in their hands.

"Go! Go!" Odd shouted as he put a foot up on the sheer strake, ready to go up and over the side. He felt something bump him in passing, and once again Bragi Shipslayer was there, vaulting over the sheer strake beside him and onto the other longship, amazingly nimble for a man built like a barrel. He wore no mail, no helmet, and his only weapon was a four-foot club he had fashioned from a spare boat oar.

Bragi hit the deck with both feet. The man nearest him turned and raised his shield and thrust his sword as Bragi lifted the club over his head and drove it down. The tip of the blade was an inch from Bragi's gut when the club came down on the man's head and just kept going. Even over the mounting din of the fight, Odd could hear the sickening sound of the man's skull caving in.

Then Odd was up and over the side and landing on the deck of the other ship. His foot hit the edge of a frame and he stumbled and went down on one knee. Instinctively, he held his shield up over his head, and was rewarded with the jarring sensation of a sword bouncing off the wood.

He lifted the edge of the shield and peered under it, found he was looking at leggings and the hem of a tunic. He slashed sideways with the seax, making a line of torn cloth and lacerated flesh. The legs buckled and staggered away and Odd stood, shield up, seax in hand.

Skidi, one of the fishermen, was beside him, having launched himself into the fight, but it was not going well. He seemed to have dropped his sword and was holding his shield in both hands, holding it up over his head. The warrior he was fighting raised his sword and slammed it down on the shield's face, and the shield shattered under the impact and broke in half.

Skidi seemed unsure what to do next. He was all but frozen, holding the half of the shield that remained, when Odd twisted sideways and thrust the tip of his seax at the warrior's neck. The man sensed the strike coming and turned, bringing his shield across his chest and hitting Odd's forearm with the rim. The impact knocked the seax from Odd's hand and sent it spinning away. Then Odd swung his own shield down and to the right, catching the warrior's sword and pushing it aside as the man lunged for Odd's stomach.

Odd stepped back, two steps, and pulled Blood-letter from its scabbard, sweeping it sideways as it cleared the leather and parrying the blade that was coming at him again. He saw more movement to his right and he twisted sideways and brought his shield up in time to catch the tip of another sword, striking like a snake. He hacked at this second opponent, felt Blood-letter bounce off the man's shield, then turned back and slashed at the first.

There was shouting now from the far side of Halfdan's longship, and through the press of fighting men Odd saw Arnor leading the second wave of fishermen up and over the larboard side.

Arnor's men were shouting as they came aboard, trying to sow maximum confusion and fear, and it was working. Halfdan's men seemed to be taken completely by surprise by these new arrivals. They glanced over their shoulders to see who was there, but most dared not turn and face them. They were hemmed in now on both sides.

The fight did not last long after that. Arnor's men slammed into the back ranks of Halfdan's warriors, who turned to meet them, but the shock of the fishermen's sudden appearance was enough to knock the fight out of most. One by one they started throwing shields and weapons away and holding their hands up in surrender.

Some died anyway, cut down by the fishermen, who were in battle frenzy. But Arnor shouted for them all to put up their weapons, and Odd and Ragi joined in, and soon the fighting dropped off to nothing, and the only sound was the moaning of the wounded and the creak of the ships grinding against each other.

Odd took a few deep breaths, enough to regain his equilibrium. "We must hurry now!" he called, once his head had cleared. He turned to a knot of Halfdan's men who still had their hands partly raised. They were weaponless and scowling, but if any were frightened of what would come next, they did not show it.

"You lot," Odd said, pointing with his sword. "Get your wounded in the boats alongside. Your dead, too. Hurry, or by the gods, it's overboard with all of you!"

For a moment they just stood there, but before Odd could speak again, Bragi Shipslayer stepped up. He grabbed one of Halfdan's men by the tunic and half-flung him across the ship, and called, "Are you bastards deaf! Do I need to knock the stuffing from your ears?"

That seemed to wake them up. Suddenly they were all moving at once, grabbing up the dead and wounded, lowering them over the side into the fishing boats.

Odd and the others had planned for this, what to do with prisoners if they came by them. There were three choices: let them go, cut their throats, take them hostage. Happily for Halfdan's men there was little appetite for wanton slaughter, and it was decided that hostages would be more trouble than they were worth, so letting them go won out.

Odd left them to it. He looked around for Bragi. The next task was to take the captured longship in tow.

He saw Bragi up by the bow of Halfdan's ship. He and Huginn and Muninn were lashing a towline to a heavy cleat there and running it over to their own ship.

The last of Halfdan's men disappeared over the rail and down into the boats. Odd looked over the side. They had cut the lines that held the boats fast to the longship, and were already twenty feet away and drifting. And they would continue to drift, since the fishermen had thrown all the oars overboard, a fact that Halfdan's men would soon discover, if they had not already.

"Odd, ship's made off," Arnor called. He and Bragi and Huginn and Muninn had carried the tow line back aboard the first ship and made it fast in the stern.

"Very well!" Odd called back. He looked around the newly captured ship. Some of the fishermen had pulled the shattered oars in and stacked them on the deck. Others had pulled intact oars from the larboard side and were ready to run them out the starboard row ports, once there was room enough.

Good, Odd thought. He stepped up onto the sheer strake and back onto the first ship. "Cast off those grapples!" he shouted. The seal-hide ropes were let go and the two ships drifted apart. On Bragi's command the men ran out their oars and started an easy stroke, building speed and momentum with each subsequent pull.

Odd looked back toward the town of Fevik. There was a handful of ships tied up at the docks there, and more at anchor. He thought he could see one ship, at least, moving, pushing off from the dock, but he could not be sure.

"Pull, you bastards!" Bragi called. He looked back over his shoulder, at the other ship at the end of the tow line. They had left six men aboard, pulling three oars on each side, to help with the effort. "And you lazy bastards back there, you pull, too!"

The two ships made their way southeast, leaving Fevik in their wake. Odd climbed up on the sheer strake at the stern, one hand on the backstay for balance, and stared back at the town. He could see now that there was definitely one ship coming in pursuit, its oars moving in unison as it pulled away from the waterfront. He guessed that more would follow.

"They're going to collect up the boats," Bragi called from the tiller, as if he could hear Odd's thoughts. "They won't send a ship after us!"

Odd knew better than to reply, but he did it anyway. "Why not?"

"Because they're afraid of me, of course! When they learn of the slaughter I made among those bastards, they'll piss their leggings and hide under their beds."

This time Odd did not reply, just kept his eyes on Fevik. The ship that was underway did in fact seem to be heading for the fishing boats they had set adrift, but that did not mean they wouldn't also come after the two stolen ships. They could not possibly ignore such an outrage.

Odd kept his eyes on the enemy astern until at last the town and the bay disappeared from sight behind a headland. He climbed down from the sheer strake and leaned against the ship's side and looked forward. There was another headland on the larboard bow, about half a mile away. On that heading, they would just brush past it, after which they would tuck in behind.

The afternoon was getting on as they skirted that point of land and turned north into a small bay that opened up ahead of them. The fleet of fishing boats was there, floating just off the shore, riding at their anchors. They were fully manned — close to a hundred armed fishermen — all those who had not joined in the ambush of Halfdan's ships.

Bragi kept the longship on that heading, then fifty feet short of the cluster of boats he pushed the tiller over and swung the ship up into the wind. The oars came out of the water, and forward Huginn and Muninn lowered the stone and wood anchor over the bow. One hundred feet away the newly captured longship came to anchor as well.

"Let's get some food and drink for the men," Odd said to Arnor, once the ship was settled and the anchor holding. "With any luck our work is not done today."

He looked over at the rocky headland they had just rounded. It rose a hundred feet above the water to where it leveled off into a stretch of brush and stunted trees. He could see a figure standing there. That man, he knew, was watching another man on the next headland, who would signal when Halfdan's ships were on their way.

Because Odd was sure they would come. And when they did, the wolf pack would be ready to pounce.

Chapter Fifteen

It's ill for men
to endure old age;
it snatches from them
sight and sense.

The Saga of the Confederates

Thorgrim, despite his determination, did not sail the day after coming awake in Gyda's house in Ribe. It was not through any fault or choice of his own.

He was ready to get underway. He could barely walk, but that did not dissuade him. His weakness was not the problem; rather that *Sea Hammer* was still in need of repair. They had found some rot in the garboard while trying to stop up the leak, and now a new section of plank would have to be scarfed in.

That, at least, was what Harald and Hall told him. He was not certain he believed them.

He slept the night on a straw mattress, his sleep deep and dreamless. Harald and Starri found beds on the platforms against the other side of the house, and Gyda retreated to the walled-off room at the far end. By the time Thorgrim awoke, the sun was up, and Gyda was stirring a porridge in her iron pot, and Starri and Harald were sitting on benches near the fire, waiting like dogs for feeding time.

Thorgrim pushed himself up as best he could, involuntarily groaning, and Harald and Starri were there in an instant, helping him sit up and get to his feet. They guided him to his seat on the bench and set him down and Gyda distributed bowls of porridge all around.

"How goes the work on *Sea Hammer*?" he asked.

"Good, good," Harald said. "We've got the fresh plank fitted and the holes drilled for the roves. Should be mostly done today."

Thorgrim scrutinized the boy, looking to see if he was obfuscating, playing for time to let the old man heal up a bit more. Harald was not a good liar, and he did not seem to be lying now. That meant he was telling the truth, or his skills at deception had improved. Either was possible.

"I'm glad to hear that," Thorgrim said, his tone emphasizing the seriousness of his words. "We don't have the time to be lazing around here. Your brother's in trouble. We don't know what sort of trouble, but whatever it is, we need to get to him."

"I understand, father," Harald said, and his gaze, in turn, did not waver.

Starri finished his bowl of porridge; Harald finished his and two more. Then they took their leave, Harald to help with repairing *Sea Hammer*, and Starri to do what, only the gods knew. Starri was no shipwright, or much of anything else, save for a fighting man.

"You're looking better," Gyda said, once the men had left. "Your color is better."

"I'm feeling better," Thorgrim said. "Much better. You must be a skilled healer, to have brought me back the way you did."

"No, not really," Gyda said. "I don't really do so very much. I won't drain a man's blood or fill him full of this or that potion. I know something of healing plants, I suppose, and poultices and such, but mostly I just let the gods do their work. I don't try to do it for them."

"You give all the credit to the gods?"

"Most of the credit. I've found that if you leave the gods and spirits to it, the chances are better than even that they'll bring about a cure. That's my secret. That's why I have more success than most of the ones who call themselves healers."

"I see," Thorgrim said. He thought of Morrigan, an Irish woman he had known. Morrigan, with her dried plants and poultices and various concoctions. She was a skilled healer, just like this Gyda seemed to be. Skilled, despite her protests.

It was better than two years past since he had been with Morrigan. It felt like twenty.

"Still, it's a good secret," Thorgrim said. "The folk here must seek you out."

"Some do. Most don't. Some think I'm a witch, bent on doing evil. They'd probably kill me for it, if they weren't afraid to try."

"When my men asked for a healer, you were the one the folk here sent them to."

Gyda smiled at that. "You're strangers in Ribe. And you're Norwegians. Not merchants, Norwegian raiders. A lot of folk here don't care for either. That's why they told your men to seek me out. They weren't trying to help you."

Thorgrim smiled too. "Well, won't they be sorry." He sat a little more upright, then added, "You're not a Dane." It was a statement. Her accent did not seem right for a native of Ribe.

"No. I'm Norwegian. From Kaupang."

"How do you happen to be in Ribe?" Thorgrim asked. He was not generally very curious about people, but he was curious now.

"I married a Dane," Gyda said. She stood and took a step toward Thorgrim. "Do you think you can walk? Perhaps we should try, just a bit."

"Yes, I think I can walk," Thorgrim said, though he was not as certain as he made himself sound. Gyda came over and slipped a hand under his arm and helped lift him to his feet. His head swam and he felt dizzy and for a moment he thought he was going down again. He stood motionless, Gyda's arm wrapped around his, and waited until his head cleared.

"Here we go," he said, but before he could take a step Gyda brought his arm around her shoulder so that she might better support him. It was a good fit, with her shoulder tucked right under his arm, his arm draped around her shoulder.

Together they moved down the center of the room as far as the door, then turned around and walked back. Thorgrim was tentative at first, but with each step he felt his strength returning, felt his head clear. He was sure he could walk without Gyda's support, but still he did not remove his arm.

They took two more turns up and down the length of the house, which was no great distance.

"There, how do you feel?" Gyda asked.

"Good," Thorgrim said. "I feel good."

"You should rest now."

"I've been resting for seven days. I don't think I'll ever need to rest again. I'm going to walk down to the water. I have to see what state my ship's in."

Gyda stepped out from under his arm and appraised him skeptically. Thorgrim wondered if he was in for a fight here, but Gyda said, "Very well. I'll come with you."

Iron-tooth was lying on the platform next to the table on which Thorgrim had been laid out — Thorgrim had looked for it almost as soon as he had come awake — and now he crossed the room unaided and strapped it on around his waist, adjusting the hang of the sword and the set of the seax in front.

Gyda dug around inside a wooden chest on the floor and came up with a wool cloak. She brought it over to Thorgrim and draped it over his shoulders, then pinned it with a fine silver brooch at his shoulder.

"There you go," she said, patting the fabric into place.

They stepped through the door and into the cool of the late summer morning. Thorgrim paused and looked around. For the past day he had been hearing the muted sounds of Ribe coming through the wooden walls of Gyda's house, but this was the first time he had seen the town since he and Ornolf had passed that way years before.

It was bigger than he recalled, and busier. Ribe, it seemed, was prospering. Gyda's home was fronted by a patch of open ground with a small garden planted in raised wooden beds, a profusion of green overgrowing the sides. A short wattle fence separated Gyda's property from the wide dirt road beyond: the market street, Gyda had said, Ribe's central thoroughfare.

It was crowded with men and women and oxen and wagons. Flocks of sheep and small herds of cows were driven by boys with long sticks, who shouted and wielded their prods like swords in battle. The road itself was dry and mostly even, though Thorgrim could see that it had been rutted and beaten flat, rutted and beaten flat, over and over again through the years. A worn and dirt-covered plank road ran down the center to make the going easier in wetter times.

Both sides of the street were lined with buildings of various shapes and sizes, some bigger than Gyda's, some smaller. Some were plank-built, others wattle and daub. Most were covered by thick roofs of thatch, with smoke roiling out of the gable ends. There were smiths' shops and woodworkers' shops, where craftsmen labored under roofs of canvas or thatch stretched over their yards. There were bakers, too, and brewers, and goldsmiths, and all manner of trade taking place.

"Ribe's grown quite a lot, as of late," Gyda said. "Are you impressed?"

Thorgrim smiled. "I was in Frankia not long ago, in a great, walled house. Before that, in the king's palace in Wessex, where I was nearly burned at the stake. I've seen the ruins that the Romans left behind. I've seen Dubh-linn. Ribe's not so impressive to me."

"A man such as you…I might have guessed that he would not be impressed," Gyda said, with an edge of teasing in her voice. "How are you feeling? Do you still feel strong enough to walk?"

"I do. Lead the way."

They stepped out into the street, into the stream of people and animals, and Gyda took Thorgrim's arm, though Thorgrim did not actually feel the need for support. They walked slowly, more slowly than Thorgrim, who was eager to get to his ship, might have wished. He suspected that Gyda was purposely slowing the pace, keeping him from overexerting himself, which he likely would have done.

"You said you married a Dane," Thorgrim said, as they made their way past shops selling bread and cured meats. "Is he a merchant, off to sea? Off raiding?" Thorgrim had seen no husband, nor any sign of one.

"No," Gyda said. "He's dead."

"Oh. I'm sorry."

"Hmm," Gyda said.

"You seem to do well, for a widow."

"Since my husband stopped spending all our silver on drink, and then beating me when there was no more? Yes, I've managed to get by."

"I see," Thorgrim said. "So what became of him?" The question surprised him, even as he asked it. He generally did not inquire into people's affairs.

"Don't know," Gyda said. "They found him on the road, some ways out of town. His head was bashed in. There was never any notion of who might have done it."

"Hmm," Thorgrim said.

They paused at a sword-maker who had some of his wares laid out on a table by the road. "Finest steel," the craftsmen said, gesturing toward the weapons before him. "Perfectly balanced. You seem like a man who knows of such things. Please, see what you think."

Thorgrim picked up one of the swords and slid it out of its scabbard. He held it straight, then made a short, slashing motion.

"Good," he said. "Good balance, like you said." He flipped the sword around and offered it to Gyda to try. She smiled and took the grip and held the weapon up and crosswise in front of her. She did not look at all uncomfortable holding it.

"Very nice," she said. "But too heavy for me."

"Try this one," Thorgrim said. He picked up another sword, a shorter weapon, more an oversized seax than a sword. He offered the grip to Gyda, who slid it out of its sheath and gave a half lunge at an imaginary enemy.

"Better!" she laughed. Thorgrim turned to the swordsmith.

"We'll take this one."

"Oh, no, Thorgrim," Gyda protested. "I don't need a sword!"

"Do you have a sword?"

"No."

"Then you need a sword. You have very dangerous men staying in your house."

Thorgrim and the swordsmith haggled a bit and settled on a price. Thorgrim fished in his purse for a piece of silver of the agreed upon weight — a small fraction of what was in there — and paid the man. They continued on down the road, Gyda holding her new weapon under her arm.

"Why do they call you Night Wolf?" she asked, after they had walked a bit farther.

"Because there's some who have come up with some strange notions about me," he said. He, too, could be evasive if he chose to be. And he usually did.

"I can see how that might happen, that stories are told. Most men talk of nothing but themselves, but not you. Harald said your home is in Vik?"

"That's right. My farm's there. At least it was when I sailed, better than two years past. If it's still there now, I don't know."

They walked on a bit more. Thorgrim could see the masts of the ships rising above the roofs of the buildings, though he could not distinguish *Sea Hammer*'s from the rest.

"You've been gone more than two years," Gyda said. "You must miss your wife."

"I do," Thorgrim said. His normal inclination would be to add nothing to that, but for once he felt otherwise inclined. "She died a year or so before we sailed. Honestly, it's the only reason I was talked into going raiding again. I thought I'd left that behind in my younger days."

"I see," Gyda said. Thorgrim felt her grip tighten a bit on his arm, but she said nothing more, and he was grateful for that.

The country around Ribe was marshy and flat as a shield, the coastline mostly mudflats cut through with channels here and there. Ribe itself was situated several miles inland, on a wide river that ran like a Roman road to the sea. The houses and shops were pressed up close to the river's edge, where fishing boats were pulled up for repair, and nets spread out for mending, and racks of split fish drying in the sun. Docks thrust themselves out over the water, with longships and knarrs and various other vessels from all over the northern countries, and Frankia and even Engla-land and Ireland, tied alongside. The shore was lined with more ships and boats of all sizes pulled up on the muddy bank.

Thorgrim could see *Sea Hammer* now, just upstream of where the market street ended at the water. She was unmistakable to him, with her familiar figurehead and the sweep of her sheer and the blue-painted upper strake.

"Here's my ship," Thorgrim said, nodding. "*Sea Hammer.*"

"She's lovely," Gyda said.

"Do you know about ships?" Thorgrim asked.

"Not in the least," Gyda said.

Sea Hammer was drawn well up on the shore and tilted onto her larboard side, and boards had been laid in the mud to form a stable platform. Thorgrim's men, as promised, were hard at work on the garboard, the lowest plank and closest to the keel, on the starboard side.

Hall — Thorgrim was fairly sure it was Hall — was squeezed in under the ship, a hammer in hand, and there were a few others with him. He did not see Harald, and guessed he was at work onboard, down in the bilge. Harald was a good shipwright, and there was no chance that he would miss out on work such as this.

"Almost there, Harald!" Hall called, his voice muffled by the bulk of the ship. "Give it a few more blows!" From inboard a hammer rang out once, twice, a third time.

Unseen, from the other side of the planks, Harald called, "That looks good to me!"

Thorgrim led Gyda out along the planks to where the men were working. "How goes it?" he asked. He was happy to hear that his voice carried its old authority, his words sounding as much like a command as a question.

Hall rolled over on his back and looked up at him, squinting against the daylight after having been jammed in under the hull.

"Ah, Thorgrim! Good to see you up and about!" His arms were covered in mud and he held a hammer. "We're setting the last of the roves now. Should be solid and tight. When the tide comes in later, we'll float her off."

Harald's head popped up over the sheer strake. "Father! You're walking! Good day, Gyda!"

"Good day, Harald," Gyda said.

"You should come aboard, father, inspect the repair we've made."

Thorgrim reached up and put his hands on the sheer strake, ready to hoist himself up and over, but Gyda put a hand on his arm and stepped in close.

"If you try to pull yourself up onto that ship, I swear by the gods, I'll take my new sword and run you through."

"That's your way of keeping me from injury?"

"I'd rather cause you to bleed out than watch you do it to yourself."

Thorgrim nodded. He took his hands off the sheer strake. "I'll just see what Hall's done here," he said to Harald.

With some difficulty — the wound in his shoulder was aching and stiff — Thorgrim knelt down and worked his way in close enough to see the fresh plank Hall and the others had installed. It melded perfectly with the others, and only the color of the new-cut wood set it off. Thorgrim looked over the plank and the neat line of rivets, fore and aft, then crawled out again. Hall and Gyda helped him to his feet, and much as he wanted, like a petulant child, to shake their hands off his arms, he resisted.

He spent some time engaged with Hall and Harald and the others concerning the maintenance of the ship and her seaworthiness, and that of the rest of the fleet — the most enjoyable discussion he had had in some time — then he and Gyda made their way back to her house. Inside, he eased himself down onto one of the benches and gratefully took the cup of ale that Gyda offered.

The day was getting late, the sun low in the west, and inside the house it was growing dark. Gyda stoked up the embers in the hearth and added more wood, until the fire was burning brighter, putting the dark to heel. She lit a few oil lamps and set them around. She sat and looked at Thorgrim.

"You're tired," she said.

Thorgrim was vacillating about whether or not to deny it when they heard a knock at the door; a tentative and uncertain sound. They froze and looked at one another. There was no reason that a knock should seem menacing, but somehow it did. Thorgrim stood and nodded in the direction of the door. Gyda nodded in return and crossed the room.

"Yes?" she said, leaning her shoulder against the door.

"Is this the home of Gyda Ketilsdottir?" came the voice from outside. Thorgrim stepped closer, his hand resting on Iron-tooth's grip. Gyda looked at him again, and again he nodded.

"Yes."

There was a moment's pause, then the voice again. "May I come in? I have business, I think."

Gyda looked over at Thorgrim. Thorgrim nodded. Gyda lifted the latch and swung the door open. The man standing in the doorway was younger than Thorgrim by about a decade, with dark brown hair hanging long over his shoulders and a beard to match. He had the unkempt appearance of a man who had been traveling, and the stains on his tunic, which looked very much like tar, suggested a man who had been traveling by sea. He was well-armed, of course, but then it would have been strange had he not been.

He stepped in through the door and another man, similarly clothed and armed, followed behind. He nodded to Gyda, then looked around the room. His eyes settled on Thorgrim and his expression seemed to change, the tension seemed to go out of him.

"Thorgrim. Thorgrim Ulfsson," he said.

"Yes," Thorgrim said. The man looked vaguely familiar, but that meant nothing.

"I'm Eyvind Bjarnason. From Vik." He nodded to the man behind him to close the door, which he did. "Thank the gods we've found you!"

"You found me," Thorgrim said. "Now, what do you want?"

"It's not what we want. It's what Odd wants. Odd, your son. He sent us to find you. To bring you back. He needs you. Now. He needs you very much."

Chapter Sixteen

On both sides, men on benches
greeted me kindly, while I,
wringer of verses, wished each
and every man there good health.

Gisli Sursson's Saga

Thorgeir Sveinsson was cursing as if he had gone mad, and spinning around in frustration. Skorri was not sure if he was really that angry or just pretending to be, to distract from how great a mess he had made of things.

"Bastards!" Thorgeir shouted.

It was not until the trap was well sprung that they had even realized there was a problem. *Dragon's Claw* had come limping in after some apparent mishap, or worse. Thorgeir had sent *War Hammer*, with oars double-banked, out to meet her: not to fight, but to tow her in. There was nothing threatening about *Dragon's Claw*; indeed, it seemed as if her crew could hardly move the ship on their own.

War Hammer had pulled easily out to the stricken vessel, half a mile off the waterfront, and come alongside. All seemed well. And then the shouting started, and the ring of steel on steel, the clash of shields against shields, faint over that distance, but unmistakable to men who knew the sound.

"Seems *Dragon's Claw*'s no longer part of your fleet, Thorgeir," Skorri said.

Had the situation been just a bit different, had it been Skorri who sent *War Hammer* out so unprepared, then he would certainly have been as enraged as Thorgeir was. More, perhaps. But this was Thorgeir's fault. Thorgeir's complete failure. Both the loss of *Dragon's Claw* and now this surprise attack on *War Hammer*. Thorgeir had sent the ship out with men who were not ready for a fight because he did not have the imagination to see that there might be a fight.

He, Skorri, had felt in his gut that there was something wrong. He had kept his mouth shut, because it had been too late to call *War Hammer* back, but he had been correct.

Thorgeir made no reply, he did not even look at Skorri, as if he had not heard. Instead he shouted, "Ingolf! Get your men and get underway, now! Go help that idiot Bardi, he's rowed right into a trap!"

Ingolf was master of one of Halfdan's three remaining ships. He waved to acknowledge the order, but the bulk of his crew, unfortunately, were ashore, set to various other tasks, and not ready to get underway. Some were nearby, however, and they heard Thorgeir's words, and with no further instruction raced down the dock to where their longship was tied.

"Bardi didn't row into a trap," Skorri corrected. "You sent him into a trap."

Thorgeir certainly heard that. He glared at Skorri, lips pressed tight, but he said nothing. It was bad enough that he seemed to have lost *Dragon's Claw*. If he lost *War Hammer* too it would not go well for him. Halfdan the Black did not like to lose ships. They were much more costly than warriors to replace.

The sound of Ingolf's men scrambling to get their ship underway — to get oars down from the gallows, gear moved clear for the rowers, the dock lines singled up — blanketed the sound of the fight taking place down the bay. Those on shore could do little but watch and try to divine, over the distance, what was going on. There seemed to be a mighty struggle taking place on *War Hammer*'s deck, some undefined action surging fore and aft.

There was movement on the water as well, and Skorri guessed that there had been boats hidden around *Dragon's Claw*'s far side, with more armed men aboard, and now they were pulling into the fight, the men ready to swarm up *War Hammer*'s side behind those struggling to defend her. Skorri shook his head as he watched.

You can kiss my ass, that was well done, he thought.

Odd Thorgrimson might still lose this fight, but even so, this trap was masterfully set and sprung. Had this disaster been Skorri's responsibility, he would have felt quite differently and he knew it, but as it was, he could only admire the boldness and execution of the thing.

Ingolf's men were still getting the ship ready when it became clear that something had changed. The chaotic fight on *War Hammer*'s deck seemed to be over. There was a crowd of men still aboard the ship, and people moving back and forth, but whatever was happening did not have the frenetic quality of a battle, as seen from far off.

That, at least, was how it seemed to Skorri. He was not sure if the others were seeing the same thing. Then Thorgeir spoke up, and his voice sounded optimistic.

"There," he said, "It looks like the fight's done. Bardi must have butchered those traitorous swine."

Skorri smiled. *There's wishful thinking, you dumb bastard*, he thought. Someone, it seemed, had come out victorious, and though it was not yet clear who, Skorri's silver was not on Bardi. He could see men stepping back onto *Dragon's Claw*, while others remained aboard *War Hammer*, dealing with the aftermath of the fight. Others seemed to be climbing back down into the boats floating alongside.

"Cast off!" Ingolf called from the end of the dock, and the lines holding his ship in place were let go and tossed ashore. Oars were run out the row ports and they pushed off and the ship drifted clear. For a moment it floated motionless as the rowers sorted themselves out, then the oars moved as one and the ship began to gather way.

The two ships out on the bay were moving as well. The boats, seemingly full of men, had been cast free, and now *Dragon's Claw* was underway, all oars manned and pulling. But they were not making for Fevik. They were heading in the other direction.

"Doesn't look like Bardi's butchered anyone," Skorri said. "In truth, it looks like you've lost another ship, Thorgeir."

"You can keep your mouth shut if you've nothing helpful to say," Thorgeir snapped. Skorri guessed he must be picturing his own head on one of Halfdan's pikes, for him to say such a thing, to forget himself in such a way. Skorri let it go, made no reply. He was enjoying himself too much.

Dragon's Claw was gathering momentum, pulling away from *War Hammer*, when a few oars appeared from *War Hammer*'s side, and a tow rope lifted up out of the water. Then, a moment later, *War Hammer* was underway as well, towing behind *Dragon's Claw*, adding a bit to the effort with the six oars she had manned. The two ships were heading for open water.

Ingolf's ship was a hundred yards off the dock, underway and pulling for the other two vessels, but Skorri could see it was time to put an end to this folly. He wondered if his voice would carry that far. He hoped it would.

"Ingolf!" he roared, and waved an arm. He saw Ingolf turn and wave back. "Get those boats and bring them back! Let those two ships go!"

"What are you saying?" Thorgeir demanded, but Skorri ignored him.

"Don't chase those ships!" he shouted again. Once more Ingolf waved acknowledgement, and Skorri hoped the man genuinely understood what he said.

"What do you think you're doing?" Thorgeir asked. "You'll just let them sail off, with two of the king's ships?"

"He had the guts to come in here and set that trap, half a mile from shore, and he was clever enough to pull it off. You think he didn't guess you'd send more ships after them? I'll bet he's counting on it."

"Who is 'he'?"

"Odd Thorgrimson," Skorri said.

"You think that was Odd Thorgrimson, in command there?" Thorgeir asked.

"Yes, I do."

"You think he's clever enough to pull that off?"

"He's more clever than you. By far."

Thorgeir ignored the jibe. "And you'll just let him go?"

"If you want to send more ships into his trap, feel free. Once they're all gone you can return to Grømstad and tell King Halfdan all about it."

Thorgeir made no reply. A moment later *Dragon's Claw*, with *War Hammer* in tow, disappeared around a headland, and the two ships were lost from sight. Ingolf's ship reached the scattered boats and drifted to a stop, going no farther. Thorgeir turned and stormed off, and Skorri, once again, smiled.

It was late afternoon, and the weather was starting to change, as Skorri and Koll led their men back to Ornolf's great hall. The skies had been clear most of the day, as they had been for the past week or so, but they turned a milky gray as the day wore on, and dark and ominous clouds rolled up from the west. Skorri pulled his cloak farther up on his shoulders as he rode at the head of the column, up the hill out of Fevik.

He had remained in Fevik long enough for Ingolf to tow the boats to the dock, long enough for Bardi to explain how he and his men had been surprised by the warriors crouching down in the bottom of *Dragon's Claw*, and the boats hidden around her side. How they had not been prepared for a fight, and had been quickly overrun. Skorri could barely stand to listen.

A hundred warriors had been left behind to guard the town, with orders to quarter themselves in whatever homes they found agreeable, and to continue their patrol. They were to make sure that no one entered the town or left it, and to quench any spark of resistance, if such were to flare up.

Thorgeir remained in Fevik as well. He commandeered a few of the buildings closest to the waterfront to house himself and his men. He claimed that he did not want to leave his ships unattended, which was likely true, in part, but Skorri knew it had more to do with not wishing to be in the company of the rest of the army. Not after the humiliation of losing two ships through his own incompetence.

The first drops of rain were starting to fall as the warriors came in through the big gates in the earthen wall surrounding Ornolf's compound. Stable hands came out to take the few horses they had with them, and Skorri and his men filed into the massive hall.

Fires were blazing in the hearths on the floor, and lanterns and candles were lit, throwing light around the cavernous room. The warmth and the light struck Skorri first, and then the smell of food cooking. His warning that the servants had best have a feast prepared had not gone unheeded. Pigs and sheep were turning on spits. Somewhere, bread was baking. A fish stew bubbled in a big iron cauldron. Servants were rushing fore and aft, setting platters and cups and pitchers out on the tables that ran half the length of the building down either side of the great hall.

Ornolf's high seat, a throne in all but name, stood at the head of the tables, on a dais that raised it a foot off the floor. It was a huge, oak affair, the sides ornately carved with various beasts that melded into twin dragon heads rising above each shoulder. A table was set up in front of the high seat, extending out on either side far enough to provide seating for a dozen of the most important men in the hall.

Skorri took his place on the high seat. He called for Koll and the other captains to sit flanking him, and for the servants to bring them drink immediately or face the consequences. Koll and the others climbed onto the dais and sat at the table, the places of honor. Mead was brought to them by servants with eyes averted; mead not in cups or horns, but in silver chalices studded with jewels. Chalices that Ornolf the Restless had likely plundered from some church in Englaland or Frankia in his younger days.

Skorri looked out at the hall, down the long tables where his warriors had found their seats on the benches and had started in on the food and drink. They were smiling and laughing as they lifted their cups, shouting to one another, recounting this or that moment of the day. They were boisterous and happy. It made Skorri happy in turn.

"What think you of today, Koll?" Skorri asked. He had to speak loud over the din of the men in the great hall, nearly four hundred warriors who were becoming increasingly drunk.

"I think you did well, Lord Skorri," Koll said. "You've already done most of what King Halfdan sent you to do. And I think Thorgeir proved himself a useless pile of goat shit."

"I agree," Skorri said. He gestured toward the men at the tables. "They're in good spirits?" The answer seemed obvious, but he wanted to hear what Koll had to say.

"Very," Koll said. "They plundered the traitor Thorgrim's hall. They plundered the rabble here in Fevik. They're much wealthier for it now, and not so much as a black eye for the effort!"

"Good," Skorri said. He drank and stared off into the dark recesses at the far end of the hall and turned Koll's words over in his head.

The traitor Thorgrim…

What had Thorgrim done? Far from being a traitor, he did not even know what was taking place in East Agder. He probably was not even alive, rumors of his return notwithstanding.

For that matter, what had the people of Fevik done? He had suspected they were harboring Odd Thorgrimson and his followers, but apparently he was wrong.

Those strange thoughts, coming from where, he did not know, led him down the path to another consideration.

Odd Thorgrimson…

It was bold and clever, what he had done that day. Skorri had to admire it, despite himself. And now Odd had two ships to his name, and an untold number of men under his command. He was out there, somewhere, and more men would rally to him. He was a problem that had to be addressed.

But not just then.

Skorri looked away from the dark corners and around the well-lit part of the hall, at the tapestries that hung from the walls, the lovely, intricate carvings on the posts that supported the roof, at the furs and blankets on the platforms on either side, chests full of all manner of riches. Chandeliers with arms forged to look like twisting serpents, each holding a blazing candle in its mouth, hung from the ceiling. Each was worth more than a farmer or fisherman might make in a year. This was the sort of place that a worthy man, a leader of men, should enjoy.

And was he not a worthy man, and a leader?

A servant girl passed by, a pitcher in hand, and Skorri recognized her as the one who had protected Thurid from his wrath, who had stopped him from running her through.

"You!" he called, and the girl stopped and looked over at him. He could see the uncertainty — fear, even — on her face. "Come here."

She gave a hint of a curtsy, stepped closer to the dais, and stood with eyes downcast. She was gripping the pitcher hard, and Skorri guessed it was to stop her hands from shaking.

"Look at me," Skorri said, and the girl looked up, looked him in the eye. She was a pretty one, a bit taller than most, light brown hair spilling out from the cloth tied around her head, her face heart-shaped, with cheekbones slightly pronounced. Her clothing was finer than that of the other servant girls, and she wore strings of beads around her neck. Skorri guessed that she enjoyed a position of some greater importance than most, perhaps as Thurid's personal maid.

He wondered if that had made her off limits to Ornolf, because, if not, that boisterous old dog would most certainly have tried to hump her.

"I told you to see that a decent feast was laid out for my men, and I see you did as you were told. Did it very well."

The girl curtsied again. "I just told the others of your wishes, Lord, and they saw it was done." She did not look down at the floor that time, did not shift her eyes away from his.

"Good," Skorri said. "I'm pleased. And as a reward, now you may serve me. Come stand here, so you can be ready as I need you." He pointed to a spot next to the high seat, but the girl hesitated, and looked uncertain. The confidence he had seen flickering in her face was gone.

"Come along," Skorri said. "Do as you're told and no harm will come to you."

The girl nodded, then she stepped up onto the dais and around the end of the long table and stood where Skorri had indicated. She paused for a moment, then bent over and filled his silver chalice from the pitcher she held in her hand. Skorri nodded his approval. He lifted the chalice and held it up, and once the others at the table had lifted their cups as well, he drank.

The servants had prepared great quantities of food, roasted half a dozen animals, baked dozens of loaves of bread. But, plentiful as it was, it all disappeared as the hours wore on, until the spits were empty, the tables and floor scattered with bones and the remnants of loaves of bread. Bowls and wooden plates were strewn around, some still upright, some capsized. It was like the aftermath of some great battle, pitting food against man, with man the clear victor.

The barrels of drink, however, seemed bottomless, so no one objected, or even seemed to notice, when the flow of food slowed to a trickle. Skorri wondered how much more food and drink there was in Ornolf's storehouse, how long he could continue hosting this army in such a manner.

That was a thing he would need to know, because he would need to keep these men happy. Despite his years of loyalty to Halfdan, his laboring as king's overseer, making certain that the wealth of the region continued to pour into Grømstad, Skorri himself was not a wealthy man. He did not have the means to maintain even a small hird, never mind one of five hundred men. Until he could find further opportunities for plunder, he would have to use the resources he had there in Ornolf's hall to keep these warriors well-sated.

But that was a concern for the morrow. Tonight would be given to celebration. Which led to another thought. He turned to the servant girl.

"What's your name?"

"Gunnhild, Lord."

"Well, Gunnhild, are there musicians here?"

"There are, Lord."

"And where are they?"

"Hiding, Lord, I do believe."

Skorri smiled. That was hardly a surprise. "Go find them. Tell them they'll have silver if their playing pleases me."

"Yes, Lord," Gunnhild said. She looked surprised, and Skorri imagined it was his offer of silver that surprised her. She had seen him strike Thurid, nearly kill her, and she probably did not reckon him as a generous sort. But the mead and the good spirits and the pleasure he was taking in these great trappings of wealth were doing wondrous things to his mood.

Gunnhild curtsied again and hurried off, as if afraid that Skorri, a rabid dog, could turn on her at any moment.

Not long after that she returned with the musicians, who took their place between the two rows of tables and played with all the enthusiasm they could muster. The sound of their instruments was largely drowned out by the voices of the men, some singing along with the tunes the musicians played, some singing other tunes, some arguing or laughing, but the music was loud enough that it added greatly to the atmosphere.

Skorri had been to many feasts in his life, in many halls, big and small, wealthy and otherwise. He could not recall any that were as fine as this.

His feast. In his hall.

The festivities were still going on sometime later when Skorri decided it was time for him to be off to bed. He stood to leave. Koll, sitting beside him, stood as well, and held up his chalice. In his commanding voice he called out, "Men!"

Almost instantly the hall fell silent, as if the noise was a flame that Koll's breath had blown out.

"Let us drink to Lord Skorri!" Koll shouted, and with that the men roared their approval and stamped their feet to make the floor shake. They snatched up their cups and drank. And Skorri lifted his chalice and drank as well, and that led to further cheering. Then Skorri put his chalice down and turned to Gunnhild.

"Come with me."

He led the way off the dais, confident that she was following behind. He walked down the length of the great hall, past the long tables where the warriors raised their cups to him in passing. He continued on toward the far end of the building, where the sleeping chambers were sectioned off by a wall built not of wattle, but of wooden planks, planed smooth.

He stopped and turned. Gunnhild was a few steps behind him. She had picked up an oil lamp on the way and held it in her hands like an offering. In the light of the flame Skorri could see the fear on her face.

"Which of these is Ornolf's bed chamber?"

"Well, this one, Lord," she said, nodding to the first door in a series of four that ran along the length of the wall. "It's more my lady Thurid's, I should say, what with Lord Ornolf gone these two years or more."

"Is she in there?" Skorri asked. He realized he had given Thurid no thought since the moment Gunnhild had stopped him from killing her. He did not even know where she was.

"No, lord," Gunnhild said.

"Where is she?"

"The baker and his wife have rooms off their bakery, Lord. My lady Thurid's sent them to bed down in the stables and has taken that place."

"Hmm," Skorri said. He did not actually care where Thurid slept, as long as it was not where he wished to sleep. "Come."

He opened the latch to Ornolf's chamber and swung the door open. It was cave-dark, but Gunnhild followed him in with the lantern, and the weak light revealed part of the room: a large, carved bed, a table, chests on the floor, more tapestries on the walls.

"Light those candles," Skorri said, nodding toward the tall iron candlesticks standing near the bed. Gunnhild lit one set of candles, then walked around the bed and lit the other. The light filled most of the room, so that Skorri could see all but the upper reaches of the ceiling, and those corners where the light would not reach.

Gunnhild had told the truth: the bedchamber was Thurid's now. There was a decidedly feminine quality to the place. No shields or weapons hung on the walls. The tapestries depicted florid gardens and creatures of a gentle sort, deer and such, not scenes of battle, or ships loaded with spear-bearing warriors. There was a vaguely sweet smell to the air.

"This will do. For the present," Skorri said. A large silver basin with elaborate gold inlay stood on the table near the bed. He looked in it. It was empty.

"Go fetch some water," he said to Gunnhild. "Warm water. And a cloth. And be quick."

"Yes, lord," Gunnhild said. She could not hide the reluctance in her voice, but neither could she object in any way. She hurried out the door. Skorri stood for a moment and breathed deep. Then he unbuckled his sword belt and carefully laid sword and seax on the edge of the straw-stuffed mattress where they would not interfere with his sleep, but where he could snatch them up quickly, even in the dark.

He pulled his tunic up over his head and dropped it on the floor. He could feel the stabs of pain from his half-healed bruises and many lacerations, the aching soreness of his muscles from the beating of weeks before, and the brutally hard day he had just endured. He considered taking his shoes off but knew bending over that way would be a very painful proposition. Instead, he eased himself onto the bed and carefully stretched out to full length. He closed his eyes and let his breath out slowly and felt himself relax.

He heard footsteps on the floor, soft and hurried. Gunnhild, he guessed, and he knew he should open his eyes, sit up, and make certain, but he could not summon the energy. The door creaked open, then closed, and Skorri heard the sound of water pouring into the basin by the bed.

"Take my shoes off," he said.

"Yes, Lord," Gunnhild said. He felt hands like a bird's wings fluttering against his feet, and then a firmer grip pulling the shoes away. It felt marvelous.

"You see the bruises I carry?" Skorri asked.

"Yes, Lord." Skorri could hear nothing in her tone; no surprise, no revulsion, no pleasure. Resignation, perhaps.

"Take the cloth and wet it and apply it to the bruises and the cuts. Gentle, now. And wash my face and hands."

"Yes, Lord."

He heard the cloth dip in the water, heard the water splash as she squeezed out the excess. Then the cloth was on his face, wiping gently down, across his forehead, and then down his nose to his cheek and neck. She continued on, dabbing at his injuries, moving gently over the tender places. The water was warm, but still cool enough to be soothing, and Gunnhild applied exactly the right pressure, enough that he could feel it, not enough that it hurt. Skorri felt his head swimming with the sensation.

She moved over his shoulders and chest, and along his stomach. She came to his waist and the upper edge of his trousers, the last of his exposed skin, and he felt the cloth lifting away. He opened his eyes.

Gunnhild was standing beside him, the limp cloth in her hand. She was lit by the flames of the candles; soft, yellow light and deep shadow. She was looking at him. There was no expression on her face.

"Remove my trousers," he said. His voice sounded hoarse, as if he had not spoken in years.

Gunnhild bent over and untied the strip of cloth that bound Skorri's leggings around his waist. Her expression still did not change. She still looked as if she was resigned to her fate, would endure whatever came, to the extent that she could. She slipped her fingers under the edge of his trousers and eased them down his legs and over his feet. She picked up the cloth and dipped it in the water again, squeezed it, and began dabbing it on the wounds and bruises on his legs.

Skorri closed his eyes. He imagined Gunnhild had expected to find him aroused, ready, like a buck in rut. But he was not. He was relaxed. The sensation he was experiencing was something beyond arousal.

Is she surprised, I wonder? Does it bother her?

She finished at last, running the cloth over his feet, washing the dried sweat away. Skorri opened his eyes again. She was at the foot of the bed, more lost in shadow now, with less of the light from the candles reaching her there.

"Come closer," Skorri said, making a weak beckoning gesture. Gunnhild stepped closer. Skorri looked her up and down. She was beauty and strength and resolution. Even her loose apron and dress could not hide the shape of her body. The flames that lit her face only augmented her features, the texture of her skin.

"Take your clothes off."

He saw the hesitation then, the pause. The flicker of fear and disgust. But still there was resolution, and acceptance of the inevitable. She bent over and pulled her shoes off, then reached up and slipped the cloth off her head and shook out her hair. She unhooked the simple metal brooches that held the shoulder straps of her apron. She let the apron fall around her feet and then pulled her dress up and over her head.

Then she stood, motionless, arms at her side, as if she did not know what Skorri expected her to do next. And, as it happened, that was true. She did not know.

"Lay down beside me. Here." Skorri indicated the side of the bed opposite where his sword and seax lay. Gunnhild eased herself onto the bed, and laid down slowly by his side, as if she was getting gingerly into a hot spring. He put his arm around her shoulder and he felt her tense, and he pulled her tight to him as she did.

They lay like that, Gunnhild pressed against him, his arm around her. She was trembling, he could feel it through the rough palm of his hand.

"Now, now…that's fine," he whispered. He felt the luxurious sensation of her skin against his, even more wonderful than the warm, wet cloth she had wielded so expertly. He felt…good. He felt full. He felt better than he could recall feeling in a very long time. Ever, perhaps. He was aware of the rise and fall of her chest as she breathed. And then he was asleep.

Chapter Seventeen

It's a very roundabout route to a bad friend's house,
even if he lives on your way;
but straight roads lead to a good friend,
even if he's gone further away.

The Sayings of Hávi

Thorgrim looked the two men up and down. *Eyvind Bjarnason*, he thought. The name sounded familiar. The man looked familiar. But he could not be sure.

"We've met?" Thorgrim asked.

"Yes," Eyvind Bjarnason said. "Not often. Two or three times, perhaps. Twice, I recall, at Amundi Thorsteinsson's hall. And we were in a hunting party another time. Many years back. I don't recall exactly. There were about a dozen of us."

Thorgrim nodded. It was entirely possible.

"But see here, Thorgrim, what I have to say…" Eyvind began, taking another step forward, but Thorgrim held up a hand.

"Hold a moment." He turned to Gyda. "Send someone to my ship to fetch Harald. Have them tell Harald to bring the other ship masters with him. Whatever this fellow has to say, I would have them all hear it."

Gyda hurried out the door and Thorgrim gestured for the two men to sit. They sat, and he sat across from them. "How long have you been in Ribe?" he asked.

"Two days," Eyvind said. "We've been looking for you. Like I said."

"And you found me, like I said."

"Which was no easy thing. We had to be careful. We didn't dare ask too many folk if they knew of you. We didn't want it known that you might be here. There are others who are seeking you out. Others who are no friends of yours."

"I don't make friends easily," Thorgrim said.

They sat for a bit in awkward silence, then the door opened again. Gyda came in, followed by Harald and Gudrid, Asmund, Halldor, and Hardbein, the masters of the ships in Thorgrim's fleet. And of course, Starri Deathless, who always appeared when such a gathering was taking place, whether he was wanted or not.

Eyvind and the man with him stood as they came in.

"Harald!" Eyvind said, like this was a happy and unexpected reunion, but Harald just looked at him and squinted, as if doing so might help his recall.

"Do you know this one?" Thorgrim asked. Harald studied the new arrival a moment longer.

"Yes, I remember you," he said, finally, addressing Eyvind. "We were in a hunting party together. Years ago. I was just a boy. But I don't recall your name."

"Eyvind Bjarnason."

"Yes," Harald said. "That's it." Thorgrim was not sure if the name really meant something to Harald, or if he was just saying that.

"You men sit," Thorgrim said to the others, and they found benches and sat.

"Eyvind has come looking for us," Thorgrim continued. "He has news from home. From Odd." He did not try to hide his skepticism. He turned to Eyvind. "Go ahead with what you have to say."

Eyvind cleared his throat, shot a look at his companion, then looked back at Thorgrim. "As I said, we got here in Ribe two days back. We came looking for you…"

"How did you know we'd be in Ribe?" Thorgrim asked.

"We didn't. But we heard you were alive, and trying to return to Vik. A fellow who'd met up with you, he came back with news not long ago."

"Who?"

"A man named Bergthor. Bergthor Skeggjason. From Fevik."

"Bergthor Skeggjason…." Thorgrim repeated. He could hardly believe the man was still alive, never mind safely back in Norway. "What did Bergthor have to say?"

Eyvind shook his head. "I never spoke with him, or any of his men. But he came back and told others of seeing you. Sailing with you.

And that you were on your way back to Vik. Word got around. Your son Odd got the news."

"Where is Odd now?"

"He was in Fevik, when I left him."

"You were with him? How is he faring?"

"Not well," Eyvind said. "Have you heard of the troubles he's had with King Halfdan?"

Thorgrim nodded. "We've heard some tales."

"Well, I can tell you, the situation is bad. Odd's in hiding, along with the few who are following him. Halfdan has sent hundreds of warriors and his best ships to hunt them down. The people are ready to rise up, to join in with Odd, but they're afraid to do it. I can hardly blame them. Me and my men, we were with Odd, in hiding. When Odd heard you might be returning to Vik he sent me to look for you."

"You said you didn't know we'd be in Ribe," Harald said. "Yet still, this is where you came."

"It was a guess, no more," Eyvind said. "A gamble. But most ships going north or south, they stop here. We hoped you might stop here as well, because otherwise we'd never find you. And it seems the gods gave us good luck."

Thorgrim considered that. It made sense. But still there were many questions unanswered.

"Why did Odd want you to find us? If he already knew we were on our way home, why did it matter?"

"Because Odd's not the only one who knows of your return. Word has spread. Halfdan knows. We…those of us fighting Halfdan…we have people in Halfdan's hall. People who tell us things. So we know that Halfdan's heard about your coming back, and he's afraid of it. Afraid that the people will rally to you. So he's set a trap at your farm in Vik, figuring that's where you would go. Odd sent me to warn you."

Thorgrim looked over at the rest of his men. He could see the doubt was running thick as tar, and he felt the same. He looked back at Eyvind. "So what would Odd have us do? Meet him in Fevik?"

"No. Halfdan's sent ships and warriors to Fevik, looking for Odd and his men. You'd be walking into a trap there, as much as at your farm. But there's a small harbor, west and south of Grømstad, where you might go in undetected. Odd has men keeping watch there. He begs me tell you to make landfall at that place, and he'll meet you. He told me to act as pilot for your fleet."

Eyvind held Thorgrim's eyes for a moment, then he reached into a leather bag on his belt and pulled out a silver arm ring, which he handed to Thorgrim. "And Odd asked I give you this, as proof of what I say."

Thorgrim recognized the arm ring as soon as Eyvind pulled it out, and knew as soon as it was in his hand that it belonged to Odd, his son. The small dragon's head at one end of the open hoop, the tail at the other, the finely engraved scales along its back — the little silver beast was turned in nearly a complete circle, its open mouth trying to bite the tip of its tail. Thorgrim had given it to Odd on his wedding day. Thorgrim's father, Ulf, had given it to him, a prize from the first raid in which Thorgrim had taken part.

The sight of the arm ring brought such a mix of emotions, Thorgrim did not know what he felt. He had been ready to dismiss this Eyvind as a spy or a fraud, but now he was not so sure. As he examined the shining silver dragon he felt a renewed longing to get back to Vik, to come to Odd's aid. He could taste the fear that he was too late, and the longing to be with his sons and his daughters, back on his farm, and he ached for the happy days when Odd was young, and Harald was young, and Hallbera was alive, and he, Thorgrim, was done with raiding and fighting.

He handed the arm ring to Harald. Harald held it close to his face, examined it, nodded in recognition.

"Very well," Thorgrim said to Eyvind. "Maybe I believe you, maybe I don't. But I'll seek the council of my men, and then we'll send for you with our decision."

Eyvind stood and the man with him stood. "I understand, Thorgrim Night Wolf. Of course, you must be cautious. But please, don't be long in deciding. The need is urgent. Your son's need is urgent." They nodded to Thorgrim, nodded to the others, and took their leave.

"Well," Thorgrim said to his men as the door closed. "What say you?"

"That arm ring he showed you, did that convince you?" Asmund asked.

"It's Odd's, there's no doubt about that," Thorgrim said. "Now, whether Odd gave it to him, or he took it off Odd's corpse, that I don't know."

"Either way, we're bound for East Agder," Gudrid said. "Just a matter of whether we make landfall at Thorgrim's farm, or we go where this Eyvind claims Odd wants us to go."

"I never meant to go to my farm," Thorgrim said. "I decided that long before Eyvind Bjarnason showed up, to steer clear until we know what's going on. We have no idea what we're stepping into."

The others nodded agreement. They talked some more on it, debated the various possibilities, the advantages and disadvantages of heeding Eyvind Bjarnason's warning. Finally, Thorgrim had heard enough.

"We'll sail as soon as we can," Thorgrim said. "On the tide tomorrow. We'll sail in Eyvind's company. Better to keep him close. We'll have five days or so, before we reach East Agder, to decide if the man's to be trusted."

That was the last word on that. There was still the question of whether Thorgrim was fit enough for an ocean passage, but every man there knew better than to ask. Instead, they shared more ale and sat by the dying fire and talked of various things and ate the bread and cold meat that Gyda offered them. Finally they took their leave, save for Harald and Starri, who, it seemed, were still insisting on staying by Thorgrim's side.

The four of them sat up a bit longer, then drifted off to their beds. Gyda helped Thorgrim onto the platform opposite where Harald and Starri were sleeping, then eased him down onto the mattress. She checked the wound in his shoulder, and assured him that, despite his best efforts, the gods had kept it from opening up again. She touched his face, gave him a bit of a smile, then made her way to her own bedchamber at the far end of the house.

The fire was still burning low, illuminating the lower half of the main room, while the rest of the house, higher up toward the roof, was lost in darkness. Thorgrim lay on his back and listened to the night, but there was little to hear. Animals scurrying nearby, inside or out, it was hard to tell. Owls hooting off in the distance, the buzz of insects from the nearby marsh. Beyond that, Ribe seemed to slumber, and soon Thorgrim, too, was fast asleep.

He came half-awake to something jostling him, but even in the stupor of sleep he understood it was no reason for alarm. He heard a voice, just a whisper, saying, "Shhhh…shhhh…" and Gyda slipped in under the covers and pressed herself against him. He wrapped an arm around her, ran his hand down her side. She was still wearing her fine woolen dress, but she had shed the tunic she wore over that. Her hair was undone from its braids and falling over her shoulders and back.

She put her arm over his chest, well clear of his wound, and pulled herself closer to him, and he held her a bit tighter. He could feel the deep sword thrust in his shoulder faintly throbbing; not pain, exactly, but he could feel it. He said nothing.

"Don't move," Gyda said, her voice like a breath. "I just want to be close to you, just for a while. Tomorrow you sail, and then I'll never see you again."

"Hmm…" Thorgrim said. He was not sure what else to say to that.

It was warm and lovely there on the bed, with Gyda pressed up at his side and the thick furs covering them. He reached out his free hand and ran his fingers over Iron-tooth, lying by his side, a thing he did frequently, and without really thinking about it, when he was in bed. Then he wrapped his arm around Gyda once more and applied the slightest of pressure to pull her close.

They seemed to fit well together, like mortice and tenon. His head was full of the smell of her; the faint scent of the soap she used, a bit of a tang of woodsmoke, the stew she had made for dinner. Comforting smells, all. He felt his head swimming in fatigue, and luxurious sleep washing over him, and then he was out.

And then he was awake again, sitting bolt upright, his hand wrapped around Iron-tooth, his eyes open to the faint light, even before he knew what had torn him from sleep. It was something loud. Feral. Starri Deathless, screaming his battle cry. Men moving across the floor. Cool air blowing in through the door, which had been barred, and was now smashed open again.

Thorgrim tried to swing his legs around and found he could not, and he realized that Gyda was beside him, blocking him from getting off the platform.

"Stand clear!" he shouted, but by the time he finished she had pushed herself off and jumped to the floor and was lost in the shadows. Thorgrim swung his legs around, found the floor with his bare feet,

Iron-tooth held by the scabbard in his left hand. Someone was coming at him from the direction of the door — Thorgrim could see only the dark shape outlined by the glow of the coals in the hearth, and the orange light glinting off a blade of some sort.

Thorgrim pushed himself off the platform and launched himself into the figure coming at him. No time to draw his sword, he hit the man full on, chest to chest, and grabbed a handful of his tunic. The man toppled backward, shouting. A flailing arm caught Thorgrim around the neck and held him tight as the two of them, together, tumbled for the floor.

But not the floor. The man fell, back first, onto the hearth and the thick, healthy bed of glowing coals, and Thorgrim came down on top of him. For a moment they struggled, then Thorgrim pushed himself up, his left hand, still holding Iron-tooth, on the man's chest, his right hand in a fist, which he drove into the man's face again and again.

More people were rushing past, on the left and the right, but Thorgrim was only vaguely aware of them. He and the man under him struggled against each other for the briefest of moments, before the coals burned through the man's cloak, through his tunic, and began their work on his flesh. He paused in his struggles — Thorgrim felt his whole body tense — and then his eyes went wide and his mouth opened and he shrieked, a horrible, high-pitched shriek.

Thorgrim could smell the awful odor of burning flesh as he pushed himself off and the man in turn pushed him away, trying to get free of Thorgrim's weight, trying to get off the searing coals. Thorgrim rolled clear of the hearth and up onto his feet. He pulled Iron-tooth free and tossed the scabbard away, as his former opponent stood screaming and staggered away, beating at his clothing which was engulfed in flame.

Eyvind Bjarnason, you traitorous whore's son, he thought. Instinct had told him that Eyvind was a liar, that he should cut the man down where he stood, before he could pull any tricks. But he had resisted, and now they were paying the price.

He looked around at the shadowy images of the people in the little house. Nearly a dozen, it seemed, and only three of them were friends. The others had come to kill them all.

A few feet to his left, Harald was engaged with two men: ax-wielding, big and clumsy, too stupid to be aware of anything that was not right in front of them. Thorgrim took the closest out with a single thrust, straight and true, coming in right under the man's arm. He pulled the blade free, let the man drop, screaming and writhing. The man's partner, confused, turned away from Harald to look, and when he did, Harald finished him off.

Thorgrim bent over and scooped up one of the axes. He held it in his left hand, Iron-tooth in his right. He sensed someone coming up behind him, and turned to face the man. This one had a sword, but it might as well have been an ax, for all the finesse he displayed. Up went the sword, over his head, for a chopping stroke, and up came Thorgrim's ax, taking the man in the belly before he could even start his attack.

The sword fell and the man went down on his knees. Thorgrim kicked him aside and took another step forward. Starri was flailing with his twin axes and the men he was fighting were not fighting back, just trying to get away.

The light from the hearth seemed to spread down the length of the room now. Thorgrim could see Gyda fighting too: the sword he had bought her in one hand, a heavy iron pan in the other. She stabbed at the man in front of her, and when he flinched she swung the pan around, caught him on the side of his head and sent him flying across the room, his skull likely stove like a ship on a rock.

That was well done, Thorgrim thought. But it was not enough. The door to the house lay just beyond where Gyda stood, and there seemed to be more men pushing their way in. Gyda saw that too, and came rushing back toward Thorgrim as their attackers all but filled the narrow space.

Someone lunged at Gyda as she went running past, a seax thrust at her neck, but Thorgrim was there first. Iron-tooth caught the man's extended forearm and tore on through. The seax fell and Thorgrim twisted the blade sideways and pulled it back. The man stumbled and fell and Gyda neatly sidestepped him as he sprawled on the floor.

Gyda pressed herself against Thorgrim's chest and Thorgrim put an arm around her and Gyda shouted in his ear, "It's on fire! The house is on fire!"

She was pointing, Thorgrim realized, and he turned and looked behind him. The man who had fallen into the coals and ignited his clothing had run to the back of the house and crashed into the wattle partition. His burning corpse was laying on top of the wreckage of the wall, and the dried wattle had gone up like kindling. Now the fire was taking the platforms on either side of the room and working its way up the tapestries on the walls to the thatch above.

This was going to be a problem. Thorgrim looked across the room. Harald was standing nearby, Oak-cleaver in hand, the light of the fire glinting on the blood that coated the blade. Their eyes met and they nodded to one another. Mutual understanding: they had to get out of that building, and it had to be now.

They both turned and looked toward the door. There were a dozen men there at least, not counting the three who were still struggling with Starri Deathless. They formed a human wall of sorts, weapons ready, a wall that he and Harald and Gyda and Starri would have to get through before they choked to death on the smoke or were consumed by the flames.

Thorgrim looked at Harald again. "Right at them! We hack our way through, or we'll meet in the corpse hall!"

Harald nodded. He raised his sword and gave a bit of a smile. There was not a trace of fear on his face, and Thorgrim felt a deep pride. And he felt blood, warm and sticky, running down his side, under his tunic. His wound, it seemed, had opened up. The least of his problems.

"You stay behind me," he said to Gyda, "but if you can use that deadly pan of yours, do it. Bash in all the heads you can!"

Gyda nodded, and Thorgrim readjusted his grip on Iron-tooth and stepped forward. He could feel the heat of the flames on his back, and the room, which moments before had been barely visible, was now brightly lit.

The men they faced held weapons ready, a motley assortment of axes and swords and seaxes. They did not seem to be warriors of any great status — they wore no mail or helmets — but still there were a dozen or more of them against three men, one wounded, and a woman with a frying pan. Even if Starri Deathless, in his berserker rage, was worth five fighting men, they were still badly outnumbered.

"Here we go!" Thorgrim called. He stepped off, moving with caution, eyes everywhere, when suddenly surprise and panic seemed to sweep over the men ahead of them. Those in the center of the line staggered forward, the men on either side tried to shove their way clear: why, Thorgrim could not tell. From the front, Starri plunged screaming into their ranks.

Thorgrim stopped, held up his hand, unsure of what he was seeing. And then he understood. Some others had come in through the door at the killers' backs and they were laying into them, an attack from behind. He saw spears flashing left and right as the newcomers drove into the men blocking the way, trapping them between their deadly surprise assault and Starri's manic flailing axes. The line crumbled as if it was made of sand as men fell screaming, twisting to the floor, and others lurched aside in terror.

That was all Thorgrim needed to see. He ran forward, Iron-tooth leading, and thrust and slashed at men who did not know which way to turn. Harald was beside him, Starri in the middle of it all. He caught a glimpse of Gyda swinging first her sword, then her pan, at the head of a man who had gone down and was trying to get back up. He heard the sound of pan hitting skull, even over the shouting and the flames, and doubted the man would ever get up again.

The fight was brief. Very brief. A few moments at most, and then Thorgrim was standing half doubled over, gasping for breath, Iron-tooth's tip resting on the floor. He could feel that his chest and stomach were swathed in blood.

Finally he straightened and looked to see who it was who had come through the door at that last moment. He expected to see Gudrid, or Asmund. One of his ships' masters. But he did not. Before him, also breathing hard, sword in hand, stood Eyvind Bjarnason.

"We were late, Thorgrim," Eyvind said. "Forgive me."

Thorgrim took another deep breath. "Why did you come? How did you know?"

"I told you, we're not the only ones looking for you. I had a couple of my men watching the house, in case of trouble. But I thought maybe one or two would come for you, not a full crew. My men had to send for help. It slowed us up."

Thorgrim nodded. He looked around. He had seen the aftermath of more battles than he could recall, but in that confined space the heaps of dead and wounded looked particularly horrendous. Behind him, he heard something collapsing in the flames.

"We had better go," Eyvind said. Thorgrim nodded again, too winded to do more.

They made their way out the door and into the small yard, the night considerably cooler than the burning home they had just left. A crowd of people were in the street, and already the cries of "Fire!" were ringing out around Ribe, with people rushing here and there to respond. Gyda's house was beyond saving, but a blaze like that could take out half the town if it was not contained.

Eyvind stopped at Thorgrim's side. "The gods know that you'll do as you see fit, Thorgrim Night Wolf, but if you're ready to sail, right now might be a good time to do it. The tide and the moon should serve to get us to sea, and there's a good chance that more enemies are lurking on land."

Thorgrim did not say as much, but he was inclined to agree. He had been eager to be gone since waking from his death-sleep. He turned to Harald. "Are we ready to put to sea?"

"Yes," Harald said. He did not hesitate.

"Good. Let's go." Then he remembered Gyda, standing right behind him. He looked back at her house. The roof was fully engulfed, the flames rising an impressive twenty feet above the thatch, illuminating the road and the nearby houses. It filtered through Gyda's long, blond hair that fell in disarray around her shoulders. Happily, Njord, god of wind and seas, had decreed it be calm that night, and the flames had yet to leap to the neighboring roofs.

"You've lost everything," Thorgrim said. "That's your reward for caring for me. I'm sorry."

"I'm sorry, too," Gyda said. "Such is the will of the gods. Capricious bastards, all."

"Come with me."

"Come where?"

"Vik. My farm. If we make it there alive, you'll want for nothing."

Gyda looked him steadily in the eyes. What she might be thinking, he could not tell. Then she nodded. Just nodded. She made no other reply. And Thorgrim felt a strange and anomalous sense of relief wash over him.

"Let's go," he said, meaning Gyda, Harald, Starri, any who wished to join him. He pushed through the collected press of men, on toward the market street, toward the river and the sea, certain that the rest were following behind.

Chapter Eighteen

I got drunk, got extremely drunk,
at the house of wise Fjalarr;
in that case the best ale-feast
is one where each man gets his faculties back.

The Sayings of Hávi

In his younger days, Hallbjorn Osvifsson had been known as Hallbjorn Deer's Bane. He had been a hunter then, a tracker, a man who seemed able to read the thoughts of deer and other game. He knew where they would go, what they would do. He could move silent as a cat through any landscape, be it forest, or tall grass, or muddy earth.

Those skills had served him well for years. He liked hunting. But he liked eating and drinking, too, perhaps more than hunting. The seasons passed and he grew fatter and less able to move with stealth and ease, and less interested in doing so.

He earned good money selling game, with little time to spend it, and in that way managed to accumulate a respectable hoard. He was a jovial man, and well-liked in Fevik, so when he grew weary of hunting he bought a tavern and became known as Hallbjorn Ale-slinger. He didn't mind that. He thought it funny. His tavern prospered, and so did he.

Now, he could only wonder if that prosperity had come to an end.

He was standing behind the counter in his tavern, looking out at the men drinking his ale. He would not call them customers, because customers paid for what they drank, and Hallbjorn realized pretty quickly that these men had no intention of doing so.

They were the crews off the longships that had come in a few days before. King Halfdan's men, sent to root out Odd Thorgrimson and the rebels who followed him.

When the longships arrived, the warriors on board had swarmed over the waterfront, overrunning the few taverns there. They were loud and unruly and demanding, in the way of men who are strangers to a town, and who know there is no one who can stand up to them. They did not pay anything like the worth of what they took, but they did pay. Hallbjorn did not think they would do that again.

Things had changed that afternoon. More men came, under the command of Skorri Thorbrandsson, the king's former overseer, now, apparently, the king's man for hunting down traitors. Unlike the longships' crews, Skorri's men had not simply overrun the shops and taverns, taking more than they were willing to pay for. They had plundered the town, torn though every home and workshop, destroying what they pleased, stealing what they pleased, beating anyone who dared resist.

They were looking, supposedly, for the rebels, but even after it became clear that the rebels were not to be found in Fevik, they did not stop. The town might as well have been some monastery in Englaland or Frankia for all they cared.

Hallbjorn was stunned. His neighbors were stunned. No one knew quite what to say. It was disorienting, like a fever, or a blow to the head. A spirit of oppressed outrage swept through the town. Men and women muttered curses under their breath and to one another in muted voices when they dared.

Night came, and with it, rain, and most of Skorri's men marched off. Word went around that they had taken over the great hall of Ornolf the Restless, a man loved and honored in that country, now more than two years gone. Skorri had left a hundred or so men behind, as well as the crews of the longships, who numbered another hundred at least. They were enough to continue inflicting misery on the people of Fevik. On Hallbjorn Ale-slinger.

Some of the men off the ships, as many as could fit, once again crowded into Hallbjorn's small tavern. They demanded ale and wine and mead, whatever he had. They drank their fill and then some, toasting their conquest, roaring out with song, eating the food Hallbjorn had on hand, while outside the rain came down in sheets and the wind shook the little building.

The evening passed, and the men's exuberance tapered off, as it was wont to do, the drink and the day's exertions at long last having their effect. Some had even fallen asleep, heads down on the tables, amid a scattering of cups and horns and gnawed bones. No one seemed to be paying attention to Hallbjorn, or seemed likely to demand anything more of him.

He reached under the counter and rolled out a small firkin of mead he had been hiding there: the good mead, not the swill he allowed to Skorri's men. He held it under his arm and pulled his hood up over his head and grabbed up four relatively clean cups. He stepped around the end of the counter and headed for the door. He tensed, waiting for one of the men to call to him, to demand something more, to ask him where he was bound. But no one spoke. With all the food and drink in them, no one seemed to care.

Hallbjorn stepped out of the tavern and closed the door behind him. He was immediately assaulted by the wind that tugged at his hood and tunic, and the rain that soaked quickly through his clothing, as if he had jumped into the ocean. Ten feet away, barely visible in the dark night, stood a smaller building, a little storehouse that Hallbjorn used to house his barrels of ale and wine.

He pushed his way through the storm, found the latch with his one free finger, and pulled the door open. The wind caught it and slammed it against the side the building, but luckily it remained intact.

Inside the storehouse three men sat at a table, an oil lamp placed between them. They leapt up as the door swung open and raced over to help Hallbjorn. One took the firkin from under his arm, another the cups. A third stepped outside and with some difficulty shut the door and latched it. Incredibly, the lantern had not gone out.

"Thought we'd die of thirst," said the man who had taken the cups. His name was Thormod and he was a woodworker who lived one street over from Hallbjorn's tavern. He set the cups on the table and sat where he had been sitting before.

Hallbjorn pushed his hood off his head. "Bastards in there wouldn't stop," he said. "Every time I tried to leave it was 'fetch me this, bring me that.' Sons of whores. I'll see all their heads on a pike."

"Come, have a drink," said the man who had taken the firkin and set it on the table. He was Olaf, a goldsmith. He picked up one of the cups and filled it, but rather than hand it to Hallbjorn he took a drink himself, then sat and gestured toward the small barrel. "Help yourself."

"You're a generous bastard, Olaf, I'll give you that," Hallbjorn said. He sat and poured himself a cup. When he was done, Thormod filled his, and then the third man, whose name was Storolf, did as well.

Storolf was Hallbjorn's oldest friend. They had been hunting partners in the younger days, but now Storolf worked as a butcher.

"So, what do you hear, Hallbjorn?" Storolf asked.

"I hear a lot. A lot of blather and horse shit. A few things of interest. The vermin who've infested my tavern, they're off the ships. Best I can figure, Thorgeir Sveinsson, the king's new overseer, commands the ships, but Skorri's in command of all."

"Skorri Thorbrandsson." Olaf spit the words, like they tasted bad in his mouth. "There's one vicious whore's son. I thought that he turned on Halfdan, that he was disgraced."

"I did, too," Thormod said. "But apparently not."

"Seems it's true that Halfdan sent him here to hunt for Odd Thorgrimson," Hallbjorn said. "That what I picked up from the drunk swine in the tavern."

"Hunt for Odd Thorgrimson," Thormod said, with thick disdain. "Is that what they called it?"

"Well, they did a thorough job," Hallbjorn said. "They took everything of value. I guess they wanted to be sure Odd wasn't hiding under any of it."

The men nodded. They drank. Hallbjorn turned to Olaf. "How did you make out?"

"Could have been a lot worse," he said. Olaf always had quantities of gold and silver in his shop, to use in the intricate rings and brooches and necklaces for which he was famous in that country. "They took everything I was working on. My raw stock I keep well hidden. They couldn't find it. But once they figure that out, I'm sure they'll be back to beat me until I tell them."

"My ale and wine I couldn't hide so well," Hallbjorn said. "Three nights and they've all but cleaned me out. Before they came, we wouldn't have all fit in this storehouse."

"Odd's been in hiding for a long time," Storolf said. "I thought Halfdan had given up on him. He doesn't seem to be much of a threat."

"I don't think Halfdan will ever let that go," Olaf said. "As long as Odd's alive. And now we hear Thorgrim Night Wolf's on his way back, and that has to put a fright in Halfdan."

"Thorgrim Night Wolf," Thormod snorted. "It's just stories."

"It was Hallbjorn who heard it," Storolf said. "Heard it from Bergthor."

"Ah, Bergthor Skeggjason," Thormod said. "The only man who could go off raiding and come back poorer than when he left. And even Bergthor said it was months ago that he saw Thorgrim, and across the narrow seas. Still, folks heard that, they started thinking the Night Wolf would come back like Thor riding in on his goat-drawn chariot, swinging Mjölnir and striking their enemies dead. And now look where we are."

They nodded and drank again. Hallbjorn wanted to argue, to suggest some reason they should have hope, but he could not think of any.

"Bergthor may not be a lucky man," Storolf said, "but I don't reckon he was lying about seeing Thorgrim in Engla-land. And if anyone could live to come home, it's Thorgrim Night Wolf."

"Sure," Thormod said. "But there's not much profit in just waiting around to be saved. What do we do to save ourselves? Save all of Fevik?"

"What of Gest Heggsson?" Olaf asked. "He styles himself jarl around here, since Ornolf seems to have sailed off the edge of the earth. What might he do?"

"He'll bow at Skorri's feet," Thormod said. "Already has. What else can he do? He's not strong enough to fight Skorri. Even if all the men in Fevik joined him, we'd still have no chance. Skorri has five hundred men with him, and they're the best of Halfdan's army."

"There's someone who's beat Halfdan. And Skorri. Did it today," Hallbjorn said.

"Who?" Thormod asked.

"Odd Thorgrimson. He led a rebellion once. Escaped from Halfdan. Seems to have raised an army. He has a longship, and he just took another, right under Skorri's nose."

Just that morning the men had watched the strange fight across half a mile of water from Fevik. One ship ambushing another, or so it seemed. Later, when Skorri's men had come back to the dock, rumors spread. Odd Thorgrimson, apparently, had tricked Skorri once again.

"And from what I gather," Hallbjorn continued, "listening to the bastards in my tavern, that crippled longship was Halfdan's, too. Seems it ran aground on something, and Thorgeir left it behind, and they think it was Odd and whoever he has with him took it. No one knows what happened to the crew. Butchered, maybe."

"Impressive," Thormod said. "But what good does it do us?"

"If we're going to fight Skorri, and Halfdan, the best we could do is join up with Odd," Storolf answered. He and Hallbjorn had hunted together for so many years that they no longer needed words to understand one another.

"Exactly," Hallbjorn said.

"But we don't know where he is," Olaf pointed out. "We saw them sail off. Hours ago. They could be many miles from here."

"My brother-in-law came in from fishing, just before this rain," Storolf said. "He said he saw them, heading north along the coast. Two longships and a whole fleet of fishing boats. A couple hundred men, he reckoned."

"Then they couldn't have gone far," Hallbjorn said. "Once this weather blew in they sure as Thor's ass would not have wanted to be out on the water."

"There's the harbor just up the coast from here," Thormod said.

Storolf shook his head. "Too exposed in this wind. And besides, they were already north of there when my brother-in-law saw them."

"Just a couple miles farther there's that big harbor," Hallbjorn said. "Better protected from any wind. Lots of islands. They might have gone there."

"Could be," Thormod said. "But we're trapped here, sitting on our asses. We can't join Odd if we don't know where he is, and even if we did, Skorri put a hundred men outside the town. No one's getting in or out."

"Hallbjorn could get out," Olaf said.

Hallbjorn shook his head. "Hallbjorn of fifteen years ago could have got out," he said. "This Hallbjorn couldn't."

"Maybe not in daylight," Storolf said. "But now? In the dark, and in this rain?"

Hallbjorn frowned, but he did not argue the point.

"Slip out of town, find Odd and whoever's with him," Olaf said. "Find out their plans, let them know what's happening here. It might be that more of us could find a way to leave Fevik, join them, if it seemed we could help in the fight. If there's going to be a fight."

Still Hallbjorn did not reply. He took a deep drink and set his cup down. He looked from one man to the other. They were each looking at him, waiting on an answer. Finally he looked Storolf straight in the eye.

"I'm not going alone," he said.

Chapter Nineteen

The skillful hardener of weapons
that peck wounds gave eloquent
Egil in reward three shells
that rear up ever-silent in the surf.

Egil's Saga

The wind was fair, *Sea Hammer*'s big sail was full, and the ship was rolling along with that pleasing rhythm of a vessel in a moderate sea, with a steady breeze coming from aft of the beam. The water was washing down the sides, singing its water song, and every once in a while, when ship and sea got out of sync, it would give the hull a gentle thump, as if to tell the vessel that it was in the ocean's realm now, and it had best remember that.

The other ships of the fleet were spread out on either side of *Sea Hammer* and a bit astern, each with its sail set and drawing in the fair wind, under the blue sky.

That part, at least, was what Thorgrim assumed. He couldn't see the other ships, because he was laying propped up on the deck, on top of a bed of old canvas, and Gyda was standing over him, a bucket in her hands.

"This might be a bit cold," she said, and with that she started pouring the sea water over his chest and right shoulder, a steady stream hitting him about neck-level and running down over tunic and trousers and onto the deck.

Hall, at the helm, stepped away to avoid his shoes getting wet in the spreading water. Thorgrim glanced up at him and Hall looked quickly away, but not quickly enough to hide his suppressed smile. Thorgrim pressed his lips together, struggling not to react to the cold, and keeping in check the words he wanted to say, words that would not have been helpful.

"Your own fault," Gyda said as she poured out the last of the water. "Now, we'll let that work a bit."

Thorgrim was not happy about the dousing, and he did not think it was his fault, or anyone's fault, really. After the fight at Gyda's house, after the sudden appearance of Eyvind and his men, with the dead laying scattered around and the fire consuming the place, it was immediately clear that leaving Ribe, and quickly, was their best option. For Thorgrim, it was not a hard choice. It was the very thing he was aching to do.

He led them down the main street to the waterfront. No one paid them any attention. Gyda's house had become a great inferno, and the folk in Ribe were thinking only about stopping the flames from spreading to the rest of the town.

They came at last to where Thorgrim's fleet and Eyvind's ship were pulled up on shore, their bows just nestled in the mud and long lines run to posts to keep them in place. His captains; Gudrid, Asmund, Halldor, and the rest; were gathered near *Sea Hammer.* They could see the flames rising up over the town from there, and they could hear that some sort of panic had broken out, but they seemed unsure as to what they should do about it.

"Thorgrim!" Asmund called, as Thorgrim and others appeared out of the dark. Asmund was smiling, a rare thing indeed. "We didn't know what was going on there."

"Nothing good," Thorgrim said. "We were attacked. Eyvind and his men showed up to fight with us, and it was a good job they did. Ships ready for sea?"

"*Oak Heart*'s ready," Asmund said.

"*Black Wing*'s ready," said Halldor, and the other captains chimed in as well, all ready for sea.

"Good," Thorgrim said. He turned to Eyvind. "You coming with us?" Eyvind nodded. "Ready to get underway?" Eyvind nodded again. "Very well," Thorgrim said.

He looked up. The moon was well above the horizon and nearly full, and the tide was high and still rising. Ribe was several miles up a river from the sea, but in those conditions they should have no problem navigating to open water, despite the dark.

"Let's get under way," he said next. "*Sea Hammer* will take the lead. Follow in the order that you're pulled up here on shore. Eyvind, fall into line where you can. And don't anyone run into anyone else, or I swear on Odin's horse's ass I'll rip your lungs out."

With that encouragement, the rest disbursed to their various ships, and Thorgrim led Gyda over to *Sea Hammer*'s side. "Let me help you aboard," he said, but Gyda shook her head.

"I can get aboard, and you've torn your wound open enough as it is. With the blood you've lost, I expect you'll drop like a rock any moment now." With that, Gyda put her hands on the sheer strake and hefted herself up and over the side in a flurry of clothes. Thorgrim started to pull himself up after her, but she put a hand on his shoulder to stop him.

"Starri," she said to Starri Deathless, who was at Thorgrim's side. "Don't let him do that. Help him."

Starri looked at her, looked at Thorgrim, and with a resigned and apologetic expression linked his fingers and held his hands down for Thorgrim to use as a step. Thorgrim, resigned as well, put his foot into Starri's hands and stepped up and on board, which, admittedly, put considerably less pressure on his wounded shoulder.

He made his way aft and stood at the tiller as the men, larboard and starboard, took the oars down from the gallows and settled at their rowing stations on the sea chests lashed to the deck.

"Shove off!" Thorgrim called forward, and half a dozen men, unseen under the bow, put their shoulders against the ship and pushed it out into the river, and then came swarming up over the sides. A few more commands, and the oars were run out and down. The rowers pushed and pulled and the ship spun around until the bow was pointing downriver toward the sea. Thorgrim sent Vali up to the bow to direct their course down the twisting waterway.

They moved slowly against the last of the incoming tide, and one by one the other ships fell in astern. The sounds of shouting from Ribe faded away, and soon there was nothing to hear but the dip of the oars in the water, and the squeak of the looms in the row ports, and the sound of insects in the fields off to larboard and starboard. Every few moments Vali would call aft to indicate which way the river was bending as it wound to the sea.

"You've opened up your wound," Gyda said. She was standing close by Thorgrim on the small afterdeck, and she spoke softly. "You should let me tend to it."

"I will," Thorgrim said. "But not until we're clear of this river and out to sea."

Gyda did not argue. Thorgrim reckoned that she knew him well enough to know how futile that would be, even after their short time together. And he appreciated it.

They kept on downriver. Thorgrim could see *Oak Heart* astern of *Sea Hammer*, and sometimes, as they went around a bend, he could catch a glimpse of the other ships strung out astern. There was nothing else moving on the river. Whoever had tried to murder Thorgrim and Harald and Starri in their sleep had apparently made no contingency plans if they failed.

Sometime later — Thorgrim had no sense for how long — the banks of the river passed astern, and Thorgrim could see nothing but dark water all around, the moonlight glinting off it. Vali called aft, "I think we're out of the river now, getting to the sea!"

"Good," Thorgrim called forward. "But we're not clear yet. You keep a sharp eye out for mud banks."

"Sharp as my sword!" Vali called back, and he did not disappoint, watching the way the water rippled over the shallow parts, which was his only clue as to where the mud flats were lurking. In that way he managed to bring the longship through, until at last they were in genuinely deep water, with the dark, open ocean ahead.

Thorgrim continued to lead the fleet west, rowing in a straight line directly away from the coast, and then, as the sun started to illuminate the eastern sky, and Frisia became visible as a low, thin, line on the horizon, he turned north. Astern of *Sea Hammer*, and spreading farther apart as they gained sea room, he could see the other five ships of his fleet, and Eyvind's ship as well.

Hall came aft. "I can relieve you at the tiller, if you like," he said.

"This might be a good time," Gyda said, nodding toward the wide patch of dried blood on Thorgrim's tunic. She had been standing beside him since they got underway.

"Not just yet," Thorgrim said. "I want to wait to see if the wind comes up."

"And that won't happen unless you're standing here watching?" Gyda asked.

"No," Thorgrim said. "Njord does nothing without asking my advice."

He marveled that Gyda could say such a thing, and in such a tone that it made him smile and joke, and not snap at her in irritation. Thorgrim did not usually think of himself as the joking sort, and he suspected most of his men would agree.

"It won't be long," Thorgrim added. He hoped that would mollify her some, but in truth he was a bit concerned. All the signs pointed to wind, and Thorgrim was usually right with such things. But he feared that his joke about Njord might have ruined his luck.

But it did not, and soon he could feel the first stirrings of a breeze on the side of his face. He looked over at Gyda. Wisps of blond hair that had escaped her braids were lifting and twisting in the wind.

"There, just as I said." Thorgrim smiled at Gyda. "Njord favors us."

He let the wind build a bit more, then ordered hands to set the sail, and told the grateful rowers to unship their oars. Soon *Sea Hammer* was rolling along nicely. Astern of her, the sails of the other ships sprouted like flowers blooming in spring.

"Now?" Gyda asked. Thorgrim nodded. He called for Hall to come and relieve him at the tiller, then he stepped across the narrow deck to where Gyda stood. She looked closely at the great swath of dried blood on the front of his tunic. She pinched the cloth between thumb and forefinger and tugged gently, and Thorgrim could feel his skin lifting with the cloth.

"As I feared, the blood has pasted your clothing to your skin," Gyda said. "If I pull too hard it will open the wound again."

"So what will you do?"

"We'll have to soak it, so it'll come free." She turned to a knot of men standing just forward of the afterdeck and told them to fetch something for Thorgrim to lie on, and a bucket of sea water. They did as instructed and soon after Thorgrim, propped up by a pile of old canvas, was clenching his fists against the cold of the salt water soaking into his tunic and shirt.

Once she had emptied the bucket on Thorgrim's chest, Gyda helped Thorgrim move to where he could sit on the edge of the afterdeck, legs hanging down. She stood in front of him and pulled gently at the cloth, frowning as she did.

"Well?" Thorgrim asked.

"We'll wait a bit, see if the cloth comes free," she said, and sat beside him. "If not, it's another bucket."

"Just so we understand," Thorgrim said, "I'm not the sort of man who'll let a wrong go unavenged."

"Meaning?"

"Meaning one of these days I'll pour a bucket of sea water on you. Except you won't see it coming."

"Hmm," Gyda said. "I wish you luck."

They let a few moments pass, and then Gyda tried the cloth again and found that it pulled easily away from Thorgrim's skin. "The best thing would be for me to cut your tunic and shirt away from the wound," she said.

"I think not," Thorgrim said. He was a frugal man, and could not tolerate ruining good clothing just for the sake of his ease.

"Very well," Gyda said. She had Thorgrim raise his arms, slowly, and eased the tunic up over his head, and then the shirt. She had washed and mended the garments back in Ribe, and though her stitching was still intact, the clothing was once again soaked through with blood. She spread it out on the deck to dry as much as they could, then carefully unwound the bandages she had wrapped around him two days earlier.

Thorgrim looked down at his chest and stomach. His pale skin was washed pink by the diluted blood, as were the few white hairs that lurked among the dark ones on his chest.

Gyda stood and asked the men nearby for another bucket of sea water and some rags. When they were delivered she stood in front of Thorgrim once more and dipped a few of the rags in the water and began gently wiping the blood away from the wound. She leaned in close, studying the injury as best she could, and gently poking with her finger.

"Well?" Thorgrim asked. The breeze was cool on his wet, bare skin, and it was raising gooseflesh.

"You managed to tear my stitching," Gyda said. "And you bled a fair bit. But it looks like it's mostly closed up again." She leaned closer still and sniffed the wound. "Doesn't seem any rot's set in."

"Good," Thorgrim said. "The gods are not always kind, but I hope they'll let me get back to my home, and help my son."

"If your end comes soon, I don't think it will be because of this," Gyda said. She picked up a few of the still-dry rags and began tearing them into long strips for bandages. "It's lucky it's no worse than it is. All of my healing things went up in flames. Along with everything else."

"I'm sorry," Thorgrim said. "I'm sorry you had to pay such a price for helping me."

"Hmm," Gyda said. "Well, Ribe was my home, but not because I had any love for the place. I just had nowhere else to go, and no way to get there."

"Still, I'm sorry you lost all that you had."

"I still have my sword," Gyda said, with a bit of a smile. "The one you bought me."

"And your frying pan?"

"No. I dropped that somewhere."

"Then I'll get you another frying pan. You seem to be deadly with one of those. You laid that one whore's son right out, as I recall."

"Oh, yes," Gyda said. "You can have your swords and seaxes, but give me a frying pan, and stand clear. Anyway, let me tell you, it was a pleasure, caving Galti Grimolfsson's head in."

"Who?"

"Galti Grimolfsson. That bastard I hit with the frying pan. Breaking his head was a pleasure."

"You knew him?"

"Certainly. He was from Ribe. Him and the scum that were with him. They'd leave from time to time, doing whatever they'd do. Make everyone hope they were gone for good. But then they'd come back, like a plague. Why do you ask?"

"It surprises me," Thorgrim said. "I thought they were strangers to Ribe."

"No, not strangers," Gyda said. "But now their home is in the realms of Hel, and she's welcome to them."

Gyda finished tearing the rags into strips, and then wrapped them around Thorgrim's wound, binding it good and tight. That done, she helped him back into his shirt and tunic. The clothing had managed to dry a bit on the warm planks of the deck, and Thorgrim was grateful for that, but he could see that nothing would remain dry for very long. Dark clouds were building to the southwest and spreading out over the dome of the sky, bringing with them the threat of strengthening winds and rain. Already Thorgrim could feel the breeze veering, and growing stronger and colder.

He stared at the clouds and frowned and felt his anger building like the storm. At the start of the day his fleet had been enjoying an easy run north, rolling along with sails full, closing with Norway, and Odd. There was no means on earth by which men could travel faster than they were then. Had the weather held, they would have reached home in just a few days.

But not now. Soon this storm would roll over them, and they would be forced to put their ships on the beach to ride it out. It made him wild with frustration.

Had it been him alone he would have told the gods to kiss his arse. He would have sailed on through any weather, let Njord and Thor do their worst. But it was not him alone. It was all the men under his command. It was Harald and Starri, who could not be allowed to end their lives by drowning. It was Gyda. He could not let them all die as the seas overwhelmed their ships, or smashed them like eggs on a rocky shore.

He wanted to shout, to punch something in his fury. But instead he just clenched his teeth and stared out to windward at the mounting storm.

Is this because I mocked Njord? Thorgrim wondered. He pushed the thought aside. He could not consider it, because the idea made him even angrier still.

The fleet plowed on north, and the clouds overspread the sky, and the wind continued to veer and build. Thorgrim's anger was pushed aside by thoughts of keeping *Sea Hammer* and the others alive in the wild seas. The motion of the ship was growing noticeably more pronounced and more chaotic; more like clinging to an unbroken horse than riding one trained to the saddle.

He ordered the sail lowered and the bottom edge reefed to lessen the amount of cloth spread to the wind. He looked astern, off to larboard, then starboard. The other ships were laboring as well, their bows rising high and smacking down and sending spumes of spray up in the air, which quickly blew away to leeward. *Dragon*, Harald's command, and *Fox*, the two smallest ships, were falling behind, and making heavy weather of it.

Thorgrim sighed and looked forward. His men were shooting furtive glances his way, and he knew they were wondering if he meant to get the ships out of that weather, or if he was driven enough, and mad enough, to just keep going and hope the gods would forgive such foolish hubris. And well they might wonder, because Thorgrim was still not entirely certain himself.

With the wind veering from the southeast to the west, the coast of Frisia had become a lee shore, so Thorgrim led the fleet farther and farther off to gain enough sea room for safety. Now the land, several miles away off the starboard side, looked to Thorgrim like little more than a low, dark, irregular shape on the horizon. He ran his eyes along the shore, searching for some spot where they might beach the ships, but the coastline looked entirely featureless to him.

"Starri!" he called over the mounting wind. Starri was standing on the sheer strake amidships, one hand on a shroud, staring out at the shore. The ship was rolling and plunging and bucking under him, but he was standing there as if in an open field on a summer day. It was madness. But then, it was Starri.

He turned on hearing Thorgrim's voice, gave a little wave, and hopped down from his perch. He ambled aft, past the men sitting on the deck, huddled against the side of the ship, seeking some little shelter from the wind.

"Yes, Night Wolf?"

"We need to get out of this weather. There are harbors on this stretch of coast, but they all have narrow channels to get in, and we'll never find them. A beach will be our best chance. Can you go aloft and look for a beach that might work?"

Starri smiled. "Of course, Night Wolf!" Starri had eyes like a hawk, and he was the only one aboard who could make it to the masthead with the motion of the ship as it was. Besides, he enjoyed doing those things that normal men would consider insane.

He turned and jogged forward, and without breaking stride grabbed onto one of the windward shrouds and began scrambling up, hand over hand, legs wrapped around the rope. He swung violently side to side as the ship rolled, and was nearly flicked off as the shroud went slack and then snapped tight again. But soon he was at the top, clinging to the mast and looking out at the lee shore.

For a long time he said nothing, just hung on as he scrutinized the land. Finally he called down.

"There, Night Wolf!" He pointed to a spot just off the starboard bow. "When we come up on a wave, I can see it! A wide strip of beach! As good as we're like to find, I think!"

"Very good!" Thorgrim called back. It would have to do. The weather was going downhill fast; if they hoped to go ashore at a place of their choosing, they would have to do it now. He turned to Hall at the tiller. "You saw where Starri was pointing?"

"I did."

"Start falling off some, heading that way. But not right at the shore. The wind and seas will set us down where we want."

Hall nodded. He pulled the tiller toward him a bit, and *Sea Hammer*'s bow began to swing away from the wind, turning more toward the shoreline to starboard. Thorgrim ordered the sail trimmed to the new course, then looked at the other ships astern. They had seen *Sea Hammer*'s change of course, and they were following her lead.

Thorgrim kept eyes on the coastline as they closed with it, and more and more of it become visible to him. There was still not much to see. Frisia was flat and marshy and featureless. Good for farming, but not much else. He looked at Gyda, and she looked grim.

"How are you doing?" he asked. "Is the motion making you sick?"

"No, no, I'm fine," she said and tried for a weak smile. "Your ship…these waves aren't too much for it?"

Thorgrim nearly laughed, but he stopped himself. He could see that Gyda was genuinely concerned. "No, the ship is strong. It's been through much worse than this." He nearly added that there was no possibility of the seas destroying *Sea Hammer*, but he thought better of it. "If Njord decides to be kind, we'll get to shore safe as can be," he said instead.

The wind continued to build as *Sea Hammer* closed with the land, the reefed sail bellying out and straining at the sheets. The seas were rolling under her larboard quarter now, lifting the ship and setting it down with a corkscrew motion. Thorgrim glanced over at Gyda again. She was staring out toward the coastline, her mouth set, her hair whipping around, but she did not have the stupefied look of one who was suffering from seasickness.

Well, if this won't make her puke, nothing will, Thorgrim thought.

The low-lying coast was now only a mile or so away. Thorgrim waited until a wave lifted the stern high and then looked out past the bow. He could see it now, the pale strip of sand right at the juncture of sea and shore. It seemed very much like a beach from that distance, a decent place to bring the ships ashore. But first they had to land there in one piece, and that would not be so simple.

"You men, get that sail in!" Thorgrim called forward, putting all the voice he had into the command, so that he could be heard over the howling wind. "Get the yard fore and aft and down and lash that sail up! Then get ready with your oars!" He could feel his wound throb with the effort of shouting.

Forward, the men staggered around and slipped in the water rushing over the deck boards as they swung the yard around and dipped the end in behind the shrouds until the spar hung along the centerline of the ship. They lowered it the rest of the way, and men grabbed up handfuls of the sail, which was snapping and filling and trying to jerk free of their grip as they lashed it to the yard. Even without the sail, under the one bare pole, *Sea Hammer* plowed wildly along.

"How does she feel?" Thorgrim asked Hall.

"A little sluggish. Not bad. She doesn't like to steer with the seas like this and the sail stowed."

Thorgrim nodded. He wanted very much to take the tiller himself, but he was afraid he would tear open his wound again if he tried. And worse, after his wounding, his long death-sleep, his loss of blood, he had a vague fear that he might not have the strength for it.

"We'll close with the beach," Thorgrim said to Hall. He was all but yelling, though Hall was only five feet away. "Get the rowers in place. When we get close, on my word, you'll turn up into the wind and the rowers will pull like their lives depend on it, 'cause they will. With any luck we can ease our way stern-first onto the sand, instead of being driven onto it."

Hall nodded, his eyes fixed forward, his body leaning into the tiller. He was not looking forward to this, Thorgrim guessed, and he was not alone.

With the sail down, the rowers took their places on the sea chests, while others struggled to pull the oars down from the gallows and pass them along without being flung across the pitching and rolling deck. Thorgrim called for Bjorn and Onund.

"You two," he said, after they had come staggering aft. "I want you to get the anchor ready. We're going stern-first onto the beach. When we get near the breakers and make our turn, you toss the anchor over and then take a strain on the cable. It might hold, it might not. But if you can, try to keep the bow up into the seas."

The two men nodded and headed forward. Thorgrim called out to the rowers at their stations. "Keep your oars inboard, but ready to run out in an instant! Every man on the oars. When I say pull, you pull with everything you have, if you hope to live through this!"

He leaned over the sheer strake and looked astern. The other ships had also taken their sails down. He wished he had some means to tell them what he planned, but he did not. He could only hope they'd figure it out on their own.

With the wind driving them, and the mounting seas flinging them land-ward, *Sea Hammer* closed rapidly with the shore. Thorgrim stood on the aft deck, larboard side, his eyes fixed ahead. They were close enough now that even he could see the waves breaking on the sand, the long stretch of beach running for miles in either direction. It still looked like a good place for what he intended, and he could only hope there were no dangers hidden from view.

"Get ready," he said to Hall, then shouted forward to the rowers, "Get ready!" He braced himself, feeling the rise and fall of the ship underfoot, judging the speed with which they were closing on the shore. He felt the stern rise and then fall again into the trough between waves.

"On the next rise!" he shouted to Hall. He waited while *Sea Hammer* twisted in the saltwater valley, waited as the stern began to rise again, and then shouted to Hall, "Now!"

Hall leaned into the tiller, pushing it forward, his feet braced against the wet deck boards. Thorgrim heard him grunt with the effort and *Sea Hammer*'s bow began to swing to larboard, the ship turning up into the wind and seas. For a sickening moment she lay broadside to the waves. *Sea Hammer* took a great roll to starboard, nearly knocking the rowers off their seats. Shields were lifted from the shield rack amidships and sent spinning away down wind.

Come on, come on… Thorgrim thought. If the ship did not continue her turn they would be flung sideways onto the beach, or rolled like a barrel in the surf. He looked over at Hall, saw that Hall still had the rudder hard over. He looked forward.

Here we go…

Sea Hammer was still turning, rising up as the next wave met the ship on her larboard bow. Foot by painful foot she turned. Thorgrim could feel the wind on his face now, not the back of his head: he could see it was blowing nearly down the centerline of the ship as the bow crested the next roller.

"Rowers! Now!" he shouted "Now! Run out and pull!"

The rowers, braced for that command, ran their long sweeps out the row ports and lowered them just as the bow took a sickening plunge down off a wave. The stem hit with an impact that sent a shudder through the entire ship, and a great spume of spray rose, like some monster from the deep, and rained down the full length of the ship, but no one seemed to notice. As one, the men leaned forward and pulled back on their oars, lifted, leaned forward, pulled again.

Sea Hammer was moving astern fast. The sea had her in its grip and was flinging her back toward the land. Hall had shifted the rudder amidships and now he clung to the tiller, the ship beyond any control he could exert.

"Cut that lashing away!" Thorgrim shouted, pointing at the rudder shaft. The head of the rudder was lashed to the side of the ship with a leather strap. If the lashing was cut free, it would allow the rudder to pivot, and that might keep it from shattering when the ship went aground.

Hall nodded, let go of the tiller and pulled his knife from its sheath. Thorgrim looked forward again. The rowers were soaked with spray and red-faced as they heaved at the oars. The bow lifted up so Thorgrim was looking at the gray, roiling clouds, then dropped, and he was staring into the face of the next wave rolling down on them. Up in the bow, Bjorn and Onund threw the anchor over and took a turn of the anchor cable around a heavy wooden bitt.

Thorgrim looked astern. They were all but on the beach now, and he was surprised that they had not yet hit. Then the next sea passed under and dropped the stern down on the sand with a bone-jarring impact. Gyda gave a short cry, leapt up and grabbed on to the side of the ship. She looked wildly around, as if waiting for *Sea Hammer* to fall apart under her feet.

The seas lifted the hull again and flung it farther up the beach, and once again dropped it so that the entire vessel shook, stem to stern. And then the next wave came, but this one did not lift *Sea Hammer* at all. It barely made the ship move as it broke around her bow and swirled inland over the sand. They were there. And they were still whole.

One by one the other ships came in on either side of *Sea Hammer*, and each did as Thorgrim had done, backing stern-first onto the sand, the rowers pulling for their lives, so their grounding might be slower and controlled. Only *Fox* got sideways to the seas, driving beam-on toward the beach, rolling so hard that the on-lookers were certain she was going right over.

But she did not. Just as she was turning on her beam ends, the bottom hit the sand and the ship stopped dead. She rolled upright as the water pulled back, then the next wave washed her farther up onto the sand, high and dry, but still in one piece.

"Let's get the awning up!" Thorgrim called forward as the first of the rain started blowing in sideways. They were on the beach now. They were safe from the sea. And only the gods could tell how long they would be stuck there, while many leagues away to the north Odd battled on without them.

Chapter Twenty

One doesn't bear a better burden on the road
than great common sense;
better than wealth it seems in a strange place;
such is a poor man's means of existence.

The Sayings of Hávi

It was not long after Hallbjorn Ale-slinger agreed to make his attempt to leave Fevik that he and Storolf stepped out of the little storehouse and into the blowing rain. They wore heavy wool capes with hoods over their tunics and cloaks. The capes kept the rain off, but they had no illusions that they would continue to do so for long. Oiled canvas bags were slung over their shoulders, and Hallbjorn carried the firkin, now empty, under his arm.

They stepped into the road and looked around, but they saw no patrols, or much of anything at all, through the storm. They continued on, moving down streets so familiar there was no need for them to see more than a few feet ahead to find their way. They skirted through alleys and along the edge of the wattle fences that separated yards from road.

They saw no one. If any of Halfdan's men had been ordered to keep watch over the town, they were choosing to disobey those orders. Hallbjorn could hardly blame them. No one would want to be out in that weather, if there was some way they could avoid it.

At the very northern edge of town, a block up from the water, Hallbjorn and Storolf made their way down a narrow alley that separated two of the houses. They paused where the alley yielded to the open ground beyond. There was still nothing to be seen out in the dark, but that did not mean there was nothing, or no one, there.

Skorri, they knew, had ringed Fevik with men, and ordered them not to let anyone in or out. Hallbjorn figured that the guards in the town itself might let their vigilance lapse in the middle of that storm, but he did not think those watching the roads and fields would. Skorri was not likely to forgive that sort of negligence.

And Hallbjorn knew better than to take Skorri's men for granted, despite the cover provided by the dark and the rain. These were not farmers carrying their fathers' old, rusted swords. These were the best of Halfdan's hird, trained warriors who knew how to follow orders and knew how to remain vigilant, even in those conditions.

"Let's go," he said to Storolf, and he headed out into the open.

It was slow going, their feet sinking into the wet ground, their capes now soaked through and heavy. They walked through waist-high grass that pulled at their wet clothing. They were heading for the stand of trees they knew was there, though they could barely make it out.

"Hold there!" The voice came out of the dark, from off to the right. Hallbjorn and Storolf stopped where they were and blinked in the direction from which the voice had come. A moment later two of Halfdan's warriors seemed to materialize in front of them. They wore helmets and mail shirts, which were visible under capes hanging open.

"There you are!" Hallbjorn called, all but yelling to be heard over the rain. "Sons of bitches don't make this easy."

"Who are you?" one of the guards asked, his palm resting conspicuously on the pommel of his sword. "Where do you think you're going?"

"Your captain sent us. Told us to bring you food and drink," Hallbjorn said. He half-raised the firkin so they could see it.

"Food and drink? On a night like this?" the other guard asked. "What captain was it who sent you?"

"How should I know? Some big bastard. Nasty piece of work. Said to bring food and drink to all you whore's sons guarding the roads. He sounded like he was in command." Hallbjorn noted that the chin straps on their helmets were unbuckled and hanging down on either side of their necks.

That's a help, he thought.

"What do you have there?" the first guard asked, nodding toward the firkin.

"I've got mead. I've got bread and meat."

"And you don't know who sent you?"

"Look, do you want this or not?" Hallbjorn said, like a man whose patience had run out. "You think I want to be out here on such a night, bringing mead to the likes of you?"

"Very well," the guard said, his desire for a drink apparently outweighing his suspicion. Before he could say more, Hallbjorn set the firkin down and turned to Storolf.

"Do you have those cups?"

"Yeah. Here," Storolf said, and dug into his oiled canvas bag.

"I've got bread, too," Hallbjorn said. He opened his own bag and reached inside, pulling out what looked very much like a small loaf of bread, but was in fact a rock. He took half a step toward the closest guard. His left hand lashed out and knocked the guard's helmet off his head as his right hand, holding the rock, came swinging around.

The guard made a grunting sound, barely audible, and fell sideways as the rock struck. Hallbjorn looked over just in time to see the rock in Storolf's hand hitting the other guard's helmetless head, and he, too, went down. They were silent for a moment, listening, looking around. Nothing.

"You kill yours?" Storolf asked.

"Don't know." Hallbjorn nudged the motionless man with his foot. "Don't think so. You?"

"Don't think so."

Hallbjorn cleared his throat and spit on the crumpled figure at his feet, not the most effective protest in the pouring rain, but it pleased him. He tossed his rock away. Storolf did, in fact, have two cups in his bag, and he pulled them out now and dropped one by each guard.

They could have killed the men, of course, at least as easily as they had knocked them out, but the murder of two of Skorri's men would certainly bring terrible retribution on the town. This way, when the guards were found unconscious, with cups and an empty firkin, it might be assumed they drank themselves into oblivion, their protests to the contrary not believed. Just as likely, the two would rather admit to getting drunk than being fooled by townsfolk and letting two unarmed men escape.

"Let's go," Hallbjorn said. He trudged off toward the stand of trees, tense, waiting for another challenge, not sure what he and Storolf would do if it came. They were out of firkins and rocks. If challenged, they would have to rely on their hunting knives.

But they were not challenged, and they reached the trees and stepped in among them, where the rain and wind were not so brutal. They stopped for a moment, catching their breath, reorienting.

"Isn't this grand," Storolf said at last. "Like the old days."

"Like the old days," Hallbjorn agreed. "That's why I was happy to kick the old days in the teeth and buy my tavern."

"You remember how to do this?"

Hallbjorn knew what Storolf meant by *this*: move over land in the dark. Find their way despite the driving rain. Keep an eye and an ear and a nose out for any danger. Those skills had once been as natural as breathing, or walking.

"Yeah, I reckon."

They headed out again, emerging from the trees on the far side and into open county. Happily, the terrain was not difficult, mostly low, rolling hills covered by open fields and stands of trees. They moved slowly nonetheless, since the dark and the lashing rain made it hard to see. They moved by instinct, the old senses kicking in, a feel for place and direction deeply ingrained.

They walked on through the night, and eventually the sky to the east grew lighter, a barely discernable easing of the blackness, though the rain did not let up in any way. Soon after, dawn began to assert itself, undeniably, the country around them growing grudgingly visible, fields and trees and the distant sea all rendered in shades of gray, and black, and brown.

Hallbjorn paused and surveyed what he could see. He grunted. "We seem to be where I thought we were."

"You sound surprised."

"I am. Some. Guess we had better take more care now, in case Skorri's sent patrols out."

He did not think it likely, but it was possible that the guards had been found and they had told the truth about what had happened to them. It was also possible, likely even, that Skorri was as eager as he and Storolf were to find where Odd Thorgrimson had gone, and had sent riders out searching.

"I'd hate for us to get caught now," Storolf said, "just when we're starting to have fun."

They moved down the sloping field and into a wooded area that seemed to run north for about half a mile, good cover in that country. They continued north, working their way through the trees and the bracken, roughly following the coast. They were close now to where they thought Odd might be, though they were well aware that it was only a guess.

They came at last to the north end of the woods and paused there to look out over the countryside beyond. From where they stood the land sloped away for half a mile before it yielded to yet more trees. Beyond that they could see the wide harbor and the scattering of islands in the distance.

"You see any longships?" Storolf asked.

"No," Hallbjorn said. "But then, bad as my eyesight's grown, I'm lucky that I can see you."

"I don't see any either," Storolf said. "And I wouldn't expect to. If Odd's here, he'd be a fool not to keep the ships well hidden."

They took another moment to look over the open ground, to see that there was no one moving, no riders in the distance, then they headed down toward the trees and the water. Hallbjorn's legs were growing weary and his cape seemed twice as heavy as it had been when dry.

They reached the woods and plunged in and kept moving, more motivated now that they had all but come to their destination, even if they had no idea whether or not they would find Odd there. They moved with caution, looking and listening, the old senses sharp. Soon the trees began to grow thin, and they could catch glimpses of water between them. They slowed their pace and moved in a crouch, until at last they found themselves in tall grass, with the harbor spread out before them, and the rocky shore to the left and right.

"Look at those idiots," Hallbjorn whispered, nodding to his left. A hundred feet away, two men were standing huddled against the rain. They were wearing helmets and mail and capes, with the hoods pulled up over their heads. They had their arms crossed on their chests and they were staring miserably at the ground, where their spears were laying.

"Guards, I reckon," Storolf whispered back. "Odd's, or Skorri's?"

"Odd's. Farmers dressed up like warriors. Skorri's men would not be such useless buggerers."

"Got to admire their vigilance."

"We should go cut their throats, just on principal," Hallbjorn said.

But they did not. Instead, they worked their way along the tree line, unseen, closer to where the guards were standing, then stepped out into the open twenty feet in front of the two men.

"Good morrow," Hallbjorn said. The guards looked up and visibly started. One made a choking sound of surprise and tried to untangle his cape and draw his sword, while the other scrambled to pick up his spear.

"Relax," Hallbjorn said. "We decided not to cut your throats." The guards paused in their attempt to take up arms and stared warily at the strangers.

Hallbjorn and Storolf stopped ten feet short of the men. "I'm guessing you're not Halfdan's men," Hallbjorn said.

The guards glanced at one another, clearly unsure if they should answer, or how. "No," one said at last.

"Where'd you get the helmets and mail?" Storolf asked.

"Took them," the other guard said. "From Halfdan's men."

"You're with Odd Thorgrimson," Hallbjorn said. It was not a question.

Once more, the guards did not know how to answer. Finally, the first one spoke.

"What business is it of yours?"

"We came from Fevik," Hallbjorn said. "We escaped. Skorri Thorbrandsson's taken over the town, in the name of King Halfdan. They sacked the place. Looking for Odd. We escaped, and now we need to talk with him."

"I'm not so sure Odd wants to talk to you," the guard said. "He…"

"Enough," Storolf said, wearily. "There's only two of us. I'm sure Odd has men enough to put our heads on pikes if he doesn't like what we have to say."

The guards paused. They looked at one another. Then the one said, "Very well. But you'll have to wait."

Odd and the men and women with him, it turned out, had not made camp on the shore of the harbor, but rather on one of the larger islands to the north, a thoroughly sensible decision, Hallbjorn thought. The guards on shore had a boat to go back and forth, but they could not leave their post, nor were they willing to give the two strangers the use of it. So there was no choice but to wait until two more guards rowed over from the island to relieve them.

The rain, happily, was tapering off. Hallbjorn and Storolf sat on the rocks to rest after a long night. They answered the guards' questions about the goings-on in Fevik, and the guards in turn answered theirs as to who the people were in Odd's company, and what exactly had happened in the taking of the longship the day before. They even warmed up to Hallbjorn and Storolf enough to share some ale and bread and cheese with them.

It was not long after that that a second boat arrived, rowed by another two men in mail, and after the first guards were properly relieved they led Hallbjorn and Storolf over to where their boat was hidden in a little rocky cut in the shore. The two guards hopped aboard and bailed the eight inches of water out of the bilge, then gestured for Hallbjorn and Storolf to climb in.

Hallbjorn did as he was told, fearful that he and Storolf might be asked to row. He was very tired at that point, and had always been fairly inept at pulling an oar. But the guards had said that they were fishermen, and that became obvious by the ease and skill with which they handled the faering. They did not ask for help.

The two rowed the boat across the half mile of water to the largest of the many islands scattered around the harbor, a long, low stretch of land, grass-covered, with trees here and there. They pulled around the western side, which was hidden from any ships passing up or down the coast. There, Hallbjorn saw dozens of fishing boats pulled up on a thin strip of gravel beach. Farther off, two longships were likewise run up on the shore. A scattering of tents was set up on the island, a ways back from the shore.

The two men rowing kept a course parallel to the island. Then, with an expert twist of the oars, they turned the vessel and ran it bow-first onto the beach, nestled up among its brethren, and the four men climbed out.

"Follow us," one said, and they led Hallbjorn and Storolf across the beach and up the short slope to the level ground above. They could see that what had looked like a few tents from the water was in fact a few dozen, some small, some quite large. The tents were circled around a big firepit, where a fire was blazing despite the soaking rain of the night before.

"Looks like you're here to stay," Hallbjorn said to their guides, who were leading them in the direction of the firepit.

"Don't know," one of the guards admitted. "After we captured that longship at Fevik, we set a trap in a cove to the south, laid in wait. Odd reckoned Skorri would send more ships after us, and we were going to ambush them. But no one ever appeared. So when the weather turned on us, we came here, set up the tents we brought. Don't know what the plan is, don't know how long we'll stay."

They reached the place where a handful of women were tending the fire, building it up into a warming blaze, and the guards led them to one of the tents just beyond. A few men were sitting on benches outside one of the larger tents, deep in discussion. Hallbjorn recognized one: Bragi Shipslayer, a man who spent considerable time in the various taverns on the Fevik waterfront. He was not sure that Bragi's presence was such a good omen.

"Odd?" one of the guards called, and the men looked up. "These two, they're from Fevik. Said they escaped. Said they wanted to talk to you."

One of the men nodded. He stood up and stepped closer. "I'm Odd Thorgrimson," he said.

Hallbjorn looked Odd up and down and nodded. Odd's name had been on people's lips so much the past year it was interesting to see the man in person. A young man, but his face showed the hard use he had endured. His beard was light brown, his hair long and braided behind. He had the look of one who was comfortable with command. Hallbjorn could definitely see traces of Thorgrim Night Wolf in his face.

"I'm Hallbjorn," Hallbjorn said. "This is Storolf. From Fevik, like he said."

"He's not lying," Bragi said. "Hallbjorn Deer's Bane. I know him from old. Drank a fair amount of his ale."

"Bragi," Hallbjorn said, nodding to him. "Not too late for you to pay me what you owe me for that."

"Seems I've lost my purse," Bragi said. "But once I find it, I'll settle with you, to be sure."

Hallbjorn ignored him, turned back to Odd. "Good to meet you at last. It was me who first got the news of your father coming back. It gives the people hope, I can tell you."

Odd frowned. He looked as if he did not understand Hallbjorn's words. "My father coming back?" he said.

Hallbjorn opened his mouth, but he was so surprised by this that no words came at first. Then he found his voice.

"By all the gods, you haven't heard?"

Chapter Twenty-One

The horsemen of the sea
could well have waited
for other sea-skiers
to pile rocks over me.

Egil's Saga

Thorgrim's men managed to wrestle *Sea Hammer*'s awning — an old sail they'd recruited for that duty — up and over the lowered yard, just as the rain started blowing in. They hauled the corners out to the sides of the ship and lashed them tight, then lashed down the edge of the cloth. At the windward end of the makeshift tent, flaps that reached down to the deck were secured to block the wind. The awning twisted and bucked, as if fighting against the restraints.

"Let's get out of this," Thorgrim said to Gyda. He led her forward, under the flogging cover. It felt suddenly calm there, despite the awning's mad thrashing. Thorgrim guided her over to one of the sea chests and gestured for her to sit.

"Are you all right?" he asked. She seemed a bit stunned, her eyes still wide, her mouth partially open. She looked up at him, looked around, looked back at him. She nodded.

"Sit for a moment," he said. "Just sit and catch your breath. That was not much fun."

Gyda gave a weak smile. "No," she agreed.

Thorgrim made his way forward, where a handful of his men were just finishing the lashings on the awning. Others were setting the oars back on the gallows overhead, and straightening out the jumble of gear that had been tossed around during their chaotic ride through the surf.

"Looks like we're here for some time," he said to the men in general. "Hard to say how long it'll be before this blows itself out, but my guess is, it won't be soon. So once everything's put to rights, break out some food and drink."

"Say, Lord," Ulf said. "That…ah…that was a good job. Getting us through the surf like that." He sounded almost apologetic for saying it. The other men mumbled their concurrence.

"Thank you," Thorgrim said. "You men broke your backs at the oars. That's what brought us safe here." He took a deep breath. They sounded like a gaggle of women praising one another's weaving, talking like that, and he was ready to be done with it, so he changed the subject.

"I'm going to go check on the other ships, make sure they fared as well as we did," he said.

"I'll go," Hall said, quickly. The wind was making the awning balloon out, then collapse again, then flog like a pennant. The rain was loud as it beat down. Hall cleared his throat. "Please, Lord Thorgrim. Let me go."

It was a request, but it sounded more like a statement, which Thorgrim found irritating. He understood that Hall spoke with the best intentions, that he wanted to spare his captain the exertion of climbing on and off the ships in that terrible storm. He found that irritating, too.

He looked around. Men were watching expectantly. Some were nodding their heads.

"Oh, very well," Thorgrim said, exasperated. He turned to Hall. "See if there's any damage to the other ships, see if they're in need of help. Tell them to hunker down for the time being, and tell the masters that we'll gather when the storm has blown through."

Hall nodded and ducked out from under the awning, and Onund and Vali joined him. Once they were gone, Thorgrim returned to Gyda and sat down beside her. She was looking considerably better now.

"What was that all about?" she asked, nodding toward where Thorgrim had been addressing the men.

"That? Oh, my men. They treat me like I'm their feeble old grandfather."

Gyda smiled, something Thorgrim had not seen her do since she poured a bucket of salt water over him. "They care about you. They love you."

"Love me? I think not."

"Oh, yes," Gyda said. "I can see it. You may not be an easy one to love, but I think it's possible."

Thorgrim grunted. He did not agree, but he did not care to argue the point.

The storm raged on, and the men of *Sea Hammer* remained huddled under cover. Someone managed to get a small fire going in an iron pot, which was enough to partially illuminate the inside of the tent, but not enough to cook, so they ate cold, dried fish, and bread, and cheese, and washed it down with the ale they had stowed aboard in Ribe.

Their meal finished, some leaned against the side of the ship and slept, and some gamed, and some tended to weapons or carved pieces of wood or bone. Hall and the others returned, as wet as if they had jumped into the sea. They reported that all was well with the other ships, beyond a few broken rudders and oars. *Fox* was so far up on the sand that it was going to take a lot of effort to get her floating again, but other than that, the ships and men were intact.

The storm continued, unabated, all through the daylight hours, and did not ease as darkness fell. One by one the men drifted off to sleep, laying furs and blankets down on whatever patch of deck they could find. Only the middle third of the ship was covered by the awning, and the men were crowded in. Still, a wide area aft was reserved for Thorgrim alone. Whether that was out of respect, or out of fear of sleeping near him lest one of his wolf dreams come, he did not know or care. He was just happy to have the room.

He opened his sea chest and pulled out a sheepskin blanket and a bear skin that was starting to show signs of hard use, and laid them out on the deck. He looked over at Gyda who was sitting on a sea chest nearby. He wondered if he would have to invite her to join him, but he could see by her face, softly illuminated by the low fire, that he would not.

He took Iron-tooth out of the chest and laid it down beside the bed, then took off his belt and shoes and lay down himself. Gyda came over to him and removed the cloak she wore around her shoulders and lay down beside him, her back pressed to his chest.

"Is that all right?" she asked, her voice nearly a whisper. "Does that hurt your wound?"

"No," Thorgrim said. "No, that's fine."

He put his arm around her waist and pulled her a bit tighter against him, and she grabbed the edge of the sheepskin and pulled it over them, then rested her hand on his. Thorgrim breathed in the smell of her, reveled in the warmth of her body pressed against him. He had not felt this sensation, bedded down aboard his ship, a woman drawn close, since Failend had left to go back to her own people.

Failend…

She was much smaller than Gyda, more bird-like. It had felt different, holding her close, as if he was wrapping her up in himself. Gyda was more substantial than that, more solid. More of a presence on her own. He doubted that Gyda could match Failend's skill with a bow, but Gyda could wield an iron pan that Failend would have strained to lift with one hand.

He drifted off to sleep with those thoughts tumbling around in his head, and he slept soundly, despite the rain beating on the awning, and the animal howling of the wind.

The gale was still blowing strong when he woke the next morning, the rain still coming down. At some point Gyda had extracted herself from his arms and climbed from their bed. When he opened his eyes she was there, sitting near him on the deck. Beside her, a wooden plate full of bread and cheese, and two cups full of what he guessed was ale.

"Good morrow," Gyda said.

"Good morrow."

"It's still raining," Gyda said.

"I can hear that. If it was in my power to make it stop, I would."

"I'm sure you would." She handed him a cup and he drank, gratefully. He was very thirsty.

"We won't put to sea in the rain?" Gyda asked.

"If it was just the rain, then yes, we would," Thorgrim said. "But the wind's still westerly, and blowing like it means to kill us. I doubt we could even push the ships off the beach in this, never mind row against it."

Gyda took a drink from her cup. Her eyes never left him. "I'm sorry," she said. "You're worried, I know."

"Hmm," Thorgrim said. He would not have said *worried*, but he could see how she might think that.

"Tell me about your home," Gyda said. "What's it like?"

Thorgrim gave a bit of a smile and stared off into the gloom of the tent and let his thoughts wend their way back to the sprawling farm at the foot of the hills in Vik. He thought of it often, more so in the past few seasons, and sometimes he wondered if his memories were true, or if, in his long absence, he had created them in his mind.

"My home?" Thorgrim said. "There are rolling fields that run off to the mountains in the north. There's a great hall with a roof of wooden shingles, room for a hundred men. Warm, even in the winter, when fires are blazing in the hearths. Good, fertile fields. We grow barley, oats. Onions and carrots. Sheep, pigs, cows."

"It sounds nice."

"It is. It's very nice." Thorgrim was getting wistful, despite himself. "The farm was given to me by my father, when I was a young man. My father was named Ulf of the Battle Song. A great warrior. The farm wasn't much then, just a small farmhouse and some other buildings. About a dozen acres. It wasn't my father's home, he'd been given it by someone. I forget who. Anyway, I wasn't much interested in farming then. I was young, and fighting and raiding was all that interested me. I went off a'viking for a number of seasons. Got decently rich from it. Built the farmhouse into a proper hall, bought more land.

"Then I started raiding again with Ornolf the Restless, and he was a great one for that, I can tell you. We made our fortunes. When we got back after the third year I married Ornolf's daughter, Hallbera. We moved to the farm, built the hall even bigger. Put up more buildings, got servants and farm hands and thralls."

"You didn't go a'viking again?" Gyda asked.

"No. I was done with that. And I came to love farming, to tell the truth. We had four children. My son Odd, that I'm trying to get back to, who's in some trouble now. A daughter, Hild. My son Harald, who you know. And another daughter, we named Hallbera, after her mother. My wife died giving birth to her. The girl lived, but my wife died."

Gyda nodded. She did not speak.

"After that, Ornolf asked if I'd go raiding with him again. I never had any intention of going a'viking again, but…I could hardly think. I was grieving. Odd was married and off on his own. So was Hild. Harald was eager to fight and raid, like a man should. I left little Hallbera with Odd and sailed away."

They were quiet for a long moment. Thorgrim could not recall the last time he had spoken so many words at once.

"But now you're ready to go home?" Gyda asked.

"Yes. If Odd needs my help, nothing will stop my returning. But I pray to the gods that I can help Odd and then go back to my farm in peace and never leave again." He smiled at Gyda. "You'll be happy there."

"Did you ask me to come to your farm because you want me to, or because you feel responsible for me losing my home?" Gyda asked.

Thorgrim had never considered that question. There had been little time, and he was not much given to introspection in any event. He tended to act as his spirit told him to act, and for more than four decades that had served him pretty well.

But now, with Gyda asking him outright, he did consider it. And he did not know. And he would not lie to Gyda.

"I don't know," he said. "Asking you was the right thing to do. I just felt it." He paused, tried to read her expression, but he could not. "You will be happy there," he said again. "And if you're not, I swear I'll help you find a place where you are."

Gyda took a deep breath and exhaled. "That's fair," she said.

They finished their breakfast and Thorgrim found his heavy wool cape in his sea chest, wrapped it around himself, then patiently endured Gyda's adjusting it. He ducked out the back of the tent and made his way to *Sea Hammer*'s afterdeck. The wind was still howling, and the cape beat at his legs, and strands of his hair pulled free of the leather thong that bound it and whipped out to leeward. He stepped up onto the afterdeck, bracing himself with a hand on the sheer strake.

Thorgrim had set a watch, which he changed frequently, so that no one had to suffer long in that weather. Just then a man named Oleif was taking the duty. He nodded his greeting and stepped aside as Thorgrim came up on the afterdeck. Thorgrim nodded back and looked around.

The seas were huge as they rolled in from the west, great heaps of gray water marching off to the horizon. They curled over white as they closed with the land, and then flung themselves at the beach, exploding in a welter of water and foam and spray. They surged up the sand, breaking around the six stranded ships as if they were outcroppings on a rock-strewn shore.

What he had said to Gyda was absolutely correct. There would be no getting the ships out to sea through that.

He turned his gaze from the surf to the vessels run up on the sand off his larboard side. Like *Sea Hammer*, they were bow-out, pointing into the wind and seas, and had awnings rigged over their yards. All save for *Fox*, which was sideways to the surf and farther up on the sand. Each wave that rushed under her hull lifted it a bit and made it rock, and Thorgrim figured it must be giving the men aboard an uncomfortable time.

He frowned as he watched the small ship getting knocked around by the waves. He could not blame Hardbein — landing stern-first was a difficult maneuver to pull off in those conditions. It was surprising that *Fox* was the only one of the fleet that had gotten sideways in the surf. But this would mean a lot of effort, and a lot of time wasted, getting her floating again, and he was not happy about it.

He turned and looked off to starboard. *Blood Hawk* was the closest ship to him, about a hundred feet away. Thorgrim could make out the hulking shape of Gudrid, her master, on the afterdeck, apparently doing the same thing he was. Thorgrim lifted an arm in greeting and Gudrid did as well. Neither of them tried to yell over the wind.

The next ship past *Blood Hawk* was the one belonging to Eyvind Bjarnason. He did not know its name, and he had never taken a very good look at it. He looked now, as much as he could with *Blood Hawk* in the way, and what he could see impressed him. She had an elegant, sweeping bow that rose up and curled over to terminate in a figurehead of some beast, a dragon or a serpent or some such, that stared defiantly out to sea. The hull came down in a long, pleasing sweep until it was lost from sight behind Gudrid's ship. The mast looked freshly oiled, though it was hard to tell in the rain, and the rigging was taut and black with tar.

Nice, Thorgrim thought. *Now, how does Eyvind come by such a ship?*

Thorgrim knew almost nothing about Eyvind, other than Odd had supposedly sent him to hunt them down in Ribe, with a message concerning their return. There was a great deal more to discover.

He looked past Eyvind's ship to the others beyond, a line of vessels drawn up on the beach and hunkered down in the foul weather. He could see some figures moving about on the decks, but not with much enthusiasm. Beyond that, as far as Thorgrim could tell, the men of the fleet might have been the last people on earth. He turned to Olief.

"Have you seen anything?"

"No, Lord Thorgrim. Men on the other ships show themselves sometimes. Haven't seen anything moving on shore."

"Good. Keep a sharp watch. I'll see you're relieved soon."

He ducked back under the awning, happy to be free of the wind and spray, not happy at all to confirm they were stuck on the beach for the near future, and nothing they could do about it.

The rest of the day was spent much like the day before, the men eating, drinking, gaming, sleeping. Thorgrim could see they were getting restless, which was never a good thing. He was feeling restless and irritable himself. He figured they had one more day of inactivity at best before things started to get ugly.

Time dragged by, and finally, when the sun went down and the fire in the iron pot gave off only enough light to differentiate men from gear or barrels, Thorgrim and Gyda headed off to sleep, curled up on the bear skin, pressed close. Their shared warmth was a comfort in that comfortless place. Once again Thorgrim reveled in the way Gyda fit against him, like parts of a ship crafted to perfectly interlock. He let that feeling, and the smell of her hair and her skin, envelop him.

By the time he woke to the early morning light, she was up and had fetched breakfast. Again. He could tell from the sound and movement of the awning that the wind had dropped considerably, and he could tell from the buffeting of the ship that the seas had not. It was what he had expected, that the wind would die away much quicker than the waves. It was the way of such thing.

No matter. There was work to do, and now it could be done.

Chapter Twenty-Two

"I have had no evening meal, nor will I do so until I join Freyja. I know no better course of action than my father's. I do not want to live after my father and brother are dead."

Egil's Saga

Odd Thorgrimson looked around the low, flat, scrubby island on which his tent, and dozens of others, were pitched. Things had changed, that much was clear.

They had come there as the first of the storm began lashing the coast and driving spitting rain before it. The seas started to build as they crawled northeast along the rocky shore, so that Odd feared for the men in the faerings. But they were expert boat handlers, and seemed to hardly notice the rollers moving in from the open water.

By the time they were tucked in behind the island, with the boats and the two captured longships safely beached, the rain had started to come down in earnest. They struggled to heft the tents ashore and set them up, and haul up barrels of dried fish and ale, enough for a few days at least, and then they hunkered down to wait it out.

Odd had set guards at various points around the island, and when the weather permitted, sent men to the mainland to keep a watch there. He did it because he knew it was foolish to not take that simple precaution. He did not think anyone was likely to attack them in that weather. And he was right. No one came.

For nearly two days the renegade fishermen and Odd and his folks remained huddled in place, venturing out only to take their watches on guard duty, to find food or drink, or to relieve themselves. Odd and Signy shared a tent with Amundi and Alfdis; tight quarters but good company, and the crowding offered a modicum of warmth. They talked when they could, though it was not easy with the constant hammering of the rain, and the wind making the canvas flog. Mostly they slept.

Two days, and then the rain let up, and the folk, like animals emerging from their dens with the first inkling of spring, came crawling out. The sky was still gray and low, but the rain had become more of a heavy mist than a genuine downfall. Some of the tents were tilting at strange angles, their stakes unable to hold in the soft ground. Here and there around the island, pools of water stood like a chain of miniature lakes where the thin soil covering the granite could absorb no more.

A few of the women had had the foresight to collect firewood when they first came to the island, and they had kept it under cover, and now it was dry enough that they were able to start a blaze in a firepit that the fishermen dug near the center of camp. The mounting fire was one of the most welcome things Odd had ever seen, and the others felt the same, judging by how quickly they congregated around it. Iron pots were hung from tripods and porridge set to cook. Benches were hauled up from the longships and set around the fire pit.

Odd and Amundi and Ragi, Arnor and Bragi Shipslayer and a few others sat on the benches, stared into the flames, and began the first tentative discussion of the question that was on everyone's mind: what now?

There were, of course, many opinions. None seemed to meet with universal acclaim.

They were not long into that discussion when Odd saw the two guards he had earlier sent ashore approaching, and with them, two men he did not know. Hallbjorn and Storolf, it turned out, come from Fevik. Not young men, but not as old as, say, Amundi either. Men who had seen hard use in their younger days. Odd could see that on their faces.

He did not know what to make of them. Were they who they claimed to be? Or Halfdan's spies? Or something else entirely? But Bragi knew them, and they knew Bragi, which at least meant they were genuinely folk from Fevik. And Hallbjorn seemed to not care much for Bragi, so that, too, was in his favor.

Then Hallbjorn spoke the words that made the earth shift under Odd's feet: *It was me who first got the news of your father coming back.*

At first, Odd could hardly make sense of what the man was saying. He asked Hallbjorn something — he could not recall what. Something foolish. He saw the surprise on Hallbjorn's face, incredulous that Odd had not heard. Thorgrim Night Wolf was coming home.

Odd invited Hallbjorn and Storolf over to the fire, cleared some spots on the benches for them, called for cups of ale to be brought over. In front of the other men they told their story, about how Bergthor Skeggjason had returned to Fevik after having sailed with Thorgrim in Engla-land. How Bergthor said with certainty that Thorgrim was on his way back to East Agder, how his only thought was to return home. How he was in command of six ships and more than three hundred hardened warriors.

Odd could only listen and try to get his thoughts organized. It was Amundi who asked the first question.

"Bergthor last saw Thorgrim and his men in Engla-land?" he asked. "How long ago?"

"Not sure, exactly," Hallbjorn said. "Mid-summer?"

"Hmm," Amundi said, and Odd was sure they were all thinking the same thing he was: why was Thorgrim not there yet? Hallbjorn seemed to have read their thoughts.

"Bergthor said Thorgrim and his fleet were bound for Frankia first, something about sailing in company with men from Wessex." He took a drink of his ale, looked around. "Wherever he is, he better get back here fast, or there won't be anything to come back to," he continued, and from there he proceeded to tell them about the fate that had befallen Fevik, the sacking of the town, Skorri setting himself up in Ornolf's great hall.

"Skorri Thorbrandsson," Ragi said. "May crows eat his liver. I thought he died going over the cliff after burning my hall."

"That bastard's too mean to die, I suspect," Amundi said.

Odd felt sick as he took it all in, sick in the pit of his stomach. His thoughts were trying to swim in this flood of information, and they were going under. He found himself wishing that his father was there just then. He was sure that these considerations were beyond his poor powers, but Thorgrim Night Wolf would know what to do.

He shook his head, trying to drive those thoughts away. Hallbjorn saw the gesture, misinterpreted it.

"I know," he said. "Too terrible to think about. I don't know what's actually going on, what Skorri is doing. I can't see how Halfdan told him to do any of this, to set himself up like a jarl in Ornolf's great hall. And I have to wonder, could Halfdan really be such a son of a bitch that he'd give his men leave to sack Fevik?" Now Hallbjorn shook his head.

"Don't know," Ragi said. "Halfdan's surprised us before, with how much of a son of a bitch he can be."

"That's right," Amundi said. "We saw what Halfdan did to Odd, when Odd was his prisoner. Doesn't seem to be much limit to what he's willing to do to hang on to power."

The discussion turned then to Hallbjorn and Storolf, and how they had managed to get out of Fevik and find Odd's camp. About how, if they could find Odd's camp, it was possible that Skorri could as well. About just how precarious their position was.

"We can run, or we can fight," Odd said at last. "And running accomplishes nothing, beyond keeping us alive a bit longer."

"I don't reckon the fishermen even have that choice," Arnor said. "If we just go back to our fishing grounds, I don't think Halfdan's going to forget what we did to his longship anytime soon."

"Skorri's got hundreds of men. Trained men," Bragi said. "Now, me, I'm worth at least a hundred men in a fight, but even so I don't reckon we have anything like as many men as he does. Or their weapons. Or their skills."

"There's men in Fevik," Hallbjorn said. "Men out in the country. Some experienced raiders, some warriors. All of them ready to stand up to Skorri. That's why we came here to find you."

"There's men in Fevik," Odd said, "but they're trapped in Fevik."

"Maybe," Hallbjorn said. "Maybe not. We got out. Others could, too."

"People know people," Storolf said. "You know that, Odd. You live in these parts. Word will spread. It's spreading already. Like the rumor that it was you who took Halfdan's ships, which turned out to be true. Those rumors gave people hope, made them want to fight back. So did the rumor that your father was on his way home."

There was silence for a moment, then Odd said, "If we're going to be strong enough to fight Skorri, we need to be together, a single army," he said. "Us, the men in Fevik, the men in the countryside. Gathered together. Do you think you could get back into Fevik, encourage others to slip out? Get word out into the country?"

Hallbjorn and Storolf looked at one another. "Right now?" Hallbjorn asked. "We've been walking all night, and we're not young men."

"Tonight? After some sleep and a good meal?"

The two men exchanged glances again. Hallbjorn shrugged. "Why not? If we drop dead in our tracks, that will save us from having to worry about any of this."

They left a few hours before sunset — Hallbjorn and Storolf and a few of Arnor's men who were nimble trackers and hunters. The weather had turned decent over the course of the day, the mist drying up, the sky turning from gray to white, and the cloud cover finally breaking apart to reveal the blue sky hidden behind.

The next day was the same, the storm just a memory, and the world growing dry under the warming sun. And that meant the time to hunker down under shelter was over, and the time to turn the rabble into an army had begun.

"These fishermen, they're as tough as old leather, but they've got no training," Ragi said, when the discussion of how to confront Halfdan was taken up again.

"So we should train them," Odd said. "You should do it, Ragi. You and your men. You're the most experienced fighters here. You should turn them into warriors."

"Training will keep them busy. Give them hope," Amundi said. "Worst thing is for these men to be sitting around the camp with no work to do."

Ragi looked skeptical. Quite skeptical. Odd could see the protest forming in his mind, and disappearing just as quickly. "Very well. I'll do what I can."

They gathered the fishermen, and Ragi and his warriors demonstrated the use of the weapons they had. Next, they divided the nascent army up into companies and began working with those smaller groups and their assorted swords and axes and spears and shields. The fishermen were not much experienced with weapons, that was true, but neither were they completely unskilled and hopeless. Odd felt a vague sense of encouragement as he watched them, and he could see on the faces of the others that he was not alone.

They kept at it all through the afternoon hours, until the sun started sinking into the west and the fire was stoked up against the coming night. They ate náttmál, coarse oat bread and bowls of the fishermen's beloved fish stew. The conversation around the camp was reduced to the murmured talk of tired men, and soon they were off to their beds.

Odd was not long behind. He stepped into his tent, suddenly aware of how tired he was. He unstrapped Blood-letter and set the sword down beside his bed. Amundi and Alfdis were already asleep. Odd could hear their soft, rhythmic breathing.

Signy was at the far end of the tent, kneeling, a small pot of herbs smoldering on the ground in front of her, a bronze statue of Freyja in front of that. She was saying prayers, softly, and the smell of the burning herbs filled the tent.

Odd untied his shoes and pulled them off, then lay down on the fur and pulled the blankets over his legs. He was nearly asleep when Signy lay down beside him and slipped her legs under the covers and pressed herself against him.

"What do you say, husband?" she asked in a soft voice.

"I say…I don't know what to say."

"What will you do?"

"I don't know that either."

"Hmm," Signy said. Odd did not think she would ask further questions, and he was right. Soon she was asleep, and soon after that sleep came for him as well.

He woke sometime later — he did not know how much later — to the sound of someone just outside the tent. His hand came down on Blood-letter's hilt and he sat up, eyes open, mind alert.

"Odd?"

Odd paused for a moment, waited, but there was nothing else.

"Yes?"

The flap of the tent was pulled aside. Thorlak, one of the fishermen, was standing there in a crouch, a lantern in his hand. "Something's happened," he said.

Odd stood, stepped out of the tent. He expected to find Thorlak in a near panic, come to report that some disaster was unfolding. Instead, Thorlak looked a bit confused.

"I'd just come off watch ashore," he said, nodding in the general direction of the point of land west of the island. "We'd changed over and were just about back here when…some people showed up."

"People?"

"They said they were from Fevik, and from the country around. Men, mostly. They had weapons. They said they'd come to join us."

"I see," Odd said. "Did you bring them back with you?"

"No," Thorlak said. "Couldn't. There were dozens. And they said more was coming."

Chapter Twenty-Three

That's also the case with the one whom you mistrust
and whose disposition you suspect:
you must laugh with him and mince the truth;
there should be like repayment for gifts.

The Sayings of Hávi

Thorgrim and Gyda ate their breakfast, and by the time they were finished, all of the men aboard *Sea Hammer* were moving about. Thorgrim stood, and he felt a surge of strength such as he had not felt in a while, as if his blood was pumping harder, his muscles taut again. Two days of forced rest, and Gyda's ministrations, seemed to have done him considerable good.

"Listen here," he called down the deck. "Have your breakfasts, then meet me out on the beach. Bring any shovels, picks, anything like that that we have on board. There's work to be done." He saw a few heads nodding, but not much reaction beyond that.

He turned to Gyda. "Would you like to go down on the beach?"

"Well, I've come to love this awning so much, and the smell of all these men packed together, I hate to leave it. But maybe some fresh air will do me good."

They ducked out the aft end of the tent and looked around. The cloud cover had broken up and there were patches of blue sky to be seen through masses of white and gray. The wind was still blowing, but it was closer to a breeze than a gale. The waves, too, were less ominous than they had been, but they were still rolling in, tall as the tallest man, and crashing down on the beach, keeping the ships pinned where they were.

Gyda stood beside him, her arm linked through his. She looked out at the surf, and the waves flinging themselves against the sand. She looked, if not frightened, then at least concerned.

"Will you try to get the ships out through that?" she asked.

"No," Thorgrim said. "That surf's too big. We'd be thrown back on the beach before we could get clear."

"So we're stuck here still?"

"I figure the seas will keep settling down as the day goes on, but then the tide will be out. High tide tomorrow, I think that'll be our chance." He found his frustration growing even as he said the words.

"I see," Gyda said. "I'm sorry."

They climbed down off the side of the ship, and Thorgrim took more care than was his habit to see that he did not open up his wound again, because he knew Gyda was scrutinizing him. He helped her down, and together they walked up the sloping sand, away from the surf, the first time they had been off of *Sea Hammer* in two days. Up and down the beach, men were climbing down off the other ships, checking how deep in the sand their vessels were stuck, looking to see if they had sustained any damage in coming ashore.

I'll leave them here, Thorgrim thought. *If any of these ships aren't fit for sea, I'll leave them behind, let them make repairs and catch up.* He was done waiting.

Soon the men from *Sea Hammer* were following Thorgrim and Gyda off the ship, milling about on the sand. Some carried shovels, some picks, and some other tools they thought might help. Thorgrim sent a few of his men off with orders for the other ships' captains to arm their men with shovels and send them over.

When all the crews had gathered, Thorgrim named off two dozen men to arm themselves for a fight and take a position on the high, grassy bank that marked the juncture of beach and open country beyond. He had not forgotten the ugly surprise they received before reaching Ribe, in a situation much like this, and he did not intend to let that happen again.

Once those men were off, he addressed the rest of the crews.

"Listen here!" he called, and the buzz of conversation dropped away. Men were leaning on shovels, or standing with arms folded. Some were already sitting on the sand. Two days of idleness had done them no good.

"Wind's backed off," Thorgrim continued, "and I reckon that the surf will settle down enough by high tide tomorrow morning for us to get through. I mean to be underway then. So you need to get your ships ready for sea. Check if there's any obvious damage. But first we need to get *Fox* to a place where she'll swim again. So half of you, go dig out under the bow, and half dig out under the stern, and we'll see if we can pivot her around and get her pointed right."

He stopped. Looked around. No one moved, as if they were waiting for more.

"Go!" he shouted, and that got them moving, though not quite as quickly as he would have liked. They lifted shovels and picks and wandered off toward *Fox*, still high and dry.

"Harald, come here," Thorgrim called, waving his son over. He hated to do it. Harald seemed to be the only one moving with any degree of enthusiasm, but he handed his shovel to another man and hurried over.

"Yes, father?"

Thorgrim turned so he was facing the sea, and Harald did as well. "I haven't had a chance to talk to you about this," Thorgrim said. "But what do you think of this Eyvind Bjarnason?"

"Eyvind? The one who showed up in Ribe? That Odd sent?"

"Yes. What do you think of him? His story?"

"Well, it's a good thing he found us. If Odd's in trouble, needs our help, then it's good he's here to tell us that. A fellow we know from back home."

Thorgrim nodded. Harald wasn't telling him what he thought, he was telling him what he thought his father wanted to hear. Agreeing with him, without saying as much. And why wouldn't he? Had Thorgrim ever asked Harald for his true opinion?

"Harald," he started over again. He met Harald's eyes with an unwavering stare, and he was happy to see Harald returned it with his own. "I'm asking you as warrior. And as a man I trust. What do you think of Eyvind Bjarnason?"

"I think there's something not right about him," Harald said. "All of the words that come out of his mouth sound right, but they don't feel right."

Thorgrim nodded. "He had the arm ring."

"He did," Harald said. "And it was Odd's, there's no doubt about it. And he and his men did show up to fight with us. Honestly, if they hadn't, I think we would have been killed. And that makes it hard for me to say it, but I still have my doubts about him."

Thorgrim made a grunting sound of agreement.

"The other captains, they seem ready to take him at his word," Harald continued, as if he was trying to talk himself out of his own opinion.

"They do," Thorgrim said. "That's why I wanted to ask you alone."

They were quiet for a moment, looking out at the sea, the rollers that marched their way toward the shore. "He's got a fine-looking ship," Harald added. "I'll give him that."

"Yes…yes, he does," Thorgrim said, and that was another thing that was nagging at him. "What do you make of his owning such a ship?"

"Well…" Harald said, drawing the word out as he searched for an answer to that open question. "A man would need some wealth to own a ship like that. Maybe Eyvind Bjarnason's a wealthy jarl. Rich as a king. I don't know anything about him. But we've met him before, in that hunting party we were all in together, so he has to live not too far from our farm. Or at least he did once. Knows Amundi."

They fell silent again, and Thorgrim waited for Harald to take the next step in his thinking. "A man that rich, who lived in Vik," Harald said at last, "I'd think we'd have heard more of him."

Thorgrim smiled. He enjoyed watching Harald muddle through and reach his conclusion. And even narrate the process.

"I think you're right," Thorgrim said. "Another riddle."

"So, what do you mean to do, father?"

"I don't know, son," Thorgrim admitted. "I haven't decided yet. I hope the gods will give me a hint."

He turned around to check on how the work on *Fox* was progressing. The ship was a hundred yards away, and it took Thorgrim a moment to understand what he was seeing. Men sitting. Men leaning on tools. Maybe a third of them taking desultory stabs at shoveling. Thorgrim squinted and frowned and felt his fury rising like water boiling over the sides of a pot.

"Father, let me…" Harald started in, but Thorgrim was moving before he could finish, walking as quickly as he could through the soft sand. He would have run, but in his current condition he was not sure he could cover that distance, and he did not need to be heaving for breath when he got there. He would need his lungs.

A man from Halldor's crew, leaning on his shovel, watching the work taking place, had the bad luck to be the first man Thorgrim reached. He turned at the sound of Thorgrim's steps and opened his mouth to speak, but Thorgrim was on him by then. He grabbed the man by the arm and spun him back around and planted a shoe in the small of his back. With a push of his leg he sent the man sprawling onto the sand, and shouted, loud enough to be heard up and down the beach.

"What do you think you're doing, standing here with your head up your ass? Son of a bitch!"

He looked around. Now no one was working. They were frozen in place, staring at him. But his violence toward that one fellow had not been cathartic, it had not dissipated his fury. Rather, he felt all the anxiety, and frustration, and anger at being thwarted again and again in his quest to get back home come flooding in, overshooting the bank, sweeping away all in front of him. He could hardly see, he was so angry. The red rage, normally reserved for battle, was on him now.

"Every one of you sons of bitches, start digging now!" he shouted, advancing toward the men closer to the ship. "If you don't have shovels, dig with your hands, and you best be doing it before I reach you!"

Those words were like a bow-string released, the men like an arrow. The ones gathered at the bow and stern began furiously digging, flinging sand over their shoulders like spray from pounding surf. Those not digging ran and stumbled and regained their footing and ran some more to get in on the effort. Fore and aft they clawed at the sand under *Fox*'s either end.

"Dig, you bastards!" Thorgrim shouted. It took every bit of self-control to stop himself from grabbing the nearest man and beating him bloody. Had he seen any man giving less than everything he had, that would have been his fate.

"Enough!" Thorgrim shouted a few moments later. "Hold up!" They had dug deep enough by Thorgrim's guess to turn the ship on its keel. "Starboard bow! Push! Larboard stern! Push!" The men struggled to find their places at the ship's sides. A few climbed aboard and found ropes and made them fast and tossed them down to eager hands below.

"Heave!" Thorgrim shouted. "Heave, you miserable bastards, heave!"

A collective sound of effort rose up from the sand as the men pushed on bow and stern and heaved on the ropes. They leaned against the hull and dug feet in the sand and pushed for all they were worth, and slowly, foot by foot, *Fox* pivoted around.

"Heave!"

Men fell as they lost their footing, and shuffled forward as the ship swung beyond their reach. Thorgrim watched the ship turn and waited for his anger to abate, but it did not, not in the least.

"That's well!" he shouted. The men stopped pushing and they looked at him, mouths open, red-faced, breathing hard, but Thorgrim was not ready to let up, not for a moment.

"Everyone to the stern! We're going to push this whore's son down to the water. Get those ropes led forward, and every man had better have his hands on a rope or the hull or by all the gods he'll lose them both!"

The men rushed off to find their places, pushing at *Fox*'s aft end, or heaving on one of the lines run off her bow. It was ridiculous to think that even that many men could push the ship through soft sand, but no one dared point that out.

"There's a beitass onboard *Fox!* Get it down here!" Thorgrim shouted. Half a dozen men clambered aboard and hefted the beitass — a twenty-five-foot pole, big around as a small tree — out and over the side.

"Jam that in under the bow, athwartships! There's a beitass on every one of these ships, I need men to go get them! Now! Go, go!"

Handfuls of men raced off to carry that order out. The rest braced themselves against *Fox*, or tailed onto the ropes.

"Heave! Heave!" Thorgrim shouted. The men pushed, digging in their feet and straining at the ropes.

"Heave!" Inch by agonizing inch *Fox* crept forward, her keel and hull dragging through the sand. The bow rode up on the beitass as the ship was pulled forward, lifting it a bit, leaving less of her hull in contact with the sand.

"*Heave*!" The ship moved a bit more that time, six inches, a foot. They pulled again and it moved even farther. Each foot of keel that passed over the beitass lifted more of the ship from the sand. A gang of men arrived from *Blood Hawk,* carrying her beitass between them, and Thorgrim had them lay it just under *Fox*'s bow, and told the others to heave again.

With a slow, jerking motion, the ship slid down the beach, moving faster as more of her keel rode on the smooth wooden spars, rather than dragging through the sand, until at last she was entirely up and out of the beach's grip.

"Get that last beitass, move it around to the bow!" Thorgrim shouted, and hands lifted the first spar, now astern of the ship, and shifted it around until it was first again.

After that, it did not take long to move the ship the rest of the way to the surf. The men gave up the drag ropes as the bow reached the water, and all hands went aft to push from the stern, heaving until they were up to their thighs in the water, the seas rushing in around them.

"That's well!" Thorgrim called. *Fox*'s bow was all but floating now. "Get her secured. Get the beitasses back to their ships. See to your own vessels."

The men hurried off in various directions, none of them daring to seem anything less than eager to obey. "Harald!" Thorgrim called, and his son, who was hurrying back toward *Dragon*, stopped and hurried back.

"We'll be underway soon," Thorgrim said, when Harald was in front of him. "After that, I won't have a chance to speak to the other captains before we make landfall again. So I need you to give them my instructions. Each one, on his own. And privately. All but Eyvind."

"Yes, father."

Thorgrim gave Harald his instructions, had the boy repeat them back, and then sent him off. That done, he turned and walked off, up the beach, toward the dunes. His anger had turned to something beyond anger, a stew of exhaustion and determination and resolve. He was done now. Done with everything. He was going home.

Chapter Twenty-Four

She saw a hall standing far from the sun, on Nástrond,
the doors face north;
venom-drops fell in through the roof-vent;
that hall is wound with the spines of snakes.

The Prophecy of the Seeress

It was Skorri's habit to rise just before dawn. It had been his habit for so long that he needed no servants or rooster to wake him, regardless of the time of year. He just came awake. But that morning he did not.

When he did finally wake up, he did so instantly, and he did so in a state of great confusion. Wherever he was, it was dark. Completely dark, so that he could make out no details. He was lying on a mattress that was softer than any he could recall sleeping on. The air smelled strange, like flowers. He was naked, and there was someone pressed against him. A woman, he guessed, from the size of her body and the smoothness of her skin.

Then it all came back to him, and with it, a vague sense of regret. What he had experienced the night before was behind him now, and he doubted he would ever find it again. If he had just died in his sleep, passed on to the next world, the same way he had fallen into that profound slumber, would that have been so terrible?

A man like me does not die in bed, he reminded himself.

He lifted his head a bit. The room was not, in fact, completely dark. He could see thin lines of light leaking in around an imperfectly fitted door. He could hear sounds on the other side of the door. Nothing alarming. Servants talking. Some work taking place: cooking or cleaning or washing. Servants' work. He could hear louder voices farther off.

Gunnhild stirred and propped herself up on one elbow. Skorri could just make out her outline and a hint of her features in the weak light.

"My Lord," she said, in a throaty voice, half awake.

"Get your dress on and go fetch a lamp," Skorri said.

"Yes, Lord," Gunnhild said. She climbed off the bed, then walked around the other side and felt on the floor for her dress. Skorri could just barely make her out as she pulled the dress on over her head, like a moving shadow in the dark. A moment later she opened the door, just a crack, just enough for Skorri to catch a glimpse of her and that end of the bedchamber, and then she closed it behind her.

Skorri lay down again and stared up into the dark, and in his mind he was back at the feast, watching over the festivities from the high seat on the dais. And then Gunnhild was soothing his wounds with the damp cloth, and he could feel her smooth skin pressed against his body, battered and abused. He sighed a deep sigh.

A few moments later Gunnhild was back, a lit oil lamp in hand. Most of the candles in the candle holders had melted down to nubs, but she lit the ones she could. Skorri swung his feet over the edge of the bed. He stood and felt his head swim. He steadied himself against the bed for a moment, until everything settled.

"What part of the day is it?" he asked.

"Dagmál, lord. Mid-dagmál."

"Help me dress," he said. He did not really need any help, he just enjoyed having Gunnhild tend to him, relished the feel of her hands on his body.

Gunnhild knelt down and picked up his trousers. She held them open and he stepped into them and she adjusted the legs so they were not twisted. Then she found his shirt and tunic and helped ease them over his head. Skorri held his arms out as she tugged the cloth into place and smoothed it out.

The morning was cool, so Skorri called for his cloak. Finally, he strapped his sword belt around his waist.

"Go see to my breakfast," he said, then stepped out of the room and into the great hall. He paused and looked around, assessing the state of things. The damage wrought by the night's feasting had been set to rights, the remnants of food cleaned up, the cups and wooden platters and such cleared away. Clusters of men were sitting at the long tables, eating or gaming or tending to weapons.

The servants and thralls were bustling around, working hard enough to avoid a rebuke or a kick, but no more. If any of them objected to having a new master, they knew enough to keep it to themselves. Such was the survival instinct of servants and thralls.

Skorri did not worry about any sort of uprising among them, not when he had five hundred warriors with him. Even if he had just five warriors with him he would not have worried about it. He did, however, wonder if any of the servants had managed to slip away in the night. If so, where might they go?

Would they run off and join with Odd? Would they know how to find him?

Servants and thralls sometimes knew these things, these secret places and hidden knowledge. How, Skorri did not understand. Word seemed to drift through the air like a scent, one only the lower sort could smell.

The last Skorri had seen of Odd and his followers and their fleet of boats and two stolen ships, they had disappeared from sight around the headland southeast of Fevik. Where they were now, he had no idea. He did not think they had gone very far. The storm would have kept them ashore. Besides, Odd's people were here. The fight was here.

At some point he would have to hunt them down. But not just yet.

He walked down the length of the great hall, back toward the dais and the high seat, the visual and spiritual center of the building. It was still raining outside, and raining hard. He could hear it. Koll came hurrying up to him as he walked.

"Lord Skorri, good morrow," he said, falling in beside him. "You're well this morning?"

"Yes," Skorri said. He guessed that was true enough.

"I've sent men to patrol the grounds here, make sure none of the people are up to any mischief," Koll said. "It doesn't seem Ornolf kept warriors in his household at all, not that I've seen."

"Ornolf would have taken his men with him. And no one would swear an oath to his miserable wife. She's probably too cheap to take on any fighting men who'd work for silver. And why would she need warriors? They're under the king's protection here."

"Exactly, Lord," Koll agreed, and continued on with his report. "I sent others to check on the storerooms, see how much food and drink is here. Also to collect up anything of value, so that it doesn't wander off."

"Good," Skorri said. They had reached the dais and Skorri stopped there, but did not step up.

"What orders do you have today, Lord?" Koll asked.

Skorri was not sure how to answer. He had been thinking quite a bit about all that had happened thus far, but he had not really considered what he would do next.

Before, in Grømstad, he had it all worked out. His plan had been to take Fevik, where he was sure he would find Odd Thorgrimson and the rest of his band. Five hundred warriors, coming in by land and sea; they would scoop the traitors up, fish in a net. Then he would return to Halfdan with the prisoners in chains, and receive the reward that was coming to him.

But it had not worked out that way. And his failure, ironically, was not because he was wrong, or that he was too late. It was because he was too early. He had been right about Odd going to Fevik, but Skorri and his men had arrived in Fevik before Odd and the rest. He had realized that while watching Odd's attack on *War Hammer*. If not for Thorgeir's idiocy in leaving *Dragon's Claw* behind, Odd might still have stumbled into Fevik, into Skorri's eager arms.

Instead, Odd and whoever was with him — and it was not just Amundi and Ragi Oleifsson and his men now, there had to be hundreds more — had captured the stranded *Dragon's Claw* and discovered Skorri's plan. And then they had used *Dragon's Claw* to capture *War Hammer* as well.

Now Skorri held Fevik, but Odd was gone again, slipped through his hands like an eel. They would have to start all over, hunting him down, luring him out, doing battle. It was tiresome just thinking about it.

Skorri looked around the great hall. The fires were roaring in the hearths on the floor, the flames leaping and twisting four feet above the logs burning there. At a second hearth, where the flames burned lower over a deep bed of coals, a pig was already turning on a spit, the savory smell of its roasting flesh filling the room. He could see Gunnhild approaching from the far end, a platter in one hand, a chalice in the other.

"Send a company of men to Fevik to relieve the guard there," he said to Koll. "The men who're relieved can return here and refresh themselves. Keep guards posted around the compound, and on the walls, so we have no surprises. But see that they're relieved often. No need for any to stand out long in this miserable weather."

"Yes, lord," Koll said. "Will that be all?" He looked a bit uncertain. Surprised, even, as if he expected more. By reputation alone he probably thought Skorri would send warriors out scouring the countryside, plundering all the farms nearby in search of the rebels, a relentless quest to bring Odd and the rest to bay. He probably figured Skorri would lead the search himself.

And not so long ago, he would have been right. Skorri had driven himself nearly to madness hunting Odd. But he no longer felt so driven, so motivated. Not with the rain coming down and the food and drink and warmth of the great hall to enjoy. And Gunnhild.

"Yes, that will be all. The men who aren't on watch are free to pass their time in the hall as they wish. The servants will attend to them."

Koll hesitated, just a heartbeat, and then said, "Yes, Lord." He turned and walked off just as Gunnhild arrived.

"There," Skorri said, pointing to the table in front of the high seat. Gunnhild nodded, stepped up on the dais, and laid his breakfast down. He ate, then spent time in conversation with some of the other captains, and ordered Gunnhild bring him warm, mulled wine. When Koll returned from Fevik, after relieving the men there, and after he had dried himself by the fire, Skorri questioned him as to the state of things.

"It's quiet, lord. The folk are going about their business. The rain keeps them in. They don't seem happy to have your men there, but they know better than to say anything. Or do anything."

"Good," Skorri said. "What of Thorgeir?"

"Just sitting on his ass. Nothing to do. His ships are tied up and his crews are idle. He does send men to help keep the peace in town, but that's about it."

"Very well," Skorri said.

"One thing, Lord." Koll's tone suggested he had something to say that Skorri would not like. "My men have tried to keep anyone from coming into the town, or leaving, as you told them to. But we have only a hundred men at Fevik, and it's hard to guard every way in or out, especially at night. My men think there are some slipping away. They're sure of it, in fact. They've chased some, but couldn't catch them. The people, they know the country around here, and my men don't."

"Yes, of course," Skorri said. Koll might think this would make him mad, but it didn't, because he had already reckoned on its happening. "It's no surprise folk should slip away. They're cowards, and weak. And I don't much care. But their homes are in Fevik. Where could they be going?"

"I don't know, Lord," Koll said. "Maybe just trying to get away from the king's warriors. Live in the woods. Maybe they have people in other villages."

"Maybe…" Skorri said. His thoughts went back to his earlier musings, wondering if the servants here in Ornolf's compound were slipping off, finding their way to Odd's camp, wherever that might be. He had thought it likely. For the folk in Fevik to run off and join Odd was more likely still. These local folk, they were Odd's people. Word of Odd's hiding place might filter into the town, and they would know how to find it.

"You say your men chased some of these traitorous curs who were sneaking out of Fevik?"

"Yes, Lord, but they lost them, and they dared not get too far afield."

"Do you have hunters among your men? Men who are good at tracking? Following game?"

"Yes, lord. A few."

"Good. We can make use of them."

They discussed a few more matters, none too pressing, then Koll went off to attend to the men, and Skorri spent a leisurely day eating, drinking, conversing with some of the warriors, who seemed to be enjoying Ornolf's bounty as much as he was. He could not recall the last time he had spent a day in such a manner. He liked it, he had to admit.

That night they feasted again. When things began to quiet down, Skorri led Gunnhild back to his bedchamber, and again had her undress him and tend to his wounds. After she had finished with that, he told her to remove her own clothing. He watched her as she did so, and considered having her do more this time than just lay at his side, considered using her the way the gods meant for a man to use such a woman.

But in the end he did not. Rather, he contented himself with having her pressed up against him, and relished the sensation of her smooth flesh on his weary body. And once again he slept, deep and untroubled.

The next day proceeded much the same, with the rain coming down in torrents. The weather did not clear until the day after that, the rain tapering off to nothing, the dark gray sky becoming light gray, then white, then breaking up like ice on a spring-time fjord. The sun came out and glinted off all the wet world, and Skorri decided he would ride to Fevik and see for himself what was going on. He called for his horse to be made ready, for Koll to join him, and to assemble a ten-man guard to accompany them.

Soon they were underway, riding through the gate in the earthen wall and down the muddy road to the town. The countryside was newborn, wet with the rain and bright with the sun. They could hear birds and insects where, for the past few days, there had been only the monotonous beating of the rain. The air smelled clean and heavy, the sun warming and drying the cool, soaked earth.

They rode slowly over the few miles downhill to Fevik. Soon they could see the ocean off in the distance, the long bay that led out to open water, and then the steep thatched roofs of the town. As the ground leveled out a quarter mile from the edge of the village, Skorri could see that there were guards on the roads, guards out in the fields that surrounded the town, guards presumably in the few stands of trees that stood like islands in the grass here and there. That pleased him.

They continued on, and the guards parted and smiled and held weapons up in salute as Skorri rode past. They came into the town, where the people seemed to be emerging from their homes like animals coming out of hibernation, blinking in the sun and starting the work of cleaning up. Soaked clothes and bedding were hanging out to dry. Some of the wood and canvas lash-ups that had served as shelters over smiths' forges or woodworkers' benches had blown down in the wind and the rain, and now folks were fishing them out of the mud and setting them up again. Others were up on roofs, replacing the thatch that the storm had pried free.

They stopped and stared at Skorri and Koll and the guard as they rode past, their expressions neutral but their hatred evident. It troubled Skorri not in the least.

And where are the able men of the town? Skorri wondered. He could see women, he could see children and old folk, but there seemed to be few men of fighting age. Skorri did not wonder too much, however. He had a pretty good idea of where they were.

Skorri and his men came at last to the waterfront. Thorgeir's ships remained tied to the dock, their crews busy on board, bailing out the copious water that the sky had dumped in the bilges, setting up rigging, and letting their soaked sails hang from the yards to dry in the sun.

Thorgeir himself was on the dock, walking slowly beside Ingolf as they inspected the ships. He stopped when he saw Skorri, and waited for Skorri to come to him. He made no sign of greeting, said nothing as Skorri approached.

"Lord Skorri," he said at last.

Lord Skorri, Skorri thought. *He fears me now, after losing two ships.*

Skorri looked at Thorgeir, then turned away. He looked over the ship tied up to his left, and then the one to his right. There was no damage that he could see. He turned back to Thorgeir.

"Are you ready to get underway?"

"Once the ships are bailed out and the rigging set to rights."

Skorri nodded. Thorgeir waited for him to say more, but he did not, so after a moment Thorgeir said, "Will we be going to sea? We've been sitting on our asses for days now. At least we have here in Fevik. I understand you've been having a grand time of it in Ornolf the Restless's great hall. Drinking, feasting, and whatnot."

"What I do is none of your concern."

"Catching the traitors is my concern, and we don't seem to be doing much of that. King Halfdan gave you five hundred men. He didn't give them to you just so you could take your pleasure in some great hall that you seem to think is your own."

Skorri's eyebrows came together and he frowned. He did not expect such boldness from Thorgeir, and he did not care for it. If he kept this up, Thorgeir's time among the living might be shorter than he expected.

"Bold words for a man who's lost two of the king's ships without a single thing to show for it," Skorri said. "But see here, you can bleat away about this or that. It doesn't matter to me. All I care about is that you have your ships and men ready to go. And I mean ready to go in an instant. The very moment I send word."

That seemed to get Thorgeir's attention, to rouse his curiosity. "And why is that? Is there something in the wind?"

"Soon, perhaps. You just be ready."

That was all that Skorri meant to tell Thorgeir, and it was as much as Thorgeir needed to know. But there were indeed things in the wind, plans resolving in Skorri's mind, pieces moving around the gaming board. Thanks to the trackers among Koll's men, Skorri Thorbrandsson now knew where Odd Thorgrimson and his band of traitors could be found. And he was ready to act.

Chapter Twenty-Five

Then all the great powers, the most holy gods,
went to their doom-seats and deliberated about it:
whether the Æsir must pay a great penalty,
or all the gods must have offerings.

The Prophecy of the Seeress

Magnificent…magnificent, Halfdan thought.

His head turned slowly right to left as he tracked Valkyrie, his gyrfalcon, soaring high above the walls of his massive compound at Grømstad. The hawk appeared as little more than a small, dark, fast-moving shape against the blue sky. To anyone else, she would be indistinguishable from any other bird of prey. But Halfdan Gudrødson could certainly tell a gyrfalcon from any of its lesser brethren, and he could tell Valkyrie from any other gyrfalcon.

He held the thin rope of the lure in his right hand, and twirled it in a slow, wide, vertical circle. He gave no thought to the effort. He had been luring flying falcons for thirty years. His eyes and his mind were on the bird as she made her deadly patrol of the perimeter of the compound. He turned with her as she circled around, and he knew her eyes were on the lure and she was waiting for her moment to strike, that perfect synchronization of man and bird, each focused on achieving one goal: the meeting of talon and leather lure in midair.

Valkyrie turned and her wings came in and she began her dive, moving faster, perhaps, than any other living thing on earth could move. One more turn of the lure and Halfdan let it fly, paying the line out through his fingers, the leather bag soaring up and away from him. His eyes were on the bird and he could see that once again the timing was flawless, their coordination impeccable.

Valkyrie's wings flared as she slowed, just a bit, her unstoppable attack, and her talons hit the leather bag with an audible thud. Bird and lure landed on the grass, the gyrfalcon perched on top of her prey, and she let out a squawk of triumph.

"Well done! Well done!" Halfdan said. A servant was standing behind him, holding a bowl with chunks of raw meat. He handed one to Halfdan and Halfdan held it up between gloved thumb and forefinger. Valkyrie immediately abandoned the lifeless lure and flew to the king's leather-clad arm and settled there. For a moment her wings beat at the back of Halfdan's head, then she folded them in and eagerly grabbed the meat in her dagger-sharp yellow and black beak.

It was only in the past few days that he had felt his tension ease, his restlessness abate. Before that, the rain had come down like the gods meant to drown the world, the wind had torn and buffeted all that it touched, and Halfdan had been cooped up in the great hall, just him and his servants and the handful of jarls and such who happened to be in Grømstad, paying homage or taxes.

The weather broke in the night, and the following morning Halfdan had stepped out into the sunshine and looked around the grounds, the glistening world, and felt in his gut that something was not right. Things did not look the way they usually looked. It took him a few moments to realize what it was. The place was practically deserted.

Generally, the grounds were all but overrun with warriors: his hird, and the men who made up the bulk of his army, and the crews of his longships. There was never a time that they were all there, of course; men had to be sent to this place or that to enforce the king's laws and his peace. Men were garrisoned in smaller fortifications scattered around the kingdom to which Halfdan laid claim. But that still left a lot of men, who would generally be busy exercising with weapons or training horses or polishing swords or mail, or attending to any of the many other things that occupied a warrior's day when he was not doing battle.

But now, a few servants were moving around, a smith's hammer was ringing out, a handful of guards were walking the top of the walls, and beyond that, nothing.

It made sense, of course. Halfdan had sent five hundred men off with Skorri and Thorgeir to hunt down Odd Thorgrimson, to finish that business once and for all. And then, when word reached him that Thorgrim Night Wolf himself might be on his way back, he had sent another five hundred south to lay a trap for him and his raiders. Now, between those two armies sent off, and the other men scattered around various posts in the kingdom, there were very few warriors still in residence at Grømstad.

And that meant he had room to fly his gyrfalcon. This was the only time that Halfdan could recall flying Valkyrie, or any bird, within the walls of his compound. Normally, with all those men, all that activity, there was too much distraction. To go hawking he would have to assemble a guard and servants and ride out to the open fields beyond the walls. But now, for once, there was no need for all that fuss, and for the past few days he and his bird had enjoyed the relative peace of the open grounds.

He reached his left hand behind him for another piece of meat, and when the servant pressed it into his palm he fed it to Valkyrie, who gobbled it down.

"You're getting fat," Halfdan said. "Soon you won't be able to get off the ground." He felt calm, his mind felt at ease, for the first time in a long time. Man and bird: he loved this above all things. It made him happy. And that in turn made him anxious, sure that something was going to come along and ruin it all.

"Shall we have another go at this?" he asked the bird. He started to lower his arm, to toss Valkyrie into the air, when he saw his overseer, Grim Grimsson, hurrying toward him. He was moving with a determination that suggested something was wrong, which meant it was almost certainly something that was going to ruin his mood.

There was someone else as well, walking behind Grim. Halfdan could not see for certain who it was, but he had an idea it was Thorgeir Sveinsson, which meant things were likely very bad indeed. Thorgeir would not have dared abandon his task in Fevik otherwise, not even for the single day it would take him to get to Grømstad and back.

"King Halfdan, my lord!" Grim called as he and the other one approached. Halfdan watched them for a moment. Yes, it was most certainly Thorgeir following behind.

He waited until they were a dozen feet away, then said, "Hold there!" The two men stopped in their tracks and Halfdan launched the bird into the air. He watched her fly as he coiled the lure's rope in his hand, ignoring the men who had come to speak with him. It was a petty thing to do, and counterproductive, but he could not help himself.

Grim and Thorgeir stood silently as Valkyrie once again made her great circle around the compound and Halfdan drew her back in with the lure. She hit the bag with the same exquisite timing she had displayed before, but for Halfdan, the joy was out of it now. He felt only irritation as the bird flew to his arm and accepted a chunk of venison.

"What is it?" he said at last, turning to the two men.

"Lord Halfdan, Thorgeir's come back from Fevik, with news of Skorri and his hunt for Odd Thorgrimson. And I fear it's…it's…"

"A mess?" Halfdan supplied. "A pathetic mess?"

"Well, I suppose…" Grim stammered.

"Of course it is. What else could I expect?" Halfdan snapped. "It's what I get for sending traitors and incompetents to do the job." He wondered if there would ever be just one day when he didn't have to undo someone else's disaster. He was starting to wonder if he was a king or a nursemaid.

For a moment neither Grim nor Thorgeir made reply. The servant stepped closer and set a tall perch beside Halfdan, and Halfdan held Valkyrie up and let her step on to it. The bird only weighed three pounds, but even that grew heavy after a while. He turned back to the men.

"Well, what's the nature of this mess?" Halfdan snapped.

Grim half turned and made a small gesture for Thorgeir to take over, feeling, no doubt, that he did not care to endure Halfdan's wrath for something that was Thorgeir's business. Halfdan could see Thorgeir visibly gathering his nerve to address his king.

"My lord, the problem, I fear, is Skorri Thorbrandsson," Thorgeir began.

Yes, of course it is, Halfdan thought. *The traitor, not the incompetent. Never your fault, which is why you've come running to tell tales.*

"And what is the problem with Skorri Thorbrandsson?" Halfdan asked.

"He's turned on you, I fear," Thorgeir said. "Again. Once again he had Odd in the palm of his hand and he let him go. Odd and his gang of traitors. They were hiding in Fevik, just as you thought they would be. I sailed my fleet there directly, the way we had planned. If Skorri had marched there as well we would have had them all. But instead he spent a day and a night sacking Thorgrim Night Wolf's farm. Which is your farm, now."

Halfdan stared at Thorgeir, wondering at the truth of this. Thorgeir was warming up, his speech coming with more confidence, and Halfdan had to guess there was some kernel of truth to his words. How much was the question.

"After he was done with Thorgrim's farm, he became like a dog that's tasted blood. He took Ornolf the Restless's great hall, and let his men sack that, too. When he finally bothered to bring his warriors to Fevik, he let them plunder it as if it was a Frankish village, and not one of your majesty's possessions. By then Odd had slipped away. Worse, Odd and his rebels attacked one of my ships, and when I tried to send more ships to crush him, Skorri stopped me. He insisted just one ship be sent, and so of course Odd managed to capture that one as well."

Halfdan felt his eyes narrow. "You've lost two ships? Odd has taken two of my ships?"

"We would have lost none, Lord, and we would have taken Odd and his men as well, were it not for Skorri. I don't know what Skorri's playing at, but I don't think it's for your benefit."

For a moment Halfdan did not respond. There was clearly more to this than Thorgeir was letting on. He had lost two ships, and so he had hurried to Grømstad to make his excuses before Skorri could tell his version of the tale. But that did not mean that everything Thorgeir said was a lie.

"The last I heard, Odd had just a handful of men," Halfdan said. The situation was becoming clearer to him. "A dozen at most. And now he took two of my ships. He did not do that with a dozen men."

"No, Lord," Thorgeir said. "There seem to be more who have rallied to Odd."

"More? Enough to take two ships manned with my finest warriors?"

"Yes, Lord, so it seems," Thorgeir said. Then, apparently realizing, correctly, that this was the last thing Halfdan would care to hear, he added, "This might have all been prevented if Skorri had acted as you wished."

"Where are Odd and these… followers now?" Halfdan asked.

"We don't know, Lord. Run off to the east, the last we saw. Skorri has done nothing to hunt them down. He's set himself up in Ornolf's hall, and he's living there like he's some grand jarl. Or perhaps he thinks he's king. He seems to have no interest in hunting for Odd."

"And you've done nothing either?"

"Other than argue with Skorri about how we should be following your orders? No, Lord. I'm subordinate to him. There's nothing I can do without his permission."

Halfdan frowned. Thorgeir was getting bold now. He knew he should stamp that ember out, but he had more important things to consider. How much of a problem was this? Had Skorri genuinely gone rogue, or was Thorgeir setting him up to be knocked down?

He needed time to think. There were too many factors, too many unknowns.

It had all seemed fairly straightforward at first, but that was how these things usually went. Halfdan had felt confident that Skorri would do as he was told, and do it well, once he had brought the man to heel. Skorri Thorbrandsson was nothing if not dogged. And he was not stupid.

But he was ambitious, and that could be a problem. Once, Skorri had seen service to his king as the fastest way to achieve his ambitions. But perhaps the man had changed his mind.

Thorgeir, of course, was ambitious as well, and jealous of Skorri, because he knew that everyone considered Skorri the better man. That was why Halfdan had put them together. They would keep each other in check. Two forces opposing one another.

Yes, it had seemed quite straightforward. And then, out of nowhere, word that Thorgrim Night Wolf might appear over the horizon, with six ships and hundreds of warriors, and suddenly Halfdan had another threat to consider.

He had worked out a plan: one of his captains, Eyvind Bjarnason, knew Thorgrim, but not well. Not enough to have any loyalty to the man, but enough that Thorgrim might genuinely believe that he had been sent by Odd to search for him. The arm ring Halfdan had taken from Odd when Odd was his prisoner would give the story a nice shine of believability.

Send Eyvind off to find Thorgrim, have him convince Thorgrim to sail to a small harbor to the south, ostensibly to meet up with Odd, but in fact to meet up with five hundred of Halfdan's best warriors. It was a good plan. If it worked.

But would it? Would Eyvind find Thorgrim? Would Thorgrim believe him, and sail blindly into a trap? As Halfdan was waiting to find out, five hundred of his best men were sitting on their asses, eating Halfdan's food, collecting their pay, doing nothing, possibly for no reason, when they could be sent to deal with Odd, and now Skorri, run amok.

Halfdan needed time to think.

"I'll speak with Skorri and discover the truth of this," he said to the two men who had been waiting, silent and increasingly nervous. "Thorgeir, you return to Fevik and tell Skorri that it's my command he return here tomorrow to give me the particulars of what's going on. Grim, you go with him, and you find out what exactly is taking place there in Fevik."

"Me, Lord?" Grim said. He looked on the verge of panic.

"Yes, you. Return here with Skorri tomorrow. I need to know the truth of this matter." He looked at Thorgeir, daring the man to argue, but Thorgeir was wise enough to keep his mouth shut.

For a moment no one moved. "Do you two need to crawl through the gauntlet to get you moving?" Halfdan asked. The two men bowed, turned, and hurried off as quickly as they could, while still maintaining a bit of dignity.

Over Halfdan's shoulder, Valkyrie squawked for another piece of meat.

Chapter Twenty-Six

Almost nothing is worse
for the burner of shields
the spender of sea-fire,
than to be versed in evil.

Gisli Sursson's Saga

We have to move, Odd thought. *This won't do. We have to move.*

He was standing at the southwestern end of the island that had been their home for nearly a week now, on the edge of the flat ground that sloped gradually down toward the gravel beach below. He was looking out at the mainland beyond, the wide bay, the point of land where his guards were stationed, the rolling green hills beyond. He could not see it, but just a few miles beyond that point of land was Fevik, and the beleaguered people there, and Skorri Thorbrandsson's army.

The camp with its firepit and circle of tents was a few hundred yards behind him. Beyond that were the open fields where Ragi and his men were putting the fishermen through their drills. Odd could hear them perfectly well: the clash of steel on steel, steel and iron on wooden shields, men calling orders, others grunting and shouting with the effort of mock battle.

They were doing well, Odd thought. He could see the men's skills improving, the way they handled their weapons, the way they moved together, fighting as units, like warriors in formation and not like sailors in a tavern brawl.

Still, they lacked a great deal by way of weapons and armor, and they lacked experience. The only shields or mail or helmets they had, and most of the swords, were what they had taken from the crews of the two longships they captured. It was fine equipment, but it was only enough to outfit about six score men.

As to experience, the fishermen were certainly not strangers to conflict. Theirs was a hard life, which often involved fighting, and not just with wind and waves and nets. But that sort of brawling — fists and knives and whatever else came to hand — was something quite different from actual battle.

Odd, of course, was no expert in such things either, and he was well and painfully aware of that fact. He was a farmer by trade, not a warrior.

As the son of Thorgrim Night Wolf, grandson of Ulf of the Battle Song and Ornolf the Restless, he had been raised to weapons and fighting: sword and shield, battle axe, seax, spear, fist. Over the past year and more he had gained experience leading men in every sort of fighting, from surprise attacks with a handful of warriors to open combat against hundreds. Fighting on foot, fighting mounted, fighting on shipboard, he had done it all. And he still felt like a fraud.

Deep down, unspoken, even to Signy, he felt sure that at any moment the others would realize that he was in no way qualified to lead them in this fight. And then what? Would it all collapse? Would Halfdan have all of East Agder and beyond under his heel?

Odd had no idea. And he could think of nothing to do but keep plowing on, and hope that he did not make too much of a hash out of it all.

And that was what he was doing, standing on that point of land, looking out over the mainland. Plowing on. Trying to imagine what the next step might be.

An army was gathering around him, an army big enough to matter. Just a few nights before, Thorlak had come to tell him that men had arrived from Fevik, and since then they had continued to arrive. About thirty that first night, seventy the next. Another seventy or eighty after that. And still they appeared, even during the daylight hours. The fishermen brought them over in their boats, housed them where they could, got them drilling with Ragi and his men.

But they were too many for the island. There were not enough tents or food for everyone. And they were vulnerable there, should Skorri or Halfdan ever discover where they were.

We've got to move, Odd thought again. But where? Were they ready now to take the fight to Skorri and his men? The uncertainty was driving him to madness.

And then he heard his father's voice, clear as a bell ringing out at first light.

Don't hesitate…

Odd stood up straighter, and despite himself he looked to his left and his right, as if he might see Thorgrim standing there, but of course he did not. Still, he heard his father speaking, the words coming to him through the fog of years.

Don't hesitate when making a decision. It might be the wrong one in the end. But when you're leading men, a wrong decision is better than no decision.

They had been on a hunting party, a dozen men and Odd and his brother Harald, hunting a wolf pack that had decimated local herds. Thorgrim had organized the thing, but at the last moment had left it to Odd to decide how they would approach the wolves' lair: divide the men up, come on all at once? From what direction? And Odd had been torn, unable to decide.

Don't hesitate. That was what his father had told him. Odd could not recall what decision he had made. But in the end they had two men slightly wounded, and a dozen wolves dead.

The words, as he considered them now, brought with them a profound sense of relief. It was not the uncertainty that was tearing at him, it was his unwillingness to decide. It was his need to find the perfect solution, and to be certain that everyone else agreed. But he could not wait for those things to happen, because they never would. He understood that now.

Odd smiled, something he had not done in a long time. He smiled, and he knew, once again, that the old man was right. He could not hesitate, not anymore. Time to move.

That was when he saw the boat.

It was one of the fishermen's boats, one of the faerings, he was fairly certain, pulling away from the point of land on the near shore. Nothing terribly unusual about that, but still it caught his eye, and made him wonder who it was in the boat. It might have been the sentries coming back, but Odd was fairly certain that they had just relieved the watch not long ago. It may have been more refugees from Fevik or the lands around, but Odd had not seen any boats going over to pick them up.

He walked slowly along the shore, watching the boat approach. The distance between the island and the mainland was not far, and soon Odd could see that there were two men at the oars, and they seemed to be wearing mail, which meant they were probably the sentries. There were also two other men in the stern of the boat, and one in the bow, and they, too, seemed to be wearing mail and helmets, which meant Odd had no idea who they could be.

When the boat finally ground up on the beach, near where the other boats were pulled up, Odd was standing on the top of the low bluff above. He had been right: the men at the oars were the sentries, in their mail. The other three were indeed wearing mail as well, and two wore helmets. All five men stepped out of the boat at once and waded ashore. The two men wearing helmets had swords drawn.

What by all the gods? Odd wondered. He heard a bell ringing out a warning in his head, but faintly, and he ignored it. Mostly he was curious as to what these idiots were about. If they meant to kill the sentries they could have done that long before they reached the shore. If they meant to attack the folk on the island, they were a bit outnumbered.

The two sentries led the way up the now well-worn path, up toward where Odd was waiting, and as they approached Odd felt a spark of recognition. The big man, last in line. No helmet, no sword in hand. A thick, blond beard and a tangle of blond hair, like seaweed clinging to a rock. Odd felt sure that he knew the man, but he was still too far off to tell for certain.

He stayed where he was, watching, as they came up the path. They were still fifty feet away when Odd finally realized who it was, and the recognition increased his confusion and surprise fivefold. He squinted, and tried to make sense of what he was seeing. He tried to think of how he should react to this, but he was too taken by surprise for thoughts to coalesce.

The sentries approached, their expressions more apologetic than anything. They had no weapons, the scabbards that had once held swords and seaxes were empty.

"Odd, we're sorry about this…" the one on the left stammered, but Odd paid him no attention. His eyes were on the man behind him.

They stopped where they were, the five men looking at Odd, Odd looking at the five men. Odd spoke first.

"Skorri Thorbrandsson," he said. "I'll own I didn't expect to see you."

Skorri looked Odd up and down. At first he seemed unsure as to who he was looking at, but then he nodded and said, "Odd Thorgrimson. You've lost weight."

"I have," Odd agreed. They were silent for a moment, then Odd spoke again. "Tell me why I shouldn't kill you, right here and now."

Skorri shrugged. "You could try. Mind you, if I'm not back at Ornolf's great hall by sundown, then your grandmother and all her people will be burned alive. There's one reason. The other is, I suspect you're curious as to what I have to say."

They were good reasons, Odd had to admit. The first was not an empty threat. He knew Skorri was perfectly capable of having his captives put to the torch, and would only regret that he was not there to watch. And, to be honest, Skorri's second reason was valid as well: Odd was indeed curious as to what he had to say.

"Very well," Odd said, "we'll hear you out before we kill you. You can sheath your swords," he said to Skorri's men. He turned to the sentries.

"You two, where are your weapons?"

The two men glanced at one another, glanced at the ground, then looked up at Odd. "Bottom of the boat," one said.

"I see," Odd said. "Well, get back to your post, and see that no one else sneaks up on you like these three seem to have done." He turned to Skorri and his two guards. "Come with me."

He turned and walked back toward the camp and the fire ring at its center. The fishermen and the men from Fevik were still out in the field, drilling, and Odd knew that Skorri's eyes were everywhere, taking in the number of men, the weapons they had, their skill at using them. Whatever reasons Skorri had for coming to the island, spying was certainly one of them.

Odd had considered not letting Skorri come any closer, but by the time he thought of it he knew it was too late. Skorri had seen enough. Odd did not think Skorri would find what he was seeing at all intimidating.

As he approached the fire ring, Odd beckoned to one of the women. "Pray, go fetch Ragi and Arnor and ask they come here," he said, and the woman nodded and hurried off.

Amundi was sitting on one of the benches by the fire, and he stood as they approached. Odd could see the surprise and confusion on his face.

"Amundi Thorsteinsson," Skorri said. "An old man like you, I would have guessed you'd have dropped dead by now."

"No, I live on," Amundi said. "And I thought we'd seen the last of you going over that cliff. Reckoned you'd been wandering around the underworld all this time."

Skorri looked around, then looked back at Amundi. "I'm not sure I haven't," he said.

How did Skorri find us here? Odd wondered. He considered asking, but then realized that asking would make him look foolish. In any event, dozens of men had been slipping out of Fevik, making their way there. It would not be very difficult for Skorri's men to follow and discover where they were going. From the mainland they could see the longships pulled up on the beach, the array of tents on the flat, all but treeless island.

"Men have been leaving Fevik, coming to join us," Odd said instead. "And that means you've been letting them escape the town."

"Hmm," Skorri said, by way of acknowledgement. "Well, I suppose every one of these miserable bastards who comes here is someone you have to feed and I don't have to guard." He nodded toward the men out in the field, and gave an ironic smile. "But I see you're turning them into a formidable army, so maybe that was my mistake."

The jibe struck home, and Odd felt a flash of anger, which he struggled to keep from his face. Before he could think of a reply, Ragi and Arnor approached, with Bragi Shipslayer, who had not been invited, following behind.

"Well, look at what some seagull has shit out on our island," Ragi said, as he looked Skorri up and down. There was no humor in his words. "I may have to shove your head in that fire there, to thank you for burning down my hall."

"Forgive me," Skorri said, "that was your hall? I thought it was some dilapidated barn. And I fear you were no match for me even before you became an old cripple."

"I still have one hand," Ragi said. "And that's enough to rip your heart out and eat it in front of you."

"Well, this is great fun, this talk, I must say," Bragi Shipslayer said. "Now, I'm guessing you all know each other?"

"This is Skorri Thorbrandsson," Odd said.

"Ah, yes! King Halfdan's lickspittle!" Bragi said. "His little toad! Yes, I've heard of you!"

"No doubt," Skorri said. "Now, if we're done with pleasantries, I'll tell you why I came here alone, to talk. Instead of with my army."

"Go ahead," Odd said. It was, of course, the thing he most wondered about.

Skorri looked around at the assembled men, and his expression seemed to change, just a bit, the haughtiness seeming to dissipate. "I've been Halfdan's man for some time, that's certainly true. I've done his bidding, made sure the tribute kept flowing. I've seen what he's done to his own people. I was the instrument of a lot of it."

He looked around as if expecting someone to argue, but no one did. They were listening.

"This whole thing, this *rebellion*, started when Halfdan tried to take Thorgrim's farm," Skorri continued. "He had no right to do that. I know it, you know it. But I stood with him, because I was his man. I stood with him when you men rose up against him, even though I knew you had every right to do what you did."

Ragi turned and spit on the ground. "Do want our sympathy? Do you want our forgiveness? What do you want?"

Skorri looked at him, but did not answer. He turned to Odd. "I'm out here with five hundred men. My men. I've made sure that their loyalty is to me. You must have…what? Another three hundred out there? And more will join you. Between us, we're strong enough that we don't have to do what Halfdan commands. We can force him to strike a bargain. Isn't that what you wanted all along, to stand up to Halfdan and make him see reason? Well, you'll never do it with that mob you have out in the field. But with my men and your men together, the whole countryside rising up to join us, Halfdan will have to listen."

For a long moment, no one spoke. The five men stared at Skorri, and Skorri, in turn, looked from one to the other. It was quiet. The men in the field had stopped drilling.

"You want us to join you?" Odd said. "Or you join us? Against Halfdan?" It was so extraordinary and unexpected he had to be certain he had heard correctly.

"Yes," Skorri said.

"And you expect us to trust you?" Amundi asked.

"No," Skorri said. "But I'm willing to give myself up as a hostage. If you agree to join with me, I'll give myself up to you. You can kill me at the first sign of betrayal."

This was followed by another moment of stunned silence. Then Ragi asked, "Why would you do this?"

"As I said, I can see what Halfdan's become. I don't want any part of it. And, to be honest, I don't see any other way I'll ever be free of him. But if we stand together, you'll show Halfdan that freemen are not to be treated like thralls, and I'll be free to set myself up in my own great hall, with my own army. There would only be one loser, and that would be King Halfdan."

Again, for a long moment, no one spoke. "This is not a decision to be made quickly," Odd said.

"Neither can it wait very long," Skorri said. "If we're to strike at Halfdan, we must do it soon. Before he sees it coming."

"What would you have us do?" Amundi asked.

"Me and my men are at Ornolf's great hall. Send word there. Tell me you'll join with me, and I'll come back and give myself up as your hostage. And then we'll figure how we move on Halfdan."

"If we agree to accept your offer, we'll send word on the morrow," Odd said. "Either way, I expect my grandmother and her people won't be harmed."

"I don't expect I'll have to harm them," Skorri said. "I'll wait for word. Just bear in mind...you can have me as a friend, or as an enemy. And you don't want me as an enemy." With that he turned and headed back toward the beach, his two guards following behind. Odd and the others just stood there and watched him go.

Finally, Amundi broke the silence. "Well, I did not expect that."

"He's a lying pile of dung," Ragi said. "We'd be fools to trust him."

"Maybe," Bragi Shipslayer said. "Or maybe he's telling the truth. This is the best chance for all of us to be free of Halfdan. He's not wrong about that."

"Odd, what do you say?" Amundi asked.

Odd did not know what to say. In his gut he knew better than to trust Skorri Thorbrandsson. On the other hand, Skorri had been clear that he was acting out of self-interest, and that made his proposal believable. Had he tried to convince them that he wished to join their cause because it was right and just, it would have been an obvious lie.

Also, Odd found himself agreeing with Bragi — if they hoped to force Halfdan into bargaining with them, the addition of Skorri's five hundred trained men would go a long way.

Questions, questions. The sort of questions that Odd could spend days wrestling with, and still not come up with an answer that he would not second guess. But he was not going to do that.

Don't hesitate...

"I say we can't stay here on this island, not one more night. I want things packed up, ready to go. But not so anyone watching from shore could see it being done. We'll take the tents down once it's dark, load everything in the boats and the longships. The tide's dropping now, so take care the boats and ships don't get stranded. Bragi, what will the moon be tonight?"

"Half moon. Should rise just before sundown."

"That'll do," Odd said. "We're underway by early *elding*, once the sun is well down. Come dawn I want to be miles from here."

"That's no easy thing," Amundi said. "All these people, and boats, moving at night? And the longships. Wouldn't it be better to wait until dawn?"

"It would be better if we had that luxury," Odd said. "But we don't. We leave tonight."

He looked around at the other men. They were nodding, ready to follow his lead.

Chapter Twenty-Seven

The fir-tree that stands in a farmstead withers,
neither bark nor needles protect it;
so it is with the man whom no one loves:
how is he to live for long?

The Sayings of Hávi

There were dozens of boats on the beach, and Skorri chose one of the smaller ones for him and his men to take back to the mainland. The two warriors who had accompanied him out to the island were not so pleased to have to row back, he could see that. Not when there were so many of these miserable fishermen around who could easily be forced to take them. But Skorri did not care to waste time hunting anyone down.

They pushed the boat into the water and climbed aboard. The two guards picked up the oars and Skorri took up the tiller. Soon the boat was making way through the short chop, leaving the island in its wake.

"Thoughts?" Skorri asked. His two guards were named Grimar and Aki and they had not been chosen at random. They were favorites of Koll, and since joining Skorri's bodyguard they had proven themselves smart and loyal.

"Bunch of fishermen and comb-makers and carpenters," Grimar said as he pulled the larboard oar. "Did you see them at their drills? What they called their drills? They'll run at the first sight of a real warrior."

"Maybe," Skorri said. "Aki, what do you think?"

"Not much impressed. But there's a lot of them. Near as many as we have, now that we lost the crew from *Dragon's Claw*. And it was the fishermen, most likely, who took *Dragon's Claw*, so they got some balls."

"Hmm," Skorri said. He did not offer his own opinion, but his thoughts were more in line with Aki's. The fishermen might be untrained, but they were not weak or cowardly men. Halfdan had been trying to clear them out of the islands near Grømstad for years, and yet there they were.

They could be useful in battle, Skorri thought. Put them in a line in front of his men — the real warriors — and the fishermen could absorb the first waves of attack. After that, Halfdan's men would have to stumble over their bodies to get at Skorri's. Useful.

Skorri had not been lying to Odd and the others, not entirely. On balance, he did hope they would take him up on his offer to join forces. That would help Skorri clear the path in front of him.

If not, that would be all right as well. He still had three excellent longships and nearly five hundred elite warriors. He could crush Odd, and then force Halfdan to come to some sort of arrangement.

All of these machinations, all the fighting, if it came to that, were all about achieving a single goal: making Skorri Thorbrandsson a powerful jarl, with land enough to provide him a massive income, and men enough to defend it from all comers. Because, after what Halfdan had done to him, and after tasting what it was like to be a powerful man, lodged in a great hall and in command of a powerful army, he had no intention of going back to being Halfdan's lickspittle, his little toad.

There was a time when Skorri had hated Odd Thorgrimson more than any man in Midgard, but he was past that now, his hatred directed elsewhere. Given a choice, he would rather fight with Odd than against him. It would be easier that way. He would prefer that Halfdan's men be killed in battle against the rebels, rather than against his, Skorri's, men. But he would do it with the help of Odd Thorgrimson, or without.

And, of course, there was another consideration: Thorgrim Night Wolf. Skorri had heard the rumors of his return, and while he did not believe them, there was always the possibility that they were true. And if they were, he wanted Thorgrim and his warriors on his side, even more than he wanted Odd.

"We'll see what comes of this," Skorri said by way of an answer. "But don't forget my words. You tell no one where we went, or what we talked about. If there's anyone who needs to know, I'll tell them."

"Yes, Lord Skorri," the two men said in unison.

"Good. Loyalty is rewarded. Rewarded well." He let them guess for themselves what disloyalty earned them. He imagined that they guessed correctly.

The boat ground up on the shore where the two sentries, who they had captured earlier, were standing guard. Pathetic bastards, they had been half asleep and staring off in different directions when Skorri and Grimar and Aki had walked quietly up to them and relieved them of their weapons at sword-point. It was Skorri's first hint as to what he was facing with Odd's rebel army, and he was not impressed.

Grimar and Aki climbed out of the boat and pulled it up onto the gravel, and Skorri climbed out after them. The sentries were alert this time, and had their hands on the hilts of their swords, and Skorri had to smile at that.

"Be calm," he said. "You don't want to draw your weapons, believe me. And don't make us take them from you. Again."

The sentries said nothing, just glared at him.

"I trust our horses are where we left them. If anything's happened to them, it'll go bad for you." Still the sentries did not reply, so Skorri walked past them, up the trail that led into the woods near the shore, Grimar and Aki following behind. A hundred yards in, they came to a clearing where their horses were staked out, just as they had left them. They mounted and rode off south, back the way they had come.

Another quarter mile and they found the rest of the guard, eighteen mounted warriors, though they were not mounted just then. Rather, they were sprawled in the grass, sleeping, or sitting on the ground eating or gaming. They spotted Skorri coming from some ways off, jumped to their feet, gathered their horses, and were in some sort of respectable order by the time he rode up to them.

"All quiet?" Skorri asked one of the guards, a man named Vegeir, whom he had left in command.

"All quiet, Lord Skorri," Vegeir said. "Saw some of the bastards from Fevik sneaking around, but we let them be, as you said."

Skorri nodded. "Good. You can mount up. We're done here."

Vegeir turned and relayed the order and the men swung themselves up into their saddles. Skorri led the way back to Ornolf's great hall — *his* great hall — over open fields, skirting the deep gullies and sundry stands of trees. Off in the distance, here and there, were the small farms of freemen who held no great wealth or influence. They were likely the sorry bastards who had flocked to Odd's banner, hoping to gain some small advantage by upsetting the natural order of things, the order in which men like Skorri Thorbrandsson sat perched at the top of the hierarchy.

The afternoon was wearing into evening when Skorri finally saw the great earthen walls that enclosed his new hall rising up out of the ground. The walls had stood so long they were mostly covered in grass now, and only the wooden palisade on top made them stand out from the green fields around them.

The guards saw them coming, and the big oak gate swung open as they approached, so that they did not have to break stride as they rode through and onto the grounds within. As he led his men toward the stables, Skorri looked for anything out of the ordinary, any sign that something had changed, that some intrigue was afoot. But he saw nothing. Servants were going about their business, guards were walking their patrols, clusters of his men were sitting on benches outside the great hall, drinking, eating, enjoying their spoils.

My men, he thought. *My men*. They would not betray him.

He saw Koll hurrying toward him from the great hall, moving like a man with something of consequence to say, and Skorri felt that little dagger-prick of concern. He climbed down off his horse, and his twenty-man guard did likewise, and they handed the reins to the servants who came for them. Skorri dismissed his men, told them to get food and drink.

"Lord Skorri," Koll said as he approached. "You were successful?"

"Yes," Skorri said. Koll did not actually know what Skorri had been doing that morning, only that it required horses, a guard, and secrecy. And he would not ask, which was one of the reasons Skorri liked Koll.

"Good," Koll said. He nodded toward the great hall. "We have guests."

"Guests? Welcomed guests?"

"Not welcomed by me, and I don't think they'll be welcome by you. Thorgeir and Grim Grimsson. Halfdan's man from Grømstad."

Skorri frowned. This was unwelcome news indeed. Thorgeir was no surprise. He was ostensibly second in command, and would be wondering at Skorri's plans. But Grim's being there meant that Halfdan was involved, that the king was starting to stick his nose into Skorri's business. Skorri knew he would have to reckon with Halfdan eventually, but first he needed to eliminate Odd, either by usurping his ridiculous army or crushing it.

"They're waiting inside?"

"Yes."

Skorri headed off to the great hall, Koll beside him, Grimar and Aki following behind. They stepped into the dim interior, with its now-familiar smells of woodsmoke, and meat cooking on a spit, and ale, and many men. The usual clusters of warriors were sitting at the various long tables, servants were moving busily around, musicians playing softly at the far end of the hall. A couple dozen men, who did not seem to be doing much of anything at all, were seated at one of the tables nearest the center of the hall.

And, on the dais, Thorgeir and Grim. Skorri didn't see them at first. He didn't look toward the dais, because he did not imagine they would have the audacity to seat themselves there. But they had; Thorgeir sitting in the high seat, one leg draped over a carved armrest, Grim half sitting on the table.

Their eyes met, and Thorgeir gave a bit of a smile, and Skorri had the impulse to pull him from the chair and beat him bloody, right then and there. He headed toward the man, not certain what he would do when he reached him. But Thorgeir, sensing the danger, perhaps, stood and stepped down, unwittingly or not saving himself from a beating. Grim followed behind.

Skorri stopped, rested his hand on the pommel of his sword. He realized that the twenty or so men seated nearby were not among the warriors who had taken up residence in the great hall; they were from the crews of the longships. Thorgeir's men, or the closest that Thorgeir had to his own men. Skorri wondered what they might do if it came down to him and Thorgeir.

He turned to the two waiting on him. "Well?"

"You've set yourself up nicely here," Thorgeir said, gesturing toward the great hall in general. "Made yourself at home. Like you think this hall belongs to you."

"I think I'll decide what does or does not belong to me," Skorri said.

"Will you, indeed?" Thorgeir asked. Skorri did not like his tone. It was the tone of a man with a secret that worked to his own benefit.

"Tell me," Thorgeir continued, "what you've done to find Odd and bring him to the king's justice. As I recall, that's why you were sent here, and yet you seem to do nothing about it. You don't even know where Odd and his people are."

"You mean I don't know where they went after they took the second longship from you? Actually, I do. I was speaking with them this very morning."

That news seemed to take the two men aback, and for a moment no one spoke. "You were speaking with Odd this morning?" Grim asked at last.

"Yes."

"To what end?"

"To resolve this whole thing," Skorri said. "To see if we can bring an end to all this without bloodshed. If there's fighting, then Halfdan will most certainly lose men. Surely he would rather not." Skorri was not at all certain why he was explaining this in such reasonable terms. He had already realized that this meeting was unlikely to end well.

Thorgeir laughed, a short and ugly sound. "'Bring an end to this without bloodshed'? You must be joking. There's already been bloodshed. More bloodshed than Halfdan's willing to forgive. The king doesn't just forget wrongs that have been done him. Maybe you remember that. Maybe you remember crawling on hands and knees through the gauntlet while your betters kicked you and spit on you and beat you with their swords."

Skorri clenched his teeth and tried to keep his face expressionless, though he guessed his cheeks were flushing, and that thought made him madder still. No, this most certainly was not going to end well.

"See here," Grim said. He was sounding bolder now. Thorgeir's arrogance had bolstered his confidence, Skorri guessed. "King Halfdan is concerned. He thinks you've lost sight of why you were sent to Fevik. You were charged with finding Odd and putting a stop to this rebellion, not sacking the town and setting yourself up in Ornolf's great hall, like you're jarl of the lands around."

Skorri felt a calm settle over him, a calm that he knew from past experience was the next step beyond rage. "Where do these concerns of Halfdan's come from?" he asked. "How does Halfdan know what's going on here? I've sent no messenger to report to him."

Grim's eyes flicked over at Thorgeir and Thorgeir stood a bit straighter, tried to assume a more imposing look. "You've betrayed your king. Once again. It's clear. As Halfdan's loyal subject, I felt it was my duty to make him aware of that."

Skorri locked eyes with Thorgeir. He felt the rage boiling under the calm. *You filthy worm*, he thought. *You pile of cow dung.*

"So, you crawled off to Halfdan when my back was turned?" Skorri asked.

"Thorgeir did his duty," Grim said. "He did what was right by his king. And now we find you've snuck off to meet with Odd, and the gods alone know what sort of treachery you've planned. I'd say Thorgeir did the right thing. I know Halfdan thinks Thorgeir did the right thing."

Thorgeir half-turned toward the longship men seated at the table. He nodded toward them and they stood and took a few steps toward the center of the great hall. They did not fan out or draw their weapons or do anything else that might imply threat, but still it made Skorri's anger flare anew.

"Halfdan commands that you return to Grømstad and give him an account of what you've been doing," Grim said. His tone was reassuring, as if he was trying to keep a mad dog from biting. "We were sent here to tell you that. The king's not angry, he just wants to be certain that his orders are being followed. He wants to know how you plan to crush Odd and this rebellion."

"Yes," Thorgeir said, his words close to a sneer. "Halfdan would like very much to hear from you. Actually, he insists on it."

And that was it for Skorri — Thorgeir's sneering, taunting tone of voice — the end, the bursting point. There were twenty armed men backing Thorgeir up, and Skorri did not care in the least. He took a step toward Thorgeir, drawing his seax from its sheath as he did. Thorgeir looked confused, as if not certain how seriously to take this threat, and Skorri drove the foot-long blade up into Thorgeir's stomach and under his ribs until the hilt stopped him from driving it up any farther.

Thorgeir's eyes went wide and his mouth hung open and he made a gurgling sound in his throat. Skorri twisted the blade, grunting with the effort. Thorgeir's eyes went wider still and Skorri held him there, impaled on the seax, relishing the way the man's face looked as he died in unimaginable pain.

Thorgeir made another sound, a gasping sound, and blood began to run from his open mouth. Skorri pulled the blade free and pushed Thorgeir away, even as Thorgeir collapsed to the floor.

Behind him, the longship men were moving, drawing swords, but Skorri had no thought for them. He turned to Grim, whose eyes were as wide in terror as Thorgeir's had been in agony. Skorri took two steps in his direction. Grim's hands were up and he was talking. Skorri heard "Halfdan" and "forgive" and "no need" but he was not really listening.

He brought the seax backhand over his shoulder. The blade, and his hand, and the sleeve of his tunic, were soaked in blood, which glinted on the steel of his weapon. He swung the blade horizontally. The tip caught Grim's throat and opened it wide as it sliced right through, the cut deep enough that Skorri thought it might take the man's head clean off.

The force of steel on flesh spun Grim halfway around. He fell, arms flailing, and lay there on the floor kicking out the last seconds of his life. Skorri turned to the longship men, snarling as he switched the seax to his left hand and drew his sword with his right. Beyond Thorgeir's men, Skorri's men were standing as well, also drawing swords. It was an ugly, internecine fight that was shaping up, but Skorri was well beyond caring who died now: him, the longship men, his men, anyone.

But no one moved. The longship men were staring at Skorri, and they seemed unsure as to what they should do. The same was true of Skorri's men behind them. Then Koll stepped forward.

"Put up your swords! Put up your swords! These two..." he indicated the two dead men, laying on the floor in spreading pools of blood, "would have you betray Lord Skorri, and betray your king."

Collectively, the men in the hall seemed to relax. Swords were not sheathed, but they were lowered, and the men who had assumed a fighting stance stood straighter.

"If you'd stand with Lord Skorri," Koll continued, "and follow him to greater riches, even greater riches than what we've already seen, then let me hear it now, from your own mouths!"

There was silence at first, and then a single voice from the back of the hall called, "Lord Skorri!" It was followed, almost instantly, by the sound of every other man there, swords raised, shouting with a pulsing, thunderous rhythm, "Lord Skorri! Lord Skorri! Lord Skorri!"

Skorri looked out over the cheering men and nodded and let them yell for another few moments. Then he turned to Koll, and gestured toward the two dead men on the floor.

"Find some servants to clean up that mess."

Chapter Twenty-Eight

One should be a friend to one's friend,
to him and to his friend;
but no one should be a friend
of his enemy's friend.

The Sayings of Hávi

Thorgrim Night Wolf held fast to the tiller, though *Sea Hammer* was beyond the point where the rudder was going to do any good. The next wave moved under the stern and gently lifted the ship and drove it forward. The bow made its familiar crunching sound on soft sand, and the ship shuddered a bit as it ran up on the shore and came to a stop.

The oars came in and were laid down lengthwise while a handful of men leapt over the side and into the shallow water below. Another wave lifted the aft end again, pushing the vessel farther up onto the sand, but that was as far as those small seas were going to move the heavy ship. Hall and Onund, up in the bow, tossed coiled seal-hide ropes to the men on the beach to hold the ship in place.

Gyda, standing just forward of the afterdeck on which Thorgrim stood, picked up the short length of line used to lash the tiller in place and handed it up to him. Thorgrim gave her a bit of a smile and nodded his thanks as he passed the lashing around the worn oak shaft.

Forward, a few of the men still on board were gathering up the oars and stacking them on the gallows. Most of *Sea Hammer*'s crew were lifting their shields free of the shield rack and taking up spears and following the first men over the side. There was no obvious threat to be seen on shore, but Thorgrim knew better than to leave his ships and men exposed with no defense ready.

He looked down at Gyda. "Come with me?"

Gyda nodded. Thorgrim hopped down from the afterdeck. He landed flat-footed and felt a stab of pain in his lacerated shoulder, but it was a trivial thing. The wound was mostly healed now, thanks to his strong constitution and Gyda's care. Still, Thorgrim could not help but think that such wounds — and he'd suffered plenty over a lifetime of fighting and raiding — had healed up much quicker in his younger days.

They made their way down the centerline of the ship, skirting around the mast and the massive step in which it sat. There were still a few men on board, and they moved silently out of the way as the two headed forward.

Off the starboard side, about fifty yards away, *Oak Heart* was next ashore, following *Sea Hammer* onto the sand. Thorgrim glanced at the ship as it ran up onto the beach, but it barely registered as he and Gyda made their way toward the bow.

They stopped where the sheer strake began its upward sweep to form the ship's tall, elegant bow, and where the side of the ship was still low enough to easily climb over. At one time Thorgrim would have stepped on a sea chest, and then onto the sheer strake, and launched himself over the side to the beach below. But that no longer seemed like a good idea, particularly with Gyda behind him, ready to admonish him if he risked opening his wound again. So instead he swung one leg over the side, then the other, then slipped down to the wet sand on which the ship rested.

Gyda swung her legs over the side as well, and Thorgrim took her by the waist and lifted and set her down easily. Thorgrim offered her an arm and she took it and the two of them walked up the slight incline of the beach. Neither one of them spoke.

Fifty feet from the water's edge, Thorgrim stopped and looked around. Those of his men who were armed were formed up in a loose line, facing landward. Some others were burying anchors in the sand, to which they would make fast the seal-hide ropes. Thorgrim was aware of them all, but he did not really see them. Rather, he was looking past the beach, inland, to the country beyond.

The coarse sand ended a hundred feet away at a grass-cover berm that rose up like an earthen wall. Past that, Thorgrim could see rolling countryside, meadows and stands of trees. Farther off, some miles inland, stood ranges of mountains like broken dragon's teeth along the horizon.

Beautiful country, Thorgrim thought. He breathed deep. He could smell the salt water, and the wrack, cast up and drying on the beach, and a hint of tar and linseed coming off the hull of his ship. But he could smell the land as well: the earth, warm in the sun, the grass, and the spruce and pine.

He closed his eyes and let the smells wash over him. He could hear that more ships were running up on the beach, their crews spilling over the sides, but he did not turn to see them. He just stood for a moment with his eyes closed, then slowly opened them again.

Beautiful…

In truth, this beach did not seem so different from a hundred other beaches he had run up on since he and Ornolf had set sail to go a'viking. Ireland, Engla-land, Frankia, Frisia. Every country had its own unique features, but few of them looked so terribly different from one another. And that was true as well of this land on which he now stood.

But this land *was* different, despite how it appeared. Because it was not one of those other places. This was East Agder. It was Norway. He was home.

Gyda, by his side, squeezed his arm tighter and leaned her head against his shoulder. She did not speak. She seemed to understand what this meant to him, and that the spirit of the moment was not to be intruded upon with words.

Thorgrim was silent as well. Even if he had felt inclined to speak, he would not have known what to say, and he would not have trusted his voice. He hardly knew what to think. So many miles under the keel. So much fighting and bloodshed and death. So many hopes dashed, plans frustrated. Fortunes won and lost and won again.

So many people left in their wake. Ornolf the Restless and Godi Unundarson. Aud and Jorund and Fostolf. Hrapp, and the entire crew of *Falcon*, swallowed up by the merciless sea on their unplanned crossing to Engla-land. And so many others, their bodies left to molder on foreign soil, their spirits off to the Allfather's feast hall.

Louis de Roumois and Failend.

And for all that time, one force alone drove Thorgrim harder than all others; the aching desire to get home. And now he was there.

Or, at least, he was in Norway. His actual home, his farm in Vik, was still some thirty miles away, along the tricky, rock-bound coast. They had come ashore in a harbor south of there, clear of the bloody fighting that Eyvind Bjarnason had assured him was taking place to the north.

Thorgrim heard footsteps in the soft sand, and then Starri was standing beside him. Their eyes met and Starri nodded his head and then joined Thorgrim and Gyda in looking out over the country beyond.

Are you home, too, Starri Deathless? Thorgrim wondered. After all this time, he still did not know where Starri was from, or what place he considered home. If any. If Starri had just been created fully-formed out of dust and rocks and trees and wind, Thorgrim would not have been surprised.

More steps in the sand, and Harald appeared on Thorgrim's other side. He, too, nodded to Thorgrim and joined the three of them in their silent vigil. After a moment Thorgrim looked over at his son. He wanted to say something, but he was afraid that his voice might crack if he spoke, and he did not want that.

He took another moment to collect himself, then reached over and gripped Harald's shoulder. He recalled doing the same thing, years before, when he first told Harald that he would be allowed to go a'viking with his father and grandfather. How different the boy's shoulder was now! Broad, muscular, powerful. Harald had grown in many ways. He had done things and seen things in those few years that most men would not do over a full lifetime. He had left Norway as a boy, ignorant of the wider world, hiding his fears and trying to play the man. He was coming home as one who truly was a man, in command of his own ship and crew. Harald Thorgrimson. Harald Broadarm.

"We're home, son," Thorgrim said. His voice remained steady, and he was happy for that.

"Yes, father. Yes, we are." Harald's face had a wistful look that Thorgrim had a hard time reading. Was he, like his father, happy to be home? Or was it something else?

"It's been a long time," Thorgrim said.

Harald nodded. "It has. A long time. A lot of miles. But it's good to be here at last, since Odd needs us now. It's good to be here for him."

"It is," Thorgrim agreed. He wondered if there was some deeper meaning behind Harald's words. Was he telling the old man it was time to stop daydreaming and wallowing in sentiment and get to the bloody business at hand? Possibly. And he was not wrong.

As if prompted by what Harald had said, the four of them turned and looked back toward the surf line. All seven ships were run up on the sand now; the six in Thorgrim's fleet and Eyvind Bjarnason's longship that was sailing in company with them. They were stretched out along fifty yards of beach, and hundreds of men were swarming over the sand. Some were securing the vessels, and others were carrying supplies ashore. Most were under arms, standing ready for trouble. Waiting on orders.

A figure was walking in their direction, a half-dozen men behind him, and Thorgrim was quite certain it was Eyvind. Eyvind, he knew, would be eager to speak with him now, to find out his plans, whereas his other captains would not. They knew better than to ask Thorgrim what he had in mind. They knew by now that Thorgrim would tell them when he decided it was time to tell them, and not before.

Twenty feet away Eyvind — it was Eyvind — raised a hand in greeting. "Thorgrim!" he called as he and his men approached. "I wish you joy on your landfall, and your getting back to Norway. You've been gone a long time."

"A long time," Thorgrim agreed.

"It's just..." Eyvind said, then rethought what he wished to say, then started again. "This is not the harbor that Odd said we should meet him at. I tried to let you know that, while we were underway. I guess you didn't understand what I was trying to signal. But I fear we've come ashore in the wrong place."

"It's not the harbor you talked about back in Frisia, that's true," Thorgrim said. "That harbor's a few miles to the north of here. But it's not the wrong place. This is the harbor I meant to come to."

Eyvind frowned and shook his head a bit, like a man who did not understand. "But...Odd wished us to meet up with him at the other place."

"Did he?"

"Yes, he did."

Thorgrim nodded thoughtfully. "I see. You know, I've long admired your ship. Very well built. Lovely lines. Looks like the sail's had little use. Honestly, it's the kind of ship a king would be proud to own. How do you come by a vessel like that?"

"What?" Eyvind asked. "Why would you ask such a thing?" He sounded genuinely offended by the question, but then, any man sent on a mission to deceive would have to be a good liar.

"I ask because I want to know."

"I have some means," Eyvind said. "But if you must have the truth, my uncle is a wealthy man. I told him I wanted to go raiding, and he supplied the ship in exchange for some share of any plunder. But then I decided that helping Odd…your son…in his fight was more important than raiding."

"Who is your uncle?"

"His name is Thorleik Eglsson. He lives far from Vik. And in case you forgot, I risked a great deal defying the king, doing as your son asked, coming to find you. I saved your life, and yours as well," he said, pointing to Harald and Starri. "And I don't much care for your suspicions."

"Yes, you saved our lives," Thorgrim said. "But who was it, do you suppose, who attacked us?"

"Who? Halfdan's men. Who else? If I could find you in Ribe, then they could too, I don't doubt."

"But Gyda here says they were not Halfdan's men. She says they were men from Ribe. Scum. Men who would kill for hire."

"Yes, that's probably true," Eyvind said. "So, Halfdan didn't send men to kill you. He sent one man, who hired others to kill you. That makes sense."

"Explains why there were no other king's ships there on the riverbank with us," Harald said.

"Exactly," Eyvind said. Then he knitted his eyebrows and said, "Hold on, are you suggesting my ship is one of the king's ships?"

Before Harald could answer, there was a shout from down by the water's edge, then more shouting, and a voice calling an order. Thorgrim could not make out the words, but he had a pretty good idea of what was being said. He and the others turned toward the commotion, which was taking place fifty feet up the beach, where Eyvind's ship was pulled up on the sand.

There were a few hundred men collected there: the crews of *Sea Hammer*, and *Oak Heart*, and *Blood Hawk*, and Thorgrim's other ships. They had weapons drawn, swords out, shields on arms, spears leveled. They were standing in a loose circle around Eyvind's men, about sixty in all, who had their own weapons drawn, at least those weapons they had on them. They had not come ashore expecting a fight.

But Thorgrim's men had. They had left their ships well-armed, in part to be ready for any surprise attack from beyond the beach, but mostly to launch this surprise attack of their own.

Back in Frisia, before leaving for that last open-water crossing to their homeland, Thorgrim had given his captains the orders they were following now. On coming ashore, they were to have their men move unobtrusively toward Eyvind's ship and surround the crew. Then, on Gudrid's command, draw weapons, close ranks, and demand that Eyvind's men surrender.

The men had followed those instructions, and with such discretion that Eyvind's men did not even realize they were being herded together until the weapons came out. Now their shouts of surprise and outrage were rolling up the beach.

Eyvind turned to Thorgrim. His face was red with fury. "What by all the gods is this? What do you think you're doing? I'm trying to help your son, keep him and his people from being slaughtered, and this is how you reward me?"

"This is not a reward," Thorgrim said. "And it's not a punishment. We're just going to find out if you are who you say you are. Nothing more. No reason for an honest man to have any fear. Come with me."

He headed back down the beach, toward the men clustered near the bow of Eyvind's ship. Gyda and Harald and Starri were at his side, Eyvind and his half-dozen men trailing behind.

Thorgrim's eyes were on the stand-off ahead. It was a strange sight; the crew of Eyvind's ship clustered together, facing out, swords drawn, and Thorgrim's men making a circle around them, like a human fence penning in half-wild beasts. A volatile situation.

"Listen here, listen here!" Thorgrim called as he approached the circle, and the men who had been eyeing one another looked at him instead. "We don't want any bloodshed today. But we want to get to the truth of what's happening here. Eyvind tells me that you men are fighting with my son Odd. That you came to find me, to bring me back so I might come to his aid. Me and my men. Is that right?"

He searched the angry faces of Eyvind's men. They had the look of warriors about them. He saw defiance, but no fear. And he thought, if those were really the sort of men flocking to Odd, then Odd was in a good position to drive Halfdan into the ground.

"Well, is that right?" Thorgrim asked again. One by one the men began to nod, though not with any great conviction, it seemed.

"Yes, that's right," a single voice called.

"Anyone wish to say anything different?"

The men stared back at him. No one moved.

"Very good," Thorgrim said. "But still we have to get to the truth of this. So for now, I need you all to give up your weapons."

A loud shout of protest came up from Eyvind's men, a defiant sound, and Eyvind, standing beside Thorgrim, said, "We don't give up our weapons. Not to you, or anyone."

"I said we don't want any bloodshed today, and I meant it," Thorgrim said, addressing Eyvind and all of the men there. "But there will be bloodshed, and soon, if you don't do as I say."

Thorgrim let his words hang. Eyvind's warriors were glancing around at the wall of men facing them on all sides, four times their number, men wearing mail and helmets, carrying shields, leveling a multitude of spears at them, or with swords or axes drawn. They themselves were clad in tunics, and armed with swords and seaxes and not much else. No shields, no spears. It would not be bloodshed, it would be slaughter.

It was quiet for a moment, quiet enough that the loudest sound to be heard was the lap of the surf, and the soft grinding of the ships' bows on the beach. Then, with a grunt and a curse, one of Eyvind's men spit on the ground and drove his sword down into the sand. He stepped back, scowling, and folded his arms. Then the man beside him did the same, and two more, and a moment later they were all standing with arms folded, swords stuck upright before them.

"Good," Thorgrim said. "Now, let's get some food and ale down off the ships. Get a fire going. Starri, Harald, Brand, Vali, come with me."

By the time the sun touched the mountains to the west, the fire was burning well, a massive affair built up from the copious driftwood they found on the beach. There was beef that they had salted down in Ribe, and that went into the massive stew pot, along with whatever else they had on hand — onions, carrots and the like. Barrels of ale were rolled ashore and broken open.

It was a subdued gathering, with Eyvind's men sitting in a sullen group under heavy guard, and the rest mostly quiet, lost in their thoughts. Still, the men were in a buoyant mood, save for those who had been stripped of their weapons. There were a few Swedes and Danes among Thorgrim's men, and one Irishman, but for the most part they were Norwegians all, and many from East Agder. And they, like Thorgrim, were home.

And, thanks to the Franks and the good raiding they had enjoyed over the past year, they were returning as wealthy men.

"What do you think?" Thorgrim asked Gyda as she handed him a cup of ale and sat beside him on the driftwood log he was using for a bench. "You're from Norway. Like me. Do you feel you're home?"

"Hmm…home…" Gyda said, as if trying the word out for the first time. "Norway was home once. When I left with my husband, I thought Ribe could be home, but I was wrong. I don't know if any place will ever be home."

"That's too bad," Thorgrim said. "Home is important. Maybe this land will be home again. I hope it will."

Gyda leaned her head against Thorgrim's shoulder and put her hand on his arm. Her skin looked smooth and soft in the light of the fire, her fingers delicate, belying the strength that Thorgrim knew was there.

"Perhaps, for me, home is not a place," she said.

Out in the dark, someone started singing, the song slow and melodic. A few others joined in, and then a few instruments as well; a couple of flutes and a tagelharpa, with its haunting notes. More songs followed, all of a kind. Finally, the musicians fell silent and the men began to drift off to bed.

Gudrid stepped around the end of the log on which Thorgrim and Gyda sat. "What would you have me do with Eyvind's men?" he asked.

"We can't let them go onboard their ship," Thorgrim said. "They'll have more weapons stowed there, and I don't want them getting ideas. You can let a handful go onboard under guard to collect up blankets, and then they can sleep on the beach. Keep guards posted around them, have the guards relieved through the night. Weather's good and the fire's warm. They'll be comfortable enough."

By the light of the flames he could see Gudrid smiling. "You're getting downright considerate of your fellow man, Thorgrim, now that you've reached home."

"Am I?" Thorgrim asked. "How about I shove your sword up your ass and we'll see if you still think that?"

"Maybe I'm wrong," Gudrid said, but he was still smiling as he turned away and disappeared again into the dark.

Thorgrim and Gyda made their way back aboard *Sea Hammer*, climbing wearily over the side and picking their way past the few humps of sleeping men on the deck. Back aft they found that someone in the crew had lashed a line from the sternpost to an oar set upright against the afterdeck, and draped a tarp over the line to form a sort of tent, a rare bit of privacy on what was essentially an open boat.

"Look at this," Gyda said. "It's like a jarl's great hall. Jarl Thorgrim."

"Jarl Thorgrim. That suits me. And I don't need any great hall finer than this."

They ducked in under the flap of the tent. It was cave-dark, but they found that whoever had set up the shelter had also spread out the furs and blankets they used for their bed. Thorgrim unbuckled Iron-tooth and set it down on the deck, then pulled off his shoes and his tunic and shirt and dropped them next to the furs. He laid down and stretched out and felt the tension ease from his muscles. He realized then how tense he had been, but that did not surprise him.

He heard Gyda shuffling around in the dark, getting ready for sleep. As his eyes adjusted he could just make out her shape as she knelt beside him, then eased herself down and lay partway across his chest. He felt her warm, smooth skin against his, her bare arms reaching up to his shoulders and he realized that she had taken off more than her shoes and her apron. That she had, in fact, taken off every article of clothing.

He ran his hand up her smooth, strong back and through her hair, which was now cast loose from its usual twin braids and hung in long, thick strands down her back and shoulders. She shuffled up higher on his chest, high enough that their lips could meet, and they kissed, a long, deep luxurious kiss, a kiss that went on and on as they lost themselves in one another.

Thorgrim shifted his arm, intending to roll over, to position himself on top of her, but she pulled her lips from his and said in a breathy voice, "Uh-uh…" and pushed him back down.

"What?" Thorgrim whispered.

"Your wound."

"It's healed. You healed it."

"Maybe," Gyda whispered. "But if it opens up now, the absurdity will kill me. Don't worry. You won't be deprived."

She pushed away and began easing slowly down his chest, kissing him as she moved. He felt her hand gliding over his stomach, her fingers finding the cord that bound his leggings around his waist. With a deft tug, the cord was untied, and with Thorgrim's assistance Gyda slid the leggings down and over his feet.

After a few moments she moved back up along his chest, and once again pressed her lips to his. He ran his hands over her skin, her lovely, lovely skin, smooth and pliant as anything he had ever felt. And she ran her hands over him, over his chest and his shoulders, touching the all-but-healed wound lightly with her fingertips, over his stomach and the various places where skin yielded to hard scars. She eased her leg over his waist until she was straddling him and he felt the glorious sensation of their coming together.

He slept after that, deep and dreamless. He slept peacefully, more than he had in a very long time. All, at last, seemed right: Gyda half on top of him, his beloved *Sea Hammer* below him, her keel resting on his native land.

When he woke in the dark of the tent, he had no notion as to what part of the day it was, or who or what was waking him. He opened his eyes and looked up and saw only blackness, and he imagined the night was moonless, the skies so clouded over that the stars could not shine through. And then he remembered the tent. And Gyda, who was easing herself off him.

"Father?"

It was Harald's voice. Had he been calling out for some time? Thorgrim had no idea. He could just barely make out Gyda, pulling her dress over her head, and he waited until she was settling it in place before he called, "Yes?"

There was a pause, as if this response did not make sense. Then Harald said, "We're back."

Back…

Thorgrim remembered now. He had sent Harald and Starri and a few others he trusted north, told them to make their way to the harbor where Eyvind had said they were to meet up with Odd. There they were to find out what was really going on. And now they were back.

"Hold a moment," Thorgrim said. He realized it must be daytime, since there was a trace of light creeping in around the tent flap, enough for him to see Gyda passing him his leggings. He pulled them on, then the shirt and tunic she handed him, then he tossed the tent flap aside.

It was early morning. Fore and aft, men were just starting to push themselves to their feet. Harald was standing at the break of the afterdeck, waiting patiently. His eyes moved over to Gyda, then back to Thorgrim, but he showed no reaction.

Thorgrim crawled out of the tent and hopped down and stood beside Harald. "Any problems?"

"No. There was a decent road north. We followed that until we got near the harbor, then we took to the countryside. Nothing to see at first, but once we worked our way around the far side we did find there was an army waiting. But not Odd's, as far as we could tell. There were plenty of fine tents. And banners. Lots of men fitted out with mail and swords. Not an army of regular folk rallying to a cause, it didn't seem."

"King Halfdan's?"

"Most likely. We weren't close enough to see for certain, but the banners looked like Halfdan's white and red with the black gyrfalcon. We brought a prisoner back. He can probably tell you."

"He didn't tell you?"

"He didn't seem much interested in talking, and we didn't have time to convince him."

"We should be able to convince him now," Thorgrim said. "We'll see." He put his hand on Harald's shoulder. "Good work, son."

He sent Harald back to the beach and resumed dressing, putting on shoes, belting on his sword and seax, and a cloak over his shoulders, fastened with an elaborate silver brooch. That done, he and Gyda made their way to the beach as well.

Most of the men ashore were up and moving about, strapping on weapons, stumbling off to relieve themselves, the various rituals of waking. Eyvind's men were still clustered together and still well-guarded by a ring of men with spears and shields. Harald's prisoner was seated on the sand some distance away, his hands bound behind his back, a few of Harald's men standing guard over him. Harald and Brand were seated on a log nearby, eating.

Thorgrim grabbed a spear that was thrust into the sand and carried it over to the fire, laying it down so its iron tip was resting on a heap of coals. He left it there and strolled over to where Harald and Brand were seated. The two young men stood as they saw him coming.

"This is your prisoner?" Thorgrim asked, nodding toward the man on the ground. On closer look, Thorgrim could see that his tunic was torn, his hair was hanging in tangles, and he had a variety of bruises on his face. It seemed he had not come so easily.

The man glared up at Thorgrim. "Yes," Harald said.

Thorgrim nodded to the men standing guard, and they bent over and hefted the prisoner to his feet. Thorgrim looked him up and down. His clothing was made from good linen, not rough homespun stuff, and he wore several silver arm rings. He had the look of a warrior.

"I'm Thorgrim Ulfsson," Thorgrim said. "What's your name?" He stood for a moment while the man continued to glare at him in silence. "Very well," Thorgrim said. "Come with me."

He led the way back toward the place where Eyvind's men were waiting, and the guards pushed the prisoner along behind him.

"Eyvind, come here," Thorgrim said. Eyvind looked up at him. He seemed to hesitate, considering, as if he had a choice, then stood and walked over.

"Yes?"

Thorgrim turned to the prisoner. He nodded toward Eyvind and asked, "Do you know this man?"

The prisoner looked Eyvind up and down and then looked back at Thorgrim. His face was nearly expressionless, but Thorgrim could see the uncertainty there as he wrestled with which answer would serve him best. "No," he said at last.

"You don't know him," Thorgrim said. "Who do you serve?"

This time the prisoner just looked into Thorgrim's eyes and let the anger on his face answer for him.

"Do you serve King Halfdan the Black? Why was the army camped where it was?" Still no answer.

"Very well," Thorgrim said. He bent over and lifted the spear off the ground. The tip was glowing red now, and tendrils of smoke were rising off it. He moved it closer to the prisoner's face, and he could see the struggle in the man's expression as he tried to remain impassive.

"Next question," Thorgrim said. "Left eye, or right?"

Chapter Twenty-Nine

An old stay-at-home
finds satisfaction
in talking chiefly
with intelligent men.

The Saga of the Confederates

Ragi Oleifsson sat on the faering's middle thwart, on the windward side, enjoying the late-morning, late-summer sun. There were four other men in the boat, fishermen who had volunteered to bring him to Fevik. The trip made an interesting diversion, and all five men were grateful for it.

They had left, not long before, from the army's new camp, situated in a small harbor about three miles due south of Fevik, hidden in a channel between a pair of islands. The islands were two of the many thousands that littered the coastline, humps of granite jutting up from the ocean, tall enough to give an observer at their peak a decent view of the mainland.

Unlike many of their brethren, those islands boasted enough topsoil that they were mostly covered by tall grass, brush, and even some trees. Odd's people would be well-hidden there, considerably more so than at their former encampment.

They had shifted to the new camp two nights before, and had spent all the dark hours moving that short distance. By Ragi's estimate, Odd now had close to five hundred men under his command, and they had been in one place long enough that breaking camp and humping it all into the boats was no simple thing. Add to that Odd's insistence that it be done as quietly as possible, and done after dark, so that no one watching from shore could see what they were about, and it had become a serious logistical challenge.

The longships, loaded with men and women and stores, led the way. The vessels were crowded to the point where it was difficult to walk fore and aft, and the oars were double- and triple-banked, mostly to provide more men with places to sit.

As to the fishing boats, they were so loaded down that anything save for the smallest chop would have threatened to swamp them. Happily, there was no wind that night, and the seas were mostly flat.

Odd, it seemed, had found a new determination, a new drive to move things along, to force this standoff with Skorri to a head, and Ragi was glad of it. Shifting their camp to a new, hidden place had been the first step. This mission that Ragi was now on was the second.

They had decided that morning, at a council of war.

"It's time for us to act," Odd had announced, as Arnor and Bragi and Amundi and Ragi gathered around, sitting on driftwood logs that had been arranged in a tight circle on the beach. "We're equal in strength to Skorri now. Time to confront him." The others all nodded their heads. Ragi was the first to speak, because he had questions.

"Skorri…that whore's son. Does he still fight for Halfdan? Or has he gone off on his own? I swear by the gods this thing has become as confused as a herd of drunk goats."

"I don't know," Odd said. "According to Skorri's own words, he's done with Halfdan. Wants us to join with him in fighting the king. You all heard that yourselves."

Arnor spit on the ground. "Skorri…miserable bastard."

"So, do we believe him?" Amundi asked. He looked around at the others, but no one offered a response.

"I'm hard-pressed to trust Skorri Thorbrandsson," Odd said at length. "But even if he's trying to trick us, we might use this to our advantage. Skorri's men hold Fevik. I mean to start there. Take it back. But maybe we can be more clever about it. Something more than just a frontal assault."

"Like what?" Ragi asked.

"I'm not sure. But we told Skorri that if we were going to take him up on his offer, we'd send someone today. It's worth playing along, at least for a while. See what he has in mind. Which is why I'm going this morning to meet with him."

The others sat more upright. Ragi and Amundi frowned. Bragi laughed. "Well, it's been interesting knowing you, young Odd!" he said.

Ragi shook his head. "No. You can't do that."

"Someone has to go. Of course there's a risk. Maybe a big one. Which is why I'm not going to ask anyone else to do it."

"If we had hostages to secure your safety, then perhaps," Amundi said. "But we don't. So there's no reason on earth for Skorri to not take you prisoner then and there. Sell you to Halfdan, or use you to get back in his good graces. And then all this…" he gestured toward the camp and the people around them, "…collapses."

They were quiet for a moment after that. Then Odd said, "Well then, what…"

"I'll go," Ragi had said. "I know Skorri of old. He won't fool me. And I'm of no consequence. There would be no point in him taking me prisoner."

"I imagine Skorri's still angry about the way you fooled him with your tunnel," Amundi said. "He may be happy to take vengeance on you."

"So, let him. I'll die with a sword in the one hand I have left," Ragi said. "But Skorri's waiting on our reply. There's not much point in him killing the messenger, is there?"

Once again they fell quiet. Odd seemed to be searching for some reasonable objection, some reason that he, not Ragi, should go. But he found none.

"You should go soon," he said.

Arnor had found a boat, and informed the four fishermen that they would be volunteering, but they did not seem too put out by the task. It was a fine morning, sunny and warm, and the tolerable breeze from the west meant no rowing — they should be able to sail there and back with little effort — whereas staying in camp would mean they were put to some odious work or other, or made to participate in more exhausting and repetitious military training.

The fishermen were not alone in enjoying the trip. Ragi was well sick of sitting around in camp, or drilling men who were little used to arms in how to wield spears and shields and axes in battle, or how to form a shield wall or a swine array. It grew quickly tedious. After a youth spent raiding and seafaring and adventuring around the watery world, most things grew quickly tedious.

He leaned against the side of the boat and looked up at the wool sail, full but not straining at its boltropes. A square sail, like a child's version of a longship, but big enough to drive the twenty-foot faering, with its four-man crew and single passenger, at a respectable speed.

The boat pitched up and down in the small chop, with a quick and jerky motion, and rolled a bit with each flaw in the wind, quite different from the solid feel of a longship underway, but more exhilarating in that light air.

Ragi took his eyes off the sail and looked forward, past the bow. They had rounded the headland that marked the southwest end of the long harbor, at the head of which sat Fevik, and they were standing north toward the village. He could make it out now: the various homes, and shops, and the ships at the wharves, appeared as distant, brownish-gray shapes to his aging eyes. Ragi was not as old as say, Amundi, but he had seen harder use, and he was feeling it more and more with each passing season.

He scanned the harbor north to south. No boats, no ships moving that he could see.

"You know these waters?" he asked the other four in general.

"Some," said the man sitting by the starboard sheet on the leeward side.

"I don't see any boats out," Ragi said. "Much fishing around here?"

"Usually. Usually pretty decent fishing around here. And a lot of boats out of Fevik. But we keep to our grounds, and they keep to theirs." He was quiet for a moment and glanced around some. "Don't know why no one's out now. Lazy, I guess."

They sailed on, and slowly the brownish-gray shapes on the horizon began to resolve, in Ragi's eyes, into individual buildings and ships' hulls. They were still too far off to see anyone moving around on shore, if such there was, and he still could see no other sails on the water.

Now, what am I going to find here? he wondered, as he looked at the town at the head of the harbor. *What have you made of this place, Skorri Thorbrandsson?*

The faering covered the last of the distance quickly, the harbor growing more narrow, the town more distinct.

"If you boys want to leave me off to the east or the west of the town, that's fine by me," Ragi said when they were still half a mile or so distant. "I can't say what's going on here, or how friendly Skorri's men will be. I can't promise it's not a trap."

Ragi was betting that he could talk his way through Fevik and on to Ornolf's great hall, where Skorri was making himself at home. But maybe not. Maybe he would be taken for a spy and killed on the spot.

It was a risk he was willing to run, but he would not insist that these young fishermen run that risk as well.

Now the four of them exchanged glances, each apparently waiting for one of the others to make the decision. Finally, the fellow at the starboard sheet took it upon himself.

"I reckon we've got no problem bringing you right into town. Skorri's turds won't bother us. We're just harmless fishermen, innocent as lambs." That garnered a chuckle from the others, but no objections, so they sailed on.

As they came up with the village, Ragi could count three longships tied to the wharves, presumably the remaining vessels from Halfdan's fleet, those that Odd had not yet taken. There were a few men at work on those, and some others standing around on the wharves, or seated on barrels. They were the first and only living persons Ragi saw in Fevik. A few seemed to have cups in their hands.

The fishermen did not land at the wharf, but rather stood on to the beach at the head of town. Twenty feet shy of the surf line, one of the men eased the halyard and dropped the sail, while two others brought it in as it came down. Their timing was flawless, and the boat ground up on the sand with the last bit of its forward motion.

Ragi made to stand, but before he could, the fishermen obligingly hopped out into the low surf and pulled the faering further up on shore, allowing Ragi to step out onto dry ground. He adjusted his sword and seax, stretched, and looked around.

About fifty feet away there was a longship run up on the beach, but it was clearly not one of Halfdan's. It had been there some time by the look of it, half filled with sand and water and stripped of anything that might be of use. Ragi smiled at the sight.

Good to see there's someone who's even worse about caring for their ships than I am, he thought. He wished Bragi Shipslayer could see that neglected wreck; it would make him so mad his head would break open like some overripe fruit. Bragi seemed to feel that he alone had the gods' permission to destroy a ship, and Ragi found it very amusing.

He turned his eyes toward the town, expecting to see a company of warriors rushing down the beach with swords drawn, demanding to know who they were. But there was no one. He turned to the four men with him.

"Don't know how long I'll be," he said. "I should be back before nightfall. If I'm not, that likely means things haven't gone well, and I probably won't be coming back at all. If you don't want to tarry here, I can understand that. Maybe best you head off, come back around sunset if it seems safe, and see if I'm here. If I'm not, head back to the island."

The four fishermen looked around them. The one up in the bow said, "Don't look too dangerous here to us. Reckon we can take our leisure. If we see trouble we'll get underway. Come back for you at sunset, like you said."

"Good," Ragi said. "Thank you."

"Happy to oblige," one of the others chimed in. Ragi had noticed the firkin of what he guessed was ale stowed down under the thwart. He hoped that of these four, at least two would still be sober enough to row or set the sail by the time he returned. He himself was not much good at either, not since the day a Frankish sword had taken his left hand off at the wrist.

"Very well," Ragi said. "Be safe."

He left them there and walked up the gently sloping beach to the road that ran along parallel to the sand. Ragi did not know Fevik well, but he knew it well enough, having been there perhaps a dozen times before. From what he could see, walking along the road toward the town, it had not changed much. A few more buildings than the last time he was there, perhaps, and one of the wharves was new-built. But other than that, it was pretty much as it had been.

Only one thing seemed markedly different: there was no one around. The streets and the waterfront, which he remembered as being crowded with people, carts, horses, wheelbarrows, all the frenetic activity of a busy port town, were nearly empty now, save for the few men he had seen on the wharves.

He ambled on, and as he got closer to where the houses and shops were more concentrated he did, at last, start to see others: women standing in doorways, children darting here and there. There were armed men, warriors, here and there, though it was hard to say what they were doing. If they were meant to be patrolling the streets, they did not seem to be taking their duty too seriously.

Ragi had expected to be challenged on coming ashore, but it was not until he was nearing the head of the main road through town that anyone seemed to notice him.

"Hey, you!" The voice was gruff and demanding. Ragi stopped in his tracks, turned toward the sound. One of the warriors, one of

Skorri's warriors, he imagined, wearing mail, a sword on his belt, shield on his back, coming down one of the side roads, four other armed men following behind. Ragi waited patiently as they approached.

"Who are you?" the warrior demanded.

"Ragi Oleifsson," Ragi said, matter-of-factly, and then said no more. That seemed to throw the man off balance. Ragi imagined he was ready for some sort of convoluted story or obfuscation, and was not sure what to make of that simple and direct answer.

"Well, *Ragi Oleifsson*, what's your business here? And why are you walking around armed?"

"'A wayfarer should not walk unarmed, but have his weapons to hand: he knows not when he may need a spear, or what menace meet on the road.' Those are the words of the High One, are they not? Who am I to argue?"

"Best not be too clever, old man," the warrior said. "It might get your head separated from your body. No one but Lord Skorri's men walk around with arms, that's the law."

"I didn't know that. I just arrived here, and I've gone unnoticed until now. But you mentioned Skorri Thorbrandsson, and that's who I'm here to speak with."

"What business do you have with Lord Skorri?"

"Business that's of great importance to him, but not for your ears."

They held one another's eyes, Ragi and this warrior, who was once in the service of Halfdan the Black, but now seemed to be Skorri's man. Neither moved, neither looked away.

"Lord Skorri's not here," the warrior said at last.

"Lord Skorri told me to look for him at Ornolf the Restless's great hall."

Another pause for consideration, and then the warrior said, "Very well. I reckon an old cripple's little threat to Lord Skorri and his men. We'll walk you to the edge of town."

Old cripple, Ragi though. *This old cripple would have your throat split open in a heartbeat.* But he kept those thoughts to himself, and said only, "Lead on."

They made their way down the road through the center of the village, past the various workshops — the blacksmith and the woodcarver and the silversmith — Ragi and the warrior walking side by side. Ragi tried not to look overly curious, but he took in as much as he could, gauging the state of things in the town. From what he could see, they were not good.

The shops were idle, no craftsmen working at their trades, and the buildings themselves seemed battered and in want of repair. Ragi guessed that some of that — the thatch ripped from roofs, the lean-tos fallen over, the small gardens beaten down into the mud — were caused by the storm they had just suffered through. But some of it seemed to be the work of men, raiders tearing the places apart in search of loot. Ragi knew what that looked like.

As they walked on, he saw more folk, women and children, mostly, watching in silence as they passed. They wore the haunted look of people who had suffered sudden violence, and were not yet free of its threat. Ragi knew what that looked like, too.

There were a few men among them as well, but only a few, mostly very young, just past childhood, or very old, or disabled in some way.

Have all the men from here fled to Odd's camp? Ragi wondered. Since Hallbjorn and Storolf had first arrived, and then gone back to Fevik to spread the word, the men had been showing up by the dozens. Some had brought their women and children with them, but most had not, because they were not joining Odd to escape, they were joining him to fight. And Skorri, apparently, had let them go.

There were other men in Fevik, of course. Skorri's men. Elite warriors, but they seemed quite undisciplined as they wandered around the streets, talking loudly amongst themselves in half-drunk voices, laughing, paying little attention, it seemed, to anything around them. They were supposed to be patrolling the town, he guessed, but there was something very haphazard about it.

He saw others digging through carts, or outbuildings, or chests dragged out into the daylight. He saw women and children pushed out into the road so their homes could be rifled through undisturbed. The armed men seemed to be searching for loot; any little thing they might have missed the last few times they had scoured the place.

"Are you men guarding the town?" Ragi asked. "Who are you guarding it against?"

"Shut your mouth," his escort said. They walked a few more steps, and then he added, "I guess you know full well who we're guarding it against."

"I have an idea," Ragi said. But it was clear that the folk in Fevik were in more danger from the guards than from anyone else.

They came to the end of the road, where the last houses in town yielded to trampled, open ground, and then fields of tall grass beyond that, and patches of woods running slowly uphill. There were more of Skorri's men on the road, and they at least seemed to be paying more attention to their duty than the men in town were.

"You know where Lord Skorri's to be found?" the man at Ragi's side asked.

"He's made his home in Ornolf the Restless's great hall, I understand."

"You understand right. You know how to find it?"

"I do."

They continued on until they met up with the men standing guard on the road.

"This one says he has business with Lord Skorri," Ragi's escort said. "We'll let him continue on. Not much harm he can do."

The men on the road looked Ragi up and down, and then nodded and stepped aside. Who was in charge of whom, Ragi could not tell. It did not seem that anyone was in charge in Fevik. There did not seem to be any sort of order at all.

He turned to his escort. "You're not going to come with me?"

"No," the man said. "Just promise me that when you get there you won't kill Skorri and the lot of them single-handed. Which I guess is how you'd have to do it."

The man laughed. The other guards on the road laughed. Ragi laughed.

"No, fear not," Ragi said. "I'm not going to kill you all. Not yet."

He pushed past them and continued on up the road, which was dry now, after several days of fine weather, but still showed marks of having been churned to mud. Deep, parallel ruts ran along either side, and in the low places horses' hooves had done their damage. But the walking was easy, and Ragi enjoyed watching the birds making their short, frenetic flights through the tall grass, and he enjoyed the sound and feel of the breeze that had driven their boat to Fevik as it gently tugged at the branches.

The road he was on led uphill and inland, and right to Ornolf's great hall. Ragi approached, unchallenged, until he was close enough to see the handful of men walking a slow patrol along the top of the wall, outside the palisade. Two guards were stationed on the wall just above the big gates, but they said nothing until Ragi came to a stop just below them.

"Well, who are you? What do you want?" one guard said.

"My name is Ragi Oleifsson. I've come to speak with Skorri Thorbrandsson."

"*Lord* Skorri," the guard corrected.

"Lord Skorri," Ragi said. The man in Fevik had used that honorific as well, and Ragi thought it strange. He still did. He wondered if Halfdan had bestowed it on Skorri, or if Skorri had bestowed it on himself.

"What's your business with Lord Skorri?"

"I'm sent by Odd Thorgrimson to speak with him."

For a moment neither guard replied, they just stared down at Ragi. Then Ragi could see them exchanging words in a low voice, debating, no doubt, if it was worth calling someone of greater authority. They seemed to conclude that a lone man, with a beard that was mostly gray, did not justify the effort. The guard who had spoken turned and called down to someone on the other side, and a door in one of the oak gates, just big enough for one man to pass through, swung open.

Ragi nodded and stepped through the door and onto the grounds surrounding the great hall. It looked the same as he recalled from the few times he had visited before: stables, smith's shop, storehouse, butcher, scattered around the open space, while the hall itself sat in the center of the circular wall, a great, slumbering sow surrounded by her brood.

There were four men bearing spears waiting to greet Ragi as he stepped through. One took a step toward him and said, "Here, come with me," and without waiting for a reply he turned and headed off toward the great hall.

They crossed the grounds together, Ragi following a few steps behind the man, and once again his eyes were everywhere. There was more activity than there had been in Fevik: servants hurrying back and forth, livestock grazing at the sparse grass, women plunging clothes into massive tubs, others working at sundry tasks. The butcher and his assistants seemed to be hard at it. But for a place that supposedly housed the bulk of an army, there seemed to be precious little military activity going on.

Ragi was surprised by that. He would have expected to see men drilling with sword and shield, or tending to horses, or sharpening or repairing weapons. But there was none of that. The men walking the walls were the only ones bearing arms that he could see. There were men lounging around at various places on the grounds, a few sitting in a circle around a fire, others on benches near the walls of the great hall, but if they were warriors or not, Ragi could not tell. They wore no mail, carried no weapons, save for the swords they wore on their belts.

He considered asking his escort about it, but decided he was not likely to get a helpful response, so he kept his mouth shut.

The main door to the great hall, at least, had guards stationed outside, with helmets, mail, spears. They opened the door as Ragi and his escort approached, and the two of them walked right through into the twilight-dim interior.

It was like stepping from one world into another as they came through the door. Outside, the sunshine and fresh air of the open grounds, with the faint smells of earth and animals and vegetation, and then into a world that smelled of cooking meat and spilled ale and stale smoke roiling off the cooking fires and hanging under the roof overhead. There were loud voices, shouting, laughing, singing. There were musicians playing somewhere off at the far end of the massive space.

Ragi continued following his escort halfway down the length of the building, and as his eyes adjusted he could see that a bulk of Skorri's men were there, at the tables, or on the platforms that lined the sides of the building. Men were eating, or drinking, or gaming, or sleeping. Ragi had been in many mead halls over the course of his life, and most had been filthy and disreputable places. Ornolf's great hall reminded him of those, but on a grander scale.

The high seat was positioned on a dais near the center of the floor, back to Ragi as he approached. The escort led the way around the front of the dais, and it was only then that Ragi saw that Skorri Thorbrandsson was seated there, a half-eaten meal on the table in front of him, a very pretty young woman, one who had the look of a thrall about her, seated on the floor at his feet.

"Lord Skorri?" the escort said. Skorri turned his head slowly in his direction. His eyes moved over to Ragi and he looked him up and down. "This man says he's sent by Odd Thorgrimson to speak with you."

Skorri nodded and made a gesture that the man should go away, which he did, after a quick bow. Skorri stood, slowly, and stepped down off the dais so that he and Ragi were at eye level.

"Ragi Oleifsson," Skorri said.

"Skorri Thorbrandsson," Ragi said.

"*Lord* Skorri," Skorri corrected.

Ragi nodded. "That's what they seem to call you."

"When Odd said he'd send someone, I thought he'd send some nameless messenger. Not you. Now I'm wondering if I should gut you, here and now, for what you did back at your hall." He lifted his hand slowly and rested it on the hilt of his seax.

"Maybe I should do the same," Ragi said, putting his hand on the grip of his own seax. They stood there like that, looking one another in the eyes, waiting to see who might make a move first. Then Skorri dropped his hand and smiled.

"No need for this. We have greater concerns. Tell me why you've come. Has Odd decided to take me up on my offer that we join forces? Wisely decided?"

"Perhaps," Ragi said. "You offered to give yourself up as a hostage. Does that offer still stand?"

"It stands. But there's no time for that now. Things have changed. Halfdan is gathering his army, and he'll march on this place soon."

This was news to Ragi. He frowned and shook his head. "I thought *you* were Halfdan's army."

"I was. Now these men are mine. Loyal to me. I have five hundred men and five ships. Three ships, now. But do you think these are all the men Halfdan has under his command? He's pulling men in from all the outlying territories, twice the number I have here. When he has them, he'll fall on me and my men, and then you and Odd on your island, and that will be an end to it."

"How do you know this?"

Skorri let out a breath, a sound of exasperation. "By all the gods, Ragi Oleifsson, you were not born yesterday. A man like me has ways. People who tell him things. I know what Halfdan's up to. And that's why I know that my army and yours must join together, or we are certainly all dead men."

Ragi thought about this. He looked off into the far end of the great hall. A fight seemed to have broken out, half a dozen men flailing at one another with fists and jugs and one with a small bench. Others were staggering in their direction, but whether to break it up or join in he could not tell. He turned back to Skorri.

"So what do you propose?"

"Bring your men here. There's room enough. We join our armies, and make ready to meet Halfdan when he comes for us."

At that, Ragi smiled. "Here? You mean, within these walls? March them in the way you'd drive deer into a trap?"

"You don't trust me?"

"I don't trust anyone. Least of all you. You say you're no longer Halfdan's man, but we have only your word to go on."

"Indeed," Skorri said. "Well, I'm sure you know Thorgeir Sveinsson?"

"I do. Halfdan made him sœlumadr, after he decided you'd turned traitor."

"Yes. That's the one. And Grim Grimsson, Halfdan's overseer?"

Ragi nodded.

"Well, those two are certainly Halfdan's men. And I'm close with both of them. Here, come." He led the way around to the far side of the dais, where an elaborately carved wooden box was pushed up against the platform. Skorri reached down and unfastened the hasp and flipped the lid back. "There you go."

The stench was familiar — Ragi had smelled it often enough before — but it was still like a gut punch. He clenched his teeth, pressed his lips together. He heard the thrall make a gagging sound and heard her footsteps as she raced away. He stepped forward and looked down into the box. He knew full well what he would see there, but he looked anyway.

The heads were side by side, skin waxy and white, mouths open, teeth barred in two horrible grins. Dull eyes staring straight up, the jagged and rent flesh around the stubs of their necks black with dried blood. Their hair seemed to spill together, their beards splayed out from lifeless jaws. Thorgeir Sveinsson and Grim Grimsson. Barely recognizable, but it was them, to be sure.

Ragi stepped back. "You're close with them, indeed."

Skorri closed the box with his foot. Ragi was still taking shallow breaths, but as the smell dissipated he took the risk of drawing in more air.

"So you see I have…severed my ties with Halfdan." Skorri smiled at his play on words. "I'm my own man now. And I'd like to keep on being my own man, and a living one. That means defeating Halfdan in the field. And for that, I need Odd and his men. And frankly, if you and Odd and your army of fishermen and shopkeepers want to keep living, you need me and my warriors."

"I see your point. But there's no chance we'll just march into this compound. Even if we join you, it doesn't mean we trust you, not entirely. What else do you suggest?"

"I'll move my men down to Fevik. We'll make camp just outside the village. You bring your men by water. I know you have enough ships and boats for that. I'll be on the wharf to meet you. If you want to take me hostage then, that's fine. As long as our armies are joined, and you take my council when it comes to fighting Halfdan."

Ragi considered that. "It's not for me to agree or not. I'll tell Odd what you've proposed here, let him decide."

"Be quick about it. There's little time. Halfdan will march soon. If we don't join together before he does, then we'll all end up in the box with Thorgeir and Grim."

Ragi gave a shallow bow, because he figured Skorri expected it, and took his leave. He stepped out of the smoky, dim great hall and back into the sunshine and fresh breeze of the open ground. He blinked and breathed deep to clear the putrefaction out of his lungs. He walked quickly toward the gate.

He was not sure what to make of Skorri's offer. He could not tell if Skorri was lying, if it was a trap, or if he really thought that joining with Odd's army was his only way of saving himself from Halfdan's wrath. There was only one thing he knew for certain: Skorri Thorbrandsson had gone completely mad.

Chapter Thirty

Generous, brave men live best,
they seldom nurse sorrow;
but a foolish man fears everything,
a niggard is always nervous about gifts.

The Sayings of Hávi

It was not Ragi Oleifsson who returned the following day, bearing word of Odd's decision. That did not surprise Skorri. Ragi, messenger-boy and spy, had seen all that he needed to see, and would have reported it all back to Odd. No need to send anyone of any value after that.

The fellow Odd sent in his stead was some old fool from Fevik who called himself Hallbjorn. As sorry an example of mankind as he was, he still managed to find the right balance between respect and boldness, so that Skorri did not feel the need to send his head back to Odd in a sack, which would not have been terribly productive.

Odd and the others had agreed to Skorri's terms. That was what this Hallbjorn had been sent to say. They would bring their men ashore at Fevik if Skorri would bring his to the fields just outside of the town. The two armies would keep their distance. The leaders would figure how best to counter Halfdan's forces when they marched from Grømstad. Once it was over, and assuming they were victorious, then they would reckon on how to proceed.

"Very well," Skorri said. He had remained in the high seat this time, looking down at Hallbjorn, Gunnhild sitting at his feet. "And when does Odd propose this happen?"

"Odd says he can land his men tomorrow. Midday. If that meets with your approval."

Did this bastard address me as Lord Skorri? Skorri thought. He tried to remember. *Did he use my name at all?* He did not intend to let anyone show him any disrespect, but he could not recall now what this Hallbjorn had said. And then he realized the man was waiting for a reply.

"Midday?"

"Yes, Lord Skorri."

Lord Skorri…good, Skorri thought. *Good.* Then he made himself consider what Hallbjorn had said. *Midday?*

"Midday's acceptable," he said.

"Yes, Lord," Hallbjorn said. He frowned and glanced around. He squeezed the fingers of his left hand with those of his right, and seemed quite unwilling to say whatever it was that he intended to say next.

"What?" Skorri said. He had never been a patient man, and he was feeling much less so these days.

"Odd said that you had agreed to be on the wharf when he arrived. He said you had agreed to…" Hallbjorn seemed to struggle to find the words, so Skorri gave them to him.

"Agreed to give myself up as a hostage?"

"Yes, Lord. He said that's what you agreed."

"So I did. Tell Odd I'll be on the wharf, as promised."

Hallbjorn nodded. He seemed relieved, as well he might be. He had come that far, and his head was still attached to his body.

For a moment the two of them just looked at one another. Finally Skorri said, "Is there anything else?"

"No, Lord," Hallbjorn said.

Idiot, Skorri thought. "Well then, you had best be back to Odd and tell him what I said."

"Yes, Lord," Hallbjorn said. He bowed, turned, hurried off.

Idiot, Skorri thought again. *The lot of them. Idiots.*

He looked around the dim, cavernous interior of the great hall. There were probably three hundred men in there, but the place could easily have held twice that number. Some were eating, some sharpening weapons. Some had dragged servant girls onto their laps. Nearly all of them were drunk, loud, and boisterous.

It was not by accident or neglect. Nothing Skorri did was by accident or neglect, including letting these men have free rein here, and making few demands of them. This was the life they loved, a glimpse of the Allfather's feast hall, and it was Skorri's gift to them. Like men born with a strong taste for drink, they had quaffed from that cup and now they would want more, and their loyalty would go to the man who could give it to them. Skorri had won their devotion, and now it was time to put it to use.

He stood, so abruptly that Gunnhild looked up with surprise and a touch of fear on her face. "Lord?" she asked.

"Nothing. Clean this food away." He stepped down off the dais and walked quickly out the main door and into the yard. It was just past midday, the sky was all but cloudless, and Skorri had to blink and wipe tears away.

He could not recall the last time he had left the great hall. Not since making his visit to Odd Thorgrimson, holed up on his pathetic island. Since then, he had preferred to remain sitting on the high chair, brooding, drinking, or lying in bed with Gunnhild pressed against him. He had recoiled at the thought of venturing outside. He was not sure why.

He turned to the guards who were standing on either side of the main door and trying to look attentive, now that he was there. "Go find Koll and tell him to come to me," he said. One of the guards nodded, hurried off.

Skorri walked slowly across the open ground, watching the activity there. The butchers were still at work, and had been almost continuously since he and his men arrived. Five hundred warriors went through a lot of meat. Skorri wondered how much of the herd was left, if he was going to have to send men out into the countryside to round up more livestock.

The traitors around these parts, they've probably driven off what cattle they have, Skorri thought. But it did not matter. Men like that, farmers with their sorry little plots of land, it was not too hard to convince them to reveal where things were hidden.

He saw Koll hurrying over, not running, but not strolling either, and Skorri stopped where he was. There were no others around, and that was good. He did not need anyone hearing what he and Koll were discussing. Not for their ears. The rest could stay drunk and well-fed, until it was time for them to be otherwise.

"Lord Skorri?" Koll said. Unlike most of the men, Koll was wearing mail, sword, and seax, and had his shield slung over his back. He lacked only his helmet to be ready for battle.

Koll hated the lack of discipline that Skorri allowed. Skorri was well aware of that. But, good subordinate that he was, Koll had said little about it.

Still, Skorri could see it on his face, the way he looked at the men who were doing little but eating and drinking and taking their leisure. The way he struggled to keep his mouth shut when Skorri told him there was no need to force the men into drills, or to attend to their weapons. Koll was a good man, but he lacked Skorri's profound understanding of how to bend men to his will. As did Halfdan. As, indeed, did nearly everyone.

"What of Odd and his little make-believe army?" Skorri asked

"They're still on their island, lord. They're still sending a few boats out every day, fishing and spying on Fevik. But they haven't made any move, and they don't look to be getting ready to do so."

"I see," Skorri said. "Good."

Odd and Ragi and that sorry bunch thought that they were far more clever than they actually were. They had gone to great lengths to break their camp on the first island, the one to the north, in the dead of night, fires low, voices hushed. They thought they could sneak away with him, Skorri, never knowing where they had gone.

Idiots…

Skorri had men hidden on the smaller islands that surrounded their camp, watching and listening. He had men on every headland for miles up and down the coast, men well used to hunting and woodcraft, men who could bring word quickly back to Skorri in his great hall.

It was one of the few things Skorri had ordered done that Koll approved of, so Koll was enthusiastic about implementing those orders, selecting the most able men in the ranks, closely overseeing their work. And they had not failed. Odd and his fisherman army had done nothing, could do nothing, without Skorri's knowing about it.

"I've had word from Odd, just now," Skorri said. Koll nodded. He already knew that, of course. Koll knew most everything that went on in the great hall. "He says he's willing to join his army with ours. But he won't bring them here. I agreed to meet with them in Fevik. We'll make camp in the fields just outside of town."

"Very good…" Koll said, but his tone suggested he did not think this was very good at all. Skorri had told Koll little about his earlier meeting with Odd Thorgrimson, and what he hoped to achieve with it. He had hinted at the idea of joining forces with Odd, made a feint at the thought of opposing Halfdan the Black and establishing himself as, if not a king, then at least a powerful jarl, with the men now under his command forming the loyal core of his army.

He had said none of that explicitly, because he was not sure how Koll would react. Koll was a good man, a loyal man, but he lacked imagination and vision, which was why he could lead warriors, but could not inspire them. He lacked the ability to see how things could be, and the initiative to make them so.

But Koll still had some sway with the men. Skorri knew he had to approach Koll with care, the way he would approach a dog that might be friendly, or might be very much otherwise. He hoped Koll would remain loyal, and would embrace Skorri's vision of what could be. He hoped he would not have to put Koll's head in the box with the others.

"What happens once Odd and his people are in Fevik?" Koll asked.

"That's mostly up to Odd and his people," Skorri said. "Look here, it's only fair that I tell you what my plans are. Halfdan sent us here to capture Odd and break up this rebellion. And yes, we could simply crush it underfoot if we wished. But what Halfdan really wants is peace in his kingdom. If we just crush these folk, whoever's left will keep fighting, keep resisting. It just goes on and on. But if we convince them to give up, to think they're joining with us, then they'll stop fighting, and take up our banner. And then there'll be real peace. That's what I'm thinking."

"I see," Koll said. "They would take up the king's banner...."

Skorri nodded, though he had not actually said *king's* banner. He could hear the skepticism in Koll's voice. Men like Koll were never good at hiding their true feelings. "And what of Odd?"

"Once his people are with us, we can take him prisoner to Halfdan, and no one will say a word in protest."

"I see," Koll said again. He frowned, as if he was struggling to keep up with Skorri's machinations, which was likely the case, so he started in on a different tack.

"You'd have me move the men to Fevik? When?"

"Now. This afternoon."

Koll looked over toward the great hall, where a number of the men were taking their ease in the sun. They did not look ready to move: they looked about as far from ready as conscious men could look. "It'll take some effort to get this lot going," Koll said.

"And that's why I rely on you," Skorri said, bringing a brotherly hand down on Koll's shoulder. "Feast time is over for these men. Now I put them back in your tender care. Arms, food, ale, tents, I want it all ready to move out well before the sun is down. I want to have camp set up outside Fevik by nightfall."

"Very good." For the first time in some time Koll seemed genuinely pleased by the orders Skorri was giving him. That was hardly a surprise. He had been chafing at the inactivity, and worse, the lack of discipline, since they had arrived at Ornolf's great hall.

His great hall. Lord Skorri's great hall.

"What of the watchers?" Koll asked. "Shall I call them in?" There were close to fifty men from Skorri's army now employed watching from the headlands and the islands, and carrying news of Odd's activities back to Skorri and Koll.

"No, no," Skorri said. "We need to keep our eyes wide open. I'm not such a fool as to take Odd at his word. We'll see what he does, if he actually does what he says he'll do. One hint of betrayal and we crush him."

"As you wish," Koll said, and again he seemed to approve of the order. He bowed, hurried off toward the great hall. The men lounging around turned to look as they saw him coming. Skorri watched, amused by the sight. Koll was yelling, though Skorri could not make out the words, and gesturing with both arms in a very animated way. The men, who a moment before had been perfectly idle, now leapt to their feet and started scattering like sheep attacked by wolves.

This is good, this is good, Skorri thought. Even he felt the men were getting soft, maybe too used to these easy ways. Time to make them remember who they were: warriors, not the village drunks.

Skorri thought about what he had said to Koll, that it would be better if they could make peace with Odd, rather than fighting him, and that was true. It was also true that Skorri would be just as happy to turn Odd over to Halfdan. If Halfdan was willing to let him rule over Fevik, and the country around, and to take Ornolf's great hall for his own, in exchange for Odd Thorgrimson, there would be no need to go to war, a war that was certain to be bloody. He and Halfdan could both get what they wanted, and it would spare the lives of a lot of good men.

Skorri made a sound in his throat, half sigh, half shout of frustration, as he thought of the many things with which he had to contend. He suddenly felt sorry for himself. It was very complicated, a great puzzle. So many things to consider.

Plunge in, just plunge in and see, Skorri thought. Sometimes in battle it was best to just send your men into the fight and take advantage of whichever way things turned. Maybe Halfdan was putting an army together. Maybe Odd would join his men to Skorri's, maybe he would try to play some trick. There was no telling.

Skorri felt suddenly naked, a strange and unsettling feeling. He was not sure why. He looked down at his tunic and leggings and understood at once what was lacking. Mail. A helmet. A shield on his back.

First and foremost, Skorri Thorbrandsson was a warrior; it was time to outfit with a warrior's kit. He headed back toward the great hall, his stride long and confident. A lovely calm swept over him as he thought of donning his mail, Gunnhild strapping his sword and seax over it. Skorri was a man of action, and it was time to act.

Chapter Thirty-One

'We two have seven hall-houses, full of swords,
on each of them is a hilt made from gold;
I know that my steed is the best, and my sword the sharpest,
that my bows are bench-worthy,
and my mail-coats are made from gold…'

The Lay of Atli

The first two boats to approach the night-dark beach held fifteen men each, the most that the faerings could reasonably carry. They were dressed in mail, and well-armed. Ragi was in one of the boats. Beside him sat Hallbjorn Osvifsson, once known as Hallbjorn Deer's Bane. Arnor Knattarson was in the other.

It was well into elding, the darkest part of the night, and there was no moon, so what feeble light they had came from the stars alone. The men at the oars pulled gently, barely making headway. They could not see well enough to know when they would touch land.

Then, at last, they did, running their bows up on the unseen, soft-sand beach. Grounding out like that, they made barely a sound as they eased to a stop.

The warriors climbed out first, eleven men who were not fishermen and were not at the oars, moving with great care to keep their mail from making its jingling sound, and their weapons and shields from thumping against the sides of the boat. The rowers followed, and they all pulled the boat farther up on shore, lifting the bow to keep it from dragging on the sand.

Ragi and Hallbjorn climbed out last of all. Ragi's muscles were stiff and his backside was sore and he pressed his lips together to keep from groaning. He arched his back and stretched, happy for the cover of dark. He had been sitting on the boat's hard stern thwart since just before sunset, and he was finding that he could not endure such things the way he had in years past.

"Come," he said to Hallbjorn, his voice barely louder than a breath. The two men took a few steps up the beach, toward the granite ledge and woods just inland. They stopped and listened. They could hear the small surf lapping the sand, and, from the men behind them, the occasional soft cough, or footstep, or jingle of mail, or a few muted words. They were the source of most of the noise that Ragi could hear, despite making every effort to remain silent.

He turned his ears toward the woods. He tried to ignore the sounds from behind him and concentrated instead on what was out there. He could hear insects and the breeze shuffling branches. He heard the sharp hoot of an owl, loud and intrusive in the still night air. He could hear nothing else. Nothing that alarmed him.

"Hear anything?" he asked Hallbjorn.

Hallbjorn remained silent a moment longer, still listening. "Nothing," he said at last.

The beach had been chosen by Arnor and Bragi Shipslayer, for the same reason it had been up to them to pick the island on which Odd's army was hidden: they knew that part of the world, where land met sea, better than anyone else in camp. And once again they had chosen well.

This stretch of sand was only half a mile east of Fevik, up a narrow, tree-lined cove that hid it well from the shore. It was wide, half-moon shaped, and big enough for all the boats to comfortably land, with trees and soft ground to muffle the sounds of the landing.

Ragi heard the swishing sound of footsteps in the sand, and a shape resolved out of the dark, which he took to be Arnor. For a moment the three men stood there, listening to the night.

"What do you hear?" Arnor whispered.

"Nothing," Ragi said. "Nothing that concerns me."

"Me either," Hallbjorn said.

Arnor was silent, listening, and then he said, "Neither do I."

It had taken considerable discussion and planning to come to that place, an empty beach on a moonless night. When Ragi left Ornolf's great hall and returned to their camp on the island, he delivered Skorri's news, that Halfdan was gathering an army to march on Fevik. He also delivered the offer Skorri had extended: join their two armies, defeat

Halfdan, and negotiate a peace. To assure there would be no betrayal, Skorri would give himself up as a hostage.

Ragi did not hold back in describing to the chief men in the camp what he had seen. He told them how Skorri had let his men sack Fevik, news that they had heard already from the many folk who had fled the town. He told them of the lack of discipline among Skorri's men, and the free rein they were given to debauch themselves. He told them about the heads in the box. He told them how he was convinced that Skorri had gone insane.

"Making an alliance with a madman?" Amundi had said. "That doesn't sound like the prudent course."

"If his men have become nothing but useless drunks, they'll have no fight in them," Bragi had argued. "Let's go ashore and kill them all. I'll kill them all, with my fists alone."

"Just because Skorri's mad, and his men are drunk, it doesn't mean the fight's out of them," Ragi said. "And it doesn't mean Skorri's not dangerous. It's the mad ones, I've seen, are often enough the most clever."

Odd listened to the council, which was far-ranging. He said little, just allowed the debate to play out among the others. Finally, when that was done, he spoke.

"Skorri's a mad dog, we can see that. And you handle mad dogs with the most caution of all. And you certainly don't ignore them, or turn your back on them."

"Which means?" Arnor asked.

"Which means we join with Skorri. If we have him hostage then there's not much he can do to betray us. We'll fight Halfdan's army and see where the bones fall."

"I agree," Ragi said. "But I'm still worried about landing all our men in Fevik, right at Skorri's feet, with him waiting for us. It could well be a trap. If Skorri had you as his prisoner, Odd, he would be in a good place to bargain with Halfdan."

"You're right," Odd said. "So we won't land all our men at Skorri's feet. We'll split the army in two. Half will move out tonight, in the boats, after dark. We'll have to find some place close to Fevik where they can land without being seen. Some place they can stay hidden. If Skorri's honest with us, those men can join us in Fevik. If he springs some sort of trap on us, that second part of the army can attack from the flank. If the gods will it, we'll take Skorri by surprise and finish him on the battlefield."

The others had agreed with that, and the men were organized into their two divisions. Ragi and Arnor were selected to lead the night party. Hallbjorn was sent with them because they needed someone who knew the countryside well, and who could act as a scout in the night woods.

And so far, Ragi had to admit, things had gone well. Arnor and the other fishermen had deftly navigated the shoreline in the dark, bringing the little flotilla to within half a mile of the designated beach, before Ragi and Arnor had gone ahead to make sure it was safe to land.

Now they stood by the edge of the woods and listened for a few moments more, but still they heard nothing from the country beyond the beach; no challenge, no cries of alarm, no crush of vegetation as some sentry raced off to announce their presence.

"What say you?" Ragi asked the other two, still keeping his words barely audible.

"I say I go into the woods, have a look around," Hallbjorn said. "Make sure we're really alone here."

"While he's off, I'll send word for the others to come ashore," Arnor said. "We have little time to waste."

"Yes," Ragi said. "Good. We'll get the men ashore now, but we'll wait until Hallbjorn returns before we move inland."

Arnor walked back down to the surf to send his boat crew off to the rest of the fleet, floating out there in the dark, and tell them that the way was clear. Hallbjorn moved in the other direction, toward the trees. Unlike the others, he wore no mail or helmet, carried no shield or sword. For weapons he had only a seax and a hunting knife on his belt: moving quickly and unencumbered was his primary goal.

Once the other two were gone, Ragi stepped closer to the tree line, the stump of his left hand pressing against his sword so it did not thump against his legs or mail shirt. He stared off into the dark woods. He listened. He heard nothing, until he heard the soft shush of feet in sand behind him.

He turned. He could see the dark shapes of a few men standing a dozen feet behind him. Instinct more than recognition told him that one of the men was Asgeir Refsson, chief among the dozen warriors from Ragi's household who had escaped with Ragi when Skorri had attacked his hall. Asgeir and the others, experienced fighting men all, had come with Ragi and Arnor in the first boats ashore.

Ragi took a few steps in his direction. "Is there news, Asgeir?" he asked.

"No, nothing, Ragi," Asgeir said. "We're just waiting. Like you."

"Very well," Ragi said. "Keep quiet." He turned back and faced the woods again.

There was an entire beach on which Asgeir and the others could wait, but Ragi knew full well why they chose to stand where they did. They were his household warriors, and they were protective of Ragi, sometimes to the point where it grew annoying. To the point where he felt like a feeble old man.

Ragi remained where he was, motionless, listening, until at last he could hear the drip of water off the blades of oars, the all-but-silent sound of the boats running up on the beach.

"Keep watch, and stay quiet," he said to Asgeir, then walked back to where the faerings were pulling up, around twenty in all, carrying some two hundred men between them. These were less than half of the men Odd had, but Odd would need to arrive in Fevik with a substantial army in his company, and the men Ragi had under his command should be enough to launch a surprise attack on Skorri, if need be.

He walked along the surf line, talking in a whisper to the men. "Carry your boats up the beach a ways. Don't drag them, carry them. Keep silent. Once your boats are ashore, gather up by the tree line."

He could barely see the men as they carried out his orders, dark shadows on a dark beach, hauling the faerings farther up the sand where the tide would not carry them away. When that was done, and the men were moving up the beach, Ragi joined them, his shoes sinking in the fine sand as he walked.

Arnor was standing between the tree line and the men, and Ragi joined him there.

"Hallbjorn's not back," Arnor whispered, and Ragi made a soft sound of acknowledgement. They continued to wait, continued to listen, and suddenly there was a dark form moving in front of them. Ragi startled, just a bit, and hoped the night had hidden that reaction.

"There's a field yonder where I thought we might bed down," Hallbjorn said, his voice barely audible. "I scouted the woods between here and there, and beyond, to the outskirts of Fevik. There are guards on the roads into the village, and some in the fields. But we reckoned on that."

"The woods?" Arnor asked.

"Nothing..." Hallbjorn said, but that time he did not sound so certain.

"What is it?" Ragi asked.

"There was something moving. Very small sound. Nothing unusual, really. An animal of some sort, I'm sure. That was it."

The words hung there for a moment. Ragi spoke next.

"Is this something to worry us? Does it change things?"

"No, no, I don't think so," Hallbjorn said. "An animal. A fox, or the like."

"Good," Ragi said. "Then we go."

The two hundred or so men had been told what to expect, what they would be expected to do, well before they climbed into the boats. Now Ragi moved among them, reminding them, *sotto voce*, what the plan was.

"We're going into the woods. Single file. Keep eyes on the man ahead, and not a sound. We don't have far to go, and then we bed down for the night, see what the dawn brings."

That done, he gave Hallbjorn the word and Hallbjorn headed back toward the tree line, Ragi just behind him, the rest of the men falling in behind Ragi, a long serpent of warriors snaking onto the trail that Hallbjorn had found. It was slow going; what little light they had from the stars was mostly blocked out now, and to Ragi's eyes, Hallbjorn, in his linen tunic, was no more than a slightly less dark figure against a thoroughly dark background.

Hallbjorn, happily, had sense enough to move slowly, and Ragi was able to keep up, and he could only hope that the men behind him were keeping up as well. He could hear the occasional snapping of a twig, or the rustle of a branch brushing a mail shirt, or the thump of a sheathed sword against something. He could even hear the occasional muted curse. He knew the men were being as quiet as they possibly could, but still they sounded to Ragi as loud as if they were plundering a Frankish monastery.

He did not know how long they walked, but, concentrating as he was on every step, it seemed a very long time. Finally they came to a place where the woods thinned and started yielding to a small field of tall grass. Hallbjorn kept going, and as they stepped out of the trees and into the open ground, under the sweep of stars, it became a bit easier to see.

Halfway across the field, Hallbjorn turned and whispered, "We'll stop here."

Ragi turned to the man behind him and whispered, "Hold up, and pass word down the line," and soon the sound of two hundred men trying to walk quietly faded away to nothing, and only the sound of the night forest remained.

Arnor, who had been bringing up the end of the line, now appeared at Ragi's side.

"This is where I reckoned we could spend the night," Hallbjorn said. "There's another stretch of woods beyond, and then Fevik is beyond that. So we're close, but we're hidden here."

"Good," Ragi said. "In the morning we can move closer, maybe keep to the woods, see if Odd needs us in town." The other two grunted their acknowledgement.

"We'll need sentries out in the trees, all around this field," Ragi continued. "To make certain that no one comes walking up in the night."

"I'll find men for that," Arnor said. They discussed a few more details, then Ragi and Arnor spread the word that each man should find some nice patch of field and bed down in the tall grass for the night. They would need their rest. At first light they would be up and at it again, which might entail simply walking into Fevik, or might mean fighting their way in.

Once Ragi was satisfied that all was well, that the men had made their beds and the sentries were in position, he looked around for a place where he, too, could lie down. He heard a voice call in a hoarse whisper, "*Ragi! Here!*"

He could just make out Asgeir beckoning to him. He stifled a sigh and walked over, then laid down in a spot near where Asgeir and the others were bedded down. The ground was not particularly comfortable, but there were no roots or rocks, so it was not the worst that Ragi had experienced. It would have been better still if he was not wearing mail and sword and seax, but he had no intention of going to sleep less than completely prepared for battle.

He laid his head on his shield and closed his eyes, and eventually the weariness of the day won out over the discomfort and concerns, and he managed to sleep, if fitfully.

Sometime later he woke, gazing up through stalks of tall grass. They were black-looking against a sky the gray color of the sea just before a storm. He had no idea where he was.

Field… he thought, as it started coming back to him. He was in a field, just outside of Fevik. Hiding. Standing ready in case Skorri should betray them.

It's not dawn yet, he thought next. Judging from the muted light above, Ragi guessed the hour was a little shy of sunup. And that was good. That was when he liked to be up and about, even if he had no particular reason to be up at that time. That morning, however, he did.

He pushed himself up to a sitting position and then up onto his feet, happy there was no one else awake to see that struggle. For an awkward moment he thought his knees might buckle under him, but they held and he stood to his full height and worked the kinks and cramps from his muscles.

He looked around. Everything in the pre-dawn light was washed in tones of gray and black. He could see Asgeir five feet away, sprawled out on his bit of flattened grass, snoring, mouth open, and the rest of his men nearby. Beyond that, he could see only the open field and the dark stands of woods all around. He could hear only the morning song of countless unseen birds, and the guttural, animal sounds of dozens of snoring men.

Ragi adjusted his sword and seax, picked up his shield off the ground and slung it over his back, then headed off toward the woods. Asgeir would be annoyed, he knew, when he found Ragi had gone off unaccompanied, but Ragi was eager to enjoy the dawn's quiet, and to see that the sentries were still alert.

He walked through the tall grass, like walking through waist-high water, until he came to the edge of the trees. He stopped to relieve himself, then stepped into the cool dark of the woods. It had grown noticeably lighter in the brief time he had been awake, and now he could see well enough to make his way through the trees and brush without a path to follow.

He moved slowly, stepping around trees, over fallen trunks, taking care not to catch his sword or shield in the undergrowth. He looked and he listened, but he saw nothing but woods, heard nothing but birds.

Ragi was not sure where the sentries were posted, but if Arnor had taken care to put a sufficient number in place, then Ragi figured he would not have to go far before finding one. He was eager to hear what they had to say, what they might have seen or heard in the night. He was eager to know if there was any reason for concern.

Something caught his eye, not too far off, twenty feet or so, something different from the dark greens and browns of the woods. Not a man crouched and watching, which he expected to see, but something else. Smaller. Ragi moved in that direction, eyes on whatever it was that had caught his attention.

He was ten feet away when he realized it was a foot. A man's foot in a light brown calfskin shoe, toes up, and a leg bound in windings of a similar color. The rest of the man was hidden in the brush. A sentry, fallen asleep, was Ragi's first thought.

Son of a bitch... He took two steps closer. He wanted to give the man a swift kick to wake him up, but feared he would yell in surprise, so he reconsidered. He was still thinking on it when he parted the brush and saw the rest of the man; arms spread, eyes wide, throat open in a wide gash of torn and bloody flesh.

"Son of a bitch," Ragi said in a loud whisper. He put his hand on the hilt of his sword, pivoting as he did, and peered through the trees. He heard a twanging sound, a familiar note, and before he even realized what it was, he saw the flash of the arrow as it shot past the spot where his chest had been a heartbeat before. He heard a thud, saw the arrow embed itself in the trunk of a pine tree ten feet away, and then he started to run.

Chapter Thirty-Two

And it seemed to me
those hands of the ring-goddess,
blood-red, were bathed
and drenched in gold-breaker's gore.

Gisli Sursson's Saga

Ragi crashed back through the trees, following the trail of trampled bracken he had left on his way in. He heard another bow string twang and felt a pull on his left arm, as if someone had tried to grab it, and he was thrown off stride. He saw the arrow fly past in a tumbling, uneven flight, and then he felt the burning sensation in his upper arm where the arrow had torn through chainmail, and linen, and flesh, and muscle, on its way through.

"Ahh, bastards!" he shouted through clenched teeth as the pain shot up and down his arm, but he did not slow his pace. He came bursting out of the tree line and onto the grassy field. There were a few dozen men on their feet, scattered all around the open ground, but they did not seem in any way alarmed, just waking up as the sun rose behind them.

"To arms!" Ragi shouted as he ran. "To arms, to arms, they're coming now!" He saw heads turn, men turn, more men getting to their feet. But no more movement than that. They were still too taken with sleep, too surprised, it seemed, to understand.

"To arms! Make a shield wall! Form up! Shield wall!" he shouted as he ran.

Asgeir, fifty feet away, was the first to react. He charged back toward the other men, waving his arms and shouting, pointing, calling orders, in some cases actually shoving men into place. More men rose up from the grass as if conjured from the earth. They were putting helmets in place, those who had helmets, and those who had shields were slipping them over their arms.

"Here!" Ragi called, stopping near the middle of the field. "Form up on me! There, and there!" He pointed with his sword, which was in his hand, though he did not recall drawing it.

He stabbed the sword into the ground and slipped his shield off his back. He put his left arm through the straps, and tightened the thong he had rigged so he could hold it secure despite his missing hand, then took up his sword again. Pain from his bleeding wound shot through him, and he allowed himself a muted cry of agony between clenched teeth.

Men were running in his direction, taking their place on either side, shields locked, swords up. Ragi had put himself in the center of the shield wall even though he was not certain he could hold his shield with his wounded arm. But he knew from past experience that pain often disappeared when the fighting started, and he was counting on that.

Asgeir stepped up on his left side, pushing the man who had been standing there out of the way. "You're hurt!" he said.

"Bastards got me with an arrow," Ragi said.

"How many?"

"Don't know. Never saw one of them. I found one of the sentries dead. That was all I saw before they loosed an arrow at me."

"Well, we'll know soon enough," Asgeir said.

And he was right. Ragi's men were still forming up when Skorri's warriors came out of the woods a hundred feet in front of them. And they kept coming, hundreds of men, charging into the open field. And unlike Ragi's men, they all had shields, all had swords and mail, and many with spears as well.

"Stand ready!" Ragi shouted. "You men with shields, interlock them! You men with spears, get behind the shield wall and kill the bastards as they come!"

He looked back across the field, hoping that Skorri's men were going to make a wild and disorganized charge. It might be the only way that Ragi and his men could hope to stand up to them. But no such luck. Whoever was in command there, he had stopped their headlong rush and was getting the men into a wedge-shaped formation, a swine array, a potentially lethal attack against a shield wall.

"I hoped they wouldn't do that," Asgeir said, speaking Ragi's thoughts out loud.

"I don't think they have as many men as we do," Ragi said, hopefully. And it was the truth. There were perhaps a hundred and fifty men to Ragi's two hundred. But they were experienced warriors all, it seemed. And that mattered more than numbers.

It was suddenly quiet, oddly quiet, just for a moment, and then, with a shout, Skorri's men began to move forward. The one who had formed them up was now at the point of the wedge, the rest of the men streaming back on either side. Like a massive rock come loose and rolling downhill they started their advance slowly, moving at a quick walk, no more. Then yard by yard their speed built, and with it their shouting, until, with the pounding of feet on the soft earth, and the clash of shields and mail, and the shouting, there seemed to be a solid mass of noise coming across the open ground.

"Stand ready! We'll kill these bastards!" Ragi shouted. He looked left and right down his own line. He saw three men throw their weapons away and turn and run for the woods behind them. He wished he had archers to shoot them down as they ran, but he did not.

He looked straight ahead: fifty feet between their lines and closing fast. Ragi could see faces under helmets, the texture of mail shirts.

When Skorri's men hit, it was like a battering ram against an oak door, a blow powerful enough to nearly shatter the boards, but not quite. The warrior at the point of the swine array slammed hard into Ragi's shield, and Ragi shouted, part battle cry, part scream of agony, a cry that came up from his gut as the fury and the pain in his wounded arm rolled over him.

The man had his sword held straight up and back, as if he was trying to keep it out of the way, but as the lines hit and Ragi was driven back a step, the sword came down and darted out over the man's shield, over Ragi's shield, driving at Ragi's head.

The move was swift and well-timed, but it was not a surprise. Ragi knew it was coming, knew it even before their shields hit. He ducked his head and lifted his shield up with a sudden motion, knocking the man's sword with the iron rim. Then with his own sword he thrust up and under his shield. He felt the tip hit and he thrust harder and the man he was facing twisted and tried to step back, but he could not, crowded as he was by the men behind him.

Ragi tried to drive the sword home, but he was at the end of his reach. The man brought his shield down and knocked Ragi's blade aside as Ragi drew it back. A spear point came in at him from the left, but Asgeir's sword was there, hacking down on the shaft, knocking it aside. Asgeir recovered, thrust, and took the spearman in the neck. There was a spray of blood and, as the spearman stumbled back, a gap opened in their shield wall, but it was filled in an instant.

Up and down the line men were shouting, screaming, voices cutting through the clash of shields on shields, iron on iron. The sensation of fighting in a shield wall — Ragi had known it many times, but it had been a long while since last he felt it. He remembered now. It was horrible and wonderful all at once.

The warrior he faced in front of him lashed out with his sword. Once again, Ragi twisted his head out of the way and counter-thrust. He realized that he knew the man. He was sure of it. His face was half obscured by his helmet, red with exertion, shouting, but Ragi was certain he knew him.

And now he hoped to kill him. He darted his sword out, over his shield this time, not under. He saw it hit the side of the man's helmet and bounce off. Half an inch to the left and that would have been an end to it, but no such luck.

"Hold the line! Hold!" he heard Asgeir shouting, and he realized that the shield wall was being pushed back, bending in the middle where the swine array was putting the most pressure, like a beam with too much weight loaded on.

"Hold!" Ragi shouted as well. "Push them! Push them!" He dug his back foot into the dirt and shoved forward, pressing his shield against that of the man in front of him. Again the man's sword came over the top of his shield, and this time Ragi ducked his head behind his own shield and slashed at the man's legs. If he could drop this man, or push hard enough against the center of Skorri's line, get them moving back, it was possible that the enemy would break first.

But it was no good. The pain in his left arm was overwhelming. Ragi felt his head spin, thought he might actually pass out. He took a step back to relieve the pressure. Asgeir reached across with his sword, thrust at the man Ragi was facing, and the man did not see it coming until the last second. He turned his head and Asgeir's blade ran along his cheek, opening up a bright red gash just above the line of his beard, then deflecting off the nose-guard of his helmet.

Ragi saw the man's mouth open as he cried out in pain, but he could not differentiate the shout from the rest of the chaotic noise along the line. The man turned to look at Asgeir, bleeding, distracted by this new attack, and that left him one easy thrust away from dying on Ragi's sword.

Ragi cocked his weapon arm, eyes on the man's face. He was just starting to thrust when he felt himself knocked back, felt the entire shield wall knocked back, as Skorri's men together gave a shout and drove forward, slamming shields on shields, hacking with swords, thrusting with spears, working together to break the deadlock in the middle of the field.

And it worked. Ragi saw men in his line go down left and right. He saw another turn and run, and then another after that.

"Hold! Hold!" he shouted. "Stand fast!" But he knew already that it was useless. He had won fights in shield walls, and he had lost them as well, and he knew what losing looked like. It looked like this.

He shouted again, in pain and frustration. He lowered his shield a few inches and hacked with his sword: unsubtle, uncoordinated, just hacking, again and again, and all the man in front of him could do was hold his own sword up to take the blows, and try to drive Ragi back.

"Hold together! Fall back! Hold them and fall back!" Ragi shouted. The shield wall was done, and the best they could do now was retreat back into the woods in some disciplined way and fight man to man. Maybe get back to the boats. Maybe die there among the trees.

He took a step back and Asgeir did as well, as did the man on his right. They stepped again, holding with their shields, hacking with their swords and axes and thrusting with spears. Ragi stole a glance at either flank. Most of the shield wall was still intact, holding, moving back. Three steps, four steps.

A few more men turned and raced off for the trees. And then a few more behind them. And then it was over, and all of Ragi's men were turning and running and throwing weapons away as they fled.

"Let's go! Let's go!" Asgeir was shouting, pulling at Ragi's arm while simultaneously flailing at Skorri's men with sword and shield.

Ragi looked at him, looked at Skorri's man with the bleeding cheek facing him. He slashed at the man, and then, with a shout of fury and despair and pain, he, too, turned and ran.

They ran side by side, Ragi and Asgeir, stumbling over the uneven ground, running for the woods and the trail down to the beach. Ahead,

Ragi could see the others, all fleeing headlong in the same direction. The ground was littered with the shields and spears and axes they had thrown aside in their flight.

No, no, no! Ragi thought. He had hoped they might make a defensive line in the woods, where the trees would stop Skorri's men from advancing in a shield wall, but he could see now that was not going to happen. He could shout orders until he dropped dead and no one was going to listen. The panic had taken hold of them. And even if they did listen, they no longer had weapons with which to fight.

He could hear Skorri's men behind them, the pounding of their feet, the thumping of their shields and weapons. They were moving fast, but not running, not matching the headlong flight of Ragi's men. They were more disciplined than that, better trained. Whoever was commanding them understood the importance of not letting his attack devolve into chaos. When the fight resumed, Skorri's men would be ready to hit their enemy with a single, mighty blow.

They were in the woods now, charging down the trail that Hallbjorn had led them up the night before. The branches pulled at their shields, which, unlike the others, they had not tossed aside. Ragi could feel blood running down the stump of his left arm and soaking into the shirt he wore under his tunic and mail.

At last they came out of the trees and stumbled down onto the beach. Ragi had figured the others would have raced for the boats and shoved off, pulling as hard as they could to get out of the archers' range. But to Ragi's surprise, the men were still there, gathered by the surf, milling about like a herd of sheep.

He and Asgeir ran across the sand and came to a stop twenty feet from the rest. They doubled over, breathing hard. Ragi heard several voices at once, shouting, angry and afraid.

"The boats! The boats are gone!"

He looked up, still gasping for breath. He could see the gouges in the sand where the faerings had been pulled up, and where apparently they had been pushed back out again.

"There!" someone shouted, pointing. Heads turned. A few hundred feet off, drifting away on the falling tide, the boats were being swept out to sea.

Ragi shook his head. *Fools. What fools we are…*

They thought they were so clever, sneaking around on Skorri's flank, but they had not been sneaking anywhere. Skorri knew full well where they were, what they were doing. Enough so that he sent his men around to set their only means of escape drifting off on the tide.

A hundred feet back, the first of Skorri's men began to emerge from the woods and make their way cautiously down to the beach. They were taking their time, not making some wild and disorganized charge. There was no need for them to do that. There was no danger of their enemy rowing away to safety.

"Where's Arnor?" Ragi asked, then called, "Arnor!" He looked around the crowd of men by the surf, but he could not see Arnor among them, and he knew he might well be one of the dead they had left back on the field in the woods.

"Son of a bitch!" Ragi said to himself. He felt a sense of despair, hopelessness, but behind it came a strange sort of calm, a profound resolve. "Asgeir, listen here," he said. He pointed with his sword to the woods at the far end of the beach. "Lead the men there, see if you can't make an escape that way. Could be Skorri has men waiting. You can try to fight your way through."

Asgeir frowned. "What are you going to do?"

"Makes no difference what I'm doing. You take charge of this lot. Get them out of here. If Odd still lives by the end of the day, try and join with him again. Keep fighting."

Asgeir was shaking his head. "Whatever you're thinking, I won't allow it."

Ragi raised his sword, the point at Asgeir's throat. "By the gods, Asgeir, I love you, but if you don't do as I command I'll kill you here and now."

They held one another's eyes, neither moving, neither speaking. There was a shout from back by the woods as Skorri's men made ready to advance.

"Go," Ragi said.

Asgeir nodded. "We'll fight again, side by side, and feast when it's done." He turned, lifted his sword and shield and yelled, "Everyone! To the far woods! Run, run!"

Ragi watched until the first of the men started to race off, and more and more followed. He turned toward the woods. Skorri's men were charging across the sand, led by the man with the bleeding cheek, a less organized charge than before, but now they were running after fleeing men who were mostly without weapons.

Ragi refreshed the grip on his sword and started jogging toward the men who were coming at him. No need to run now, he preferred to save what little breath he had. The man with the bleeding cheek was fifty feet away and making right for him, which was good, because he was the one Ragi wanted.

They met shield to shield, slamming into one another. The pain ripped through Ragi's arm, but there was something cathartic about it this time. His face was a foot away from the other man's, their eyes fixed on one another's.

Koll Thorvaldson, he thought. That's who it was. He had known the man for years. A good man. It was too bad it had to end that way.

Ragi raised his sword and slashed down in a sideways blow at Koll's head, but Koll's sword was up and took the blow with a ring of steel on steel. Ragi shoved, trying to get space to fight, and brought his sword back for another blow. He was aware of men coming around the sides now, some racing past Koll, trying to get to the others.

Koll thrust and Ragi jerked his head to the side and felt the blade slicing through his ear. He heard Koll yell, "No!" and did not know what he could mean by that, and then he felt the tip of a spear ripping into his side, through his mail, and everything seemed to burst into a lightning strike of agony. For an instant he could not move, could not think, he could only stand there, consumed by pain.

He started to turn toward the spearman when another spear hit him from the other side, higher up, ripping into his chest. He felt blood coming up his throat. His eyes met Koll's and he saw that Koll had a strange look on his face. Sorrow. Pity. Koll shook his head, just a bit, then stepped back, brought his sword backhand across his chest, and swung it at Ragi's neck.

It was just before dawn, the gray light yielding to full morning, when Skorri heard the first sounds of the fight. Or at least, he thought he did.

He sat up a little straighter in his saddle and turned his head toward the wood line. The enemy, such that it was — the part of Odd's army that had been sent around to flank Skorri's men — was only about half a mile away. At that distance, the battle would have been easily heard, if not for the trees between it and Skorri.

As it was, Skorri was not absolutely certain of what he was hearing. It should be fighting. It had best be fighting.

Idiots... Skorri thought.

Word of the landing had been brought to him in the dark hours of the night. He was awake then, laying on his bed in the big tent in the field outside Fevik, the rest of his army in smaller tents surrounding it. A messenger from Koll had brought the news: about two hundred of Odd's men had come ashore a few miles east of Fevik, pulled up on a beach earlier in the night. Well-armed, at least by the standards of Odd's ridiculous band of fishermen and shopkeepers.

This did not surprise Skorri. He had guessed all along that Odd would make some bumbling attempt to trick him, to get the upper hand. That was why he had told Koll to keep the watchers in place, the men who had eyes on every part of the coastline thereabouts. Men who could move unseen and unheard through the woods and fields. And it had paid off. Now it was time for Skorri to go to work.

He made his way out of his tent and onto the grounds, where he found Koll conferring with a few others.

"Well?" Skorri asked.

"About two hundred men," Koll said. "Landed by boat, moved inland. There's a field of tall grass between here and the cove where they landed. They're bedded down there for the night."

"Who's in command?"

"I don't know, lord."

"Do they have guards? Sentries?"

"They posted sentries in the woods, lord. A dozen, maybe, ringing the field. The rest of them are asleep."

"Sentries might be a problem," Skorri said.

"Not anymore. My watchers killed the lot of them. Never made a sound. I hope that's what you wished."

"Yes, good, good," Skorri said. "I won't find fault with you killing any of those vermin. And now what do you intend?"

"I just passed the word for my men to make ready for battle. I mean to get them into the woods now, close to the field. I don't think Odd's people will move before dawn. We'll catch them just as they're waking, kill them all as they're having their morning piss."

Skorri nodded. "I want them all dead. I don't want any to escape. Do you have any men who could get around behind them, get to that cove where they landed and burn the boats?"

"I do, lord. But burning might give us away. The tide'll be ebbing soon. If we pushed the boats off they'd be carried out to sea."

"Very well. Do that," Skorri said. "And I'm counting on you to follow through on this attack. No one lives."

"Yes, lord," Koll said. He sounded like a man who was trying to appear sincere, rather than a man who genuinely was. Skorri doubted that Koll was up for the level of brutality needed in this situation, but there was nothing for it now. The coming fight was a sideshow, a distraction. Skorri could not be bothered with it, so he let Koll take command, gave him a hundred and fifty men, more than enough to kill all the fishermen and shopkeepers sleeping in the tall grass. The rest he kept for himself.

The real action would take place there in Fevik, once Odd and the bulk of his army were lured ashore. He hoped that Koll's business would be done by then, and Koll and his men would be back for the big fight. But if they were not, it would not matter. The men that Skorri had with him, and the surprise that he had in mind, would be enough to grind Odd into the ground.

Skorri spent the rest of the dark hours on horseback, patrolling the streets of Fevik and the country nearby. As the sky started to grow lighter, he returned to the camp. He rode to the edge of the woods and sat motionless in his saddle, ears turned in the direction where the fight should be.

Every now and then he heard a sound that made him sit more upright, something that might be shouting, or weapons clashing, but he could not be sure. He was about ready to give it up, convinced he would not be able to hear the fighting from there. And then he did.

It was muted and far off, but unmistakable: the sound of men shouting, the clang of weapons on weapons, the thump of shields on shields, cut through here and there by the screams of the wounded. He sat and listened, his head turned in the direction of the sound. It was like hearing through plugged ears, but Skorri had seen and heard enough battles to know he was hearing one now.

The fighting did not last long, and when it ended, it ended abruptly. Skorri's first hope was that Koll and his men had killed them all in that short skirmish, but he knew that was unlikely. It was more probable that Odd's men had run off, and now Koll's warriors were chasing after them. Koll would have to run them to ground before he could slaughter them.

Skorri dismounted, found some bread, meat, and ale. When he was done, he told the men in his personal guard, the only ones awake at that time, to rouse all the others in camp, quietly, and tell them to make ready for battle. Odd was not expected to arrive at the waterfront before midday, but they needed to be in place well before that.

The sun was above the trees by the time Koll and his men came walking out of the woods and back into the camp. Some were wounded, with legs or arms bound in bloody bandages. Some were being carried in makeshift litters, the dead with their shields over their chests and faces. But there were only a few dead or wounded. Mostly, they looked like men returning triumphant from a not-too-difficult fight.

Koll led the way, and Skorri was there to meet him. He had a nasty cut along his cheek, and a swath of dried blood which had flowed down his flesh and into his beard, but he looked otherwise intact. He held a cloth bundle in his hand. The bottom half of the bundle was soaked through with blood.

"What do you have there?" Skorri asked, nodding toward the bundle. Koll let go of one edge of the cloth. The head that tumbled out rolled onto the ground and came to a rest on its side, face toward Skorri.

Skorri stared down at it. The skin was pale as could be, mouth and eyes wide open, the long hair and cropped beard more gray than dark.

"Ragi Oleifsson," Skorri said at last. "Looks like he made some bad choices, when it comes to loyalty."

"He died well," Koll said. Skorri looked from Ragi's face to Koll's. Skorri had ordered Koll to bring him the head of whoever was in command of Odd's men, but he did not think Koll was particularly happy about it.

"What's that?"

"Ragi. He died well. A warrior's death. Attacking, with his sword in his hand."

"Well, good for him," Skorri said. "And now he'll make a fine addition to the collection in my box. What of the fight?"

"They were just waking when we attacked. They met us in the field. They made something like a shield wall. It didn't hold long. We chased them back to the cove."

"And the boats?"

"They were off on the tide. Half mile off by the time we got there. So we ended it there on the beach."

"Ended it? You killed them? Killed them all?"

"We did," Koll said. "Some got away, but we killed most."

Skorri studied Koll's face. The man claimed to have slaughtered the enemy, then in the next breath admitted that some got away. He was not even sure Koll was telling the truth about killing most. But there would be time later to get to the bottom of that. They had more pressing matters.

"So, that's taken care of," Skorri said. "Good. Get your men something to eat and drink, and then we'll get in position. You recall what I said?"

Koll nodded. "We'll spread the men out through all the buildings lining the chief road through town, keep them out of sight. Odd arrives about midday, and you'll lead them down the road to the camp. Once Odd's men are spread out along the road, we'll fall on them, hit them on both flanks."

"Exactly. Kill them all, just like before. But not Odd. Odd'll be at my side, so I'll see to him."

"Very good, Lord Skorri," Koll said, though there was a quality to his voice that suggested it was not so very good, at least not with him. But again, there would be time later to deal with that. Skorri's only interest now was in crushing Odd's rebellion. And this time, he would be there to make certain Koll was acting as remorselessly as the situation called for.

In some ways, it was too bad. If Odd had been willing to join forces, it would have been easier for Skorri to take on Halfdan and win. Close to a thousand men would be better than just five hundred, even if half of them, Odd's half, were largely just fodder for Halfdan's swords and spears.

But that was not to be. Odd had tried to betray him, just as Skorri suspected he would. And now there was *wergild*, blood money, to pay.

Chapter Thirty-Three

I know it, the sixth: if a warrior wounds me
on the roots of a strong tree
— so too with that man who provokes my hatred
— harm will devour him, rather than me.

The Sayings of Hávi

It was enormously frustrating, not knowing. But there was nothing for it. Odd understood that.

He was standing on the afterdeck of his longship, which had once been Halfdan's longship, the name of which he did not know. The ship was floating now, in the narrow channel that ran between the islands on which he and his people had made their camp, and it remained tied by a single line to a rock on shore.

Odd was staring out at the water, but his thoughts were elsewhere.

Ragi and Arnor and the men with them had landed safely on the beach the night before, he was fairly certain of that. If there had been a problem — a trap, or something else unforeseen — they would have returned to the island camp. If they had been attacked after landing, at least a few boats would have escaped and made their way back, he had to imagine.

But none had. And Odd took that to mean that the landing, and Hallbjorn's scouting the trails, and the men's clandestine approach to Fevik, had all met with success.

"I'm impressed," Bragi Shipslayer said. He, too, was standing on the afterdeck.

"What?"

"Well, the water was too low for us to get our ships out of here, but you've been staring at it for half the morning, and it seems, through the force of your magic, you've made it rise. That's some power you have there." Bragi gave a shallow bow.

Odd frowned. He resisted making the reply that first came to mind. He was not in much of a joking mood, and could not recall the last time he had been. And he could not recall the last time Bragi had been in any other sort.

"Is the water high enough now," Odd asked, "or do I need to keep staring at it?"

"High enough, I should think. We wait only your word, Lord Odd, to be underway."

Odd looked past Bragi, out toward the other vessels in his strange fleet. Close to half of the fishing boats had gone off with Ragi and Arnor; the twenty or so that remained were manned by the rest of the fishermen-cum-warriors. The longships were crowded as well, the oars double-banked, and more men were standing or sitting amidships and fore and aft.

Next, Odd looked up at the sun, which seemed to be nearing its midday high. Time to go. He turned back to the men in his longship and those in the other vessels.

"Listen here!" he called, in a voice that could be heard all across the small cove. The general buzz of noise dropped away as all heads turned toward him. "Time to get underway. My ship will lead. Second longship behind us, and the faerings behind that. If things look right, I'll go ashore, and you men follow. If things don't look right, you'll hear it from me. Keep alert, look to me for orders."

He looked around. Heads were nodding. No one said anything.

"Very well, Bragi Shipslayer, off we go," Odd said.

Bragi grinned. He was already at the tiller, and now he shouted his orders forward. Huginn let the bow line go, the rowers dropped the oars and pushed, and the longship started backing away from the shore. Once mid-channel, Bragi gave the orders that had the ship deftly spin a quarter-turn, then begin moving ahead.

Odd leaned over the side and looked astern. The second longship was now doing the same, following right behind.

He was sorry not to have Ragi in command of that ship. After Bragi Shipslayer, Ragi was the most experienced ship driver among them. And he certainly had the most experience in battle, both on land and sea. But that was exactly why Odd needed him to lead the other men around Skorri's flank, and be ready to launch a surprise attack if Skorri had some treachery in mind.

In Ragi's stead, Bragi had suggested Muninn take command of the second ship. Odd did not argue, since he had no one else in mind. Now, watching Muninn getting the ship underway, it seemed a good choice.

The tide was still rising, the current against them, which made it slow going as they pulled out between the two islands. They moved into the wider channel that ran through the scattering of islands around them, and then into open water beyond. The wind was steady and from the southwest, and would have made for excellent sailing, but Fevik was less than three miles away by water, and it was hardly worth setting sail for so short a distance. And, of course, the faerings would have been left far astern.

There was little talking onboard, only a few conversations in low tones here and there. They were heading into a very uncertain situation — possibly a trap, possibly a grand battle against King Halfdan and his army — and every man seemed to feel the weight of that.

They moved along an open stretch of coastline and rounded a point of land to the west, and as they did, the wide harbor, with Fevik at its head, opened up before them. Odd looked astern, to make certain the second longship was with them, and, of greater concern, that the faerings were able to keep up. But there seemed to be no problem. The smaller boats, rowed by fishermen well used to the work of pulling oars, were maintaining the pace just fine, and probably with less effort than that required of the men rowing the ships.

"It's going to make me cry, you know, wasting this beautiful breeze," Bragi said. "A sailor never wastes a fine breeze. You'd know that if you weren't a sheep-herder at heart."

"By the time you get the sail set, stumbling over the crowd of men we have aboard, we'll have run aground in Fevik," Odd said, and the truth of that was so obvious that even Bragi could not argue, and only grunted in reply.

They pulled north up the harbor, and soon Fevik came into view, half a mile away: the ships tied to the wharves, the buildings, with their steep thatched roofs, crowded on shore. A few thin columns of smoke were rising here and there, cooking fires or forges, Odd imagined. Nothing unusual, nothing alarming.

"Amundi, please join us," Odd said. The older man was standing just forward of the break of the afterdeck, and he climbed up and stood at Odd's side. Odd nodded toward the town right ahead of them. "I see no cause for alarm yet."

"No," Amundi said. "But then, if it's a trap, Skorri would take care to hide it well. Until it's too late."

"We won't just blunder ashore. And if there is a trap waiting for us, we have Ragi and his men in place to back us up."

"I guess that's the best we can do," Amundi said. "That, and hope that the gods are with us."

"Gods my ass!" Bragi all but shouted. "Bragi Shipslayer is with you, and that's all you need!"

Odd wanted to grimace, but he held it in check. He did not care for Bragi's taunting the gods, particularly not as they were rowing into what might well be grave danger.

"Well," he said to Amundi, "keep your eyes open. Look for any hint of betrayal. We won't go ashore until we're satisfied. At least, as satisfied as we can be."

They closed quickly with the town, the oars double-banked, the wind astern. They could make out more details as they approached — a few smaller knarrs riding at anchor or tied to the wharves, three longships tied there as well. Halfdan's longships: Odd could see the king's long, pointed, white banner, with its broad red border and the silhouette of a gyrfalcon in flight, rippling at the mastheads. He could see the beach where they would land, and the workshops and houses and taverns in the town. But no people. They could see no one moving about.

"Do you see anyone?" Odd asked. "Any living soul?"

"No," Amundi said. "Of course, my eyes aren't what they used to be."

"I don't see anyone," Bragi said, "and my eyes would make an eagle weep with jealousy. But of course there's no one to see. Every whoreson bastard in Fevik's run off to join us."

"Skorri said he'd keep his men on the outskirts of the town," Amundi said. "And any town folk remaining there are probably hiding. So I suppose it's only right that we don't see anyone."

"That's true," Odd agreed. But still, he found it unnerving: this town, perfectly intact, and not a living soul there, as if a plague had wiped them all out.

The longship was a hundred yards off the end of the wharf when they finally saw someone, a single figure, striding with determination out along the wooden planks. Skorri Thorbrandsson. Odd was quite sure of it. He recognized the man's stride and his bearing. And, of course, this was the time and place they had agreed to meet.

"Here's our welcome!" Bragi said. "He better be ready to wash our feet, and serve us bread and honey and ale. I'm very fond of bread and honey and ale."

"Bragi, get us in close enough that I can talk to this bastard," Odd said. "But not so close that they can pull any tricks on us."

"As you wish, Lord Odd," Bragi said. He pushed the tiller over and called orders forward. The pace of the rowing slowed by half, and the longship's speed dropped away.

Skorri reached the end of the wharf and stopped, waiting with arms folded, his red cloak waving a bit in the wind, his mail shirt catching the sun and reflecting little pinpricks of light. Odd was wearing mail as well, but it had a much duller patina. It had been a long time since polishing chainmail was any sort of a priority for him. His sword Blood-letter, however, hanging at his hip, was perfectly maintained.

"Skorri!" Odd called across the fifty feet of water that separated them. The longship had come to a stop, the rowers resting with their blades in the water. "You're here, I see, as promised."

"Of course I am," Skorri called. "More to the point, so are you. Now, come along. Time is short. Halfdan could be on the march as we stand here blathering like idiots. Get your men ashore and let's make ready."

"Where are your men?"

"They're camped in the field just outside town, as I said they would be. Half of them, anyway. The other half are still up at the great hall. Which means you outnumber us now, in case you had any fears."

"You mean for us to come ashore here, go join with your men in the field?" Odd asked.

Skorri let out a sigh loud enough to be heard over the intervening space. "That's what we discussed. That's what we agreed to. See here, I'll meet you on the beach. Just me. So you'll have me as a hostage. If you think I'm betraying you, feel free to cut my throat."

"I will, depend on it," Odd said, then, quietly to the others, "Well, what do you think?"

"It is what was agreed to," Amundi said. "So far it seems Skorri's keeping his end of the bargain."

"Bragi?"

"I suppose even a serpent plays fair once in a while. But not often. And not for long."

"Very well," Odd said. He turned back to Skorri, ready to agree: they would meet him on the beach, land their men, march through town. Then something caught his eye, something moving through the air, high overhead. His first thought was *bird*, but it was flying too fast, too straight, for that.

He looked up, tracing the high, arched flight against the blue sky. He followed as it reached its apex and then began its descent, falling back to earth, and finally striking and embedding itself in the wharf, ten feet away from where Skorri stood.

An arrow, the lower end of its shaft wrapped in burning cloth.

"What…?" Skorri said, scowling as he looked at the strange sight, standing upright as it burned.

"That's a sign from the gods, Skorri!" Odd called. "A sign that you mean to betray us! Bragi, let's be gone from here!"

It was a sign, to be sure, but not a sign from the gods. Hallbjorn Deer-slayer, former hunter and tracker, had been sent ashore with Ragi to scout out the approach to Fevik from the east. Hallbjorn's old hunting partner, Storolf, equally adept at moving unseen through woods and fields, had been sent to scout things out from the west, to see if there was any treachery in the offing.

A hunter of long experience, Storolf could put an arrow pretty much wherever he wished, including at the end of Fevik's wharf, even from a place of concealment well away from there. And that was what he had promised to do, if he saw that Skorri was laying a trap for them.

"Starboard, pull! Larboard, hold your oars!" Bragi shouted and the men along the starboard side leaned back into the stroke and pulled and the longship began to spin around. Bragi turned to the other longship astern of them. "Muninn! Get your fat ass out of my way! And turn that tub around if you don't want your guts ripped out!"

Skorri's gaze moved from the flaming arrow, back in the direction from which it had come, and then out toward Odd's longship, as if he was trying to figure out what had happened. Whether he did or not was unclear, but he most certainly understood the implications: Odd and his men had been within his grasp, and now they were not.

"Bastard! You treacherous son of a bitch!" Skorri screamed. He turned and looked back down the wharf, toward the town. "Turn out! Turn out! Get down here, now! All of you! Koll, get them down here!"

"Look at that," Amundi said, dryly. "Apparently his men weren't on the outskirts of town after all."

"Larboard and starboard, together now, pull!" Bragi called, and the longship, now stern-to the wharf, began to gather way, heading back out to sea. Muninn's ship had turned as well, and was just making headway. The fishing boats were already pulling for all they were worth.

Odd and Amundi were leaning over the sheer strake, looking back toward Fevik. They heard a new sound, feet pounding on wooden boards, and then they saw men racing down the length of the wharf, men outfitted for battle. Dozens of men. Many dozens.

"Treacherous bastard," Odd said. "Can't say I'm much surprised." He wondered where Ragi and his men were, if they were nearby. They would have to attack in the next few moments if they hoped to be of any help.

The wharf was a couple hundred feet astern now, the distance between it and the longship opening up quickly, but Odd could see they were still far from safety. Skorri was shouting orders as his men leapt aboard the three longships tied to the wharf and started pulling oars down from the gallows overhead. The sound of cursing and running feet and oars thumping on the sheer strakes came at them over the water, louder even than the groan of their own oars in the row ports and the water rushing down the ship's sides.

"We'd do well to row as fast as we can," Odd said to Bragi.

Bragi frowned and looked astern. "Oh, that sheep-biter," he said. "We should have taken all his ships, not stopped at just the two."

"But of course there's no need to worry, right, Bragi?" Amundi asked. "There's no chance that Skorri or anyone could catch you at sea."

"Of course that's right," Bragi said, "if we were under sail. But we wasted that fine breeze, and now it's nearly dead against us." He scowled, glanced astern again, then forward. "Once we get clear of this cursed harbor we can set sail and Skorri can kiss our asses, one at a time. But until then it's just a matter of who can row faster."

Who can row faster, Odd thought. *There's the question. Skorri's fresh warriors, or our men who've already been at the oars for half the morning?*

He looked back at Fevik and the waterfront, now half a mile behind them. One of Skorri's ships was still made fast to the wharf, but two others were already underway, their oars seeming to go up and down in that strange way oars do when viewed from head-on. Then the third ship pushed off the wharf, drifted clear, and its oars came down and it was underway as well.

"Listen here, you bunch of lazy kitchen thralls!" Bragi called down to the rowers forward. "You best pull like wolves are chewing your asses, because they are! Any of you standing around, if you can triple bank an oar, then do it. Anyone feeling tired, you give up your place to someone who's fresh. It's that, or we turn and fight these whores' sons in our wake, and I don't reckon any of you want to do that!"

The men heard him. Where there was room enough for a third man at an oar, people squeezed in to join in the rowing. A few others, red-faced, sweating, breathing hard, gave up their seats to anyone who had not pulled an oar that morning. The longship was cutting through the water as fast as it was likely to go. But it was not clear if that would be fast enough. Not clear at all.

Odd leaned on the sheer strake on the larboard side, looked straight ahead, and willed himself to not look astern again. He lined up one of the shrouds with a point on shore to gauge the ship's speed. They were making solid way, though they would have been moving faster if they were not rowing straight into a headwind. Of course, Skorri's men would have to contend with the same wind, so that was something.

On either bow, and about a mile ahead, were the two headlands that marked the entrance to the narrow harbor. If they set sail right then, with the wind as it was, they would be driven ashore before they could round the headland to the southeast, the downwind point of land. The best they could do was keep rowing as fast as they could, set sail once they had sea room enough to clear the point, and count on Bragi's magic ship handling to get away. Not much of a plan, but it was all they had.

Odd was no longer able to resist: he turned and looked astern. The second ship, with Muninn in command, was about a hundred feet back and matching their pace. The fishing boats were there as well, spread out on either side of the longships, two men at each boat's oars. Skorri's ships were still a half mile astern and pulling hard.

Are they gaining? Odd wondered. He tried to picture how far astern they had been at the start of this race. They looked closer now, but it was hard to tell.

"I know, I know!" Bragi shouted.

Odd turned back. "You know what?"

"That bastard Skorri. He's gaining on us."

Well, there's my answer, Odd thought.

"His men might have been rutting with goats all morning, but they haven't been pulling oar like ours have!" Bragi continued. "They're fresher. That's just the truth of it."

Odd did not reply. It was not like Bragi Shipslayer to start making excuses so far in advance, and Odd did not take it as a good sign. He tried to gauge how much farther they would have to row before they could set sail and clear the headland. Half a mile more, at least, he figured. He considered asking Bragi, but decided he did not need that aggravation.

Amundi, however, seemed more willing to endure the abuse. "When will you set sail, Bragi?" he asked.

Bragi made a grunting noise. "Another half mile? Once that headland to the southeast is bearing just forward of the larboard beam, then we should be able to weather it."

Bragi's eyes were moving from shore to shore, looking to windward and down at the rowers, and occasionally aft at the ships astern. He seemed too distracted even to mock Amundi's question. Odd did not take that as a good sign, either.

They pulled on for some time more, their world narrowed down to the oars grinding and splashing in a steady rhythm, the water gurgling down the length of the hull, the timbers of the ship's fabric creaking with the strain. The rowers were breathing hard and giving the occasional gasping curse from the exertion. Their faces were red and dripping with sweat. Exhaustion was overtaking them, Odd could not deny it.

Skorri's ships were just a quarter-mile back, now. A quarter mile. They had halved the distance. Odd looked out at the headland to the southeast. If they set sail now, they might make it around the point and out to sea. Or they might not. If they didn't set sail, they had no chance at all.

"Time to set sail," Odd said, turning back to Bragi.

"Set sail…" Bragi repeated. "A fine notion, but there's a problem with that, Lord Odd. We need to stop rowing to set sail, and if we do that, those bastards will be on us before that miserable yard is halfway up the mast."

Odd felt his stomach twist. Of course Bragi was right, and he felt like a fool for not realizing it. With the oars run out and the rowers in place there was no room to set the sail. They needed a much bigger lead than they had to give them time enough, and there was little chance of their getting that.

"So, what do you suggest?" Odd asked. "Either of you?"

"Two choices I can see," Bragi said. "We turn and fight these sons of bitches, and die like men. Or we try to run the ships ashore and scatter like rats. Me, I've always been fond of rats. They seem like sensible creatures."

"I thought you were fond of fighting," Odd said.

"I'm fond of fighting and winning. Not so fond of losing. Particularly not when losing a fight means losing my head." He leaned over the side, looked astern. "You better decide quick, or Skorri'll decide for you. They're just a few ship lengths away from chewing on Muninn's ass."

Odd looked astern as well and he saw that Bragi was right. In truth, it was probably too late already for them to get ashore and get away.

"Oh, by all the gods…" Odd muttered. The first of Skorri's ships was maybe a hundred feet or so astern of Muninn's, and overtaking fast. If Muninn turned now and headed for shore, he would certainly be intercepted before he reached land. If they had to fight, then they would do well to take the fight to the enemy, rather than let the enemy run them down. Time to decide.

"We're going to turn and attack these whores' sons," Odd said. "Maybe we can hurt Skorri enough that we can get ashore and get clear."

Bragi laughed out loud. "That's the stupidest thing I ever heard!" he said, but for the first time in a long time, he was grinning.

Chapter Thirty-Four

Óðinn let fly and shot into the army — that was still the first tribe-war in the world; broken was the board-way of the Æsir's stronghold, the Vanir bestrode the plains with a battle-spell.

The Prophecy of the Seeress

"Listen here!" Odd called forward to the men at the oars. "We can't outrun these bastards! We're going to turn and fight! Keep rowing until I say the word, and when I do, you just run your oars in, just leave them there, grab your weapons and go! Get aboard Skorri's ship and start killing whoever's in front of you and you can't go wrong!"

The men were looking back at him, red-faced, wide-eyed. Some nodded. No one cheered, no one spoke. They were too winded to speak.

"All right, Bragi, let's be at them," Odd said. He grabbed his shield and leapt down off the afterdeck and began pushing his way forward. Behind him, he heard Bragi give a beastly howl of excitement as he pulled the tiller aft. Having realized there was no escape from the coming fight, Bragi seemed to have welcomed the idea with his usual enthusiasm.

The ship heeled a bit to starboard, coming around in a great, wide turn. Odd stumbled as the ship tilted under him, and he saw a few men standing amidships do the same. Muninn's ship was ahead of them now, off the larboard bow, and Odd could see that they were turning as well, Muninn having reacted instantly to Bragi's move.

Odd regained his footing and continued stumbling forward, making his way to the bow. When they hit Skorri's ship, Odd intended to be in the lead, the first over the sheer strake and into the fray.

By the time Odd reached the forward end, just fifty feet separated his ship from Skorri's as they raced at one another, bow to bow. Close enough: Skorri's men were still rowing and there would be no avoiding a collision.

"Run in your oars! Weapons! Take up your weapons! Oars in!"

Odd did not fear damaging the oars, but he did not want them to drag in the water and slow the ship's momentum, or get in the way of the two ships hitting. On either side the men pulled the oars in and laid them down, then leapt to their feet. They grabbed up shields, and took up swords and axes and spears, whatever they had to wield. They crowded the larboard side, facing Skorri's ship, with which they were closing fast.

Then, from the stern, came Bragi's voice, loud like a thunderclap, as he called a chant: "Odd! Odd! Odd! Odd!" And suddenly the rest of the men were chanting as well, yelling as loud as they could, banging swords and axes against shields or the side of the ship. "Odd! Odd! Odd! Odd!"

Odd could feel the energy radiating out, like the heat from a massive fire. "Odd! Odd! Odd!" And then the ships struck.

They did not hit bow on. At the last moment Bragi pushed the tiller over, just a bit, so that the two ships ran up against each other side to side, giving Odd's men more space to board. The air was filled with the sound of Skorri's men shouting, and Odd's men chanting, and the snapping of Skorri's oars as Odd's longship ran them over, crushing them one after another.

The two ships hit beam to beam with a rending, crushing sound. Sheer strakes were stove in as the hulls ground together, and Odd could hear nothing but shattering wood and shouting men.

Skorri had three longships to Odd's two, and Odd did not know which of the three Skorri was aboard. He looked aft, and with a wave of relief saw Skorri was there, sword drawn, shouting orders forward at his men. If Odd was fated to die in this uneven fight, he meant to take Skorri Thorbrandsson with him.

Skorri's men were just then leaping to their feet, grabbing up shields, drawing swords. Odd could not imagine why Skorri had kept his men at the oars right up until the ships hit, but now they would pay the price for his doing so.

"Go! Go! Go!" Odd shouted, and he put a foot up on his ship's damaged upper plank and half-stepped, half-leapt across the space and onto the deck of the other ship. He slashed at the man in front of him, who was struggling to get his shield on his arm. The man fell back to avoid the arc of the blade, and Odd took that instant to look around.

His men had followed him over the side and onto Skorri's ship, screaming like tortured souls. They plunged ahead, spears thrusting, axes rising and falling, as Skorri's men were still scrambling to take up their shields and get swords clear of scabbards. Men dropped, bleeding, cursing.

The second longship, Muninn's ship, was passing down the other side of Skorri's, making for the ship astern.

And that was all the time Odd could give to anything beyond what was right in front of him. The first man he had slashed at was still down, trying to regain his feet, but another was coming up behind him. Odd had only a vague image of a mail shirt, a shield painted yellow and red, a big beard under a bright helmet. And a sword, thrusting straight at his chest.

Odd twisted, swung his shield sideways like opening a gate, caught the sword and knocked it aside. He counter-thrust, but the man had his own shield up and Odd stabbed straight into it. Blood-letter's sharp point pierced the thin wood and drove several inches in.

Odd jerked back hard to free the sword, and realized to his horror that it was stuck fast. He saw the bearded man grin as he, too, realized it. The man twisted his shield sideways, the sword still caught in the wood, pulling Odd off balance, and Odd forced himself to let go. He saw and heard the man roar with laughter as he brought his own sword up over his head for a lethal stroke.

He was too late. Odd leapt forward, drawing his seax with well-practiced ease as he did. The man's expression changed from laughter, to surprise, to panic, and Odd drove the seax up under his chin, and kept on driving, until the crossguard stopped him from driving it any further. The man's eyes rolled back and Odd let the seax go and the man crumbled backwards to the deck.

He grabbed hold of Blood-letter's grip, put a foot on the dead man's shield, and pulled the weapon free. He looked around. His men had fought their way to the centerline of the ship and were still fighting. But Skorri's men had recovered from the surprise of the sudden attack, and now they were offering serious resistance.

And not just resistance. Skorri's men were gaining momentum, driving Odd's back, cutting them down. Swords and mail and helmets, shields and training and discipline, were proving their worth over the makeshift weapons of an *ad hoc* army. Men were bleeding on the deck, thrashing or laying still. Odd's men and Skorri's men. But mostly Odd's men.

Skorri himself was still on the afterdeck, still shouting orders, pointing with his sword. Between him and Odd stood a phalanx of Skorri's men; men Odd would have to fight his way through to get at Skorri, and that would be no easy feat.

He took two steps aft, and that was as far as he got, stopped by the wall of defenders. In front of him, one of Skorri's men, shield up, sword arm cocked high, ready to drive the point of his weapon in over the top of the shield. Odd raised his own shield to chest height, shouted, loud and from the gut, and drove into the man, pushing off hard with his back leg, slamming recklessly into him, shield to shield.

The man stumbled back, thrown off balance by the unexpected hit. Odd slashed low, under the bottom edge of his shield, catching the man's legs with Blood-letter's sharp blade.

The man screamed, his legs crumpled under him. He went down and Odd left him there. Alive or dead it did not matter, he was out of the fight. Odd took another step in Skorri's direction. Some of his men had worked their way aft to join him in the chaotic brawl. All down the length of the ship, men were slashing at one another, axes and swords rising and falling, shields crashing against shields.

Odd stole a look forward. His men had hit Skorri's by surprise and driven them back, but Skorri's men had recovered now, rallied, and were driving into Odd's men, pushing them toward the larboard side over which they had come. Men were falling under their swords, dying on the ends of spears. Some were abandoning the fight, scrambling back aboard their own ship. It did not look good.

"At them! Push them!" Odd called, though he doubted his voice could be heard over the din. He turned to the pack of men in front of him, his men and Skorri's, hacking at each other in a brutal and ugly way. He pushed forward, Blood-letter rising and falling, darting in and out, looking for a vulnerable place to strike amidst the mail and helmets and shields.

He heard shouting from forward, a different tone. Something was happening. He slashed with his sword, darted his eyes toward the bow. Men were coming over the far side of the ship, the starboard side, vaulting to the deck with weapons ready. It was Skorri's other ship,

Odd guessed, the third one, come to help. And that would be the end of it.

But it was not the other ship. The men coming over the side were not wearing mail, not carrying shields. And they did not come to help Skorri's men; they came to fight them. With axes and spears they laid into the better-equipped warriors, who were taken by surprise by these unseen attackers. Some of Skorri's men fell, some roared in surprise and outrage as they turned to face this new threat from behind.

The fishing boats! Odd realized. The men in the faerings had come along the starboard side of Skorri's ship, up over the rail, and plunged into the fight. The surprise alone might be enough to win the day. But Odd had more immediate concerns, as he and his men on either side were driven back, fighting for their lives.

Skorri's men came surging across the centerline of the ship, their shields interlocked in a short shield wall as they advanced. Odd stepped back, Blood-letter parrying their thrusting and slashing blades. His foot came down in a pool of blood and he felt himself slipping as he staggered to keep his balance.

He was vulnerable, and the men in the shield wall saw it. One pushed forward, shield low, sword up. Odd, off balance, tried to raise his own shield in time to block the stroke. And just as he realized he could not stop the fatal thrust, the man with the sword was shoved aside, and in his place stood Skorri Thorbrandsson, helmetless, sword drawn, shield on his arm.

"I'll kill this one!" Skorri roared. "No one else!" He took a wild swing at Odd, but Odd had recovered his footing enough that he was able to twist clear of the blade. He heard the whirring sound of its passing, inches in front of him, and he lunged while Skorri was still in mid-stroke.

Blood-letter hit Skorri just below the ribs. Odd felt the resistance as the blade connected with mail, and then tore on through, but Skorri jerked sideways as it did, and the point was knocked free before it sunk to a fatal depth.

Skorri roared again, furious with the wound, and no doubt feeling it as well. He took a step toward Odd, slashing with his sword, and all Odd could do was back away and fend off the attack with sword and shield.

Skorri was a powerful man. Odd had always known it, and he was reminded again as he felt the strength behind every blow, every push of his shield. Skorri's long, blond hair was in a wild disarray, his mouth and eyes wide with fury as he mounted his attack. The fighting on the deck seemed to devolve down to just the two of them: two men, and one of them would be dead very soon.

This won't do, Odd thought. Skorri was in control of the fight now, and if he remained in control, then it was Odd would soon be dead. Time to fight back.

Skorri thrust again, and Odd knocked the sword aside with a powerful swipe of his shield. Skorri recovered, raised his sword and hacked down, and once again Odd's shield was there to stop it. Skorri cursed with anger, frustrated that he could not get his sword on Odd.

He began hacking up and down, too furious now for any subtlety, just slamming the steel against the shield's wooden boards. He struck again and again, exhausting himself in the effort. Odd twisted the shield back and forth to catch the blows, and bit by bit the shield began to fall apart under the onslaught.

By the time Skorri stopped, his face and beard soaked with sweat, his mouth open as he gasped for breath, the upper third of Odd's shield was nothing but splintered shards. Odd held it low and let Skorri take one last, feeble thrust. As the blade came at him, Odd swept it aside, counter thrust, and felt Blood-letter's point once again tear through mail and flesh.

The pain was enough to revive Skorri. He stepped back, roared, swung his sword in a wide, horizontal stroke. Odd ducked low, and he felt the wind of the blade passing over his head as he stabbed Blood-letter under Skorri's shield. The tip ripped through Skorri's leg windings, his leggings, the flesh of his calf. Blood sprayed out and Skorri screamed. Odd leapt up and jumped clear as Skorri's sword slashed through the space where Odd had been an instant before.

Odd lifted the remains of his shield, braced himself to attack, when suddenly the deck shuddered and rolled under his feet, and the sound of shouting men and clashing weapons was blanketed by that of wood grinding on wood. Then came a new wave of shouting, louder and more energetic than before, and despite themselves, Odd and Skorri both turned and looked forward.

Dead and wounded littered the deck. Odd's men, the handful who remained, were pressed back against the larboard side, fighting for their lives. The arrival of the fishing boats had not changed the tide of battle.

And now another longship had smashed into the starboard side, a longship filled with warriors who stood ready with shields and mail and helmets. The two ships were still grinding against one another as the newcomers started to leap over the side and into the fight.

It was Skorri's third ship. It had to be, Odd thought. Who else could it be? Three ships against two, they had come to Skorri's aid, and that meant this whole thing would be over soon.

And with that realization, Odd recalled that he was still in a fight for his life, and he understood that the only thing he could hope for now was to take Skorri down, and then die with Blood-letter in his hand.

He turned back to Skorri, and in that instant he saw that he was too late. Skorri had turned first and thrust. Odd swung Blood-letter up and over in a desperate attempt to parry the attack. He caught Skorri's blade with his and for an instant they stood with swords pressed against one another. Then Skorri slid his sword down the length of Blood-letter's blade, over the crossguard, and deep into Odd's right hand, the razor-sharp steel slicing through skin and muscle.

Odd shouted, dropped his sword, and heard it clatter on the deck. The agony in his hand was blinding, and blood was already dripping off his fingers.

He looked up at Skorri and saw the smug triumph in his eyes as he drew his sword back for the final thrust. But the confidence on Skorri's face was like red-hot metal pressed to Odd's flesh; agonizing and infuriating. He felt the spirit of Ulf of the Battle Song, and Ornolf the Restless, and Thorgrim Night Wolf, and all the warriors who had gone before him, welling up inside.

He did not retreat; rather, he took two steps in Skorri's direction — too close for Skorri to use his sword — and saw Skorri's look of triumph turn to surprise as he grabbed the edge of Skorri's shield with his bleeding hand and jerked it out of the way. He could no longer feel the agony of his deep wound as he let go of the shield, grabbed the collar of Skorri's mail shirt, and jerked Skorri close. His left hand reached down and found the grip of the seax on Skorri's belt and he pulled the weapon free.

Skorri realized in that instant what was coming. He shouted, tried to push Odd away, but Odd held tight, the fingers of his wounded hand locked on the chainmail collar. With his left hand he drove the seax up under Skorri's mail, up into his gut, and he kept on driving it in.

Skorri's shout turned to a scream, and his eyes went wide, and still he tried to push Odd away, and still Odd held tight. Odd pulled the seax free and then drove it in again, and then again. The screaming turned to a strangled, gurgling noise, and the blood ran out of Skorri's mouth and down his long yellow beard.

Their eyes met, though Odd was not sure Skorri could even see him. He unclenched his fingers and pushed, and Skorri fell to the deck, dropping his sword and shield as he did. He lay there, hands clutched to his gut, his legs making weak jerking motions.

Odd staggered back, unsure if he could keep on his feet, or if he, too, was about to collapse to the blood-soaked deck. He could still hear fighting. He looked forward, figuring on seeing the last of his men slaughtered.

Blood-letter... he thought. He had to pick up his sword. The enemy would be on him in an instant, and they would cut him down, and he had to have his sword in his hand when they did.

He took a step forward, his feet unsteady, his eyes on the fighting that was still surging along the deck as he lifted his sword with his left hand. The battle was fierce and chaotic, but it was not clear to Odd what the newcomers were about. He had expected them to be butchering his men, but it was Skorri's men they seemed to be attacking.

Not far from where he stood, near the base of the mast, one of these new men was trading blows with two of Skorri's warriors. A young man, blond hair, using his sword and shield with remarkable skill as he fended off the attacks and drove the two men back.

Odd stared at the yellow-haired warrior, helmetless, a poor excuse for a beard on his face, quick and powerful despite his youth. There was something familiar about him, but not entirely. Like someone he had once known, one who had changed with the passing of time.

And then a thought materialized, ghost-like, in his mind.

Harald?

Chapter Thirty-Five

There you can choose shields and smooth-shaven ash-spears,
gold-plated helms and a horde of Húnar,
silver-gilt saddle-cloths, foreign-red tunics,
lances, spears, bit-champing steeds.

The Lay of Atli

In the end, Thorgrim Night Wolf did not have to burn his prisoner's eye out with the red-hot spear tip. The glowing iron was still six inches from the prisoner's right eye when the man suddenly became very talkative.

There was a lot he did not know, as is often the way with foot soldiers. But he did admit, with a touch of pride, that he was part of the army of King Halfdan the Black. He said that he and his fellows, around five hundred men, trained warriors all, had been sent to where Harald had found them to lay a trap for some enemy of the king.

Who that enemy was, he did not know. Some army that posed a grave threat to the kingdom. They would be coming by sea in six or seven longships. That was all he had been told, and all he needed to be told. Anything more than that was the business of captains and jarls and kings.

By the time the man shut his mouth, the tip of the spear had cooled and turned black again, so Thorgrim shoved it back into the coals. He looked back at the prisoner, and saw that the man had not missed that gesture. In truth, Thorgrim did not think he would need the hot iron any more.

"Do you know who I am?" he asked. The man shook his head. "I'm Thorgrim Ulfsson. Known as Night Wolf."

Thorgrim saw the flicker of recognition in the man's eyes, the surprise and uncertainty, which he kept admirably in check. "Do you know of my son, Odd?"

For a moment the man did not answer, as if weighing which would be more dangerous — speaking or remaining silent. Thorgrim glanced down at the spear tip in the coals and then back at the prisoner.

"I know who he is," the prisoner said.

"Where is he now?"

"Don't know," the prisoner said. Thorgrim figured that was true. He also figured that the man had some idea, which he was keeping to himself.

"Where does Halfdan think he is?"

The prisoner glared at him, mouth set, once again wrestling with what course of action would be most to his benefit. His eyes flicked over to Eyvind, just for a heartbeat, and then back to Thorgrim.

"Don't look at him," Thorgrim said. "He's not the one who's going to burn your eyeballs out with that spear tip. I am."

The prisoner frowned at Thorgrim for a moment more, but at that point it was just face-saving defiance, not the real sort. "Fevik," he said at last.

That was all Thorgrim needed to hear. The man was well-motivated to tell the truth, and what he said was exactly what Thorgrim would have guessed.

"If Halfdan thinks Odd's in Fevik, what's he doing about it?"

"Odd's leading a rebellion. Halfdan sent men to put it down."

"Halfdan sent his men here. To lay a trap for us."

At that the prisoner gave a hint of a smile. "Halfdan's a king. You think we're the only warriors he commands?"

Halfdan sent men to put it down. Thorgrim considered the prisoner's words. He felt his stomach twist.

It was not likely that Odd's rebels were trained, well-armed men. Maybe some of the wealthy freemen had brought their house warriors, but more likely Odd's people were farmers, craftsmen, just folk who were tired of Halfdan's rule. They would not be able to stand up long to Halfdan's army. Halfdan had already sent men to Fevik, and that meant Thorgrim and his fleet were probably too late.

Most of the men from Thorgrim's six ships were gathered around, enjoying the fun. Thorgrim turned to them. "Get everything aboard the ships and get them ready for sea. We leave immediately."

The men did not hesitate. They scrambled as if they, too, were in danger of having their eyes burned out, and Thorgrim found that very satisfying, found that it eased his fears just a bit. He walked over to where Eyvind and his men were standing, sullen and quiet.

"You men, you're Halfdan's warriors, is that right?" He looked from man to man. No one spoke.

"I don't find fault in your loyalty to the king," he continued. "I'm loyal to the king, too. Always have been. Now I've come back to see if he still deserves that loyalty. I've heard things. Just rumors, but it does seem there's some truth in them. Halfdan went to a lot of trouble trying to kill me and my men when we returned. So now I have to find out why, and set it right."

He searched the men once more. Still no reaction.

"I may be loyal to the king, but I'm more loyal to my son," he continued. "My loyalty will always be to my family first. So I'm going to sail to Fevik, and I'm going to find the truth, and if I have to fight Halfdan at my son's side, so be it. I won't punish you for being loyal to your king. But I can't have you joining him against my son."

"Your son did nothing wrong." The voice came from somewhere among the sixty men who had sailed with Eyvind, but Thorgrim did not see who spoke.

"What's that?" Thorgrim asked.

One of the men took a step forward. He looked older than the rest, his dark beard shot thought with hints of gray, his long hair hanging in a braid over his shoulder. There were crow's feet at the corners of his eyes that suggested years of standing on a ship's deck, squinting out at the sea.

"I said your son did nothing wrong. Halfdan tried to take your farm, because he grows ambitious. And greedy. He reckoned if he could take your farm, it would show the other freemen he could take theirs, too, and so they had best bend the knee in every way. Your son Odd, he felt different. So did a lot of the other freemen. But Odd was the only one with the balls to do something about it."

"I see," Thorgrim said. He did not ask this man why he still followed Halfdan. He understood. A man needed to live, and being in the king's service was a better living than most. Then someone else spoke.

"We all know who you are, Thorgrim Night Wolf. We know your reputation. No one told us it was you we were sent to Ribe to find." At that, heads started nodding.

That took Thorgrim a bit by surprise, and he was not certain what to make of it, so he continued on with what he meant to say.

"I believe you. But, like I said, I can't have you helping Halfdan fight my son. If any of you want to swear an oath to me, fight with me and Odd, I'll welcome you. You can have your mail and weapons back. But remember, you might have to raise them against men who were once your fellows. Any of you who want to remain with Halfdan, I'll let you go here. But first I'll have your weapons, your mail, your shields. And your shoes."

In the end, only a dozen or so were willing to give up weapons and shoes and begin the long, painful, and humiliating walk back to Grømstad. Eyvind was among them, though Thorgrim doubted very much he would return to Halfdan's hall and admit to his abject failure. The rest swore an oath to Thorgrim Night Wolf, and Thorgrim hoped very much that they were sincere in that. They would be good men to have, if they were genuinely willing to fight with him.

But he would not trust them entirely, not yet. Not until they had proven themselves. So he spread Halfdan's erstwhile warriors among the various ships' crews, putting only a handful with each. He gave command of the seventh longship, Halfdan's former ship, Eyvind's former command, to Hall. It was still well before midday when the fleet finally pushed off the beach, bound for sea.

It had all worked out as well as Thorgrim could have hoped, but that, it seemed, was an end to his good luck. There was little breeze when they shoved off, so they took up the oars for the pull northeast along the coast. Soon after, the breeze started filling in from the east, not quite dead against them, but close enough. They could not sail into it, and it made the rowing vastly more exhausting.

Forty miles by sea to Fevik. With a good westerly breeze they could have covered that in half a day. As things were, there was no telling how long it would take them to crawl that distance.

All through the afternoon they plodded along northeast, the broken granite coast, with its blanket of pine and fir, passing slowly down the larboard side. *Sea Hammer* took the lead, the other ships, by Thorgrim's orders, clustered close astern. He did not want any of his captains to get beyond the reach of his voice. That was true for all of them, but it was Harald, with his lighter, quicker ship, and at times excessive enthusiasm, who he had primarily in mind.

By the time the sun began to approach the western horizon, they had covered less than half the distance to Fevik. The shadows were getting long, the rowers staring down at the deck to keep the setting sun out of their eyes, when Thorgrim finally, and with great reluctance, made his decision.

He knew of a beach half a mile off *Sea Hammer*'s larboard bow, and he knew that it would do for the night. As he turned the ship north, the men at the oars looked up, relief on their faces. The change of course could only mean that their labor at the oars would soon end. They seemed to row with a renewed enthusiasm, which annoyed Thorgrim considerably, but he said nothing.

Soon all seven ships' bows were run ashore, fires were lit, food cooking, ale served out. Thorgrim and Gyda sat by the fire and ate and drank, not because Thorgrim craved company at all, but because he thought it was only right that he join his men. He would have much preferred to be alone. Alone with Gyda, who knew when to talk to him and when not.

Thorgrim was up before dawn the following day, and he saw to it that the rest of the men were as well. They shoved the ships off just as the sun broke the horizon, bathing the coast with enough light to safely navigate. The morning was calm, the seas mostly flat, and that made for easier rowing than the day before. And it gave Thorgrim hope as well. He understood how the weather worked in that part of the world, and he saw the signs that it might well turn in his favor.

And he was right. They had not been underway for long before he felt the first stirring a breeze at his back, the cool air on his neck, the slight tug of wind at his hair and beard. Not enough to fill the sail yet, but he did not doubt that that would come.

By the time the men at the oars were ready to be switched out, the westerly breeze had filled in enough that Thorgrim was certain it would drive *Sea Hammer* faster than the rowers could. He ordered oars in, the yard swung around, the sail set and hoisted. Just astern, the other ships followed his lead.

The sail snapped, ripped and filled as the yard was hoisted up the mast. In no time *Sea Hammer* was rolling along, the water singing its water-song down the ship's sides, the shrouds and mast creaking under the strain of nearly a thousand square feet of sail. Thorgrim felt as if the hands of the gods, which had been holding him in check, had suddenly let him go.

They plowed along through the morning hours, keeping to open water, half a mile or so to seaward of the outermost islands. Thorgrim kept a close eye on the distant shore, and he watched it change from something vaguely familiar to something quite familiar indeed. He felt a strange sensation in his gut as he watched the well-known points of land pass slowly by. Nearly three years he had been gone from his home. It felt like thirty.

"This place, the land here, it's familiar to you?" Gyda asked. She was standing by him now, joining him in watching the coast passing down their larboard side.

Thorgrim smiled. "Oh, yes," he said. "Where we made landfall, two nights ago? That part of the coast I know pretty well. Well enough to take us to the beach I wanted, not the one Eyvind wanted to take us to. I knew about the beach we spent last night on as well. But this part of the coast? Yes, I know it like I know my own farm."

"We're close then? To your farm?"

"Yes." He pointed forward, broad on the larboard bow. "Do you see that group of islands there? There's the big one on the right, and then the cluster of smaller ones on the left?"

"Yes."

"If you work your way through those islands, then you find yourself in a long, narrow bay. On the western side is Grømstad, where King Halfdan the Black's great hall sits. It was an impressive place, last time I saw it. I imagine it's more impressive now. At the head of that long bay is Vik. That's where my farm is."

"But that's not where we're going?"

"Not yet. My son Odd is in Fevik. At least that's what Halfdan's men said. So that's where we're bound."

"And when will we reach Fevik?" Gyda asked.

Thorgrim looked up at the sail, which was bellied out full. *Sea Hammer* was rolling a bit, side to side, as she drove through the seas. Every once in a while, when she hit a swell just right, spray came flying aft over the bow.

"Soon," he said.

As they passed the mouth of the bay at the head of which sat Vik, Thorgrim turned the fleet a bit more northerly, heading for a channel between a cluster of islands ahead. It was something he would not have done on an unfamiliar coastline, bringing his fleet in through that narrow, rocky passage, but here he knew with absolute certainty they could pass safely through, and cut many miles off their race to Fevik.

They left the islands astern and headed out across an open stretch of water. Ahead, fine on the larboard bow, was a point of land and two small granite islands. Those landmarks made up the southwestern point of the wide, deep bay that led north to Fevik. Once around that, they had no more than a mile to cover before they reached the village.

Starri Deathless was at the top of the mast, as was his wont, but he slid down the shroud, hopped down to the deck, and came walking aft, pulling his tunic up over his head as he did. He arrived at the break of the afterdeck and threw the garment aside, leaving only his leggings and his shoes and the two axes shoved in his belt.

Around his neck, hanging from a leather thong, Starri wore a split arrowhead which had once embedded itself on the blade of Thorgrim's sword, an artifact from an earlier battle that seemed to Thorgrim to have been many ages ago.

Thorgrim had pulled the arrowhead free and tossed it away, considering it just one of those strange things that happens in battle. But Starri had snatched it up, certain that it brought good luck, and that it was a sign Thorgrim was blessed by the gods. He had worn it ever since, and ever since had remained at Thorgrim's side.

"Getting ahead of yourself, aren't you, Starri?" Thorgrim asked.

"How's that?"

"You're making ready for a fight, but we don't know what we're going to find."

Starri cocked his head and gave Thorgrim a quizzical look. "You don't hear that?"

"What?"

Starri pointed with his thumb back over his shoulder. "The battle."

Thorgrim frowned. "What battle? I don't hear anything."

"You're getting deaf as a rock in your old age, along with going blind. There's a battle going on, just around that point of land."

Thorgrim looked past the bow, in the direction that Starri was indicating. He turned his head a bit and listened. He heard the creak of his ship's hull, and the mast. He heard the lap of the water. He did not hear a battle.

"Any of you men hear a battle going on out there?" he called forward. He turned to Armod, who was at the tiller. "Do you hear a battle?" He turned to Gyda. "Do you?"

Armod shook his head. Gyda shook her head. Some of the others were shaking their heads as well. No one claimed to hear what Starri heard.

"Ah, the lot of you. Deaf as stumps. But mark my words."

Thorgrim did mark Starri's words. As mad as Starri might seem half the time — most of the time, actually — he was generally right about such things. His eyesight and his hearing often proved as extraordinary as his prowess in battle, and Thorgrim was not in a mood to take chances.

"You men forward!" Thorgrim called. "Take up your weapons! I want you ready for a fight the moment we round the point!"

The fleet stood on, closing quickly with the two islands, and the men pulled swords out from where they were stored and strapped them on, along with knives and seaxes. They lifted their shields out of the shield racks and set them down where they could be grabbed up quickly.

The point of land with its twin islands drew abeam, and Thorgrim ordered Armod to start turning *Sea Hammer* north. More and more of the bay opened up before them, but Thorgrim could see nothing, save for the wide stretch of blue-green water and the hilly, wooded shore on the far side.

He continued to turn, and the men braced the yard around as *Sea Hammer* charged along, the rest of the fleet right on their heels. Thorgrim's eyes were everywhere, but he saw nothing to cause alarm. And then, as yet more of the bay was revealed, he did.

Ships, seemingly locked together, half a mile away. They looked like wrestlers holding one another in their unbreakable grips. Two clusters of them, one consisting of two ships, side to side, the other of three, and there seemed to be smaller boats everywhere. Thorgrim could make out a swarm of activity on the ships' decks, and though he could not see in any detail what was going on, he had seen enough fighting, ship to ship, to be sure he was looking at that now.

"Well, well, what do you know?" Starri asked. "So, who there's fighting who?"

"I don't know," Thorgrim said. "That's the problem. Don't know who's fighting who. Can you see anything?"

Starri scrambled up onto the afterdeck, then up onto the sheer strake, one hand on the tall sternpost for balance. The sail had been braced around, so he was able to see past the edge of the cloth to the fighting in the distance. For a long moment he said nothing, just stared at the ships.

"Three of the ships have banners at their mastheads," he said at last. "I can only just make them out. But they look like the pointy sort of banner…mostly white. Like the ones me and Harald saw when we snuck up on that army that was lying in wait for us."

"Halfdan," Thorgrim said. "Halfdan's banner." Which meant that, unless every rumor he'd heard, every confession regarding what was taking place here was a lie, he was witnessing what could be his son's final battle. And he might already be too late.

"Ease those sheets some, spill some wind!" Thorgrim called forward. He recoiled at giving those orders that would slow *Sea Hammer* down, but he needed to communicate with the other vessels.

One by one they drew up on either side, *Blood Hawk*, *Oak Heart*, *Black Wing* and the rest, and as they did Thorgrim called his orders across the narrow strip of water that separated them. There was not much to say, because he did not really know what was taking place. He relayed to his captains his best guess: that Halfdan's three ships were doing battle with Odd's two. He told them to go in fighting, and hope that they could tell friend from foe. If not, they should put a stop to the battle, and sort it out after.

That done, he called for his men to sheet *Sea Hammer*'s sail in again, and the ship drove ahead once more. Gyda held up Thorgrim's mail shirt, offering it to him, but he shook his head. He had watched an enemy once being dragged under by his mail, while he, Thorgrim, wearing no mail, lived. He had not forgotten that lesson.

Gyda set the mail down, handed Thorgrim his sword and seax and he strapped them on. "Stay here. Stay clear," he said to her, and kissed her. He turned to Armod at the tiller.

"We'll sail right past these two ships closest to us, leave them for the others. You see those three ships beyond? You aim to put us right between two of them, just drive us right in there. You got that?"

Armod nodded. Thorgrim took up his shield and hopped down off the afterdeck. *Sea Hammer* was charging down on the other ships now, heeling hard to starboard, pounding through the short chop. Thorgrim made his way forward, addressing his men as he did.

"We're going to run right into these bastards, board wherever the fighting is. You heard what I said to the others. We're not going to know who's friend, who's enemy. Look for the warriors with mail, swords, helmets and such — they're most likely to be Halfdan's men. Odd's people might not have much armor, might be fighting with spears and axes. Might not have shields. Don't kill anyone if you can't tell what side they're on. We can just put a stop to the fight, figure it out later."

By the time he reached the bow, they were up with the first two ships, passing down the starboard side, just fifty feet off. The fighting was desperate, Thorgrim could see that. The ship nearest them was swarming with men engaged in the chaotic hacking and stabbing and one-on-one struggles of a battle that had devolved into a bloody brawl. Who was winning, who was losing, who was who, Thorgrim could not tell.

Starri was already forward, standing on the sheer strake, his eyes on the ships they were closing with, his arms doing that strange jerking motion they did when battle was in the offing and the berserker spirit was taking over.

"Starri, listen here," Thorgrim called up to him. "We've got to try and figure who are Halfdan's men, and who are my son, Odd's. Look for the men wearing mail, they're more like to be the king's men."

Starri was still staring out ahead. He made no acknowledgement of Thorgrim's words.

"Starri, did you hear me?"

Starri turned and stared at Thorgrim for a moment, but he seemed to show no comprehension. Then he nodded and looked forward once more. Thorgrim let out a breath. He could not tell if Starri had heard or understood him, but there was nothing he could do now except hope for the best.

He leaned on the sheer strake and looked past the bow. The three ships they were heading for were a hundred feet away, and with the mounting breeze *Sea Hammer* was closing fast. He turned and yelled aft.

"Get ready to haul that sail up! Stand by the sheets and clewlines!" he shouted. *Sea Hammer* was moving fast and carrying considerable momentum. If they hit the other ships at that speed, it might well stove them all in and send them to the bottom, which would do no one any good.

Thorgrim watched the distance close, calculating how long *Sea Hammer* would keep making headway once the sail was taken in.

"Now! Let the sheets fly! Haul away!" he called. Behind him, men eased the sheets quickly away while others hauled on the clewlines, pulling the heavy sail up to the yard. *Sea Hammer*'s speed dropped away quickly, the ship standing more upright and settling down into the water. But she still had speed enough to run hard aboard the other ships.

"Ready!" Thorgrim shouted, as *Sea Hammer* drove into the space between two of the ships, which were bound together with lines and grappling hooks. She came to a shuddering halt as her bow jammed in between the other two, with a groaning, creaking sound. But Thorgrim was barely aware of any of that.

His eyes were on the ship at the center of the three, where the fighting was taking place — a wild and brutal scene. Dead and wounded were thick on the deck, which meant the battle had been going on for some time, at least by the standards of fights such as these.

He saw, roughly, two lines of men, one in mail and helmets, and bearing swords and shields, the other in leather armor, or just tunics, and they were carrying spears and axes and such, some with shields, some without. It seemed his guess had been right, as far as who would be well-equipped, and who would not.

The ships were still grinding together when Starri launched himself off the rail, shrieking and jerking the axes from his belt in mid-leap. He came down in a crouch on the other ship's deck, and then he was up again, plowing into a knot of sword-wielding warriors, axes flailing, as men turned in shock and wonder.

Thorgrim considered leaping across as Starri had done, but he thought better of it. He swung a leg over *Sea Hammer*'s side and onto the other ship and pushed himself aboard, pulling Iron-tooth as he did.

"Odd!" he shouted. "We fight for Odd!" Farther aft, his men were pouring over the rail, onto the deck, and into the fight. Thorgrim kept shouting, "Odd! Odd!" and some of the others took up the cry.

It had the intended effect. The warriors in mail and helmets turned to this new threat, meeting swords with swords, shields with shields. Beyond them, on the far side of the ship, the fighting men were more ragtag, more ill-equipped, and considerably less in number. Odd's men — they had received the worst of it, that was clear.

Thorgrim looked fore and aft, hoping to catch sight of Odd, but he saw no one who looked like his son, and there was time for only a glance before he was confronted with a sword making a vicious slash at his head. He lifted his shield and felt the blade slam against the wood. He thrust around the edge of his own shield, Iron-tooth's tip neatly passing the other man's shield, tearing though his mail and into his chest, just below his right shoulder.

Thorgrim pulled the sword back as the man turned sideways, screaming, and falling against the warrior to his right. He glanced around again, still looking for Odd. This ship or the other, Odd had to be on one of them, fighting with his makeshift army. But even if he was there, it did not mean he was still standing. Perhaps he was among the many dead or gravely wounded, scattered over the ship's deck.

Thorgrim felt the fury, the red rage, coming over him, sweeping him up as it had not done in some time, as he turned back to the fight. Two of Halfdan's men were coming at him now, shoulder to shoulder, shield overlapping shield. Thorgrim snarled, and the snarl built into an animal sound, part roar, part howl. He flung himself forward, pushing off hard with his back leg, slamming his shield into the two shields in front of him, sending the men reeling back with the violence of the attack.

Thorgrim had a fleeting glimpse of bearded faces, mouths and eyes wide with surprise and panic. He slashed left and right with Iron-tooth, feeling the blade bite, hearing the shouts, watching the men trying to stumble clear. He lifted his foot and put it against the face of a shield and kicked, and the man went back and down. Then Thorgrim stepped up on the shield like it was a flat stone in a river, pinning the man underneath, and drove Iron-tooth straight down into his neck.

He pulled the point free, swung shield and sword to his left as yet another came at him. His shield knocked the threatening sword aside, twisting the man off balance as it struck, with a force that seemed to catch him by surprise. Iron-tooth found the gap where the short sleeve of his mail shirt hung loose under his arm, and Thorgrim drove it in.

The man roared, twisted, as the blade plunged through his side, just under his arm. Thorgrim kicked this man too, as much to yank Iron-tooth free as to push him to the deck. He was almost blind with rage. Everything he saw seemed to be rendered in shades of black and red. Everything seemed to move very slowly.

His shield felt suddenly like a great encumbrance and he threw it aside. A sword darted out at him. He side-stepped, and the blade missed his neck by an inch, no more. He reached out with his left hand and grabbed the sword-man's shield and jerked it aside, pulling the man with it, then stabbed Iron-tooth in and back, in and back.

He was still making that howling noise as he charged ahead, hacking left and right. Iron-tooth bounced off shields and rang off swords lifted in defense, and men fell in front of him, or stumbled out of his way, as he cut through the crowd: him, a reaper, his enemies stalks of wheat.

And then there was no one around him, and he stopped, gasping for breath, Iron-tooth's point resting on the deck. He could feel the sting of sweat wicking into his eyes, and colors seemed to reappear in his vision.

He looked around. *Blood Hawk* and *Black Wing* had run up on the far side, their men joining in the fight. Thorgrim had not even noticed their arrival. Halfdan's warriors, those still standing or kneeling, had hands raised in supplication. His own men stood loosely guarding them, as did the others, the men carrying spears and axes and wearing sundry bits of armor.

"Odd?" Thorgrim called. "Where's Odd?"

He looked from man to man, but in the immediate aftermath of that bloody fight, no one seemed able to answer.

"Where's Odd?" he demanded again, all but shouting, but his own men did not know and the others just stared at him with stunned expressions. Then he heard a voice, calling from across the water.

"Father? Father!"

Not Odd's voice. Harald's. Calling from the other ship, where he must have taken *Dragon* to join the fight. Thorgrim stumbled to the side and looked across the fifty feet of water that separated the two clusters of ships. He could see his son standing there, his blond hair bright in the sun. He was holding his sword straight up. The fighting there was over as well.

Thorgrim wondered if that was why Harald was calling, to let him know they had won their fight. But he noticed there was another man standing close at Harald's side. A bit taller than Harald, his beard a light brown.

"Father!" Harald shouted again. "See who I have here!"

Thorgrim looked at the other man once more. And he saw who it was. He gave a weak smile, all he could manage, as the sight overwhelmed him.

Harald…Odd…my boys.

Chapter Thirty-Six

King Halfdan never had dreams, which appeared to him an extraordinary circumstance; and he told it to a man called Thorleif Spake (the Wise), and asked him what his advice was about it.

Halfdan the Black's Saga
Heimskringla

King Halfdan Gudrødson was in a rage. Not the sort that comes like a knife-thrust, a sudden and violent emotion. It was a fever-rage, building over time, increasingly disorienting and all-consuming. Burning him up.

It had been an intolerably long time, and he had heard nothing. Skorri had sent no word, no indication that he had found Odd and crushed and scattered the mob that followed him. Only Thorgeir Sveinsson had returned to Grømstad, and he had come with news that Skorri, far from doing Halfdan's bidding, had betrayed his king once again.

In another time, a simpler time, Halfdan would not have endured the torment of waiting in impotent frustration for word of what was taking place. He would have ordered his horse saddled up, and his hird under arms and mounted. He would have ridden out and dealt directly and personally with such problems. But that was a long time ago.

His kingdom was much bigger now, thanks to his own cunning and ambition, and his responsibilities greatly increased. Rents, duties, taxes, the machinations of jarls and other kings, the maintenance of an army spread far beyond Grømstad — his problems had expanded with his territory. The days of roving the countryside and leading men in battle — his finest days, the days he recalled most fondly — were gone. He longed for the freedom he had felt back then, in wild youth. But it was over.

Or perhaps not. Perhaps, out of necessity, such action was needed again. Because he seemed to be experiencing chronic levels of incompetence and betrayal.

Skorri Thorbrandsson was running amok. Halfdan had sent Thorgeir back to Fevik to bring Skorri to heel, and to order him to return to Grømstad to explain himself. He had sent Grim Grimsson off with him, to see that things were done in accordance with his king's wishes.

That was a week or more past, and there had been no word from Skorri, no word from Grim, no word from Thorgeir, just mounting uncertainty and frustration. If this sort of failure persisted, Halfdan knew he would have no choice but to ride out and personally see that things were set to rights.

All of this he considered as he stood on a raised platform on top of the wall surrounding his great hall, and stared out at the country beyond. The walls were of earth and palisade construction, and Halfdan had built them taller, longer, and more substantial with each passing year. From his observation post he could see his hall and his various outbuildings on one side, and the lands around the compound on the other, as far as the glittering blue water of the bay a few miles distant.

He was watching warriors on the move, men coming in from every direction, congregating at the royal compound at Grømstad. It was the first thing he had seen in days that mitigated his anger somewhat, rather than stoking it further.

The real source of his anger, he knew, was this feeling that he could not act, that he was blocked at every turn. Even if he wanted to ride out himself and personally beat these disloyal dogs into submission he did not have the men to do it. But he was changing that.

Halfdan had warriors garrisoned all over his increasingly expansive kingdom; men to keep the peace and collect the taxes and stop any other kings or jarls with similar ambitions from encroaching on his territory. But now he was calling them in, sending messengers far afield to order his warriors back to Grømstad. The outer reaches of his kingdom could take care of themselves for a while. In Fevik he had more immediate concerns: an open rebellion at his gate, something he had never encountered before.

He watched as a dozen warriors came riding up to the gate, and tried to comfort himself with their appearance. They were hard and seasoned men, well-armed, and they rode with the confidence that came from that. And he had more like that, many more. Even if the five hundred who had gone with Skorri had all turned traitor, he had enough men left to crush them, and Odd's rabble as well.

But they were not there at Grømstad, not all of them. Another five hundred were sitting idle and useless in the woods by some cove a hard day's march to the south, waiting for the possible return of Thorgrim Night Wolf and his men.

He wished Grim was there to give advice. The man was greedy, conniving, and cowardly, but he was not stupid, and he knew that the better he served his king, the more it profited him. Halfdan could use Grim's unique insights just then. But Grim's whereabouts, like everything else it seemed, was some great mystery that he had no means to unravel. It made him want to scream. It made him want to beat someone bloody.

The day was getting on, the sun heading toward the western horizon, and Halfdan felt no more clarity than he had when the sun first came up. He needed wine. Or mead. They seemed to offer the only relief he was likely to find. Then he caught sight of something that drove thoughts of drink from his head.

Riders, heading toward the gate. He had been watching riders approach for much of the day, coming in from various directions, answering his summons. Those men, a dozen or so at a time, had been moving at the steady, unhurried pace of men covering distance. These newcomers — and there were only three of them — were riding at a flat-out gallop. And they were coming from the direction of Fevik.

Halfdan frowned as he watched them approach. He had an uneasy feeling, but he also felt a sense of relief. Whether they carried good news or bad, at least they would bring news, and that, more than anything, was what he craved.

He climbed down from the platform and then down off the wall. He walked quickly across the open ground to the main gate through which the riders would come. The warriors he encountered gave shallow bows as he passed, and he said to one, "Go find Thorodd Valbrandsson and send him to me."

With Skorri, Koll, and Thorgeir off doing only the gods knew what, command of the men had fallen to Thorodd, next in trust and seniority. Halfdan could only hope that Thorodd would not fail him as well, but he was starting to think that was too much to wish for.

Forty feet from the main gate, Halfdan stopped and waited with arms folded. He heard the man on the wall challenge the riders as they approached, heard the muffled reply of one of them calling, "We would speak with King Halfdan! On urgent matters!"

Halfdan let out a breath. He could not miss the tone of the man's voice: it did not sound like that of someone come to announce a resounding victory.

The big gate swung open and the three riders came in at a trot. They wore mail shirts which were rent in various places and stained dark with dried blood. One had a bandage wrapped around his head, another had one around his hand, where apparently a few fingers were gone. Their leggings, too, were bloodstained and torn.

They saw Halfdan as they approached, reined to a stop and slid down to the ground. "My lord," they said, nearly in unison, and bowed low.

"Stand," Halfdan barked. "What do you have to say?"

They straightened and glanced from one to the other, as if trying to decide who should be the bearer of the news. Finally the man with the missing fingers took a step forward.

"King Halfdan, we come from Lord Skorri's army. From Fevik," he said, all but choking on the words. "There's been a battle, highness. Horrible battle."

Halfdan waited for more, but a moment passed and nothing else seemed forthcoming, so he said, "Well? What of it? Who fought? Who won?"

"We fought the rebel, Odd, highness," the wounded man continued. "Lord Skorri had a trap set for him in Fevik, once he came ashore. But he…I mean, him, Odd…got wind of it, highness, before he and his men got out of their ships. They tried rowing away, but we…that is, all Skorri's men that were there in Fevik…we got in the longships and went after them. Caught 'em, too, and made a real slaughter of them. But then…there were more longships that showed up and came to their aid."

"More longships? How many more?"

"It was hard to tell, highness, in all the confusion. But six or seven, at least."

Halfdan felt as if his stomach had been dropped from the top of the wall. *Six or seven longships? Who might bring six or seven longships into this fight?* He had an ugly feeling that he knew the answer already.

"Who was this, in the six or seven longships, who fought with Odd?"

"Well…" the man said, and now he clearly did not want to be the bearer of this news.

"It was Thorgrim Ulfsson," said the man with the bandaged head. "Thorgrim Night Wolf, come back from the dead."

Those words did not surprise Halfdan, though they were still a punch in the gut. "You're certain?"

"Yes, highness. I know his features well. And we were face to face. He gave me this." The man pointed to his bandaged and bloody head.

Halfdan stared off into the distance, ignoring the men, letting those words turn in his head. They churned up all sorts of sediment that had long ago settled. Sediment that he wished would remain settled.

After all that time he had convinced himself that Thorgrim really was dead, but Bergthor had torn that belief to shreds. And despite having sent five hundred warriors south to ambush him, Halfdan had made himself believe that Thorgrim would not really show up on those shores. And now, here he was.

Thorgrim Ulfsson. Halfdan knew all the stories. Everyone in East Agder did. Thorgrim Ulfsson. Kveldulf. Thorgrim Night Wolf. A man blessed by the gods, who could take on the form of a wolf and prowl the night. But not a real wolf, one that could be killed with arrows and spears. Something else. Something not quite of this world.

Halfdan felt a little tremor run through him as he thought about that. Even if he killed Thorgrim while he was still a man, would that kill the night wolf as well? Or would it turn him into something even more frightening? Something that might hunt him for life, or beyond?

If Thorgrim returned, there was also the possibility that the people of East Agder would rally to him, that he could lead them against their king. That enough people would join him that even the king's trained men could not beat them all. It was a concern, to be sure. But it was not at all what scared Halfdan the most.

He heard the sound of hurrying feet, and Thorodd appeared at his side.

"My lord?" Thorodd said, forcing Halfdan from his unwelcome thoughts.

"These three men say they've come from Fevik. They were part of Skorri's army. They say there was a battle. At sea. They say that in the middle of it, Thorgrim Night Wolf arrived with six or seven longships."

"Thorgrim Night Wolf?" Thorodd said. Halfdan ignored him, turned back to the three.

"So what happened, after Thorgrim Night Wolf arrived?"

"They came straight into the fight, highness, and that was pretty much an end to it. They had hundreds of men. Tough bastards. The first one aboard, he was like a spirit of death. No mail, no shield. Not even a tunic. Ax in each hand." The man visibly shuddered at the memory.

"So you were defeated?"

"Yes, highness. Our people were butchered."

"Yet you three escaped," Thorodd pointed out, his words heavy with accusation.

"There were a lot of boats there, as well as the longships," the one with the bandaged head replied. "Some of Odd's men, I think they were fishermen. Anyway, we managed to get in a boat and get away. Reckoned it was more important to get word back to the king."

"I see," Thorodd said, though it was clear he did not believe it. No matter. Halfdan did not care in the least what these men may or may not have done.

"I take it you know nothing of what happened after the battle? If Thorgrim remained in Fevik?"

"Don't know, highness," said the man with the missing fingers. "Last we saw, it was just after the end of the fight, all the ships were still lashed together. But there was a lot of dead and wounded. A lot of damage to the ships. I don't think they could have sailed off, even if they wanted to. Most likely went ashore in Fevik."

"No one to stop them going ashore there," the other man added. "Nearly all of Lord Skorri's men were in the fight, and they're dead or prisoners now."

There were many feelings vying for prominence in Halfdan's mind, but foremost, strangely, was relief. Here at last was news. Bad news, but news that let him know what he now must do. He turned to Thorodd.

"Saddle up my fastest horse, the black stallion, you know the one. Find your best rider. Send him off to the men we sent south, the ones waiting to trap Thorgrim. Tell them I command them to start marching at first light on the morrow. I want them back here by end of day at the latest. Is that clear?"

"Yes, highness," Thorodd said. He gave a quick bow and hurried off, all but running to carry out his king's command.

Halfdan took a deep breath as he watched him go. He felt sick with this news, but he also felt both calm and elated, sensations that had been absent a long time. Finally, there was no doubt as to what he had to do. It was time to go to war.

Chapter Thirty-Seven

From there come maidens, knowing many things,
three [maidens], from the sea which stands under the tree;
they laid down laws, they chose lives for the sons of men,
the fates of men.

The Prophecy of the Seeress

One way or another, the day was bound to end in feasting. Thorgrim knew that the moment he had seen the ships locked in battle, his own fleet charging down on them. The day would end with some men feasting in victory, and some men feasting in the Allfather's great hall in Valhalla. He could imagine no other outcome.

His feast, it turned out, would be in their earthly realm of Midgard. But even with the battle won, there was considerable work to be done between fight and feast.

The dead and wounded were strewn around the decks, amid swaths of blood and discarded shields and weapons. The prisoners were kneeling, hands held out to show they were empty. The ships were drifting on the tide, creaking against one another. Starri Deathless, still alive, was in a heap, weeping bitterly.

There were a thousand things to do, and the men of *Sea Hammer* and *Blood Hawk* and *Black Wing* were looking to Thorgrim for orders. And Thorgrim could think only of Odd and Harald, just fifty feet away.

He shook his head and made himself consider the next task, and the next after that. Gudrid, captain of *Blood Hawk*, and Halldor, who commanded *Black Wing*, were standing on the opposite side of the newly captured ship, where they had led their men into the fight. They were still holding their broken shields and dripping swords. Gudrid had blood on his face, and Halldor's mail shirt was torn, but they seemed to be hale enough.

"Gudrid! Halldor! Take charge here," he called. "Take the prisoners' mail, their weapons, whatever they have. Arm rings, purses. Pile it all by the mast. Have our men tend to our wounded, Halfdan's men can tend to theirs. And get a couple of anchors over the side, if it's not too deep."

Gudrid and Halldor nodded and began calling orders, and Thorgrim was grateful that they did not ask what he was going to do. He looked over the side of the ship. He had noticed a faering tied there as they had come charging in, and he was pleased to see it was still there, and had not been crushed or sunk.

He grabbed the painter and pulled the boat toward him. He heard a voice, soft, feminine, incongruous in that setting. "You're alive. I'm happy to see it."

The first thought to flash in his head, just for an instant, was that the Valkyrie were talking to him. He looked and saw Gyda standing on board *Sea Hammer*, just across from him. He felt a flush of guilt that she had slipped his mind.

"Yes. And you," he said. "You're not hurt?"

"No. There was no one aboard *Sea Hammer* but me." She nodded toward the boat. "Are you leaving?"

"My son, Odd, is on the other ship. Odd and Harald. Come with me."

"There are a lot of wounded men that could use my help," she said, glancing over at the deck of the captured ship.

"There'll be time for that. Come." He swung a leg over the side of the ship and lowered himself into the faering, then pushed it off and let it drift over to where Gyda was standing. He helped her aboard, settled her in the stern, then sat on the center thwart. He took up the oars, and with two dozen strokes pulled them over the stretch of water and alongside the other ship.

As they came abeam, Thorgrim pulled in the oars and looked up. Harald was there, Odd beside him, both looking down at him and smiling. In that moment they looked to him the way they had looked a decade before: two rambunctious young boys, running amok on the farm, battering one another with wooden swords and sapling spears.

Thorgrim stood, helped Gyda to her feet. "Here, help Gyda get aboard," he said. She grabbed onto the sheer strake and hoisted herself up, and the boys gently pulled her up the rest of the way. Then Thorgrim pulled himself up and over.

He looked at Odd, looked into the young man's face. He did not know what to say. A face he had loved for twenty-two years. The same face, but different now. Older. Weary. More drawn. Thorgrim felt tears filling his eyes.

"Son…" he said. He took a quick step at Odd, put his arms around him, squeezed him tight. He felt Odd returning the hug. They stood like that for a moment, embracing, then Thorgrim held Odd out at arm's length and looked him up and down.

"You're wounded," he said. Odd held his hand up. It was bound in a strip of cloth, brownish-red with drying blood, as was his sleeve and the front of his tunic. Odd looked at the hand as if he had just noticed it, and then shrugged.

Thorgrim turned to Harald. "Are you hurt?"

"No. The gods fought with me."

"Good, good." He turned back to Odd, then gestured to Gyda. "This is Gyda Ketilsdottir. From Ribe." He was not sure what else to say.

Odd gave Gyda a bit of a smile and a nod of the head. "A pleasure to meet you, Gyda."

"And you, Odd Thorgrimson," Gyda said with a slight curtsy. "I've heard a great deal."

It all seemed so strangely familial, there amid the aftermath of battle, the groans of the wounded, the blood sprayed fore and aft. Forward, someone gave a muffled cry and a curse, and that brought Thorgrim back to the present, and the many things that required attention.

He looked past the boys, along the deck toward the bow. There was another longship grappled alongside the one they were aboard, and grappled onto those two were *Oak Heart* on one side and *Fox* on the other, while *Dragon* was jammed in between Halfdan's ship and Odd's: an island of ships slowly turning with the tide.

Asmund, master of *Oak Heart*, was amidships, on the larboard side. He and his men had had to climb over Halfdan's ships just to get into the fight. Thorgrim looked around for Hardbein, *Fox*'s captain. He saw men he recognized from Hardbein's crew, but no Hardbein. That did not bode well, but Thorgrim had other things on his mind.

"Asmund!" he called, and Asmund looked up and gave him a wave. "Get a couple of anchors down, if they'll reach the bottom. Get your men and Hardbein's to tend to the wounded. Also, get the mail, the weapons, purses, whatever, from the prisoners, and have them tend to their own wounded."

Asmund nodded and waved again. He wiped his sword on the tunic of a man lying at his feet, sheathed it, and began calling orders. Thorgrim turned back to Odd.

"I've been hearing things about you," he said. "As far away as Frisia. I hear you've been quite a thorn in your king's side."

Odd gave a crooked smile. "The Norns weave a long and twisted thread."

"I've seen that myself," Thorgrim said. He gestured toward the men and ships around them. "These are Halfdan's men you fought?"

"Yes," Odd said. He paused. "I think. You recall Skorri Thorbrandsson?"

"The king's overseer."

"Yes. Or he was. He…I'm not sure. He's nothing now, at least not in this world. That's him, there." Odd pointed to a body sprawled out on the deck, fifteen feet away. The face was turned from Thorgrim, but Thorgrim could see Skorri's long yellow hair, and the rich fabric of his tunic under his mail shirt. He was lying in a wide pool of blood, some of it smeared from his thrashing about.

"Did you do that?" Thorgrim asked.

"I did," Odd said.

Thorgrim nodded. "I see."

Skorri was a warrior of some renown, and he had fifteen years of experience, and five inches and two stone on Odd. Yet he was the one lying gutted on the deck. Thorgrim was impressed.

"Skorri was Halfdan's overseer, like you said," Odd explained. "But I think he turned on the king. These are his men, but I don't know if they were loyal only to him, or if they were still loyal to Halfdan."

"A long and twisted thread, indeed," Thorgrim said. "Seems like Halfdan has a hard time making friends."

He heard a voice call across the deck. "Thorgrim Ulfsson!" He looked up at the man coming toward him, dressed in mail over a red tunic, his hair and beard gray and tousled. He was just a few steps away before Thorgrim recognized him.

"Amundi Thorsteinsson!" he called. He moved to meet the man, and embraced him just as he had embraced Odd. "Are you part of this whole bloody mess?"

"I am," Amundi said, stepping back and looking Thorgrim up and down. "All of us old men, we came in support of your son. Who has become quite the leader in his own right."

Before Thorgrim could say anything to that, another man pushed his way up to where they were standing. He was shorter than Thorgrim, and wider, more the proportions of a barrel than a man. He wore no mail, no sword, no seax. His hands, or his knuckles and fingers at least, were red with blood, and there was blood on his face and his faded blue tunic.

"This must be the great Thorgrim Night Wolf!" the man said. He grabbed Thorgrim's hand in both of his and shook.

"Father, this is…" Odd began, but the man released Thorgrim's hand and waved Odd's introduction away.

"No need, Odd Sheep-herder," the man said. "I know of the legendary Thorgrim Night Wolf, and I have no doubt he knows of the great Bragi Shipslayer! That's me!" he said to Thorgrim, pointing at his own chest. "Now you've met me at last!"

"At last," Thorgrim agreed. "And I long to hear your tales. From all of you. But right now we have urgent matters to attend to."

They discussed those matters, the group huddled there. Then, reluctantly, and with a final hug for both boys, Thorgrim and Gyda returned to *Sea Hammer* and the other ships with which she was bound.

Gudrid and Halldor had managed to get anchors down and they seemed to be holding, mostly, their floating island no longer being carried out to sea. The prisoners were stripped down to tunics and leggings and sat in a sullen group under guard, or were tending to their wounded, or piling their dead near the mast. The crews of *Sea Hammer*, *Blood Hawk*, and *Black Wing* were likewise looking to the dead and wounded, and once Gyda came aboard she took charge of the latter effort, issuing orders with the ease of one long used to command.

Soon the destruction of battle was set to rights, as much as it could be, floating there in the bay. Thorgrim ordered the anchors raised and the ships underway, and one by one they untangled themselves and ran their oars out and followed *Sea Hammer* north to Fevik's harbor. Thorgrim piloted his ship up alongside the wharf, and one by one the others tied up as well, or ran themselves up on the beach once there was no more room to tie up.

Thorgrim stepped off *Sea Hammer*'s shear strake and onto the thick planks of the heavy-built wharf. He stopped, his hand resting on Iron-tooth's hilt, and looked around. The village of Fevik seemed deserted. Nothing moving. Nothing human, anyway. He could see only a few sundry chickens and dogs. He listened, but his ears did not tell him anything different.

"Gudrid!" he called. Gudrid had brought *Blood Hawk* to the side of the wharf opposite *Sea Hammer*. "Keep your men here, guard the prisoners. Asmund, get your men under arms and join us. Sea Hammers, with me. Swords, shields." There was another ship tied up astern of *Blood Hawk* and it took Thorgrim a moment to realize it was Odd's.

"Odd," Thorgrim called. "You and your men, take up arms and come with me."

Even as he said that, he realized that he was assuming command, even though Odd might rightly consider himself to be the leader there. But Odd said nothing, and a moment later he led his men, with their strange assortment of weapons and armor, onto the wharf and over to where *Sea Hammer*'s men were gathered.

Starri was there as well, still alive, and having recovered from the disappointment. He appeared to be horribly wounded, his face, chest, and hands painted with blood, but Thorgrim knew the blood was from those who'd had the bad luck of getting in Starri's way.

Starri's tunic was in his hand. He pulled it over his head and down and tucked the edge in behind the two axes in his belt, a sure sign that the berserker rage had passed. "Well, that was a fair morning's work, Night Wolf!" he said with enthusiasm.

"It was," Thorgrim agreed. He and Starri turned at the sound of steps on the wooden boards, and saw Odd hurrying toward them.

Starri spread his arms in a welcoming gesture, and called in a loud voice, "This must be Odd Thorgrimson, of whom the gods sing!"

Odd seemed unsure what to say to that. He muttered, "Uh…" and then Starri leapt forward, threw his arms around him, and hugged him tight.

"I am so pleased for Night Wolf that you're still alive," Starri said into Odd's shoulder.

Odd turned confused eyes to his father, and Thorgrim said, "This is Starri. Starri Deathless. We've…been through quite a bit, him and me."

Starri let Odd go. Odd said, "I'm honored to meet you, Starri." But he still sounded a bit uncertain.

Thorgrim gestured toward the town. "What do you reckon we'll find here?"

"Not sure," Odd said. "I think most of Skorri's men were on the ships. I don't think there'll be many left on shore to oppose us. Skorri took over…" He paused, frowned. "Where's Grandfather Ornolf?"

"Dead," Thorgrim said. "Two years gone. He made a good end. Died with Oak Cleaver in his hand, saving your brother's life."

Odd nodded slowly. Thorgrim recognized the emotions playing on his face. Sorrow, but also a warrior's understanding that death would come for them all, and there was no better death a man could hope for than such a one as Ornolf's.

"Skorri took over grandfather's hall," Odd continued. "Treating it like his own, playing at being a great jarl. He probably left a few men there. Not many, I don't think. I'm afraid he sacked your hall and farm as well, father. And the town of Fevik."

"What of your grandmother, Thurid?" Thorgrim asked.

"Alive and well, as far as I know. Skorri was holding her hostage, to use against me."

It's a wonder the old crone didn't singlehandedly kill the lot of them, Thorgrim thought, but he said only, "Let's hope he's kept her safe."

With the men assembled on the wharf, Thorgrim led the way slowly toward the town. His eyes moved from building to building as he advanced, but still he saw nothing to suggest a trap, or any cause for concern.

"Look there," Starri said, pointing to a spot farther along the dock.

Thorgrim could see what he was pointing at, something lying near the end of the wharf, but he could not make out what it was. "What is it?" he asked.

"A head, if I'm not mistaken," Starri said.

He was not mistaken. They approached carefully, as if it might present some sort of threat. They were ten feet away when Odd said, "Oh! That bastard!" Thorgrim could hear the grief in his voice.

"You know the man?"

"Ragi. Ragi Oleifsson." They came closer, and Thorgrim could see that Odd was right. He had not seen Ragi in years, but he knew him well, well enough to recognize him even with his features distorted as they were.

"Ragi was with you?" Thorgrim asked.

"He was. Saved our lives. All of us. He lost his farm, his hall, his ship. All because he joined with us."

Bragi Shipslayer pushed past them, a piece of cloth in his hand. He carefully lifted Ragi's head, held it at eye level, and looked at it, face to face. He shook his head.

"You were a good one, Ragi Oleifsson," he said. "A good one, indeed. Young Odd here killed the one did this to you, and I'm sorry for it, because I would have liked to kill him myself." With that he bundled Ragi's head up with the cloth and held it at his side.

They continued on to the end of the wharf and then into the town, moving down the main road, past the seemingly deserted homes and workshops, the empty tables where merchants had once sold their wares.

A voice called out, a female voice, calling from a home they had just passed. "Kalf!"

Thorgrim turned at the sound, saw a woman running, arms up, from a small house by the road. One of Odd's men broke from the rest, ran over to her, and scooped her up in his arms as they met.

With that one name, shouted in joyful recognition, it seemed as if some demon's spell was broken. Suddenly more women, and children, and a few old men, appeared in doorways and on the beaten paths leading from the houses. Names were shouted back and forth, men abandoned the ranks to race to their wives, woman ran toward the road to embrace their husbands.

"I think the fighting's over, Night Wolf," Starri said. He did not sound happy. But he was right. They scouted the remainder of the town, and did not find one of Skorri's men left in Fevik. So then the real work began.

There were dozens of wounded who needed shelter and care, dozens of dead who needed burial. Happily, with their prisoners from Skorri's army, Thorgrim and Odd had a great many laborers at their disposal.

Under guard, the prisoners were set to work offloading the wounded and getting them to their homes ashore, or finding folk to care for them. A tent, fashioned from one of the longships' sails, was set up on shore, and Skorri's wounded were housed under that. A hundred more of Skorri's men were sent to the fields beyond the town to start digging graves, a task that took them until the afternoon began to settle into evening.

As all this was going on, Thorgrim called together fifty of his men, and Odd called fifty of his, and they were sent off under Amundi's command to Ornolf the Restless's great hall. They were sent with instructions to secure the hall, to take as prisoner any of Skorri's men still there, and to see that Thurid and the rest of the people were safe. They were to tell Thurid that Thorgrim had returned, and that they were to make ready to host his men and Odd's: six or seven hundred in all.

Word came back some time later that Thurid and her people were safe. News of Skorri's defeat had reached the great hall earlier in the day, and the handful of his men who had been left on guard lit out immediately, taking with them all the loot they could carry. Not one of them was to be found when Odd's and Thorgrim's men came through the gate.

It was getting dark by the time the graves were dug and the dead transported to the burial field. Thorgrim ordered a bonfire kindled, and soon it was built up into a great tower of flame that threw its light all over the grounds, casting shadows behind the mounds of earth next to each open grave.

Earlier, Thorgrim had ordered that a bull be brought to the field, and now the animal was slaughtered next to the fire, the blood from its rent throat let to drain in a big wooden bowl that Starri held under the dying animal. Two intact wolf skins were found, and Thorgrim and Starri each draped one over their heads. With Starri carrying the bowl of bull's blood, Thorgrim went from one corpse to the next, dipping a pine bough in the blood and shaking drops on each of the dead; his men, Odd's, and Skorri's as well.

That done, each body was lowered into a grave, and each of Thorgrim's and Odd's dead was provided with weapons: swords or axes, shields. Hardbein, it turned out, was among the slain, thrust through with a spear as he came over the side of Skorri's ship. For his good service, Thorgrim ordered him buried in mail and helmet, with sword, spear, seax and shield.

"We'll fight side by side with this one again," Starri said, as he and Thorgrim watched the weapons being placed in Hardbein's grave. "In Valhalla, we'll fight with Hardbein again."

"And all these good men," Thorgrim said. "And all the ones before." He had buried a lot of men over the past years. He was tired of burying men.

They interred Ragi as well, or what was left of him, with all the weapons a true warrior could want. Bragi Shipslayer wept unabashedly, and insisted that he and Huginn and Muninn shovel the dirt into Ragi's grave.

Skorri's men — Halfdan's men — being the enemy, were not buried with swords or mail. But they had fought well, and died well. For that reason, Thorgrim would not send them to the next world bereft of weapons, so each was buried with a spear to see them along.

All, save for Skorri Thorbrandsson. He was stripped naked, and his body tossed into the nearby woods. From King Halfdan's overseer, to self-proclaimed jarl, to vanquished foe, to carrion, it was a long fall for one man to take, but no one felt moved to mourn.

Finally, with night fully on them, the weary men began the long, uphill walk to the great hall that once belonged to Ornolf the Restless. It was a walk that Thorgrim knew well, and even in the dark, and after all the time that had passed, he still recalled every turn in the road, every outcropping of granite along the way.

They came to the tall gates, unchanged since Thorgrim had seen them last. The walls were outlined with the light of the fires burning on the grounds, kindled for cooking the great quantity of meat needed to feed all those men. Thorgrim could smell the roasting beef and pork, along with the wood smoke, and he realized how hungry he was.

The gates swung open as they approached, and Thorgrim and Odd and Harald led the way in. Thurid was there to greet them, her servants standing behind her in a swine array. She stepped forward, kissed Thorgrim on both cheeks, looked him up and down, then stepped over to her grandsons and kissed them each in turn.

"I never thought to see one of you alive again," she said. Then, almost as an afterthought, she added, "Your men told me Ornolf is dead. They did not say how." Thorgrim guessed this news had not come as a surprise, that she had long ago embraced her widowhood.

"He was killed. In Ireland. Two years back. He died a good death, Oak Cleaver in his hand. Saving Harald's life."

Thurid nodded. "Foolish old man," she said.

"I've been carrying Oak Cleaver since Grandfather's death," Harald said, half-pulling the sword from its sheath. "But if you'd like it, of course I'm happy to give it up."

"No, no," Thurid said. "Ornolf would want you to have it. Now that he's in Odin's feast hall, drinking and whoring, just as he's always dreamed of doing. Just as he always did in life."

She led the way into the great hall, which was just as Thorgrim remembered, a cavernous affair, built to house the kind of feasting and debauchery that a man of Ornolf's wealth and appetites would require. And it was well that it was so big, since Thorgrim and Odd had between them six or seven hundred men, all ravenous, all craving drink, all ready to celebrate the fact that they were still alive at the end of the day when so many others were not.

Thorgrim was given the high seat, Gyda beside him, with Odd to one side, Harald to the other. Beside them sat Thorgrim's captains, and Amundi, and Bragi Shipslayer, and some of the chief men among the fisherfolk. The rest were spread out at the tables that ran fore and aft along the great hall's stunning length. The servants, grateful to be free of Skorri and his men, struggled under Thurid's sharp direction to keep the food and drink coming.

It was a boisterous affair, but short lived. Exhaustion swept like a malevolent spirit among the men, and one by one they stumbled off to find some place to bed down, or simply slumped over on the tables, or dropped to the floor. Thorgrim and his sons, who knew the great hall nearly as well as their own farm, directed the men at the head table as to where they might find beds, then they themselves stumbled off to their familiar sleeping quarters.

The following day, just after daybreak, Thorgrim sent men out to scout the countryside, to discover what they could about the goings-on in East Agder, and to spread the news of his return and Skorri's defeat. Soon after, men began arriving at the great hall, coming in from all around, drawn by word that Thorgrim Night Wolf had returned, and wanting to know what that portended.

Among them were two men leading a band of a few dozen warriors. One was named Asgeir Refsson, whom Odd introduced as the leader of Ragi Oleifsson's house guard. The other was Arnor Knattarson, leader of the fishermen who had joined with Odd.

Odd had earlier explained why Ragi's head had been found on shore, that he and his men were sent to keep an eye on Skorri, and to attack his flank if he was setting a trap in Fevik. Asgeir and Arnor now completed the tale of how Skorri had found them out, set their boats adrift, attacked them at dawn and driven them back. They told how the warriors had dispersed, all save for Ragi, who had led a one-man charge straight at the enemy, and in doing so earned his brutal death and his place at Odin's table.

In the late morning, Thorgrim called for horses, and he and his sons rode back to Fevik to check on the wounded, and to see that the prisoners were in no danger of escaping. They found that Gudrid, who had been left in charge, had loaded Halfdan's men aboard two longships and anchored them thirty feet away from the wharf, with no oars or sails: a trick they had first tried in Hamtun and found worked well. Gudrid had stationed archers along the wharf and the shoreline in case any of the prisoners felt like taking a swim or trying to let go the anchor line, and that had done the trick of keeping them from any mischief.

They returned to the great hall in the late afternoon, where preparations were underway for another feast. Thorgrim wondered how much longer Thurid's food and drink would hold out, particularly since Skorri and his men had, by all accounts, not been sparing in their consumption.

One more night, he thought. One more night of feasting at Thurid's expense and then it would be time to move on, back to his home, his farm. The idea made him happy. And it made him afraid.

For more than two years he had yearned to get back to his farm, but the closer he came, the more he dreaded it. He was tired near to death of the peripatetic life, but feared the memories the farm would bring swirling up from the muck: the loss, the grief. He wondered sometimes if he should have set the course that Starri Deathless had, and tried to be slain in battle. He had certainly fought often enough over their years of raiding, but so far he had met with no better success in leaving the world than Starri had.

He had his sons now, and his daughter Hild, who was married, but lived not too far distant, and that would help him. And he had his little daughter Hallbera, who would hardly remember him. He wondered if she was growing to look like her mother, her namesake.

And he had Gyda. Even with his children at his side, he was not sure he would have had the courage to return, if not for her.

No, there was really no choice. On the morrow he and his men would board their longships for one last time. They would sail from Fevik to Vik, and Thorgrim would march them a short ways inland to his farm and find what Skorri had left him. He would feast his men at his own expense and then they would say their farewells and be off to wherever they wished to be off to, to spend their riches however they desired, and he would settle in on his farm and swear an oath to never leave it again.

Skorri was dead, his army was scattered. With those men lost, and Thorgrim back, Halfdan would, with any luck, be willing to talk. Peace restored, lives resumed.

It was all very simple, a smooth, wide road laid out at his feet, but Thorgrim knew too much of the ways of the gods to think it would actually play out the way he imagined. And so he was not very surprised at all when, the following morning, his scouts returned to say that King Halfdan the Black had gathered his army, and they were ready to move.

Chapter Thirty-Eight

Hear a great wonder,
hear of peace broken,
hear of a great matter,
hear of a death,
— one man's or more.

Gisli Sursson's Saga

This is it," Thorgrim said, twisting in his saddle as he spoke. He was unaccustomed to riding, and was trying to find a position that was not so hard on his backside and thighs. "This is where I mean for us to make our stand. I thought for certain we'd be late to the feast."

He looked over at Harald, riding beside him on his right. Harald had not done much riding of late either, but he was naturally graceful and coordinated, surprisingly so for one as stocky-built as he was, and he seemed to take it in stride, as he did most things. Odd was riding on Thorgrim's left. Unlike him and Harald, Odd had spent considerable time in the saddle over the past few years, and it showed.

"It does look like we got here before our hosts," Odd agreed.

They were about two miles west of Fevik, moving along the road that ran from that village to Vik and Grømstad and beyond. Thorgrim and Harald and Odd were mounted, as were the captains of Thorgrim's ships. Behind them rode Harald's shipmate, Brand, holding a flagstaff from which fluttered a green pennant with a prominent red wolf's head. The banner of Thorgrim Night Wolf. Thorgrim did not fly it often, but now seemed like the right time to do so.

Behind the riders marched Thorgrim's army, such that it was. Close to four hundred raiders from his seven longships, the remnants of Ragi's house guard, and the disparately armed and trained men from the fishing camp and from Fevik and the farms around. Six or seven hundred men, a little over half of whom could genuinely be called warriors. They had been on the move for hours, marching at a moderate pace, in fine weather, lightly encumbered: the calm between two storms.

Thorgrim's scouts had returned to Ornolf's great hall a few hours after sunrise that morning, having ridden from Grømstad in the half light. It was not a long ride, about five miles, and they had covered it quickly, because they had news that they knew Thorgrim needed to hear.

The night before, about five hundred men had arrived at Halfdan's compound from the south. They were warriors, for certain, the king's men, marching under Halfdan's banner. They had set up camp in the fields just outside the walls. At first light they turned out and were clearly making ready to march, with horses harnessed to wagons, mounts for the chief men saddled, the men outfitted for battle with shields and mail and helmets in place.

And they were not the only warriors under Halfdan's command. There were more inside the compound as well: the scouts could hear them getting ready, shouting orders, moving gear. How many, they could not tell. Enough that the new arrivals had to camp outside the walls, and that could mean a lot of men indeed.

Thorgrim called a council of war, which seemed like an army in its own right: him and Harald and the rest of the fleet's captains, Odd and Amundi and Arnor, Bragi Shipslayer. Starri Deathless, of course. Thorgrim was not much in the mood for discussion, and would have had little patience for debate, but luckily there was no debate. They were all of a single mind. It was time to make a stand.

They would have to confront Halfdan, and every man there knew it. Thorgrim and his men had heard the tales of Halfdan's on-going effort to crush the rebellion and keep the freemen under his heel, and it was as clear to them as it was to Odd that Halfdan would not stop until he was made to stop.

It was clear as well that this was the time to stop him. They would never have a bigger army than they did just then, and the men would never be better motivated than they were after having defeated Skorri Thorbrandsson and his warriors. With luck they could even pick the ground on which they fought.

The plans they made were simple, because Thorgrim knew that being too clever was the quickest means of being defeated. That done, they gathered the men, had them break their fast, and got them in marching order. Then Thorgrim and the others on horseback led the way out of the gate and down the road toward Grømstad.

Thorgrim had in mind the place where he hoped to make his stand, but that meant getting there before Halfdan did, which would be hard, if it was even possible at all. He and his men had scrambled to get underway just that morning, whereas Halfdan had most likely been preparing to move for some time now. Thorgrim doubted they would steal a march on the king, but apparently they did, because when they arrived at the place of Thorgrim's choosing, they were alone.

The road from Fevik had come through a series of tree-covered hills and down into flat, open country. A few hundred feet south of the road was the head of a long, narrow bay that ran down to the sea, the bay on which Ragi Oleifsson's farm had stood before Skorri burned it to the ground. That bay, Thorgrim figured, would serve to anchor the left end of his line.

To the north, also a few hundred feet away, stood the edge of a forest that extended a mile or so inland, and which Thorgrim was relieved to find was still where he remembered it to be. That would serve to anchor his line's right flank. And so it was there he would make his stand.

Thorgrim raised his hand to signal he was stopping, then reined his horse in. Harald, Odd, and the other mounted men did the same, and behind them the column came to a ragged halt as well. The riders gathered around Thorgrim, a council of war on horseback.

"Here's the place I reckoned we'd make our stand," Thorgrim said to the collected leaders. "Looks like we got here first." If Halfdan meant to bring his army to Fevik, and it seemed a near certainty that he did, he would have to march them along this road. But there was no sign of him.

"Halfdan doesn't travel light," Odd said. "He'll bring wagonloads of supplies. His big field tents, wine, fine food. You can depend on it. His army won't march faster than his supply wagons."

"He probably doesn't feel the need to hurry," Amundi said.

"Probably not," Thorgrim agreed. "Well, so much the better for us. We'll get the men in place and wait for word of Halfdan's approach." Scouts had been sent out ahead of the column, ordered to ride toward Grømstad until they caught sight of Halfdan's army, then report back. So far they had heard nothing from them.

"Me and Harald and our ships' crews will take the center of the line," Thorgrim continued, pointing to a spot roughly midway between the bay and the stand of trees. "You other ship captains, get your men in line on either side of us. Odd…your people, the town folk and the farmers and fisherfolk and such…those who have shields can stand in the shield wall, too. Have the rest form a second rank with spears and axes, whatever they have. Arrange them however you see fit, but have them ready to move, to shore up any weakness in the shield wall. The men can rest for now, eat what they brought, but see that they're ready to form a shield wall in an instant."

The others nodded as they listened. They had no questions.

It did not take long to get the men in place, a line of warriors stretching from the shore to the woods, a human barricade across the road to Fevik, a shield wall many hundreds of shields in length. Once they were in place, they sat in the grass, talking, sleeping, eating and drinking the provisions they had brought with them.

Thorgrim remained in the saddle so that he could move quickly up and down the line and better see what was going on. Harald and Odd also remained mounted, and by his side. Thorgrim knew that Harald would never sit or rest as long as his father was not. He guessed that Odd felt the same, with the added sense that this was all his responsibility, and he could not relax his vigilance even a little. Thorgrim was proud of them both.

They were discussing the possible weak spots in the shield wall when Starri stepped up to Thorgrim's horse. "Riders coming," he said, nodding west down the road.

Thorgrim looked in that direction. He squinted in hopes that it might improve his vision. He thought he could see movement, but he was not sure.

"He's right, father," Harald said. "And they're riding fast."

"Let's hope it's our scouts coming back," Thorgrim said.

They watched for a moment more, and then Starri said, "There's four of them."

Thorgrim frowned. Four riders. That was not good. He had only sent two.

The riders kept coming, close enough that Thorgrim could see them clearly. Four men on horseback, mail glinting in the morning sun. They were not Thorgrim's scouts, so they had to be Halfdan's.

Thorgrim wondered what had become of his men. He did not imagine it was good.

"Everyone, keep down, keep down!" he called, so that all the men already sitting could hear him and stay where they were, partially hidden. No reason for them to let Halfdan know any more than they had to.

The four riders reined to a halt a couple hundred feet down the road and came no closer, their horses prancing restlessly.

"Think they've come to talk with us?" Odd asked.

"We'll see," Thorgrim said. They continued watching until, a moment later, the riders turned and raced off the way they had come.

"Reckon not," Harald said. "Should we get the men in the shield wall now?"

"No," Thorgrim said. "Not yet." There was still no telling how far off Halfdan was, and there was no point in having the men standing in their shield wall, tiring themselves, and growing increasingly nervous, for some unknowable amount of time. Halfdan's army would come that way, they had no choice, and they would have to cover at least a mile of open ground before the two sides met. It was not as if they were going to sneak up on Thorgrim's line.

Halfdan's army, it turned out, was quite a distance behind its scouts. It was nearly *hádegi*, midday, by the time the head of Halfdan's column appeared around the bend a mile to the west. They were moving at a deliberate pace; not charging into battle, but not strolling, either.

"Up! Everyone up! Form your shield wall!" Thorgrim had dismounted, but now he climbed back into the saddle and rode up and down the line, calling orders. As he did, hundreds of men stood up from the grass and locked their bright-painted shields together: a surprising and intimidating sight to the oncoming army, or so Thorgrim hoped.

"They seem to be moving faster now," Harald said, nodding to the approaching warriors.

"Probably left their wagons behind once they knew we were here," Odd said.

The king's column continued its steady approach, until they were close enough that Thorgrim and the others could pick out the individual warriors, their shields and banners and horses. Then the column stopped, with something like six or seven hundred yards between the two lines, and everything was silent.

Thorgrim could hear voices, men shouting orders, presumably, but he could not make out the words. Then, a moment later, Halfdan's men began to move from column to line, forming a shield wall, north and south, facing Thorgrim's. Halfdan's line, also flanked by the water and the trees, was no longer than Thorgrim's, but it was two and three deep, a thousand men at least, and none of those men were farmers or fishermen.

I hope the gods are with us, Thorgrim thought. *That's the only advantage we're like to find.*

The men in Thorgrim's shield wall shifted nervously in place, digging feet into the dirt, their overlapping shields thumping against one another.

"Stand ready and hold your ground!" Thorgrim called up and down the line. "Let them come to us!"

For long moments no one moved. Then a gap appeared in Halfdan's line, and a half dozen horsemen rode though. They were wearing mail and helmets and their horses appeared to be clad in armor as well. One was holding Halfdan's banner aloft. They rode to a place halfway between the two lines and reined to a stop.

"I guess Halfdan wants to surrender," Odd said.

"Could be," Thorgrim said. "We had best go find out. Brand! Get that banner and mount up!" They were not going to match Halfdan's regal trappings, but they could try.

A moment later Thorgrim's line made a gap and Thorgrim rode through, with Odd, Harald, Amundi, Hall, and Asmund flanking him. Brand followed behind, with Thorgrim's banner streaming from its staff. They trotted over to Halfdan and his men, and pulled to a stop ten feet away.

"King Halfdan," Thorgrim said, giving a little bow and then looking the man up and down. He had not seen Halfdan in years, not since his wife, Hallbera, had died, well before he and Ornolf had sailed. He did not look much different. Worn down a bit by care, if not by hard labor. More gray hair, more lines etched in his face, but generally the same.

"Thorgrim Ulfsson," Halfdan said. "You've returned to us."

"I have. Not without considerable difficulty, but I have returned. And in good time, it seems."

"There's been trouble, I'll admit it," Halfdan said. "And I fear your son, Odd, here, has been the cause of it."

"Hmm," Thorgrim said. "Not what I hear. I hear there's blame to go around. And that being the case, perhaps we can find a way out of this, without anyone having to die."

Halfdan smiled. "Do you think I'm here to negotiate a peace? You think I'm trying to avoid battle? I can see why you might not want to fight, with your army of farmers and tradesmen and cripples, but I'm perfectly happy to settle this at the end of a sword."

"Not all my men are farmers," Thorgrim said. "Most are warriors who've been plundering Ireland and Engla-land and Frankia for near on three years. And they'd be happy to do the same to Grømstad."

"And yet here you talk to me about making peace. As if you were afraid to fight."

If Halfdan's words were meant to cow Thorgrim, they had the opposite effect. He felt the anger surge through him, the red rage growing, and it was in his voice as he growled, "I don't fear fighting you or any thousands of your warriors. The gods have brought many men to their death at the tip of my sword, Iron-tooth."

Halfdan's face blanched a bit, and the arrogance was replaced by something else. Surprise? Fear? It was subtle, and gone in an instant, but Thorgrim did not miss it.

"Yes, well…" the king stammered, trying to regain his footing. Thorgrim offered him a hand.

"See here, your highness," Thorgrim said. "I've never been anything but loyal to you. You know that. You also know I won't turn on my own son. But he and the freemen are no threat to you and your rule. Let us find a way to make peace that will satisfy everyone."

Halfdan's eyes moved from Thorgrim to Odd and back to Thorgrim. He seemed to be wrestling with the question. But he did not wrestle long.

"That time is long past," he said. "I will not ignore this insurrection, and I will not forgive it. I met here with you to give you the chance to surrender, before we butcher your entire mob. So, what will it be?"

"A stupid question, from a stupid king," Thorgrim said, the anger back again. "I've never in my life surrendered, but I've torn the throats out of plenty of men who hoped I would. So let's be on with it now."

He saw it again, the uncertainty on Halfdan's face, but Thorgrim was done talking, and he knew in his gut it was pointless in any event — Halfdan would consider any negotiation a sign of weakness that he could not afford. He pulled his horse's reins over and turned the animal around, turning his back to his king. He kicked the horse's flanks and took off at a gallop. He heard the others riding hard behind him.

The men in his shield wall stepped aside to make an opening as he approached, but Thorgrim did not ride through. Instead he stopped twenty feet short of the line and stood up in his stirrups.

"King Halfdan has no interest in anything, save bloody slaughter!" he shouted, looking right and left. "And he thinks his victory will come easy! But the gods favor us, because we stand here and laugh at his threats! So, bold men that you are, fight for your homes, fight for the man beside you! We'll kill the lot of these bastards, or we'll go to the Allfather's feast hall with our weapons in our hands!"

They did not cheer. Rather, someone down the line let go with a manic howl, rising in pitch and volume. The cry of the wolf. It was taken up immediately by another, and another. Thorgrim wanted to make them stop, but more joined in, until he knew he could never make himself heard over that wild noise.

He spurred his horse, rode along the length of the shield wall. He pulled Iron-tooth from its scabbard and held it up and the howling redoubled. Thorgrim turned the horse, rode down to the other end of the line, and the noise was like a storm rolling over the field. Then he sheathed his weapon and rode in through the gap in the line, and the shield wall closed up again, and the howling died away.

It was only then that Thorgrim saw the riders coming. Half a dozen or so, riding hard down the road they had just taken from Fevik. He turned to Odd, who was riding beside him.

"Any notion who this could be?" He nodded toward the approaching men.

"No," Odd said. They fell silent as the riders drew closer. They were forty feet away when the man in front raised an arm and shouted.

"Ha! Thorgrim Night Wolf! That would explain that lunatic howling!" He reined to a halt ten feet from Thorgrim's horse, his face red and running with sweat, his hair and beard soaked, his chain mail shirt dull with road dust. He was grinning.

"Vifil Helgason," Thorgrim said, recognizing the man at last. He looked at the rider beside him. "And Thorgeir Herjolfsson." He smiled, despite himself.

"Looks like the tales of your death weren't so accurate, Thorgrim," Thorgeir said. He was smiling, too. Thorgrim had known those men for many years, and Odd had told him how Vifil and Thorgeir were among those who stood up to Halfdan and fought at Odd's side.

"And you, Odd," Vifil said, nodding toward Thorgrim's son. "Here you are having all this fun and never inviting us."

"I was on my way to Fevik to try and raise the army again," Odd said. "But I didn't make it."

"Still, you're not too late, as you can see," Thorgrim said. "You may only be six swords, but I know that you're worth sixty."

"Not just six swords," Vifil said. "We have near three hundred warriors, about half a mile up the road. We left them behind so we could ride ahead and find you. Vigdis is there, too, and most of the men who were in Ulfkel Ospaksson's hird. And some others. Good men, the lot of them."

"Three hundred warriors?" Thorgrim said. That was welcome news indeed. It turned a hopeless situation into one that was at least a bit less hopeless. "I'm well pleased to hear it. Let me suggest you bring them up as quick as you can."

Vifil turned and gave orders to two of the men behind him, and they wheeled their horses and charged back the way they came. He turned back to Thorgrim. "Now, if only Halfdan will be considerate enough to wait for them."

But he was not. Thorgrim heard cheering from across the open ground. He turned his horse and looked out over the men's heads, out toward Halfdan's army. They were moving now, eight or nine hundred men at least, advancing in a uniform line, their shields bright spots of color, their helmets glinting in the sun. They would slam into Thorgrim's shield wall like a wave from a gale-whipped sea, and Thorgrim wondered how long his men could stand against it, if they could at all.

Chapter Thirty-Nine

There lie on the earth almost all
of your kinsmen, turned into corpses;
you couldn't prevent the battle, for you it was decreed
that you were the source of strife for powerful men.

The Second Lay of Helgi Hundingsbani

Halfdan's men were not advancing in a straight line. It took Thorgrim a moment to realize that. As they moved across the field, their momentum building, he could see that the center was getting out ahead, forming a human spear-point, a swine array many hundreds of men in length. It was a shallow point, the center not so far in front, but enough that they could hit the center of Thorgrim's line like a hammer-blow, with the rest sweeping in behind.

"Harald!" Thorgrim called. "They'll hit the center of the line first! You and your men, brace yourselves! If they break through, it's over!"

Harald had climbed down off his horse as soon as they had come back through the line. His men, the crew of *Dragon*, were in the center of the shield wall, and he meant to stand with them. Now he turned quickly and gave Thorgrim a wave to acknowledge his words, then turned back to face the enemy.

Odd was dismounted as well, and getting the men who had followed him from Fevik into the line, forming them into a second rank a little north of where Harald was standing. Thorgrim spurred his horse over to him.

"Odd!" he called, and when Odd looked up, Thorgrim pointed to the center of the line. "They're making a swine array, they're going to hit first where Harald's men are standing! Get some of these men behind them, strengthen that part of the line!"

Odd nodded, then began gesturing and shouting and shifting his men south, to where they could stand behind the Dragons and help absorb the coming shock.

Thorgrim rode back to where Vifil Helgason and the others were sitting their horses. "Seems Halfdan will not do you the courtesy of waiting for your men to get here," he said. "If there's still a fight going on when they arrive, put them in wherever it seems they're most needed."

"That I will do, Thorgrim," Vifil said. He was smiling, and he seemed to be genuinely enjoying himself. "Ah, we're going to murder these bastards!" he added. "The gods are with us, I can feel it in my gut!"

Thorgrim smiled as well, and nodded, though he was not feeling so confident as Vifil seemed to be. His two boys were holding the center of the line, and he feared for their lives, despite his efforts to pretend otherwise. He turned his horse and rode back to the shield wall.

The crew of *Sea Hammer*, Thorgrim's men, were next to Harald's, and Thorgrim wanted very much to stand with them. He even started to climb down from his horse when he realized he was better off where he was, mounted, able to see the battle more clearly, and move quickly up and down the line.

He saw a spear that had been left sticking upright in the ground and he snatched it up. That, at least, would give him some means of joining the fight.

Halfdan's men were just a few hundred yards away now, and moving fast. They were not running; they were too disciplined for that. Rather, their advance was quick, steady, and organized, their line still whole.

"Stand ready!" Thorgrim shouted up and down the line. "Dig in! Hold your ground and push back! Kill them as they come!"

Halfdan's warriors were still in a wedge formation, the center of the line coming right at Harald's and Odd's men. Halfdan and his mounted guard rode behind them, banners snapping above their heads. Thorgrim had a sudden impulse to plunge his horse right through his own line, right through Halfdan's, and take the fight to the king, sword to sword, man to man.

Could I make it? he wondered. *Or would I be pulled out of the saddle?*

"Father!" He looked down. Odd was standing nearby, pointing off to his left, shaking his head in confusion. "What is the matter with Starri?"

Thorgrim looked where Odd was pointing. Starri Deathless was standing a few feet back from the line, bare-chested, spinning in place, his arms out and making their strange jerking movements.

"Nothing's wrong," Thorgrim said. "He's a berserker. I told you. The madness is coming on him."

"Should I get him a shield, so he can stand in the shield wall?"

Thorgrim smiled at that. "No, he won't stand in the shield wall. He'll…."

But Thorgrim did not have to explain what Starri would do, because just then the battle-madness came full on him. He stopped spinning and started in with his berserker scream, the sound, terrifying and unearthly, building as he ran at the back of Thorgrim's line.

Harald's men heard the familiar shriek and opened a gap to let Starri through, but Odd's men, standing between them and Starri, forming the second rank, did not. They turned to see what this noise was about, and Starri leapt off the ground as he came at them. His feet found men's arms and shoulders as he vaulted over Odd's line, knocking his men to the ground, and racing through the gap left by Harald's.

"What is he doing?" Odd shouted the question in surprise as Starri raced across the open ground, right at the point of Halfdan's human wedge. "He's a dead man!"

"That's his hope," Thorgrim said, "but it hasn't worked yet. Now watch this. He's about to do us a great favor."

The lone, shirtless figure continued his charge at the hundreds of warriors coming at him, and the men in Thorgrim's line began shouting their encouragement as he ran. The two battle axes were out of his belt now, and held over his head. A spear came sailing at him from Halfdan's line, and then another, and he sidestepped them neatly, never breaking stride.

Thorgrim watched him run, and it occurred to him that Starri might actually die this time. In all their time fighting together, he did not think they had ever faced an enemy as well-trained, well-equipped, and disciplined as this. If Starri threw himself at Halfdan's line, or attempted to go over it, he would meet with a dozen swords, protected by a dozen shields and wielded by elite fighting men. If Starri could indeed be killed, he might well be killed now.

Thorgrim pressed his lips together. He did not want Starri to be killed, and he figured it would be a very bad omen if he was.

But once again, Starri did something Thorgrim did not foresee. He did not hit the line head on, and he did not try to go over it. Rather, he dropped to the ground ten feet short of the first man in the wedge, went down on one shoulder and tumbled sideways, slamming into the surprised man's legs and sending him sprawling into the dirt.

The men behind him in Halfdan's line could not stop in time, and they stumbled over the tangled forms of Starri Deathless and their fallen comrade. Two or three of them staggered and went down themselves, and then another few behind them. Thorgrim caught a glimpse of Starri in the middle of Halfdan's line, upright, axes already flailing, and then he was lost from sight in the press of men.

"Ha!" Odd shouted. Starri's attack had thrown the point of Halfdan's wedge into chaos. Some men were still charging, some were stumbling over the downed men in front of them, some were turning to fight the wild man suddenly in their midst.

"Dig in! Dig in! Here they come!" Thorgrim shouted. Halfdan's line was still advancing, not so organized as before, but still a force with terrific momentum behind it. They were shouting as they ran, a wild cacophony of guttural yells, curses, and battle cries, a wall of force and noise rolling down on Thorgrim's men.

But Thorgrim's men were braced and ready, back feet set, leaning into their shields, their swords, axes, and spears poised. They were yelling, too, a wild cry, rippling up and down the line, to match the shouting of the men charging at them. And then the two lines hit.

The air was filled with the crash of shields smashing into shields, the ring of iron on iron, the grunt of men heaving against each other. Swords and axes reached through the lines, and some were knocked aside by shields or blades, and some claimed the first screaming victims of the fight. Thorgrim's men were driven back a step, and then another, by the force of Halfdan's warriors slamming into them, but they yielded no more than that.

"Hold! Dig in!" Thorgrim shouted. He spurred his horse and rode down the line, calling out to his men as he did. A length ahead, he saw some great brute of a warrior, Halfdan's man, wielding a battle axe as if it was a twig. The giant hacked down at a man named Vefrod, from

Blood Hawk, and before Vefrod could react, before Thorgrim could react, the axe split helmet and skull. Vefrod crumpled under the force of the blow, and a gap in the shield wall opened up.

The big axe-man pushed his way through, shield in front, axe rising again. He looked up and seemed surprised to see Thorgrim there, on horseback, and seemed more surprised still when Thorgrim's spear darted out over the rim of his shield and drove through his throat, just above the collar of his mail shirt.

The man's eyes went wide and he stumbled back, and Thorgrim pulled the spear free. The man fell, and the Blood Hawks in the shield wall closed up the gap, just in time to meet the second rank of Halfdan's men, coming forward.

Thorgrim rode up the line, driving his spear in where he could, shouting encouragement, looking for breaches in the shield wall. He saw none. Up and down the line his men and Odd's men were pushing back against Halfdan's, shields slamming against shields, swords and spears darting in and out, axes rising and falling. There were men stumbling back from the line, clutching wounds, men dropping to the ground and writhing or laying still, but every time there were others to take their place, others grabbing up discarded shields if they had none and stepping up into the front rank of the fight.

This can't go on, Thorgrim thought, even as he drove his spear at another trying to break through the shield wall. The two lines were hammering away at one another, like two drunk men in a tavern trading blows until one fell. At some point one or the other line would break. Perhaps it would be Halfdan's men. Perhaps they would break, turn, and run. But Thorgrim did not think so.

Or perhaps his own line would collapse, and the fight would devolve into a thousand individual brawls. Thorgrim did not doubt that Halfdan's men would win that fight. His own warriors, he knew, could stand and match the king's men sword for sword, but he did not think Odd's farmers could.

He looked out at the water to the south but he saw nothing there. He looked back over his shoulder, hoping to see Vifil Helgason's men riding toward the fight, but the road was empty. He cursed himself for a fool. Vifil's men would not be there for some time more, if they arrived at all.

There was a burst of shouting toward the southern end of the line, and Thorgrim could see a bulge as Halfdan's men drove a portion of his shield wall back: a bulge that threatened to break and open up a hole in the line. Thorgrim wheeled his horse and drove his spurs in, racing toward the threat.

"Odd! Odd!" he shouted, reining to a stop. His son was standing just behind the shield wall, Blood-letter in hand, its blade glistening. Thorgrim pointed south to the bulge in the line. "The shield wall's being pushed back there! It's going to break! Shift your men down there, fast!"

Odd glanced down the line, looked back at Thorgrim, and nodded. He began calling orders, grabbing men to get their attention, and Thorgrim spurred his horse forward again. He charged down the line just as the first of Halfdan's men broke through, and the warriors in Thorgrim's shield wall stumbled as they were pushed back, and died under the king's swords.

Thorgrim roared out in fury as he came pounding up. The first of Halfdan's men to make it through the line turned to face him, and Thorgrim hurled his spear. The throw was hard and true, but the king's man managed to get his shield up in time. The spear point hit the thin wood boards, embedded and stopped. The man looked at the spear, looked up at Thorgrim, and grinned.

With his left hand, Thorgrim pulled back on the reins. With his right, he drew Iron-tooth and slashed at the man with a backhand swing of the weapon. The sword hit the man's helmet, just above the ear, and knocked it off, like flicking a crumb. Then Thorgrim swung back the other way, and Iron-tooth's sharp blade took the top of his head right off; neat, clean and bloody.

Thorgrim kicked his horse's flanks to drive it into the fight. He knew nothing of the beast, had never seen it before that morning, but he could tell now that it was battle-trained. It did not shy from the noise and fighting — rather, it charged in, front feet rising and kicking, twisting side to side as Thorgrim lashed out with Iron-tooth.

Thank you, Ornolf! Thorgrim thought, as he continued to slash away. His blade bounced off a raised shield. He drew it back for another blow, and the horse lashed out with its hoof, catching the man with the shield in the thigh. He howled in pain, staggered, and Iron-tooth finished him.

Thorgrim glanced to his right. Odd was leading a few dozen men at a full run down the back of the shield wall, even as more of Halfdan's warriors pushed their way through the widening gap. Thorgrim drove his horse into them, slashing left and right, hoping to pull their attention away from Odd and his men.

It seemed to work; Halfdan's men seemed taken by surprise as Odd drove into them, shield raised, Blood-letter coming in over the top. The men on either side of him were carrying spears, and they fanned out as they ran into Halfdan's men, the long, iron tips looking for openings past shields, helmets, and mail.

"Form up the shield wall!" Thorgrim shouted to the men on either side of the gap. They were Halldor's men, Black Wings, and Halldor was a little ways to the south of them, standing in the defensive line.

"Halldor! Close the gap!" Thorgrim shouted. He was not sure that Halldor heard him through the chaotic din, but then he raised his shield, took a blow from a sword on its face, and looked behind him. He seemed to notice for the first time that the shield wall had been breached, and he certainly recognized the danger that posed, as Halfdan's men swarmed in behind his. He began to shout at the men on either side of him, working them sideways, closing up the gap, even as they fought the men in front.

Odd's men had taken Halfdan's by surprise, spears first, and behind them came men armed chiefly with axes — battle axes, and axes made for splitting cordwood on a farm, which worked just as well for killing. Between those men, and Odd with Blood-letter, and Thorgrim's horse, and Iron-tooth, Halfdan's men were overwhelmed. A moment later they were mostly down, dead or wounded, or stumbled off, and the gap in the shield wall closed.

"Well done! Well done!" Thorgrim called to Odd and the others. He was breathing hard, and could feel the sweat running down his face. The shield wall had nearly been breached, Thorgrim's line nearly overrun. But they had stopped it, fought off the king's men, plugged the hole. Thorgrim did not think they could do that forever.

He was looking out at the water again when a new sound caught his ear. It came from the northern end of the battle line this time, a rise in the pitch of the shouting, a new tone to the noise. He stood up in the stirrups and looked up the line, toward the woods where the right flank was anchored. There was something happening there, but it was not clear to Thorgrim what it was.

What, by all the gods? he thought.

There were men coming out of the woods about a hundred yards away, racing out of the tree line in a chaotic rush, coming at Thorgrim's shield wall from behind. It took Thorgrim a moment to realize what had happened, and when he did, he cursed himself.

Oh, you motherless fool! he thought. He had imagined that the forest would anchor his right flank, that Halfdan would not send men into the woods, where it would be difficult to move, but rather would use all his men in a frontal attack. And he had been wrong.

All the time that Halfdan that had seemingly been getting his men in order for their advance, he had been sending others around the right end of Thorgrim's line. Now Thorgrim's men were caught between Halfdan's shield wall and these new arrivals, and they were paying the price for his foolish assumption.

"Odd!" Thorgrim shouted down at his son. He pointed north with Iron-tooth. "They've come around the end of our line, getting behind our men!"

Odd looked to where Thorgrim was pointing. "Oh, the bastards!" he shouted, then started calling to his men and pushing them in that direction.

"Get all your men up there!" Thorgrim shouted. "If Halfdan breaks the line there, we're done for!" With that, he spurred his horse forward, riding hard behind the battle line, the surging mass of men banging shields against shields, heaving against those opposed them, flailing iron against iron.

"Vifil!" Thorgrim shouted, and pulled back on his reins, as he approached Vifil Helgason and the men with him. Like Thorgrim, they had remained on horseback, riding up and down the line, adding their weight to the shield wall where they could. Vifil had pushed his horse in behind some of the Sea Hammers and was thrusting at Halfdan's men, but now he pulled the horse back and turned toward Thorgrim.

"Halfdan's sent men around the flank!" Thorgrim shouted, pointing with his sword. "Come with me! All you men on horseback, come with me!" He spurred his horse again, until the animal was charging flat out at the increasingly wild brawl taking place on the right flank.

That end of the line was held by the men of *Oak Heart*, Asmund's men, and Thorgrim was thankful for that. They were as battle-hardened as they came. They would not flinch in the face of this new threat, a threat that would soon send lesser men running in panic.

The king's men had come out of the woods piecemeal, unable to maintain order as they worked their way through the trees. Now they were racing at Asmund's men from behind, forcing the Oak Hearts to turn and fight them even as they were going at it shield to shield with the men in front.

"Right into them! Right into them!" Thorgrim shouted. He was calling to the riders behind him, and to himself, but mostly to the horse under him. And the horse seemed to understand. It did not break stride as it slammed into a knot of Halfdan's men charging toward the line. Thorgrim saw men flung to the ground by the collision, and he held tight as the horse rose up on hind legs and brought its front hooves down on the men scrambling to get clear.

Thorgrim leaned sideways, Iron-tooth in hand, and began slashing left and right, sometimes finding air, sometimes finding mail or shield, sometimes finding flesh. He meant to kill and wound who he could, but mostly he meant to break the momentum of this new attack, to slow it down until Odd's men could run the length of the line and join in.

More horses appeared on either side, Vifil Helgason and the others, and they, too, were slashing with swords or thrusting with spears. But Halfdan's men were still coming out of the woods, and they were surrounding the riders. Thorgrim's horse half-turned, just in time for Thorgrim to see a spear hurled at him, straight and true. He jerked his shield upright and the rim caught the spear and knocked it away, a heartbeat before it would have pierced his mail and kept on going.

Thorgrim urged the horse forward, and the spearman leapt out of the way. He looked back over his shoulder. Odd was leading his men along the line, grabbing more as he passed them by. They would add considerable weight to the counterattack; they would also be winded by the time they reached the fight, and that was not good.

To his left, Thorgrim could see the men in Asmund's shield wall turning to meet the threat at their backs, leaving gaps, and the men in Halfdan's line were pushing through. Whereas a moment before there had been two lines of warriors locked in stalemate, now the lines were breaking down, devolving into a hundred individual fights, just as Thorgrim had feared. If it kept up, the entire shield wall would collapse, and his men would be overrun.

With a shout of rage and frustration, Thorgrim began hacking at the men around him as they, in turn, tried to close in, jabbing with spears, slashing with swords. The horse pranced and kicked and turned in place in its strange dance. Vifil Helgason was nearby, dancing the same dance, his sword a blur as he swung left and right. Then, suddenly, Vifil pulled the reins over, turned his horse, and began riding clear of the fight, leaving it behind.

"Vifil!" Thorgrim shouted. Vifil, it appeared, was abandoning the fight, running off, but that seemed unimaginable to Thorgrim. He swiveled around and saw, just up the road, men running toward them, men with shields and helmets. Vifil's men, arriving at last, and Vifil riding off to lead them to where they were most needed.

Thorgrim still had his eyes on Vifil when Odd and his men came charging in, about a hundred men whom Odd had scooped up along the way. They came with spears leveled, shouting as much as they could after running that distance.

Thorgrim urged his horse forward, Iron-tooth knocking swords and spears aside, looking for any vulnerable target. Just to his right, a man held a spear low, and thrust it up at Thorgrim's gut. Thorgrim swept his blade sideways to knock it away, but the man who wielded it deftly dropped the point and let Iron-tooth sail right over. Then the spear was up again and the point tore through the windings on Thorgrim's calf, and through his flesh, and into his horse's flank.

The horse screamed and reared and kicked and the spear point was jerked free, the spearman knocked backwards by the frantic animal. Thorgrim pulled back on the reins and the horse turned and charged off, but, well-trained animal that it was, only ran clear of the fighting men and stopped, still bucking and twisting, but not racing away.

Thorgrim clung on as the horse settled. Vifil rode past, his men following behind, and they surged into the fight, throwing themselves into the dozens of skirmishes spread out over the field. It was chaos now, fighting one on one, two on one, pockets of men hacking away for any advantage. Asmund was down, dead or wounded, Thorgrim could not tell. But Odd was still up, fighting, calling orders, standing bold in the melee.

My boy… Thorgrim thought. If Odd or Harald or both died that day, he knew at least that his grief would be tempered with pride. And he knew as well that if they did not survive, he would take care that he did not either.

The horse was calmer now, and Thorgrim took advantage of that to survey the field. He started to stand in his stirrups and felt a bolt of pain shoot through his calf. He fell back in the saddle and looked down at his right leg. He had forgotten the wound, had not even felt it until then, but the windings were soaked through with blood, and the torn flesh was suddenly agonizing.

"Ahhh!" he shouted. He pushed the pain aside and looked along the line of battle, and what he saw was not good.

To the south, where the left flank was anchored on the shore, the lines were still intact, his shield wall standing up to Halfdan's, each surging forward and back as they fought for advantage. But at the northern end, where Odd and Vifil were fighting the men who had come out of the woods, the line had collapsed. There was no cohesion now, and it would not be regained.

Worse, it was bound to spread, the line crumbling, north to south, and there was nothing he could do to stop it. In no time at all the fight would become exactly the one he did not want, the one he did not think he could win.

He clenched his teeth and felt the fury surging through him again. He renewed his grip on his shield and on Iron-tooth, ready to plunge back into the battle. Then he looked up, over the men's heads, out over the deep blue water that ran up to the shore, and he saw what he had been looking for since Halfdan's army had first charged forward in their swine array: longships.

Chapter Forty

Wound fires burned in bloody gashes,
Where the long-beards lifted against the lives of warriors
The sea-of-wounds surged high around the sword's edges
Ran the stream-of-arrows…

Hákonarmál

"You know, Arnor," Bragi Shipslayer said, "if we come through this alive, you and me, we should be friends. Forget old misunderstandings."

He was standing at the helm of the first longship they had taken, the one that had run up on the wreck of Ragi's ship. Arnor was on the larboard side, and nearly a hundred warriors were forward. They had been sitting for the past few hours as the ship made its way south, and then north again, but they were standing now. They were close, and the men were ready.

"No misunderstanding," Arnor said. "I understand just fine. You took near a full summer's catch and ran off with it."

"See, that's the thing," Bragi said. "And you never let me explain. I took the catch to market, like we agreed. Drove a hard bargain for it. But then I was robbed, and there was nothing for it."

"Robbed?" Arnor said. "My men, the ones I sent with you, you set off on an island and left them there. That was the last any of us saw of you. You forgetting that part?"

Bragi considered. "Yes, I guess I did forget that. But there's a good explanation for that, too."

"You know, there's a lot I hate about you, Bragi Shipslayer. But I'd say it's your mouth I hate most. Of course, I'm hoping Halfdan'll save me the trouble of killing you. But if you want to make sure I do it, then you just keep talking."

Bragi nodded. He looked over the larboard side. The second longship, driven by Huginn, was nearly abeam of them, sail set taut, water curling around its bow and swirling white along its long, low side.

Lovely, lovely, Bragi thought. In his mind there was nothing, not even a fine-looking woman, more beautiful than a well-built ship running fast before a quartering wind. He wondered why, then, he so enjoyed wrecking them. He wondered if it was related at all to the way he seemed to always turn his personal affairs into so much flotsam.

He pushed the thought aside. Not the time for such introspection.

"What do you see?" Bragi said to Arnor, nodding toward the bow. Arnor bent low and looked under the foot of the sail.

"Half a mile to go," Arnor said. "It's Loki's own mess there. Might be we're not too late, but sure as my ass we're not too early."

"But the fighting, you reckon it's where Thorgrim meant it to be?"

"I reckon. The bastards are right down by the beach, like he said."

Thorgrim...Bragi thought. *Clever son of a whore*.... This had been Thorgrim's idea, though even he was not so sure of the wisdom of it.

He had laid it out at the council of war. He knew of a place where the road ran close to the head of the bay, with thick forest just inland of that. They would make their stand there, the ends of the shield wall anchored by wood and water. They would meet Halfdan's army on its way to Fevik and slug it out on that stretch of ground.

It was a decent plan, with one serious flaw — no one thought that ad hoc army could defeat Halfdan's warriors in such a fight. But if they could spring a trap, throw something unseen into the stew, that might change it up. And Thorgrim had an idea for the trap as well: send part of the army around by water, and land it behind Halfdan's line. If the timing was right, they could throw Halfdan's men into confusion and roll them up.

It was a risky plan, terribly risky. It carried far more chances of failure than success, and Bragi loved it. The entire thing rested on the ships getting to the fight in time, but one look at the sky and the clouds told Bragi that the wind would be near perfect for that: brisk out of the northwest, which would drive the ships fast on a beam reach down the bay from Fevik, and then up the other bay to where Thorgrim meant to fight.

Arnor had agreed with Bragi's forecast. And Thorgrim, who Bragi was coming to grudgingly acknowledge knew more than a little about the mariner's trade, agreed as well. Two hundred warriors had been dispatched to man the two longships in Fevik, and they had sailed even as Thorgrim's army was still getting ready to march.

And now here they were, their timing near perfect. Thorgrim Night Wolf had a reputation as a lucky man, blessed by the gods. So far, Bragi had seen nothing to suggest otherwise.

He leaned low, looked under the sail himself. A ragged line of men ran from the edge of the water up toward the woods inland. Behind that line, well back from the fight, he saw others mounted on horses, banners flying — the king and his more important underlings, Bragi had no doubt.

As he studied the fighting on shore, he realized it was as if two different battles were going on. At the southern end, closest to the water, the two armies seemed to be fighting shield wall to shield wall, locked against one another, surging a few feet one way, a few feet the other, looking for some advantage. But further inland the lines had fallen apart, the shield walls collapsed, the battle devolved into hundreds of small fights. That was not good. This little surprise they were throwing at Halfdan would not be nearly so effective if the fighting was just a disorganized brawl.

"You're right we're not too early," Bragi said. "I just hope we're not too late." He thought about shouting some instructions forward, something about the men directing their attack at the back of Halfdan's shield wall, but he kept his mouth shut. They were warriors, they knew what to do, and they had been thinking on this moment since the early morning hours.

The longships were closing fast with the beach, heeling to larboard in the stiff breeze, their sails straining at the sheets that held them down. Both ships had been emptied of everything aboard — food, water, spare sails, stores — to make them as light and fast as they could be, and to keep them from running aground until they were as far up the beach as they could go. And that was paying off now, as the sharp hulls came charging into the fight, fast as stallions, silent as birds of prey.

Bragi gripped the tiller hard. The beach was just a few hundred yards ahead, the distance dropping rapidly away. He could see the fight more clearly now, could see the place where the warriors he was bringing to battle would hit the back of Halfdan's line.

He felt the excitement building, and he shouted, "Oh, we're going to give Halfdan an ugly surprise!" It seemed that no one on shore had even noticed the longships loaded down with shield-bearing warriors racing toward them. No one seemed to be reacting to their arrival at all.

"Yeeaaaaahaa!" Bragi shouted, with the sheer exuberance of the moment. He could not contain himself. The ship seemed to fly over the last few yards and he braced for the moment they would hit.

"Let those sheets go!" he shouted forward, and the men there cast them off. The huge red and white sail flogged off to leeward just as the bow ran up out of the water and buried itself in the sand. The ship staggered to a stop and Bragi felt himself thrown against the tiller. He saw Arnor stumble a half step, and others as well, but they had been ready for this, and they managed to keep their feet.

"All right, you whore's sons, over you go!" Bragi shouted. "And scream like madman, make 'em piss their trousers!" If the men ashore had not yet seen the longships, they would soon, and Bragi wanted maximum surprise and intimidation.

He grabbed up his cut-down length of an oar's loom, his new weapon of choice, and raced forward, Arnor beside him. The rest of the men were crowding toward the bow, vaulting over the side, and running up the beach. To his left, Bragi caught a glimpse of the ship Huginn was driving. It, too, was up on the beach, the men aboard just going over the side.

"Get out of my way, you bastards, get out of my way!" Bragi shouted to the men in front, but no one was listening to him and he had to push his way through to get to the side of the ship. He stepped up on a sea chest, up on the sheer strake, and jumped. He came down in a foot of water, then waded fast as he could up to dry land.

The men from his ship and the men from Huginn's ship were charging up the beach toward the grassy field where the battle was being fought. There was no attempt to organize the attack or to advance in a line — they were there for surprise, and that meant hitting hard and fast. And from what Bragi could see, they had achieved the surprise they sought.

Half a dozen of the men on horseback, Halfdan's chief men, had peeled off from where they were watching the fight, and now they were riding toward the shield wall, gesturing, shouting. Alerting the men to this new threat, Bragi guessed. At the same time, the men in the second rank of the battle line were turning to face this attack from the sea, an attack they had not seen coming,

All of that Bragi took in as he ran up the beach and directly at the fighting. He had been one of the last off the ship, and he was not a man built for speed in any event; the others were already leaving him behind. He cursed and picked up his pace as he reached the end of the sand and the edge of the knee-high grass.

The first of the men from his ship were already slamming into the back of Halfdan's line, and Bragi could hear the renewed shouts of surprise and fury. He was searching for where he might best join in when he saw motion in the corner of his eye, off to his left: three of Halfdan's mounted men riding hard toward the battle line, spears leveled, hoping no doubt to get in among these fresh warriors and cut them down.

"Oh, this looks like fun!" Bragi said. He changed direction, ran off to intercept the horsemen, shouting and waving his cut-down oar. "Here, you sheep-biting dwarves! Over here!"

He did not go unnoticed. Two of the horsemen turned and charged at him, side by side, spears held low, shields on their left arms. The rider on Bragi's left shifted his spear over, so he was holding it crosswise on his horse. They meant to pass on either side of Bragi, both spear points driving for his chest.

Bragi stopped running. He waited, club resting nonchalantly on his shoulder, as the horsemen rode down on him. Forty feet, thirty, twenty, he could hear nothing but the pounding of the horses' hooves, could feel the slight tremors underfoot. The two black, iron points came flying toward him, as Bragi lifted the club and swung it in a circle. He felt the wood connect with the spear shafts and knock them up and away. He spun to his right as he let the momentum carry him around, and slammed the club into the small of the rider's back as he passed.

The horses thundered past, and the rider whom Bragi had struck was leaning back and sideways in an unnatural way, and slumping over as the horse ran off. But the second rider wheeled his mount around and was already racing back toward Bragi, his spear level.

He won't fall for that again, Bragi thought as he stood firm, club ready. The horseman did not have as much speed this time, having just changed direction, and that was good. Bragi rested the club on his shoulder and waited as the single iron spear tip came sailing in at him.

The horse was ten feet away and building speed when Bragi stepped right in front of it and swung the club in a wide arc. The horse tried to swerve away; Bragi hit it hard on the neck as it passed, and the animal shied and whinnied in pain.

The rider pulled back on the reins as the horse twisted and bucked, and now it was Bragi's turn to charge. He took three quick steps, winding up with his club as he did. The rider was just regaining control when Bragi swung the club under the rim of his shield and hit the man on his left leg, catching his knee between club and saddle. Bragi could hear the sound of the bone snapping, and then, almost instantly, the rider screaming in agony.

"Good luck getting off the horse!" Bragi shouted, as the horse trotted off with its rider slumped over in the saddle and still screaming. He turned toward the fighting in the shield wall. The arrival of the longships had done just what they had all prayed to the gods it would do: it took Halfdan's men by surprise and threw them into confusion. The king's men were fighting enemies front and back, and they were dying under their swords and spears. The semblance of a line remained, but it could not be called a shield wall. It was quickly becoming a slaughter.

"You bastards! Save some for me!" Bragi shouted. He raced off toward the crowd of struggling men, his sawed-off oar held over his head. A warrior with bright mail and helmet stood in his path; Halfdan's man, turning to meet the threat from behind. The warrior raised his shield to chest height, his sword above that. He almost looked confused as he watched Bragi coming at him with no real weapons at all, and wearing nothing but tunic and leggings and his wide, red cap.

Bragi swung the club sideways, swung it with such force that it crushed the edge of the shield and slammed into the warrior's helmet. The helmet rang like a bell and the warrior was lifted off his feet and flung motionless to the grass. Bragi grinned, looked around, then plunged into the fight, his club swinging, his heart singing with joy.

It was an astounding sight. Thorgrim was certain he had never seen the like. Two longships run up on the beach, behind the lines of fighting men, and, engaged as they were in their bloody battle, no one even noticed. Not until the warriors from the ships came charging in, screaming like madmen.

A moment before, the battle was lost. Now, it seemed there was at least a chance, but Thorgrim knew the gods were capricious. They could give him this glimmer of hope and then stomp it out just as quickly. He knew better than to think that victory might be at hand. All he could do was fight on, as best he could, and hope that the gods were pleased.

He looked around him, even as he worked sword and shield, the horse turning and prancing among the knots of fighting men. Odd's men and Vifil's men were fully engaged with the remnants of Halfdan's shield wall and the men who had come out of the woods. It was too confused to know who was winning, and probably would be until one side or the other threw down their weapons, or had so many killed or wounded they could not fight on.

There was nothing he could do about the fighting at that end of the field, no way he could bring any order or cohesion to the scattered combat. But to the south the situation had changed. The shield walls were still intact, and now the men from the longships were charging in at the back of Halfdan's line. Some of the horsemen who had been standing with Halfdan were on the move, giving orders and joining in the fight, no doubt. From his vantage on horseback, Thorgrim could see the confusion in Halfdan's line, the order falling apart.

There, at least, was opportunity. If Thorgrim could keep his men together, maybe get the center of the line to swing around and fall on Halfdan's flank, then they might well turn the tide of battle. If Thorgrim's men could crush that section of Halfdan's army, the rest might well call for quarter, or run.

He pulled the reins over, kicked his horse, and felt the pain from his wounded calf shoot through him again. He had a fleeting image of Gyda, what she would say, how she would tend to his wound, if he lived that long. He pushed thoughts of her aside, ignored the pain as best he could and rode down toward where Harald and his men were still standing in the shield wall.

The chaos at the northern end of the line was spreading. What was left of the shield wall ended just about where Harald and the men of *Dragon* were making their stand, with half of Gudrid's men on one side of Harald's, and Thorgrim's own men, the men of *Sea Hammer*, on the other. They were good, dependable men, all of them, hard men, and that would help.

Thorgrim rode down the line, clear of the fighting, his only thought now on getting to Harald and urging the men there to swing around Halfdan's flank. It was hard to find his son in the wild scrum of men, but Thorgrim finally recognized his broad shoulders, the yellow hair spilling out from under his helmet, as he drove against Halfdan's shield wall, slashing and stabbing with Oak Cleaver.

Thorgrim urged his horse forward, right into the line of battle, just a few yards from where Harald stood near the ragged end of the shield wall. He cut and slashed at Halfdan's men in front and beside him, glancing over when he dared.

"Harald! Harald!" he shouted again, and finally Harald heard him and looked up. His mouth was open, his face was red with exertion. There was blood smeared on his cheeks and in his scruffy beard. He looked surprised: surprised to see Thorgrim there, surprised to see that most of the shield wall had collapsed and he was now near the end of the line.

"Push them that way!" Thorgrim shouted, pointing with Iron-tooth toward the south. "Let's turn their flank!" He doubted that Harald had seen the longships or knew of the change in circumstances, but as long as the boy understood, he would obey. "Push them hard!"

Harald nodded that time. He turned back to the line and let loose with a battle cry that seemed to ripple up and down the line, and the cry was taken up by the men around him as they pushed off hard with back legs and slammed shields into the weary enemy in their front and hacked with swords as they drove forward.

Thorgrim urged his horse deeper into Halfdan's men at the end of the line. He threw his shield aside and pulled a battle axe that was hanging off his saddle, and with that in his left hand, Iron-tooth in his right, he began cutting his way forward. The horse pranced and kicked and Thorgrim swung left and right, his blades hitting shields, helmets, and flesh.

Halfdan's line was wavering. Thorgrim could feel it. He could always feel it when a line was on the edge of breaking. The men were backing away, and what had been a stalemate — two shield walls, like men of equal strength, heaving pointlessly against one another — was turning in his men's favor.

Harald's men were pushing hard, pushing with a renewed vigor, and the madness caused by the warriors from the longships was starting to spread. The men in Halfdan's line could sense that something was wrong, something had turned against them, and it was giving their enemies a drive and purpose.

Thorgrim shouted again, leaned over and thrust. Iron-tooth found its way past a raised shield and down, ripping through mail, through flesh, causing the shield-bearer to scream, to twist aside. Thorgrim turned to look for someone on his other side, but there was no one there. Halfdan's men were backing away, not grudgingly yielding one step at a time, but moving back two and three steps, driven back by the pressure from Harald's men, and by the mounting confusion around them.

"Run, you bastards! Run!" Thorgrim shouted. He waved Iron-tooth above his head, and all around him, men turned and ran.

Thorgrim Night Wolf…

King Halfdan the Black sat upright in his saddle, lips pressed tight together, his eyes on Thorgrim Ulfsson, a hundred yards away and also mounted. Halfdan had been watching Thorgrim for the bulk of the fighting. Despite the battle raging before him, spread over hundreds of yards of open field, a battle that he well understood could determine the fate of his kingdom, his eyes had been mostly fixed on the Night Wolf. He could not help himself.

Thorgrim was everywhere. While he, Halfdan, had remained pretty much in one place, surrounded by his lead men and his personal guard, directing the fighting from a place where he could see all, Thorgrim had been racing up and down the line. He had plunged into the fighting at the center of the field, and when Halfdan's men had come out of the woods to the north, Thorgrim had been off to join in there. It was bold, it was admirable in some ways, but it was no way to command in battle.

Halfdan was no stranger to battles, large and small. He might have inherited a kingdom from his father, Gudrød the Hunter, but that kingdom was just a fraction of the lands he controlled now. He had acquired some of his new territory through diplomacy, but most of it had been won on the battlefield. For Halfdan, battle was as much a part of life as feasts or harvest festivals.

He understood the rhythm of battle, the feel of battle, how to identify strength and weakness. For that reason he knew at first sight that Thorgrim had made a big mistake, thinking the right end of his line would be protected by the woods beyond. And he knew as well that Thorgrim would not launch an attack against the king's clearly superior warriors; he would wait for Halfdan to advance. And that left plenty of time to send men around through the woods, where they could fall unseen on Thorgrim's flank.

The rhythm of battle. Halfdan had played that rhythm today as if he was playing a drum. Watched his men come out of the woods, watched Thorgrim's line collapse around him. Watched Thorgrim charge into that part of the fight long after his presence there could do any good. He smiled as he watched it. He smiled despite the uneasy feeling in his gut.

Thorgrim Night Wolf... King Halfdan was the most powerful man for hundreds of miles, and yet Thorgrim Night Wolf had always made him uneasy. A man, blessed by the gods, who became a wolf when the sun went down? He had heard the stories for years, as everyone in Agder had, and he had not believed any of them. He had seen no proof of it, and he knew of no one personally who had. He did not think Thorgrim himself believed it. But still the stories persisted.

Halfdan had spent little time in Thorgrim's company. They had had occasion to meet once or twice a year, if that. Still, Halfdan had felt an undeniable sense of relief when Thorgrim sailed with Ornolf, even more so as it started seeming likely he was not coming back. Taking his farm was like the final step in eradicating the man, stomping out his memory.

At the heart of all this was a simple truth: Halfdan was frightened of Thorgrim Night Wolf. It was a truth he would admit only to himself, and even then just barely. But it was, in fact, the truth. And it bothered him a great deal.

It was also the reason for his profound sense of relief as he saw Thorgrim's line falling apart, and Thorgrim himself mounted and fighting for his life. There, at last, unfolding on the battlefield before him, was the final answer to that problem. Thorgrim was not immortal, he was not blessed by the gods. He had made a foolish blunder and Halfdan had taken advantage of it, and now Thorgrim's army, and the army of his miserable son, Odd, would be crushed and scattered. Thorgrim dead, Odd dead, Harald dead. The rebellion crushed. It was the rhythm of battle, and it made Halfdan want to sing.

"What, by all the gods?" The voice, surprised, even a bit disconcerted, came from right beside him. The speaker was Kjotvi

Sighvatsson, a jarl who had brought the bulk of his hird to join in the fighting.

Halfdan swiveled around, annoyed, to see what had so grabbed Kjotvi's attention, and he, too, felt the same unwelcome surprise. Two longships run up on the beach, their sails still flogging in the wind, their crews, hundreds of men, leaping over the sides, running toward the fight.

"Thor's ass, who's this?" one of Halfdan's captains said, as all heads turned to look at these new arrivals, charging ashore, shields on arms, swords and axes flashing. Halfdan had no idea who they were. And then he did.

"Thorgrim's men," Halfdan said, and thought, *Clever, clever bastard*, but he would not say that out loud. "Thorgrim. He sent the ships around to get his men in behind our lines."

For a moment no one spoke as they watched the armed men racing for the back of the shield wall. Halfdan was the first to recover his wits.

"Go tell the men in the shield wall they're about to be attacked from behind! Go, you idiots, go warn them!"

Six men dug spurs into their horses and the animals leapt forward and charged off toward the shield wall, their riders shouting warnings as they did. Halfdan remained where he was, still watching the battle unfold, but suddenly it was all different, the rhythm changed to something beyond his control.

I trick you, Thorgrim, you bastard, and you trick me, Halfdan thought. *I suppose we're even.* But Halfdan did not wish to be even. He did not wish for any outcome save for his own unqualified victory. Nothing else was acceptable.

He looked on in silent rage as these men from the longships charged at the back of his shield wall, trapping his own men between two forces, hammer and anvil. And because Halfdan was no stranger to battle, he understood that unqualified victory was not always to be had.

He could see immediately how this would play out, and it did, right before his eyes, just as he envisioned. By the time his men realized there was an enemy in their rear, Thorgrim's seaborne warriors plowed into them, cutting them down where they stood. Some turned and fought, some kept pushing back against the shield wall in front. Some fell under the onslaught. And then more and more fell.

Halfdan searched the field for Thorgrim. He found him, still on horseback, still up by the woods, but with the longships' arrival, he rode back down the line, back to the center of the fighting. Halfdan watched him drive his horse into what was now the ragged end of the shield wall, saw him gesture with his sword, directing his men. Thus urged forward, Thorgrim's warriors began pushing Halfdan's back, threatening to turn the flank and envelope his men.

One of the jarls to Halfdan's left shouted, "Fight back, you cowardly bastards!" Halfdan gave a grim smile. A bold command from a man who was watching the fighting from a perfectly safe distance. But Halfdan's men were in fact fighting, and they were losing.

Halfdan had lost battles before. No one achieved victory every time. But he had never lost a battle where the stakes were so high, because he had never fought such a battle. In the past, if he lost, it meant only that he failed to conquer the territory he craved, and he could always try again.

But this was different. He had thrown the last of his warriors into a fight against rebels who threatened his very kingdom. If he lost this battle — and it was starting to look very much as if he would — he was not sure what it meant. Exile? Ruin? Death? There were no good outcomes.

And that meant he could not lose, or at least that he had to do all in his power to prevent it. He could not make his men fight any harder, and he could not destroy Thorgrim's army by himself. But if Thorgrim was killed, it might well take the fight out of his men. Thorgrim Night Wolf was the linchpin to all this, and it was time he was removed.

"There's Thorgrim Night Wolf," Halfdan said, pointing and speaking loud enough for his guard and the jarls to hear. "Do you see him? On horseback?" The men acknowledged, with various grunts and yesses, that they did.

"We must kill him," Halfdan said next. "We must ride in and kill him. If he goes down, maybe his men will lose heart. It's our only hope now." He did not say the other thing he was thinking, that they had to prove Thorgrim was indeed human, and not blessed by the gods. That he, Halfdan, had to rid himself of this creature that so frightened him.

His shield was slung over his shoulder and he pulled it off and settled it on his arm. He pulled his sword from its sheath.

"Let us go," he said. He kicked his horse and flicked the reins, and the horse leapt forward, from a standstill to a trot and a gallup. He did not bother looking to see if the others were with him. He had no doubt that they were, and he would have continued this charge even if they were not.

Thorgrim's intention, clearly, had been to turn Halfdan's flank, to crush the shield wall, and he had achieved that. The order was falling apart, and Halfdan's men were pressed on all sides, with Thorgrim driving them on. The battle was over, as far as the men on the field were concerned. Now it was Halfdan's fight.

His eyes were on Thorgrim, who was not yet aware of the horsemen charging toward him: Halfdan and the jarls and his personal guard, fifteen mounted men who could drive through the line and overwhelm the Night Wolf. Even if Halfdan lost the battle, lost his kingdom, he would see Thorgrim Night Wolf die. He would drive that demon out. For the first time since seeing the longships coming up on shore, Halfdan felt a touch of hope.

Chapter Forty-One

She saw Valkyries, come from far and wide,
ready to ride to the god-realm.
Skuld held a shield…ready to ride the earth —
Valkyries.

The Prophecy of the Seeress

Harald could feel the strength draining out of his arms and legs, and he cursed himself for a weakling. He pushed against the men in front of him, Halfdan's shield wall, a blur of faces and beards and helmets. He hacked down with Oak Cleaver, groaned as he lifted the blade, and hacked down again.

He had been fighting there for a long time, it seemed, a very long time. The moment when he had locked shields with his neighbor, watching Halfdan's men charging across the field, seemed like a strange memory, more like a dream. A wash of feelings had come over him: anger, excitement, a touch of fear. The image floated in his head of a sword or an ax coming down on his shoulder, right at the base of his neck, and cutting deep — the old, irrational fear that had always haunted him at such moments.

He stood firm as Halfdan's line closed, and the men charging at them became individual faces, individual mouths open and screaming. He waited as Starri Deathless, predictably, launched himself at the head of the wedge and disappeared under the press of men. He braced himself as Halfdan's warriors crossed the last hundred feet and slammed into the shield wall.

After that it was chaos and brutal fighting, shields pushing against shields, swords and spears and axes looking for advantage. Men yelling, shoving, a foot ahead, a foot back, two lines locked in combat, like bucks fighting in rut that have tangled their antlers one in the other.

And there they stood, hacking, pushing, bleeding, dying. Harald had killed or wounded some who faced him, had received a deep cut in his upper arm, which he could no longer feel, another across his right hand. Men had been slain on either side, only to have the shield wall close up again, like the sea rushing in.

Now he was starting to tire, which he never thought could happen. He expected every man around him to drop with exhaustion before he felt a hint of strength ebbing from his arms. But he was wrong. And that made him feel weak, and angry.

He heard his name being called from above, and, numbed as he was from exhaustion, he thought that the Valkyrie were calling to him, that he had actually died on the field, a noble death, and they had come to choose him. He heard it again, and he realized it sounded like his father's voice, and he thought maybe his father was in Valhalla already, and calling down to him.

He looked up. His father was there, not in Valhalla, but on a horse, driving the animal into the shield wall, hacking with Iron-tooth. The horse was lashing out with its hooves, as deadly as any of the spears or axes. His father was shouting.

"Push them that way!" He pointed with Iron-tooth toward the south. "Let's turn their flank!"

Harald was not sure what he was looking at. And then he realized that the opposing shield walls to the north of them had collapsed, that between his men and some of Gudrid's and the woods beyond, there was only open fields where hundreds of men were engaged in a sweeping, wild melee. What had happened, he did not know.

He looked to the south. Something was happening there, too, but caught in that tight-packed crowd, he could not tell what it was. He could sense, however, that Halfdan's men had lost their resolve, that their line was wavering. And now his father was urging them to push forward, to drive the line back. He did not know what had changed in that moment, but something had. And then he remembered the longships.

In all the madness, they had gone completely out of his mind. His father had a plan to send two hundred men around on longships to land behind the lines. It seemed madness to Harald, though he would never have said as much. He wondered if it might actually have worked.

Harald felt the energy surging through him again. This was his father's genius, this ability to see what would bring victory, riches, and glory, and to inspire other men to believe, and to follow. It was a genius that Harald dreamed he might someday possess, and feared he never would. But for now, he felt the force of his father's spirit energizing him and the men around him, urging them to fight, and to win.

He shouted and pushed hard against the man in front of him. He hacked down again and again with Oak Cleaver, and felt not the least bit of weariness in his arms and legs. He saw his adversary take a step back, and another. He could see the exhaustion on the man's face as he fended off Harald's attack, his movements dull and slow as he tried to deflect Oak Cleaver, missed, and died at the end of the sword.

He fell, and a hole in the shield wall opened. Another of Halfdan's men stepped up to close it, but not before Sten of *Dragon*, fighting at Harald's side, thrust his sword into the gap and tore a nasty gash in the new man's arm. The man held his shield up, chest height, but his sword arm hung limp, and Harald did not think he would last a moment before he, too, was cut down.

Halfdan's men were falling back. Thorgrim was still on horseback, Iron-tooth in hand, hacking away, and he was pushing his men to envelop the end of Halfdan's line, to hit them from in front and on the side, and collapse whatever defense they had. And it was working. Halfdan's line was finished. Harald could feel it.

He heard a new sound, a familiar sound, though it took him a moment to recognize it as horses' hooves, many horses, approaching fast. He looked around but he could not see the riders through the press of men. He pushed against the man in front of him, thrusting as he did, and suddenly a horse seemed to appear behind the man, a massive gray horse looming over his shoulders, carrying a rider with helmet, mail and shield, sword raised.

The horse careened into the shield wall, knocking Halfdan's men and Harald's men aside indiscriminately. It slammed into Harald's shield and knocked him back. As he went down, the rider took a broad swipe with his sword, but Harald had already fallen clear, and the blade missed him by inches.

Harald came down hard on his back and the horse thundered past. For a moment he just lay there, partially stunned, looking up at blue sky and more horses and riders, breaking through the line. Through the fog in his brain he recalled glimpses of Halfdan and his men sitting their horses a hundred yards back from the shield wall, and he wondered if that was who was attacking them now.

His head cleared and he grabbed Oak Cleaver from where it had fallen in the collision and pushed himself to his feet. The shield wall was well ahead of him now, as his men and the Sea Hammers drove Halfdan's men back. The stalemate was over; Halfdan's line was collapsing.

He looked to his right. Where Gudrid's warriors were making a stand, the horsemen had shattered the line and now they were whirling and hacking at whoever they could reach, crowding each other as they tried to converge on a single point. They were wearing bright mail and helmets, their shields wonderfully painted. Wealthy men — the jarls and the king's personal guard. And, incredibly, Halfdan himself.

The king's horse was now at the center of the fight, Halfdan twisting the animal side to side, slashing at someone Harald could not see. Harald looked through the legs of the horses and men. He sucked in his breath.

It was his father, kneeling, sword in hand. He was swinging the blade left and right as he fended off attacks from the surrounding horsemen. He must have been knocked from his mount, but he would never let go of Iron-tooth. Harald could hear the ring of steel on steel as Thorgrim desperately countered attacks from all sides.

Harald felt sick with fear, in a way he never had before. He shouted and raced forward. One of the horsemen blocking his way turned to slash at him. Harald held his shield up, felt the blade bounce off, then he drove the tip of his sword into the horse's rump. The horse shrieked, bucked, leapt clear, and Harald ran through the gap.

"Gudrid! Help!" he shouted.

Gudrid was ten feet away, also doing battle with the mounted men. "Coming!" he shouted, then started fighting his way in Harald's direction.

"Father!" Harald called. Halfdan had turned his horse in a circle and was once again raising his sword. As Harald came charging in he swung Oak Cleaver underhand, catching Halfdan's sword on the upstroke as it was coming down, and knocked it clear. He stabbed at Halfdan's horse and hit only its armor, but that was enough to drive the animal back a few steps. Halfdan pulled on the reins and Harald dropped to a knee at Thorgrim's side.

"Father!" he shouted again, their faces inches apart. His father's face was bathed in sweat and blood.

"My leg," he said. "Help me." He put his arm over Harald's shoulder. Harald threw his shield aside and took Oak Cleaver in his left hand. He stood, his arm around his father's waist, and Thorgrim stood as well. Harald could see his father's right calf was soaked with blood, and he was putting all his weight on his left leg.

The riders were on them again, on all sides, still crowding each other as they tried to charge in. Harald shouted and hacked at his closest attacker. It was an awkward, left-hand blow, but a powerful one, his arm driven by the animal fury he felt at what these men had done, dropping his father to the ground in that way, swarming him, trying to kill him.

Steel was ringing out to his right as the horsemen came surging in and Thorgrim fought them off. One of Halfdan's guards charged through the pack, sword raised, yelling as he came. The yell turned to a shriek, and the man twisted in the saddle and slumped sideways. Gudrid burst through the cordon of riders, pulling his sword from the guard's back as he did.

He slashed at another of the horsemen as he worked his way to where Harald and Thorgrim were making their stand. He pressed his back against theirs and the three of them stood in their defensive circle, three men, a dozen horsemen circling, making their attacks. Harald could see nothing now but horses, armor, blades, surrounding them. And foremost, Halfdan the Black, slashing with a wild abandon as Harald and Thorgrim fought him off.

So far...we came so far...

The thought floated through Harald's head, misty and indistinct. All the battles, all the storms, all the raiding over those past years. They lived through it all, only to die on their native soil, not five miles from home.

But they had to die sometime, and Harald knew he could ask for no end greater than dying with sword in hand, shoulder to shoulder with his father. Thorgrim Night Wolf. Harald Broadarm. They would feast with the Allfather that very night, and they would feast well.

*   *   *

Starri Deathless was not dead. He opened his eyes as that realization came to him. He found he was staring at grass, inches from his face. He pushed himself up and looked around.

The battle was not over. There were clusters of men fighting up by the woods, but that seemed to be tapering off, with dead and wounded strewn all over the field, and those still standing going at one another with waning strength and enthusiasm. There were more men to the south, and they seemed to be in some semblance of order, the last vestiges of a shield wall that had mostly fallen apart, but not entirely. But around Starri, there was no one.

"This is very strange," he said out loud. He realized that he must have been knocked unconscious and left for dead. It was not the first time that had happened in battle, but now it was different. Usually he woke with the berserker rage passed, and in its place a profound grief at finding himself still in Midgard, still among the living. The Valkyrie, he was sure, were choosing their men, and they would not choose him, because he still lived. That knowledge would move him to tears.

But he did not feel that now. There was no grief. Far from it. He felt a certain lightness of spirit, a kind of radiance, as if his whole existence was moving toward its culmination.

He wondered if he was, in fact, dead, but he dismissed the idea. His head ached, and he was bleeding from half a dozen lacerations, and he could feel bruising on his arms and legs. Surely if he was dead, he would not be in so much pain. So what could be happening?

He stood slowly and picked up his two battle axes that were lying beside him. He continued to scan the battlefield, and saw something he had not noticed before: a cluster of horses, circling, charging in and back, crowding together, like too many riders trying to get at too few enemies.

"This is very strange," he said again. The cluster of horses was like an island, alone in a sea of grass. None of the men fighting to the north or south seemed even to notice them. He frowned. He could not take his eyes from the scene. It seemed to call to him, to draw him in. It was as if the Norns had woven his fate in with that strange equine dance.

He started to run. His head thumped in pain, and his many wounds and bruises were agony as his feet hit the ground, but with each stride the pain seemed to dissipate, and the strength seemed to grow in his arms and legs. The spirit of the berserker was no longer on him, his mind was clearer than it had ever been, and yet he felt an extraordinary power surging through him. The split arrowhead he wore around his neck thumped off his chest as he ran.

The mounted warriors, turning in their tight circle, seemed not to notice him as he ran toward them, or if they did, they paid him no attention. He was twenty feet away when one of the horsemen turned in his direction. Starri could see the surprise on his face as he lifted his shield and sword. The horseman opened his mouth to shout something, but he never had the chance.

Five feet from the horse's side, Starri leapt, never breaking stride. He rose up off the ground as if he was flying, hit the warrior's shield with his shoulder, and the two of them kept on going, right over the far side of the horse. They hit the ground hard, the horseman first, Starri on top of him. Starri rolled away, came up on his feet and hacked down at the dismounted warrior. The battle axe went through his mail and through his chest like they were rotten wood, and the blood sprayed as Starri pulled the axe free.

He looked around the circle, and was surprised to see Thorgrim and Harald and Gudrid at its center, but he paid them no attention, as if they were just a vision, and not really there. Another of the riders charged in, leaned forward and lunged. He seemed to move so slowly that Starri could have paused for a cup of ale in the time it took the man's sword to reach him. With an almost casual stroke, Starri knocked the blade aside with the axe in his left hand, then with the one in his right he took the warrior's sword arm off as he rode past.

It was glorious, it was otherworldly, like nothing he had ever experienced before, even in the depths of a berserker rage. His every movement seemed guided by the gods themselves. The horses were swirling around him, the swords coming from every direction, and yet his battle axes found them all. They could not touch him as he pulled the riders from their mounts, or left them dying in their saddles.

There were fewer riders now, far fewer, but they were still charging in, and now they were not getting in one another's way. Starri smiled as he danced and whirled, horses front and back. A rider came charging in, sword high, and took a broad stroke at Starri's neck. Starri leapt back, clear of the blade. He swung one axe, which buried itself in the man's arm, then the other, which took his hand off at the wrist.

There was another rider at Starri's back, he could sense it. He started to turn, and he felt something ripping through him. He felt pain such as he had never felt before, like a burning spear right through his body. He looked down. The end of a sword had burst from his chest, gleaming and dripping with blood. He felt the pain wash over him, but that, too, was glorious, glorious, like easing into warm water. He turned, pulling the sword free as he did, looking up at the rider who had driven it through him. The man had his shield up, sword drawn back again.

Starri swung his battle axe and it hit the shield, and to his surprise it bounced off, rather than shattering the wood. Then the rider thrust again, and Starri could do nothing but watch as the tip of the sword sailed toward him, drove into his chest, and kept on going through.

He saw a burst of blood where the sword had pierced him, like a wave hitting a granite shore, and once again he felt the glorious rush of pain. He heard a voice calling his name — it was Thorgrim Night Wolf, his friend, a man blessed by the gods. Someone raced past him, shouting, and Starri saw it was Harald, brave Harald, who drove his sword into the rider's gut and sent him toppling over.

Starri felt the battle axes slip from his hands, and he felt his knees giving way under him. He fell sideways onto the soft grass. He could not move, but the pain was gone now. He closed his eyes and for a moment he was still, as still as he had ever been in all his life.

And then he was running, running. The ground moved swiftly under him, trees flew past on either side, and he knew that he was not alone. There was another figure beside him, running too, keeping pace, as they ran swiftly on, effortlessly through the dark forest. Not a man. Something else. Something like what Starri was now.

Night Wolf…

They ran on and on, leaping over fallen trees, bursting through the bracken, and then Starri realized he was alone again, and he pulled to a stop. He turned. His companion was there, behind him, but he was no longer running. He had stopped, and he was watching Starri with burning eyes, and Starri knew that Night Wolf could go no farther, but he himself could not stop, that he had to keep running. But it was all right. He could run on alone. He knew it. It would be all right.

He turned, and again he was rushing through the forest, and now the trees were not so close together, the bracken not so thick, and he could see light ahead, working its way through the trunks and the leaves.

He did not slacken his pace, and soon the woods were behind him, and he was in a wide, grassy field and the light was all around. And standing in the middle of the light, as if it was radiating out of her, as if she was the burning source of that brilliance, stood a woman, more beautiful than any Starri had ever seen, or would have ever thought could exist. And she was beckoning him.

He felt something stirring inside, spreading outward from his very core. It filled him until it seemed to spill out of him, a cup flowing over, the same way the light was spilling out of the beautiful woman. He had never felt it before, but he knew what it was. Joy. Peace.

He paused for a moment, then ran on.

Chapter Forty-Two

Sat there the liege-lords with swords brandished
With shields shattered and shredded mailcoats
Not happy in their hearts was that host of men
As to Valhalla they winded their way.

Hákonarmál

Thorgrim stood over the body of Starri Deathless and he wept. Only once in his life had he wept at a man's death — when Ornolf the Restless had given up his life to save Harald's — but he wept now. It was foolish, and he knew it. This was what Starri wanted, what he had always wanted: to die in glorious battle, weapons in hand.

And his death had been glorious indeed. He had appeared like a god, flying over the mounted riders, taking the nearest man down to the ground. He did not even seem aware of Thorgrim and Harald and Gudrid as he went through the mounted warriors like a scythe through barley. One by one he killed them, maimed them, drove them off. Sent them fleeing in terror from this otherworldly creature that seemed untouchable as he slayed all who came at him.

Halfdan, to his credit, had been one of the last to run. He kept to the fight, charging at Thorgrim, charging at Starri, until there were only a few of his mounted warriors left. He and the last three of his guard turned and raced off just moments before Starri met his end.

Thorgrim's arm was around Harald's shoulder, and Harald was weeping as well. Starri seemed small, lying at their feet, bathed in blood that was mostly his own this time, leaking from two vicious wounds and soaking into the earth.

Gudrid stood with them, and he was the first to speak. "The Chooser of the Slain will lift him off the field today. Before any of the others, they'll choose him." Thorgrim could only nod. He did not trust his voice.

They stood like that for a moment more, then Gudrid pulled the fine cape off one of the fallen horsemen and draped it over Starri's form. Thorgrim looked up from where his friend lay sprawled on the grass, looked out over the battlefield. He felt that he had regained control enough to see to other matters.

The fighting was done, both to the south, where the men from the longships had joined the battle, and to the north, where Odd's men and Vifil's men had stood up against the flanking attack from the woods.

It was not entirely clear which side, if either, had won. Men were standing in postures of exhaustion, men were sitting, hurt and defeated. Men were lying strewn out on the field. Quite a lot of men. More than Thorgrim had ever seen in the wake of a fight.

"Get us horses," he said, and Harald and Gudrid nodded and hurried off. The riderless mounts of Halfdan's guard, too well trained to run off, were standing nearby, and they rounded up three of them and led them back. They helped Thorgrim up onto one horse, and mounted the other two. Then Thorgrim led them toward the northern end of the battlefield.

His only thought now was to find Odd, and he felt a cold dread as he considered how he might find him. Laid out perhaps, bleeding into the ground the way Starri had. He did not think he could endure it.

He searched the living, the wounded, and the dead as he rode slowly toward the tree line. He saw that the men who were still standing, standing with weapons drawn, shields on arms, were not Halfdan's men. Not the men in fine mail. They were the ragged men who had come with Odd, and men from his own fleet as well. The victors, it seemed.

He saw three men, mounted, and they wheeled their horses and rode toward Thorgrim as he rode toward them. One of the riders was Vifil. The second he did not recognize. The third was Odd.

"Father!" Odd said, as he reined to a stop. "Harald!" He was smiling, but his eyes flickered down to Thorgrim's blood-soaked leggings and the smile faded. "You're wounded."

Thorgrim did not speak at first, too taken by his relief at seeing Odd alive and unhurt. Then he said, "A lot of men are wounded. I don't think I'll die of mine. Starri Deathless was not so lucky."

"Starri's dead?" Odd said. "I'm sorry…"

"He made a good end," Harald said. "Died saving us, with his axes in his hands. He died the death he wanted to die."

Odd nodded. He seemed not to know what to say.

"I don't know this man Starri," Vifil said, "but I'll tell you, he also died victorious. Halfdan's men threw down their weapons, and some gave up and some ran off. Those that were still able to run. The day's yours. And Odd's."

"Halfdan?" Thorgrim asked.

"Don't know," Odd said. "We saw him gathering some of his men and heading west, but we weren't able to go after them. Might be running back to Grømstad. I don't know."

Thorgrim surveyed the field once more. So many wounded, so many dead. He turned to Vifil. "Any men who are fit enough, have them strip Halfdan's men of weapons and mail, then gather the prisoners up and set a guard over them. The rest can see to our wounded. Halfdan's men can care for their own wounded, if they wish."

"Very good," Vifil said.

"Odd, come with us," Thorgrim said. He rode off to the south and found the situation there the much the same: many of Halfdan's men run off, many dead, wounded, or surrendered. Halldor, captain of *Black Wing*, was there, and though he was wounded, he was still upright, still in command. Thorgrim put him in charge at that end of the field, told him to do the same as he had told Vifil.

Next he told Gudrid to find some men and gather up all the horses wandering around the field of battle. That done, he sent riders under Gudrid's command to scout to the west, to see if Halfdan and his men had truly run off, and to bring back Halfdan's supply wagons if they were to be found. Then, finally, Thorgrim gave in to his sons' persistent nagging, dismounted, and allowed them to tend to his wounded leg.

The boys dressed and bound the wound, with only minor squabbling as to how it should be done. Then the three of them mounted up again, so they could more easily move from one place that demanded their attention to the next. The day wore on, the sun moving slowly toward the west, and the scene of bloody slaughter and chaos was slowly transformed into something more resembling order.

The shadows were growing long when Gudrid and his riders finally returned. They had seen no sign of Halfdan and his surviving men, but they had found the supply train abandoned on the road, and had come back with the wagons trailing behind. Food, ale, tents, weapons: Halfdan did not want for anything in the field, and now Thorgrim's men would not either.

Feasting, however, would wait. First, preparations were made to send off to Valhalla the many bold warriors who had fought their last battle that day. Great quantities of dried wood were scavenged from the forest and along the shore, and a massive bonfire built up near the water's edge. On one of the longships, run up on the shore, a tall pyre was erected at the base of the mast, and others at various places around the ship. A bull was found at a nearby farm, which the owner gladly yielded up for a handful of silver.

Finally, when it was full dark, the bonfire was lit, and soon it was throwing its light all across the field and the white sand and the dark water. It lit up the bow of the longship and the mast and the yard, lowered to the gallows. It fell on the hundreds of men gathered to witness this solemn event.

Thorgrim led the way, a wolf's skin draped over his head. Behind him came the men of *Sea Hammer*, and *Oak Heart*, and *Black Wing*, and the others, bearing their dead. Asmund was among the draped corpses, and Vali, and Hall, and many others with whom Thorgrim had fought so many battles, sailed so many miles. Arnor, chief of the fisherfolk, had been cut down, as had many others from the ranks of the farmers and fishermen. But first in that grim line was Starri Deathless.

Each man was sent off to the Feast Hall armed for battle. They wore mail and helmets, with swords at their waists and spears at their sides. All but Starri. He would never have tolerated such niceties. For him, a simple tunic, and gripped in his hands and crossed on his chest, his two battle axes, which had served him so well. Which had saved the lives of Thorgrim and Harald and Gudrid. Lying between the two ax heads was the split arrowhead that Thorgrim had once plucked from the edge of his sword.

Starri was laid out on the big pyre by the mast, the others arrayed around him. The bull was brought to the bonfire and its throat was cut, and Odd held a bowl under the neck of the dying animal to catch the blood that spurted and flowed from the gash. It was a ritual that Thorgrim had performed many times, but he could not help but think how, since their paths had crossed, it had always been Starri there by his side.

Once the bull bled out, Odd stood, bowl in hand, and followed Thorgrim back aboard the longship. There Thorgrim called on the gods to look with favor on the bold deeds of the men laid out on their pyres as he dipped a pine branch in the bowl of blood and sprinkled it liberally around. Behind them walked four men with flaming torches, and once the bowl of blood was emptied, the men set the various pyres ablaze. They climbed back ashore, and with a signal from Thorgrim two dozen men heaved the ship off the sand and into the dark water.

The tide was just starting to ebb, and the sea carried the longship farther and farther from shore as the flames climbed up the mast and spread along the furled sail and across the open deck. Thorgrim stood at the water's edge, his sons on either side, the hundreds of men who had followed him into battle arrayed behind him. He watched the flames consume the ship, rising higher and higher, a dark bowl in the water filled with bright fire, and once again the tears ran down his cheeks. Someone began singing, a mournful dirge, and hundreds of voices joined in, and they all watched as the ship burned down and was at last swallowed up by the sea.

They ate and drank after that, but with little enthusiasm or energy. They had captured a great number of tents from Halfdan, but there was no will to set them up. Rather, each man found a spot in the grass where they dropped to the ground, and soon all were fast asleep, and the only sound was the owls and the insects, snoring men and the groans of the wounded.

They rose just after dawn on the following day, because there was still much to do. They broke their fast, and the wounded were loaded on the wagons they had taken from Halfdan and sent back to Fevik. Those men who were still able to march were told to take up arms and be ready to move, because this was not over, it was not resolved, and Thorgrim did not mean to stop until it was.

The prisoners, now clad only in tunics, leggings and shoes, were bound with hands behind their backs, a long rope running one to the other, and placed near the middle of the line of march. By midmorning the army was on the road, in the wake of Halfdan and the few men still with him. Thorgrim, Odd, Harald, and the other chief men led the way on horseback, with two columns stretching out behind.

There were still seven hundred or so men under Thorgrim's command, and they were a more impressive-looking force than they had been before. The mail and helmets, swords, axes and spears they had taken from Halfdan's elite warriors had been distributed among them, and now most were outfitted more like king's men than fishermen. Despite the bloody work of the day before, the price they had paid in dead and wounded, the men's spirits seemed high as they followed in loose lines behind Thorgrim and the rest.

They marched west, and soon passed the road that led north to Thorgrim's farm. Thorgrim looked wistfully at that familiar way as he rode by, and every bit of him longed to pull the reins over and make an end to this long journey. But he did not, and knew he could not until this business was done.

Another hour's march brought them to Grømstad and the massive walls surrounding Halfdan's great hall. They had seen no sign of the king or his men on their march, so Thorgrim had to assume that Halfdan had retreated to this place, his stronghold. He could not imagine what else he might do.

His assumption proved correct. As they approached the huge oak gates in the earthen wall, Thorgrim ordered his men to spread out in a line abreast, shields up, an impressive and intimidating display. Behind them, the hundreds of bound prisoners stood angry and dejected. A guard was standing at the top of the wall, but he just watched in silence. Moments later, Halfdan himself appeared.

"Ah, Thorgrim," Halfdan called down. "Have you come to name yourself king? You were lucky on the battlefield. I don't think you'll be so lucky trying to breach these walls, and take on the army behind them."

"Army?" Thorgrim said. "There's your army." He pointed to the bound prisoners behind him. "I've talked to some of these men, and they tell me they're the last of the warriors you command, that you have no one left, save for the handful who fled the battlefield with you."

"Is that what they say? Well, I suggest you make an attempt against these walls and find out."

Halfdan was making a bold stand, but Thorgrim knew he was lying. He had indeed spoken with some of the prisoners, and persuaded them it was in their best interest to be forthcoming. He knew that Halfdan had lost most of the men he sent with Skorri to hunt down Odd, and many more in yesterday's battle in the open field. He could not have a hundred warriors behind those walls, if that.

"We've had a bellyful of fighting," Thorgrim said. "You, me, these men. We'll batter down your gates if we must, and find the truth of what you say, how many warriors are in there. But I told you before, I'd rather we find some other means to resolve this. You didn't listen the first time. Maybe you will now."

"Resolve it? How do we resolve it? By me giving up my crown to you?"

Thorgrim sighed. "I don't want your crown. You couldn't pay me silver enough to take your crown. I…we…just want to be left in peace. It's all any of these men have ever asked. So here's what I say. You open the gate and we march in. Then we sit down and come to an agreement; you, me, Odd, all these men. If all are satisfied, you keep your crown, I give you back the prisoners, and we leave."

He let that offer sit for a moment, and then continued. "If you don't open the gates, then we'll break them down and we'll come in anyway, and find out if you really have men enough to stand against us. If you're defeated like the last time, then we sack your hall, and we keep these prisoners for thralls and sell the rest in Frisia. And I let my men do with you as they will. The choice is yours."

Halfdan was silent as he stared at Thorgrim and considered his choice. "I must think on this," he said at last. "Come back on the morrow."

"You have as long as it takes us to fashion a battering ram," Thorgrim said. "Not a moment more."

But Halfdan did not need that long. He stared at Thorgrim and frowned and looked as if he meant to reply. Then he turned and called down to someone on the ground below.

"Open the gates," he said.

They heard the sound of the bar being lifted from the gate, and a moment later it swung open and Thorgrim led his warriors through, followed by the prisoners. Thorgrim's guess had been about right: Halfdan seemed to have about a hundred men left under his command. Even with the return of the prisoners, it would be years before he could build his army back up to the strength he had enjoyed when this all started.

It would cost Halfdan a fortune just to replace the mail and helmets and swords Thorgrim had taken from his men — Thorgrim had no intention of returning any of it — and Halfdan no longer had a fortune, he no longer had the wealth to support the many hundreds of warriors he had once commanded. Most of his treasure had been spent in fighting Odd's rebellion, and the freemen of Agder would not be much inclined to pay more taxes. Nor did Halfdan have the means to compel them. Thanks to his own foolishness, King Halfdan Gudrødson was little more than a shrunken version of what he had once been, and it would be years, if ever, before he was anything else.

They met in the great hall; Halfdan, Thorgrim, Odd, Vifil, some of the more prominent men from Fevik, and a handful of the jarls who had fled the battlefield with their king. The talks did not take long. Halfdan had little with which to negotiate; even less now that he had let the enemy into his walled compound.

Reparations for the damage Skorri had done sacking Fevik, a promise to respect the rights of freemen, to impose no new taxes and to seek no vengeance against any of those who had stood up for themselves, and to leave the fishermen to do their work in peace. And in exchange, Halfdan to keep his crown, to have his prisoners and longships returned, and to be allowed to collect taxes and require service just as he had before the troubles; it was all discussed and agreed upon.

Thorgrim was satisfied. Halfdan had given his word, and that, along with the fact that he was now largely toothless, was enough for him. The people of Agder had come together as an army, fought as an army, and they could do so again. He knew it, Halfdan knew it. And Halfdan knew that he, Thorgrim Night Wolf, was back, and he was watching.

When all parties were in agreement, they left off talking. Thorgrim and his boys mounted up, and once again the ad hoc army formed a loose line behind them and they rode out through the gate, leaving Grømstad and Halfdan behind. They rode east, and then turned onto the road running north. They came at last to the smaller road that continued on to Thorgrim's farm, and this time they did not march past it, but turned that way, that dry and rutted way, the last mile. After so many miles, they turned onto the last mile home.

Epilogue

Sword-wielder, feller of blood oaks,
rider of Sea Stallions,
go now, to the land of your father's father
where fate will weave its thread for you.

Egil's Saga

It was a strange rush of emotions that Thorgrim felt as Skafti Hrappsson greeted him at the gates in the wall surrounding his great hall, tears streaming unabashedly down his weathered cheeks.

Thorgrim reined his horse to a stop and looked around. He felt an overwhelming sense of relief, and apprehension as to what he might find. And weariness. Profound weariness. He was home, his raiding was done, Odd was safe, but his concerns were not over. Far from it.

"Welcome home, Lord." Skafti managed to choke the words out.

"Thank you, Skafti. It's good to be home." He nudged the horse forward and rode onto the grounds.

The farm looked just as he remembered it, save for the strange lack of activity. The few servants and thralls still there rushed out to take Thorgrim's horse, and Odd's and Harald's and the others'. They did what they could to accommodate the nearly seven hundred men who had suddenly appeared in the yard.

Skorri had sacked the great hall, and made off with everything he could carry, so there was little left to eat or drink. Thorgrim sent men to collect up the supplies, taken from Halfdan, that they had left behind. With those stores, and what Skorri had not stolen, and what they could buy from the neighboring farms, there was enough to keep the army in food and drink, at least for a little while.

They feasted that night, and the next morning they turned to, ready to address the thousand issues that confronted them. Thorgrim sent Harald and a handful of armed men to what was, to him, the first concern — retrieving Gyda from Ornolf's great hall, bringing her back to the farm in Vik, and seeing her settled into what he hoped she would be pleased to call her new home. Another contingent of armed men, under Gudrid's command, was sent to Fevik. There they retrieved the great quantities of plunder, stored under guard aboard *Sea Hammer* and the other ships, which Thorgrim and his men had won in the course of their raiding in Ireland, Engla-land, and Frankia.

Day by day the number of men in Thorgrim's great hall dwindled. Those from Fevik returned to their homes, and the fishermen to their camp. The homes of many who had sailed with Thorgrim were nearby, and those men were given their share of the plunder, which was considerable, and horses, if needed, and bid farewell. Thorgrim gave *Blood Hawk* to Gudrid, *Oak Heart* to Bragi Shipslayer and *Black Wing* to Halldor, with the agreement that they would first use the ships to carry home the other men who lived in farther flung towns and villages.

Harald returned with Gyda, and she was well pleased with the farm and the great hall. Thorgrim explained that it had been sacked, assured her it would be returned to what it had been, but she seemed unconcerned. Still, as it happened, nearly all that had been stolen from Thorgrim's hall was still at Ornolf's, where Skorri had meant to keep it as his own. It took several wagon trains, back and forth, to return it all, but it was done, and Gyda busied herself in overseeing the effort to put everything to rights.

Soon after, and before all of the men from Thorgrim's fleet who meant to depart had done so, Thorgrim and Gyda were married. The neighbors were invited, and the feasting was raucous and several days long.

A month passed, and soon it was only Thorgrim and Gyda and Harald in the great hall, along with the servants and thralls and the forty men Thorgrim maintained as a hird, men whom he had come to think of as brothers over their years of voyaging together. More servants and farmhands were hired, the crops came in, the livestock was replenished. By the time the weather turned cold, the frenetic activity that surrounded Thorgrim's return had tapered off, and life took on a certain quiet routine. It was the quiet routine that Thorgrim had longed for, and he was not disappointed.

The snows came and blanketed Vik, and winter storms buffeted the farm, but there was wood enough to keep the fires roaring and the massive hall warm. With the food and drink they had stored away they could have kept the crews of all Thorgrim's fleet well fed and full of ale and wine and mead through all the long winter, which meant there was more than enough for those on hand.

It meant as well that, when the midwinter celebration of Yule came around, and the gods kindly gave East Agder a reprieve from winter storms, Thorgrim could invite his neighbors to his great hall, and feast them in a way that a wealthy and generous man might be expected to do. And after he had downed several horns of mead, and after much prompting from his friends, Thorgrim regaled them all with tales of their adventures.

He had once been known as a skald, skilled with verse, and though he had not composed or recited in a long time, he found pleasure in doing so again, and his neighbors and the men and women in his household found pleasure in listening. Gyda found pleasure in listening, too, and in most things in her life with Thorgrim, and that made him profoundly happy. She proved a gracious hostess, and an excellent head of the household, a patient, loving, if a bit headstrong wife, and that made him happy as well.

The Yule celebrations passed and Thorgrim's guests went home, and the weather continued to be unseasonably mild. One morning, a week after the feast, while Thorgrim and Gyda and Harald were breaking their fast, Harald said, "I think I'll make a visit to Odd."

Thorgrim nodded. He had noticed a certain restlessness in the boy, and it was hardly a surprise. He was eighteen, and had spent the past years raiding and voyaging, seeing more and doing more than most men did in a lifetime. One could get a taste for that, the way one got a taste for drink, and it could be just as hard to give it up as it was ale or mead. Then there was nothing for it but to give in to the desire, and hope you lived long enough for it to pass. No one knew that better than Thorgrim Night Wolf.

"It would be good to see your brother," Thorgrim said. "I'm sure he'd be happy to see you again."

Harald had spent much of the autumn on Odd's farm, helping him make it livable through the winter. Odd's hall had been burned down, and the brothers struggled to get a suitable shelter built before the snow flew. There was little firewood, little food or drink laid in. Odd and Signy had spent the past year or more running from Halfdan's vengeance. There had been no time for domestic concerns.

Halfdan, happily, had been true to his word in paying reparations, and some of that had gone to Odd, which meant he could purchase that which he could not supply himself. Thorgrim had helped as well, as had Harald, from the abundance they brought back from Ireland and Engla-land and Frankia. But mostly Harald had lent his strong arms and back, and his insatiable desire to work, and for the time it had tamped down his need for something beyond his father's farm.

"Any reason you want to see Odd?" Gyda asked, as she refilled Harald's cup.

"None in particular," Harald said. "I could use some fresh air. Exercise. I'm not much accustomed to being indoors so long."

Breakfast done, Harald wrapped himself up in a long sheepskin cape and settled a fur hat on his head. He slung a sack over his shoulder and took up his skis. Thorgrim and Gyda followed him to the door and stepped outside with him, into the brilliant winter morning.

The sky was perfect blue, the sun low in the horizon, as it always was at that time of year. But the air was not so cold, and the long icicles that hung from the edge of the great hall's roof were dripping, making a slow, irregular drumbeat on the ground. Gyda knelt down and helped Harald bind his skis to his fur-lined shoes.

"I should be back in a week or so, if the weather holds," Harald said.

"Give our love to Odd and Signy and the children," Gyda said. They embraced, then Thorgrim and Gyda stood with arms around one another and watched Harald head off on the day-long trek to his brother's farm.

"A fine day," Gyda said.

"A fine day," Thorgrim agreed. They were silent for a moment, enjoying the morning.

"Are you home?" Thorgrim asked. Gyda did not answer right away.

"I'm home," she said at last. "Are you home?"

Thorgrim did not have to think on that question. "I'm home," he said.

He watched Harald make his way through the big gate in the wall. He understood the boy's restless nature. Understood it perfectly well. And he felt none of it. A thousand tides, a thousand sea-miles, a thousand battles, had washed it all clean away. He was home. And home he would remain.

*   *   *

Odd Thorgrimson took advantage of the fine weather to split firewood. They had gone into the winter with a short supply, so he took every chance he could to lay in more. There was little he could do about food or drink at this point, save for bringing in more water or hunting or trapping, which he did when he could, but he was generally able to find the time to split wood.

It was not just the lack of wood that drove him out into the yard. The house they lived in was only as much house as he and Harald and a few friends and hired men were able to build in the short time they had in the autumn months. It could not compare to the hall that Halfdan had burned to the ground, and it often felt cramped and stuffy, filled with smoke and the smells of cooking and damp clothes and the cries of children, joyful cries sometimes, and sometimes otherwise. It made Odd feel agitated at times. It made him want to breathe fresh air and work his muscles.

His daughter Thorgid was four years old now, her younger sister Hallbera just over a year. Ornolf, his boy, was five. During most of the time that he and Signy were in hiding, and fighting Halfdan, the children had been hidden away at Signy's brother's farm, far from Fevik, and there they had remained safe. The reunion of parents and children had been a joyous one, but one that required adjustment all around. They were still settling in from the great upheaval of the past year and more.

Odd wrapped his cloak around his shoulders and let Signy pin it on. He picked up his ax and stepped out into the perfect winter afternoon. The sun was bright, and ice was starting to drip, but Odd knew better than to think this was a harbinger of spring. This was one of the gods' tricks, this false promise of coming warmth. Winter would hit them again, and hit them hard, at least a few more times.

He took an oak log off the pile and set it upright on the stump, swung his ax back with a familiar stroke and brought the blade down on the wood. The log was still frozen, and split easily in two with a satisfying *pop*. Odd set half the log back up and split it again.

One by one he took logs from the pile and halved them and quartered them, and as he did, his mind went back to the times when he had swung Blood-letter in much the same way, bringing it down on flesh or mail, more yielding than oak or maple. These visions always came to him now when he split wood, and he dreaded them and he relished them. In his head he heard the battle cries of furious men, the screams of the wounded, the clash of steel on steel. He did not know what to think. It confused him.

"Father! Father!" The voice startled him and made him jump. It was little Ornolf, who had no doubt pleaded with his mother to be let outside, away from the company of his sisters. Odd turned around. The boy was halfway between the house and the woodpile, dressed in a cloak and wool hat and reindeer boots. He held a small wooden shield on his left arm, a wooden sword in his right hand.

"Look, I'm a great warrior, just like you! And like Uncle Harald and Grandpa!"

Odd smiled and nodded. *Great warrior…* he thought. Harald had been fighting and raiding those past years. Grandpa Thorgrim was a legend. Could he stand in that company? He had led a rebellion against the king, had fought a few bloody battles and won. Won with the help of his father and brother. Before that, he had been wrestling pigs, and soon he would be again.

"That's good, son," Odd said. "You can go and practice on the post while I split some more wood." He turned back to his axe and his logs, and soon he could hear the tap, tap, tap of Ornolf attacking the upright post in the yard with his wooden sword, and banging it with his shield, as if it was standing opposite him in a shield wall.

One by one the logs were split and the pile of cordwood rose higher and Odd's arms grew weary with the effort. He paused now and again to correct Ornolf's technique, just as his father had once corrected his. He leaned on his axe and breathed deep and looked at the long, oval, hump of snow that covered the charred remains of the great hall that Halfdan had burned. He sighed, and felt a wave of concern wash over him.

He could not raise his family in the sorry house that he and Harald had built. It was fine for a winter, but the children were growing fast, and the son of Thorgrim Night Wolf, grandson of Ornolf the Restless and Ulf of the Battle Song, could not live his life in such a place. He could not be a man of any consequence, able to feast his neighbors, in such a home. But when or how he might ever replace his fine hall was beyond him.

When Odd had split as much wood as he cared to split that afternoon he carried it all inside, with Ornolf eagerly helping, one small piece at a time. The house seemed close and oppressive after being outdoors, but it smelled wonderfully, too, of the stew that Signy was cooking in the big pot over the fire.

They were just sitting down to eat when they heard a knock on the door. Odd and Signy exchanged glances. They had no reason to think danger might be coming for them, but after running so long, it was hard to believe, deep down, that they were safe. Odd stood and crossed to the door. He glanced down at the sword propped up beside it — not Blood-letter, but a perfectly serviceable weapon. Just in case.

He swung the door open, and standing there, smiling, ruddy-faced, was his brother.

Odd smiled as well. "Harald!" he said, and from behind him came little Ornolf's voice, calling "Uncle Harald!" And then Thorgid and Hallbera shouted the same, or some reasonable attempt.

Signy appeared at Odd's side. "Harald! This is a surprise and a pleasure! Come in! You're just in time for náttmál."

"Of course he is," Odd said. "Harald has a great ability to show up when the food's being served."

They welcomed him in, took his hat and cloak and sack, leaned his skis against the wall. The children attacked him like dogs on a bear until Signy shooed them back to their seats. Then Harald sat and Signy set out another bowl of stew and a spoon and Harald dug in with the appetite of an eighteen-year-old who had just skied over many miles of hilly country.

They peppered Harald with questions as he ate: how were things with Thorgrim and Gyda, what was taking place on the farm? in Vik? Had Harald heard any news that Odd and Signy had not? That would be pretty much any news at all, since they heard very little indeed.

Harald told them all was well, that their father was still pleased to spend his days at farm work, or exchanging stories with his men. He told them that Thorgrim had started composing skaldic verse again, and that Gyda was enjoying her new life there. He told them of the great festivities they had hosted for Yule. Signy told Harald that they had spent their Yule celebrations as a guest at a neighbor's hall, since things were too close to the bone for her and Odd to host their own. Odd said nothing.

Finally Signy forced the children, against their will, to go to bed, though Harald had so worn them out that they were soon asleep. Signy made up a bed for Harald, kissed him and kissed Odd and retired herself. The two brothers remained at the table, cups of mead in front of them.

"So, really, how is it with you?" Harald asked. He spoke in a soft voice, and Odd was not sure if he did not want to disturb Signy, or if he did not want her to hear what he had to say. Or both.

Odd shrugged. "Things are fine. The house does well enough. The children are in good health."

For a long moment, Harald just stared at Odd, in a way that Odd could not recall him ever doing before. It gave him a strange feeling, as if Harald was looking straight into him.

Finally, Harald spoke. "Can I show you something?"

Odd nodded. Harald stood and fetched the bag he had carried over his shoulder. He dug inside and pulled out a rolled-up vellum scroll. Odd had seen such things before, but only rarely. Harald moved the cups and set the scroll down on the table. He unrolled it, and Odd saw that it was folded in two. Then Harald unfolded it.

Odd stood so he could see the whole thing at once, though he had no idea what he was looking at. The surface of the vellum was mostly white, with patches of blue; strange shapes that did not look like anything Odd recognized. There were blue lines as well, crooked and branched like bolts of lightning, and thin, dark lines in crescent shapes at regular intervals. There were runes of some sort in various places, clearly meaningful, but nothing Odd recognized. It made Odd uncomfortable, as if it was possessed of some magic.

"What is it?" Odd asked. He spoke in a whisper.

"It's a map," Harald said.

"A map?"

"Have you ever seen a map before?"

Odd nodded. "Once. A map of East Agder. Halfdan had it made."

"So you know what a map is?"

"I know what a map is." Odd was starting to get annoyed.

"Well, this is a map of the whole world," Harald said. "Or most of the world. I took it from a Frank named Felix. But it's very old."

"The whole world?" Odd said.

"See here?" Harald pointed to an irregular shape near the upper left corner, rendered in white, surrounded by blue. "That's Engla-land, where we were raiding. And that's the narrow sea, where we crossed to Frankia. And there's Frankia. And Frisia."

"Blue is water, white is land?" Odd asked

"That's right."

Odd stared at the map, and it slowly dawned on him what Harald was telling him, though he had no way of knowing if anything Harald said was correct. "Where's Norway?" he asked.

"The ancient people who made this, they didn't know about Norway. None of our lands are on this map. But just look at how much of the world is."

Odd frowned. It was becoming clearer to him. "How do you know it's right?"

"I don't know for certain. But as we were making our way home, I looked at the map, and I looked at where we were, and it seemed what was on the map was just as it was in the world. The way the coastlines trended. Where the rivers were."

"These are rivers?" Odd pointed to the crooked lines.

"Yes. Big ones. Some wide as fjords. I saw them as we sailed north. And there are cities on them, such that you can hardly imagine."

Odd felt a strange excitement growing in his gut. He was beginning to understand why Harald found this so very fascinating. And at the same time he felt a twinge of envy. Harald had seen these places. He had not.

"What's this?" he asked, pointing to another irregular blue shape.

"That's a sea that they call *Mediterranean*," Odd replied. "That's what Felix said. And he said there were great cities there. Cities spilling over with silver and gold and all manner of riches."

Cities of gold...Odd thought. "This is a great curiosity," Odd said. "Thank you for showing me."

Harald shook his head. "Don't you see?"

"What?"

"This map tells us where to find these riches. Places no one else knows of. Things even father hasn't seen. A couple of bold men, with longships full of warriors...they could make their fortunes. There's more wealth to be had, more adventure, than anyone could ask in three lifetimes."

Odd looked down at the map once more. He felt that stirring in his gut again, but stronger this time. Irresistible. The blue, the white. It called to him, in a voice he could not ignore.

"A couple of bold men?" he asked.

"I think I know of two," Harald said. "They come from a long line of famous warriors. They have longships at their disposal, and reputations such that the best fighting men in the country would be eager to sail with them."

Odd pressed his lips together and looked his brother in the eye. He saw, in his head, like the most vivid dream, himself on the afterdeck of a longship, bowling along through blue seas, the ship's figurehead staring out at the mouth of a wide river to which they were bound.

He saw a new great hall rising up from the ashes of his last, but bigger, finer by far, built with the wealth garnered from those foreign lands which were now rendered before him in ink on vellum.

"A couple of bold men," Odd said. "I think I know them as well."

The End

Coming in 2026:

Book I of *The Brother's Saga*

The Brothers' Saga is coming in 2026! For a heads-up on new releases, as well as preview sample chapters and other good stuff cheap (actually free) visit our web site and sign up for our (occasional) e-mail newsletter:

www.jameslnelson.com

Other Fiction by

James L. Nelson:

Blood, Steel, and Empire:
Novels of the Buccaneers of the Caribbean
The Buccaneer Coast
The Tortuga Plantation

Also:

The Brethren of the Coast:
Piracy in Colonial America
The Guardship
The Blackbirder
The Pirate Round

The Samuel Bowater Novels:
Naval action of the American Civil War
Glory in the Name
Thieves of Mercy

The Isaac Biddlecomb Novels:
Naval action of the American Revolution
By Force of Arms
The Maddest Idea
The Continental Risque
Lords of the Ocean
All the Brave Fellows

James L. Nelson

The Falmouth Frigate

The Only Life that Mattered:
The Story of Ann Bonny, Mary Read and Calico Jack Rackham

Nonfiction by
James L. Nelson:

Reign of Iron: The Story of the Ironclads Monitor *and* Merrimack

Benedict Arnold's Navy: The Battle of Valcour Island

George Washington's Secret Navy

George Washington's Great Gamble

With Fire and Sword: The Battle of Bunker Hill

Glossary

adze – a tool much like an ax but with the blade set at a right angle to the handle.
Ægir – Norse god of the sea. In Norse mythology he was also the host of great feasts for the gods.
Allfather - foremost of the Norse gods. See **Odin**.
Asgard – the dwelling place of the Norse gods and goddesses, essentially the Norse heaven.
athwartships – at a right angle to the centerline of a vessel.
backstay – a rope running from the top of a ship's mast to the stern, used to support the mast.
beitass – a wooden pole, or spar, secured to the side of a ship on the after end and leading forward to which the corner, or clew, of a sail could be secured.
berserker – a Viking warrior able to work himself into a frenzy of bloodlust before a battle. The berserkers, near psychopathic killers in battle, were the fiercest of the Viking soldiers. The word berserker comes from the Norse for "bear shirt" and is the origin of the modern English "berserk."
bitter end – the end of any length of rope.
block – nautical term for a pulley.
boss – the round, iron centerpiece of a wooden shield. The boss formed an iron cup protruding from the front of the shield, providing a hollow in the back across which ran the hand grip.
brace – line used for hauling a yard side to side on a horizontal plane. Used to adjust the angle of the sail to the wind.
bride-price – money paid by the family of the groom to the family of the bride.
byrdingr – a smaller ocean-going cargo vessel used by the Norsemen for trade and transportation. Generally about 40 feet in length, the byrdingr was a smaller version of the more well-known knarr.
cable – a measure of approximately 600 feet.
clench nail – a type of nail that, after being driven through a board, has a type of washer called a rove placed over the end and is then bent over to secure it in place.

clew – one of the lower corners of a square sail, to which the sheet is attached.
dagmál – breakfast time, roughly 7:00 am to noon.
double-banked – an oar pulled by two men.
dragon ship – the largest of the Viking warships, upwards of 160 feet long and able to carry as many as 300 men. Dragon ships were the flagships of the fleet, the ships of kings.
dubh gall –Gaelic term for Vikings of Danish descent. It means Black Strangers, a reference to the mail armor they wore, made dark by the oil used to preserve it. See fin gall.
elding – the last part of the night, after the night meal.
ell – a unit of length, a little more than a yard.
eyrir – Scandinavian unit of measurement, approximately an ounce.
faering - double-ended, clinker-built boat, generally twenty or thirty feet long, designed for rowing and sailing
félag – a fellowship of men who owed each other a mutual obligation, such as multiple owners of a ship, or a band or warriors who had sworn allegiance to one another.
figurehead – ornamental carving on the bow of a ship.
fin gall – Gaelic term for Vikings of Norwegian descent. It means White Strangers. See dubh gall.
firkin – a small cask usually holding about nine gallons of liquid.
forestay – a rope running from the top of a ship's mast to the bow used to support the mast.
Frisia – a region in the northern part of the modern-day Netherlands.
Freya – Norse goddess of beauty and love, she was also associated with warriors, as many of the Norse deity were. Freya often led the Valkyries to the battlefield.
gallows – tall, T-shaped posts on the ship's centerline, forward of the mast, on which the oars and yard were stored when not in use.
hack silver – pieces of silver from larger units cut up for distribution.
hall – the central building on a Viking-age farm. It served as dining hall, sleeping quarters, and storage. Also known as a longhouse.
halyard – a line by which a sail or a yard is raised.
Haustmánudur – early autumn. Literally, harvest-month.
Hel – in Norse mythology, the daughter of Loki and the ruler of the underworld where those who are not raised up to Valhalla are sent to suffer. The same name, Hel, is given to the realm over which she rules, the Norse hell.

hersir – in medieval Norway, a magistrate who served to oversee a region under the rule of a king.
hide – a unit of land considered sufficient to support a single family.
hird – an elite corps of Viking warriors hired and maintained by a king or powerful jarl. Unlike most Viking warrior groups, which would assemble and disperse at will, the hird was retained as a semi-permanent force which formed the core of a Viking army.
hirdsman – a warrior who is a member of the hird.
hólmganga – a formal, organized duel fought in a marked off area between two men.
jarl – title given to a man of high rank. A jarl might be an independent ruler or subordinate to a king. Jarl is the origin of the English word earl.
Jörmungandr – in Norse mythology, a vast sea serpent that surrounds the earth, grasping its own tail.
knarr – a Norse merchant vessel. Smaller, wider, and sturdier than the longship, knarrs were the workhorse of Norse trade, carrying cargo and settlers wherever the Norsemen traveled.
league – a distance of three miles.
lee shore – land that is downwind of a ship, on which a ship is in danger of being driven.
leeward – downwind.
leech – either one of the two vertical edges of a square sail.
léine – a long, loose-fitting smock worn by men and women under other clothing. Similar to the shift of a later period.
Loki – Norse god of fire and free spirits. Loki was mischievous and his tricks caused great trouble for the gods, for which he was punished.
longphort – literally, a ship fortress. A small, fortified port to protect shipping and serve as a center of commerce and a launching off point for raiding.
loom – the middle part, or shaft, of an oar, between the blade and the handle
luff – the shivering of a sail when its edge is pointed into the wind and the wind strikes it on both sides.
Midgard – one of nine worlds in Norse mythology, it is the earth, the world known and visible to humans.
Mjölnir – the hammer wielded by the Norse god Thor as a weapon and a divine instrument.

Niflheim – the World of Fog. One of the nine worlds in Norse mythology, somewhat analogous to Hell, the afterlife for people who do not die honorable deaths.
Njord – Norse god of the sea and seafaring.
Norns – in Norse mythology, women who sit at the center of the world and hold the fate of each person by spinning the thread of each person's life.
Odin – foremost of the Norse gods. Known as the Allfather, Odin was the god of wisdom and war, protector of both chieftains and poets.
perch – a unit of measure equal to 16½ feet. The same as a rod.
Ragnarok – the mythical final battle when most humans and gods would be killed by the forces of evil and the earth destroyed, only to rise again, purified.
rod – a unit of measure equal to 16½ feet. The same as a perch
rove – a square washer used to fasten the planks of a longship. A nail is driven through the plank and the hole in the washer and then bent over.
sceattas – small, thick, silver coins minted in England and Frisia in the early Middle Ages.
seax – any of a variety of edged weapons longer than a knife but shorter and lighter than a typical sword.
sheer strake – the uppermost plank, or strake, of a boat or ship's hull. On a Viking ship the sheer strake would form the upper edge of the ship's hull. See strake.
sheet – a rope that controls a sail. In the case of a square sail, the sheets pull the clews down to hold the sail so the wind can fill it.
shield wall – a defensive wall formed by soldiers standing in line with shields overlapping.
shroud – a heavy rope stretching from the top of the mast to the ship's side that prevents the mast from falling sideways.
skald – a Viking-era poet, generally one attached to a royal court. The skalds wrote a very stylized type of verse particular to the medieval Scandinavians. Poetry was an important part of Viking culture and the ability to write it a highly regarded skill.
sling – the center portion of the yard.
sœslumadr – official appointed by the king to administer royal holdings. Similar to the English shire reeve.
spar – generic term used for any of the masts or yards that are part of a ship's rig.

stem – the curved timber that forms the bow of the ship. On Viking ships the stem extended well above the upper edge of the ship and the figurehead was mounted there.
strake – one of the wooden planks that make up the hull of a ship. The construction technique, used by the Norsemen, in which one strake overlaps the one below it is called lapstrake construction.
swine array – a Viking battle formation consisting of a wedge-shaped arrangement of men used to attack a shield wall or other defensive position.
thing – a communal assembly.
Thor – Norse god of storms and wind, but also the protector of humans and the other gods. Thor's chosen weapon was a hammer. Hammer amulets were popular with Norsemen in the same way that crosses are popular with Christians.
thrall – Norse term for a slave. Origin of the English word enthrall.
thwart – a rower's seat in a boat. From the old Norse term meaning "across."
Ulfberht – a particular make of sword crafted in the Germanic countries and inscribed with the name Ulfberht or some variant. Though it is not clear who Ulfberht was, the swords that bore his name were of the highest quality and much prized.
unstep – to take down a mast. To put a mast in place is to step the mast.
Valhalla – a great hall in Asgard where slain warriors would go to feast, drink, and fight until the coming of Ragnarok.
Valkyries – female spirits of Norse mythology who gathered the spirits of the dead from the battlefield and escorted them to Valhalla. They were the Choosers of the Slain, and though later romantically portrayed as Odin's warrior handmaidens, they were originally viewed more demonically, as spirits who devoured the corpses of the dead.
vantnale – a wooden lever attached to the lower end of a shroud and used to make the shroud fast and to tension it.
varonn – springtime. Literally spring work in Old Norse.
Vik – an area of Norway south of modern-day Oslo. The name is possibly the origin of the term Viking.
wattle and daub – common medieval technique for building walls. Small sticks were woven through larger uprights to form the wattle, and the structure was plastered with mud or plaster, the daub.

weather – closest to the direction from which the wind is blowing, when used to indicate the position of something relative to the wind. Something "upwind" is considered "to weather".
wergild – the fine imposed for taking a man's life. The amount of the wergild was dependent on the victim's social standing.
yard – a long, tapered timber from which a sail was suspended. When a Viking ship was not under sail, the yard was turned lengthwise and lowered to near the deck with the sail lashed to it.

Acknowledgements

My thanks as ever, to the crew: Steve Cromwell for his excellent work on the cover, and Chris Boyle for the maps. Once again, bringing the production to another level. And thanks to Nathaniel Nelson and Stephanie Nelson for their adventures in copy editing.

Thanks to Felicity Fern Lockard and Victoria Rose Lockard for being so cute.

And, as always, thanks to my family, my bedrock: Elizabeth Lockard, Patrick Lockard, Nathaniel Nelson, Jonathan Nelson, Abigail Nelson, and Stephanie Nelson. And of course, my shipmate, my partner, my wife of thirty-two years, Lisa Nelson.

Fair winds and deep water to all.

Printed in Dunstable, United Kingdom

70440646R00251

Tales Round the
Cauld

Paddy S

CAPALL BANN PUBLISHING

www.capallbann.co.uk

Tales Round the Cauldron

ISBN 186163 0468

Cover design by Paul Mason

Published by:

Capall Bann Publishing
Auton Farm
Milverton
Somerset
TA4 1NE

Contents

Introduction and Acknowledgments

This is a series of short stories which I have written over several years. They are mostly about animals and encounters with the God and Goddess whom I have had to privilege to meet on quite a few occasions.

One or two, however, have been based on other experiences, little or nothing to do with magic except in the broadest sense.

I have been helped by two friends with the illustrations, because I cannot draw for toffee. The ones for the Fox and the Moon were done for me by Constance Clarke, when I first had the idea for the book. She lived near Oldham and died suddenly just before I sent her the rest of the stories.

I tried to find another illustrator but it was difficult to match the words to the pictures until my son suggested a friend of his, who did most of the rest. The rather simpler efforts were my own.

Memories

I danced around the stones when I was young
My joy so light that I could only sing.

The work my father's fathers had begun
Was now complete. The great stone ring.

I walked around the Stones when I was grey,
The Ring was set in time, the Earth was pure

The Moon rose darkly over darkly setting day,
The thought would last forever, we were sure.

I swirled around the Ring when I was gone.
Time had forgotten why the Ring was made.

The work my father's fathers had begun
Was meaningless and lifeless and afraid.

I danced about the Ring when I returned.
Once more the Stones were vibrant with the rhyme.

The work my father's fathers had begun
Was now at work, recaptured, out of time.

The Right of Poetry

There was once a very young man, who had so many wonderful attributes that one would have thought he would easily have reached his one, burning ambition. He wanted to be a bard. He studied composition and music, the sagas of his ancestors and all the botany and wildlife he could. He was a model student, everyone said so. His tutors sighed and wished that all young men would apply themselves a he did.

But, and there is always a but, he lacked the one ability to grace his chosen profession. he wished to be a bard, but he could not write poetry. This is an essential for bardship. His prose was beautiful and as a storyteller he kept his audience spellbound, from the lord on the high table to the warriors who even left the serving wenches alone and those at the bottom of the table who would normally have preferred bashing one another with quarter staff or mace.

He could draw such music from the harp that tears would fall down the cheeks and soak the beards of the strongest knight. He could play the pipes and the small birds would cease calling from the top-most boughs, the small animals would come out of their burrows and sit quietly beside foxes and badgers, even wolves and wild boar listened enchanted while the music lasted, then sportingly gave their prey time to get away, or as far as they could while the memory of the music lasted.

But the moment he tried to speak in verse, the hounds began to howl and the young at the bottom of the table began to throw bread, the warriors made the sort of rude noises warriors make best and mayhem ruled in the hall until he played his harp again.

He travelled the land, sitting at the feet of the great bards whose poetry soothed the savage breast, learning all he could, but his verse remained doggerel and not fit for the halls.

In despair he took the long ode to the hills and became lost in the mist, sad, cold and alone. he walked for days until even the birds deserted him, except the rooks who mocked from the bent over trees, seeming to screech "You'll never be a bard, you'll never be a bard".

And in depair he agreed with them.

He had wandered into an ancient forest, which tripped him with its roots and made him slip and fall over huge boulders. He slid down a long bank and saw a thin path climbing up the far side of a small valley. As he climbed, the air grew thin and the mist closed in again. Up and up, higher and higher until just at the tree line he came out onto a plateau. He could not see how far it stretched, he could make out no features; there just seemed to be nothing to shelter him from the thin keening wind. Wet, cold and muddy he fell exhausted to the ground.

He slept for many hours, dreaming muddled dreams, waking suddenly in fear and dreadfully uncomfortable in his wet robes on the damp ground, then falling asleep again.

Eventually he woke to find that night had come. A clear, starlit night, scented and warm. Above him the sky appeared to be revolving and he thought he was delirious. He did not know this word of course, he thought that he had been bewitched. The stars seemed to be coming closer until they looked like a spinning silver wheel. The moon was nearly at the full and shone down bright and clear to show him that it was indeed a sacred grove into which he had stumbled. There were stately oaks, interspersed with apple trees and rowan, all crisp and silver in the moonlight. These he knew were not ordinary apple trees, but those of legend, for they bore both blossom and fruit and the sacred herb mistletoe.

The young man looked about him enchanted, he now felt no discomfort from his sore legs and damp clothes. These had become warm and dry and his grazes had heale with no scars. Never had he felt safer, more rested or closer to a mystery, but what that mystery was, he did not yet know.

All the time the spinning circle of stars came closer and music such as he had never heard came with it. The music of birds singing, small children laughing, gentle waves breaking and a soft wind chiming in the frosted branches of the trees.

He noticed a great flat stone on the other side of the grove and upon it a large iron cauldron, steaming and smelling of herbs. The young man approached, but before he could reach the stone, the great silver circle came to rest, surrounding it. he stood transfixed as the figure of a woman appeared on the far side of the altar. Her hair was bound with stars and her robe was of softest silk. Her eyes shone kindly in the moon and starlight.

He did not know if he heard Her speak, but words in the most melodious voice imaginable spoke clearly into his mind.

"Drink, oh seeker, of the Cauldron of Inspiration. Your way has been long and hard, but this shall be your reward."

He took the bowl She offered him and drank deep, falling into an ecstacy as he did so. As he fell asleep he could hear the voice of the Lady.

"Those who seek shall find. And those who drink of the cauldron Awen shall be inspired."

The figure faded.

The great wheeling circle swung away back to the heavens, the moon set and as day broke the young man awoke. He had little in his pouch but spring water and a little bread, but he felt no hunger. He poured some water onto the stone as a libation, then took a sip, he took a bite of the dried bread and crumbled the rest for the small birds. The water tasted like the best wine he had ever drunk and the bread was delicious.

He had nothing to give in return for this blessing except the gift of his music. He began to play his harp and soon he began to sing and the poetry he sang was the most beautiful ever heard.

As he ran for joy down the hillside, he sang his songs at the farmsteads and his fame went before him. He did not return immediately to the halls of the mighty, but wandered over the land he had traversed in his searching, giving pleasure and solace to the poor and the destitute and the unloved.

Such talent cannot be hidden for long and his fame spread even into the halls. Soon he was the most revered bard in the whole land and he became a great teacher, never forgetting those who had listened to him first. His fame spread to other realms and bards came to gather the crumbs from his table of wonder.

Long after he died, his songs were sung and his poetry remembered, with love and honour and the willingness of those he taught to teach.

The Fox and the Moon

New Moon

It was a chilly late afternoon when the sound of scrabbling came from deep underground. The earth had not yet woken from its winter sleep and brambles were bare, only the sad stalks of some of last year's nettles lay round the half-hidden hole.

A thin crescent, now riding down to the southwesterly horizon, showed that this was the first day of the new moon.

The scrabbling came clearer, closer to the mouth of the earth and suddenly a small red head with a pointed snout popped out of the hole. A little reddish brown figure hopped neatly over the rim and shook itself. She was a tiny vixen cub, smaller than her brothers but far more adventurous. They were content to stay down in the cosy bed made by their mother, they did not wish to venture out into the chill evening.

The little cub shook the loose earth out of her coat, sat down to scratch and stood up, looking about her. This was all very new. She sniffed the air and coughed because of the chill, the touch of frost in the air. She walked round the earth, and squatted to make a mark then she look wonderingly around her. Why she knew that the faint mark was a path she did not know, but she jumped daintily down from the bank and trotted in a rather ungainly way along it. She was after all a very young cub and this was the first time she had ventured so far.

She followed the path, sniffing new smells and scenting as she went. A small woodmouse crept out of hiding and she

pounced, but having caught the creature she was not sure what to do with it and it slipped away. The path led to a gate. This worried her and she darted back the way she had come, but not far. Several times she approached the gate and finally crept slowly up to it, sniffing at the very strange scents rubbed on the wood.

Some were high up and she stood shakily on her hind legs to investigate those. She dropped down quickly, puzzled. None of these had been in the earth and her mother never smelled of them.

There were strange prints in the wet earth too. Large paw prints, deep round prints that did not smell like animal although there was a smell of animal about them. Then there were different ones, both large and small to us but huge to her, which had a very frightening and unpleasant smell. She wondered what kind of creature made them.

Then her gaze was caught by the silver light of the crescent moon and she sat staring. This was something very new and she sat for a long time watching as it sank down into the trees. She wondered if it would come back but it did not and she became cold and shivered, for the frost was taking hold of the wood now.

A cough, sharp and cross, made her look over shoulder and she could see the shape of her mother standing by the gate. Her mother was angry and yapped at her to come quickly, she was chivied back along the path and down into the earth. Her mother gave her a nip and made it very clear that she was not to do anything of the kind again. Not for a long time, Her brothers and sisters pushed her away. They did not want to feel their mother's anger, besides her fur was cold and she smelled bad. Soon though they settled down to sleep in the deep litter of dry leaves, rabbit fur and grasses.

Full Moon

It was mid-summer and the great full moon shone across the long meadow clearly showing the figure of the vixen as she trotted carelessly away from the wood. There was no need for stealth at this time of the year. The nights were warm, smelling of wild roses and meadowsweet, which mingled with the honeysuckle in the hedges.

The vixen was happy, her time was her own. Her cubs were well grown now and able to look after themselves. There was plenty to eat and nothing hunted her. Life was good.

She sat looking at the moon, remembering yesterday. A day of excitement and a little fear. She hadn't been really hungry, it was just that she had come across the hen house. Just out of curiosity she had walked round it and found a hole in the fence. The night was hot and the farmer had not closed everything up properly. His fault really, if he didn't take care of his stock who would.

The hens began to stir, fussing about inside the house. One of them clucked and the vixen froze. She stayed absolutely still for some time, well down wind of the silly creatures, for a time after they had settled. She was still only curious, so crept silently back to the roost. This time nothing stirred. She slipped into the house and was startled by the very odd smell, so investigated further. She was at the far end when something disturbed the hens and they set up the most abysmal din. They jumped down from their roost and flew about clucking and squawking. The vixen hated noise and tried to stop it. She did this by biting heads. The birds were in a panic and the vixen lashed about her, snapping and biting.

She became very frightened and grabbing one of the hens slid out of the house. Just in time. Lights came on in the farmers house and angry voices shouted. A large figure raced out of the door, yelling and she heard the sound of a gun. She had heard one before and it told her to get out of there as fast as she could. She slipped out of the wire and shot across the orchard hearing something pattering behind her. She didn't stop running until she reached the wood but she had kept hold of the hen. The cubs fed well the night.

She sat watching the moon until it went down behind the trees, which bordered the meadow. She remembered the taste of the hen but would not go back that night.

She stretched and yawned. She did not go back to the earth but slept under a bramble patch.

The Last Quarter

It had been a long chase. There were times when the vixen had waited for hounds to get her scent again and they kept losing it. It was one of those days. She stopped again, she was feeling tired but she had plenty of time, hounds were a long way behind her and she had time to rest. Not a good place to be though. The side of the hill was covered in small stones and she slipped several times.

She was clever, though, this vixen. They had tried to catch her all season and for several seasons before that. Her cubs had all dispersed and now were about to mate and find an earth of their own. She missed them sometimes, missed the warm, writhing bodies feeding and sleeping close to hers. Mostly, though, she didn't even remember them and if she had come across one she would have driven it away.

The evenings were drawing in, frost fell most nights but this kept the scent close to the ground, so even the stupidest hound got it eventually and most them were not stupid. There would be no moon this night, it had set while the pack was resting. The Last Quarter was always late.

She had been dreaming and the pack had not only got her scent strong but was closer than she thought. She found the going hard on the loose scree, but she was lighter than the hounds and reached the top of the hill with space to spare. She was tiring but just as she began to get really worried another larger dog fox shot across her trail and she found some damp marsh. They ran round each other to confuse the scent and she managed to leap over a large boulder and away down the hill. Hounds were confused, but the dogs scent was stronger. The whole pack took off in the opposite direction and the vixen laid up in briar patch.

The Dark Moon

The thinnest sliver of the old moon slid over the trees. The night was bitter. Heavy snow had fallen and a deep frost made it hard. Beneath the hedge a shadow lay, chilled and frozen and almost lifeless.

As the last trace of the old moon faded, the last trace of light left the old eyes. The oldest vixen left too, leaving her stiffened body stretched beneath the hedge she had first seen as a tiny cub.

All things are born and all things die. Nature does not sleep.

Images by Constance Clark

Fings Ain't What They Seem To Be

The small wayside caff was lit by low-powered naked light bulbs. Steam had condensed on the windows and ran down the panes in dismal drips. There were a dozen plastic-covered tables and some cheap chairs, their paint kicked and scuffed from the hard soled boots worn by the usual customers.

Eight of them were there that night, seven of them intent on a game of Dungeons and Dragons, which was now in its fourth week and down at a low level. The eight youth sat idly smoking, watching the game, and drinking from the thick white mug of surprisingly good coffee. His character had been killed off earlier in the evening, eaten by a Werebear.

A pale, thin girl behind the counter was not interested, except in the boys and over the weeks her interest in them had lessened in fear of their potential violence. They were a rough looking lot, grubby, unwashed with their hair hanging down in the dread locks favoured by their leader. He was big, dark and looked what he was, a very dangerous man, slightly older than the others but mostly very quiet. He didn't need to be loud. He was the Dungeon Master. Always. And no-one argued with him.

Outside in the forecourt there were eight powerful bikes, wet from the drizzle that had set in several hours ago. The drizzle had turned to heavy rain recently and a strong wind was blowing. The pale light from the windows barely showed the puddles and potholes and the short, fat person on the bright yellow scooter regarded the place dubiously but she had been riding for some hours and needed a cup of something hot and she was too old to be of interest to a bunch of Hell's Angels.

For a moment there was no reaction as she walked through the door but as she reached the counter a battery of hard eyes followed her progress. The pale girl looked more scared than ever, so the woman smiled at her and ordered coffee. She then turned and regarded the men coolly through her large glasses and took them off because the heat and steam had clouded them. The girl had not moved to serve her and seemed to be waiting for permission to do so.

"In the wrong place, ain't you Ma?" the leader of the Chapel asked. He was unprepared for the look of complete tranquillity or for the smile the woman gave him. She took her time answering him.

"Oh dear. Is it a private function? I do so need a drink. I've been on the road for hours. My poor little scooter is not really made for long, over-laden journeys." She laughed at the astonishment on the rough faces. They were as much astonished by her lack of fear as her clear, polished accent. "I do wish I could manage one of those monsters outside. I particularly like the B.M.W.

The girl behind the counter winced, expecting trouble and whispered, "I should leave Madam, before they get mad."

"Nonsense" the little woman replied. "I have two sons far scruffier and far bigger than them. Now let me have my coffee." Her voice though soft, was quite determined, and her look said that she was quite unused to being denied and carried over to the men at the tables, who looked down at their dice.

The girl filled a mug saying shyly "I'm afraid we don't have any cups. They break them, you see."

"Don't they just," replied the woman and wondered over to stand behind the D.M. "Now this looks interesting. I"ve

CAFE

been playing at the convention this week-end, but my character fell foul of a bugbear. Do you mind if I watch?"

The men looked up, the hardness gone from their eyes and something like shock replacing it. People were scared of the Angels and that was how they liked it. To have a middle-aged woman, not only treating them like harmless little boys but apparently not prepared to run away was something they hadn't experienced for a long time.

The leader, who had been a serving soldier, hardened in battle recognised her type and shrugged. He gave an evil grin but she didn't bat an eyelid. "Yeah, come and sit by me, Ma. Move up Sid." The thin lad thus addressed moved round the table. She sat down. "Do go on, I"m interested. Which rules do you play by?" Then she laughed, "Don't tell me. Yours."

With a quite genuine laugh, the big man replied that "Yeah. Most of the rules are mine, but we're working to some new American ideas. Which ones do you play?"

"Oh. our group is old by D&D standards. My son has been playing for years and I never could decide whether it was his character or himself talking, so I started to play too. I love it. It is a fairly harmless way to get rid of aggression. We have been told about those new rules this week-end." She did not appear to notice the looks that passed between the players. But, of course, she did. She was a very observant lady and knew exactly what she was doing. Although, at that time there was nothing to warn them that she was far more dangerous than they could ever hope to be.

The leader leaned back in his chair and looking at her sideways asked "Wanna play? Sid's playing three characters, ain't yer Sid? You won't mind the lady having one." Sid, the boy who had moved for her sneered "I've got a fourth level Barbarian. Could you play him."

"Probably", she replied. "What are the other characters and what is the dungeon.?"

The leader introduced himself and then the others round the table, giving their names or approximations and the characters they played. Then he gave a run down of the experiences to date and they began to play again.

They soon discovered that she played the barbarian with ferocity, taking risks and having the sort of luck her character needed.

Somehow, after hours had gone by, most of the characters had been disposed of, none of these, seemingly her fault. She had rescued each of them from danger several times and it was purely accidental when they died. The men were wilting but the woman looked as fresh as ever. The girl behind the counter had curled up in an old chair and was fast asleep. Then only the woman herself was left, and the dungeon Master said, "Well that's that." You had some luck. You played that like a professional."

"I suppose you could say that. I think I'll toddle off now though. Long way to go still. Thank you for a very good game. Perhaps we can do it again some time." She shrugged into her coat, picked up her helmet and left.

When she was well clear of the caff, the boy who had been watching slipped out and followed her tail light, not too close but close enough to see where she was going. The men waited for him, discussing the game and her incredible luck. One of them poured out some more coffee for them all. This was strange, because usually they would have slapped the girl awake.

The woman picked up the dimmed lights of the bike following her straight away. she made no move to hurry, there was no way that the scooter could outrun the monster he was riding. She grinned to herself. It is not actually easy to ride a heavy motor bike slowly, they are built to travel fast.

They went nearly twenty miles and came to an isolated village. The boy expected her to stop here, but she went through it and when first light came she stopped far out along a lane at a little, twisted cottage. None of it's windows were quite straight. Little dormers stuck out at peculiar angles. The walls seemed curved, giving the impression of it being round. It had been built from great oaken beams, with a cruck at each end, filled with lathe and plaster. A black and white house with two very lovely, twisted chimneys, also looking curved and it stood in a garden filled with herbs and flowers with vegetables all growing higgledy-piggledy, not in nice straight rows.

The young man turned his bike some way from the cottage and rode fast back to the caff.

Large pink roses grew round the door and there were hollyhocks on each side of the downstairs windows. If you looked carefully at the lawn you might just imagine the shape of a woman. The herbs grew in a very careful pattern, although you would need to know a lot about them to discover what the pattern was.

There were apple trees and holly, quince and hawthorn, elder and damson, a medlar and in the hedge oaks and ash. Big blue delphinium stood in front of the hedge and you could see almost every old cottage flower you could name.

The path leading round the cottage was of old, ruby brick, much worn but quite safe and at the side of the house several sheds, one of which housed a shining red Mini Cooper S and had room for the yellow scooter, which showed no sign of the long journey it had just finished. The woman went in, made

herself comfortable and went to bed and to sleep.

She woke refreshed not too early, and went about her usual tasks. The doors and windows were open and you could see a long black, oak table, some chairs and a great dresser, upon which were lots of shining blue and white crockery and an amazing collection of jugs.

Go further in and you would see a great inglenook fireplace with logs and coal set ready for the evening. Two doors opened from this room, one led into a tidy living room, much used but kept bright and clean for visitors with cosy chairs, a piano, many instruments to make music and lots of books. This room opened on to another, not so tidy. Probably the most untidy room you have ever seen, but it too smelled of lavender and polish. More books lined two walls and one other had shelves of jars, full of dried herbs and flower petals, all labelled in Latin. The whole house was full of flowers but the ones in this room were wild. Half completed drawings littered the room and books with small tabs of paper marking places.

Another door led to the kitchen which was far bigger than the outside of the cottage would have led one to suppose. A scrubbed table in the middle and herbs hanging from the beams, very much a country kitchen but the owner had most of the appliances a modern housewife would need. A little glass porch leading from the back door, where there were green wellies, riding boots, assorted macks, Barbers and anoraks.

The door stood open, at least the top half did, for it was a stable door. A large marmalade cat lay sunning himself on a blue cushion on top of the washing machine and excited yelps came from the garden.

On a much bigger lawn surrounded by another thick hedge, lay a washing basket. Some of the washing had already been pegged out and a stout, middle-aged woman was playing tug-a-war with a large German Shepherd for possession of a pair of faded jeans. The dog suddenly let go and the woman sat down with a bump, laughingly threatening the dog with dire consequences. She scrambled up and whistling quite tunefully, finished hanging out the rest of the washing which flapped happily on a line stretched between two apple trees. The dog went off to investigate the compost heap.

She watered the plants in the greenhouse and then went into the kitchen to prepare food for some guests she expected later that evening. She made soup in a large black iron pot, which she put on the red Aga and prepared a very hearty steak and kidney pie, and scrubbed nine large potatoes ready for baking. She thought about puddings but decided her guests would prefer cheese.

She then went into the room with the large black table and made certain preparations not usually made for guests. Who, at this time of day, did not even know that they would be taking the road one of their number had navigated the previous evening. Most of them were still asleep, though one or two had good jobs.

As evening drew nigh, the woman fed her cats took the German Shepherd out for a good run and fed him. She put all her preparations ready but on hold, set out paper, character sheets, dice and pencils, and lastly switched on a large percolator and collected mugs and plates and made sure that the food was ready. Then she bathed, changed into a green dress rather longer than she normally wore, thought about jewellry but decided that she should not lay temptation in anyone's path, put some Mozart on the record player and sat down with a good book to wait.

The Chapter had not intended to meet that evening, but for some reason they congregated in a caff in town, each of them faintly astonished to see the others come in or sitting at a table. "Didn't expect to see you 'ere," was the phrase most often used. "I know. Just thought I'd come in for a coffee. Can't think why. Usually have something else to do on Monday."

The Big Feller stomped in. "Tried to phone you lot, but you were all out," he yelled across the room. "As we're all 'ere, let's go for a ride."
They finished their drinks and slouched out. "Where will we go then?"

"Dunno. Just where the road takes us." So they all mounted up and roared away, much to the relief of several more staid citizens who regarded the Angels as anything but.

I will make a comment here. I once had a small accident on my motor bike. I kicked it into first gear instead of neutral at a junction, ending up sideways on the road and going round in circles until someone shouted "Turn the b.......y thing off. Which I did. I lay there bemused for some time. Several motorists shot passed me, no one tried to help. I couldn't lift the bike. Then three large and scruffy bikers came along, yelled "Gawd 'elp us." and came to my rescue. "Hurt yeerself, Ma?" they asked in real concern, when I'd taken my helmet off. They got me and the bike to the side of the road, made sure I was in one piece and tried hard to get the machine going, but it was no go.

They then decided that one of them would tow me home, a dicey business, but with remarkable balance and patience one of them did this, while the other two rode behind to prevent a car cutting me up. When we got home, rather a long way away, they insisted that I made sure all was well. Mostly I was but I had a deep gauge in my leg, which had bled quite a lot. They took me to the nearest hospital and waited six hours until I was seen to. Then they took me home, made tea and sandwiches, lit my fire even took my dog for a walk and went on their way. I"ve had a soft spot for bikers ever since.

So back to the story.

The group swished along main roads and country lanes until they came to a cottage outside a village where they called a halt. The navigator of the previous evening called to the Big Feller that this was the place the strange old bird had stopped at. "Let's pay the old girl a visit." "She'll be scared when she sees us lot," someone guffawed. They all got off their bikes and parked them at the side of the road, a nuisance to other travellers because the lane was narrow.

One or two of them wondered if there would be anything to pinch and they stood looking at the cottage for some minutes.

They were surprised when the door opened and the woman said calmly "Do come in, all of you. I"ve been expecting you." They hesitated at this. People did not usually invite a chapter of Hell's Angels into their homes. The Big Feller shrugged, and stumped into the living room, followed by the others, some looking about them speculatively, nudging each other and nodding at some rather nice silver scattered round the room.

"I expect you'd like a drink before we begin," the woman stated calmly, 'I've made some supper for later." They had not really noticed that all was prepared for a Dungeon and looked a bit dubious.

In no time at all, they had been given cups of coffee. "I would offer you beer, but perhaps you'll need clear brains for the game I have in mind. Do sit down." She indicated the seats drawn up to the table. "Make yourselves comfortable. I should take off your jackets, it is quite warm. You won't mind, I"m sure if I D.M. the game, will you." Such was her self confidence that they all agreed although only the Big Feller had done this before.

"Would you like to roll up new characters? Most of you were killed off last night." They began to roll the dice and make up character sheets. This usually takes rather a long time but in a surprisingly short time they were ready to play. The woman described the dungeon they would be exploring, at quite a deep level , but as she explained, they were all experienced players and each would look after the other. The game began.

From the beginning they realised that they were being led by a mistress of the game into realms unknown to most of them, but no-one wanted to admit being out of his depth. After three hours, when many of them had been badly mauled by some fearsome monsters, but miraculously cured by moss on the damp walls or by coloured lights coming from the roofs of passages, or even potions found in rooms, they broke for supper.

They were mostly big men and found that their appetites were hearty. Asked if they had already eaten, they wracked their brains but could not remember, though they all claimed to be ravenous. The soup, pie and baked potatoes, served with lots of butter, and most of the cheese and biscuits were wolfed down.

They even made inroads into a bowl of apples. The woman served them tea, coffee and beer and joined in the food and chat. It seemed to be altogether a very convivial gathering.

At last, having accepted offers to help with the washing up, the kitchen had been restored to it's usual pleasant tidiness, they returned, most relaxed to their game.

They were down at a level none of them had entered before. The monsters were tricky and dangerous. Two of their number were tricked by gnomes and disappeared. One went into an empty room without looking for hidden traps and went through the floor. In another room, a seemingly pleasant chamber contained a vast monkey-like thing called a Su monster with six legs and a voracious appetite, three more fell victim to this horror.

There were three of them left and they were becoming very wary indeed. Their mates had actually disappeared: it was not just a matter of the character being written off. The had not noticed how dark and cold the pleasant living room had become. They had not noticed that the woman was no longer with them.

They looked round and found that they were in a cold grey stoned corridor, dressed as their own characters. They panicked and began to run, but however many pitfalls they encountered, and however many corners they turned, they always came back to the same place. A door, that for some reason they did not wish to open. Eventually, exhausted, they tried the door. It was not locked. The Big Feller opened it slowly and looked in.

"Where's that old witch leading us to?" he asked. "It looks alright. Try for hidden traps." There were none. The room was bare and trapless, but there was a door on the wall to their left. "Just a minute. Look at the floor. A series of blue flag stones led, not to the door but to the opposite wall upon which was a large mirror.

They KNEW that this had not been there before, and the blue flagstones had appeared suddenly. "Do you think we're meant to cross by them" one of them asked. "Na. I"m going for the door. Carefully." But when he tried, it gave way, just wasn't there any more. "I really don't like this," said the navigator and he tried to go to the right. The floor rumbled and quaked and he jumped back. "We'll have to cross the blue stones. Perhaps that mirror will show us the way out."

Very carefully, one following the other they crossed the room, which seemed to be much wider than they expected. At the other side, the blue stones widened to form a sort of platform, and when they looked back the floor was fading away. They turned to look in the mirror.

Coming towards them from a long way away, they saw the woman, now very richly dressed. She came right up to the mirror and smiled a not very pleasant smile. "You had me followed last evening. You had abused the young girl behind the counter. You are a violent and thoroughly unpleasant bunch and you came here, some of you intending to rob me as you have robbed others. You are on your own. Find your own way out and learn the lessons set you. Goodbye." She was gone and so was the mirror.

No-one remembered seeing the bikes.

The Gift of Fire

For more years that we can possibly count, the man kind was without fire. He did not know this, of course, because he had never had it. His cave was cold in the winter, his food was cold all year round, but that possibly did not matter, because he had never known the comfort of hot meals and you don't miss what you have never had.

He wore very little because he had not equated the fur of the meatless carcasses he found with covering for himself. He was not altogether stupid but his mind was not quick. His clothes, such as they were, were made from leaves, which was fine in summer, but they shrivelled in the winter. The women had not yet learned to weave, but as soon as they did they began to make bigger and better looms, giving themselves the wherewithal to cover their modesty, a concept they probably would not have understood. But the cloth kept them warmer anyway and prevented sunburn.

I suppose that women have always had a liking for furs and certainly;y they began to like being warm so they searched about to find scraps left by the large predators. These possibly still had scraps of meat left on them and the women soon decided that they really could not put up with the smell of rotting steak.

They stretched the skins out to dry, hoping that the sun would so shrivel the remains, that the smell would go away. And perhaps it did, but it shrivelled the skin also, making it terribly uncomfortable to wear. They did notice though, that left in a shady place they had a little, noisy helper. Flies flocked to the skins, laying eggs and the maggots ate the scraps of meet, so that the skin, or hide, or fleece, as it may be, looked much better and naturally smelled better too.

Now, while all this was going on, man had learned to hunt. He stalked his prey, trying to use the skills he had watched larger and better animals use but he was too slow and too weak to kill anything larger than a squirrel. He picked up stones and after a lot of trial and error, learned to throw them accurately, but never quite hard enough to really hurt an animal. Sticks were pretty useless, because to use a stick, you need to be close to something. So he learned to throw the stick, but being old, dry wood it broke on the animals tough hide. One chap, either in a moment of dizzying idleness or perhaps with intent found a stone with a sharp edge. He had also learned to knap flint by this time. He sat chipping at the end of the stick and produced a point, which made him yell when he dug it into his foot.

He threw it away and to his surprise it stuck into a sapling or a friend, whatever. He strolled away into the savannah by himself to try out his invention on something that moved. He kept losing the sharpened sticks at first because the animals he hit turned and charged him. But one day, to his own astonishment as well as the khudu he had aimed at, the khudu was killed. He let out such a shout of delight that all the other men rushed to see what had happened. He pulled the sharpened stick out of the dead khudu and boasted a lot, pounding his chest in the way of his kind and making "What a splendid fellow I am" noises, which annoyed the others, who relieving him of the stick, proceeded to beat him with it.

But it was a good idea and so they all set about finding nice sharp pieces of flint with which to sharpen the ends of sticks. There was a drawback. Old wood breaks too easily and newly cut wood will fray at the point. Something was needed to harden the points.

It had been a dry summer and a sudden flash of lightning set the grass of the savannah alight. Everything ran for their lives, khudu, gazelle, giraffe and gnu, not to mention lions and hyena and of course those brave hunters the man kind.

There was even a bonus to this catastrophe. When the heat had died down there were a lot of sticks with nice, pointed ends lying about and those nice, pointed ends were sharp. There were also some pieces of cooked meat lying about, which the big cats and wild dogs would not touch. The man kind did though. Some of the meat was much too charred and eating it made them sick. They had to visit the wise woman to be doctored with herbs and she suggested that they should only eat the partly roasted meat.

They did not, at this point, think that fire was really useful. It had killed a lot of game, it had driven them from their homes and had taken the lives of those too slow to run away. But, it had given them nice, pointy spears, so when the herds came back they could kill supper more easily.

Some time went by, and the man kind had nearly forgotten the grass fire. His wife, however, had not. She kept on about how much nicer cooked meat was than the raw kind. The dangerous red flash didn't do the skins much good, and everything had smelled of smoke for YEARS, but the meat was nicer.

She talked about this so often and at such length that the man became annoyed. He stomped away from the cave or the shelter and sat down mumbling to himself. "It's all very well" he thought "sending stuff that will make the women unsettled. But who had to listen to them. Eh." He had no idea who these words were addressed to, but SOMEONE was listening.

High up in the sky, upon a great white cloud, lived some other beings, who liked to call themselves Titans. This was before the Gods. Thee was a Titan of the Sky and one of the Earth.

There were Titans of Wind, Rain, the Sea, Earthquakes, and Thunder, not to mention Lightning. They all had names but the one that concerns us most was called Hyperion. He as concerned with Fire and Lightning and at this moment he was leaning over the edge of the cloud, idly scanning the Earth below, when he picked up this stray thought.

"That's odd" said Hyperion. "There's a man kind down there and he is almost thinking"

"Nonsense" said the Sky Titan, whose name was Uranus, "They can't. Not that sort at all."

"Well, come over here and listen" said Hyperion.

Uranus shrugged his shoulders and came over to the edge. He leaned over and looked down to where Hyperion was pointing. The very scruffy specimen of man kind was still mumbling. "Yes, it's not fair. Some idiot throws a flaming spear, sets the grass on fire, makes everything run away and the women moan because he doesn't do it all the time." He paused, thinking was hard work. "If people want to chuck flaming spears about, that's fine. But why can't they be little ones with only a bit of fire, then we could catch the stuff, put it somewhere safe, and we could sharpen our spears in comfort." He went home and told his wife this happy thought.

"It's an idea" said Hyperion. "I wonder what he'd do with it."

"Destroy the planet, I should think," grunted Uranus, and wandered over the cloud to a specially soft puffy bit and went to sleep.

The Titan of the Earth, who was called Gaea had joined them by this time.

"What would he do with it," she snapped sharply. "I can tell you that. He'd kill everything in sight and make the most dreadful mess of my planet. If you must do something so very dangerous, give it to the woman. She will use it for useful things, like cooking, and making pots and warming milk for the child, not to mention the cave they live in. But," she said sternly, "You would do well not to even think about giving them fire." and she went away to tell the other Titans of this stupid idea of Hyperion's.

They all turned on him and said "Absolutely No. Don't even think about it." But they were too late. Hyperion had already sent a very small bolt of lightning, which landed close to the man kind's foot.

"Oh, that's nice, that is" he shouted, shaking his fist at the cloud. "First , you bake everything in sight, and then you try to burn my foot. Thank you very much."

Hyperion turned away in disgust. What an ungrateful beast! If he'd given that to a lion or an elephant, he would have been thanked, but this awful creature, a newcomer in the scheme of things, shook his fist.

The man kind, however, looked at the little fire the lightning bolt had made and looked round for something to carry it home in. There was nothing, so he brought everyone to the fire. Everyone was delighted, and began to think of things to do with fire. The women came up with cooking and warming the cave, from which they had just been moved, making pots that would really hold water, cooking the meat, which reminded them that the men were simply standing around. They suggested that men should not waste time during the day, but should find themselves useful employment, like proper hunting, so that the women could cook the meat.

There was a fair division of labour in those days, the men caught the meat and the women cooked it. It would take too long to list all the useful things they came up with.

The man kind went away, with newly sharpened spears and hunted; and grumbled to their fellows that women always took over, didn't they. was it on account of the babies?

So men thought and thought, and learned how to make metal, and from the metal they made points for their spears, which stayed sharp; they tipped their arrows with metal and made swords. Later on, when they had developed a bit more, they made guns and bullets, cannon and howitzers, boats and planes and tanks, great drills to make holes in the earth, and sea bed, and cars to pollute the atmosphere.

The Titans were so furious with Hyperion, what with smog and acid rain and the awful noise, especially Gaea, who said that the drills tickled her so much she couldn't sleep, that they sent him away to a rocky place lashed by the sea, where they chained him to a rock and ordered a great eagle to eat his liver every day.

Now some people will tell you that it was Prometheus who caused all this noise and kerfuffle, but he was of the second wave of Titans. But do you know, no-one ever thanked Hyperion.

Branston and the Magistrate

The cold winter had turned into a mild spring and the blossom was just beginning to show on the hedges. The little river was no longer in spate and the rocks could now be seen beneath the bridge where the Old 'Un lived. He was a very large trout and many fishermen had tried to catch him, but the Old 'Un was up to all the tricks.

There were two cottages at the point where the lane turned to cross the bridge. In one of which lived an elderly woman and her large dog. An animal very much of the Heinzes beanses variety. Any guess at parentage was met with scepticism by his owner, who would only say "Maybe" or "Perhaps" or even "Do you think so. Can't see it myself."

The villagers knew that every day the woman and her dog would climb the hill to the small village shop, which did double service as the Post Office, and she would buy such things as she needed and a large tin if the very best dog food for the being she called Branston, because, she said, he was such a pickle.

One day, however, the weather reverted to winter. Overnight a quite heavy fall of snow had made the lane slippery and Branston came to the shop himself, walked in and took a tin of his usual in his large jaws and set off down the hill to the cottage. This caused surprise but for the moment no one

thought too much, but when it happened the next day, one villager after another went to the cottage, to find that the old woman had a very bad cold. The doctor had called and had forbidden her to go out but she paid for the dog's food and all

was well. The village was small and as is the way of small villages, the population looked after it's own. The old woman received gifts of pies and soup, cakes and scones and the owner of the shop made sure her cupboard was never bare.

But even village shops change hands. The new owner changed the shelves round to make it a serve-yourself emporium but hadn't been warned about Branston. On the first morning of his tenure, he was doing something in the room at the back, the shop being empty at the time, so he did not see this very large dog walk in, walk round inspecting the shelves, pick up a tin of the best dog food and leave.

This happened several days running and always when there were no other customers in the shop. The owner began to notice that his stock of a certain dog food was less that it should be and he began to keep a watch but for some reason never caught the culprit.

One morning, however, it was probably pension day, there were several people in the shop. Branston was greeted with friendly pats and asked how his mistress was. He grinned at his well wishers, showing a lovely set of very large, white teeth. He picked up his tin and turned towards the door. The shopkeeper started round the counter, yelling "You thief, now I've got you" Branston put down his tin and showed his teeth once again, growling softly.

He was quite unused to having strange men yell at him. The shopkeeper rather wisely retired behind the counter and Branston picked up his tin and left the shop, much to the amusement of the pensioners gathered there.

"That dog's a thief" shouted the irate man. They all laughed louder and one old one said. "Not he. He always has come for his dinner, but the old lady can't come at the moment, she's not well."

Another said that she would come for her pension as soon as she could and would pay what she owed, but this did not soften the man. "I'll have the law on her then" he snapped. Everyone began talking at once, saying that"This wasn't fair" and "The dog didn't mean no 'arm." "The old lady was as honest as the day was long and that people should understand."

However, the shopkeeper knew his rights. He filed a lawsuit against the old woman who was very upset. He also lost a lot of trade, especially the pensions. They found it more convenient to catch the bus to the nearest small town to do some shopping, which they also found to be much cheaper than the village shop had become.

In the fullness of time, the lady got over her chill, the weather went back to being Spring, and she walked up the hill, greeted kindly by the villagers who all stopped to ask how she was and to pat Branston's head. She walked into the shop, but Branston would not budge over the doorstep. The shopkeeper said in a very nasty voice that he did not want her money, but that he would see her in court.

Well. The dreaded day came. The lady was driven to the small market town by a kind neighbour. She sat, with her friend with the shoplifters, petty thieves and those who were accused of speeding. Eventually her case was called.

She went into the court. She had been asked to bring Branston with her and he behaved like the gentleman he was. The case was read out and the magistrate listened carefully. The shopkeeper blustered and fussed, making much of the fact that the old lady had come to pay him, only when the court summons had been sent to her.

She was questioned. Her doctor told the court how ill she had been. Various people wanted to speak on her behalf. The

magistrate listened to everyone with the courtesy of his kind and said that he thought that the bill should be paid. The lady offered to pay there and then but the magistrate told her to pay at the desk. He did not mention charges but he put on a very stern face and said he wished the criminal to approach the bench.

The lady picked up Branston's lead and led him forward. She wondered if an order would be made to put the dog down and she was very worried. She knew, of course, that one day this would be necessary and dreaded that day coming. He was her friend and companion and, everyone in the village said that he was the kindest dog they knew.

The magistrate stood up and looked at the big dog for a while, seeing the honesty in the broad face. He leaned forward, took the big jaw in his hand and in his sternest voice said "Branston. You are a very bad dog. Case dismissed".

Pathworking

Daffodils

Get up from your chair and go to the door in the wall which appears in front of you. It is locked but you know where the key is, for it is your own key. No-one else knows about it. This door will take you to the place you wish to go.

When you have found the key, unlock the door and go through, always remembering to close it behind you and always have a good look at the other side. You may need to find this particular door among many others and it as well to be able to recognise it.

Turn round and see a flight of stairs going down. There are ten of them with a half landing half way down. They are slightly worn for they have been used many times in your journeys, there is a substantial handrail at your left hand.

Begin to go down and at the half landing pause. Then carry on to the bottom.

You are in a dimly lit passage, which has doors on each side. ignore these. you do not need them at this time and you have already opened some of them. The passage is not long but the stones are uneven and the walls are rough, so take care.

A few yards further on there is an archway. Go through it and you are in a much narrower passage which smells of earth and damp. The light is very poor. Step carefully. A little further.

Suddenly blackness and nothing. Be still.

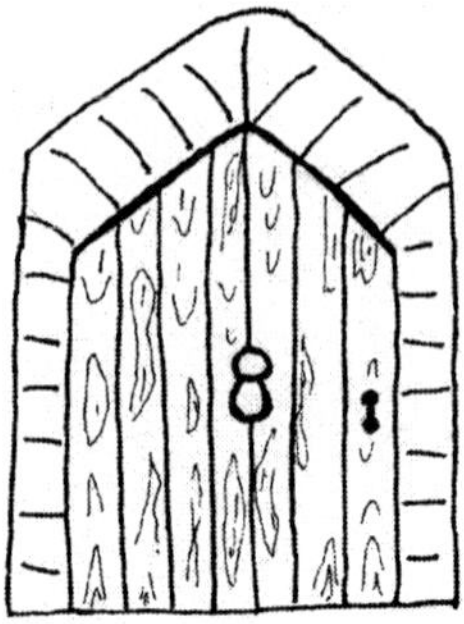

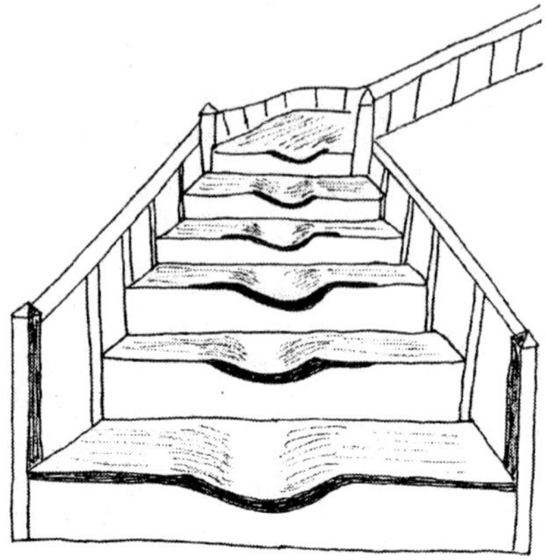

Darkness. cold. A feeling of not being. Time has no meaning.

A tingling. A feeling of being enclosed in earth. No light. No sound.

The tingling grows. You become aware of hunger and a part of you reaches down for food. Water.

Something is growing out of you, searching for and finding the food and drink you crave.

As this nourishment is drawn up into yourself, you become aware of another need and another part of you begins to push up through the darkness. as you go up it becomes not quite so cold. not quite so dark.

Then, quite suddenly, chaos hits you. Noise. Light and fierce cold. All around you is white. You try to struggle down into the dark once more. But this would be against nature. You must grow.

Your roots dig deeper. They are your anchor. They stabilise you against the wind and they keep feeding you.

You grow taller, bowing to the white snow in the bitter cold wind. The small part that is you begins to separate. You develop leaves and you keep growing. The light and the wind change constantly. Sometimes it is very bright, sometimes dark, yet not so dark as it was before you were aware.

The snow melts, taking it's icy cold water down into the earth and the world around you becomes green and brown. Some days the sun shines warm on your leaves and you have a feeling of well being, but on other days the rain beats down and you must bow your head. It is cold and wet and makes you shiver.

Then one glorious day when the sun is warm and there is no wind your bud bursts and you become. But what are you? You have heard many strange sounds as you grew. Now you can recognise some of the creatures around you. You recognise them because this is not the first time you have budded.

Not all the creatures who move about in the garden are careful. Sometimes you feel a sadness because those you recognised as brethren are broken. Some knocked over by fury beings who move about quickly with no thought of the damage they do.

Some are dug up by other creatures and others are broken off by another thing.

You hear a voice. "I must take some of these lovely daffodils. They brighten up the room. What a lovely colour yellow is. Spring is here at last.

Is that what you are? A daffodil ?

You feel an immense pride. You are tall and beautiful. Your flower is the bright yellow the voice admired. You even welcome the great buzzing thing who invades your trumpet. it frightened you at first but now it merely tickles. You know that without it's help you could not be fertile.

Some days the warm sun fails and heavy rain thunders down round you and you are splashed with wet soil. You almost wish you could hide but you must be brave. Daffodils do not hide from the rain.

You see your kind picked. They are worried about their future but this is something that happens. You can not know that they are taken away and put into a container of water in a warm room, out of their natural environment. You do not hear the voice which says 'don't mix daffodils with other flowers.

they poison the water."
This is something you do not know. You would be sad to think that such badness is thought of you and you do not know that Those flowers die in a short time and are thrown away, or that they will probably grow again in a few years.

You do not suffer this fate but one day you feel that your strength is leaving you. Your leaves no longer stand proud and your lovely yellow head no longer attracts the bee.

Gradually, the strength leaves you and you begin to draw back into yourself. The journey back is longer than the one coming out. You can feel yourself going back into the earth which is now quite warm. Your leaves and flower left behind to wither as spring draws into summer.

One day, the gardener will dig up your bulb, tie the withered leaves into a knot and you will be left with others of your kind in a dim shed until you are planted out into the garden in the autumn.

You are back in the bulb, thinking quietly of your moment of glory and then, like a light switched off -- NOTHING. UNAWARE.

You come out of the bulb and find yourself in the earthy, damp passage and before you is the archway you remember.

Retrace your steps along the earthy passage and through the arch into the dimly lit stone passage. pass all the doors and there is the flight of steps which you ascend, slowly, for you have been still for some time.

A door you recognise is in front of you. Unlock it and go through. lock it an put the key into it's safe place until you need it again. Go to your chair and sit and when you are ready--return and remember.

The Guide

There is a river, as sacred in its way as the Indus or the Ganges, which runs through the quiet water meadows of Wiltshire. It has a very ancient name - but because of the awe-inspiring respectability of a previous generation, the name is now a modern one.

It used to be lovely, gentle and clear. One could see trout, for it is a chalk stream; as well as minnows, frogs and all the other aquatic life once seen in any English river. Once upon a time, no self-respecting town was ever built without it's own supply of water. But changing values have allowed a huge town to be built and greed has allowed the lovely springs which fed the river to be drained and now it is just a series of muddy ponds connected by a thin trickle of rather dirty water. The wildlife has mostly gone.

At the time of this story however, it was still in a state of grace that seemed to touch all who ventured into the deeper shade of the water meadows.

A woman with a large dog was one such. She left her car and walked far along banks bordered by tall, waving willows and alder, meadowsweet and willowherb until she came to what looked like an old mill leet, chuckling along over round stones to enter the river presently. Sometime. No matter. No mill existed now. Indeed it is difficult to see how there could ever have been one. The countryside was flat for miles around but the ancient leet, built up on either side by old brick and knees of alder, led the way into the meadows.

It was a late afternoon in spring. The sun had warmed the lovely green of the water meadows for many hours and the earth and the water smelled of goodness and well being.
She stopped and looked longingly at the tiny animal path

running by the side of the leet. How long would it take to get there, wherever the path led?

The dog spotted it first but made no sound. She simply sat on her haunches and pointed. The woman looked. How had she come to miss that?

Sitting quite still on the other side of the little walled stream was a kingfisher. He made no effort to fly away. Just sat and looked, first at the dog and then at the woman. "Good evening, Halcyon." She said. "I apologise for disturbing you. My bitch, as you see, has better sight than I have."

The kingfisher seemed to accept the name and replied "You have been long in coming. Follow me."

He flew several yards along the leet and perched on the wall again, waiting. Waiting until the pair had picked their way carefully along the tiny path. "Too small for a badger; not smelly enough for a fox nor yet dotted with rabbit droppings. Could it have been the run of a weasel or perhaps a stoat?"

"You'll see" came a voice. Was it a bird? Or could it have been the wind?

The beautiful bird, surely the most colourful in all of old England led them on, stopping every dozen or so yards and waiting for them to catch up. The bitch had caught the feeling now, she trotted sedately just a few feet in front of her mistress, but silently. No sound was needed here.

Both the leet and the little path led deeper into the meadows. All was still.

There was only the sound of the water and the shush of the breeze in the alder and willows. Now no longer the tall weeping variety of the river bank, but the smaller stubby

sallow, decorated with the downy heads that children call pussy willow.

Occasionally, the woman could hear the sound of a bird. Marsh tits? Willow warblers? She could not see. Her boots made only soft sounds on the path.

Deeper and deeper yet. She could see in the marshy land surrounding them more trees, goat willow and delicate birch and some stands of splendid yellow flags. The sun was loosing its warmth and quite suddenly she realised that the wall enclosing the leet was no longer there, there was just a small stream with banks edged by water mint and kingcups and, just ahead, she could see where it came from.

A small lake or perhaps a large pond. Edged by osiers; in the centre of which, bubbling up, the pure water of springs, making their own sound, unique to themselves.

The kingfisher sat on a low branch, overhanging the pond and bowed to the swan, which sailed towards a little island where his wife was sitting on a nest of eggs. He hissed a warning at the dog, who lay with her nose on her paws, but the kingfisher flew over his head and uttered a sound, which few people have ever heard on mortal earth.

The swan changed direction and swam towards them, looked, then lowered his splendid head and glided back to the nest.

The beauty of the setting and of the evening caught at the woman's heart. The setting sun bathed her hair deep red and she knew that she had been to this place many, many times. The Lady of Springs and Streams came here and sometimes gave a blessing to those who had done Her bidding in a proper manner. And who had kept faith.

The guide waited. All was still.

On the island, close to the pens nest, a figure dressed in blue, appeared out of the evening light. "Welcome, my child. I see my guide found you and that you remembered the password into my realm." To the kingfisher She said "You did well, my Halcyon."

The bird bowed his bright head, looked for permission and swooped down to catch a small fish as his reward.

"How has your life been, this Earth year." Her voice as pure, like a bell underwater.

"Well, I thank you, my Lady. I have worked as you told me and have brought the results with me." The woman took from her pocket a small bundle. This she set down on an alder leaf which flowed to the island. The cob picked it up in his beak and placed it gently on the bank. The Lady of Springs and Streams held out her hand, and the small bundle opened itself. Dreams, ideas, accomplishments and music, drifted up for the Lady to examine.

"Just so and well done. Now, do you have anything to ask of me?"

"Only this, Lady. My bitch is old. I ask that you help her going. May it be peaceful and painless when it comes." The woman's eyes were full of tears. The bitch had been her companion on many an excursion into the Otherworld.

"Let her drink of the Waters of Life at her feet. Her time will come soon but I will be there to take her home." The woman watched her old dog stand up and go to the water. Her eyes were bright and her tongue lapped the sweet water from the sacred spring. She looked up with love to the blue-draped figure standing much closer now. The Lady bent and stroked the old bitch's head and the woman's tears flowed. "Thank you. My blessings to you Lady."

When her eyes had cleared, the Lady, the swans and the island had gone. Only the kingfisher remained to guide them back to the river. "Farewell, my friend and my old friend. We will meet again." He flew swiftly back along the leet.

The woman and her dog walked back through the slight mist forming over the river, back among the meadowsweet and willow herb. The sound of trout plopping in the water broke the stillness, just sometimes. Back through the setting sun and the watery, earthy smells of evening.

An Initiation

There are places on Dartmoor so unchanging that they seem to be out of time. Places where it seems possible to contact the very Old Ones of the Earth, the ancient tribal contacts.

When exercising horses across this great open wildness one comes very close to these contacts. Here are so many elements of the Earth. Basic rock of the oldest kind. Plants which are so primitive, even the flowers seem old. Water, everywhere in tiny streams, running beneath natural bridges of rock, bridges that the streams themselves have worn, the standing pools, sometimes with a standing stone in the centre and the bog.

Air all round endlessly moving, even on a hot day there is movement in the air. Gales, breezes, soft zephers, times when the snow is so heavy and so cold that the only thing to do is take shelter behind a Tor and then you can hear the wind keening, singing a song far older than time. A time when it is best to wait, cover your horse as well as you can and hope for a break long enough to get down to the road and home. This is not a time to try riding straight across moorland. But, when the wind is more gentle, it carries the sounds of running water, sheep, ponies and the lonely cry of the curlew. Stand then quietly near one of the larger pools and you can hear a sand piper, a whistling sound which is really quite from another world and always there is the song of the skylark.

Fire. A blaze in the dry heather can be a terrible thing - an elemental destroyer but it clears away the rubbish and the encroaching bracken and the regeneration of the smaller plants is swift in the clear ground.

I had spent many months riding in the lonely places, through snow and sun, rain and wind,, watching the colours changing with the passing seasons, the shadows of clouds making a valley to appear first dark then flooded with light. On this quiet Autumn afternoon I felt a great need to become one with these elements, but now was not the time. There was a place, one not yet found, a place called in my favourite book, "The Place Beyond" and when I found it, that would be the time and I would know how to accomplish this joining with and understand of, the elements.

Horses and children take up a lot of time and it was over two years before I found the place. I thought, in my arrogance that I knew the Moor, but no one ever does, there is too much mystery, so many changes of light and too many people have lived there. The echoes are thick.

Then, my children went away to school and my employers went away on holiday and I found both the time and the place appeared naturally but I was not quite prepared. I went home, dealt with the horse and then after a long shower and a quick supper, sat gazing into the log fire with the small glass of good whiskey, wondering how to set about this.

I had no idea about initiation. I knew I was a witch but had no idea that there were others about. My mother had told me that witches worked by themselves or with a few members of their family. The idea of coven and groups with set forms of what I came to know as initiation, with strange behaviour at which I know my mother would have disapproved was a closed book to me.

Some of my wood had been gathered on the shore , there are places where the moor is not too far from the sea, so it is impregnated with salt and salt can give off some odd colours. There was a bright green flame burning to one side of the fire and I watched the edge, the bit where the flame was not, and there was a djinn. Not a large one and he certainly hadn't come out of a bottle, just a being of Fire, I suppose an Elemental of Fire. I should have been surprised or scared, I suppose, but felt neither of these feelings. I was delighted to be able to listen to the deep voice which spoke to me.

As I have grown older, I have been more and more surprised by those who go into print with such experiences, talking at length of secrets best not shared. What the Genie said to me is between us but I knew what I would need to do to make contact. When he had finished he simply was not there anymore.

The next few days were cold and wet, it was early March and the wind made the horses fractious. Our rides were somewhat curtailed not just for them but for me too. Then one day Spring had come to the Moor.

I had made my preparations during the inclement weather so was ready. I took the steadiest horse, the one I could trust not to gallop off at a difficult moment and rode up across the miles to my Place Beyond.

There was a shallow dip in the ground, a small lawn of lovely soft grass, surrounded by water. A little island. On one side there was a great clump of gorse and cowslips, primroses and a little purple flower whose name I did not know. There was the stump of an ancient standing stone, with cup and ring marks, and from the south, a drift of smoke. Where that came from I had no idea, I looked carefully. The last thing I wished to do was endanger my life or that of the horse.

I had never worked naked before, never even thought of the possibility of doing so and had certainly never heard the phrase 'sky-clad', but it seemed to be right then. Luckily it was a lovely warm, sunny day or I would never have done it. I walked a rough circle round the island, and stepped over the water and with a little trepidation about ants, bees and spiders I lay down, spreadeagled. Now, since doing this I have heard many people talk about "it seeming right at the time" and unless I remember my own experience, I scoff and think what a load of rubbish. But it is so, one does what seems right at the time and blow everyone else.

I watched the small white clouds scud across a very blue sky, enjoyed the soft grass beneath me and listened to the wind in the dry heather. I was not too sure about falling asleep, it could have been embarrassing if some walker had happened that way and at first I kept an eye on the horse but strangely he made no move to trot back to his stable. In fact, he kept coming to look at me, probably wondering what the daft woman was doing now.

I watched the birds and was privileged to see a peregrine stoop to a pigeon. A fantastic sight at any time but at that moment a reminder that Nature is not always kind and gentle. At least the bird died quickly and for a good reason.

Towards evening the wind became cooler and I sat up to eat some bread and cheese and drink some water. The colours of the moor had changed dramatically. Where there had been mostly greens and yellows, there were now mauve and purples. The smells were different too and the sounds.

A badger snuffled his way close to the standing stone and inspected me in his short-sighted way. I suppose that my human scent was overlaid by the grass and the air because he stayed for some time watching me. When he left quite unhurriedly, I watched weasels and stoats chasing round the dried bracken, chasing mice I think, judging by the squeaks.

There were little plops in the water, small creatures diving in and out and then, oh joy, more insistent plops as a black cloud poured rain down. Only for a few moments though, and I did have a towel in a rain-proof bag.

When the shower was over a fox came to investigate. She snapped at me looking very annoyed at this invasion of her territory. I sat quite still. I had never sat so still for so long in my life. She lay down with her face on her paws and her yellow eyes glowing in the last fading evening light.

I lay down again but after a while the chill of the moor at night began to get to my bones. I stood up to dress and the vixen coughed a couple of times and trotted away slowly, looking back to snap at me.

I lit a small fire and fed the horse with the hay I'd brought along. He was not at all bothered about being out on the moor at night, but he settled down close to the ring of water.

I had a sleeping bag with me and snuggled down into it and slept, I'm sure until it was very dark. I was watching the stars and trying to remember which constellation was which when I became aware that there were many, many animals circling the ring of water. Then, as my eyes regained their night sight I saw a being with a wonderful head of horns, a Stag of Seven Tines, (meaning 14 points of course) standing huge and still near the stump of the old stone.

I gazed at Him and said "I remember you. We have met before."

"Indeed we have. Do you remember what happened and all you were told?" His voice was deep and quiet, it had an immediate effect on the animals. They stood and bowed. It had an effect on me too. I don't think that I have ever heard such a sexy, dark brown voice in my life.

I stammered, "Yes, I do now. Although I had forgotten. It is all coming back. Will I remember it all? "

He did not cross the water but sat at the edge. I offered Him a drink but He smiled and shook His head. We said very little but I had the feeling of learning so much. There was no need for words. How long He sat there I do not know and would not like to guess but at one point He stood and indicated that I should stand also. There was a scent drifting to me, a scent like all the flowers in the world answering the Sun and there She was. I had seen Her before too, when I was young and very afraid.

She stepped across the water. Did I say stepped? Her movements were so gentle that the word step is an infamy. Herne followed and we sat together for an eternity. Describe Her. How could I? Voice like silver bells? Eyes like velvet? There are no words to describe the Lady. We...communicated. I do not know how. We just did.

Then they were no more. The animals parted to make a path but They could not be seen. I sat for some time, then lay down until it was nearly dawn.

As soon as the sun came up again I took off my clothes and stayed quite still until I knew it was time to go. I made sure that no trace was left behind. The animals had all gone, but I could feel an acceptance. A feeling I still have when I see them. The horse had wandered off but came to my call. I towel dried his back and tacked him up and we set off in as wild a gallop as I have ever experienced. His feet hardly touched the ground but as we came down off the moor and the daily traffic made itself felt we went home at a decorous trot.

He was happy to be turned into his paddock. I gave him some feed, thanked him for his help and walked home to my cottage, met, as usual by my lovely ginger tom, who always greeted me from the same post. He made no complaint about being left for twenty four hours. I picked him up and he kissed my chin and I went into my cottage, knowing that I had been accepted. I am a witch and I am a beloved child of the God and Goddess.

The Wise One

She had parked the old banger in the shade of some oaks - well off the lane - overlooking a lovely stretch of country and thought of the cause of the gift.

She looked at the box on the back seat of the car with a rueful smile. Not too much, considering what it was for. An apology for near total disablement or perhaps her death. A bottle of very expensive bubbles and a huge and equally expensive box of chocolates from a very exclusive and expensive shop. An apology from the city banker whose father had so nearly killed her.

The old man, her temporary employer, had wanted to inspect his acres and estimate how his harvest was doing and he intended to drive his beautiful and elderly Rolls Royce in his carpet slippers. She had brought his shoes from the boot room but he could not be bothered to change.

The idea of driving the magnificent piece of machinery round fields and over ditches struck her as being not merely eccentric, the old boy was certainly that, but also hilariously funny. She suggested the alternative, a small basic runabout but the old sailor snorted "What. Drive that nasty little bit of Jap tin" and limped off to the old brick garage, stopping to croon to his ferrets on the way. Frankly, she didn't like them a bit. They stank, not having been cleaned out for some time. She followed the old boy, keeping her fingers crossed and hoping, in passing the she would not be invited to clean the cages.

Actually, of course, he was right. The Rolls had far better suspension than the Suzuki and the drive, though bumpy, and punctuated with yells to the men cutting the corn and delight at the quality of the grain, was completed without trouble.

He knew every inch of his extensive land and explained about ditches and hedges as they went. Not for him the open prairie of the agrotechnics. He liked to see trees and they were planted in stands and breaks, partly to give the pheasants cover but mostly because he hated to see bare land. They were not even conifer, but every sort of native tree, and especially crack willow. He grew these as a spare crop for cricket bats. They shared a passion for the game.

He also had the ability to find water anywhere. He was a very fine dowser and on his good days, when the debilitating disease from which he suffered allowed it, he taught her the finer points. Having seen that she could shoot, he allowed her the use of his .22 rifle.

The accident happened as the car was being put away. The wind had half-closed the doors and she got out to open them properly. He was waiting patiently but just as she stood back his foot slipped and he trod on the accelerator. At the sound of the engine suddenly revving she turned and leapt out of the way just as a ton of extremely expensive metal crashed into the Wall where seconds before she had been standing. The wall was old, so old hardly any mortar showed between the bricks and the door was falling apart - more so now.

A shower of old ruby brick and splintered wood fell round her and from the radiator came an ominous hissing. The Spirit of Ecstasy looked more than a little inebriated.

She was appaled and shaking but the old man sat in a state of shock, enough to worry anyone. "The slippers. They slipped." He gasped, and then "Better phone my son."

Two farm hands came running, drawn by the noise just as she reached in to turn off the ignition. They helped the old man into the house and she called the doctor and then his son.

She quickly explained to his secretary what had happened and then had to repeat herself to him. The explosion of fury rather shocked her. Such language from a Wickhamist. So much for "Manners Makyth Man." She thought. "I'm coming straight down. Get the doctor". Her "He's on his way" was lost in the crashing down of the phone.

Later that evening, a nurse having been installed and the doctor been and gone the son sat at the kitchen table apologising for his outburst. Never mind. Her time was up the following day, the regular housekeeper was already back and had taken over the reins at once. The bubbles, chocolates and an extra large cheque were all on the table in front of her. When she asked how on earth he had found the time to shop he grated "What the hell are secretary's for?

He looked at her for some time. "You must have had a bad shock too. My father and I hope you'll put this behind you and come again next year." This was said with great charm. He really wasn't a Wickhamist for nothing. She had been at the house for the past four years, taking over from the housekeeper when she went on holiday. A month at that salary paid phone and electricity bills, rent and whatever the car needed. Oh yes. She'd come.

Besides, she liked the house. It fascinated her. It began at one end in the Eleventh century, part of an ancient priory, and continued it's length through every type of English domestic architecture up to late Victorian. It had ghosts to spare and she liked the old man, even his predilection for raspberries, which they had almost every evening for pudding.

She called in on the old man before she left. He was full of apologies and hoped she'd come again and gave her another cheque. She refused this one but he looked so put out and said that she would help him to feel better if she accepted it, so what could she do?

The housekeeper gave her a big box of raspberries and lots of hugs. They'd always got on well.

"I hope you weren't too upset dear. He's an old fool but he does enjoy your visits"

"It shook me up a bit" she said honestly, "but I was more concerned about him"

When she left they were all there on the steps, smiling and waving. They were still there when she got to the end of the drive. She ignored the signs for the motorway, hated motorway driving. So turned right and ambled slowly through the lanes to the West.

She had another life, all bound up with the magic of the land and part of the specialness of this job was the knowledge of the old man and the journey, from the coast of East Anglia right across the Island to the deep valleys of the Old Moor.

Their generosity had been such that she had stopped for lunch at an old inn, renowned for it's food and she intended to stop for tea in Marlborough, if she got there in time. If she didn't make it home tonight it really didn't matter, there were plenty of places to stay.

With a last look at the lovely view she got back into the car and drove along lanes smelling of harvest, stopping sometimes to pick wild flowers, those she didn't recognise and some she did.

After a delicious tea, in the lengthening shadows she found herself in a lane - very narrow but quite straight. She had been wondering as she drove along if her chosen way was really the right one for her. Not the journey home, she knew her land well enough to know where she was - but the way her own life was going. Was her intense love of the Land, to the exclusion of all other forms of magic, really the right way for her?

Most of the people she knew in the craft had more tangible ways. Some were Healers, some read the Tarot, some were ardent feminists. They were Wiccans, Druids and Shamans, but she only concentrated on the Old Ones, the Old ways and the Land. This was real to her but her acquaintances in the craft talked of Religion; Sabbats, robed or not; and Moots. Their "temples" were full of 'things', they were not always clean and usually smelled of stale joss sticks. She worked alone, outside and clad in suitable clothes. Oh, she had robes and cloaks and all the paraphernalia, but she rarely used them. "What sort of a witch are you" they asked. And she would think "Yes. What sort of a witch am I?"

She was thinking of this when she became aware of a strange feeling of being watched. To her left a gate stood open, grain had been spilled from a trailer, but the field was empty. The evening was very quiet and the car seemed to be drifting along silently. She stopped and saw a large hare sitting in the gateway, watching her with soft, amber eyes.

The hare moved out onto the lane and after a deep look, lollopped slowly in front of the car, which still made no noise at all. About half a mile further on the hare turned into another gateway on the right of the lane. This field had not yet been cut. She turned, seeming to wait for the woman to catch up.

The car stopped of its own accord. They looked at one another, the woman and the hare, for several minutes. The deep wisdom in the creatures' eyes awed her.

"Am I doing the right thing, Old One?" she asked. "Should this concentration on the "Land" really be my only concern?"

She waited. The hare seemed to be lost in thought, almost as if she was listening to another, and older voice. Then she stamped her foot - nodded her head and turning, loped elegantly into the corn.

When she got home, the woman unpacked her car, took out the bubbles and the chocolates and found a small box tucked in among them. Opening it she saw a brooch. It was a silver hare with bright amber eyes and it came from the old man.

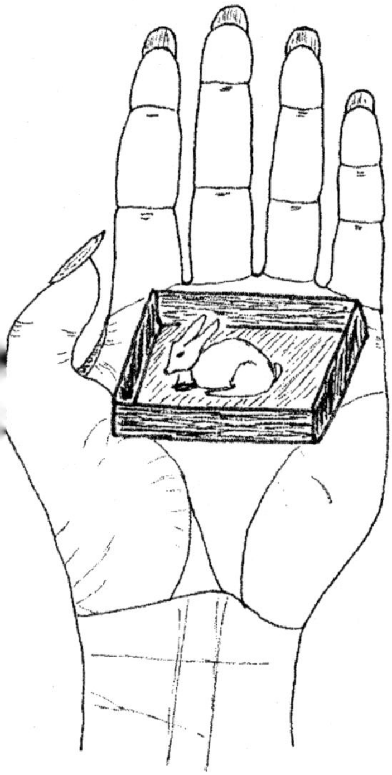

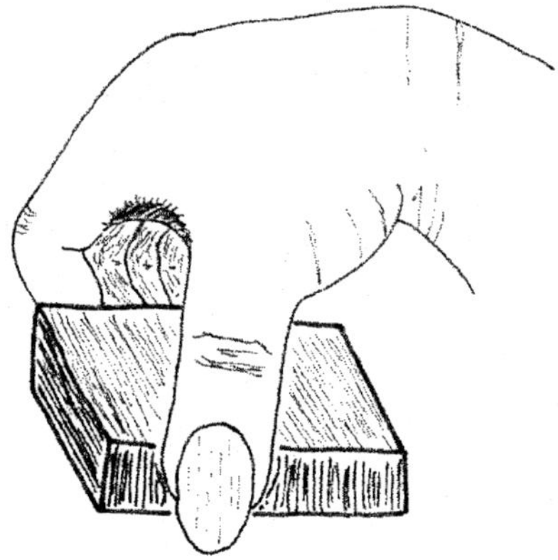

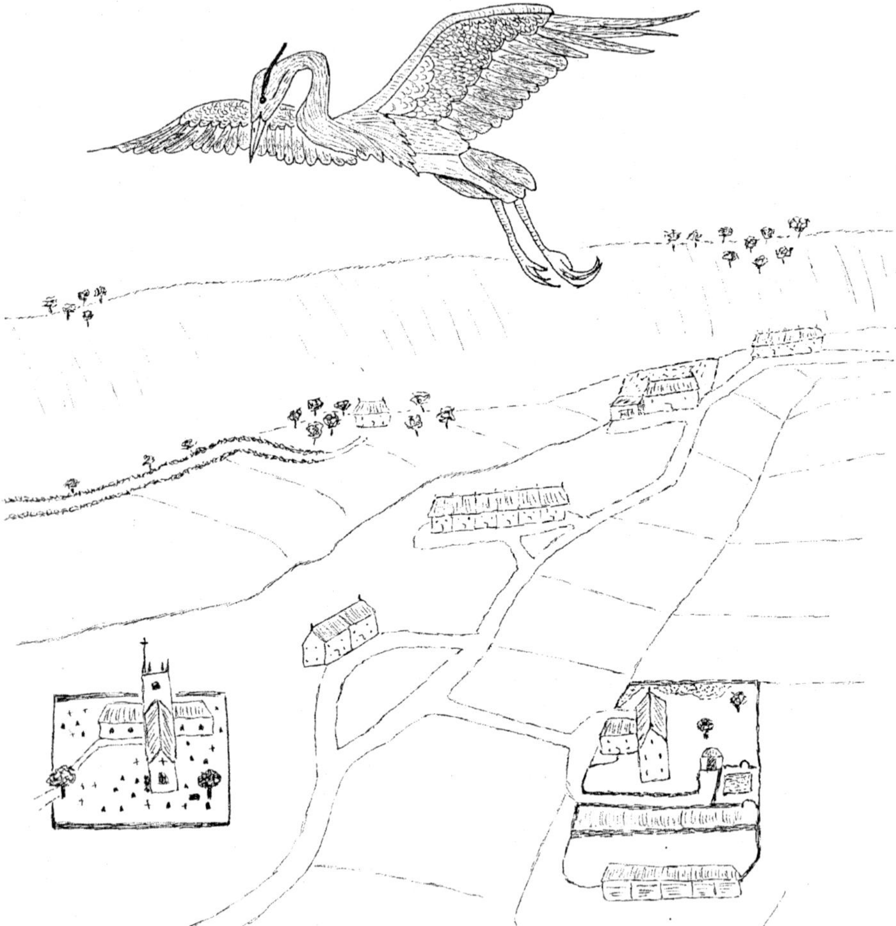

Snow, Hail and Heron

It had been a lovely morning. The Sun shone; the birds sang and the wind rustled the new leaves on the alder and willows lining the banks of the brook. There were new lambs in the fields and the bright green of new growth in the corn fields.

The great bird set off in the beauty of the morning to find a new nesting site. She could not stay with her mother. This was never allowed. She also hoped she would find a mate.

Her huge wings carried her over countryside and towns, She had heard rumours among the Heron folk that one could nest in the high trees surrounding the parks of towns, where there were usually ponds or even rivers, which meant food.

She rested for a while beside a puddle left over from the late floods, but the water was shallow and muddy and filled with objects that no self respecting heron would dream of eating.

The wind grew stronger as she dawdled and there was a sudden chill in the air. She looked at the sky and realised that the blue had gone and the clouds were grey and ragged. She took off again, into the wind as she had been taught, and people watched the great, ungainly bird with her legs trailing. As yet the wind was not strong enough to worry her, she had no way of worrying.

Beneath her she could see a place not unlike her birth nesting place and she turned into the wind once more. But now the wind was really strong and hard, huge hail stones were hammering down on her wings. She struggled on for miles, the stream always in her sights but the cold was hurting her legs and the hail chopped down on her head and beak and caused pain.

Soon, she had no more strength and fell out of the sky, a sorry lump of bird life, battered and blinded by the cold and dreadful hail. She , came to rest would be a nice way to think of the landing; a crash and a bump which knocked all the breath out of her, would be much closer. She lay in the new wheat, her head wilting, Soon it was stretched out and she closed her eyes, waiting for death.

The woman had been looking out of her bedroom window amazed at the change in the weather. She turned to her son saying " I have only seen hail like this once before. Look at the size of those stones. As big as penny pieces." The son looked and with a grin said "You are exaggerating again. Just about as big as tanners I would say."

The woman had seen something strange in the field. "What's that?"
She pointed. "I can't see anything" then he stopped, "There is something there."

They fetched the binoculars, which were never far away and trained them on the strange lump, where there should have been no lump at all.

"Some animal taking shelter" he thought.

"There is no shelter in the middle of a corn field" his mother snapped. "I'm going to see what it is." You can't go out in this" her son exploded. "Look it's coming down even harder. He was right, the hail was pelting down in a fury. "That animal is in trouble. I"m going." and grabbing her rubber boots and waterproof jacket she ran to the gate and began to stagger across the field. The wind was blowing the hail as though it wanted to ground her too.

She got to the lump and discovered it was a bird, the only one she knew of that size was a heron. She looked at the bird and she looked at the beak and knew that only one could help the poor creature. Deep within her mind she called to the Friend and Helper of Animals. Most people call him Pan and some, who do not know him, call him Devil, but she, a witch of the old kind called Him Herne. He came in the form of the Stag of Seven Tines, and as he came the hail stopped and the wind subsided. It was still cold. He changed into the God form and looking at the heron said "Pick her up and put her on my back. Come with me and we will find a place where she can rest and get warm.

He touched the bird, who lifted glazed eyes to Him. She was alarmed when the woman tried to life her, but Herne made a sound which calmed her.

The woman had been with Herne before and knew that she would be able to keep up. They flew over trees and fields until they came to the place the bird herself had chosen. There was no nest in the trees but she would be able to build that soon enough.

There was a place of long grass left over from last year. A place where there was a brook and a deep, man-made pool full of fish. Herne stood and the woman lifted the heron from his back. He turned back into the God form and helped her make sure the bird was uninjured, then made a nest of rushes and brought a fish from the pond. The owner would not have been pleased but he wasn't there to see. In any case, he would not have tackled a seven foot male with a head of magnificent horns. The fish put heart into the heron, her ride on the great Stag's back had made her warm and the nest was comfortable. Beneath the cover of the alder she settled down to sleep.

The woman turned to climb the steep slope to the village but the God, ever mindful of His followers, lifted her and carried her back up the steep, slippery slope. He put her down in the narrow lane by the field and was gone.

She walked slowly back to her house. Her son was waiting at the door.

"Who on earth was that" he asked snappishly. "I've never seen him before."

She said quietly "No-one on Earth." Her son did not understand. He was not yet knowledgeable about the old ways.

"Just a friend." she said.

The Sanctuary in the Wood

The snow is deep, but the footsteps of many travellers lead you to the inn. It is bitterly cold, but others have braved the midwinter weather for companionship and to warm themselves at the great inglenook fire. You reach the massive door and stamp the snow from your boots, push the door open and go in.

The hall of the inn is very ancient, that most early of inns, a Maison Dieu, a house of God, built to give succour to travellers in the very early years of this millennium. The ceilings are low, made of great oaken beams and they are hung with ivy, holly and mistletoe, great bunches of the stuff. The newel posts are wreathed with ivy, its bright shiny leaves reflecting the flames of the roaring fire. You have the feeling of being already in the depths of a wood. This inn is strange. It gives everyone who enters it a feeling of great love and tender care flowing over and around you. Sit down for a while with your friends and make yourself ready for your journey. It will be a long one, taking a year to accomplish.

Eat and drink, but sparingly. you cannot be overburdened with this world's food when you undertake this long walk. The name of this inn is The Herb of Grace, and as you refresh yourself you discuss the meaning with your friends. Why should a pilgrim inn, for that is what is is, have such a name? The Herb o'Grace o' Sundays, Shakespeare called it. In the old days it was planted in graveyards. It grows by the badger's sett. The Rue is a bitter-'leaved herb. Very astringent. Rue is for repentance. Astringent means contraction. "Singlemindedness", someone says. "A sort of concentration, says another. "Something you cannot do without repentance," is someone else's idea.

Someone from another table says, "With compassion, this is the root of all giving." Another says 'T.S.Eliot says' The condition of complete simplicity costing not less than everything."

This is strong stuff. You rise, pick up your coat and cross the room to a smaller door. Turn and salute your friends. They have helped you.

On a table by to one side of the door is a small blue and white bowl containing sprigs of the herb you have been discussing. Take one as you pass through the door, for now our journey through the year begins and this will help concentrate your mind for the things you will see and learn.

The door opens on to a lane, and the time is very early in the morning, it is still dark, the snow is still crisp. There are few dead leaves rustling in the hedge, the snow is melting from the thick boughs and the rank grass but there are a few snowdrops just beginning to show their heads.

Soon the lane peters out and you are walking across heath-land. Where bracken fronds are beginning to unfurl. The air seems lighter and you can smell the Spring in the air. There are great lumps of gorse blazing with yellow blossom and some bees, about early, are humming about their brightness. The sun is now up and beneath the silver birches, just coming into leaf you can see primroses and as you pass, you can smell their warm, honey scent.

The wood ahead is divided from the heath by a stream, over which there is a convenient bridge. On either side of the stream there are stones covered with brilliant fern and bright green moss. Further up each bank are larger stones thick with amber coloured lichen. The spring burgeons and soon you see primroses, violets and wood anemone. Over to your left is a marshy place where the willow shoots gleam golden in

the sun, and the alder gleams on firmer ground, still with the black cones of last autumn.

You hear the beginning of the dawn chorus.

Cross the bridge and follow the faint path which leads you through an orchard of old crab apple trees in full bloom and you stop and gaze in wonder at the beauty of the pink and white blossom in all the glory of their spring extravagance. Violets and primroses abound and just ahead of you, beneath some hazel, where a carpet of bluebells is beginning to show,are wands of greenish gold, the birches silver and the mosses and lichens are scarlet, saffron, coral and jade. Who needs a pirate's chest with these riches?

The birds are busy gathering food for their nestlings. and the sun is getting warmer.The trees are getting closer and here is the beginning of the real wood.

As the wood gets thicker you see the flash of a blue jay and a sweet piping sound tells you that a robin is close by. You stop and speak to him, he watches you with his large brown eyes and from the corner of your eye you see a wren flitting quickly through the new undergrowth. Wren are always enchanting, so difficult to see but such a bonus when you catch sight of one, even though she is supposed to represent the old year. How sad it would be if she could appear only in the winter.

Blue tits are in the trees and finches bounce on the undergrowth and there is the sound of small creatures going about their business, but these sounds only intensify the essential stillness of the wood.

As you look around you you realise that this is probably the loveliest wood you have ever seen, full of a deep peace and yet you know that it is a very direct route to wherever you are going. As you walk the hurts and anxieties of your life fade away. The air in this wood, clean and sweet as it is with the burgeoning of spring is somehow resistant, woven of a sort of heavenly loveliness which cannot be penetrated by anything contrary to nature.

The Herb of Grace gives one a defence against anything that may happen to the body but the wood is a defence against anything which may hurt or assault the soul. It has an inner safety. The Armour of the House of the Lord as those who fled from tyranny called it. This is only a courtyard and it leads to the Place Beyond.

The path suddenly swerves uphill and at the top of a grassy bank is a giant old oak, its new green leaves tipped with scarlet to whom one must pay respect before passing, for he dominates this part of the wood. You have come to one of the milestones, so sit for a while and think of your life. Think of it as a series of deaths and re-births, each an act of growing into your final self. To grow into this self you need to cleanse your soul and beneath the tree is a mass of the herb you talked about at the inn.

You know that each change in your life is pre-destined, so that as you reach each milestone, you can recognise it as something which has been waiting for you and yet each change is a matter of choice, so you come to it in the pleasure or pain of your own making. Pick another little sprig of the Rue and put it carefully with the piece you brought from the inn taking it with a dedication to the next re-birth of your life.

As you do this you hear a clear, high piping, a liquid melody of heart rending beauty. You know that you must follow but it is

now mid-morning and high summer and you are beginning to feel thirsty. Down the other side of the bank the enchantment of the silence is threaded through by the sound of running water and presently you come to it.

From a high rock a spring of crystal clear water cascades into a smooth black bowl. the water spills over the edge of the bowl in a little waterfall, the beginning of a stream. On a stone just below the bowl a tiny frog is sitting, watching you, and a silver cup stands on a ledge, and incised into the rock above it are the words "Drink traveller, for I am the refreshment given by the Goddess."

You take the cup, hold it beneath the cascade and drink. It is pure and refreshingly cold. Having drunk your fill, you pour a little on the ground as a libation. And give thanks.

The stream is quite wide and in the centre is a tiny island fringed with purple loosestrife and bog myrtle. There is a tangled mass of honeysuckle where you sit to cool your hands and face and take slow sips of the sparkling water, then resting, watch butterflies float gently down to the blossoms of rose bay and meadowsweet. You are a little bit shocked to hear the sudden shattering noise of a woodpecker whose old name was yaffingale Far away , over the river that the little brook feeds you can hear a cuckoo, but still you rest, dabbling your hot feet in the water, then before putting on your shoes you cross the stream by some ancient stepping stones, worn smooth by the feet of many travellers, so take care.

You scramble up the bank on the other side and as you stand up the piping merges with the song of thrush and blackbird and you are ready to go on.

On this side there are Ashes, great and small, their smooth skinned bark grey. Arrows used to be made from the new wood each year, a cloth-yard long. These are always the last trees to get leaves in the spring, sometimes long after the oak, so the old adage "Oak before the Ash and you'll only get a splash" is really not good country lore, because it is only rarely that the Ash comes into leaf before the oak. There is quite a lot of undergrowth here so you have to pick your way carefully.

There is another bank in front of you, the ground is getting higher. This bank is steep and you need to use whatever handholds you can find. At the top there is an archway of both hawthorn and blackthorn, and as you go through you see that the character of the wood is changing again.

You have come suddenly upon an avenue of great beeches and the quality of the wood changes. They are taking on their autumn bronze and the day is turning to evening. Through the most delicate tracery in Nature the sky is still blue but the sun is westering. There is little undergrowth beneath beeches, their canopies are too thick but you walk on beech mast and tan coloured leaves. If you are lucky you might find some delicious nuts in the mast these will allay your hunger a little. There is a crisp feeling in the air and you can see a slight mist curling round the trunks.

You can see wonderful things as you walk: a stick jewelled with scarlet moss caps; a jay's feather on a cushion of emerald moss, and the jay himself, speeding through the tops of the trees, blue and buff, with pied wings. A charm of goldfinches tossing above a clump of thistles.

At the top of another bank to your left is another ancient tree and beneath it a small cave, a badger sett and if you are very lucky you might see a stripy head and whiskers. As you cross the beechwood, you notice that an unusual number of animals and birds going in your direction. The afternoon is fading into evening and all the trees are glowing with autumn colours. There are scarlet maples and golden birches, occasionally a crab apple with bright yellow fruit and the elderberries are going black. Hawthorns are loaded with bright red clusters and there are some hollies, ancient as the conquest, their

Drink Traveller
for I am the refreashment
given by the
Goddess

berries beginning to blaze in the autumn evening light.

Two great ashes stand like pillars on either side of the path and as you pass between these the wood changes again. The trees are closer together, the piping has stopped for a moment and the stillness deepens. Sycamores have turned gold and there is real mist, through which a birch glows like a lantern. A great white owl floats by on silent wings, stops on a stump looking at you and flies on. He seems to be leading you on.

A pair of stoats, their brown coats turning white which makes the black tips of their ermine tails stand out clear, dance in front of you, standing up on their tails seem to say "Come on. Hurry up." their bright eyes seem to laugh at your slowness.

The wind gets up, roaring suddenly as an autumn gale through the trees, stripping them of leaves. You catch as many as you can, for each one caught means a happy month ahead. Then the wind dies down as suddenly as it came.

The first of the early frosts is here, bringing a chill and making diamond necklaces of the spiders webs in the bushes. Suddenly, the stillness is shattered by an enraged bellow and the clash of horns. It is the rut and the stags are competing for the leadership of the hinds. A brilliant flash of colour and a green woodpecker shoots between two oaks,

Yet again the wood changes and it is early winter. The trees are growing closer together and the stillness deepens. Beside the path is a brilliant holly bush and opposite is a clump of fern growing by a mossy rock and you see delicate hoof prints along the path. The owl appears again and just in front of you is a magnificent fox, a badger and a rabbit. You wonder at this, surely the fox must have seen his natural prey and he has, but he is waiting quietly for the rabbit to precede him.. The rabbit is quite unafraid..

Before you now, lit by a great full moon, is a solid looking rampart of hollies and brambles. There are two splendid hollies, covered with bright red berries, you cannot remember ever having seen such magnificent trees.

The path ends here, but the hollies seem to form an arch, yet you are perturbed. You stand and watch as many small animals dive through a hole in the hedge. Are you supposed to go through there?The hole is very small and it looks uncomfortable, sloping downward and the ground is moist and covered in holly leaves.

But there is nowhere else to go and you have been led here. The piping begins again, insistent, making you go down on all fours a crawl through the damp, dark, prickly opening. You loose your balance and roll, painfully and clumsily down the rest of the bank. and suddenly, you are out, in the Place Beyond, the very centre of the wood.

The bright cold light of a full moon shows you clearly the snow piled up at the edges of a clearing, yet the centre is clear, as though someone had swept it.A lawn of short cropped grass rises gently to a stream and from somewhere comes the smell of woodsmoke. All this time the piping has called you. Now it falls quiet.

There is an old building on the other side of the stream. Roofless, only parts of three walls standing. There are strange lights in the empty lancet windows as though the stained glass were still there. Giant yew meet over the broken walls and form a canopy and two blazing hollies stand guard at the door. Might this be where the holly at the inn came from?

The clearing is strangely lit and there seems to be no season. The snow is thick and yet there are primroses and violets, dog roses and honeysuckle. Dragon flies play in the irises and an otter enjoys the night. The kingfisher you saw when you first came into the wood watches you, unafraid. There are robins and wren, blue tits and lovely little black and pink long tailed tits. All the wood peckers are there together. The jay and the thrush and the owl who has stationed himself in one of the lancet windows. He hoots twice.

Music such as you have never heard fills the air. The clear, sweet piping of dreams. A rabbit hops by on three legs, his injured forth held carefully beneath him, and disappears into the ruins. A bird with an injured wing, it's flight ungainly, follows him and a fox with a torn shoulder glides like a shadow between the hollies. Hedgehogs, not hibernating here , are snuffling along, their impossibly long legs make you laugh. Many animals and birds are here, all happy and unafraid, for that is the wonder of this place, some strong influence keeps peace between friend and foe.

The rabbit returns with his leg healed and a kind of glory about him. and you feel an impulse to find this wholeness, and when the animals have all been cared for, you walk forward between the hollies.

You have come to the holy place and there beside a great stone which might have been an altar, stands the Great Horned Lord. His eyes are dark and full of humour and love, his mouth chiselled and his nose aquiline. He is a most beautiful being. The graceful curved horns associated with Pan change before your eyes to the magnificent antlers of Herne. For this is the God of Nature, the Lord of the Wild Wood, The Friend, Helper and Protector of all His younger brethren.

The wind rises and you hear his voice.

You know that from this Being you may draw strength and love; you may offer your love to Him. The music of birds, Streams and the wind make a background noise and you go forward as He beckons you and speak what is in your heart.........................

You soon begin to feel drowsy............

You wake up, refreshed, from a deep sleep, to find yourself by the rock where you drank from the cup. Through the early morning mist of very early spring, you can see your way clearly through the thinning trees.

Looking back into the shadows of the wood, something with horns moves majestically away.

Before you is the door to the inn, and you pass through, straight onto the road which you trod the night before. Or was it a year?

You have been given another aspect of the Lord of the Forest to ponder. Try to keep all He said in your heart and come to understand all you have seen.

Return to your seat and when you are ready. Return and Remember.

There is a blessing on those who serve.

Flutes Farrer

This is a story about some people who lived in a cottage, in the country, any time between the fourteenth century and the eighteenth, or as Christopher Fry put it in the "Lady's Not For Burning" "Fourteen hundred, more or less or exactly." You pays yer money and you takes yer choice.

There was a cottage standing a little way outside a small but busy village.The very special thing about this cottage was that it was actually owned by the people who lived there. This was not often the case in these times.

The legend in the village was that at some time in the very dim and distant past, someone in the family had done a great service for the Lord of the Manor, and that he, in gratitude, had given them the plot and the cottage, in perpetuity, all signed, sealed and parchmented, possibly, the villagers hinted as a safeguard. Who knows?

The family lived in the cottage, making repairs, alterations and extensions as they thought fit, without regard to laws or landlords.

As time passed the reason for the gift would have been forgotten, especially by a new lord, but the parchment was still there, carefully preserved, both in a chest in the cottage and in the muniment room in the manor.

Of course, later generations tried to reclaim both the house and the land, but the charter was always produced and, mysteriously, something always made the young lords change their minds.

At the time of which I write, the occupants were a middle aged married woman and her husband, who was the carrier.

He had a decided squint, and walked with a limp after a difference of opinion with a Shire. There were their sons and daughters and their offspring. It was, by this time, a large cottage. But the most awe inspiring member of the family was Gran, who spent most of her time sitting in the chimney corner smoking a clay pipe.

At certain times though, Gran bestirred herself, put on her high crowned hat and old cloak and went out into the woods and bushes to collect such plants and herbs as she thought fit, and sometimes visited those farmers wives who had not had the forethought to find out when this visitation might be and remove themselves, their children, their horses, carts and provisions to visit their Aunt Bet or Uncle Harry, anything and anyone to give them an excuse for these visits could be expensive.

On this particular morning, she was leaning on a gate watching a young bull romping round the meadow, when she was spotted by the farmer, who had just brought his best horse from the smithy. "Morning Gran. What you doin' then" he asked, really wanting to know.

"That's a pretty liddle bull you got there, Jarge. You "oping to breed from 'e."

Jarge knew the form, and he nodded and invited Gran up to the farm, where there might be a spare bit of bacon and a good pat of butter. "People is so kind to an old woman." Gran would say happily.

Now I would not like you to think that the family was lazy or greedy. They had a flourishing vegetable patch and kept their own chickens and a good milch cow and many good things

found their way to the cottage table. Young Gran had a way with a hare and some plums that would make anyone's mouth water. She was the village mid wife and her husband was the smith and it should be said that if any were in need, this cottage was their refuge and all were welcome to a meal, especially the poor soldiers who had been invalid out of the army. They were given dockets for their food and rest as they made their way back to their own villages, but often the elders thought it an imposition to feed them and chased them away as beggars.

They were always made welcome and often made whole as well. A short stay with this family was guaranteed to make anyone well.

Gran came back this morning laden with butter, cheese and a leg of pig. She chuckled in her usual way and repeated how good people were to an old woman. She went to sit in the chimney corner or as it was a fine day, sat under the very old apple tree in the garden. It always seemed to the family that Gran sat under the apple tree and the breeze made the tree laugh whenever some kind soul had given her a particularly acceptable present.

She had a large bedroom to herself, just off the kitchen which always smelled lovely, for her she made potions and mixtures from the herbs and flowers drying there. These were cooked,if they needed to be cooked in the old iron cauldron; not the one used for the family broth but the very old one, which had been mended and patched by the smiths, who had always been part of the family, for a hundred years or more.

Sometimes, when grandchildren were brought to visit they were allowed to peep inside, but only if Gran said so and only if they were good. Then, they might be given toffee or cashews from the smooth old tine kept by Gran's chair.

The young grandmother worked very hard and was also good at potions. As said before, she had taken over the difficult births when Gran got too old and she laid out the dead. Perhaps this was why the family was regarded with awe. Apart from being the only doctors for miles around, they were closely connected with the deep mysteries of birth and death. Even the parson spoke kindly of them, though he sometimes grumbled over their lack of attendance at church. Still, none could turn a breach birth like Young Gran and if this should happen on Sunday who knew but what these women were serving the Lord as well as he.

He was a man of gentle understanding and this was given to his flock. He was not one of your hunting parsons who only bothered with the wealthy parishioners, except, of course, when the tithes were due. His living was a poor one and he had no ambition to clamber through the ranks of the church. He enjoyed Gran's elderberry wine even more than the sack, given to him, with much condescention by the lady of the manor.

He sometimes joined the family for dinner, listening to the odd talk, which he felt should, perhaps, disturb him. The meal would be of farmer's pig or one of their own capons flavoured with herbs from the garden and such vegetables as had been grown or come by. There were often itinerant strangers and others dropping by, just in time to eat.

On Sundays, Young Gran's two daughters came over with their families and husbands. One was a smith from the village five miles away and the other, the junior and now more active partner in Granfers carrying business.

These men greeted each other with the peculiar handshake known to all horsemen and would sit outside, out of the way, on the benches beneath the windows, drinking ale or cider. talking of horses and watching the children at play in the orchard.The oldest grandson, aged six, sat behind the big rosemary bush and listened with his eyes and ears wide. He

learned more doing this than he would learn the rest of his life, about horses and their ways. "Strangely like ‘oomans is ‘horses. Understand one and you’ll understand ‘tother."

While all this philosophy was going on, the women bustled around the kitchen, preparing a nice bit of venison the old man had found lying around. And,he said, if people left things about, some kind soul would take pity on it and give it a good home. "T’was a crying shame" they all agreed, "how careless folk could be." There would be chicken and mushroom pie and apple pie for after. They had no high faluting ideas about not having pastry with successive courses.

Watching them, you would not think them a beautiful family, they were too sturdy for that, yet there was something handsome about them. They were not quite so coarsely Jutish as the rest of the villagers. Sometimes, you might see a fleeting glimpse of the Celts who had once inhabited that part of Kent and at others, even more fleeting , such as when Young Gran had helped a young mother over a difficult childbirth or when Old Gran laughed with the apple tree, or her face lit up with the joy of making a special potion for a sick child, there was something much older. Going right back to the roots of the Island, before any incomers came.

But not a trace of Norman."Never bin no Norman in this family, nor never will. Never ‘ad no truck wi’ they." And it was strange that when the young lordlings hunted down the village girls and yet another bastard brat was born bearing the features of the masters, no one such was ever born, or rather bred, in the family at Flute’s Farrer. What a strange name for a peasants cottage! "Uppitty" said the village out of earshot. "Just because it’s their own.""Aping the Gentry." and those who lived in Hawthorn or Primrose or Rose Cottage, felt that they had somehow put them in their place. But they needn’t have bothered. For if ever a family knew it’s place, this one did, and Flute's Farrer was it.

So they gathered upon certain days in the month. Often enough for there to be no special remark about it. Did they, perhaps, meet more seriously when the Moon was new, or full? When the Spring needed to be sung? Or the Harvest? Or Yule? No one bothered to enquire. People outside the village didn't and the village, as is the way of their kind "Didn't know nothin'."

Gran had been out collecting since the Sun has dried the dew. It was a beautiful morning. One that made you want to sing and dance for the sheer joy of being alive.

Washing was billowing between the apple trees, making that happiest of flapping noises and dancing with the breeze. The line was Never tied to Gran's tree. Babies lay on blankets, chuckling at the shadows on the leaves and laughing at the bees and Young Gran was shelling the very first peas of the season.

Tonight was special. The Night of the Rose Moon. Auntie Rose had come with her big slow husband and large smith son. It was her moon and her birthday was being celebrated. This year the dates actually coincided and tonight of all nights, Auntie Rose was queen. She had been since her fourteenth birthday. She looked forward to it all the year. She sat quietly, in a state of bliss. Everyone who could, came to this party and her presents were always cherished. We would probably not think much of them but life was simpler then. There had been the usual rushing around when they saw her coming down the lane, each making sure that their particular present was hidden away from sight until the magic moment.

Gran came back through the gate, laden with flowers and herbs and a "Look what I got." There were a dozen lovely peaches in a leaf lined basket. "Squire called me over. Riding that big bay mare benny shod 'tother day."

"Come up to the house" he called to me. "Got a little present for Rose on account of its her birthday." He gave me a big wink from those blue eyes of his and said "She'll have 'em later, likely!" Gran chuckled. "Later it will be. You comin' along, Squire?"

"Now Gran, when have I ever missed Rose's birthday?" and here everyone laughed for it was true. The Old Squire, unlike the young lord, kept to the old ways.

Flowers were arranged in the big crock and put in jars on the wide window ledges, until the old room looked like a bower. Buns, smelling of honey and spice were piled on the table getting cool and a particularly delicious smelling soup bubbled in the cauldron over the fire. New bread had been baked that morning and Granfer brought in two jugs, one of very special mead for later on, and one of cider strong enough to flatten the unwary.

They ate an early midday meal. Many hours would pass before the feast after the Moon greeting. The sons of the family went off soon afterwards towards the raised bank and ditch at the top of the hill, where, within surrounding trees were the remains of an ancient standing stone.

There was a good view all round and they were free from interruption. This old standing stone had about it the enormous sanctity of its kind, whenever they had always been used aright. Sadly, few were still used as places of worship, for the most vicious priesthood of the most gentle Eastern prophet had destroyed or obliterated any lingering traces of such holiness. But here, perhaps because it was small and insignificant, and really quite a long way from the village, this stone had survived and with it the gentle worship of the

Goddess and of Nature, had survived too.

The twisting of meaning which had been the lot of the old religion in other parts of the country had escaped this place, because this family had managed, through all time, to keep faith. They were helped, it must be said, in these troubled times by the Squire, the priest and even the constable, for they too had been brought up to revere the Old Things.

There was a little wood at the top of the hill, in which the oak grove stood, guarding the stone. This wood was itself guarded by a fearsome thicket of hawthorn and blackthorn, along with some carefully trained bramble.

Inside this was a circle of ash and finally the oaks of incredible age.

The entrance to all this was secret and only the family knew the way in. Even the Squire was blind-folded. Last through the gap was one of the young boys, trained from early childhood to find even the smallest thread which might betray the passage of clothing and therefore people through a gap which, by rights, should only be big enough for a badger.

The family rested during the afternoon and only the very young were given bread and honey and a drink of milk towards evening. The middle boys, aged ten to twelve, had spent most of the time wandering about aimlessly with some tough looking dogs, playing at ball or splashing in the stream, where they caught tiddlers and minnows, but let them go again. Anyone watching would have thought that they were idling away a pleasant afternoon having slipped away from their chores. But, of course, they were on the lookout, as were their uncles further up the hill. No one slipped passed their cordon when a real greeting was about to happen.
The Squire dined early and told his wife that he was just going to look about. They understood one another. The wife

was not of the Old Religion but found nothing in it to cause her distress. She would cover for her husband, if necessary. "Gone over to Well Field. There seems to be a gap in the hedge." or five miles in the other direction to look in on an old ploughman he used to employ."

Most of the village, in fact, who did not attend the Greeting, were prepared to do a grand job of misdirection should the need arise. Most of them anyway attended "Auntie Rose's Birthday."

Soon after supper, with the church bell ringing curfew, the constable found he had an important job to do at the far end of the village. He would know nothing of the figures slipping quietly through the warm, early darkness towards the fields and the hill behind Flute's Farrer.

The parson just happened to be heading that way to add to his collection of wild flowers.

Shutters in all the old cottages were closed tight, although it was a close night. At the hedge, the carefully timed crowd waited patiently to be blindfolded and led through. It was surprising just how many men there were, answering a call of nature or seeing to some job completed earlier. And how many women just happened to remember that they would need wild fenugreek or thyme for tomorrows meal.

Each waited and when their turn came was led quickly through the gap, the young boy watching to make sure that no threads were caught on the sharp thorns. Everyone looked surprisingly tidy, considering that washing was hardly part of their normal routine. Clothes had been brushed, and hair and fingernails cleaned of most of the accumulated dirt of a year. Several had even washed their faces in water, and their hands, but many thought that this was going a bit too far, even for Auntie Rose.

However, Auntie Fennel stood just inside with a bowl of lavender scented water and a rough piece of fabric for a towel over her arm and everyone rinsed hands and dried them. Squire laughed every year over this and said it was just like being back in the nursery.

The carrier son, George, called the throng together and they formed a circle just inside the trees, then walked forward until their outstretched hands touched. They they extended their hands, palm up, in front of them, while Gran welcomed them to the circle. Then they lowered their hands.

The stone had become an altar and by it stood a horn cup and a jug of mead, a small wooden plate upon which were slices of new baked bread; a sword, from which the murmurs of battle had been carefully cleaned and a wax bowl containing salt. Upon the stone, placed so that it could not hide the reflection of the moon in the water was a bowl of lovely scented roses.

Gran stood in the centre holding another cup containing water. She poured the salt into it and handed it to Auntie Rose, who carried it round the outside of the circle, sprinkling and intoning solemn words as she went.

The smith's son, Michael, took up the sword and went to Gran, who blessed it, then he carried it round, following Rose. It seemed to the company that they were enclosed in a ring of cold, brilliant blue flame. Then everyone faced towards the East where there was a small gap in the trees; and waited, hardly daring to breathe.

Gran had moved away from the centre and Auntie Rose took her place.She seemed to grow and her voice took on an authority it usually lacked. Gone was the timid little woman and in her place stood the Priestess. The Earthly spirit of the Goddess.

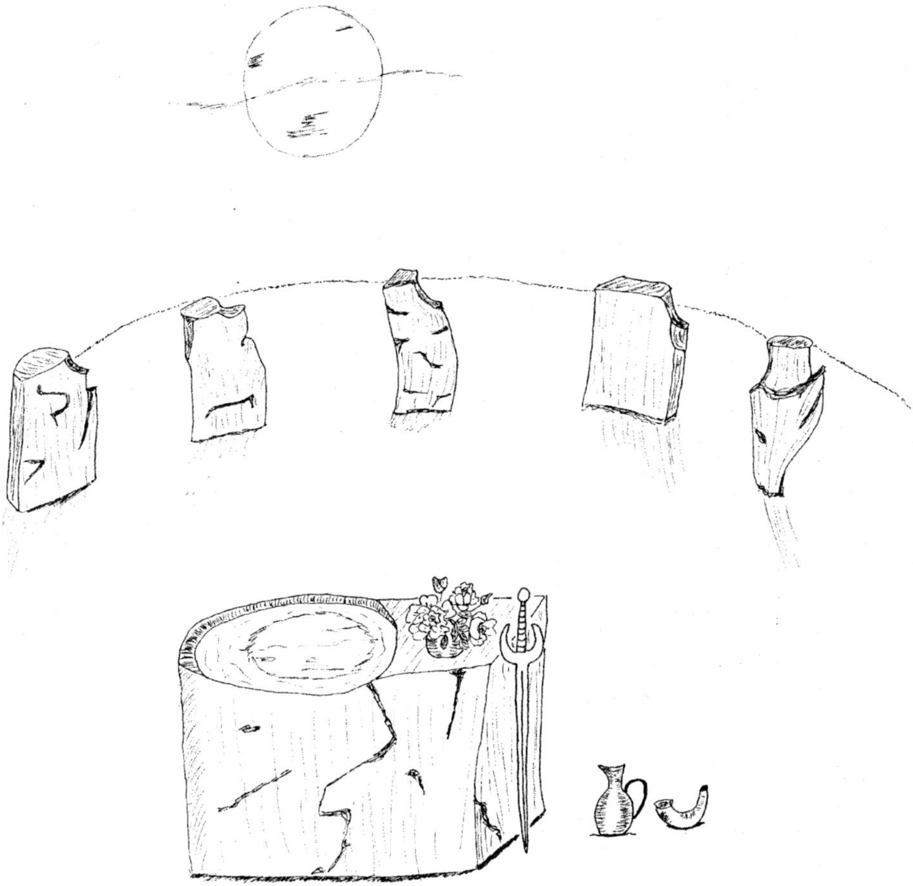

As the first slim line of light appeared she began to chant the words of praise to the Lady of the Sky, Mother of All. She spoke of how the Mother looked after her children, that She, who was before and after time, was always with them. As the Moon rose between the trees, Her light was reflected in the little pool of water cupped in the top of the stone, some of which, of course, had been used to consecrate the circle.

The Priestess raised her arms to the Moon and called for Her blessing. The whole group raised their arms in unison, and repeated the call.

Then the Moon won free from the trees and she intoned "I am She, the Changing and Unchanging Goddess."

A deep murmur came from all in the circle "Behold, the Goddess."

They stood with their arms straight up towards the Moon, while a man could count, if he could count, to one hundred. Then they lowered them and turned back to the centre of the circle, where the little stone had lost the reflection of the Moon and now showed the stars in its silent pool.

Michael stood the sword, hilt down in a little crevice and picked up the stone bottle of mead. which he passed to the Priestess who filled the horn cup and blessed it. She carried this round the circle, giving everyone to drink, pouring the remainder round the stone. Gran took up the wooden platter with the bread arranged on it, took it to the priestess who blessed it, and a little girl, dressed in white, with a pink sash round her small middle and a chaplet of rosebuds on her head, carried the plate solemnly round the circle, offering it to each person and bowing when they thanked her. She took it carefully back to the Priestess and, skipped, blushing back to her mother, who stroked her hair proudly.

Then the Priestess spoke the words of closing, offering a blessing to the Moon and the Stars, and the trees which had guarded the circle. Gran dismissed the ring of blue fire, and closed with her own words, as she always did. The people broke up and went to the little stone, offering their blessings and dipping their fingers in the water. Even the priest did this, he knew a sacred rite when he saw it. They slipped silently out of the circle of trees and through the gap in the hedge, maintaining their silence until they were back in the cottage, when laughter and chatter broke out.

The men were given stoops of ale, the women wine and the children lemonade, and they gave Auntie Rose her presents. She was no longer the great Priestess but a little lady enjoying her party. Squire gave her the peaches and a thumping great kiss, and a little something extra by way of a fur muff. She thanked him prettily and he turned to Gran and helped himself to the plentiful food, as everyone else was doing.

"You know, Gran, I always feel uplifted when I come to Rose's birthday."Then he let out a great roar of laughter and everyone joined in. Soon afterwards, the constable came in, "No trouble over there. Just a waste of time going. Still, duty had to be done." He accepted both ale and a great bowl of soup and sat talking to his cronies far into the night.

Gradually, the party broke up and the villagers slipped home, happy and contented. The Moon went down and the village turned over in its sleep, dreaming, possibly of a lovely party with good friends.

The Black Butterfly

I've heard of being pixie led but this was ridiculous. I rode a little Melody scooter and was taking some paperbacks to a second hand shop situated in a small town just North of the Ridgeway. The hill up to this ancient road was very steep and the poor little machine found it hard going, so I stopped at the top to let it get it's breath back.

I was glad to take the wretched helmet off for a few minutes and went to look for wild flowers, as is my wont.

The afternoon was baking, the smells coming off the fields to either side of the way, and the wild flowers was enough to make you pie-eyed and my boots were cooking my feet.

As I turned back to the Melody I saw something fluttering in the very lovely sainfoin plants on one side of the track. At the time, to be honest, I had no idea what the flowers were, but I looked them up later. It is a tall plant with spikes of pink flowers with a gorgeous scent.

A black butterfly, about the same size as a Peacock or Red Admiral, was browsing among the blossoms. I had never seen one quite like it. The edges of its wings were decorated with large white dots and in each centre was a smaller one of bright emerald green which seemed to be iridescent.

This was turning into an afternoon of discovery. A new wild flower to add to my collection and a black butterfly, both of which were strange to me. I tried to look more closely at this beautiful little vision but it flew off, not very far, and settled once again, this time on a patch of dyer's weld.

I followed this flying guide for a long time and although this was a time when one could leave little yellow machines lying about in the undergrowth with perfect safety, I did begin to feel that perhaps I had gone far enough.

However, the strange butterfly circled my head and I distinctly hear a voice say "Don't be silly. We are taking care of your yellow peril." At that time I was not quite so sure of "THEM" and their caretaking abilities. I know better now.

So, I continued to follow the guide, as I thought of it, far over the down. I was delighted because, for one thing, I had never walked this part of the Ridgeway, and at every pause I was shown a new plant. New to me, anyhow. The old road went over the brow of a hill, down to a small copse where there seemed to be dozens of these lovely creatures. They swirled up in clouds ,separating, coming together and swooping down to the flowers: dancing to music I could not hear. Near the bottom of the little slope beneath the trees, there was a large, smooth stone and a very small spring with clear water bubbling up from a great depth through the chalk.

I cupped my hands and drank and sprinkled a little on the grass. It seemed that the droplets became included in the dance because in small sets, the butterflies stooped to drink.

Time was no more, irrelevant. How long I stayed, watching and wondering at the beauty I was being shown, I have never really known. I cannot say that I was given some earth-shaking message. I simply drank in the beauty.

A change in temperature eventually reminded me of earth time. I stood and thanked my new friends for a wonderful afternoon and began to make my way back up to the road, half expecting my little scooter to have been taken away.
Walking back up hill and down dale, I realised how far I had actually walked away from it. I began to think that I would

never get back, that somehow I had slipped through a time warp and was back long before the days of scooters and motorised vehicles. It was strange that the whole afternoon had been so peaceful. No sound of car, plane or helicopter had destroyed the peace.

I really might have been walking the Old Ridgeway, two thousand years ago.

By the time I got back to the hollow where I had left my Melody I was tired and the evening was getting that slight chill one notices after a really hot day. I pushed the bike back to the road and looked at my watch. Heavens. It was far too late to take the books to the shop now.

I turned back down the road and eventually got back to the house where I was working at the time.

The old man for whom I worked was not happy. Why had I been so long? Had I had an accident? Where was his supper? I knew he liked it at a certain time, didn't I?

How do you explain being Pixie-led by a butterfly? Walking over downs and sitting in hollows, when you were supposed to be paying attention to an old man's whim and selling his books?

I listened to these irate questions with only about a quarter of an ear. Apologising as I made the supper. Seeming to hear tiny stifled giggles and not sure whether they were mine or some other beings. The recriminations went on most of the evening until, with real exasperation the old man said, "I don't think you have heard a thing I've said."

I could only reply "You are so right."

Pathworking

To The Herb Garden

Get up from your chair and go to the door which appears in the wall in front of you. It is locked but you know where the key is for it is your own key. No-one else knows about it. It takes you to the place you wish to go.

When you have found the key unlock the door and go through. Always remember to look carefully at the other side. You may need to find this door among many others and it is well to be able to recognise it.

Turn around and see a flight of steps going down. There are ten steps in all, five and then a small landing and five more. They are slightly worn in the middle but there is a substantial hand rail at your left hand.

Begin to go down and pause at the half-landing. Then go on down the last five stairs.

You are in a dimly lit passage which has doors on either side. The stones are not very even so take care.The walls are rough but quite dry.

There is the narrow archway you used the last time you came here but you walk past it this time. Further down the passage is a very old door, the sort once found in a monastery. This is the door you need.

It is standing open and through it you see a yew hedge with a lovely old wrought iron gate which you know will let you into the garden. There is an old brick path, well kept and weedless.

Open the gate, it creaks slightly but opens easily.

There in front of you is a beautifully tended garden set in high, old, red brick walls.There are two men with their black robes hitched up cheerfully tending the plants.

Around the walls are fruit trees, peaches and Old William pears. When you take a bite the juice runs down your arms, sticky and sweet. The taste is pure ambrosia.

There are many tall flowers lining the walls, Delphinium, Astible, Sunflower, Purple Loosestripe and Rosemary. They are mixed with the tall herbs, Lovage, Angelica, Fennel and Mallow.

One of the monks comes toward you with a smile, greeting you with the welcome “benedicte” and asking if he can be of any help. You know that he is very busy at this time of year and you reply “benedicte brother” and ask if you may just look at the wonderful display by yourself for the moment.

He is quite glad to be able to continue his work and replies that he will be happy to help should you need him to do so.

You thank him and he goes back to his weeding.

There are six large, square beds. Orientated to the compass, they are the beds of the four elements, each in its relevant corner. In the centre of the garden there are two larger beds, also square. dedicated to the sun and the moon, these are divided by small, clipped, box hedges. Between them, in round beds, divided like the spokes of a wheel by hedges of

FIRE

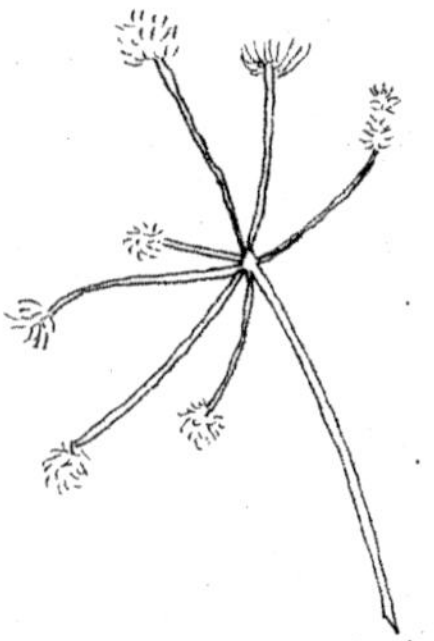

Angelica

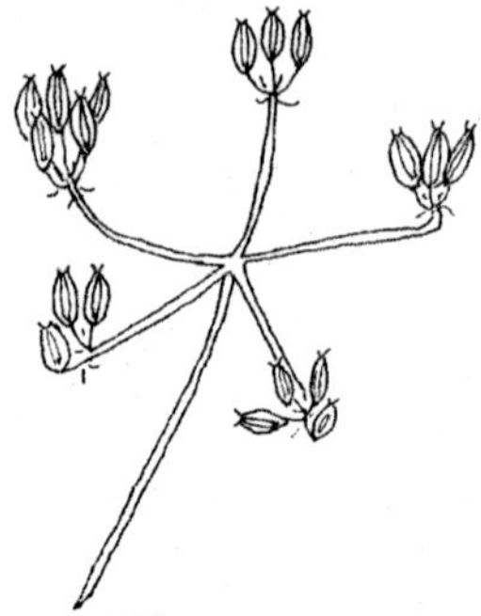

Lovage

Eyebright

Chamomile

Paeony

Marigold

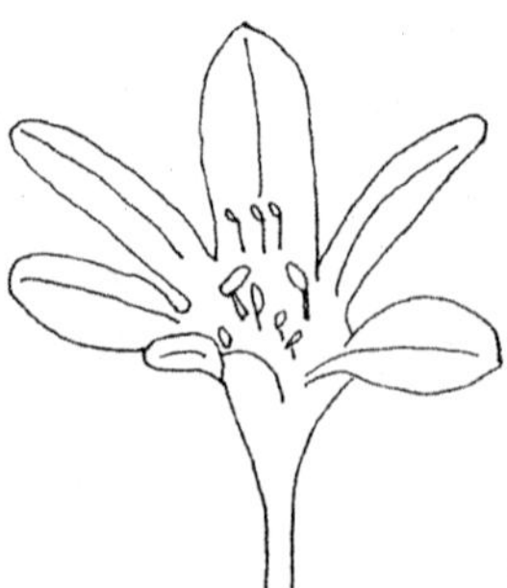

Saffron Crocus

Rosemary

Rosemary and Thyme.

The first small plot you come to, which is on your right-hand side, is dedicated to herbs of fire placed in the south corner of each corner of the garden. At the corner furthest from you is a small Walnut tree and in the other corners are the tall herbs, Lovage, Angelica and Rosemary. the bed is crossed by a beautifully kept gravel path and as you walk along it you will see edging of marigold with Camomile, Eyebright and Saffron Crocuses. In the very centre is a lovely Peony, deep red and scented.

On the opposite side there are the herbs of water. Tall herbs at the back graduating down toward the centre where there is a small pond, in the centre of which grow Stately Flags and Water Lilies. Around the edges a crop of Watercress, and in the far corners are Fennel, Fengugreek and Samphire, shading down to Figwort and Self heal and Water Betony.

The next bed you come to has herbs of Jupiter, cornered by Tarragon, Borrage and Costmary. This herb is also known as Alecost. it was used to clarify ale in the days before hops came into the country but it was most widely known as Bible Leaf because the leaves, which are large, smell of balsam, keep books smelling fresh and sweet and prevent them being damaged by damp. Close to the path is a circle of Pansies.

The next bed is again square and here we find the herbs of the sun. There are some magnificent Sunflower at the far corner and on the wall behind is an espaliered Orange tree. There are Heliotrope, Wallflowers Betony, Burnet, Centaur and Yellow Horned Poppies. The hedges are of Rosemary and near the back of the beds are St. John's Wort and Peonies. There is a new Liquidambar plant which, taken care of, will grow into a tree of great beauty. It is new to the garden and will need to be carefully transplanted. It is also known as Storax. In a little while we will learn to recognise and use all

WATER

fenugreek

fennel

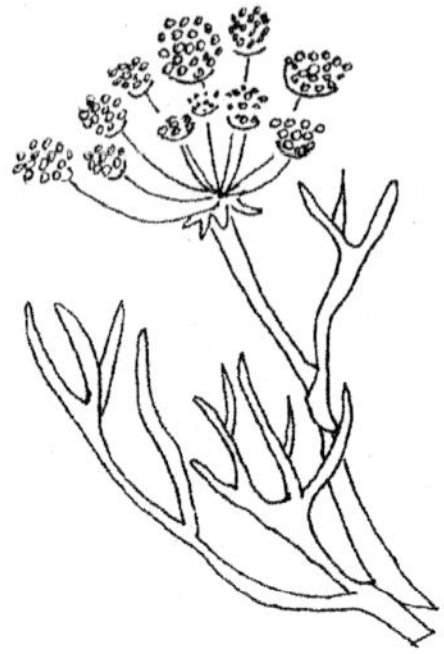

Samphire

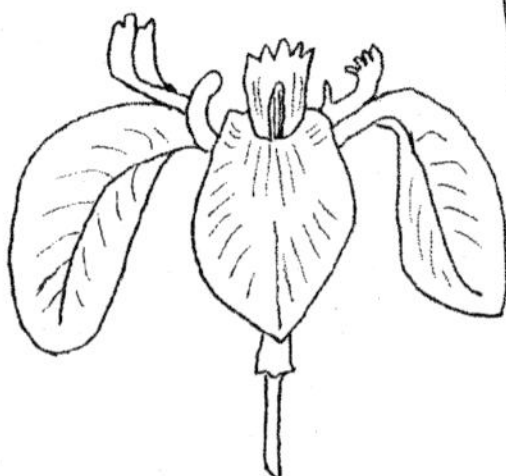

flag

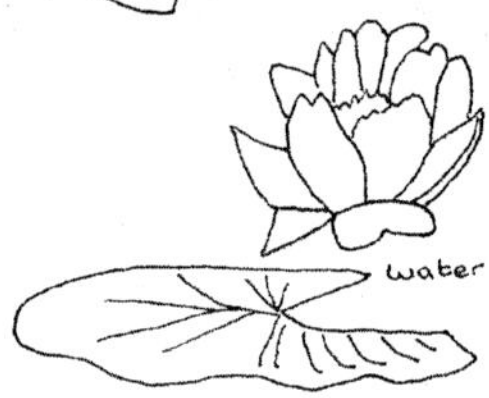

water lily

Betony

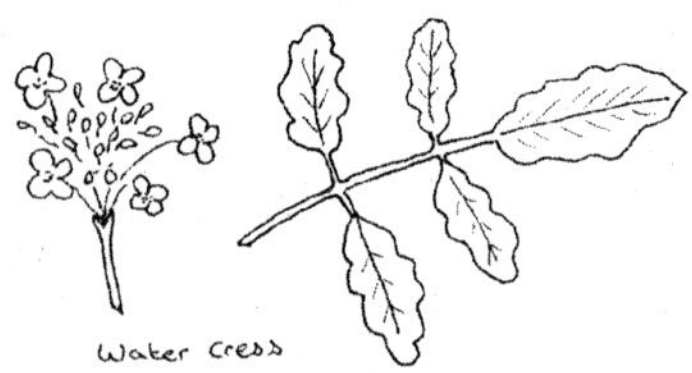

Water Cress

Self Heal

figwort

JUPITER

Pansey

Costmary
(Alecost)

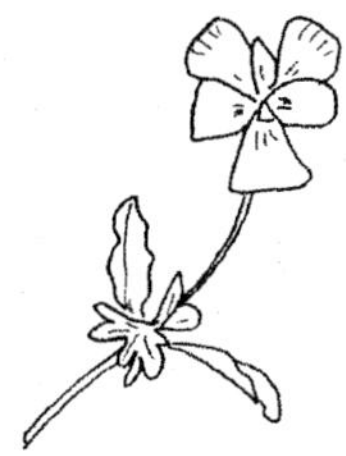

Pansey

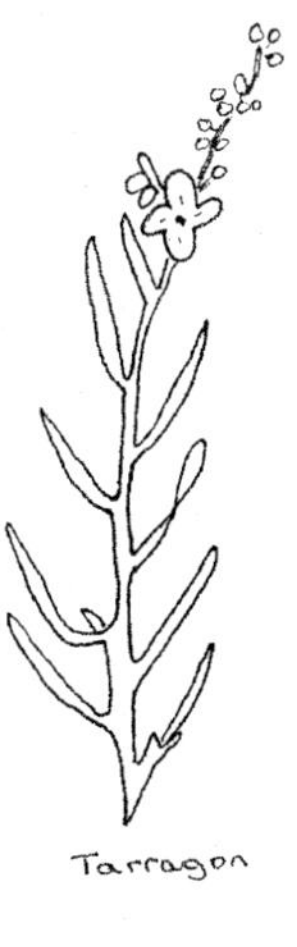

Tarragon

Borage

SUN

Heliotrope

Sunflower

Rosemary

Burnet

Betony

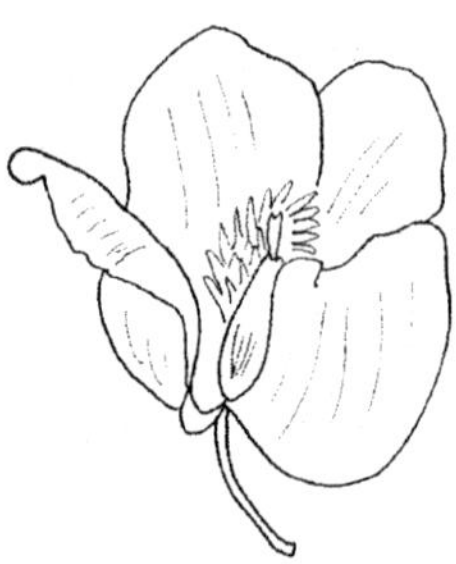

Yellow Horned Poppy

St Johns wort

SATURN

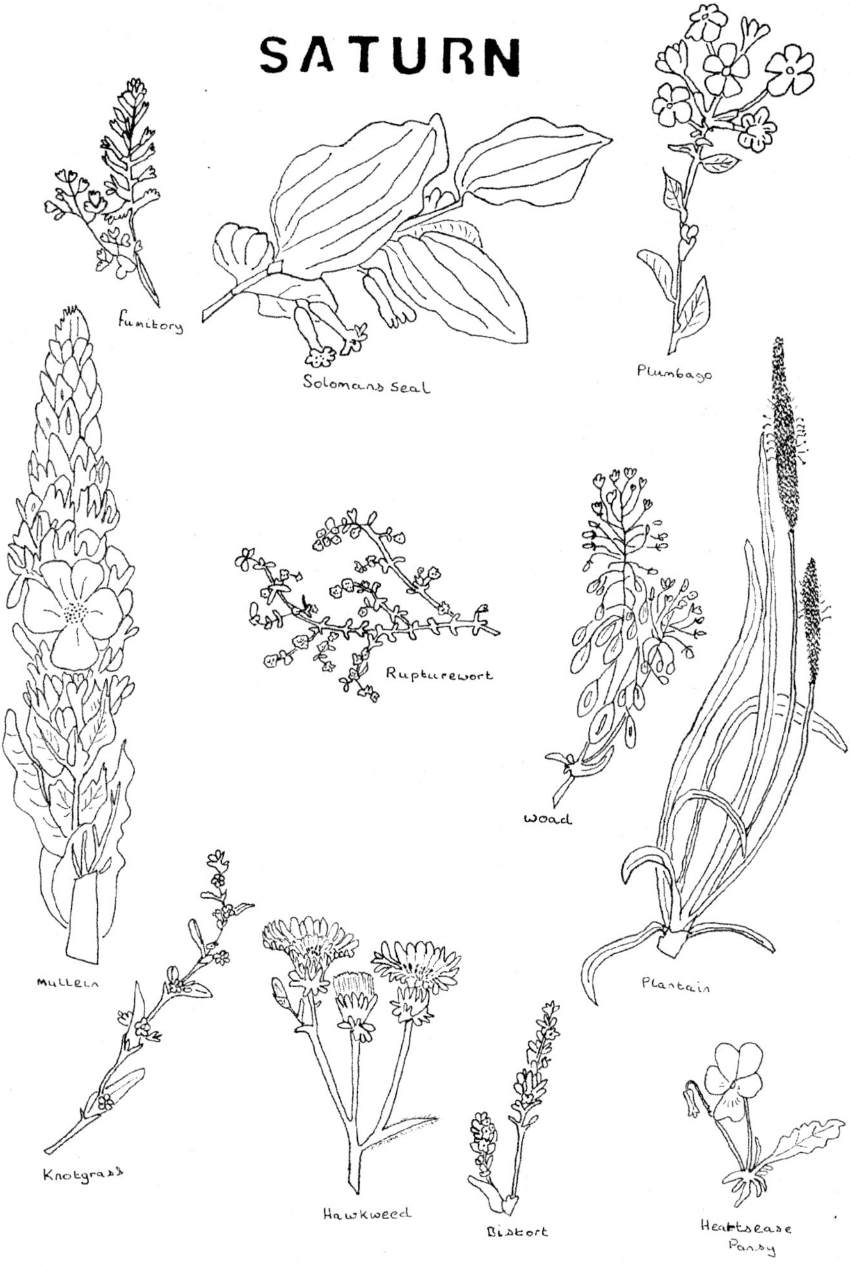
fumitory
Solomans Seal
Plumbago
Rupturewort
woad
Mullein
Plantain
Knotgrass
Hawkweed
Bistort
Heartsease
Pansy

these herbs, and those in the other beds.

The round bed of Saturn comes next. Spoked like a wheel. in the centre of the wheel is a Medlar tree which has pretty white flowers giving very sour berries. These berries cannot be used until they fall off the tree rotten, but then, oh then they are so very useful. Between the spokes, made of Plantain and Knotgrass, we find Amaranthus or Velvet Flower, Fumitory or Smoke of the Earth, Plumbago, Rupturewort, Bistor both large and small, woad, Soloman's Seal, Mullein and Hawkweed encircled by Hearts ease Pansies.

Before we move onto the next square bed we will look at the centre of the garden. here are two herbs not often grown with others because they are not compatible.

The oldest herb known to mankind, Horsetail, usually grows in marshy bed. In the times of carboniferous forests these would have been two hundred feet high and they became our coal. They now grow only to two or three feet, but they are so useful, they can stop haemorrhage and solders together the tops of green wounds and works wonders on piles. This is a herb of Saturn.

The other herb is Rue, a herb of the sun. It is said that no other plant will grow near. But I have masses of Lemon Balm, St. Johns Wort and even Hops in the same bed. It is taken, says Culpepper, in wine to promote women's courses, and is an antidote against poison. It is also known as Graveyard Dust.

Now let us go to the last square on this side of the garden. the square of earth in the far corner has some splendid Hollyhocks, pink, red and yellow. There is Comfrey, Mallow and Mullein, Loosestrife, Feverfew, Soldiers Woundwort and Motherwort, Feverfew and Endive and the very useful Wintergreen.

In the very centre of the back of the garden there is the round bed of Venus, who has so many plants that we are spoiled for choice. All the mints are dedicated to venus and at the centre is a stand of Tansey. There is Soapwaort, which makes a very soft wash for delicate fabrics and was the first shampoo. There is Ladies Mantle, Ladies Bedstraw, Columbine, Bugle, scabious and Pennyroyal, not to mention a tub of delicious Strawberries in the centre.

Silverweed, rocket, self-Heal, Coltsfoot and the very useful Mugwort, which weary travellers put into their shoes, and an edging of daisies and Hearts Ease Pansies.

But look behind this round bed of Venus. No herb garden would be complete without the plants we fear. Nightshade or Belladonna, Monkshood and Meadow Saffron, both aconite, Foxglove which is Digitalis, Bryony from which is distilled scammony resin, Hemlock and Hemblane. All very useful in very small doses, but not to be taken except under medical direction.

In the next square bed we find the herbs of the air within a hedge of Lavender. There is a Hazel tree in the far corner, balanced by Marjoram and some of the Thymes. There is Spearmint, the only mint not dedicated to Dame Venus, and here we also find Wormwoods, the Artimesias, Roman and Southernwood and Margoram. This is a highly scented area.

But we must get along, the wheel of Mercury awaits us. A great elecampane in the centre. A scruffy plant but sovereign for colds, beds of Parsley, summer and winter Savoury, Garlic Cress, which was called Sauce Alone by country people, more Lavender, more Southernwood, Carrots and Caraway and the best of the Thymes.

Cliff Meadow Rue

Varigated Rue

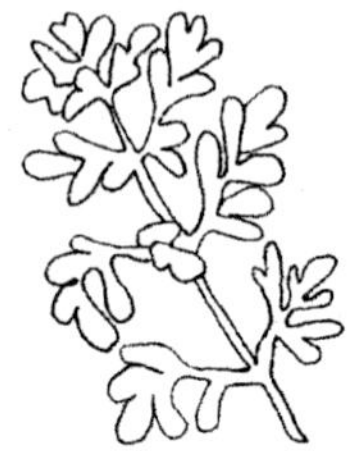

Rue

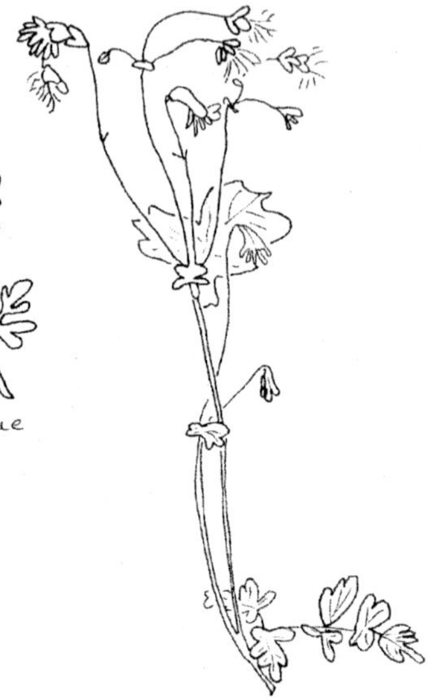

Greater Meadow Rue

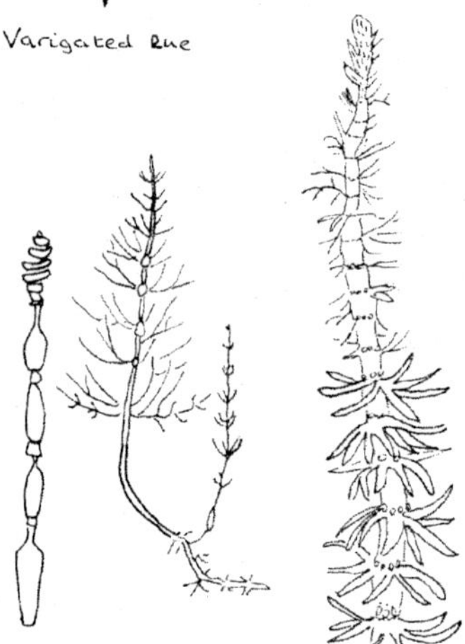

Horsetail

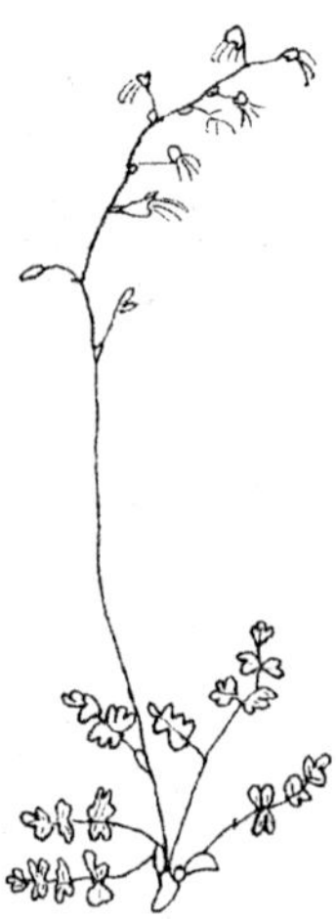

Alpine meadow Rue

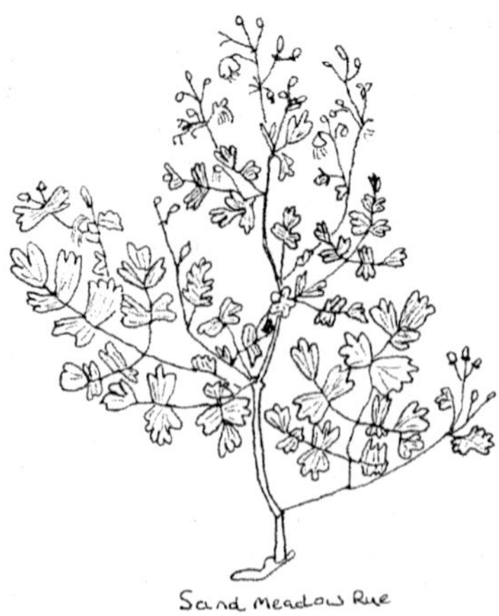

Sand Meadow Rue

Common meadow Rue

Monkshood

Deadly Nightshade

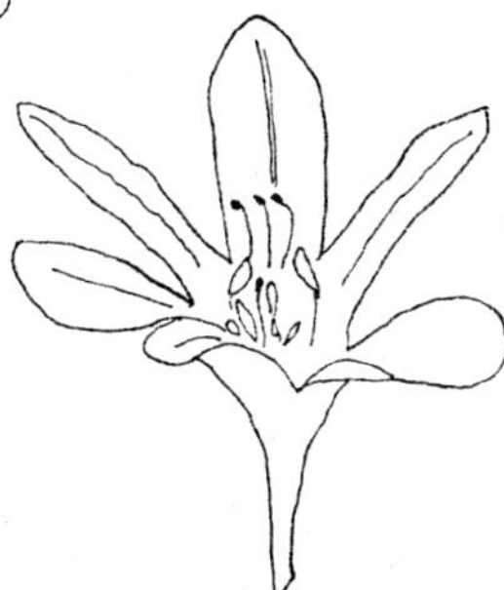

Meadow Saffron

Bryony

Foxglove

Henbane

Hemlock

EARTH

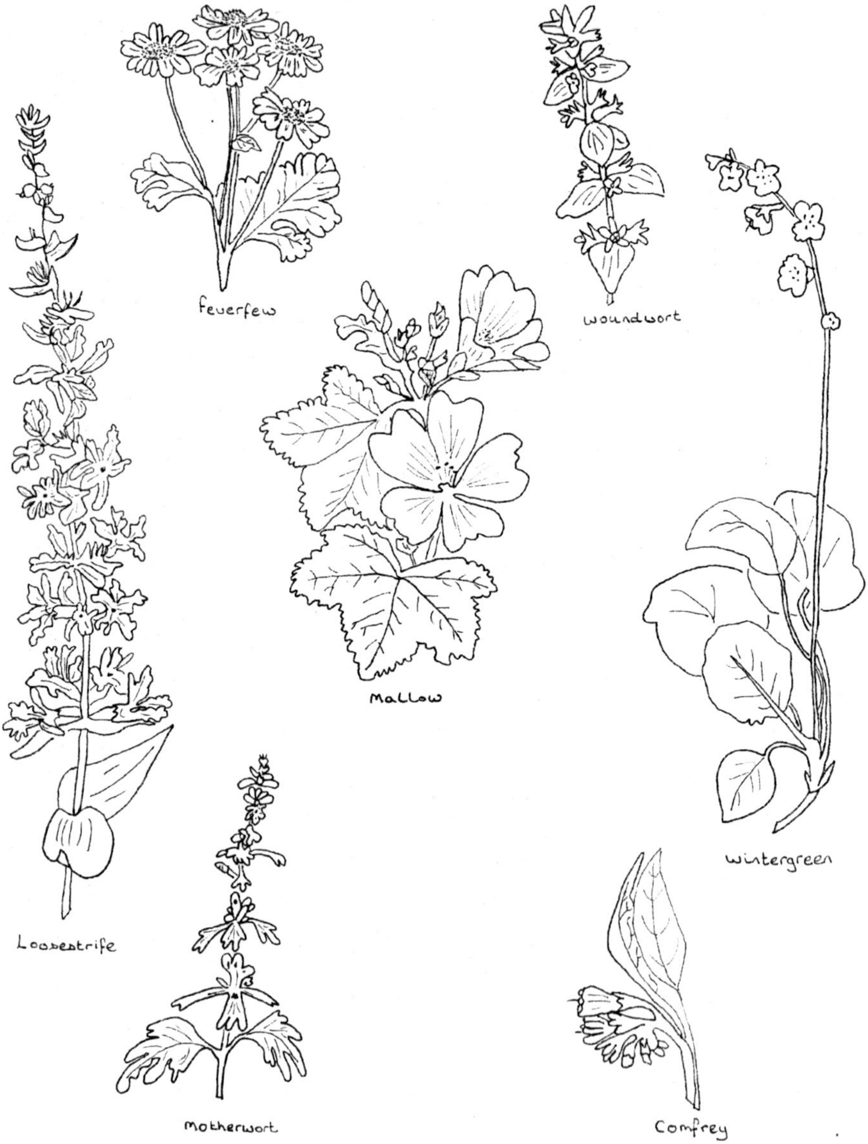

feverfew
woundwort
Mallow
wintergreen
Loosestrife
motherwort
Comfrey

VENUS

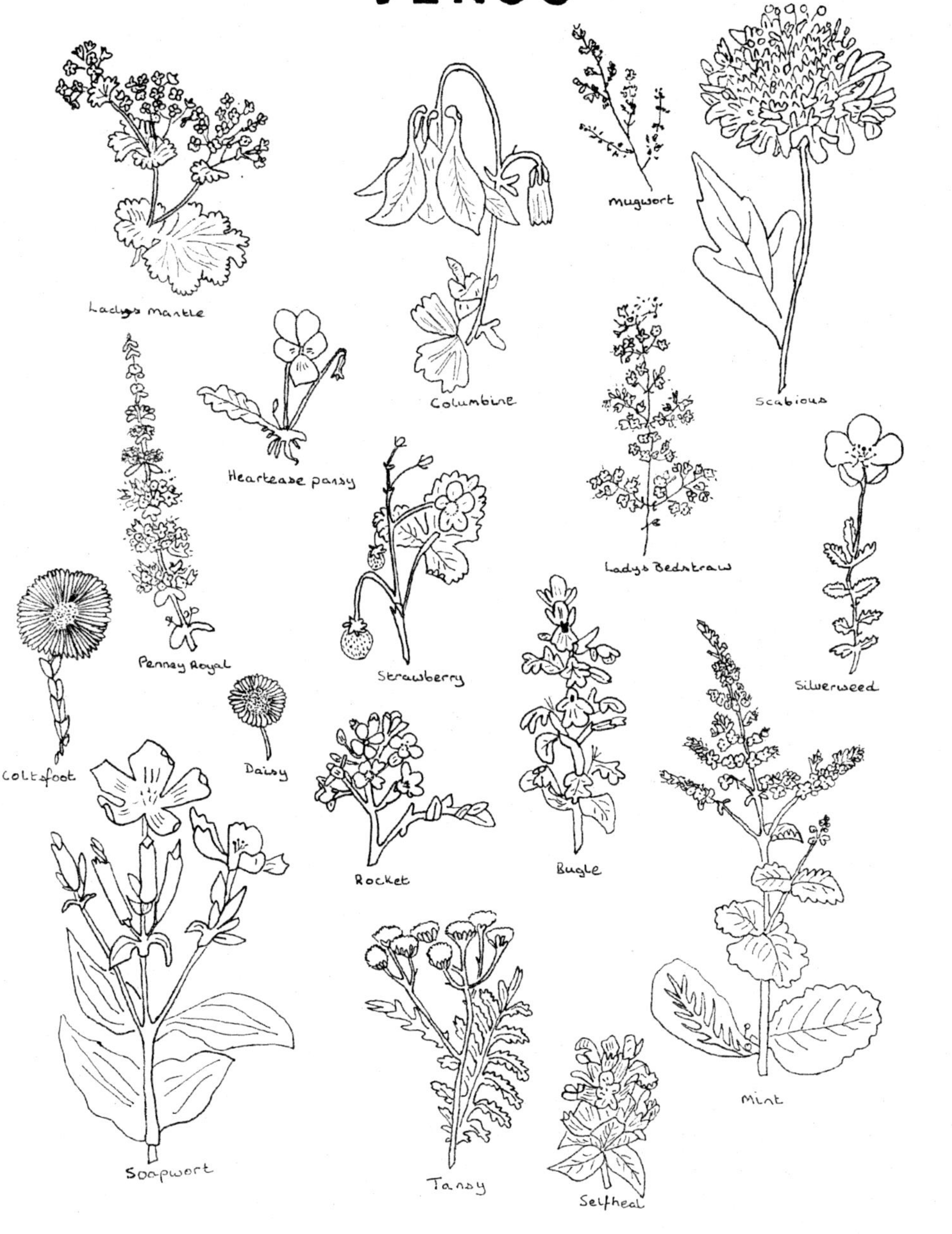
Ladys Mantle
Columbine
Mugwort
Scabious
Hearteaze pansy
Ladys Bedstraw
Penney Royal
Strawberry
Silverweed
Coltsfoot
Daisy
Rocket
Bugle
Soapwort
Tansy
Selfheal
Mint

Now we have come to the great square of the moon. At the back is a lovely white Rose, clambering over a trellis, which looks all too fragile for the strong growth.There is a lot of Cleavers growing around it, an untidy plant, but it has more than one use both in medicine and cookery.

This is balanced at the opposite corners by great stands of Fleur De Lys. There is Arrach, Chickweed, and growing up the nearer trellis are Cucumber, Clary sage, Veronica, Poppies and Yarrow. Closer to the main path is Moon Wort, Violet and stonecrop. In the small bed nearest to the path are rows of full-hearted Lettuce.

The last circular bed is that of Mars and in the centre of this is a fine crop of Rhubarb, some kept under tall clay pots to ensure colour and flavour. Here there are Lupins, Hops, some nettles kept for soups and tizanes, but only picked before June because the balance changes with the setting of the seeds. We must have Nettles in the garden or there would be no butterflies. There is Basil, Woodruff, garlic and Germander, pretty little Windflowers and Chives, some with their purple heads and some still straight grass shoots. Behind the bed is a growth of Honeysuckle, climbing the wall. All around the bed are Onions.

Go around quickly and pick what you will, for we must leave. We have overstayed our welcome and the gardeners are waiting to go to lunch.

We find our way back to the old brick path and to the wrought iron gate so lovingly made to give a glimpse of the garden. We go through it, closing it carefully behind us. it still squeaks softly. The path takes us to the yew hedge and in front of us is the ancient door. It is still open but we must close it as we go through.

You are in the narrow passage and before you is the archway. Turn into the wider passage and walk to the foot of the stairs. Can you remember?

Climb slowly to the half-landing. You will need to hold on to the rail. Count the steps, one, two, three, four, five - stop. Do you remember?

Climb to the top of the flight and there before you is your door, open it. Go through and close and lock it after you. Put the key away in its secret place. Cross the room and look at the door.

What door?

Come back now to this time and this space, to the warmth and light of this room and to your companions.

When you are ready open your eyes and know that you are not a Daffodil but yourself. Remember what it was like to be, but do not be confused, you are a human-being, not a bulb.

Salve. Bonjour. Hello.

AIR

Verbena

wild Thyme

marjoram

Southernwood

Spearmint

Larger wild Thyme

Lavender

MERCURY

Summer Savory

Carrott

Caraway

Southernwood

Elecampane

Lavender

Winter Savory

Lemon Thyme

Parsley

MOON

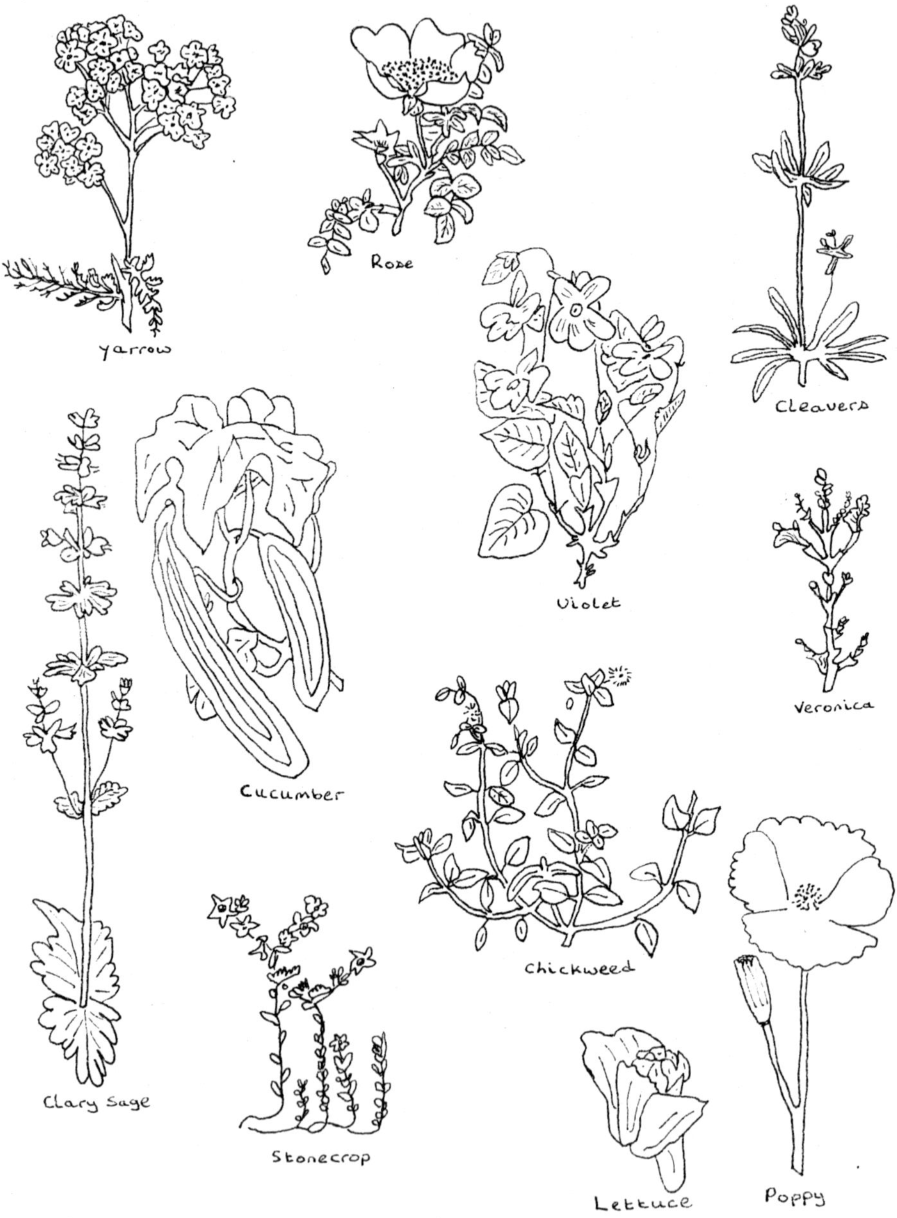
Yarrow
Rose
Cleavers
Violet
Cucumber
Veronica
Clary Sage
Chickweed
Stonecrop
Lettuce
Poppy

MARS

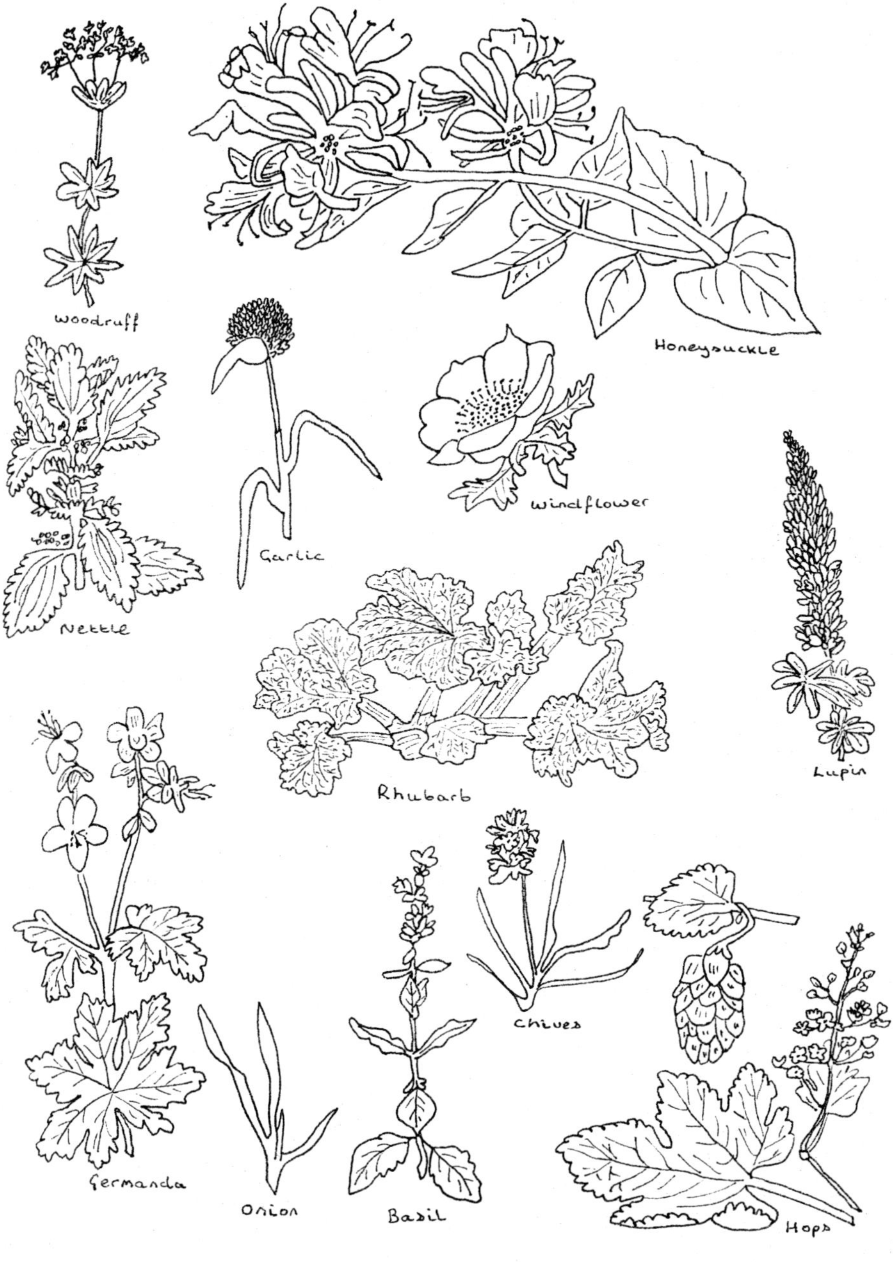
Woodruff
Honeysuckle
Garlic
Windflower
Nettle
Lupin
Rhubarb
Chives
Germanda
Onion
Basil
Hops

FREE DETAILED CATALOGUE

Fairies in the Irish Tradition, Molly Gowen
Familiars - Animal Powers of Britain, Anna Franklin
Forest Paths - Tree Divination, Brian Harrison, Ill. S. Rouse
Gardening For Wildlife Ron Wilson
God Year, The, Nigel Pennick & Helen Field
Goddess on the Cross, Dr George Young
Goddess Year, The, Nigel Pennick & Helen Field
Goddesses, Guardians & Groves, Jack Gale
Handbook For Pagan Healers, Liz Joan
Handbook of Fairies, Ronan Coghlan
Healing Book, The, Chris Thomas and Diane Baker
Healing Homes, Jennifer Dent
Healing Stones, Sue Philips
Herb Craft - Shamanic & Ritual Use of Herbs, Lavender & Franklin
In Search of Herne the Hunter, Eric Fitch
Inner Celtia, Alan Richardson & David Annwn
Inner Mysteries of the Goths, Nigel Pennick
Inner Space Workbook - Develop Thru Tarot, C Summers & J Vayne
Intuitive Journey, Ann Walker Isis - African Queen, Akkadia Ford
Kecks, Keddles & Kesh - Celtic Lang & The Cog Almanac, Bayley
Legend of Robin Hood, The, Richard Rutherford-Moore
Lid Off the Cauldron, Patricia Crowther
Light From the Shadows - Modern Traditional Witchcraft, Gwyn
Lore of the Sacred Horse, Marion Davies
Magic of Herbs - A Complete Home Herbal, Rhiannon Ryall
Magical Guardians - Exploring the Spirit and Nature of Trees, Philip Heselton
Magical History of the Horse, Janet Farrar & Virginia Russell
Magical Lore of Animals, Yvonne Aburrow
Magical Lore of Cats, Marion Davies
Magical Lore of Herbs, Marion Davies
Magick Without Peers, Ariadne Rainbird & David Rankine
Masks of Misrule - Horned God & His Cult in Europe, Nigel Jackson
Mirrors of Magic - Evoking the Spirit of the Dewponds, P Heselton
Moon Mysteries, Jan Brodie
Mysteries of the Runes, Michael Howard
Mystic Life of Animals, Ann Walker
New Celtic Oracle The, Nigel Pennick & Nigel Jackson
Pagan Feasts - Seasonal Food for the 8 Festivals, Franklin & Phillips
Patchwork of Magic - Living in a Pagan World, Julia Day
Pathworking - A Practical Book of Guided Meditations, Pete Jennings
Pickingill Papers - The Origins of Gardnerian Wicca, Bill Liddell
Pillars of Tubal Cain, Nigel Jackson
Practical Spirituality, Steve Hounsome
Psychic Self Defence - Real Solutions, Jan Brodie
Real Fairies, David Tame
Reality - How It Works & Why It Mostly Doesn't, Rik Dent